The Bison Hunters

The Bison Hunters

The Paleo-Indian Series: Folsom

Shirley G. East

To order additional copies of this book, contact:
Xlibris
1-888-795-4274
www.Xlibris.com
Orders@Xlibris.com
786501

Folsom Tool Kit

Atlatl and darts were used by the Folsom culture to hunt large animals

Awls and antler tools were used in working leather.

blades were used by everyone for a multitude of tasks. Anything a small sharp blade could accomplish. The blade was there.

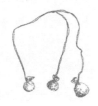

the bolas was used by both men and women alike to bring down small animals.

crude choppers were used for a variety of tasks shaping wood

sharp knives and scrapers were used for everythin from slicing the jugular to cutting thin strips of meat to dry.

the Folsom point was used by these hunters. The basal edges were ground and it was hafted to a dart. With the use of an atlatl it could be driven with considerable force. Enough to kill a bison.

the horn sheath was used as a drinking vessel, or a storage container. They were both sturdy and plentiful.

various stones were used for grinding and breaking shells. It has been discovered that the Folsom culture had a type of mano.

Side scrapers and smaller end and thumbnail Scrapers were used to remove the remaining flesh from hides and with the use of brains and urine, or tannic acid from acorns these tools broke down the fibers to soften and process hides.

Shaft straighteners were used to remove excess wood and make the dart as straight as possible.

FOREWORD

The end of the Pleistocene Era was marked with an extensive drought, called by archaeologists the Younger dryas[1]. When this drought ended a wetter or pluvial period occurred. The great Pleistocene Megafauna are no longer walking the earth. Bison became the predominant fauna of the land. The few people who survived the close of the Pleistocene had to have been driven to the very edge of survival. Now, with the increased rainfall, grass began to grow on the plain and grazing animals became abundant; a vast storehouse of food. This species is *Bison antiquuis*[2]. The animal is smaller than the great *latifrons*[3] of the Pleistocene. It had short straight horns.

The people who hunted this bison have been named the Folsom Culture[4] by the archaeologists. Their beautifully crafted points are very distinctive, but only these points and the animals they hunted separate them from the Clovis Culture[5], which existed before them. They spread over a much smaller area, basically the western edge of the Great Plains from North Dakota to the Edwards Plateau of southern Texas[6]. Their sites are associated with few animals other than bison. They moved constantly, following the great grazing herds.

Little is known of them beyond the tools they left behind that were associated with the animals they killed. At Blackwater Draw Site #1, there was an area of pure white spring sand excavated in the salvage operations of 1963[7.] Within this sand were hundreds of artifacts, including knives, blades, scrapers and points, among which were several Folsom points. (Clovis points, Milnesand, Portales, and Cody, were also present indicating that the spring was active and used for some special purpose for a very long time.) All these artifacts were polished by the sand and water action. All were broken, and both parts were present.

We can only conjecture regarding the life stories of these intrepid hunters and their families who lived and hunted, loved and died 11,000 years ago. We know they were hunters. We know they followed the herds, but little else. The imagination, therefore, has given them shape, life and hope. Everything in this book, beyond the bare facts of the archaeology presented here, is the creation of the author.

---

1. the Younger Dryas was an extremely severe time of long-lasting huge wide spread dust storms and drought all across North America. The Pleistocene Megafauna died out or migrated. Some camels migrated to South America and some to Asia. The Horse became extinct in the Western Hemisphere.
2. Bison antiquus was somewhat smaller than the great Bison latifrons of the Pleistocene. It has short straight horns.
3. Bison latifrons was the largest species of bison inhabiting North America. It lived during the Pleistocene and was hunted by the Clovis Culture people.
4. The Folsom Culture is named for the site near Folsom New Mexico. Wormington;
5. The Clovis Culture is named from the type site near Clovis New Mexico, they are called paleo Indian and lived during the Pleistocene.
6. The Edwards Plateau area of south Texas is known for the gray chert used for making artifacts by many Native American groups.
7. Blackwater Draw is the Clovis type site discovered in 1932 and first worked by Sellards of the University of Pennsylvania and is still being worked today by Eastern New Mexico University, Wormington

GEOGRAPHIC LOCATIONS

A. **The western edge of the Great Plains**. The Folsom people in this novel followed a path along the western edge of the Great Plains from the Edwards Plateau region of Texas northward along the eastern edge of the Rocky Mountains as far as northern New Mexico

B. **The Llano Estacado.** Also known as the Staked Plains. This is a high plateau area lacking any rivers. It is very flat sloping gently eastward at so slight a rate the naked eye cannot discern it. This region has changed little in millions of years.

C. **The Edwards Plateau.** The southernmost extent of the Great Plains flows into the Edwards Plateau. This area produced a wonderfully fine-grained gray chert. Native Americans prized it.

    1: **Blackwater Draw Local #1:** The Clovis Type-Site. Located between Portales and Clovis New Mexico. First excavated in 1932, it has been a continuous source of data on the Paleo-Indian. Blackwater Draw is one of the few stratified sites. It is the location of the 'Sacred Spring' depicted in this novel.

    2: **Alabates Flint Quarry:** Located north of Amarillo, Texas on the Canadian river. This was one of the major sources of workable stone material available to the Native Americans until historic times.

    3: **Palo Duro Canyon:** The location of the 'Secret Canyon'.

    4: **Folsom Type-Site:**

    5: **The Starving Mountains:** Capitan Mountains of New Mexico.

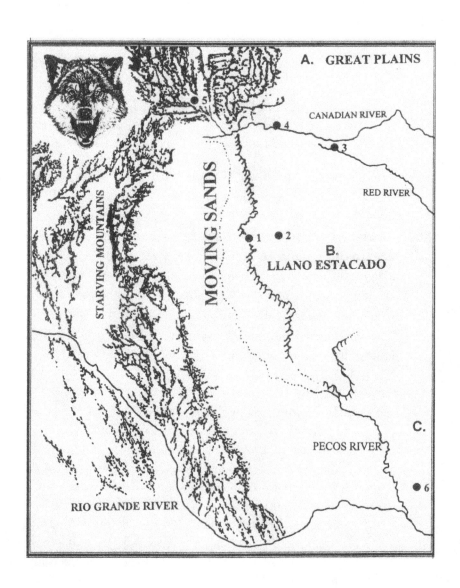

A. GREAT PLAINS

CANADIAN RIVER

RED RIVER

B.
LLANO ESTACADO

C.

PECOS RIVER

RIO GRANDE RIVER

STARVING MOUNTAINS

MOVING SANDS

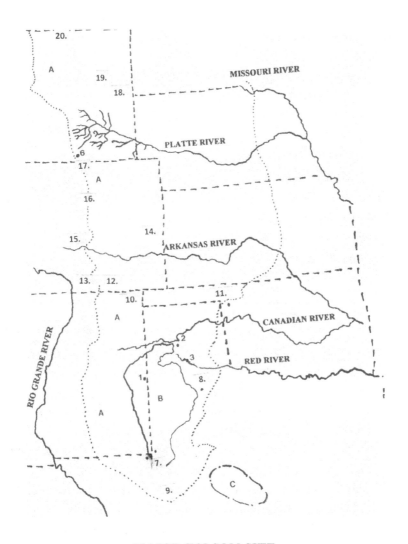

MAJOR FOLSOM SITE:

1. Blackwater Draw[1]
2. Alabates Flint Quarry[2]
3. Palo Duro Canyon[3]
4. Not Mentioned
5. Not Mentioned
6. Not Mentioned
7. Scharbauer[4]
8. Lubbock Lake, TX[5]

9. Genevieve Lykes Duncan Site, TX[6]

10. Folsom Type Site[7]

11. Lipscomb TX, Cooper, Jake Bluff, & Waugh, OK[8]

12. Steweart's Cattle Guard, CO[9]

13. Linger, CO[10]

14. Hell Gap, WY

15. Mountaineer & Reddin, CO[11]

16. Barger Gulch, WY[12]

17. Lindenmeier CO[13]

18. Agate Basin, WY

19. Carter/Keer-McGee, WY[14]

20. Hanson, WY

---

1. Blackwater Draw, NM: First excavated in 1932 by Sellards of the University of Pennsylvania, it has been an active archaeological site off and on until present. It is now owned by the state of New Mexico. Eastern New Mexico University is in charge of the site at present. It is now a National Historic Site. **Blackwater Draw National Historic Site:** 2018

2. Alabates Flint Quarry: Alabates Flint was the rock that shaped- and was shaped by cultures in the Texas Panhandle for 13,000 years. **Alabates Fllint Quarries National Monument;** 2018

3. Palo Duro Canyon: Palo Duro Canyon is the second-largest canyon in the United States. It is roughly 120 miles long and 20 miles wide and ranges from 820' to 1,000' deep. It is called the Grand Canyon of Texas. Both its size and its geologic features and steep walls are reminiscent of the Grand Canyon. The first evidence of Human habitation dates back 10,000 – 15,000 years and is believed to have been inhabited until present. Native Americans were attracted to it by the water provided by the Prairie Dog Fork of the Red River as well as the consequent ample game. Edible plants and protection from weather the canyon provided. **Palo_Duro_Canyon:** wilipedia; 2018

4. Scharbour Site, TX: Folsom as a technology is believed to have developed out of the Clovis mammoth-hunting culture. Folsom technology refers to the distinctive point with a long channel flute to nearly the tip of the point. A different technology was required for hunting bison. They are quicker and smaller than mammoth. Whereas a mammoth weighted about 27,600 pounds as bison antiquuis weighted only about 1,000 pounds. Whereas the Clovis hunters used spears, Bison hunters used a dart, cast with an atlatl. Folsom people live in small highly mobile groups traveling over large areas following the bison migration. Lithic materials have been found over 560 miles from their source. **Kris Hirst;** 2018.

   Shifting Sands, TX. The Shifting Sands site is located on the Pecos Plain along the southern portion of the Llano Estacado in Winkle County Texas. The site itself is a series of 5 to 8 meter-deep blowouts in a large dune field. The site has yielded stone tools along with many weathered bone fragments. During the past 25 years a large portion on the site has been exposed to erosion. The Shifting Sands site is important for a variety of reasons. First, it has been meticulously collected and each flake that became exposed through erosion has been catalogued and kept. Secondly no other folsom/midland site has proved the type of large-scale spatial pattering in the site structure. Third in terms of sheer numbers, the Shifting Sands site artifact assemblage is one of the three or four largest. **Westfall, 2018**

5. Lubbock Lake, TX: the first archaeological work at the Lubbock Lake site was done in 1939-1941 by what is now the museum of Texas Tech University. The Texas Memorial Museum in 948, 1949 and 1951. Etc through 1972. Lubbock Lake yielded burned bone from the first Paleo-Indian period (9883 -$^{+}$350 BP) in 1950. Lubbock Lake is a deep, well stratified site with a vertically complete cultural flora and fauna record covering the past 11,500 years defining 5five major stratigraphic units. Strata I Clovis 11,100 BP and strata 2 Folsom 10,500. **Johnson:** 2018

6. Genevieve Lykes Duncan, TX; The Center for Big Bend Studies has been documenting and investigating archaeological sites

in Brewster Co since 1999. The Genevieve Lykes Duncan site has deeply buried cultural deposits with intact thermal features dating to the late Paleo-Indian period. Two plant food preparation technologies ubiquitous across North America in the subsequent Archaic Period- the use of stones as heating elements and use of ground stone implements-as well represented within the late Paleo-Indian deposits. **Cloud, 2012.**

7. Folsom Type Site, NM; 1908 George McJunkin's discovered a point imbedded in the rib of an extinct bison. Thus began the excavation of the Folsom site and the development of the Folsom assemblage of artifacts. The site was excavated by Jesse Figgins in of the Denver Museum of Natural History in 1912. Today excavation is still ongoing. At least 32 individual Bison antiquuis have been excavated along with 26 spear points. This is only a kill site. The location of their campsite has never been discovered but must lie within a few miles. **Meltzer:** 2006.

8. Lipscomb, TX, Cooper, Jake Bluff, Waugh, OK. Three Folsom points were taken from the Cooper site in northwest Oklahoma. The Cooper Site represents a stratified Folsom bison kill site with three separate bone beds contained in alluvium is a small arroyo. Lipscomb produced 8 points and 3 tools among a bone bed in 1988. Present evidence suggests possible processing and camp activities at the northern end of the bone mass. Lipscomb has been excavated several times. In the 1939 excavation 1,000 numbers were assigned in the catalogue; in 1946 only 44. In 1986 and88 the goal was to relocate prior excavations, prepare a map of the site, determine if any archaeological area remained, assess the potential of dating the site, and study the geology of the site. As it turned out the land owners had controlled access. In 1988 evidence of intact bone beds were found. Overall the site in in poor condition due to weathering Hoffman: **1989.**

9. Stewart's Cattle Guard, CO: Located in the San Luis Valley, Alamosa County, Colorado represents a late summer or early fall bison hunting camp occupied by Folsom people circa before 6,000 BCE. The site was discovered in the late 1970's and excavated by the Smithsonian Institution's Paleo-Indian Program from 1981 to

1996 largely under the direction of Margaret A. Jodry. After the Lindenmeier Site, Stewart's Cattle Guard is the most extensively excavated Folsom site in North America. The site included three spatially and functionally distinct areas; the kill site, the butchering and residential area, and the hide processing area. The kill involved at least forty-nine bison. After the kill, the hunters probably performed preliminary butchering at the kill site before carrying portions of the bison to their narby camp for further butchering. Hides were processed in a separate area. Folsom hunters apparently performed large-scale bison kills often enough to develop specialized tools and division of labor for processing the carcasses. Higher concentrations of certain artifacts at some of the clusters suggested that they may have served as cooperative sites where men or women from several household worked together on specific tasks. Women at the camp probably processed the hides to make clothing and tent covers as used ultrathin bifaces to cut strips of meat for drying and storage. The Folsom people probably stayed at the site for about a week-just long enough to butcher and process the bison. **Jodry:** 1986

10. Linger: excavated by Jerry Dawson and Dennis Stanford in 1975.
11. Mountaineer & Reddin, CO: Mountaineer archaeological site, CO. Discovered in 1994, the Mountaineer Archaeological site consists of more than sixty clusters of prehistoric artifacts on top of Tenderfoot Mountain near Gunnison. The most significant discovery at the site has been structures dating from 9,500-5,800 BCE and associated with the Folsom tradition. The structures indicate more extensive Folsom use of the mountains than was previously thought, suggesting that the core of Folsom settlements in Colorado could have been in the mountains rather than on the plains. In 1994 the Mountaineer site was first recorded during the construction of cell-phone towers. In 2000 the top of the mountain was surveyed and mapped resulting in the discovery of more than fifteen clusters of artifacts including parts of twenty Folsom points. Anthropologist Mark Stiger of Western Colorado State University in Gunnison has led much subsequent research.

In 2000-2003 a team of Southern Methodist University graduate students under David J. Metlzer excavated a Folsom cluster at the site. The two have led additional field school projects almost every year through 2014. Researchers found a structure associated with a large number of stone tools and Folsom projectile points. The structure is a shallow basin about twelve feet in diameter, with rocks piled around the edges. It appears to be a residential structure complete with a hearth, a storage pit, and an anvil used for cracking animal bones. Bone fragments inside the structure are radiocarbon dated to around 10,400 BCE, placing it within the Folsom range. Anthropologists and archaeologists originally thought of the Folsom culture as mobile bison hunters on the plains. Recent Folsom discoveries such as the Mountaineer site and others in the Upper Gunnison Basin and Middle Park have pointed toward a modified view of the Folsom tradition involving long-term habitations in the mountains. At the Mountaineer Site, clear spatial distribution of artifacts and evidence of spatial maintenance, including an area for trash outside the structure, indicate that the structure was probably used for an extended period, perhaps over the winter. **Stiger: 2003. Andrews** 2006

12. Barger Gulch: Discovering a Folsom point while excavating a remnant from a 10.000-year-old stone age society that inhabited Colorado's Middle Park seemed remote at best. Barger Guch is a desolate spot. It is hard, parched dirt dabbled with sagebrush as far as the eye can see. However in three years of working a relatively small excavation during summer, investigators unearthed more than 18,000 artifacts, one of them a Folsom point. **Curry**

13. Lindenmeier CO.: The Lindenmeier site is perhaps the best-known Folsom site. It represents the most extensive Folsom Culture campsite yet found. The radiocarbon date 10,600-10,720 BCE. Among the artifacts-scored pieces of hematite were used to extend red ochre used as paint for their faces. In 1960 the site was dated. In 1992 the date was published. **Roberts;** 1935.

14. Carter/Keer-McGee: A decade of intensive archaeological survey in the Powder River Basin in Wyoming has revealed one stratified Paleo-Indian site. The Folsom complex consisted of several episodes occurring over several months within the same occupation events or at different times of the year. Hunting prevails using ambush methods. **Frison;** 1984.

PART I: CHARACTERS

Yucca Camp

STONE MAN: Youth wanting to find the place where the Ancient Ones hunted bison

BLUE COYOTE: Youth wanting to find the place where the Ancient Ones hunted bison

ACORN: Dreamer

RED EAGLE: Youth of 15 years, orphan. Lives at the unmated men's hearth.

BUTTERFLY: Elderly woman: grandmother of Basket

FIRE DANCER: Father of Blue Coyote. Headman of the Yucca Camp.

STAR WOMEN: Mother of Blue Coyote.

GRAY WOLF: Youth of the Yucca Camp.

BASKET: 11-year-old girl, carries the birthmark of a strange animal on her right shoulder. Granddaughter of Butterfly.

TURTLE WOMAN: Sister to Star Woman, widowed, living with the Yucca Camp again.

ANTELOPE WOMAN: Aunt to Stone Man, matron of camp.

CHIPMUNK: Unmated young hunter

COUGAR: Older hunter

MOUSE: Youngest boy of the camp 8 years old

PORCUPINE: Hunter of the Yucca Camp

JACKRABBIT: Older hunter

COTTONTAIL GIRL: 15, girl of the camp

SQUIRREL: Unmated youth
WILLOW: 17, young woman of the camp

Rabbit Camp

GRAPE LEAF: Thief of food and water
HAIRY BEAR: Thief of food and water
SQUIRREL GIRL: Laggard
MOTH: Laggard
CENTIPEDE: Man who cares

Quail Camp

ANTELOPE: Thief of food and water
SAND CRAWLER: Thief of food and water

Pine Camp

GROUND SQUIRREL: Thief of food and water

PART I
THE STARVING MOUNTAINS

CHAPTER 1

The crown of the aspen quivered violently. Three scrawny, dirty hunters crouched behind brush waiting. They each held an atlatl and a small dart. Attached to their waist thongs each had a bolas tied to a leather pouch holding an obsidian blade or knife, and a bunch of thongs. Their hair was held out of their eyes with a skin headband. The only other clothing they wore was a pair of leather and cord sandals and a breechcloth, even though it was still late winter. Over each shoulder was slung a yucca scabbard to hold more darts. Their fire blacked tips sharpened to a deadly point.

Again the tree shook, accompanied by the enraged squeal of the prey. The men, of varying ages, leaped as one and rushed into the clearing. From the aspen dangled a wiry compact mountain javalina[1] secured by one back leg. The animal kicked again with its free legs and swung wildly about, bringing the hunters into its view. Now its frantic efforts doubled, froth foamed from its mouth. Deadly, razor-sharp tusks glinted wetly in the sun as its mouth snapped open and shut.

The youngest of this group of hunters, only a span plus seasons[2] in age, rushed forward, and with a twist of his body and lightning speed, grabbed the javalina tightly by an ear, and with one slash of his obsidian blade, slit its throat expertly. The remaining men crowded around the suddenly still animal and thirstily drank the draining blood, caring not that it splattered, ran and smeared onto their grimy bodies.

Once the blood stopped draining, one of the hunters made a graceful hand movement and spoke a few brief words. Then he carefully raised the carcass while another detached the rawhide thong from the leg. While the youth carried the javalina a short distance down the clearing the other two hunters untied and reset the snare trap from a different tree along the game trail. They carefully concealed it with dirt, and then brushed away all signs of their presence.

Silently as ghosts they melted into the undergrowth, the javalina slung over someone's shoulder. A hand of time later the procedure was repeated as a second animal became victim to their deadly snare. This time however, the snare was taken with them as they hurried silently down a well-worn trail toward the base of the mountain.

Along the way they came across a shallow clear stream bubbling through the scrub. Here they stopped and washed the blood and animal manure[3] from their bodies, then slinging the carcasses once again over shoulders hurried on down the trail. It was still before midmorning and they had many traps and snares to check and far to go before their work was completed for the day.

As they returned to the camp, a rabbit flashed across the path in front of them. Like lightning, the front man cast his polished wood rabbit stick[4]. The weapon whirled through the air, spinning with deadly force toward its target. The animal leaped upward as the missile struck with lethal impact. Without breaking stride, the hunters swept by, and the rabbit and weapon were both smoothly recovered. They methodically checked all the snares to the north of the camp, finding one more sprung. They discovered no more game signs along their route, nor any roots, tubers, nuts or pine cones to gather. The women had scoured this area long ago, collecting every edible morsel of food their sharp eyes detected. It had been another long cruel winter for the people of the Yucca Camp.

Fire Dancer dropped his animal beside the fire and grinned at his mate, already busy preparing ground seed cakes for their meal. Star Woman smiled back and as soon as the cakes were roasting, she began butchering the javalina, careful to save every morsel of meat and drop of blood. First, she skinned the animal, leaving the tail and its bones with the hide. Later she would peg it out to cure and it would be added to the meager communal camp stock of raw materials. The entrails were emptied onto a slab for the dog; while the casings were set aside to be washed and later stuffed with dried berries and meat. The organ meats were carefully removed and saved for the hunters, for organ meat gave them strength.

The stringy meat of the carcass was expertly fleshed from the bones and sliced into thin strips. It was then strung over drying racks stationed above a nearby fire constructed to give off smoke from green wood to cure the meat. The bones were cracked open with a handy rock and the marrow dug out and dumped into a skin of water to which she regularly added hot stones. The feet were saved for the dog as well. Then she used a larger rock to crack open the skull and extract the brain. It went into the stew pot as well, along with a handful of ground grain and a few bits of plant fiber to produce a more nutritious meal. The tongue was cut free and set aside with the other organ meat. The hunters had already extracted the eyeballs and eaten this delicacy on the trail, while it was still fresh.

Fire Dancer handed the rabbit to Acorn, the dreamer; a most valued member of the camp. The one animal would make him an excellent stew, which would last for several meals. Red Eagle unloaded his javalina beside another hearth, leaving it for the women to butcher, for this meat would go into the camp's larder. Then he returned to the larger unmated men's fire where he lived. One of the women had prepared food for him. He scarfed the meager offering down in a couple of swallows before rejoining the others. Meanwhile, there were more snares to check. The hunters left the camp; scarcely there long enough to cause a ripple in the day's activities. They headed south, up another dusty draw. They checked their various snares, walking well into the afternoon and many hands distant from the camp. They returned discouraged and empty handed. Only one other snare had been sprung, probably by a fox. There was a bit of reddish hair caught in the chewed rawhide, but the fox was long gone.

"You had exceptional success today, Father," Blue Coyote exclaimed as he chewed on a piece of the roasted javalina, enjoying this treat of fresh meat. Beside him on a wood slab lay a cooked grain cake and a tortoise shell of stew. "This is truly a feast," he smacked his lips in appreciation. "We had no luck at all," he grimaced. "Stone Man and I went all of the way north to Buzzard Point but we did not find so much as a track. That area is all hunted out," he sighed. "On the way back, we only managed to collect a few pine cones and a handful of acorns."

"These were the last of that group of javalina. Only the spirits know when we will come across more game," Fire Dancer frowned. "Tomorrow we are going all the way to Black Bear Falls. Hopefully we will at least find a few turkeys, but we are hoping for a bear or maybe even a deer or two."

"You will be gone for a hand of days if you plan to go all the way to Black Bear Falls," Star Woman stated, "Better take an extra sleeping robe with you. It will be cold at night so high in the mountains."

"I just hope we find something," Fire Dancer grumbled, "The last pair of times we were up there, not a sign of game; even the predators have left the area. At least we were able to collect enough tubers to make the trips worthwhile. The rest of them are probably all dug by now as well. The Quail Camp has been going up there regularly all winter."

"It is the same at Beaver Pond." Blue Coyote nodded. "Why it is called that I cannot imagine, I have never seen a beaver there."

"Nor any where else I should imagine," Fire Dancer agreed. "They were all trapped out long before you were born."

"While you are there, however, you can gather some fresh cat tails[5] if there are any," Star Woman suggested.

"We pulled all of them up last fall," Blue Coyote reminded her.

"Then why do you go there?"

"We thought to get a duck or two if we are lucky, we saw some fly over yesterday; or perhaps net some fish, they are small but food is food!" He grimaced, "Either way we will search for any roots or new shoots in the forest. There should be new growth starting soon."

"It has to rain first, Son," Fire Dancer reminded him. "Not even the strongest seed will germinate without rain. That is the problem. We need rain so desperately!"

"At least we had a good meal today, thanks to you Father," Blue Coyote grinned, "I can actually go to sleep tonight without hunger cramps twisting my guts into knots!"

"It has been warm the last few days," mentioned Star Woman, "Perhaps Butterfly, Turtle, and I will go out along the moving dunes to the east and see if the lizards are out of hibernation yet. We can search for new shoots on the way. I know it will be an all-day trip, but we decided to go any way."

Their plans made, the little family banked their fire and retired to their shelter for the night, their last thoughts for once, were not centered on starvation. Above the ancestor fires twinkled brightly in the clear dark sky. Blue Coyote lay studying them, his mind alive with the possibilities of the future.

In his shelter, nearby the dreamer, Acorn, sat legs crossed before his own little fire. His stomach was also fuller than on most nights, thanks to Fire Dancer's rabbit. He had savored a full quarter of it for his evening meal, saving the rest to keep him going over the next several days. Now he poured a small amount of water into a tortoise shell bowel and settled it on a hot rock to steam. From his special wolf hide spirit pack he removed a bark packet and added a pinch of its content to the water, stirring it with a bone sliver. As the spirit drink steeped, Acorn thought back over the last seasons. Wolf helper had not contacted him in a long time. Even when he took the special spirit drink the elusive canine refused to hear his pleas. Now desperation made him try nearly nightly. His packet of special powders would soon be gone, and he had no idea where to find any more. He had not seen the Thorn Apple[6] plant now for many seasons. Like everything else in these Starving Mountains,[7] it seemed to have vanished.

*   *   *

When the tea was ready, he drank it in a single gulp, and then waited . . . Tingling in his fingertips alerted him, then slowly his world went black. He could feel the swirling as he spiraled deeper and deeper into nothingness. With all his senses he searched, straining his ears for even the faintest of sounds; seeking for the tiniest sliver of light. Far into the night, long after the effects of the drink had worn off, still he tried. Finally, realizing the futility of his efforts, he slumped dejectedly onto his sleeping robe. Frustration and failure clear to read on his deeply troubled face.

Why? Why have the spirits forsaken The People? Have I angered the Spirits? Has Wolf forsaken me? He wondered. *Or was it something The People did? Did we break some great taboo? Forget to give honor to the animals for their life-giving bodies? Why doesn't it rain?* He sighed miserably, wrapped in his sleeping robe, and stared intently at the ancient spirit hide, many questions running through his mind, but no answers. The tattered wolf skin kept its secrets. *They must be reunited!* Was the only answer he had been able to receive from it in many seasons. Who or what must be reunited? He had not a clue!

*   *   *

"We should go on up into the mountains," Blue Coyote stood skipping stones across the mirror-like surface of the beaver pond. There had been no ducks. The youths had hunkered for hands of time, in the dense brush at the far end of the pond, legs cramped, bolas poised, hoping . . . "I just can't go back empty-handed again. I have to find something!"

"We didn't go back empty-handed," protested Stone Man, "We had juniper berries, pine cones and some acorns, enough to feed at least one person."

"But there are two of us," Blue Coyote pointed out. "If we can't at least contribute food enough to justify our presence in the camp, we should have the goodness to leave it rather than be a burden on others. We are strong, young, and healthy."

"We can't provide what is not out there," reminded Stone Man with frustration. "We have done no worse than any of the other hunters."

"Father's group came in with two javalina and a rabbit yesterday; you and I a handful of pine cones," concluded Blue Coyote.

"Fine, then let's go net some grouse or dart a turkey, or maybe one of your ghost beasts!" Stone Man stalked off toward the mountain trail. "Are you coming?" He shouted over his shoulder, "Or are you all talk?"

"I'm coming!" Blue Coyote cast one more pebble then followed his friend up the trail.

"Wait! I think there is something behind that brush," Stone Man stopped, "Look, do you see that crack?" He pointed, "Let's see where it leads," Stone Man halted Blue Coyote's rapid passage forward.

They pushed into the brush and discovered a narrow opening which led into a narrow canyon. "I have never been here before," Blue Coyote exclaimed, "Look! There is a whole patch of Nettle-leafed Horsemint![8] And look at all that Thistle![9]"

"I see mustard as well!" exclaimed Stone Man. "I do not think anyone has been in this place before, or if so it was a long time ago! Come on! Let's explore! It is still early. We can gather those plants on the way back. If this canyon has not been found by others, it will be an important food source for the camp."

A double hand of time found them far up the brushy, narrow canyon. From just beyond where they crouched, they heard turkeys[10] calling to each other as the birds browsed on the scattered dried berries within the dense brush. The brush was so thick the youths could not even see the birds, and in a few breaths, they knew the prey would have disappeared and they'd not find them again. Already the distinctive clucking was growing faint. Stone Man gripped Blue Coyote's arm and pointed. The flock was starting up the canyon wall, moving now onto the more open face of rock. Stone Man slowly rose and with a mere flicker of movement cast a dart. A turkey tumbled silently down. Blue Coyote cast his dart and another bird fell. In short order nearly two hands of turkeys had been darted. Then they saw and heard no more. If there were more individuals in the flock, they had melted quickly into the brush to avoid detection.

"Come on! Let's find those birds," Stone man rose and began pushing his way to where they had hoped the birds would be. "Here is one," he called, only his backside visible as he tunneled through the brush and rocks.

"I hear one thrashing over here," Blue Coyote began working into the brush as well, "And here is another."

"Yips!" Stone Man leaped back, grabbed a rock and cast it. "Add a rattlesnake[11] to our take!" He shouted. "By the saints, there are more of them! Come here and help me, we don't want them to get away!" Blue Coyote vaulted through the brush, his turkeys flopping in a grotesque caricature of life. Soon they had added nearly a hand of large timber rattlesnakes to their larder. A movement to the left brought them quickly around and they simultaneously cast darts at a coyote in the process of stealing the last turkey darted by Stone Man. Both joined the now growing pile.

"I can see where it was, but I can't figure out where it landed!" Blue Coyote was scrambling over the canyon-side unable to locate the last turkey he had darted. "I know I got it! I'm going to climb up on the rock. Maybe I can work down from there."

"Try a little to your left," Stone Man directed, "Now a little farther."

"Yes! I can see it! Thanks!" Blue Coyote scrambled down and retrieved the bird.

"This is more food than the camp has had in over a moon!" Blue Coyote stood admiring their kill as he picked twigs from his hair and secured it once more with his headband. "We will have to return to this place again tomorrow, I just know there are more snakes here."

"It is still early so they are sluggish, a good thing for us. If it were warmer, we would be in trouble of getting bitten."

"Yes, but what a great place to hunt them." Blue Coyote began gathering up their turkeys and snakes, carefully removing the heads of the latter with a sharp blade before thonging them together with the turkeys and hoisting the load onto his back.

Stone Man carried the coyote and his own turkeys and snakes. Both now lugged a sizable load. Without the ability to transport the tubers and plants, they decided to leave them for another day. As they worked their way back to the camp, their deadly aim with stones added a span of small birds, and a rabbit. As was the custom of The People they were careful to thank the spirits of the animals for giving themselves as food for the camp. Blue Coyote was in jubilant spirits and the youths marched proudly into camp beneath their impressive loads.

"We are going back to that canyon tomorrow," Blue Coyote informed Star Woman as they nibbled seed cakes that evening. The turkeys would be added to their meager store of dried food, hopefully bringing it to a level where they did not have to worry if a day went by without food coming in.

"I will come with you and help," Star Woman replied. "There are probably many plants in that canyon you did not even notice. You say it is one you have never been in before? How can that be? I do not recognize it from your description either."

"We almost missed it, nearly walked right by. There is only a very narrow opening, almost entirely hidden by brush. Stone Man found it actually. He has a feel about things like that."

"Well, if it is a place not harvested, or at least not recently, there could be an important source of food there," Star Woman smiled at her son. "I am very proud of both of you!"

The other men of the unmated men's hearth where he had lived since the death of both parents the previous season, questioned Stone Man with equal interest.

*   *   *

The next morning the youths led a sizable band to their canyon. There was almost a festive air as people slipped through the narrow opening and into the canyon.

"Look over there!" Butterfly exclaimed. "I see trees upon trees full of cones! Basket, you start gathering them, girl," she called to her granddaughter.

"There are tubers here as well!¹²" Star Woman shouted. It was the beginning of a wonderful day of discovery. They returned to camp with fully laden baskets of tubers, pine cones, numerous small birds and rodents, two more turkeys, a fox, and a double span of large fat rattlesnakes. Day after day the camp returned to the little canyon.

But soon the secret canyon yielded no more. It had been stripped as well. The larders of the Yucca camp however, where considerably fuller.

"I am going to dig another storage pit over here at the back of the shelter," Star Woman stated. "Hand me that deer scapula would you," she took the tool from Fire Dancer. "I have just about enough stones to line it completely." A pile of dirt began to form in the middle of the shelter on a deer hide placed there for that purpose. As it filled, Fire Dancer dragged the hide outside and dumped the dirt. "There, that should be deep enough!" Star Woman stated several loads later. "Now I will line it with these stones and place the baskets of dried meat inside. Tomorrow I will fill in the old storage pit."

"Why not use it to store those skins and basket materials stacked against the shelter side? It would give us more room."

"An excellent idea and a lot less work as well." Star Woman nodded pleased with the suggestion.

*   *   *

"We are going out into the moving duns looking for lizards," Star Woman remarked to the men as she prepared to leave. "Yesterday we had good success," she stuffed a number of pebbles into her apron pocket, gathered up a cord bag and her bolas, attaching them to her waist thong as she went.

"Be sure to take enough water," cautioned Fire Dancer. "Remember there was a time that all of you thought someone else had the water skin and no one did."

"I will be sure that Antelope Woman remembers. It is her responsibility today." Star Woman assured him. "Where are the hunters going today?"

"Red Eagle claims he saw bear tracks yesterday up in the high country. As soon as he and Gray Wolf return from checking the snares we are leaving to find it."

"Maybe it is a sow and has cubs!" She looked hopefully at her mate; "We could use more meat. It seems hardly possible that all of the food from Stone Man's secret canyon is gone already."

"Well if we do not return tonight, don't worry. It could take several days to track the bear, if there is one." Fire Dancer sighed, "We seem to go farther and farther and find less and less."

"It is the rain," assured Star Woman, "Without rain the plants do not grow, without plants to eat the animals go elsewhere, and without either The People starve. We met a group of women from the Rabbit Camp yesterday. They have lost nearly a span of people so far this winter to starvation."

"It is the same with all of the camps," Fire Dancer replied.

"Where have Blue Coyote and Stone Man gone today?"

"Stone Man remembers a stand of yucca way over by Black Land. They have gone to dig for roots, and to bring back some obsidian.[13] We are getting low on that as well."

Just then Red Eagle and Gray Wolf loped into camp, and the hunters departed for the high country in one direction as the women headed for the moving dunes to the east.

*   *   *

A good span of distance to the west, Blue Coyote and Stone Man were moving rapidly toward the base of Black Land. They carried digging sticks as well as their usual assemblage of hunting tools. Since the weather was warm the youths were dressed only in breechclouts and moccasins. Over their shoulder's they carried a pack containing their tunics, pants, travois poles and water stomachs. "Where should we check for obsidian?" Blue Coyote asked, "The material at the east base is getting well picked over. I had trouble finding anything worth saving the last time I was there."

"I thought we would try the area around the bubble. That is usually a very good place, at least I have always found enough there."

"Fine, now how much farther to these yuccas? How do you know of them and I do not, we never go anywhere apart?"

"Saw them last fall when I traveled with my father to the Squirrel Camp. They are almost out of sight in the white sand. But it is not an area much frequented by anyone. I thought there is a good chance no one else has remembered them. We need obsidian, so I thought now was as good a time as any to check. It is too far to go just on the off-chance, but since we are headed in that general direction any way, it is worth checking," Stone Man replied.

At mid day they were well out into the white sand. "Look! Over there, do you think that could be them?" They had been searching for several hands of time, "Looks like something any way," Blue Coyote bounded off toward the distant dot.

Stone Man followed, frowning. He had been certain where the yuccas were growing, but once they reached the spot, now he wasn't so sure anymore. Blue Coyote hollered for him to come and the far dot began to assume the outline of a stand of tall yuccas.[14]

"Let's cut the stalk first and then sheer the leaves before we dig the root," suggested Stone Man as they stood surveying the plants.

"All right, I will boost you onto my shoulder so that you can reach the stem more easily," Blue Coyote replied.

"Closer, please," Stone Man stood balancing atop Coyote's shoulders as he attempted to reach the base of the arm long growth of the new flower stalk. "Ouch! Not that close!" he complained as a sharp tipped leaf stuck him in the belly. "There I have it," he vaulted easily to the ground, the stalk clutched in his fist. "This will make a nice meal for several people," he laid the stalk carefully beside their extra equipment. "Maybe we should strip the leaves first on the next one," he wiped dripping blood from his belly, "Those daggers are sharp."

"All right; do you want to strip leaves next then?"

"Sure, why not? We can get them cut and bundled, then cut the rest of the stalks."

"Do you think we should take all of the plants today?" Blue Coyote frowned.

"Too many for one trip," Stone Man replied, "Besides, they were here this long, it's hardly likely anyone else will find them. I would like to wait a bit on those," he nodded to a group on the outer edge of the stand. "A shame not to let the fruit stalks grow a bit bigger before cutting them. There is not much food there now. In another hand of days, they will be as big as these," he nodded toward the pile they had already cut.

"Agreed, but on the other hand, this was a long way to come. Is it worth it to make two trips?"

They were expertly slicing the leaves from the selected plant and stacking them to be tied into bundles that could be slung over their backs and carried back to the camp. "There! That is this one. I will get started digging the root while you finish yours," Stone Man laid the last of his leaves beside the rest and reached for his digging stick.[15]

Made of stout mesquite with a fire-hardened tip it would quickly loosen the soil around the base of a plant. His powerful shoulders and strong arms made short work of loosening the sandy alkaline soil from around the base of the plant. A deer scapula made pulling the dirt away easier than just bare hands. After a short while he had excavated the area around the base of the plant for nearly an arm's length of depth. He widened and then deepened his hole until it was waist-deep. Then with the sharp obsidian chopper he had brought along for this purpose, Stone Man began chopping through the tough fibrous root. He toppled the plant, then dug still deeper, cutting a further length of the root, and then he filled in the hole. He chopped through the base of the plant and added that section of root to their rapidly growing stock of stuff.

Blue Coyote was not long in catching up with his plant. The youths dug, chopped and stacked until dark, snacking on beetles and other insects they had rousted from the plants as they worked. With the settling of the sun they stretched out on the warm sand and watched the ancestor fires emerge in the darkening sky. Each had a drink from their water skin and a strip of dried meat. This is all the food they had eaten all day, for they were saving the fruit stalks and roots to share with the camp.

"What do you think is out there?" Blue Coyote motioned toward the east, "Beyond the mountains."

Stone Man frowned in the dark, "Moving sand," he replied.

"I mean, beyond the moving sand!"

"I don't know! I have never been beyond the moving sand, don't know anyone who has. Why?"

"I don't know, I just wonder . . ." Blue Coyote shifted, "Sometimes I think I can hear thunder out there, very far away. Sometimes I think I can even detect lightning. It has been so long since it has rained here."

"It's impossible to cross the moving sand. Everyone says so. There have been men who tried, but always they are forced to turn back. Besides, what difference does it make? The land beyond the sand dunes is probably no different from this."

"But how can you be sure? What if . . ."

"Go to sleep Blue Coyote, it has been a long day, tomorrow will be another, and I am tired if you are not." Stone Man Rolled onto his side and promptly fell asleep.

Blue Coyote lay with his hands clasped behind his head and studied the night sky for a long time, thinking . . .

"There, that is the last bundle," Stone Man secured the yucca leaves onto the travois they had brought along to drag home behind them. The stand of yuccas was half depleted but the youths had a substantial sled full of food and material to haul back to the camp.

"We should be at the bubble before sundown," Blue Coyote remarked as he settled the rawhide harness over his shoulder and they started north toward Black Land. "We can stash this load under brush by the mouth of the first draw and pick it up on our way back"

A lizard shot across the blowout in front of them, quickly Stone Man cast a rounded pebble, the lizard leaped into the air, landed on its back, legs kicking spastically a couple of times. Stone Man never broke stride as he scooped the lizard up and stuffed it into his waist pouch along with several more; all of which they would roast for their evening meal. Blue Coyote had a similar stash.

"That should conceal it well enough!" Stone Man stood back and surveyed their camouflaged stash. "We have made good time; I think probably there will be enough light to get all the obsidian we want before dark." He led the way toward the mouth of another arroyo, the one within which the lava bubble was located. This area was hard walking, so they were forced to slow their pace. Sharp edged chunks of lava and broken bits of obsidian discarded over the decades by stone gatherers littered the ground. Scrubby sage and a few scraggly junipers dotted an otherwise rather barren landscape. Suddenly Stone Man crouched quickly behind a bush and automatically Blue Coyote followed suit.

Slowly Stone Man reached and withdrew a dart, and smoothly, silently, fitted it into his atlatl. Blue Coyote followed suit, although he had not seen whatever it was Stone Man had spotted. Now, however he heard it. Barely perceptible, twigs breaking as something moved carefully just beyond where they crouched. When Stone Man rose and cast his dart, Blue Coyote prepared to follow. It was not necessary. In the path, a hand's distance from them laid a mule deer buck, kicking his last.

Stone Man grinned at his friend and gave a whoop of pleasure; "We will feast tonight, my friend!" Blue Coyote dug out a tortoise shell bowl from his pouch and handed it to Stone Man. He carefully severed the neck artery and caught the escaping blood in the shell, then filled his own as well. These were set heedfully aside so as not to spill. Then Stone Man opened the body cavity and they scooped the innards out onto a piece of hide. Already they were wiping blood from their obsidian knives to begin butchering the deer. Stone Man cut the hide along the belly from breastbone to stern, carefully peeling it back away from the meat. Blue Coyote was slitting the hide down each leg and pulling it back and away from the meat as well. They severed the anal opening and the tail was cut through and left with the hide. Then they split the hide up the throat and around the head. Very soon the deer lay naked upon its own hide. The innards were circumspectly separated; the intestine carried a short distance away, the contents emptied, and the casing turned inside out in the process. Then the legs were chopped off above the scent gland and set aside. The head was cut free, the tongue and brain removed, and the eyeballs quickly eaten.

It was getting dark, but Blue Coyote had a small fire started already and had gathered a goodly supply of brush and some rocks to support the tortoise shells. He found two forked sticks stout enough to support a spit, and another to serve as the spit. By then Stone Man had handed him the heart, tongue and liver of the animal. Quickly he ran the spit through them and very soon the wonderful smell of roasting venison was cleaving the air. Blue Coyote divided the brains into equal shares and added them to the now bubbling blood. He added a few bits of dry sage leaf as well. By the time the food was ready the youths had quartered the deer and set it out atop nearby brush to cool.

"That was the best meal I have eaten since I can't remember when!" Blue Coyote sighed as he set aside his empty bowl. "The heart and tongue will certainly make excellent trail food for our trip home."

"Absolutely," Stone Man agreed, "But we are going to have to hurry with the obsidian and push hard to get back to camp before the meat spoils, or we will be here for several more days processing it."

"I think we should look around a bit more tomorrow," Blue Coyote disagreed. "There could be more deer here. Maybe we could bring down another one or so."

Stone Man shook his head, "No, we had better get back to the camp. We will be returning to this area again in a few days, we can check for tracks then. It is better not to take a chance on spoiling what food we have. The yucca stalks would not keep."

"You are right, as always," Blue Coyote agreed. "I get so anxious sometimes . . ."

They were up even before the sun began to lighten the eastern sky. Luckily it took them very little time to locate enough obsidian to tide the camp over until their return in a hand of days. It was imperative that they get the venison and the plant stalks back to the camp before this precious food supply spoiled. They pushed hard and dragged their load into the camp by mid day.

They distributed their deer and yucca roots, stalks, and leaves, contributing the greater part to the communal camp stores. The stalks would have to be cooked and eaten immediately, the roots would keep for several moons before spoiling, and the leaves would be pounded and separated into fibers by the women of the camp, then stored to be used as needed. They lay about the camp for the rest of the day, resting and preparing for another trip. The obsidian was turned over to the knapper for tool making. A hand of days later they again set off toward the Black Land area.

"I think these prints are only a day old at the most!" Blue Coyote knelt studying the tracks in the sand before him. "See here. The edge is still sharp. There was a wind night before last, if they were that old the edged would be filled in with sand."

"Which means, there is at least one more deer in these lava beds," replied Stone Man. "I think we should follow the other side of the arroyo and see if we can pick up any other game signs."

"You go there, I want to go down this way, I think perhaps there is a water source somewhere over there," he pointed toward the far side of the lava bubble. "If so, not only can we refill our skins without traveling a long distance, but it will be a place for the deer to drink, and a place for us to wait for them."

"So far we have only found the tracks of one more deer," Stone Man reminded him, "But if you are right, it would explain why there are deer at all in this desolate spot. There is certainly no food for them."

"Not that we have found, at any rate. I will see you later. If I am not back here when you return, look for me down there." Blue Coyote trotted off down a dusty trail. Stone Man turned and went the other way, following his own idea.

Stone Man moved quickly up the trail, nearly a shadow as he silently slipped along the path, careful not to disturb any vegetation, nor step on twigs or dry leaves. The hoof prints were clear. He merely need follow them. So he did, to the head of the arroyo, up a trail and onto the brush-covered hillside. He signed and retraced to the point where the friends had separated. Blue Coyote was nowhere to be seen. Stone Man shrugged and loped off along his friend's trail. The farther he went, the more certain he was that Blue Coyote was right.

"Over here!" a faint whisper halted him in mid-stride. Quietly he melted into the brush beside Blue Coyote. "Look!" His friend whispered and pointed.

Stone Man carefully parted the brush and peered through. Ahead, completely sheltered by another lava bubble a minute spring bubbled to the surface, only to sink once again into the sandy soil, mere hands away. Around it however, grew the lushest group of plants either youth could remember ever seeing. Stone Man identified goldenrod, burdock and horsetail, as well as fiddlehead fern fronds[16] even from where he squatted. Lying in the shade, he picked out a whole family of javalina. It was evident that deer also frequented this watering place.

"What do you think we should do?" He whispered to Blue Coyote, "We cannot bring them all down. It would be a shame to lose so much meat for the camp."

"They are not going anywhere," Blue Coyote whispered back, "I think it would be best if we got our obsidian away from this spot, collected the yucca we came for and returned to the camp and brought back more hunters."

Stone Man frowned, "They would kill them all, and the deer as well."

"So, isn't that the idea; provide meat for the camp?"

"Right at present the camp has enough food," Stone Man replied. "I think we should keep this place to our selves and wait. The javalina will grow, if there are any fawns, they will only get bigger, as well; therefore provide more food when the camp really needs it. I saw what happened to our canyon, Blue Coyote. The camp stripped it in just a hand of days. If you and I had kept that a secret, we could have provided food for the entire camp all spring and well into the summer. Now there remains nothing to grow and mature."

"But the camp has the food!"

"Does it? I would guess that most of it has already been eaten," replied Stone Man, "And there remains not a single root, or rodent to produce more food. The People kill everything, leaving nothing for future seasons. This is part of the reason there is no more food in these starving mountains."

"You mean we should wait until the camp is out of food and then return here and take only what is necessary to keep them fed?"

"If we snare and dart all of the javalina and deer . . ." Stone Man started.

"More would take their place Stone Man, there is a dependable supply of water there; all along these animals knew it. Others must as well. They will come here also, and more after them and more yet after them!"

"Not if The People dig and gather every edible plant there, and you know they would! There are other places for animals to water; they come here because there is food as well. Take away the food and there is no reason for them to come all the way to this place."

Blue Coyote thought about his words, not agreeing, but not disagreeing either. "We might as well go get the yucca then, or do you wish to leave it for others to discover and harvest?"

"I would leave some of it," Stone Man replied as they eased away and quietly left the secluded glen.

So the two friends made a pact, they waited until the camp needed food, and then they slipped off and returned to the secret spot in Black Land. They snared only a pair of yearling javalina, leaving the sow and the rest for later. All through the summer they brought in small supplies of plants from the glen, leaving the immature to grow. They left some of the yuccas as well. The only deer taken was another young buck. The doe, faun and mature buck they left to live in the canyon until they were needed.

*   *   *

As fall approached, Fire Dancer and his group brought in a bear from far to the north, the women netted birds and brought down small rodents and lizards with rocks. A trek was made into the pinyon canyons to gather nuts. Pinecones were collected from the high mountain trees. Juniper berries and various shrubby plants added to their diet.

Early winter brought a blizzard. The camp was held captive for a hand of days as it spent its fury. Two old people froze to death. At the depth of winter, the youths brought in yet another pair of javalina, full grown now, providing much more food than they would have in early summer. Still, they kept the little glen secret.

Late winter brought about the starving period however; Red Eagle secretly followed them and discovered the water hole. He returned to camp undetected, and a few days later claimed the discovery. He led the hunters back and they killed every last one of the javalina, the doe, faun and last remaining buck. They plundered the little glen as well, leaving no living thing behind. Animals quit watering there; soon the spring dried up and was but a memory.

Acorn prayed to his guardian spirit. *They must be reunited!* No other answer came.

---

1.   Javalina: also called peccary. Javalina are a small native North American animal similar physically but not related to the wild pig.

2. A span is equal to ten. A hand is equal to five. In time measurement a finger equals 12 minutes, a hand of time equals an hour. In distance a finger equals the distance one can walk in twelve minutes. A hand equals the distance one can walk in an hour.

3. Natives Americans frequently covered their bodies with the fresh manure of the animals they were hunting to camouflage the human scent.

4. Rabbit stick: a wooden hunting tool used virtually identically in use to the Australian Aborigine's boomerang, although shaped differently.

5. Of all of the plants in North America, the cattail was one of the most widely used. Its characteristic long narrow leaves (up to 9 ft tall) were widely used to weave baskets; their fibers were broken down and used to produce rope and cordage as well. The young shoots are tender and edible, tasting much like bamboo. The young flower heads are excellent when roasted like corn-on-the-cob. The pollen was gathered and ground into flour. The tuberous roots were often roasted or eaten raw. All are an excellent source of nutrition. **Tilford** 1997: 28-29.

6. *Datura wrightii:* Southwestern Thorn Apple; extracts from this plant are narcotic, when improperly used lethal. **MacMahon** 1988: 385.

7. The Capitan Mountains of central New Mexico, in the general area of Capitan New Mexico.

8. *Agastache urticifolia;* The leaves make an enjoyable tea when brewed weakly. **Tilford** 1997: 102.

9. *Carduus species:* All species of Thistle are edible in parts. The stems and leaves provide a vegetable, and the flower heads are used to make tea. **Tilford** 1997: 144.

10. American Wild Turkey.

11. Diamondback rattlesnake

12. There were a number of plants utilized by the Native Americans including *Xerophyllum tenax,* Beargrass; *Polygonum bistortoides,* Bistort; Camassia *quamash.* Blue Camas to name only a few. **Tilford**, throughout.

13. Obsidian. Volcanic glass. Makes very fine tools with sharp edges.

14. *Yucca Torreyi:* Yucca: Native Americans ate the pulpy fruits of this and other related species. They also ate the root. The various parts of the plant were eaten raw or roasted. They also dried and ground them into meal for winter use. The coarse fibers of the long leaves were made into ropes, mats, sandals, baskets and cloth. **MacMahon** 1988: 493.

15. A digging stick was made from a stout straight branch, sharpened at one end.

16. All edible food plants.

CHAPTER 2

And the Mother of The People walked with these magical beasts,"
Pinyon made sweeping motions with his hands, demonstrating the height
of the animals. "They were special beasts; totem of the camps; and the
Mother of The People shared in their magic. She was the only one who
could claim the great beasts as her special 'spirit animal'[1]. She led The
People through times of great tribulation, away from a land filled with
blood, murder, and hate, into a new way of life. The Ancestors were fearless
hunters. In those times The People lived far to the east of here." The old
Storyteller enraptured the children with his tale once again, as he had on
countless other occasions; bringing the ancient past alive for the children of
The People. This small collection of families were existing on the very edge
of starvation; surviving on roots, nuts and grains they could harvest among
the drought-ravaged hills and open moving sand dunes of their home.

The firelight flickered over the figure of the old storyteller, and those
of his audience. There were only a few children now, where once the camp
could have boasted a Span of hands or more. They were pathetic figures,
all. The old man was gaunt, starvation aging him far beyond his actual
seasons. The children all showed classic signs of starvation. Yet no one
complained. This was their way of life here in the Starving Mountains; it
was the only life any of them knew. This last winter had been severe and
more of their number than anyone cared to think about had gone to walk
the wind. These few were the strong. They were the survivors.

"And she brought them to a place where they lived in safety. A land
of plenty . . ."

*   *   *

"What's wrong now?" Stone Man demanded. "You haven't heard a word I said!" The youth followed close behind Blue Coyote, as they hurried along a dry wash following the tracks of a desert javalina.

"Nothing's wrong," muttered Blue Coyote. "I was just thinking!"

"About what?"

"I was thinking about the Storyteller, if you must know."

"Old Pinyon; whatever for?" Stone Man stopped and stared at Blue Coyote.

"Not Pinyon, his story!"

"His story?" Stone Man gave his friend a dumbfounded look.

"All of our lives we have heard these tales about our ancestors," Blue Coyote explained. "How they were great hunters of fearsome beasts; how great magical monsters walked the land, and there was plenty of food for everyone. The People numbered in spans of hands. More than anyone could count. They lived in a land where food was plentiful, where men were actually hunters, not collectors of tubers," he swept his hand before him. "Look at us! What are we? What chance do you and I ever have of hunting any kind of game larger than a deer? Don't you ever get tired of this life? What excitement do we ever have? Wrestling the vicious Pinyon nut to the ground? What do we have to look forward to but more of the same? Have you ever seen a magical beast; or a large animal of any kind for that matter? What do we ever do, except hunt the occasional deer or rabbit, and gather plants like old women? Don't you ever yearn for something better?" Frustration etched his youthful handsome face as the gentle breeze lifted his long brown hair to caress a smooth cheek. He automatically brushed the hair back as he engaged his companion's eyes.

"What else is there?" Stone Man shrugged, at a loss to find an answer that would satisfy the other youth. "This is real life Blue Coyote," he copied his friend's hand movements. "The tales of Old Pinyon are just that, stories to entertain the children when they must go to bed with empty stomachs. He makes them up man, that's his task! We have heard those very selfsame stories, all of our lives."

"But what if they are true?" Blue Coyote leaned closer, "What if he doesn't make them up? What if there is a land east of these miserable starving mountains and moving sand dunes[2], a place teaming with animals, just waiting to be hunted? What if there really is a place where The People could grow fat and powerful again; where women still have children that don't die before their first year. What if we could go there?"

"What if we just find this javalina we are hunting? It is far more likely to fill our stomachs than dreams and 'spirit' animals." Stone Man replied, shaking his head, "You spend too much time thinking!"

"And you spend none at all!"

Stone Man shrugged, "Thinking is a waste of time."

"Don't you ever wonder...?" Blue Coyote seated himself on a large boulder. He proceeded to dig small holes in the dry dust at the bottom of the draw with the toe of his moccasin. His long brown hair hung down on either side of his concerned face, the breeze lifted it and cast shadows enhancing his concern.

Stone Man squatted beside him, "I used to," he admitted. "I lay awake at night, dreaming these very same dreams, but that is all they are, dreams! There was a time that I imagined leaving here myself, traveling heroically through the moving sands and returning to tell great tales of a wonderful land. Then my Father and Mother died, and I went to live at the unmated men's hearth. I have not had time for such dreams since. But I am sure every man of the people has had them at one time or another. Everyone yearns to do something splendid." He struck the boulder with his hand, "But this is life, it's the only one we have to live. We wake up in the morning, start out before the sunrises and hunt or gather all day. We eat only enough to keep going, and by night I am so tired I fall into my sleeping furs and no longer dream. There is so much to do. It takes all our time just to provide enough food for the families and ourselves. I try not to think on things that just yield dissatisfaction. Life is hard enough without yearning after dreams and chasing visions. If there is a better place far to the east of here, we will never get there. We have too many responsibilities here. You and I are numbered among the only fit men from this camp. There are not enough as it is capable of hunting for meat. If we ran off chasing ghosts, who would feed those we leave behind?"

"But if we found a better place?"

"And if we did not, what then? How would we justify the starvation we left behind because of our selfishness?" Stone Man asked.

"What do we do now, except share in that starvation?"

"Things will get better, once it rains . . ."

"Once it rains!" Blue Coyote snorted, "I'm not talking about some hoped-for expectation, some miracle that never happens, sometime in the future. What do The People have to look forward to NOW?" Blue Coyote jumped to his feet, "What do The People have to look forward to HERE?" He gave a sweeping hand gesture, "Just another season of failing plants and fewer and fewer animals to provide what little meat we do get. Wait for it to rain? The people are starving to death! Even the rabbits are harder and harder to find. This place is dying! Are we just going to sit here and wait to die with it?"

"You are right about one thing. Everyone is starving. The People could never make so long a journey," Stone Man stated, "Have you looked at them lately? Even supposing they would follow you, would you lead them to a sure death?"

"I don't know the answers," Blue Coyote admitted, "I don't even know most of the questions, but I have thought about it, constantly, and I have made up my mind, I am going!" Blue Coyote rose, "You are welcome to join me, I would prefer that, but regardless, I am going, almost immediately in fact, while spring is just starting. If I find a better place, then I will come back and lead the people there, because someone must do something! If we just ignore the situation, we are all going to starve!" He stabbed his digging stick into the ground. "If I do not find a better place, I will be dead, and it will no longer be a concern to me."

"The elders will never allow it," Stone Man replied.

"I don't plan to ask them," Blue Coyote admitted, "I'm just going!"

Stone Man broke a twig from a nearby tree and chewed thoughtfully on it. "You would do that? Just up and vanish, without a word to anyone?"

"If I have to! If I don't do something soon, I will just explode!" Blue Coyote ground out. "You know how it is; day after day the same meaningless round of just barely staving off starvation. We are not men! We are no better than old women! Look at us? Soon we will be as old and dried out as Butterfly."

Stone Man continued to nibble.

"We could do it Stone Man, I know we could!" Blue Coyote wheedled, "If we left now, just the two of us, traveling fast we could probably be at this grassland in just a hand of days. If it proves to be as dry and desolate as this place, at least we would have gone, at least we would have tried! We would have done something, we would know for sure, not be forever wondering . . ." Blue Coyote slumped back onto the boulder.

"You have a point. I have always wondered . . ."

"Then you will do it?" Blue Coyote leaped to his feet. "Come on, let's get this javalina and get back to the camp. We leave at dawn! No time to lose!"

Stone Man trailed Blue Coyote's rapidly disappearing form down the brush-filled arroyo as his friend followed the track of the javalina. He frowned, not exactly understanding how he had agreed to do this foolish thing. The elders would be really angry with them.

*   *   *

"What are you doing with my spare water stomach?" Star Woman demanded of her son.

"Stone Man and I are going on an extended hunting trip," Blue Coyote lied, tossing the water skin onto the pile of things he had been accumulating on his sleeping fur.

"No, you are not! You are needed here. The animals in the mountains are not fit to eat at this time of the year any way, you know that!"

"We aren't going to the mountains," Blue Coyote grudgingly admitted, "We are going east of here."

"Whatever for? There is nothing east of here but the moving sand dunes. You know that! Nothing lives there. There is no water."

"We are going beyond the moving sand dunes . . ."

"Fire Dancer! You come here and talk to your son," Star Woman shouted to her mate. "He is up to some foolish nonsense about going beyond the moving sand dunes to hunt."

Fire Dancer lay down the net he was repairing and hurried to their shelter where Star Woman confronted their only son. "What is this that your mother tells me?" He questioned Blue Coyote.

"It is nothing for Mother to make so much of," Blue Coyote replied. "Stone Man and I are just going out for a few days . . ."

Fire Dancer looked closely at his son's stubbornly determined features and sighed. "I understand Son. I have been expecting something like this.

I did it, as did your grandfather before me. We both set out to find the legendary grassland. But we failed. I walked for a span of days, dangerously far into the moving sand dunes, but all I found were more sand dunes. I nearly died of thirst before I got back. Others have tried as well, some of them, like Nighthawk, my best friend, were not so fortunate. He never returned."

"Perhaps he found the way across and just kept going!"

Fire Dancer shook his head; "He would not have done such a thing. No, he was always dreaming of a better land, a better way of life for The People. The legends fired his imagination." Fire Dancer sighed, "He went with too few supplies and not enough water. His bones are probably lying out there somewhere . . ."

"That is why I am taking all the water stomachs I can carry," Blue Coyote stated. "We are going prepared. We will travel fast; you know how fast we can go. There is a better place out there and I mean to find it, even if I have to walk for a whole moon in the sand. Father, we have all heard the distant thunder; there has been rain out there somewhere, I intend to find where Father, if not we are all going to die in this place! Every season there is less to eat. I can't remember when it rained last."

Fire Dancer thought seriously for a finger of time; frowning, he shook his head. "Two men, heavily weighted down with extra water would not travel fast, son. You would only invite disaster. You had best take the dogs and travois to carry enough supplies for at least a pair of moons or more."

"What!" Star Woman Screeched, "You surely do not mean to encourage this madness?"

"But; we cannot take the dogs!" Blue Coyote protested, ignoring his mother. "What would the families use?"

"We will get along without dogs for a moon or so," Fire Dancer assured him. "But if there is a chance, any chance, that you are right, that there is a better land beyond the sand dunes; it is important to all of us that you find it. You are right about one thing; you and Stone Man are the fittest ones, if anyone could do it, you can. I will speak to the elders."

"They will never give their consent!" Blue Coyote slumped onto his sleeping fur, amongst the clutter of his packing.

"I think they will," Fire Dancer disagreed. "We are all worried, Son. You are not the only one to correctly read the signs. The elders have talked time and again of sending someone east. Perhaps now is the time, and you are the ones."

"You really think they will stand behind us?"

"Is it not far better to take the chance of going out well prepared, with their blessing?"

"Yes, of course, I just never thought they would agree. It is a slim chance, after all, that the legends are based on fact. I have spoken to the storyteller. He assures me that they are. But even if they are not, there must be something out there! It is just that I, that is, Stone Man and I, are so desperate to do something . . ."

"The legends had to have come from somewhere," Fire Dancer replied. "I for one, think there is truth in them. I know that we have lived in these foothills since before my grandfather's time, but before that, the legends say The People were hunters of great beasts on vast grasslands far to the east. Perhaps it is time that someone, truly prepared, goes in search of that grassland. You are right about one thing; The People are dying in this place. When I was a child there was double the number that live today."

Fire Dancer turned to leave the shelter, "I am going to speak to the elders, right now."

True to his word, Fire Dancer called the council of elders and presented to them the project. All agreed. The People were desperate. All agreed that there was not enough food in the Starving Mountains to feed The People for another season. Not all agreed that Blue Coyote and Stone Man were the best choices, but the majority did, and Fire Dancer, as Headman, did not really need their permission any way, the final decision was his in the end.

*   *   *

At dawn, not the next day, but the one after that, Stone Man and Blue Coyote, accompanied by the last four remaining camp dogs, harnessed to heavily laden travois, waved a cheery good by to the silent people they left behind. The youths were high with excitement, even though they realized that they carried every spare morsel of food the camp could provide, as well as most of the water stomachs. The camp was dangerously low on both food and water now, and it was up to Blue Coyote and Stone Man to justify the faith of those left behind. They had to find the great grassland!

They moved rapidly the first hand of days, always toward the east through the moving sand dunes. They found that it was stifling hot traveling beneath the burning sun, even in earliest spring. Then the dogs began to break down. The heavily laden travois were just too much for them. Their health was just too poor.

* * *

"We have to stop for a few days to let the dogs rest." Stone Man rose from his inspection of a rapidly spreading open sore beneath the harness of the black bitch pulling the trailing travois. "This dog cannot go farther." Blue Coyote frowned, for the dog in question was Scorpion, his father's only dog.

"Then we will have to carry her share ourselves and let her range free, but stop, we cannot!" Blue Coyote stated, stubbornly. "The sun will burn us up either way. It is best to keep moving."

"I have a suggestion," Stone Man replied. "Let us rest this night and tomorrow and begin traveling again, only this time after dark. It would be cooler, and there is a nearly full moon. We could stretch our sleeping robes like a shelter using the travois poles and shelter out of the sun during the heat of the day. We would be drinking less water during the day and probably at night as well. The water would last longer."

Blue Coyote considered this suggestion for a full finger of time. "All right," he agreed. "We will rest tomorrow and start out again as the sun goes down. But we keep going well into the light hours. You are right about one thing. We can go both farther and faster traveling during the cool."

"And the dogs will benefit from the extra rest," Stone Man added.

A span of days later, the full moon had given way to the waining moon and the two men and four dogs were still traveling through the moving sand dunes. It had now been well over half a moon since they left the camp and still, the moving dunes extended before them as far as the eye could see. They had enough water to continue for perhaps a double span of days yet, but then they would be forced to turn back or choose to risk their lives going forward. Then half of their water would be nearly gone. Perhaps the moving sand dunes extended forever!

A double span of days later they sat arguing beneath the shade of their shelter. Their water supply was now half gone. The end of the moving sand was no where in sight. Stone Man stated stubbornly that it was time to turn back. Blue Coyote refused. "I am going forward. You go back if you so choose, but I am convinced that it cannot be much farther. You can hear thunder for a long way, but we have traveled a long way. It cannot be many hands farther to the end of the moving sand. I just know it!"

"And if you are wrong? What if we go on and run out of water? What then?"

Blue Coyote shrugged, "I guess we turn into an object lesson for the next crazy youth that decides to try crossing the moving sand. I don't intend to turn back Stone Man, so you only waste your time trying to convince me. What you choose to do, only you can decide, but I am going forward."

Stone Man sighed, "I didn't figure you would change your mind, but I had to try. If we don't make it, if we die in this spirit cursed place, at least I will know that I tried..."

"Stone Man! Look ahead! Do you see it?" Blue Coyote grabbed his friend's bare arm and pointed to the horizon.

Stone Man squinted into the morning sun, staring toward the east. "I think so," he agreed. "But it might just be our imagination. I can't believe I let you talk me into going forward, but if you are right and we have crossed the moving sand dunes, perhaps I will forgive you, provided we are still alive when we reach the end of this miserable land."

The small party of two men and four dogs were bone-weary, almost out of food and water well over a double moon after leaving the camp behind. At the far eastern horizon, just a dark finger of a rise in the land could be seen.

"Come on!" Blue Coyote strode forth with renewed vigor; "We can be there by nightfall!"

"No!" Stone Man refused. "I am tired, the dogs are tired, and by the spirits, man, you must be tired as well! If that is the end of these cursed sand dunes, we will be there soon enough."

Blue Coyote stopped his forward rush and sighed. "You are right as usual my friend. I get carried away sometimes. We will rest." He unloaded his pack onto the ground, which signal caused the dogs to drop to the ground where they stood, thankful to rest. Stone Man released the three dogs still pulling much-lightened loads. They shared their water with the animals and fed them sparingly, as they ate themselves. There was no game to hunt, had they had, or taken the time to do so. Everyone had lived the entire moon on their dwindling store of food and the few lizards Scorpion, the black bitch caught and brought back to share with them, frugally extending their supply as far as possible. They were also down to the last of the water skins. The two exhausted travelers settled down thankfully to sleep through the heat of the day.

"Come on Stone Man! Are you going to sleep all night?" Blue Coyote wakened his friend.

"Is it time already?" Stone Man yawned and shrugged the sleep from his body and stared toward the lowering sun.

"I have the dogs loaded already, and smell!"

Stone Man sniffed the air, "Rain?"

Blue Coyote nodded, "Thunder has been rumbling for the last finger of time. I am surprised it did not waken you."

"Nothing less than a direct lightning strike would waken me," Stone Man admitted. "I sleep like the dead when I am so tired."

Near dawn Scorpion hurried up to the men, wagging her tail and looking over her shoulder, toward the east.

"Something is out there!" Blue Coyote exclaimed, "Let's go see!"

He motioned the three hitched dogs to lie down and grabbing his atlatl and darts he fell in behind the black dog as she led the way over the nearest dune, Stone Man close on his heels. Just as the sun rose two dunes later she crouched to her belly as she approached the crest of a dune and wagged her tail. The two men crawled on their bellies to the top and cautiously looked over.

Below them in a blowout[3] a spring bubbled forth, creating a modest pond, a pond from which a small herd of antelope was drinking. Quickly the hunters rose and simultaneously cast their darts bringing down two of the startled animals. The remainder of the little herd disappeared in a flash of white rumps over the next dune, leaving their downed companions and two jubilant youths behind in the quiet blowout.

"I don't believe it!" Stone Man exclaimed. "Food! And water! We have to be the luckiest men alive!" He was already started back to where they had left the dogs and their temporary camp. "You begin dressing out the animals; I will get the dogs. With a little luck we will be on our way again in less than a hand of time." Overhead black clouds gathered, and thunder rumbled. The wind began to pick up, fresh and cool.

Already Blue Coyote was half way to the pond. He pulled the darts from the carcasses of the animals and dropping to one knee, he withdrew his stone knife and began dressing the nearest antelope. Silently he gave thanks to Spirit of Antelope for this food, before bending forward and quenching his thirst on warm rich blood draining from a carefully cut artery. Soon Stone Man joined him and drank his fill as well. They began butchering the carcass, and quickly completed their task, feeding the dogs the remainder of the blood and strips of fresh meat as they dressed the antelope. They filled all their water skins as well, for there was no telling where they would find water again.

They set up their camp right beside the pond; relaxing during the heat of the day.

"No need to keep both hides," Stone Man stated, regretfully preparing to cast away one of the hides.

"Wait!" Blue Coyote stopped him. "Do we dare chance insulting Antelope Spirit?" He shook his head, "Best take both hides."

Stone Man frowned, and then nodded, placing the hide on the travois along with the quartered animal. "You are right. We are so close to our purpose there is no need to conserve now, with fresh meat, full water skins and our goal in sight. Did you check for prints around the pond?"

Blue Coyote shook his head. "Didn't take the time," he admitted. "We should do so however, it will give us an idea of the animals living in this area. I wonder what antelope were doing so far out in the moving sand?"

"Perhaps they are not," Stone Man suggested. "Perhaps we are at the end of these dunes."

Blue Coyote was already pacing around the pond. "I think you must be right, Stone Man. There are deer, and javalina tracks as well."

"We had best be going, then."

Quickly they filed away from the pond over the next sand dune. It was the last dune. Suddenly they were descending into a brushy area traversed with game trails, and in the distance high piled black thunderheads all but concealed a rising escarpment. Lightning streaked from the underbellies of the clouds, thunder rumbled, and the breeze was cool and moist. The men grinned at one another and whooped in glee. They had done it! They had successfully crossed the moving sand dunes. Already they had found a better place for The People. Game trails abounded as far as the eye could see, mottled with a multitude of bird and small animal tracks. The trees were already green with new growth. Darkness descended quickly and they were forced to stop, but not before they had time to erect a makeshift shelter and gather a quantity of dry wood. Later they sat cross- legged before a small fire, fed steadily from the supply of wood, wonderful smells of fresh roasting antelope wafting from the spit. After eating their fill both men took great pleasure in stripping and literally dancing naked in the sudden downpour of rain beyond their shelter, washing the sweat and grime of over a pair of moons from their bodies.

The morning brought much cooler temperatures. They judged that it would take them until mid day to reach the escarpment.[4] They were correct. As they approached, they scanned the cliff. A tumble of boulders and debris littered its base. Here and there, well-worn paths led down from above. There were even more game trails here. Quickly they made camp, set up drying racks and cut the meat from the bones before it spoiled, spreading it out in thin strips to dry. Leaving the dogs, contentedly chewing on bones, to protect the camp from scavengers, the two men climbed the nearest trail to the land above.

It literally took their breath away. Before them spread a sweep of newly greening grass, as far as the eye could see, broken only here and there with dark green strips of vegetation. They set out to investigate the nearest one of these. It was a forest, an oak forest, but the strangest either had ever seen. It was also a bounty such as neither had ever seen. There was food enough here, in just this one kind of plant, to keep their camp in food for an entire season. And from the signs along the game trails, there was plenty of game as well. If this were indeed the grassland of legend, there would be vast herds of large animals to be hunted as well. Now however, they had time only to hunt a supply of meat for a return trip and figure how they were to bring The People across the vast area of moving sand dunes.

*   *   *

"We could kill enough deer and dry the meat, then carry it a hand of days out into the moving dunes, return and take the next load another hand of days beyond the first, then return for another and another. By taking each one farther, until we had traveled a double span of days into the dunes, the last load by then would take us well toward the camp. With that much food and water stored along the way, it is possible," Stone Man suggested.

They were sitting around a campfire that evening mapping out possible ways to bring the camp across the moving sand dunes. Blue Coyote munched on a chunk of deer meat, followed it with roasted Cattail bulbs and washed all down with fresh clear water. "That might work for most of the camp, but the old ones could never move at the pace we traveled at. It would take them at least twice as long." He sighed and stretched his legs out before him, "there must be another way!"

"If there is, I cannot think of it. It would be impossible to carry all the weak ones on travois," Stone Man tossed a stick onto the fire. "What good did it do us to come all this way, if we have no plan to bring the others?"

"Perhaps if we traveled north, maybe the moving sand ends in that direction and we could travel around it."

"Don't you think others, before us, have thought of that? If there were a way around the moving sand, someone would have done so long before now."

"All right, we will follow your plan. It is the only one we have, so we best get started on it. This plan will take at least another moon to complete, followed by at least part of another moon to return to the camp. Tomorrow we begin hunting deer in earnest. By the time we are ready to haul the first load the dogs will be well rested and in much better shape that when we began this journey. They will be able to carry heavier loads, and with both of us hauling travois as well, we should be able to store a lot of food, besides the return trip will be quicker and easier. We know where to go and need only carry enough food to return. By the time the next load is ready the dogs will again be rested."

"But we will not." Stone Man replied. "Can we do it? Do we have the stamina to complete such a task?"

"With a steady diet of good food and plenty of it, our strength should be much greater. Remember we were half starved when we left the camp. Already I feel stronger, and that is after only a couple of good meals. A hand of days with good food and I will have a great deal more strength." He nodded toward the meat dripping hot fat into the fire, from its place on the skewer, "See if you do not agree in a hand of days."

They discussed other strategies and finally rolled into their sleeping furs, and with a full stomach, success at hand, and visions of the future, they slept soundly.

Just before dawn the youths rose and quietly eased along a well-used trail headed north along the base of the caprock. They moved quickly, with the ease of seasoned hunters. A hand of time later they waited at the base of the escarpment where yet another spring bubbled from the ground, forming a large pond. The edge was an orderly mass of cattails, but animals had beaten a path from the other side to drink. The men hunkered down behind large boulders and waited. They had not yet had time to develop cramps in their legs before the first deer came like shadows to drink. They waited, poised; until just the right moment; then, in well-oiled precision they rose and cast their darts. A fat doe and her season-old offspring fell silently to the ground. Three other doe and their young leaped to safety and vanished into the brush. Blue Coyote grinned at Stone Man and they bounded toward the fallen animals, to drag the kill back to the camp before dressing them out.

They fed the contents of the intestine to the dogs, reversed and washed the tubes, setting them aside for later. They skinned the deer and pegged the hides out beside those of the two antelope to dry. There was no time to deal with the hides now, but when they brought the camp across, they would provide much-needed hides for new clothing and shoes.

"I will wade out and pull up the reeds and toss them to you on the bank," Stone Man was already easing barefooted into the pond.

"They will float, you know," reminded Blue Coyote. "I thought of digging some of those tubers and beginning a pile of those while you gathered the cattail."

"What do you intend to transport them in? I thought you could be making baskets while I pull more cattails."

"All right," Blue Coyote grabbed the first of the cattail reeds, expertly cut the tuberous root free, beginning a pile for these, and then sat and quickly began construction of a basket. His fingers flew in the familiar routine, and within a finger of time the basket was taking shape. By the time it was completed he had a generous pile of tubers to put into it.

"I think these are enough cattails to remove from this pond," Stone Man studied his handiwork. "We can move to that pond at the point next."

"Why not just gather the rest of the cattails here?" Blue Coyote protested, "If we leave a few they will have filled the pond again by the time we get The People across the moving sand."

"It might be a bit more trouble, but I would rather move to a different pond now. Then for sure they will have had time to grow again. Remember how we utilized that little glen in the Black Land? It provided a steady supply of food all season," replied Stone Man

"Until Red Eagle led the camp to it," Blue Coyote frowned. "It would still be a source of food, just as that little canyon would have been, if The People had not stripped both of every living edible thing. You are right, as I was about the glen. We will move to another pond," he rose and studied the escarpment and the land below. "I hope The People do not strip this land as they have the Starving Mountains. Do you remember Pinyon telling that when The People moved there, it also was a land of bounty?"

"There was even beaver there," Stone Man agreed. "But there is so much here, it would be impossible for so few people to kill this land."

"I hope that you are right. Perhaps if we speak to Father, he has much influence with the other leaders. Still, there is the entire grassland above. I cannot see how . . ." Blue Coyote mused.

"What do you think of checking out one of those caves up there for storage of these hides once they are dry?" Stone Man gestured with his head toward the escarpment. "We could block the entrance to keep out predators." Both youth were trying to come up with the most efficient way to complete their task.

"I have been thinking the same. You know if we used the baskets of cattail reeds, they would be lighter in weight than hide containers for transport on the travois. We could use them for storage in the cave as well. They are quicker to construct than hide containers, and there are lots of cattails."

"Look at all of the bean pods on these trees.[5] What do you think of gathering them once they ripen as well? If we get to them before the deer, they would provide an excellent food. The deer like them, so they must be edible, "offered Stone Man.

"There are plenty of yuccas in the area along the edge of the dunes. We can gather their roots as well.[6] I have even seen Soaptree Yucca[7]. We could certainly use their cleaning roots."

"Fine, right after we get these animals onto the drying racks we will begin gathering reeds. We can roast the tubers and make baskets of the reeds. There is plenty of pollen, and the young heads will last a long time roasted and stored in baskets. There must be numerous ponds along this cliff, so there should be plenty of cattails. We should be able to fill at least a hand of baskets in a single day. And those bushes over there have seeds as well."[8] They were processing yet another pair of deer seated beside their hearth fire, blades flashing and thin strips of meat rising in piles.

By mid day they had all the meat on additional racks to dry in the sun while they began gathering more cattail plants. They constructed several more large baskets and filled them with the roasted tubers, planning to store them in one of the numerous small caves visible along the escarpment. That night Stone Man began construction of a fine net from the cattail fibers Blue Coyote pounded free from the reed leaves. Before they retired, they had the net more than half completed.

The next morning, just as the sun just began to lighten the eastern sky, they darted two more deer, followed by a like number of antelope ambushed at another nearby pool where the water bubbled from the base of the escarpment. They gathered armfuls of cattail reeds for baskets as well. By mid day they were back at their camp quickly readying this meat for the drying racks already set up. Before the sun set on the third day, they had all the meat they could carry, plus a double hand more, water stomachs. By the full moon they had cached all this food and more; more than a double-hand of days out into the moving sand dunes.

They returned to their camp and began concentrating on other game as well. They netted quail[9] and brought down dove with rocks. They stunned countless lizards, captured desert tortoises and killed numerous rabbits with their rabbit sticks. The food supply grew and grew. They stored the lesser nutritious food in the caves, and concentrated on the fat and strengthening food to carry into the dunes. Again and again they led dogs with huge travois of food...

Both men and dogs were stronger and in better condition, a statement of the helpfulness of good food and plenty of it. As they set out on their next journey into the sand dunes, they had been at the escarpment for well over a full moon and gone from the camp for thrice that time. The load they hauled was the heaviest they had attempted. They contrived to cache half of it beyond the last cache and more still farther, then carrying only enough to make it back to their escarpment camp. They planned to move as quickly as possible, making at least a pair more trips each deeper into the moving sand, then hopefully arriving back at the Starving Mountains before the camp had given them up for dead.

So it went, for another moon and a span more trips, each deeper into the sand.

As they walked away from the escarpment for the last time, the dogs pulled loads groaning with food. The men had formed the lightest of containers, used netting and cordage to secure the travois poles, leaving all the hides behind. They carried the lightest, most nutritious of the food, yet the dogs strained in harness. They themselves carried huge backpacks and pulled travois as well. The weight came mostly from the water skins, all of which were fully filled. Even as they were emptied, the skins themselves must accompany them, for the camp did not have nearly enough skins to provide the whole group with sufficient water to make the trip, even considering the water they had cached so far.

During the time they had been at the caprock there had been numerous sand storms clearly visible in the moving dunes, now however, these storms seem to have abated. They had been caught in one and were forced to wait it out, huddled with the dogs beneath their sleeping robes. It had raged for a pair of days plus one more. Spring was over now, bringing intense heat to the moving dunes, they were concerned. It meant moving The People during the hottest part of the season, but there was no choice. Clearly, they should have left on this venture before winter had set in, by now The People would have been in the new land.

They had made a span plus trips into the dunes, each one farther than the last; each time loaded with as much food and water as they could haul. Hopefully they had stores at least halfway across the moving sand. Time and distance were hard to calculate with no landmarks to follow but the stars.

"That is the last of this cache," Stone Man brushed the sand from his bare legs. "We will be able to travel much faster now that the dogs are loaded only half as heavily, as are we. I cannot believe it took us so long to cover this distance. We can't be half way back to the Starving Mountains yet."

"I agree," Blue Coyote finished covering his cache. "But we were carrying a really large load. Each time we have brought supplies. Still, none of us is all that tired. If we rest for a day, we will make up the time by moving faster. I think another hand of days and we should be half way there. It is so difficult to judge distance and speed."

"I think we are still a double span of days from the camp," Stone Man sighed. "But in a hand of days we can cache most of this and then we will pick up speed."

Both youths were worried, for they had been gone for far longer than anyone had anticipated. They rested for the day and at evening again harnessed the dogs and took up the traces themselves and headed west. They pushed hard all night stopping only once to eat and share food and water with the dogs. They walked until the heat of the day became uncomfortable before stopping until evening. Again and yet again they had followed the same routine, another hand of trips into the sand, each farther than the last. Now they calculated they were at least half way back to the Starving Mountains and The People.

"I think we can cache the rest of the supplies here." Blue Coyote studied the sun. "I just hope the dog's noses are as good as you think. It would be too bad if we cannot find the caches again."

"We have left markers. You will see. The way will be clear."

"I must agree that the travois poles secured at the highest dune with a skin flapping on top should get our attention. In fact I do imagine that I recognize some of the dunes, perhaps we are really following the same trail. It is so hard to tell."

They again dug holes into the sides of dunes and stored still more of their supplies of food and water, keeping only enough for half a moon supply for them and their dogs. The empty water bags they had used on the way were loaded on top of the pile of food. And again, they followed the stars west.

"I think we should push on faster." Stone Man handed Blue Coyote another strip of dried deer meat as they sat resting in the heat of the day. "I just have an uneasy feeling . . . Nothing you could put your finger on . . ."

"It is so much hotter during the day, now that summer has arrived. But I understand your concern. We must get the people across these dunes and begin gathering food for winter. By the time we get them all across the summer will be gone." Blue Coyote replied. "But this land will be really hard on the old ones. I wonder how many will make it! They are already in such poor condition."

"But we have brought the most nutritious food," Stone Man reminded him. "Those quail are such good food that only a single quail will make a meal for most. Remember, we could barely eat one when we first arrived at the new place, so shrunken were our stomachs."

"I am also worried about there being time enough to gather winter supplies once they do arrive. We did not even begin to imagine that it would take us so long to cross these dunes. And with gathering food and caching it, the camp has probably given us up for dead. At least we will bring good news back with us. I just hope it isn't already too late!"

"The camp has gone through harder times," reminded Stone Man. "At least it is summer. There is bound to be food of some kind! Surely it cannot have all been eaten."

"I hope that you are right. Some of the older ones, like Butterfly, are beginning to get very frail."

"You think there is a possibility she won't make it? Blue Coyote frowned. "Surely she is not that frail?"

"Yes, but there is such an abundance of food along the escarpment, surely with what we have stored in the cave, the acorn crop, and all the game in the area . . ." Stone Man agreed, "But we do not know what animals may harvest the acorns."

"I would feel better if we left a little earlier and traveled a little later." Blue Coyote insisted. For three more nights they did so.

"What is the matter with the dogs?" Stone Man frowned. All four animals were whining in agitation and milling about uneasily. It was mid morning and they had just released the dogs from the travois harnesses, in preparation for resting during the hottest part of the day. They had traveled later, started earlier, and made better time over the last fingers of days. Both youths were satisfied that they were making the best time they could. Suddenly the black bitch leaped into the air and streaked forward over the dune before them. They called her, but their only answer was her fading bark as she sped away from them. The remaining dogs whined and fretted.

"Now what do we do?" Stone man quickly attached thongs to the pair of dogs, fearful they would also disappear.

"Well we can't take the time to follow her. She will either return to us before we leave or catch up with us when she has investigated whatever it was which drew her away. She is a good hunting dog," Blue Coyote remarked, "This is not the first time that she has gone off hunting on here own."

"I don't think she is hunting . . ."

The remaining dogs twisted and tried to break free as well. "Something is wrong!" Blue Coyote exclaimed. Almost in unison the remaining three dogs slipped their ties and followed the black bitch over the dunes barking in unison. The two youths exclaimed in disgust and started to follow their trail. One dog would catch up, but all four? They were not sure. It was hot, the heat driving all energy from their bodies. Gamely they trotted after the dogs, only silence surrounding them.

For over a hand of time they followed the trail. "What do you think they smelled?" Stone Man grumbled. "I cannot imagine there is any game of size in these moving dunes. At least there has been no sign of anything larger than a lizard!"

"It must have been game of some sort. Scorpion certainly acted oddly. She is usually the most dependable of dogs." Blue Coyote replied. "It would be something, wouldn't it, if they actually were onto game? Just think: more food to provide for the camp. But I have no idea how we would preserve it. And it would rot very quickly in this heat."

"We could always just dry it. The heat would do that very quickly. However, before we begin processing it, perhaps we should see what they have fond."

For nearly another finger of time they followed the trail of the dogs, then they heard them barking in the distance. And they heard something else; voices. Picking up speed, Blue Coyote and Stone Man all but raced over the next dun and nearly tumbled into the very center of the whole camp of The People. They were spread out in a long line straggling down into the blow out, the stronger men in front, the oldest and youngest at the rear. Fire Dancer was in the lead, Acorn, the dreamer beside him. Even old Butterfly was there with her granddaughter Basket, as were Star Woman and Little Antelope Woman, and far more of The People than their small group contained.

1. Columbian mammoth

2. At the end of the Pleistocene Era, circa 11,000 years ago, experts in the field of Pleistocene Geo-archaeology believe that there was a period of about 100-1,000 years of severe drought. (Dr. C. Vance Haynes, personal communication). This period coincides with the extinction of the Pleistocene megafauna. At the end of the period of drought there emerged a new culture, the Folsom people. They were predominately bison hunters. The area of moving sand would have extended in a north-south direction between the Capitan Mountains to the west and the Llano Estacado escarpment to the east, an area approximately 165 miles wide in the location under consideration. A single remnant of this moving sand remained until recently in the Mescalero Sands, near Maljamar N. M.

3. In active sand dune areas, the wind piles the sand into dunes and other areas are scoured out to the base soil or rock. These areas are called blowouts.

4. **Llano Estacado**: Also known as the Southern High Plains, or the Staked Plains. The Llano Estacado is a large plateau some 20,000 square miles in area, surrounded on all sides by steep escarpments. It is a hot, dry area with average January temperatures of 40 degrees F. There are no flowing streams on the Llano Estacado, and surface water is confined to a few large saline lakes or playas. These playas, and the numerous smaller, but almost always dry deflation basins, are a characteristic feature of the Llano and its principal source of topographic variety in an otherwise monotonously flat, featureless landscape of seemingly unending grasslands. **Wendorf** 1962:159-171.

   The Llano Estacado is an area of elevated plateau or tableland. It may well be one of the oldest land surfaces of the American continent. In nearly its present shape and probably at its present actual surface, this land surface has received no new material since being isolated as a tableland. It has suffered little from ordinary water erosion. It is watered entirely by rains, between twenty and thirty inches per year. A six-inch rain, which would cause a flood elsewhere, will soak into the ground here over night. Only an occasional pond will survive for a week.

It breaks off in a sudden, almost vertical escarpment along the north and west margins. This 'caprock' is more a residual mass of broken fragments of stone, basically chert. The down-percolating waters have continuously dissolved away the lime from what was once a thick limestone layer, leaving the insoluble flints and cherts behind. In various places along the edge of the escarpment springs emerge from the water trickling down from above.

There are no rivers or streams o the Llano, leaving the ponds formed in depressions where the water table extends above the surface as the only available water from natural sources.

5. *Prosopis glandulosa:* Honey Mesquite: Honey mesquite is a spiny, large, thicket-forming shrub or small trees with short trunk, open spreading crown of crooked branches, and narrow, bean-like pods. **MacMahon** 1988: 485-486.

6. *Yucca torreyi:* Torrey Yucca; Indians ate the pulpy fruits of this and dried and ground the roots for flour. The coarse fibers of the leaves were used as cordage as well. **MacMahon** 1988: 491.

7. *Yucca elata:* Soaptree Yucca: Soapy material in the roots and trunks of this abundant species has been used as a soap substitute. The leaves are a source of coarse fiber and were used by Indians in making baskets as well. **MacMahon** 1988: 492.

8. *Atriplex canescens:* Four-Wing Saltbush; a nutritious and important food source. The leaves are edible and the seeds provide raw material for flour as well as roasted or raw snacks. **MacMahon** 1988: 503-504.

9. Scaled Quail; Scaled quail live in large coveys along the edge of the escarpment and above on the Llano.

CHAPTER 3

Tell us Son, quickly, that you found the way," Fire Dancer hugged Blue Coyote, "For we are all dead if you did not. We have food for but a few more days, and very little water beyond that."

"Why are you here?" Blue Coyote exclaimed. "We did not expect the whole camp to come out to meet us. How did you know when we would return? We did not think to be back at the camp for nearly another half moon. Surely we are not that far off in our calculations?"

"Did you find the Grassland?" Acorn shook Stone Man by the arm, getting his attention.

"Yes! Yes, we did. I am sorry Dreamer, but all of this is such a surprise! We thought. . . . . That is, there was no need for . . . How far is the camp?"

"We are many days out into the moving dunes," Acorn assured him. "It was decided that the whole camp would gather as much food as they could and follow you. This is what we have done. Everyone worked exhaustively to do so, we were heavy laden when we set out, but people are beginning to tire. The heat is so intense. It has become a great burden upon many. As you can see, the word spread that we were leaving, many others have joined us. Now, how much farther must we travel to get out of this spirit cursed land of nothing?"

"It will take these many people moving as slowly as they do, more than another moon to reach the other side." Stone Man replied staring at the continuing column of people filing silently into the blow out. There were well over a span of spans of them, in his whole life he had never seen so many of The People gathered in one group. His heart sank.

Blue Coyote was also assessing the situation. He looked at Stone Man, his face a study in concern and disappointment.

"We do not have enough food," Star Woman stated bitterly. "I knew this rashness would get us all killed!"

"But we do!" Blue Coyote brashly reassured her. "That is why we were gone so long. We have hunted, carried and cached food and water all along the route. In fact, our last cache is only a hand of time from here. That is what we were doing when the dogs all took off. Little did we know they smelled you and went to find you."

"You have food?" She asked hopefully, then sighed and shook her head. "But food for two hunters will never feed this many! They were so sure we carried enough! Huh! We have been gone little more than a span of days and already we have gobbled up nearly everything. But it doesn't matter, for there was no more food to bring any way."

"Which is why we cached enough food for the entire camp," Stone Man stated bravely. "Not poor, scavenged food, but rich fat deer meat, and antelope, cattail tubers and roots. We have quail, dove and rabbit as well." Each youth removed the water stomachs still slung over their shoulder; "here is water as well. Everyone can have a drink. We have more just over there," he pointed toward their tracks. Inside he was quaking. So many people! There would not be enough. They had cached a great deal for their camp, making sure all would be well fed, but now there was almost a double span times the number they had calculated to provide for.

The water stomachs were passed around, everyone taking a drink, and then the youths turned and led the people back along their trail to where they had so recently buried the last of their supplies.

The sun was blazing down upon them without mercy by the time they reached the cache.

"Drive the poles into the sand and stretch sleeping furs over them, we have found that helps to keep the blazing sun from cooking one," Blue Coyote suggested as The People straggled into the blow out. "We will rest here through the heat of the day and travel at night."

"You have been traveling at night?" Fire Dancer nodded, "That makes good sense."

Tired though they were, Blue Coyote and Stone Man helped everyone settle down in the blow out, then they began distributing the food still on the travois, which they had planned taking along on the last leg of their journey. It was enough to feed the entire group the best meal they had eaten in many moons. But it would be the only good meal. Both food and water would have to be measured out carefully, for there was dangerously little for so many people.

"What is it like, this land you have discovered?" Star Woman asked as the family sat huddled beneath their sleeping furs, all laced together to provide a larger shade. The dreamer, Acorn had joined them, as well as headmen from the other camps.

"It is everything we have all dreamed of." Blue Coyote answered. "There are water, game and food plants in abundance," he handed her a piece of dried deer meat. "We had no difficulty in bringing down a span of deer and double that number antelope. Rabbits are more plentiful than they ever were in the foothills. There are quail and dove everywhere, and another, a bigger, better-tasting bird[1] that we have never seen in the foothills. All are fat and well fed. There is an oak forest, which even old Butterfly will have no difficulty harvesting." He chuckled, "She can finally sit down to work."

"Where the moving dunes end, a brushy area extends for about half a day's walk to the escarpment. This whole area is riddled with well-used game trails. The plants there include yucca, brittle brush, sage and mesquite to name but a few. There are numerous ponds at the base of the escarpment where the water comes to the surface. They have an abundance of cattails. The cliffs are about a span of men high. The land above is truly the grassland of legend. It spreads as far as the eye can see in all directions, a vast flat plain of grass. There are many herds of antelope that we have seen, as well as the area of the oak forest, which is teeming with small game. We did not explore the grassland at all though, so that is all I can tell you about it. We never went more than a hand of time in either direction while hunting, for there was no need. Game is that plentiful."

"What of other people?" Star Woman shifted to a more comfortable position.

"We saw no other people," Blue Coyote admitted, "And from the way the animals reacted, they have not seen them either." He looked to his father, "Now tell me, how do you come to be here?"

"Well, shortly after you left . . ."

*   *   *

"I wish to speak before this council of elders," Fire Dancer addressed the group of old men and women seated around the central fire. They were gathered specifically because he has asked for a meeting.

"You may speak," Acorn, Dreamer of The People, nodded.

Fire Dancer looked around at the group, measuring what he had to say carefully. He was still uneasy.

"Blue Coyote and Stone Man left a few fingers of days ago," he began, shifting uneasily from one foot to the other. "Since that time, I have had a strange dream. It has come to me every time I sleep. I would share this dream with you."

Acorn and the elders nodded.

"I have dreamed that they will have success," there were murmurs of surprise from the assemblage. "In my dream we did not sit idly by however but gathered every bit of food we could and in the dream at the full of the moon we all followed their path directly to the east." Fire Dancer looked about the group uneasily. "I am not a dreamer. I would ask for guidance, from you Acorn, and suggestions from anyone."

"This is indeed a powerful dream which you have had," Acorn addressed Fire Dancer. "If you were a dreamer, I would say it was a message from the spirits," he rose, "I will seek to discover the meaning of it and seek guidance from the spirits."

"Are you sure this was the entire dream," questioned an elder?

"Yes, it was very clear though. We follow." Fire Dancer sighed, "I am not comfortable with dreams; they are for Dreamers, not hunters."

Fire Dancer left the council after several more questions were answered and returned to the shelter he shared with Star Woman. "So! You told them of the dream and your foolish idea?"

"I told them of the dream that is all," Fire Dancer frowned at her. "Why do you think it is so foolish? Surely you can see the advantage to it?"

Star Woman shook her head, "I know you see advantage to it. We will see what the council and dreamer decide it means."

"And will you abide by their decision?" Fire Dancer asked. "Will you work toward that end if they agree?"

She frowned, "I will not oppose the decision of the council, but I still do not agree."

*   *   *

Acorn settled within his shelter, before a small fire and stared into the coals. *What could Fire Dancer's dream mean? Why had it come to that man and not to Acorn?* He set a small container of water to heat on a hot stone and searched among his dwindling supplies of spirit plants, finally locating the one he needed. Carefully he secreted a small amount of the spirit powder[2] into the hot water and stirred it with a bone splinter.

As it steeped, he went again over the hunter's words. Frowning he drank the spirit brew and waited for it to take effect.

Why have you abandoned us, your people? His mind searched for a spirit helper who had not answered his call in many seasons. Still, he tried. *Come to me!* He pleaded. Slowly the swirling began, turning him over and over as he spiraled into the darkness of his mind. Then, as always, only the darkness; but. . . then, a flicker of light? *Go! Follow the dream. They must be reunited!* Very faintly he thought he heard.

Long into the night Acorn went over and over the experience. *Was it a message, or was I just trying so hard . . . ?* He hoped he had the answer.

*   *   *

The very next morning the council of elders met again with Acorn and Fire Dancer. For most of the morning they sat huddled in heated discussion, and then Fire Dancer announced that indeed they were moving, they were taking the chance that Blue Coyote and Stone Man would find the legendary grasslands. Life was too precarious here to tolerate any longer. The signs were there to read. This land would no longer support the people for even one more season. This land was dead!

Butterfly could no longer work in the foothills as well as others, so while the girl Basket went with Star Woman, she remained in the camp.

There she produced baskets of yucca fiber, made new moccasins for every member of the camp, and began the process of packing the food gathered, in preparation for the move. There were no camp dogs, so the people would have to pull the travois. They planned on leaving in one full moon if Blue Coyote and Stone Man had not yet returned. The men were hunting what few animals remained, traveling far into the mountains on many occasions to find deer and javalina. They snared small game, netted birds and the women gathered eggs and cooked them, and they reaped the plants. They harvested pigweed, seeds and leaves, dug the few remaining tubers, and gathered pinecones to remove the nuts once back at the camp. Every yucca and prickly pear within traveling distance was dug and added to the store of food and fiber they would need. Every edible thing was harvested, but even then, there was pitifully little.

Word spread. The Yucca Camp was leaving the Starving Mountains. Headmen from neighboring camps spoke with the elders. Their people began preparing as well.

When they were ready, they numbered nearly a span of spans of individuals. Other camps still had a few dogs, and these were put into harness. The leaders studied all the supplies. Anything not absolutely necessary was discarded. No keepsakes, no extra clothing, no superfluous items were allowed at all; not even sleeping furs. Only food, and water, and the clothing on their backs would be going. Not even tools were to be taken. Seeds were ground into flour; mano[3] and metate were stone, far too heavy to take. The loads were lightened yet more by discarding the hide travois skins, replaced by lighter weight fiber netting. Men took their worked obsidian tools and atlatl and darts; nothing more.

Those individuals deemed as not totally fit were sent back to their camps as well. Once this group blazed a trail, once food was secured, someone would return for them. Meanwhile, every member of The People was to prepare to move. The news spread like a wildfire, throughout the Starving Mountains. Word would come as to when. Each of the camps had sent only their strongest to accompany the Yucca Camp.

On the appointed day, just at dawn, they headed, in a long column east into the moving sand dunes. Their destiny would be written on the wind. Food and water, they were instructed, were to be carefully rationed. Still the sun beat down on them mercilessly; soon people began dipping into their rations as they walked until they were ready to drop. Slowly and still more slowly they moved, day after day, always east into the moving sand. Each evening there was a council of leaders, after a span of days these responsible men spoke with concern that perhaps they had been foolish not to wait . . .

The headmen were busy getting the camp up and moving. Travois were reloaded, and people helped into the harnesses. Supplies were checked once again. People were grumbling and settling into position for the day's journey.

"Listen!" Fire Dancer hushed those about him, "do you hear?"

"Dogs," Acorn nodded, "Coming this way."

"That is Scorpion! I recognize her voice!" Fire Dancer began to grin, "They have found us!"

Fire Dancer concluded his story, "So here we are."

"We did not store enough food for so many," Blue Coyote admitted. "Still if it is handled carefully, measured out meagerly, I think there will be enough. The food we cached is much more nutritious than any in the Starving Mountains, it will go farther, and people will not need to eat as much. We had planned and provided a generous supply, making sure every member of the camp had plenty to eat, but we never dreamed there would be more people."

"What if a group of fast-moving men went on ahead and left the majority of the supplies for the slower ones?" Suggested one of the headmen, "That would conserve on food."

Everyone considered his suggestion, heads nodded.

"We left a lot of food stored in a cave," Stone Man admitted. "It could be brought back."

"Water will be more important," stated Fire Dancer. "Perhaps they could go ahead with the empty water skins and bring them back full. If they took most of the dogs with them, it would be possible to carry a lot of water back. That will be more important than food."

"Traveling at night as Blue Coyote and Stone Man have done, that will also conserve, both on water and on strength. It will be much easier on everyone to travel in the cool and rest during the heat of the day. I am surprised we did not think of that!" Fire Dancer concluded.

"Then it is decided. Those who can travel rapidly will forge on ahead, and the rest will follow."

"One of us will have to stay behind," Stone Man spoke. "We know where the food is stored. The other will go ahead with the fast group and lead the way," he looked around, "I do not mind leading the slow group if Blue Coyote wants to go ahead. After all this whole adventure was his idea. He should have the privilege of leading."

"It is a short hand of days to our first cache of food. There is more than a span of water skins and enough food for a hand of days if the people keep moving at a modest rate, but move, you must!" Blue Coyote added. "We will take only enough to get us to the next cache, leaving most for those who follow." He looked around, "Now everyone must get as much rest as possible, for we will be walking all night."

Quickly the blowout became silent,

"We will be across the moving sand in about a double span of days," Blue Coyote assured the group surrounding him. "Since we carry only enough supplies to get us to the first cache and our dogs run free, we will travel quite rapidly. We will be at the first cache in two night's travel. It will take the rest of you a hand of days. But we will leave all the food and water we can at the caches, for you. Then someone will come back to meet you with the remainder of the food we have stored and full water skins."

"We will keep moving," Fire Dancer assured him. "Stone Man and I will get the slower ones across, do not worry. Just pray the spirits guide our steps." Father and Son hugged once more, Blue Coyote hugged Star Woman and assured her all would be well, then he led nearly a third of the group away at a rapid pace.

They traveled well into the night before stopping to rest for a short time and eat sparingly and drink only enough water to keep them going. The night breeze was cooling and by now Blue Coyote was well used to moving at night. He had little difficulty following the trail. Their footprints were still quite visible. They rested briefly just before dawn, and then continued until the heat began to rise uncomfortably. They had made better time than he and Stone Man had with loaded packs. Blue Coyote was well satisfied with the progress.

Things were much slower back with the women and old ones. Without the men to help, getting underway took a lot longer. Stone Man helped secure packs, adjust travois straps and make sure everyone had a drink and some food before starting out. The weaker ones he gave a bit more food to nibble along the way, as they became tired. But he and Fire Dancer and Acorn now controlled the remainder of the food and water. There would be no more delving into the supply along the way. The extra length of time resting had helped as well. They gradually followed the trail left by Blue Coyote and his group. Several times they stopped to give the slow ones time to catch up, and then rest a bit before forging once again ahead. Spirits were high. The group began to look on the journey as a great adventure.

Valiantly the older members of the group kept up. Traveling at night did make a big difference. Everyone had more energy; they could travel farther. Sheltering beneath their robe shades during the punishing heat of the day meant needing less water during that time as well. They began to fall into a pattern as they accustomed to traveling. Muscles adjusted and stamina increased. The food they now ate was more nutritious as well, and it gave them added energy.

"I cannot take another step!" Squirrel Girl complained, "You go on and I will catch up." She sat down against a sand dune motioning Moth to go on ahead.

"But Fire Dancer said we were all to stay together," Moth protested. "I am tired as well, but there is no time to rest."

"Well I don't care! Besides, the trail is clear enough for a blind man to follow. I couldn't possibly get lost!"

"What about predators?" Moth suggested.

"What predators? We are out in the middle of a place with no water. What predator could possibly live here?"

Already they were alone in the blow out, the rest of the people moving farther and farther away from them.

"Very well, we will rest here for a while, but then we must catch up," Moth conceded.

The girls settled down against the sand and were soon fast asleep. The sun was well up before Moth woke, and realized they were far behind, they had no protection from the sun, no food and no water.

"Come on Squirrel! We are in deep trouble!" Moth shook her friend awake. "We have slept the whole night."

Squirrel Girl woke; yawned and looked about in confusion. Then she remembered. "We had better hurry," she agreed with Moth. "I do not look forward to the scolding we are in for if Fire Dancer discovers we have lagged behind."

Quickly they scrambled to the top of the next dune, to discover only a trail greeting them. Many dunes later they were sweating; their heads hurt from the sun beating down upon them, and still the empty trail went forward.

"We have to stop!" Squirrel Girl sagged to her knees, "I am exhausted."

"That is what got us in this fix in the first place!" Moth complained. "You can stay here by yourself then. I am going to catch up, and then I intend to stay with the group!" She staggered over the next dune, and the next and the one after that, not looking back to see if Squirrel Girl followed. She did not.

Fire Dancer was passing out food and handing around the water skin, getting everyone settled down to rest during the heat of the day. "Have you seen Squirrel Girl?" Little Fawn, a woman of the Rabbit Camp asked first of one person, then another, finally reaching Fire Dancer.

"No!" Fire Dancer frowned. "Come to think of it, the girl Moth is missing as well. Stone Man, have you seen the girls from the rabbit camp?"

"What do they look like?" Stone Man frowned as well. "I do not know everyone."

"About a span of seasons, Moth was wearing only an apron, Squirrel had on a cape as well as I can remember," Little Fawn replied.

"No one here fitting that description," Stone Man confirmed Dancer's worst fears.

"Someone will have to go back for them," he sighed, "I will certainly punish them for this."

"I will go back," Stone Man replied. "I am not all that tired. Give me a water skin and a packet of food and I will be on my way."

"Better take a couple of poles and a robe as well. There is no way you can travel in this heat with them."

*　　*　　*

Stone Man nodded, and in a finger of time was disappearing over the dune, backtracking. At midday he found Moth, staggering along the trail near complete exhaustion. He settled her quickly beneath the robe shelter and left her with food and a long drink of water.

"Wait for me here. I will return as soon as I find your friend," he assured her.

Moth took another drink and handed him the water skin, nodding her head.

He took the water skin from her shaking fingers and continued on. Already Moth was curled up asleep in the shade of the robe shelter. Evening was well upon him before he found Squirrel Girl, after following her zigzagging track for a long distance away from the trail. Buzzards circling overhead finally led him to her. She had been wandering nearly delirious, for hands of time moving farther and farther from the trail. Now she lay in a lifeless little heap, the birds edging ever closer as her death approached.

Stone Man knelt beside her. Her face was badly sunburned, her lips cracked with blood oozing from them. Her hands were raw and bleeding as well, for she had crawled on her hands and knees the last distance. He gave her a sip of water, then another. She grappled the skin with surprising strength. He had a time wresting it from her. She coughed, vomited up the water too quickly taken in, and then reached again for the skin. Stone Man refused it to her. Slowly, over the next hand of time he gave her sips of water followed by bites of food. Finally judging that she had enough water and food, he lifted her onto his back and headed back to where he had left Moth. By the time they reached Moth, the sun was setting, and Stone Man was staggering. The girl on his back was little more than a dead weight, a heavy one at that. They all rested for a bit. Stone Man knew the camp would be once again underway, led by Fire Dancer, Scorpion by his side, toward the next food cache. Well after dark Stone Man lifted Squirrel Girl once again onto his back and led Moth up the trail.

They reached the place where the people had camped during the day. In the trail lay another water skin, to replace the now empty one Stone Man carried. There was food as well. They ate and drank and resumed their pace. Moth did not voice a single word of protest, nor did Squirrel Girl, now walking shakily beside her friend. They pushed as hard as the girls could go but did not rejoin the camp that night.

Fire Dancer was beginning to become concerned. Again he left portions of food and water for them as the camp pushed on, still able to follow the faint trail left by the other group. About midway through the next night Stone Man slipped into place beside him. Dancer breathed a sigh of relief.

* * *

"I am fine." Stone Man replied to Fire Dancer's concern, "But those girls are not likely to give any more trouble. Rain Woman will probably still be lecturing Moth when we reach the escarpment. She was very angry and frightened when she realized the girl was missing."

Stone Man studied their position. "We should reach the cache in the morning," he assured Fire Dancer.

"I certainly hope so, for we are out of food entirely, and the water is dangerously low as well. I left the last of my share of both for you and the girls."

"Then perhaps we should push a little harder," Stone Man replied, "Just to be sure we do reach the cache before we stop." They picked up speed, the camp following, doing likewise. Just after dawn, Scorpion barked and began dragging her travois toward the pole flapping in the distance, in the rising wind.

They settled down in the blowout below the marker. Fire Dancer and Stone Man excavated the food cache. People hunkered beneath the fragile protection of their robe shelters as Fire Dancer and Stone man passed around food and water. Still, the wind rose. Stone Man watched with mounting concern. Soon sand began sifting down upon them. Now the wind began to moan as it swept across the dunes. The sun became a haze, and then disappeared altogether into a red blur of biting dust. The robes were now drawn over the heads of small huddled groups as they struggled to breathe hot but sand free air. All day, and all night the storm raged around them, shutting each small group into an isolated world striving to breathe and survive. During the following day the storm began to abate, and by evening had cleared away. Deer Stalker of the Pine Camp, and Packrat Woman were found huddled together beneath a robe, completely covered by sand; discovered only because one foot could be seen sticking out of the dune. The old hunter was stretched out on his back to face the sun on the dune top, the woman beside him. Acorn sent a prayer to the spirits for their souls and begged for guidance to the Ancestor Fires in the sky. Then it was done. They had been laid out to walk the wind.

"What do you think," questioned Fire Dancer?

"We tried to keep in a straight line as much as possible," Stone Man frowned. "But the whole land has shifted. I am afraid we will have to depend upon Scorpion and her nose from now on."

"We dare not hesitate any longer. Already we are well behind where we should be. We have lost more than just two day's traveling time."

They were lost. Somewhere during the night, they had wandered away from the now nonexistent trail. People huddled in silent worried groups as the two decided how to proceed.

They released the black bitch from the travois and watched hopefully as she circled in the blowout ahead of them. Stone Man followed the dog as they worked farther and farther north, away from the waiting group. A hand of time later she sniffed, looked back at him and barked once, wagging her tail as she headed up the next dune. With a sigh he followed.

Once Stone Man was certain that the dog had found the trail, they backtracked and brought the people once again onto it. From then on, however, Scorpion kept them on the trail. They no longer depended upon their own senses to guide. Food and water were handed out sparingly now, for the lost time had to be compensated for. Only a few bites of food and a swallow of water had to do for all but the weakest. Squirrel Girl and Moth stayed well within the confines of the group, having been chastised by their families as well as by Fire Dancer. There were no more stragglers.

* * *

Scorpion dug vigorously into the dune, sending sand flying far behind her. She sniffed, "woof!" and began digging with increased speed. Only the weakest had eaten in three days, they only the few lizards that Scorpion caught; and the last of the water had been consumed the day before as well. Quickly the men dropped onto their knees and began scooping sand away. It took them nearly half the day to uncover the cache, because they were near exhaustion, and because so much sand had moved over it during the storm.

People huddled thankfully beneath their shade covers and ate hungrily of the food handed out. Fire Dancer decided to give each one a bit extra, just this once. By now the larger group should have reached the escarpment. Hopefully someone would soon be heading out to meet them with water, but after losing the trail, he was afraid to depend upon that. They pushed on again as soon as the heat abated a bit, and pushed as hard as the weakest could go, night fading into day, turning again into night. They reached the next cache of food without further mishaps. When it was uncovered Fire Dancer sat staring at it with grave concern.

"We should reach the escarpment in a span of days or so," Stone Man assured Fire Dancer. "We have not made very good time, but we have not fallen further behind either," he sighed, "I am worried though. The forward group has taken far more of the water and food than I anticipated. I do not understand the Headmen, or Blue Coyote allowing this. He knows how far we have to go and how many of us there are." Stone Man surveyed the contents of the latest cache of food. "I do not think this will be enough, even handed out sparingly. There certainly is not sufficient water."

"It seems to me that each cache of food has been smaller than the last," Fire Dancer agreed.

"Yet all were about the same," Stone Man replied. "There should have been at least a span more water skins here, as well as much more food."

"What do you suggest we do?"

"The only thing we can do is push the people harder. We must make up the time or run out of food and water."

"Perhaps we should tell them," Fire Dancer suggested. "If they are aware of the danger, surely they will try harder."

"Some of them are trying harder than they can now. Old Butterfly is about done in. Snowflake, the elder from the Pine Camp is no better. We risk losing them, at the very least, if not more."

"I can do with less food," Star Woman stated, "Give part of my share to Butterfly."

Fire Dancer nodded to his mate and passed her by with only a small sip of water. He made sure that Butterfly got a little extra. His own portion and that of Stone Man likewise went to the weaker.

*   *   *

"I would speak with you," Centipede Man spoke quietly to Blue Coyote.

Blue Coyote was seated at the edge of the group, resting for a short time. The sandstorm had caught them before reaching the next cache of food, but now they were well beyond it. Blue Coyote estimated they would reach the escarpment in a span of days at most. They were days ahead of the other group.

A man of the Rabbit Camp had approached him. He recognized him. He and his family were all traveling with them.

"What is it?" Blue Coyote asked once Centipede Man was seated.

Centipede Man licked his lip nervously. He shifted, and then glanced toward the main group. Clearly, he was upset about something. "The water," he began. "We were rationed to one skin between four men, is that not correct," he asked?

"Yes." Blue Coyote replied puzzled at the question, for he thought he had made it very clear, "Four men to share each water skin."

The man nodded; reassured that he was not mistaken. "That is it, no extras?"

Blue Coyote nodded, "no extras. You know we take only what we absolutely need, why do you ask these questions?"

"As I have walked, I have noticed, some of the men are carrying extra full water skins."

"What?" Blue Coyote gasped, "You cannot be serious?"

"I did not want to believe it either, but I made sure," Centipede Man shook his head. "I would not mention it now, but I have counted at least a hand of them with a pair of water skins each. This means there is not enough water for those following, and my mate and daughter are among them."

"Can you point these men out to me?" Blue Coyote leaped to his feet.

"Grape Leaf of the Rabbit Camp has a pair, as has Hairy Bear; and so do Antelope and Sand Crawler of the Quail Camp. I think the other man is called Ground Squirrel, but I am not sure."

Blue Coyote was already headed away, "I will deal with this, you go back to your place, and take my thanks with you."

"What are you going to do?" Centipede Man jogged along beside him.

"Someone will have to go back with the water. There is no choice."

"I will do so," Centipede Man offered, "I will be glad to do it."

Blue Coyote nodded. He made his way to where several headmen were relaxing and settled into conversation with them. Shortly thereafter the entire group was gathered. The men in question were searched and their stolen goods taken from them.

"We are not the only ones!" Antelope protested. "Water is not all that was taken! Search the men of the Pine Camp!" Upon a further search, encouraged by others, it was discovered that a double span of men carried extra rations as well. These were also confiscated. Almost immediately Centipede Man hefted a heavy pack onto his back and led the biggest dog pulling a fully loaded travois back along the trail they had only just traversed.

"There must be appropriate punishment for this theft," Turkey Stalker, headman of the Pigweed Camp, demanded.

"What do you suggest?" Another headman asked.

"What did they intend for the followers? Let them go without food and water; let them suffer the fate they intended for the others; that is fair," Turkey Stalker shouted.

All but those accused, agreed heartily.

The final punishment for the theft was greatly reduced rations for those responsible, leaving them only enough food and water to stay alive and shunning by the rest of the group. Centipede drove himself and his dog as hard as he could in a desperate attempt to reach those following.

*   *   *

"I am sorry Fire Dancer," Butterfly sat stubbornly beneath her shelter. The rest of the camp was loaded and waiting to begin another night's walk. "You go on," her white-faced granddaughter stood beside Fire Dancer, her chin set stubbornly, her dirty face streaked with tears.

Fire Dancer shook his head.

"You can't let me hold you back any longer." Butterfly protested, "I have had a good life. I am an old woman. All I do now is endanger everyone else. I eat food better given to others, and I drink precious water. You must leave me," she stubbornly insisted, "Little Antelope Woman will look after Basket."

"We have lost too many already!" Fire Dancer protested, "More have walked the wind over the last hand of seasons than still live. Each of us is important. You have knowledge that contributes to the well being of the whole group. You are needed Butterfly." Dancer reached down and lifted the old woman gently in his arms. "You ride my travois for a while, just until you gain strength," he brushed aside her protests.

Soon another ancient one was gently added to Stone Man's load. But both men now knew that in all probability, none of them would make it. The food had run out yesterday, even with the strictest of rationing. Now they drank the last of the water. With a sigh Fire Dancer led his pathetic cavalcade from the blowout and up yet another sand dune, concluding that Star Woman had been right and his rashness had led them all to this sad end. It was still three more nights before they could possibly reach the next food cache. With the intense summer heat, none of them, not even the strongest, would make it without water. On they walked, for the whole night, with no water. They huddled in misery all day at the mercy of the hot summer sun. Again they walked into the night.

As the sun rose the next morning Fire Dancer staggered over the top of the last dune he was capable of crossing, he struggled down the side and sagged exhausted beside Stone Man, who suffered little better. His tongue was swollen inside his mouth, and even sucking on a pebble had not helped enough. Even the barking of Scorpion took time to penetrate their muddled minds. "What is it?" Dancer questioned, slurring his words. "Can you see what the dog is barking at?"

"Someone is coming," muttered Stone Man. He struggled from the travois harness and staggered across the blowout toward the approaching man and dog.

"As soon as it was discovered, I started back," Centipede Man explained. "We could not believe that anyone would do such a selfish and life-threatening thing!" He shook his fist, "but; be assured, it will not happen again. Blue Coyote and the Headmen will make sure there is no more theft of the food and water." He nodded, "The headmen will keep a severe eye on the culprits as well."

The exhausted, nearly dead group of people was now settled around the blowout, resting. They had been given small portions of food and water repeatedly until their starved bodies could tolerate it. There had, unfortunately been losses. Morning Glory of the Rabbit Camp had been lost somewhere along the trail, as had Muskrat Woman and Grass Skirt and her three-season old daughter. Old Coyote Man was gone as well, laid out to walk the wind. Each loss was deeply felt by all. The People were so few, and the loss of even one was a concern to everyone. The danger that thoughtless men had inflicted on so many was beyond the understanding of most.

There was, however, no way they could continue for some time. The jeopardy was escalating for those in the blowout. They were dangerously depleted. Most could not go for half a night, much less any longer. The food would not last, not nearly long enough for them to regain strength. Fire Dancer and Star Woman were in better shape than most. Stone Man was still strong; however, with the addition of hydrating water he would soon be recovered.

"You have enough food to last for a hand of days," Stone Man admitted, "this gives us time enough for Centipede Man and me to go on to the next cache. I will return with all the food there and Centipede Man will take Scorpion and locate the next one. They will return and meet us with that food and water. This will give us a few more days. By doing this one more time we will be across the moving dunes."

Fire Dancer nodded, "that will give us time to rest and regain strength. Even if we do not go very fast, with the two of you bringing us food and water, the rest of us can cripple-on across."

"We will start out again tonight," Stone Man replied.

"Even you cannot go on forever Stone Man. Surely you could rest one more night before leaving."

"I am fine, really," Stone Man assured him. "I am young and strong, and it doesn't take me as long to recover. Besides that, remember I have had two moons of good food behind me which the rest of you lack."

Fire Dancer and Star Woman walked with the two men and the dogs to the top of the sand dune and watched until they faded into the distance, then the pair returned to minister to the people below.

"Do you regret coming?" Fire Dancer questioned.

"No, not really," admitted Star Woman, "You were right, as usual. We could not stay in the starving mountains another season. We really had no choice. We had a chance to live this way, but the other death was assured." She sighed; "I only wish . . ." a tear ran down her dirty face.

"We are going to make it Star Woman," Fire Dancer took her by the shoulder and turned her toward him. "We must be strong. We can help the rest be strong. If we give up, they will give up as well. It is our responsibility to make sure they do not do so." He smiled, "We must live up to the image of our son. Blue Coyote will be a great leader soon, and I for one, intend to be there to see it happen."

Star Woman nodded in return, "Our son will surely be a great leader, for he takes after his father," she stiffened her back, "And it is up to me to be a mother he need not look down upon."

Amazingly, the group felt able to continue the next night. They even went longer into the night than Fire Dancer had ever hoped. The next night they walked longer. Then Stone Man was back among them with more food and water. It was agreed that rations could be increased. In another night they were at the location of the next food cache. This gave them more encouragement that they would make it across the moving dunes after all. Now Butterfly was walking again. Her place was taken by the weakest; who improved and yielded to another. So it went. Stone Man met them with yet another store of rations, and Centipede Man and five more men arrived two nights later with travois groaning with food and water. They actually had a feast.

A hand of days later there was almost an air of festivity as the group topped the last sand dune and cheered as they hurried to the pond. They had made it! No one had imagined that only a span of their number would perish in the crossing.[4] A much higher loss rate had been figured. Hunters greeted them with fresh meat; deer, antelope, quail and rabbit were waiting for them, as well as much fresh plant food. There were cattail tubers, yucca root and mesquite bean cakes as well.

They rested here for a hand of days more before making the final trek to the escarpment. They had arrived at their new home, with renewed vigor, brought about by all the good food they could consume. Most quickly recovered; Butterfly and a couple of the older women took a while longer. Quickly the various groups settled into the areas already claimed by the forward group. The Yucca camp settled where Blue Coyote and Stone Man had set up their camp. Other groups moved farther north, still others south, and some decided on the area farther out toward the moving dunes. Soon they were as scattered as in the Starving Mountains.

"We will begin the trek back at the next full moon," Deer Hunter stated. "I promised my camp they would be in this new land before winter. They are waiting for me to return and lead them."

Angry Hawk rose, "We must be sure there is not a repeat of the theft on the last journey," he stared accusingly at the men who nearly cost so many their lives.

"I will gladly lead the way," exclaimed Grape Leaf, "Perhaps that will help remove some of the shame that I have brought upon my family and my camp. For myself, I deserve what I get, but they do not."

It was decided that a span of men would cross the moving dunes to bring across the rest of The People. Those people remaining at the escarpment would be responsible for carrying food out and caching it along the way. First they went two days into the moving dunes and cached a large amount of food. Then more was all carried yet another three days beyond, and then more, farther yet. They continued caching until they had set up a route well stocked with food completely across the dunes. If only a couple of day's worth of food need be carried, people could travel faster. So group after group of men left with heavy-laden travois; returning and taking yet another load. All along, the way was well marked with poles so that the next pole could be sited from the last. There would be no chance of getting lost. There was also a limit set on how many people could cross at one time. They would not take the chance of trying to feed too many people on less than enough food and water. That lesson had been learned.

Meanwhile those not engaged in this enterprise would be hunting, preparing food and gathering stores for the winter. Yet others were erecting shelters and digging storage pits. Women spent days in the strange oak forest gathering vast quantities of the life-giving acorns. Nets captured the large fat birds from the grasslands above.[5] Rabbits were snared and taken with rabbit sticks. Quail were netted, reeds were gathered, yucca roots dug, and wild plums and apples picked. Pigweed[6] was harvested, as were the grains of the grasses above. It had been many seasons indeed since The People had so much food.

Late summer brought Grape Leaf leading the second wave of people to the escarpment. They had been waiting for him on the other side, dangerously low on even the most meager supply of food. Many were too weak to make it. There were more bodies laid out to walk the wind.

By the season of the harvest moon all The People were settled on the eastern side of the moving sand dunes. The Starving Mountains could sink into legend. It had taken only a third trip to bring the last of them across, and at least a span more had gone to walk the wind along the way. Still, those who had made it were quickly well fed and healthy. There was no lack of food for the few crossing on that last trip, nor in their new land.

The camps spread out in their new territory, learning the plants that would make food. The healers searched for those plants they were familiar with to restock their dangerously low pharmacopeia. The dreamers replenished their supplies of Thorn Apple. And the women gathered, and gathered, and gathered! The men hunted, bringing load after load of meat for the winter stores. Basket after basket of acorns were carried down from the shinnery above and stored in the numerous caves along the caprock. Reeds were cut for weaving more baskets. The starchy tubers were roasted and added to the menu. Fat grubs were dug out of the ground and roasted into a crunchy treat.

The few dogs quickly recovered from the stress of the journey and became fat and sleek. Scorpion, by far the largest of the dogs, was the first to recover. She could be seen trotting at Fire Dancer's heels as he went about the task of making sure his camp was prepared for winter. Blue Coyote was the hero of the day, and although he did walk with a stronger step, his status did not really go to his head. He was more interested in pursuits of youth!

He and Stone Man were daily off on some task of their own, or merely exploring the vast grassland above. Frequently the men of the unmated hearth joined them. This group had taken it upon their shoulders to explore the grassland. Really they were looking hopefully for the fabled 'beast' of legend. Alas! They found no signs.

*   *   *

Grape Leaf had regained his standing among the camps only by valiantly leading both the second and third groups across. The other men shamed by the water and food theft, simply vanished one night, people hoped never to be seen again. No one knew if they walked into the moving sands to die or tiring of the taint they had brought upon themselves had gone off somewhere else to live. The People did not miss them, however. Theft is not a thing to be tolerated by any group who lives at the edge of starvation.

---

1. *Tympanuchus pallidicinctus:* Lesser Prairie Chicken, live in sagebrush and short-grass prairie. At one time very common in the area, today only a few small flocks remain. *Field Guide to the Birds of North America;* 1989: 214.
2. *Datura wrightii:* Southwestern Thorn Apple; Extracts from this plant are narcotic and when improperly prepared, lethal. **MacMahon** 1988: 385.
3. Mano and Metate: Native Americans used these utensils to grind seed and grain into flour. The metate was a flat coarse-grained stone, usually worn down by use in the center. The mano was a stone held in the hand and rubbed back and forth over the seeds and they were crushed between the two stones.
4. The distance from the Capitan Mountains to the west to Elide, at the edge of the escarpment is 135 miles. People in poor health, walking through open sand dunes, carrying heavy packs, could make little more than four miles a day, or night. It would take 34 days of solid walking to do so.
5. Prairie Chicken.
6. Pigweed: *Amaranthus* species: Dozens of species grow throughout North America. The leaves and stems are tasty is salads or cooked especially if collected young. Some grow to six feet or more in height and produce large spread seed-bearing flower clusters that were harvested and processed as a grain crop. Amaranth grain and greens are highly nutritious. **Tilford** 1988: 14.

CHAPTER 4

The Yucca camp constructed their living shelters just at the base of the caprock beneath their storage cave. They used the hides of deer hunted in this new home, untanned and stitched together to produce a more-or-less waterproof covering. Until the colder season the sides would remain open to allow the fresh breeze through. There was a double hand of shelters in all, enough for the entire camp, numbering little more than a double span of individuals. The storage cave was partway up the face of the cliff, with a ledge before the entrance. There was a well-worn path leading up to it, made by countless feet on the compacted rubble from the breakdown of the escarpment.

At one time people had obviously used it for shelter, for the roof was fire blackened and there were bits of disintegrating basket at the far rear. Along one wall was a natural ledge, and there were signs of ancient fire pits in several places on the floor. The only thing living there now, however, was a packrat, the last of a long line of packrat from the size of the midden. Star Woman and Butterfly cleared out the midden, using it for firewood. The packrat, Butterfly and Basket had for their evening meal.

"The pigweed is nearly ready to harvest," Butterfly remarked as she, Star Woman, Basket, Turtle Woman, and Little Antelope Woman made their way along one of the many game trails away from the escarpment. They had their digging sticks, nets, bolas and rabbit sticks as always, and were after quail and any other creature unwise enough to cross their path.

"We should plan on doing that soon," Little Antelope Woman agreed.

"We already have more food stored than we could possibly eat in a hand of moons!" protested Basket. "Why do we need more?"

"The pigweed will not be producing seeds again until this time next season," reminded Butterfly, "Would you wait until then to eat cakes made of it?"

"No, I suppose not," Basket sighed, "It just seems to me that we are gathering far too much of everything! How can so few people eat it all? We have a hand of containers filled with acorns alone. There is at least a span of containers with dried meat, and still the men are out hunting every day. We have so many hides to process now that it will take the entire winter to do so, and already everyone has a new set of clothes. How much do we need?"

"At least we are not starving!" Turtle Woman reminded her.

"No, but the way we are digging up every last tuber and cattail bulb, it will not be long before we are," she protested.

"You are still a girl, Basket. Your memory is not as long as ours. You can only remember a few starving seasons. We have whole lives of them to remember," Butterfly remarked.

"Look! There are the quail!" Turtle Woman called; and they all hurried to stretch the net across the trail. Quickly the women circled around and soon were herding the large fat gray birds toward the net.

*   *   *

Acorn walked down the trail toward the pond, guided by the ancestor fires and a quarter moon. It was very late, but he could not sleep. His dreams since settling at the escarpment had been anything but pleasant. He woke in a cold sweat, but never could he remember the dreams, only his pounding heart and a sense of absolute fear. *Are the spirits trying to communicate with me?* He questioned himself. *I feel so helpless! What kind of dreamer am I, I have failed to help my people for seasons, yet in my youth . . . ?* He sighed and seated himself on a boulder near the pond. Perhaps communing with the ancestors would help.

Wake up Dreamer! Acorn jerked alert. *Come with me, I have heard your pleas! Follow me and I will show you the way of the future for The People.* Acorn floated upward and followed the path of the voice. Spirit Wolf joined him. High above the escarpment they flew, seeing the various camps spread out along its base. They were busy with the hunting and gathering of daily life. Then things began to change. The people became fat, so fat they no longer went out and hunted or gathered; but sat around their hearths eating in a passion of gluttony that amazed the dreamer. Again things changed. The plants disappeared, the game animals began to vanish, and the people became walking skeletons, and more and more were set out to walk the wind. *They did not learn!* The voice vibrated inside his head. *Still they waste. Still, they rape the land, leaving nothing behind to renew it. They mock the spirits of the plants and animals that provide for them. Unless they change, the spirits will not bless these people. You must find the one and reunite them; only they can save The People. So long as they are separated, bad luck will befall all! The evil one must be destroyed! The circle cannot close!*

Acorn woke! Light was just beginning to lighten the sky above the escarpment. His legs were cramped, his back pained, his heat throbbed and his heart beat in panic. His entire body was covered with sweat, yet he was nearly freezing from the cold. As quickly as he could, he scrambled down from the boulder and headed back to the camp. *Another dream?* Probably; yet he could not remember any of it. "I will try part of that peyote[1] button I traded for," he mumbled to himself.

Quickly he returned to the camp. Already people were stirring and another day had begun. "We are going up onto the plains to hunt antelope," Fire Dancer stated as he gathered up his hunting tools. "I hope we also come across those wolves who have been sneaking closer and closer to the camp. They are getting bolder every day!"

* * *

"Stone Man and I are considering a trip back to Black Land," Blue Coyote said. "We are desperately low on obsidian, and although we have searched everywhere here, there is none. No one has found any stone from which to produce tools."

"What does Cougar say?"

"Nothing which has been brought in has been suitable," replied Blue Coyote.

"I don't like the idea of the two of you going all that way across the moving dunes again," protested Star Woman. "Why can't some of the other men go if a trip must be made?" She expertly formed grain cakes and set them to cook on hot stones surrounding the fire. From a spit suspended over it, already three rabbits and a full hand of quail were roasting. Mint tea steeped in a container into which she added another hot stone, expertly removing the now cold one with a pair of sticks. As she worked, Fire Dancer completed his preparations.

"I wish we had more camp dogs," he complained, "I will have to take Scorpion all the way to the Pine Camp if we are to have a litter of pups out of her, and she will be unusable for nearly a double turning of the moon then."

"Why not breed Gray Eagle's bitch instead then?" Blue Coyote asked.

"She is too small. Her pups wouldn't be any good."

"What we need is new blood in the dogs."

"Where would we find that?" Fire Dancer questioned, "There is only a span or so of dogs amongst all of the camps, and Scorpion it the largest and best of them all."

"That is only because her mother ran off with the wolf pack," Star Woman commented.

"Perhaps that is the answer," Blue Coyote offered, "Let the wolf pack breed her."

"And take the chance they would kill her instead, or that she joins them?" Fire Dancer shook his head, "And then we would have no dog."

"I have watched the wolves in the Starving Mountains. I do not think they would kill a bitch in heat. Scorpion has never shown any inclination toward her wolf blood, she is too well trained and has lived all her life with us. Besides, she is far too devoted to you, Father."

Fire Dancer shook his head, "And I am too caring for her to take the risk."

Blue Coyote was very thoughtful as he ate his meal, consisting of an entire rabbit and a couple of quail, three roasted cakes and a large serving of mint tea. Already they were all becoming fat with all the good food, and they had been living in this new land only a couple turnings of the moon. Star Woman had developed a second chin, and Fire Dancer was much heavier than when he arrived. In the starving mountains this one meal would have been enough for more than a span of days.

His mind however was not on food; he was considering wolves!

*   *   *

"I think you have lost your mind!" Protested Stone Man. "Why on earth would we want to capture a wolf?"

"I think we could secure it with a thong, and let it get used to us. Then when it is time to breed the dogs, use him. Think how much better the pups would be!"

"What makes you think a captured wolf would breed our dogs, even if we could catch one alive, and keep it captive long enough to do so."

"What makes you think it wouldn't?" Blue Coyote responded.

Stone Man, for once, could not come up with an answer.

"So, when do you want to do this thing?" He finally capitulated. Long experience had convincing him that nothing was going to change Blue Coyote's mind once he set it on one of these hair-brained schemes.

"As soon as possible," Blue Coyote replied. "Scorpion will come into season in just a few spans of days. I have no idea how long it will take to get a wolf used to us."

"Forever, if you ask me," mumbled Stone man as he reluctantly followed Blue Coyote down the trail.

Later that day the two youths stood beside one of the few stout trees in the area. From it Blue Coyote had set a snare. "How do you intend to make sure the wolf we capture is a male?" Asked Stone Man.

"We will just have to take that chance. Besides, in the Starving Mountains the young males always are in the front of the pack."

"These wolves might be different!"

"Wolves are wolves," Blue Coyote replied.

"And once we snare him, supposing that we actually do, how are you going to get a thong around his neck and get him back to the camp without getting badly bitten in the process?"

"With this," Blue Coyote produced a net from among his piles of preparations. "We will throw it over him and truss him up with it, unhook the thong and cart him back to camp that way."

"And the first night he will chew the thong through and escape and all of our work will have been for nothing," replied Stone Man.

"Wrong! That is what I built the blockage across the small cave for. I intend to keep him in there. I will sleep on the ledge outside, every night if I have too."

"I still wonder . . . "Stone Man scratched his head.

"What do we have to lose?" Blue Coyote asked, "A few hours of time, which in case you hadn't noticed, we seem to have a lot of in this land."

"I suppose that rabbit is to lead the wolf to the snare?"

"Right; we will drag it along the trail and leave it just beyond the snare. It will work, you will see!"

Their trap set up and baited the youths hurriedly hid and waited, and waited . . .

"I told you it wouldn't work!" Stone Man grumbled as they munched on a late meal. The sun was going down, they had been squatted in cramping positions all day and no wolf had come near their trap.

"So, we try again tomorrow," Blue Coyote replied undaunted. Stone Man groaned and rolled onto his back in mock agony.

"Why do I always end up going along with your dumb schemes?"

"Because I always talk you into it," replied Blue Coyote logically as he kept on eating.

They unsprung the snare, left the rabbit behind, hoping it would at least bring the wolves into the area, and then they returned to camp. At dawn the next morning they were back with a fresh rabbit. Blue Coyote grinned! The other was long gone, and there were wolf tracks all around where it had been.

"I still think we are wasting our time," grumbled Stone Man, "but as you say, what else do we have to do."

"Right!" replied Blue Coyote.

Again they waited, and waited . . . "Sh.! I hear something!" Blue Coyote silenced Stone Man's muttering as he shifted into a more comfortable position. Suddenly there sounded a surprised yelp and a lot of confused barking. The youths leaped forward toward their snare.

"What is going on here," demanded Jackrabbit angrily of the two, "Why do you snare my dog?"

"We weren't after your dog," admitted Blue Coyote, "we were after a wolf."

"A wolf! What on earth for? They are predators, we no longer are forced to eat them, we have no need for their hide, and so far they do not threaten the camp."

"Never mind, I am sorry we frightened your dog," Blue Coyote apologized.

"Crazy boys," Jackrabbit muttered as he unhooked his frightened dog and led it away down the trail. "They have nothing better to do than snare the camp dogs! What is life coming too? They should be out hunting for meat, not fooling around and frightening people and their dogs."

Blue Coyote grinned wickedly at Stone Man, "I will surely hear about this," he chuckled. "I can just imagine what Fire Dancer will have to say."

They reset the snare and again hid. Late in the day, once again they heard something traveling along the path; they only hoped Jackrabbit was not coming back again along the path headed home.

The yelp, however, was not his dog. Dangling from their snare by one front leg was a young male wolf. The rest of the pack had vanished. "I can't believe it," exclaimed Stone Man, "It actually worked!"

"Of course it worked! Help me get this net over him." Blue Coyote was trying unsuccessfully to entangle the terrified animal in the net. Stone Man grabbed one side and in a flash they had the snapping, snarling, enraged and frightened wolf securely netted. While Stone Man held the netting tightly, Blue Coyote secured it with thongs, until the poor animal could hardly wiggle. Then he cut the snare loose and they lowered their prey to the ground.

"Let's get a thong around his nose, I don't want him biting me on the way back to camp," Blue Coyote remarked as they stood surveying their handiwork.

"Bite! The poor thing can hardly breathe we have him so tightly trussed!" Stone Man protested but secured the wolf's muzzle any way.

"I have put plenty of food and water in the cave already, and I have the blockage in place as well. All we have to do is release him inside."

Stone Man followed his friend back toward the camp shaking his head. About half way there he began to wonder just how they would get the wolf into the cave, release it and get out again without mishaps to one of them, hopefully, not a human one.

"Hold his feet!" directed Blue Coyote, "I have to get this thong around all of them and tie it in a release knot." Stone Man gritted his teeth and held the feet, "Now hold his ears so I can remove the net, all right, now slide your hands down his head and hold his mouth closed so I can replace this thong and get rid of the net. Hold him still! There I have it!" Blue Coyote tossed the net behind him and gazed with satisfaction at the wolf muzzled and trussed at their feet.

"Anything else?" Stone Man checked his fingers to make sure he still had all of them.

"No, you go outside and I will follow," Blue Coyote backed away from the now exhausted wolf lying inside the cave. Half way to the entrance he pulled the muzzle thong, releasing the wolf's head, instantly the animal began to struggle and chew on the thong securing his legs. Blue Coyote exited the cave and secured the barricade before pulling on the thong he still held in his hand, thus releasing the wolf, safely secured inside. Almost instantly the closure shuddered as the terrified animal tried to break out.

"He only shoves the blockage against the opening. It is impossible to open it outward." Blue Coyote watched his captive with satisfaction.

"He could chew through the cordage, and probably the branches as well," reminded Stone Man.

"I will be here to see that he does not," Blue Coyote replied, "And when I cannot be, you will."

"Well, I suppose that since we have gone too so much trouble to capture 'our' wolf, we should both keep watch over him," agreed Stone Man, still sure the plan would never work.

* * *

"I wish you had discussed this with me before you did it," protested Fire Dancer, "Jackrabbit is really mad, he has told everyone about your snaring his dog."

"How were we to know he would choose that very path to follow, out of all of the game trails available to him? It is not our fault!" Blue Coyote returned, reaching for another quail to add to the stash of food he was collecting. He licked the juice from his fingers and grabbed a hot grain cake to add to his platter.

"Besides, it was you who gave me the idea in the first place!" he added. "Wait until you see our wolf! He is magnificent!"

The first night and day the wolf cowered at the back of the cave growling and showing his teeth every time one of the pair moved. The second he merely glared hatred at them as he 'wolfed' down the food which they provided, the next he began to pace the small cave. By the end of a hand of days he was moving around the cave, ignoring them altogether. At the end of half a moon the animal was actually taking food from Blue Coyote's hand through the barricade. He had settled down and accepted his confinement. They were no longer literally living on the ledge. Now, when Blue Coyote brought fresh food and water the animal actually wagged his tail in greeting.

After the initial curiosity was satisfied, the camp more or less ignored the captive and his keepers, merely shaking their heads and muttering about the things that youths do.

*   *   *

"I am going inside," Blue Coyote said casually.

"Are you crazy?"

"We are friends! I have scratched his ears and petted him through the branches. He will not hurt me." He unlatched the barricade and slipped inside. Stone Man did not even have time to worry about the consequences of his friend's foolishness before Blue Coyote was petting and scratching the wolf. The wolf responded by rolling onto its back and fanning all four feet in the air[2], an expression close to a grin on its face as Blue Coyote scratched his belly thoroughly.

The wolf was young; he had not been with his pack for a hand of days when captured. Now as far as he was concerned Blue Coyote and Stone Man were his pack. Why not? He had not been hurt or badly treated after the initial capture. He had all the food he could eat, without even fighting for his share, and the Alpha of his new pack treated him with respect and kindness. Of course Blue Coyote and Stone Man had no idea of this.

Soon the wolf was barking a greeting and leaping about with anticipation when they arrived. The day came when Blue Coyote felt is was safe to let him out. Wolf leaped and ran in tight circles about them, raced a short distance away, then ran back and rolled onto his back. He was wild no longer.

The rest of the camp, however, was another thing. Wolf had not yet met Star Woman and had only seen Fire Dancer occasionally, however, since their scent was familiar to him, he cautiously accepted them, soon relaxing and becoming at home around the shelter. Wherever Blue Coyote went, people soon became used to seeing Wolf at his side. Butterfly would not come near the animal, Jackrabbit muttered about darting him if he harmed anyone, and Red Eagle glared angrily at both Blue Coyote and the wolf.

When Scorpion came into season, Wolf happily obliged. Grudgingly, Jackrabbit asked to use him when his own dog was ready. Soon the other of the camp dogs was obliged as well. Ordinarily the camp dogs would not have been bred at the end of the harvest season, however, there was so much food, no one would be hungry during this winter, and there was a great deal extra to feed the animals. By spring the pups would be old enough to begin training.

* * *

"I think it foolish to gather more acorns!" protested Basket. "We have more than we can eat now! Besides, look how far we have to go out onto the plains to get them."

"It has been decided," Butterfly replied, "The people from the Rabbit and Quail Camps are coming as well. It will be the last acorn gathering this season."

"Very well," Basket sighed, "I will go with you, but I have a bad feeling about this trip."

"You are always having 'bad feelings' about things," grumbled her grandmother.

"And usually I am right!" Basket reminded. "Remember I didn't . . ."

"Now no more of that nonsense," Butterfly complained, "I do not want to hear more about how you feel about things, it isn't natural. I certainly hope you have never spoken to anyone else about it."

"No Grandmother. I have said nothing, as you asked."

"What are you packing those for?" Butterfly questioned, "We have enough to pull on the travois without the addition of extra hides and robes and we certainly don't need heavy winter clothes. We are nearly uncomfortably hot in the ones we wear."

"Why do you care, I am the one who is pulling the travois?" reminded Basket.

"I suppose your strange feelings tell you to do that as well?"

"Yes, as a matter of fact it does!" Basket threw the extra sleeping robes and a hide shelter belligerently onto the travois and secured them, thus for once having the final word with her grandmother.

The selected group from the Yucca camp began to gather at the base of the trail. Star Woman checked over her own load, glanced at Butterfly and Basket's, frowned and returned to the shelter. She carried a pair of extra robes back, as well as a small hide shelter, adding them to her load. Basket, seeing this lifted her eyebrows at her grandmother and grinned. Butterfly snorted and stomped off toward the trail. Soon they headed across the plains, a hand of women and two men, to meet the other camps at the edge of the Shinnery Belt.

The camps and numerous wild animals had harvested all the acorns within a hand of day's journey from the escarpment. Now The People were making one last trip to collect before winter set in. They traveled slowly to the east, stopping early in the day, feasting well and turning in early. The sun was well up before they moved on, day after day.

Moth and Squirrel Girl busily rambled among the dunes, looking for quail and prairie chickens. They brought in the food for the evening meal the first few nights, then the novelty wore off and they drifted among the group of gatherers just enjoying being young and healthy and well fed.

"I must be getting old," Star Woman groaned rubbing her back, "I cannot remember when merely gathering a few acorns was such hard work!"

"We are all out of condition," Turtle Woman agreed, "The good living we have had these last several moons is beginning to show, more ways than one," she patted her substantial frame.

They had filled half of their containers and hoped soon to finish and return to the camp. Others however, were not nearly as attentive to work. Star Woman glanced worriedly toward the northern sky. "I hope that is not a storm building there," she remarked.

Basket whipped up her head and studied the sky; "We have to go, NOW!" She started dragging her basket to where they had camped. "Come on! We have to hurry!" The women looked at her, toward the sky and at one another.

"I don't understand that child!" muttered Butterfly, "She gets stranger every season. Just like her mother!"

"Do you think she might be right," Star Woman asked? "I don't like the looks of the sky either. We could be in real trouble."

"Are you going to start as well?"

"What do you mean, as well?" asked Star Woman.

"Nothing!" muttered Butterfly, "I'm just getting old, and . . ."

"Did Basket say something to you before we left?" Star Woman wanted to know.

"What if she did?"

"Why didn't you say something? I would have stopped the trip. I have not felt comfortable about this acorn gathering either. I noticed that you brought extra robes and a shelter, so you must have had misgivings also."

"Basket did, she insisted on the extra furs and clothing, since she was pulling the travois, I let her have her way. She doesn't know anything!" Butterfly insisted.

"Come on, we are wasting time!" Star Woman began dragging her container toward the camp. Turtle Woman and Butterfly followed her, all of them catching the anxiety initiated by Basket.

On the way they collected the rest of their party.

"What are you doing?" Questioned one of the women of the Rabbit Camp, as she noticed they were loading their travois and preparing to leave.

"Storm coming in," replied Star Woman, "We are going back to the escarpment while we still can."

The woman looked at the sky, back at them and shrugged. She returned to her group and continued gathering acorns. The Yucca Camp people moved out a finger of time later, pushing hard for home. They traveled well into the night, finally stopping, too exhausted and confused by the dark to go any farther. At dawn they were underway again. By late afternoon the wind had begun to rise; a bitterly cold cut to it. They began to shiver, the lightweight winter clothing they wore no protection from it. Star Woman handed the extra robe to Turtle Woman and wrapped in her own. Cougar was grateful for the protection of the small shelter hide. Butterfly grudgingly was thankful that Basket had insisted on the extra clothing and robes. She was now dressed in a warm rabbit fur lined winter shirt beneath her winter tunic. Her leggings were wonderfully warm as well. Basket dragged their travois ahead with a grim set to her expression. Jackrabbit had their extra shelter hide about his shoulders, thankful for its considerable protection.

"We aren't going to make it before the blizzard strikes," Star Woman finally stopped Basket in her headlong push for home. "We had better dig in and wait it out."

Jackrabbit glanced at the approaching storm. Already snow was beginning to come down, almost horizontally, whipped and driven by the biting wind. "I agree. This is as good a place as any. We can dig away the side of the dune and drag as much wood as possible to where we can reach it. By lashing the travois furs and our shelters together we can produce some protection. A small fire will keep the bitterest of the cold out, and we have lots of food, so at least we won't starve."

"We can melt the snow for water if we have to," Butterfly offered.

Already Cougar and Jackrabbit were digging the beginning of a hole into the dune with their scapula shovels. Quickly Turtle Woman searched out rawhide and her awl and began punching holes along the edge of the shelter hide, Butterfly started on the other, while Basket, Antelope Woman and Star Woman gathered and dragged as much sage and shinnery as they could and stacked it around the developing hole. The travois poles were driven into the soil and the hides securely attached with lacing across the front. Soon the shelter was completed, just large enough for the people, storage baskets containing their food and water, and a small fire. Its earth top and sides offered considerable protection from both the cold and the wind. Grimly they settled down to wait out the storm, only adding enough fuel to the fire to keep it alive.

"At least I can feel my toes again," Turtle Woman sighed, "And we are so packed in here our body heat almost keeps the shelter warm."

"The rest of the people are going to freeze to death out there," Basket said glumly, "I should have done something; I knew this trip was wrong! I should have insisted!"

"Who would listen to you?" Butterfly tried to console her granddaughter.

"I would have listened!" reminded Star Woman, "And I would have made sure the other did so as well."

"Then it is my fault if they die," Butterfly stated, "For it was I who insisted Basket say nothing."

"What difference does it make whose fault it was? We can do nothing about it now," Jackrabbit said. "They had as much opportunity to leave as we did. Is it our fault they decided to stay? No, I say. It is not." He patted Basket on the arm, "No one forced them to go and they were free to leave at any time. Everyone knew there was a storm coming, and it was discussed every day. Besides, we do not know. Perhaps they are just behind us."

Basket shook her head, "No, we were the only ones to be really concerned"

For a while everyone was wrapped up in his or her own thoughts. The other people caught out in the storm were not closely related, but they were known, some of them were friends. There was a thumping on the opening cover just then. "Hello! Are you in there?" Jackrabbit shoved the opening aside and Centipede Man and his daughter Moth crawled gratefully inside. "I cannot believe how fast you traveled," he said once he caught his breath, "We left just fingers after you, and have been trying to catch up with you ever since."

"What of the others?" Basket asked hopefully. Centipede Man shook his head, "We are all that followed."

With a bit of shifting they managed to scoop out a smidgen more room inside the shelter and fit the additional two people inside, luckily, Moth was small. Then they settled down to wait . . .

"I have to pass water," Moth whispered to Basket.

"Me too," Basket frowned, "We had better be quick though, it is really freezing out there."

"What are you doing?" Butterfly shouted as they began undoing the lacing at the opening

"We have to go!" Basket whispered back.

"Now that you mention it, so do I, if anyone else needs to pass water, now is the time," she announced as they quickly scrambled out, along with the entire occupancy. It was a quick job and they all prepared to crowd back inside. "I can't believe how cold it is out there!" Butterfly drew her sleeping robe closer about her shoulders. "I couldn't even see my hand in front of my face it is snowing so hard."

"While we are all moving about, we should pull more brush for the fire closer and add some to the fire, and it probably wouldn't hurt to fix some hot tea at the same time, and we probably should eat as well," suggested Turtle Woman.

"Probably," agreed Star Woman.

One of the men secured more fuel for the fire, shaking the snow from it before handing it into the women. Then they passed in a tripod and filled a cooking skin with snow. Already Star Woman had dug out the tea making materials. While they were up, they also excavated a bit more earth out to enlarge the shelter some, so at least there was room for everyone to settle more comfortably and make room for the fire.

Soon the fragrance of tea was cheering them up and the fire removed the chill of their excursion. As soon as the tea was hot, however, they let the fire burn to coals, for no one knew how long they would be stranded in their little cave.

*　　*　　*

"Listen!" Star Woman shook Butterfly awake.

"What?"

"The wind, it has stopped."

They had all been crowded together in the hastily made shelter for at least several days as far as they could reckon. They had slept as much as possible, to conserve energy, and to pass the time the older ones told stories. All in all it had not been too unpleasant, except for the infrequent, but necessary trips out into the storm. The men had gone out to drag more fuel for the fire closer in a brief lull, but beyond that, they had spent the time huddled as closely together as possible.

"I am going out to see," Star Woman stated.

"I will go with you," Butterfly said, "I need to move around a bit any way, I think my legs have gone to sleep."

"What is it?" Basket yawned.

"The wind has stopped," Butterfly answered, "We are going outside to see what it is like."

"Is the storm over?" asked Moth.

"I don't know." Star Woman crawled through the opening and stood up. Above her, the ancestor fires twinkled brightly in the sky. The temperature had risen considerably.

Everyone crawled out and stood looking about. The world had changed while they crouched inside the shelter. A full moon turned the entire plain into a pure white landscape of sculptures. Everywhere a plant had projected above the ground, a drift rose in fantastic shapes; in other places the ground swept nearly clear, only a thin covering of snow softening it. They stood wordlessly looking around.

"Storm's over," Jackrabbit broke the silence.

"We are still alive," Turtle Woman added, "I cannot believe the worst I have, are cold toes."

"As soon as we get things loaded, we had better start moving toward the camp," Star Woman said.

"It will be warmer once the sun is up," remarked Butterfly.

"I have been cramped up for so long, I need to move," Star Woman stretched, "It will be light in a short while any way, the sky is already turning. Those back at the camp will be worried. They are probably already on their way to meet us."

"I will make some tea and dig out the seed cakes while the rest of you get things ready," offered Moth, "We only need lift up the traces of our travois," she nodded toward it.

"And I will help the rest of you," Centipede Man was already dismantling the shelter cover.

By the time Moth had hot tea and seed cakes ready the travois were loaded and ready.

"How far do you think we have yet to go?" questioned Turtle Woman.

"It will probably take a little more than a pair of days, depending on how deep the snow is," answered Centipede Man. "You were really traveling fast."

"I know everyone at the camp will be worried about us," remarked Star Woman.

"Grandmother," Basket whispered and pulled Butterfly quietly away from the others. "I am bleeding." She withdrew her hand indicating the smear of blood on her fingers.

Butterfly broke into a delighted chuckle and hugged her granddaughter close. "Nothing to be afraid of, Basket, you are just a woman now. But I wouldn't say anything to anyone until we get back to camp. You know how men fret about taboos. Leave it to you to decide to become a woman while stranded in the worst blizzard I have ever lived through!"

Basket smiled back and hurried to take up the harness of their travois.

Jackrabbit, Cougar, and Centipede Man took turns breaking-trail through the deeper snow and the women followed. At nightfall they met the rescue party.

*　*　*

"We were sure that you were frozen to death," exclaimed Stone Man.

"Indeed, the entire camp was worried," modified Fire Dancer, "However, I was quite certain you were too intelligent to get caught unaware."

"We nearly were," admitted Star Woman, "We went too far and did not start back soon enough. But we dug in and waited the storm out with little discomfort."

"Unfortunately," Centipede Man sighed, "I am not so sure about the rest. They were not unduly concerned when we left. Nor did they have extra clothing and robes. I fear the worst for them."

They walked for the better part of two more days before smoke was smelled and soon they were hurrying down the trail into the Yucca Camp. Scorpion had came racing to greet them a finger from the top of the trail, Fire Dancer, Blue Coyote, Wolf and Stone Man were leading the acorn gatherers home.

"We had better send runners to the other camps and form a rescue party," Fire Dancer said. "If they are all dead, we have to lay them out to walk the wind, if not they are probably in need of help."

"I will go back with you," Star Woman offered, "I feel responsibility for them, perhaps if I had insisted harder they would be with us now."

"Squirrel Girl was with her mother," Moth suddenly began to cry; "She can't be dead! They would do the same thing we did, wouldn't they Father?" Tears ran down her face. "Squirrel Girl is my best friend, I know she isn't dead!"

"We will know when we get there, Daughter. You are to stay here with Basket and Butterfly until I return," the good man sighed. This was not going to be a pleasant trip for anyone. He went back over things in his mind, wondering if he could have prevented the tragedy he knew awaited them on the plain.

"But I want to go . . . Squirrel Girl is my friend!"

"Which is why you are staying right here," Centipede Man answered kindly. "If she is alive and well, you will know soon enough, if not, you do not need to see . . ." he sighed, searching for the right words. "There are predators out there, Moth, wolves and coyotes. What they do to a body, well you don't need to know," Centipede Man hushed his daughter.

"I will go to the Rabbit and Quail Camps and gather the hunters," Stone Man offered, "If Blue Coyote can go to the camps to the north." Fire Dancer nodded and soon both youths left the camp.

The word spread quickly. Just after dawn the next morning a group of a span of grim-faced men and three women headed out to where the acorn gathers had been. There was no laughter, and they did not loiter along the way.

They could see the buzzards circling long before they reached the acorn gatherers. Soon they began to find traces of their fate . . . A bloody arm, the fingers chewed free of flesh; part of a leg . . .

Squirrel Girl sat within a scooped-out snow cave similar to the one they had constructed; she was wrapped in all the robes her mother could collect. The rest of the acorn gatherers lay scattered over a small area. They had obviously huddled together within the shinnery in an effort to keep warm, but the only one provided with any protection from the cold, had been Squirrel Girl. Her body was still sitting upright in the shelter beside that of her mother, frozen to death protecting her.

Already wolves, coyotes and buzzards had been at the exposed bodies, ripping them open and scattering the parts in a macabre scene of carnage. One woman lay on her back, part of her lower jay exposed in a grisly grin, her eyes plucked from their sockets, and her abdominal cavity ripped open. Ropes of intestines trailed across the bloody snow, littered with bird tracks and those of wolves and coyotes. Star Woman turned away for the last she had seen of this woman she had been shrugging and laughing because the Yucca Camp was leaving. The hunters did their best to lay out the bodies and give them a proper death ceremony.

It took time to get the right pieces with the proper bodies. Beyond where the people worked, the vultures circled, waiting . . .

Centipede Man assured the party that all the acorn gatherers were accounted for and then the sad party returned to the escarpment. Ironically, Squirrel Girl had survived being lost in the moving sands only to meet her end as a victim of the harsh realities of life on the plains.

The rescue team returned to the camps at the edge of the escarpment in a somber mood. They had learned a valuable lesson about the grassland. It was deceptive, but as deadly as the moving sand.

Moth cried a lot and missed her friend. Centipede Man and his mate Water Woman discussed the situation and made the decision to leave the Rabbit Camp and join the Yucca Camp. Perhaps Moth would be happier without the constant reminders of Squirrel Girl. Centipede Man had developed strong ties with the people of the Yucca Camp during the crossing of the moving sand. He was also happier to relocate. Water Woman was somewhat reluctant to leave her close connections with the Rabbit Camp, but after all, it was hardly any distance between the camps. She would not really be cut off from her friends. Besides she had made new friends within the Yucca Camp.

They set up their new hearth in the last cave to the north, among the group into which the Yucca Camp had moved into just before the storm struck. The winter camp was now strung out along the escarpment nearly a finger's worth of distance. The unmated men occupied a small cave with a narrow path up to its entrance. Fire Dancer's family, Turtle Woman, and Cougar had moved into the supply cave. The wolf cave, by far the smallest, located very close to the supply cave, became the home of Butterfly and Basket. Others were scattered to the north.

During good days the unmated men cut and dragged as much dry wood into the camp, stacking it against the base of the escarpment, handily available for all. The hunters made a few short trips out, but mostly people sat around in one or another cave and occupied themselves with the traditional tasks of winter. Cougar worked on the dwindling supply of obsidian, carefully utilizing every scrap of it large enough to make tools from. He tried the local stone, grunted and discarded it as it proved unsuitable for even the crudest of tools. The women worked the ample store of hides. They used the water boiled from the acorns and ashes from the fire to tan the hides, rubbing the mixture into the hide with the use of a deer rib. Once the hides were softened, they were folded and stored in baskets, ready for use when needed. Rabbit skins were tanned by the numbers; some of them were cut into thin strips, sewn together, end-to-end, and woven into robes, in much the same manner as the baskets were woven from cattail reeds. Soon everyone had a rabbit skin robe, with which they could sleep, cuddle about the hearth, or throw about their shoulders when going outside briefly.

The men made darts, using their shaft straightners to produce the best darts possible from the less-than-straight mesquite wood. The end results were considerably shorter than the darts they had made in the Starving Mountains. Obsidian was in very short supply, as were materials to make proper darts. Yet food was in abundance.

Old Pinyon sat beside the fire on many an evening spinning tales, and teaching the children the stories of The People, telling and retelling the legends of their past.

------

1. *Lophophora williamsii:* Peyote; a small cactus with hallucinogenic properties, used widely by Native Americas to produce spirit trips.
2. This would be a typical action of a wolf accepting dominance from a pack alpha.

CHAPTER 5

Butterfly was gathering up the last of their things in preparation for moving into the wolf cave. They had returned from the disastrous acorn gathering trip just days previously. Now other important matters must be taken care of.

"You must take it at least a half day journey from the camp," Butterfly admonished, "Then dig a hole just as I explained to you. This is a secret thing. When you return I will have everything prepared. Go now!"

"I hope I can remember all of the right words... "Basket worried.

"You will be fine, and no one ever has forgotten. They don't have to be the exact words. It is the attitude that is important. Remember that these are 'women's spirits' and they are not nearly as demanding as male ones seem to be," Butterfly assured her granddaughter. "Just keep your mind on what you are doing and think the proper thoughts. And be sure to mark your spot so that you can find it again!"

Basket accepted her packet from Butterfly and headed out toward the moving sand. She did not really understand the need for secrecy. This was after all a 'becoming a woman ceremony', every woman of the camp went through it. It made little difference in her life except now she was old enough to mate and set up her own shelter. Most of the time becoming an adult merely meant additional work and responsibility. Basket didn't feel mature. She didn't feel any different from before her 'woman's bleed'.

She also didn't like that she needed to make the journey alone. There were predators in the breaks, wolves and coyotes. Of course they probably wouldn't attack a full-grown person, but Basket carried her atlatl and dart scabbard and bolas just in case. Besides, on the way back she might come across game. The People still had not sloughed off the constant need to bring food into the camp. There was so much now that some of it had spoiled and was given to the dogs, or just thrown away. This bothered Basket. Something deep inside of her protested as such wanton wastefulness. She worried about this as she trudged away from the camp, not really paying much attention to where she was going.

Any place will do now, no need to go farther. She studied her surroundings, selected a spot well concealed beneath a mesquite tree and dug a hole with her walking stick. She deposited the packet inside, stood and went through the ritual, just as her grandmother had instructed. She circled around one time for each season, thanked each direction for guidance throughout her adult life, lifted her eyes in prayer to where she knew the ancestor fired twinkled at night and ask the ancestors to guide her. She made a special prayer to her mother, that shadowy person she had never known, but about whom Butterfly had told her much. Then she carefully replaced the earth in her hole, brushed all evidence away with a leafy twig and headed back to camp. She of course had to be sure she remembered this place, for she would be returning here regularly once every turning of the moon, to bury her woman's flow. This was why her location had to be so far from the camp, and a secret. It would not do for her female spirit to soil a man.

"Why do I have to go up into the oak trees to do this?" Basket questioned Butterfly, "What difference does it make? I would be happier just to go to one of the small caves. It is cold up on the plains. The wind blows all the time; and what about predators? I do not know how long I will be."

"I will be nearby," Butterfly assured her. "You will come to no harm. It is necessary to make a spirit journey. You know that. How else would you come to know your protective spirit? I have your amulet bag made with all the proper things inside. There is a piece of the sacred red rock, the umbilical cord from your birth, and when you return from your spirit trip you will add special 'spirit objects' to it from time to time. Here," she handed the object to Basket, "You must take it with you, and once you have made the spirit quest you must not remove it from around your neck, except to make necessary repairs."

Basket took the small rabbit skin pouch attached with a leather thong. It was identical to the amulet bags of every other adult in the camps of The People. "Yes Grandmother," she added it to the little assemblage of preparations she had collected onto her sleeping fur. A small woven basket had been brought forth, one her grandmother had made just for this occasion. Into it she placed the amulet bag and a packet containing the mourning glory seed ground into a powder. This she would mix with hot water into a vision-seeking drink. She included a tortoise shell to mix, steep and heat, the potion, paints for her body, a rabbit skin mat for her to sit upon while taking the journey, and a small water skin.

"I am ready!" She rose to her feet and followed Butterfly from their shelter. The weather was much warmer today. At least the snow had melted, and the sun was shining. They made their way up the trail and into the shinnery. For a time they wandered aimlessly through the plants, first to one spot, and then to another, each rejected by Basket. Butterfly was beginning to get irritated with her but then she nodded. "This feels like the right place," finally she selected a spot, after having rejected so many . . .

Basket cleared away a flat area just a little larger than the rabbit fur mat, spread it carefully and smoothed it out. Then she built a small fire and began to heat a portion of water, some in a small shell and more in a larger one. While the water was heating she spread out the paints she had prepared. There was white, prepared from special ash mixed with deer fat, black, made from charcoal and deer fat, red, created from ground sacred red ochre and deer fat, and yellow, made from yet another ground rock mixed with deer fat. Then she waited until the morning glory drink had steeped. She removed her clothing and began the ritual washing of the body. Already her hair had been prepared, carefully cleansed with soaproot yucca and styled into the traditional knot at the base of the neck favored by women of The People. No longer would she wear it loose in the style of a girl. She dried with a small skin and began the painting of her body. The arms and legs were covered with the white. The area of the heart was painted in yellow. The area around her mouth, both budding breasts and the apex of the thigh was circled in the sacred red. A line of red was drawn from the mouth to this juncture. This signified the feeding, nurturing and reproductive capacity of a woman of The People. A yucca dagger was drawn in black of her right cheek, signifying the camp of her father; a feather on the right cheek signified the camp of her mother, the owl. Then she was ready. She raised the small shell and drank the entire contents in a single gulp.

*   *   *

She waited . . . The tingling began in her fingers, and then spread throughout her entire body. The cold breeze made her shiver. A spiraling of brilliant colors began behind her closed eyes pulling her into it and lifting her away. Up and up! The spiral changed. Now she was flying high above the earth. Below her extended a vast land of ice; it spread as wide and far as the eye could see. At the edge were huge areas of water, larger than any pond Basket had ever seen. Then she was swept to the west. A long thin corridor separated the glaciers. Through it people streamed in small groups following herds of animals into this land beyond the ice. They were dressed in a style reminiscent of The People, but the clothing was heavy and bulky, to suit the bitter cold. They all carried backpacks and many pulled travois. There were no dogs among these people. The animals

moved to the land beyond the glacier, now they changed as well. Basket had never seen such animals. There were few she recognized. The antelope were similar, only they had longer, heavier prongs. The wolf was larger and fiercer than those she was familiar with were. There were many animals she did not recognize. One had a stiff upright ridge of hair along its neck; they ran very fast and moved in small herds, their golden hued coats reflecting the sun. Another had a very long neck, long legs with knobby knees, ending in wide, large feet, and a hump on its back. And then there were the giant beasts with a hand full of legs. They had tusks emerging from their mouth so long that they curved and swept the ground. The last leg was like a greatly elongated nose sweeping to touch the ground. The head carried a large dome and there was a hump sloping from high on the shoulders nearly to the tail. When they ran the ground shook, and the sounds they made were akin to thunder.[1]

They stood so tall a man could not reach the top of the shoulder, not even standing upon the shoulders of another. The people hunted the animals, they gave thanks to the spirits for the animals, but they did not hunt the great beasts. They followed them but gave them honor. The people moved after the migrating herds, using the fast running animals and the large shaggy ones, and sometimes the other grass eaters for food.

There were large predators in this land as well. One kind reminded Basket a bit of the cougar from the Starving Mountains, but they roamed  the grasslands in groups, hunting the other animals and sometimes humans as well. The males had a huge shaggy mass of hair all about the head, extending down to the shoulders. Their color matched the winter grass, within which they hid. Another of their kind had canine teeth so long they extended a hand width beneath the chin. These also were grassland predators. Basket had never seen, nor even heard of such an animal.

The scene changed. Now The People were far to the south of the great ice sheet. They were gathering in a valley celebrating. They numbered many camps, their hearths burning in the valley akin to the ancestor fires in the sky. They joined in a great celebration, fire and lightning flew through the valley, and a herd of the great beasts tore through it, leaving wanton destruction in their wake. Then a group of the people went from the valley and killed the great beasts. The People went in all directions from the valley, some following and killing the great beasts, others following a woman who walked with a wolf to a place Basket recognized. It was their new home. She watched as the women taught The People how to use plants instead of the animals, for the animals were all dying. She saw the woman go to a pond beyond the shinnery and make offerings at a sacred spring. She watched as the woman walked among the great beasts. Then a terrible storm descended, a storm, which lasted for many years[2]. When it was over, the strange animals walked no more, and the people lived in the Starving Mountains.

Basket understood what she was seeing, the heritage of The People.

The scene faded and she was carried to a place where a white fog, so dense she could discern nothing surrounded her in absolute silence.

A far away sound began, then it rose and undulated until it completely surrounded her, caressing her like the ripples in a pond, then the fog lifted.

"She is here!" Rabbit called, "Someone had better call Bison or she will be upset."

"She is more understanding than others have been," Deer stated.

"She is coming," Antelope replied just as the huge shaggy beast hurried up to the gathering.

"Well, it is about time!" Bison commented, "We certainly have waited long enough for this Chosen One to be given to us. I only hope it isn't too late for us. You know the fate of those before us! We do not want to follow their example. Let's have a look at her!"

Basket stared about in amazement. She was completely surrounded by animals of all sorts, some familiar to her, others not. They were talking to each other as casually as though they were people. There were rabbit, fox, weasel, wolf and coyote; eagle, hawk, quail, dove and prairie chicken, deer, antelope and this huge beast called bison. All were studying her with the utmost curiosity.

"I suppose you are wondering what this is all about," the animal they referred to as Bison questioned?

"Yes," Basket whispered a little shakily, "I certainly am wondering."

"Then I will tell you. By the way, I am Bison, The People's spirit. Since the beginning, when the ancestors were young, there have been animal spirits protecting and guiding The People. You have just taken a journey through the times before now; times when the great mammoth guided The People. But they did not follow the spirits, they chose to hunt and slaughter the Great Mother. So a storm came down on the land, drought and sickness took the great herds of grazers from the plains. The People were forced to retreat to what you call the Starving Mountains. For a span of spans of seasons The People have lived there while the great storm raged."

"Even in the Starving Mountains, however, The People did not learn. They killed all the animals, gathered all of the plants, selfishly leaving none to reproduce and replenish. So the land of the Starving Mountains died. Now The People have returned to this place where the last Chosen One led The People and taught them the ways of plants. Still The People do not listen to the spirits, they waste, and gluttony has taken them over. They take more food than they can eat; they let it spoil and then throw it away. They kill far more animals than they can eat, leaving many for the carrion eaters; thus disgracing the spirit of the animal."

"When the vast herd of the plains died out, my kind survived. Now they multiply and spread like grains of sand over the plains. The Spirit Above All is not happy with The People. He has given the animal spirits one more chance to bring the wayward people back into proper veneration of the Spirits. The woman you saw is the Great Beast Mother or Mother of The People. She was the last 'Chosen'. We animal spirits have been given another chance, the circle has been opened, and we are assured that the pair will keep it so. We have chosen you, Basket, Woman of The People, descendent of the Great Beast Mother, herself, to speak for us. You must make The People change their ways of waste and gluttony, or like those who have gone before us, we animals and The People will be no more than the whisper of the wind over the great grasslands. The People must come to revere and respect the animals that serve them; they must learn to respect the spirit traditions. There is a great evil among you. You must find the other, and the evil one must be eliminated" The bison reached out with her horn and touched Basket on the shoulder, "I mark you, Chosen One." She lowered her great head and sighed, "It is done!"

Basket was once again enveloped in the fog as the sounds of the voices receded and again only silence remained. Slowly she opened her eyes. She was shivering with cold and the ancestor fires twinkled brightly in the sky. Butterfly sat quietly a short distance away, waiting patiently for Basket to return from her vision quest. When she saw movement, she hurried forward and added fuel to Basket's fire. The new woman however, was not through with her ceremony. She had yet to remove all the paint from her body and carefully catch the water from that removal in the shell. All must be taken to the secret place and buried.

* * *

As she removed the paint, Basket winced; her shoulder was very tender, although there was no sign of a bruise there. Her head throbbed, and she was sick to her stomach. Thankfully she donned the new 'woman's clothing' which Butterfly had made for her, the style of which she would wear for the rest of her life. On wobbly legs she followed her grandmother back down the trail and to the shelter they shared. On the morrow she would carry her tortoise shell of water and paint to the secret place and bury it beside her woman's blood. When she returned to the camp, there would be a celebration to welcome her, a chance for the entire camp to celebrate.

She lay on her bed furs unable to sleep, thinking back over her 'spirit quest'. Luckily her grandmother had not inquired as to her spirit animal. Basket could remember nothing of a vision trip, if indeed she had made one. She fingered her new amulet bag unconsciously, then uneasily as she realized she could feel the sacred red stone, her umbilical cord, and something else, something, which she had not put there. Quietly, so as not to disturb her grandmother, Basket crept to the cave opening and by the light of the moon opened her amulet bag and dumped its contents into her hand. There were the sacred stone, and the umbilical cord. And a bone figurine of an animal, perfect in all proportions, a tiny creature with a hump on its back, shaggy fur and large horns thrusting from either side of its large lowered head, an animal which Basket had never seen, an animal which she had no name for. She blinked, looked again and then with shaking hands returned everything to the amulet bag and replaced it around her neck.

* * *

"I carried these things hidden inside my clothing," admitted Butterfly. "I know that we were not to bring anything with us except food and life-sustaining things, but your mother was so insistent, she was so determined that you receive these things, she insisted that they were extremely important, so I kept them and brought them with me." She handed Basket a pouch containing a wrapped packet.

"What is it?" asked Basket.

"I don't know. It was meant for you, so I have never opened it."

"But you said that my mother died before I could walk! All these seasons, you never looked?"

"No, it is probably 'spirit' related, and I didn't want to know! Your mother said they were very old, even insisted they came from the Mother of the People herself. Feather claimed her as an ancestor you know."

"So you have told me many times. What I do not understand Grandmother, is that you obviously did not like my mother, yet you kept your word to her . . ."

"She was dying. She made me promise. I could not refuse." Butterfly frowned, "When one makes a deathbed promise, it is to be taken very seriously."

Basket fingered the pouch for a moment, thinking back to a mother she did not even remember. Only Butterfly's colorful descriptions had brought her to life for Basket, and Butterfly had obviously not liked the young woman, whom she blamed for the death of her only son. Basket knew that her mother met a violent end, but not the cause, on this Butterfly and the entire camp had been suspiciously closed mouthed. Finally Basket had tired of asking.

She untied the knots with difficulty; they had been knotted for a long time and had hardened over the seasons. When the knot gave way the packet all but disintegrated and delivered its contents into Basket's lap. There was a leather thong and a pair of well-worn white objects very much resembling the biting teeth of a dog, except these was longer than her entire hand. They had holes drilled in the base where they had been broken from the skull of some animal and the leather thong had been passed through the hole. The thong itself was little more than bits and pieces, but the teeth, smooth, white and glistening in the sun sent tingling feelings of some sort through her fingers when Basket touched them.

Butterfly made a gurgling sound and backed away from Basket, her eyes wide and round with amazement. For once in her long life, she was speechless. "What are they, Grandmother?" questioned Basket. "They must be from some truly magical beast! I have never seen anything like them!" *Or have I? A pair of them?* She shook her head, again stroking the surface, enjoying the sensation that raced up her arm. *Power!*

"I cannot believe it!" Butterfly exclaimed, "All these years I have carried them, cared for them, and I never knew."

"You know what they are, Grandmother?"

"Legend tells of them. But I have never seen them. I don't know anyone who has. And all the time, here I have been saving them for you!" she mused.

"Well, what are they?"

"The teeth; they are probably the very teeth worn by the Mother of the People, herself. I know of no others. There was a legendary animal, far larger than a wolf, a cat, like the cougar of the mountains, but much bigger and more ferocious. Legend tells that the Mother of The People killed this huge predator when she was a girl on her 'woman's quest'. All of her life she wore them on a thong at her waist, so that all would know what a great hunter she was, how powerful was her spirit animal, which legend says was the Great Beast itself."

"And now they are mine?" gasped Basket. "How can this be?"

"Ask the storyteller!" Butterfly shook her head. "I would tell it wrong. Old Pinyon knows all the legends. He is the one to tell you. But they are 'power' objects; that much I do know."

"What shall I do with them?" Basket asked.

"Keep them safe I suppose. I have never seen them before, so at least your mother did not let on that she had them. Someone would surely have killed her for so valuable a relic . . . "Butterfly floundered, "There is great power in such things, magical power."

"But Grandmother, what am I keeping them safe for?" Basket questioned.

Butterfly shrugged, "That is your responsibility to find out. Perhaps Old Pinyon will know the answer. Ask him to tell you the stories, but I would keep those" she nodded to the teeth, "A secret, at least until you have some sort of idea what your mother intended them for."

*　　*　　*

"Are you ready for the ceremony to begin?" Star Woman stuck her head into the cave; "Everyone is waiting."

"She is ready," assured Butterfly as Basket carefully tucked the relics beneath her sleeping fur. "Ouch!"

"What happened?" Butterfly questioned.

"Oh I must have hurt my shoulder. Just a surprising pain, that is all."

Butterfly frowned, pulled the girl around and studied her shoulder. "Must have, you are getting a bruise here," she tapped the spot. "Come on, we are going to be late for your ceremony, and that is bad manners."

Basket followed her down the path from the cave and the few steps to the center of the camp. Everyone was gathered to greet the new woman. Basket wore her special ceremonial clothes. The People knew the secret of making leather pure white. Each new woman was made a set of clothes of this specially treated leather, a short tunic, leggings, and moccasins. After this ceremony, they would be put away and worn again at the mating ceremony. There would be special food gathered by the entire camp, and usually a hunter provided a special kill as well. The hide of that animal was also treated until it was white and it was saved for the mating ceremony as well. The hunter honoring her with the kill would present this to her. There would be gifts for the new woman; each member of the camp giving something that signified their relationship to the new woman. Unmarried men might give a meal of dried meat, or a rabbit skin, to signify they were of an age to mate, not particularly that they were interested in the new woman, but a courtesy toward her. Unmated girls gave gifts of handiwork, a bone needle and sinew, a basket, some small item of clothing. Families gave almost any acceptable thing that was useful. A father of course would provide a large animal for the celebration; a deer was a really fine food. The mother and other relatives of the new woman provided the feast, but as Basket had only her grandmother, Fire Dancer had provided the meat. As Headman of the camp, he could do so without involving the fact that he had an unmated son of proper age. There were certain rules to be observed. Everyone shouted and welcomed Basket. She blushed and thanked each person for their gift and carefully laid them beside her in the place of honor. Basket was lucky, there was much to give in this new land, in the starving mountain land there would have been very little for gifts.

Since a man had to introduce the 'new woman', Fire Dancer did this as well, as part of his duty as Headman. All in all, it was a very satisfying ceremony. Butterfly had hopes that soon she would be adding a grandson to her hearth, a man to provide for her in her old age. There were several in the surrounding camps, and since Basket was not of the Yucca Camp, all the unmated men of this camp were prospective candidates. Basket was however, not the only female about the right age to become a new woman, and she was both small and insignificant. Cottontail had become a woman just before leaving to cross the moving sand, and Moth would be reaching the age shortly. Both far outshone the plain Basket.

It was quite late before the ceremony was finally concluded. The men had enjoyed a round of fermented brew, made for special occasions and even the women were allowed a taste since it was a female ceremony. Basket was quite happy as she crawled into her sleeping fur. A lump beneath her caused her to scramble up and remove the mysterious gift from her long-dead mother. She quickly wrapped it in a rabbit skin and tucked in inside one of her new baskets. Tomorrow would be soon enough to contemplate its meaning.

*   *   *

Acorn watched the new woman conduct herself properly during the ceremony. He had strange feelings about her, nothing he could put his finger on, just a feeling of unease. There had been nothing out-of-the-ordinary about the girl her whole life, why now was he having these strange forebodings? *Need to speak with the spirits.*

The dreamer made his way to where his shelter stood, a little apart from the rest of the camp. Inside he began the familiar ritual for cleansing in preparation for a spirit trip. *Not that it will do any good! How many spirit trips have I taken? How few times have the spirits answered? Why have they forsaken The People?* He sighed and began steeping water to prepare the Thorn Apple Spirit Drink.

As he waited, Acorn again and again went over the past trying to discover where he had gone wrong. As a youth he had been acolyte to Yucca, a dreamer of mediocre talent from the Deer Camp. But Acorn had been filled with visions as a youth. He had been the only choice to follow Yucca. At first everything had been fine; he had visions which guided The People along the path of spirit health. They had not prospered, but then the Starving Mountains had been in the grip of a drought for as long as he could remember. The old ones could remember no other way. Sometimes it confused Acorn when it was discussed, for no one really knew why there was a drought, when as long as memory went, the land had been parched. It was just the way the land was. The idea of green meadows and lush forest did not even enter the mind.

As it became time for Yucca to walk the wind, Acorn assumed more and more of the dreamer's duties. Then, the Deer Camp combined with the Fox, and Acorn moved to the Yucca Camp to replace a dreamer who had vanished mysteriously. He did his best for the Yucca Camp. But the visions began to dwindle, and soon they were no more. It had been many seasons since Acorn had been gifted with more than a flicker of a vision. Yet, still he tried. He continued to hope. As the tingling began, there was a change. The spiral was not black this time, but vividly colored, as in his youth. *Never noticed that it changed!* He mused, *perhaps that is my problem; I have not noticed many things. He was lifted up and could see the camp below him. It was a horrible sight. The people lay and lounged about their hearths, grossly fat and dirty. Acorn barely recognized them as the people he knew. Fire Dancer slumped against a boulder, his hair was thin and gray, and hanging in filthy wisps around a face so bloated that Acorn shook his head in amazement. Star Woman waddled to the fire, her huge breasts jiggling and her fat hips wobbling. Even Stone Man and Blue Coyote were lounging around the hearth, older and like everyone else in the camp, grossly over weight. Trash was everywhere. Remains of meals long over littered the ground. On spits over fires huge amounts of meat were cooking.*

But the land! As far as the eye could see it was as dead and dying as the Starving Mountains. No longer were the game trails littered with tracks. Quail and rabbits did not abound in the land. Buzzards circled a short distance from the camp, and as Acorn went there he could see a huge pile of rotting carcasses. Some type of large, shaggy beast had obviously been driven off the escarpment to their death, but The People had butchered only a few of them, leaving the rest for carrion eaters. On and on Acorn flew; observing more and more repeated piles of these animals. So much waste! No wonder the spirits have deserted The People! "This cannot be the future!" Acorn muttered, shifting uneasily in his trance. *You can change it! They must be reunited. The evil must be driven out!* The voice of Wolf Spirit whispered.

This is why the spirits have deserted The People. They have deserted the spirits! I have not seen even though it has been right before my eyes for decades. The People have shown disrespect, they have squandered, and devastated what the spirits have provided!

Acorn shivered as a cold wind swept over his body. His head throbbed and his stomach was churning. But he almost remembered . . . almost . . . He staggered from his shelter and wandered through the quiet camp. *The girl! She has something to do with it, but what?* He couldn't remember her being in his vision, but he knew . . . *the mystery of her birth!*

*   *   *

Basket passed him as she left the camp. The sun was just rising over the escarpment. The dreamer sat on a boulder beyond the edge of the camp, muttering to himself. She frowned, paused, then remembered her mission and continued. No man could touch her, not even the dreamer, until she disposed of the contents of the tortoise shell she carried. So she sighed and hurried toward the edge of the moving sand.

"It should be just over there," she chewed on her lip. She had been searching for nearly a hand of time, but still had not located the mesquite tree. "I know I marked that tree!" she muttered, "What do I do if I can't find it?" She swung around and headed back the way she had just come, backtracking once again. Finally she slumped to the ground and rubbed her head. It ached. She had to find the tree. Basket had no idea what would happen if she failed. No, one ever had, or at least they did not say so if they had. A movement of white caught her eye. Sitting in a mesquite tree no more than a dart cast from her was an owl[3], watching her with fixed concentration. Then she saw just beside the bird. The owl blinked, shifted and took wing. As she watched it go,  a feather drifted to the ground, floating to the very spot she had selected to bury her flow.

Basket scrambled to her feet and scurried to the tree. She set the tortoise shell on the ground and with shaking fingers reached out and touched the feather. A feeling of heat ran up her arm. She jerked her hand back, blinked, and reached again. The spot on her shoulder tingled and her amulet seemed to throb. An overwhelming feeling of rightness filled her. Somehow the feather was a sign, perhaps a sign from her mother's owl camp. She placed the feather in her waist pouch and quickly buried the liquid and paint. She was done.

"This had been a really strange experience, all in all," she muttered under her breath, "First the teeth, then the figurine, now this!" She got to her feet, scrubbed the tortoise shell with loose sand and hooked it to her waist thong. She marked again the special tree, and then started back to the camp. As she walked, she thought over the last day. Her mother had been keepers of the sacred tooth relics, yet no one had known. How could that be? Had they been handed down mother-to-daughter, generation after generation from the great Mother of The People directly to Basket? But why; was she, Basket, to keep them safe and hand them down to some as yet unborn daughter of her own? The spot on her arm suddenly hurt, just for a heartbeat of time, as though it did not like her conclusion. "Perhaps I am supposed to attach them to a thong as wear them just as the Mother of The People wore them!" she murmured sarcastically. The spot on her arm radiated warmth and pleasure, and *power!*

Basket stopped in the middle of the trail. She frowned, trying to fathom what had just happened. She had wondered if she were a keeper of the sacred relics and the spot pained, yet when she thought of actually wearing them, a definite feeling of rightness pervaded her whole body. "What about the feather?" she whispered, "Am I to keep it safely hidden, a personal message from my 'spirit' bird?" Again the spot on her arm pained, "Or am I to wear it fluttering from a long braid of hair?"

Just then a sharp breeze caught the pins and tumbled her hair loose from the knot she had clumsily put it into, just as if another message was coming to her. "Well I cannot return to camp with it like this!" she muttered and began gathering the long tresses into her hands. Quickly she braided her hair into one long braid down her back, securing it with a piece of rawhide. Then she turned to continue. A sharp pain reminded her; she stopped and reluctantly withdrew the owl feather and secured it at the end of her braid; a definite feeling of well being suddenly washed over her. "Well, at least the braid will not draw attention!" She muttered. Many of the women, both mated and unmated wore their hair in the same style at times. She returned to the camp without further distractions.

*   *   *

"Tell me about her!" She sat across the hearth from Old Pinyon, the storyteller, having brought him a container of sweet clover tea. "Do you think she really did all the things which the legends credit her?"

"I can tell you the stories which have been handed down over the generations, Basket, but how much truth they contain? This I do not know; why all of sudden this interest in The Mother of The People?"

"Well, Grandmother tells me that she was my ancestor," Basket began, "So naturally I am curious."

"Is that so? I didn't know you traced your line to the Bison Camp!" Old Pinyon said with sudden interest.

"Bison Camp? No, my mother was of the Owl Camp," Basket corrected him.

"Before it was the Owl Camp, it had been the Bison Camp," the storyteller replied.

"What is a bison?"

"Well, you see. That's why they changed the name. There were no more bison, so it didn't seem right somehow, so they changed the name. After all The Mother of The People had worn the owl feather in her hair," Pinyon frowned, "What you got one in your hair for?"

Basket shrugged, "I found it, I don't know, it sort-of seemed like an omen from the 'spirit's, you know, the sort of thing you would save in your amulet pouch."

"Then why didn't you put it there, instead of walking around with it where all can see?" He shook his head, "Just because you claim to be of her line, it doesn't mean you can go around copying her."

"Please, just tell me what a bison is," Basket brought the old man's attention back to the topic.

"A bison? Well, I never saw one myself, understand, but some say it was a huge grass-eating animal that once lived on the plain above. A great shaggy beast with a hump on its back and long sharp horns either side of a big head." He sighed, "Good eating so they say. Too bad they are all gone. I would like to have tasted bison . . ."

"How do you know?" Basket began to tremble.

"How do I know they were god eating? People have said so."

"That they are all gone! Just because we have never seen one that doesn't mean they can't be out there somewhere. As you said, it is a large plain; they could be out there somewhere, couldn't they?" Surely her animal spirit couldn't be one which no longer walked the earth?

Pinyon scratched his head, frowned, and replied, "I thought you wanted to hear about The Mother of The People, now you keep asking questions about bison!"

"Yes, of course, The Mother of The People."

"Well . . . they say she was a small woman, lived somewhere west of the plains as a child, grew up all by herself, no parents; no camp."

"She lived right here," Basket replied.

"How do you know that?" Pinyon shifted, "Who is telling this story, you or me?"

"Sorry, you are of course," Basket sighed and did her best to control her impatience with the old man. "Please go on."

"As I said, she grew up somewhere nearby this very place. Lived in a cave she shared with a huge wolf, not one like you know, mind you, but a really big one[4] and when she was going out on her vision journey, she killed a Long Toothed Cat."

"A Long Toothed Cat?"

"Bigger than the wolf; a lot bigger! She broke the long teeth right out of that cat's head and wore them on a thong about her waist, for everyone to see. Even the bravest hunter gave the Long Toothed Cat a wide distance. They were very ferocious you see."

"But if she lived all alone, who was there to see it?"

"Well of course she didn't always live alone. When she was about your age, she set off with her wolf to find The People. She found the Bison Camp. They took her in and she lived with them for the rest of her life."

"And the bison was her spirit animal?"

"Oh no; the Great Mother herself was her spirit animal; the most powerful animal spirit of all."

"Then how did she become the Mother of The People?"

"She has always been called that, because she saved The People. You see, in those days, giants walked the earth. Animals such as we have never seen; huge beasts with long, curving tusks that swept the ground. They were so tall that a man could walk right under them and not touch their belly. And they had a nose like no other animal . . ."

"Like another leg," Basket whispered, "So long it also touched the ground."

"Yes, well, you see, The People claimed this great beast as their special totem animal, and they treated it with great respect, never hunted it. But all that changed! A Diabolical Dreamer came into power and led The People to hunt the sacred beast. Led them all to destruction, he did."

"But we are still here!"

"Yes of course we are, because some of The People chose to follow The Mother of The People instead. They learned to eat plants, and to live as we do today. The spirits looked upon them with favor, and when the great storm came, they were spared. They moved to the Starving Mountains, and we have lived there ever since."

"I thank you for telling me the story," Basket rose and bid the old man good day. He nodded and sipped his tea.

*　　*　　*

"I will not have a granddaughter of mine making a spectacle of herself!" Butterfly shouted. "You get your hair bound properly or you do not leave this cave. And get rid of that outlandish feather! The whole camp is talking about you!"

"But Grandmother," Basket protested, "Many of the women wear their hair braided."

"And many wear it properly, just as you will." She placed her bulk before the cave door, "Now are you going to let me fix it for you, or are you going to stay inside this cave all day?"

"Cottontail and Willow are waiting for me. We are going out to hunt birds in the shinnery."

Basket sighed, knowing her grandmother's stubborn nature, and capitulated. She removed the feather from her hair and tucked it into her waist pouch along with the thong. Butterfly grunted and quickly unbraided, twisted and secured her hair into the traditional style. Basket sighed and escaped the cave, running off to join the other unmated women of the camp for her very first excursion as such, in the company of the other unmated women. Upon approaching the place where she was to meet with Cottontail Girl and Willow she was glad that Butterfly had insisted. The other women were faultlessly turned out, down to their properly laced leggings. Basket sighed and joined them.

"I am sorry to be late," she apologized, "My grandmother needed my help to finish some moving."

"We only just arrived, ourselves," Willow replied. "I have brought an extra net for you, in case you do not have one of your own yet."

"Thank you," Basket accepted the offered net, thankful she had forgotten her own in the hurry to escape Butterfly.

"We thought to go along the edge of the escarpment toward the north today," Willow explained as they filed 'properly' up the trail. "There are still quite a number of prairie chickens there, and we should be able to find some nests with eggs."

"You have gathered eggs before, have you not?" Cottontail Girl asked rather superiorly.

"Many times," Basket confessed, "Eggs are special favorites of my grandmother's. I always try to bring her some when they are available."

She merely nodded. "For now, however, we will concentrate on bringing down a few birds, first. We can mark where the nests are and collect the eggs on our way back."

They followed the edge of the escarpment for several fingers of time, each of them expertly bringing down the plump birds with either rabbit stick or bolas. The nets were for carrying the birds back to the camp. After midmorning they turned back and gathered as many eggs as each could carry, arriving at the top of the trail well satisfied with their trip. The older women were distant but polite to Basket. She was, after all the newest to join their ranks. It was their place to be more adult and reserved toward her. It was in this rank she would be spending her time until mated. It was essential that she fit in and get along with the others. There was little room in the strict code of social behavior for those who did not 'fit in'.

*   *   *

"I think we should check out the pond beyond the far point," Blue Coyote suggested. The hearth of the unmated men was planning an extended hunting trip; the last before winter really set in and they were confined to the camp. "I saw tracks there just the other day."

"What is wrong with the grassland?" Squirrel asked. "I would rather hunt antelope than deer."

"I think we would be better off searching for usable stone," Gray Wolf recommended. "We have all the food we can possibly eat for this winter. Workable stone is much more important. Cougar said that we are going to run out of stone before the winter is over."

"We have been all up and down the escarpment, and no one has found any stone worth bringing back to him," Stone Man replied. "Since you are the apprentice to the knapper, perhaps you have better ideas of where to look. After the loss of the acorn hunters so fresh, I for one do not want to go up onto the grassland when there is any chance of another storm."

Finally, when no one could agree on a destination, they agreed to forget the whole idea. Squirrel went off on his own, looking for antelope, Gray Wolf wandered down to the storage cave and spent the day with Cougar. Stone Man suggested that Red Eagle, Blue Coyote and he make a run to the pond at the point, but the others were no longer in the mood. Blue Coyote wandered off with Wolf and Red Eagle disappeared as well. Stone Man, alone and with time on his hands, wandered down and spent time helping old Pinyon settle into the cave he was sharing with Jackrabbit, and Porcupine, and his son Chipmunk.

"I wish I could move to the unmated men's cave!" Chipmunk muttered as his father gave him yet another order on how to arrange his things. "Soon I will be old enough! After all I completed my vision quest seasons ago. Father insists, however, that as long as Blue Coyote remains at his father's hearth, I must do the same." He sighed, "I don't suppose there is any chance . . ."

"Soon," Stone Man replied, "Blue Coyote is moving in the spring; besides there is hardly room in the cave for more of us. We need a bigger cave next winter."

"But once we have moved back into the summer shelters . . ." Chipmunk grinned, "I can wait that long, but it will be a long winter."

"So spend your days with us, just as Blue Coyote does. Your father can hardly protest that!"

"No, that he cannot!" The youth sighed, "I can hardly wait to establish hunting brothers. All my life it has been just my father and me. He may be an excellent hunter, but as a father?"

"Where do you want these, Pinyon?" Stone Man grinned at the other youth and carried the hides to where Pinyon indicated. "We are going to begin gathering fire wood soon, where do you men want us to stack your supply?"

"At the base of the trail," suggested Porcupine.

"On the ledge just outside," remarked Jackrabbit.

"Anywhere that is convenient," replied Pinyon.

"Since I am the one who will be fetching it," Chipmunk said, "Don't you think I should have a say in where it will be stored?"

"You have a point there," Pinyon agreed, "Where do you want the wood?"

"Actually, both at the base of the trail and on the ledge make sense," Chipmunk replied, "But I can always bring it up to the ledge so that you older men do not have to go so far if I am not around."

"I have been climbing steeper trails than this since before you were born!" protested Pinyon.

"Which is why you should not have to do so anymore times than necessary," soothed Stone Man.

"Well we are through here with the moving in, so why don't both of you go and get some of that wood you are talking about, we could use a fire to warm this cold cave," Jackrabbit stated, "We can finish settling our things in here. Go on, both of you," he shooed the youths off. They needed no more encouragement.

"Let's drag that old stump in from beyond the camp," Chipmunk suggested, "I have been going to do that for a hand of days. This cave is the closest to it, and it is so big we don't want to drag it any farther than necessary."

"Fine with me," Stone Man agreed. "Let's get some cordage and do it!"

They rummaged through a container not yet carried up and found just what they were looking for. Soon they had the log roped and were dragging it toward the escarpment. By sundown they had accumulated a sizable pile of deadwood for the cave. Chipmunk thanked Stone Man, and the latter nodded and made his way to the unmated men's cave. Red Eagle had wandered off to one of the southern camps and was still nowhere to be seen, but Gray Wolf and Squirrel had returned.

Over the next several days, the unmated men made a point off providing dead wood for all the caves. This would be their assigned task over the winter moons.

That night Fire Dancer brought up the subject of 'working stone' at his own hearth. "We are going to run out of obsidian before spring."

"I think we should leave right away and travel to the Black Land," Blue Coyote stated.

"Not until winter is spent," Fire Dancer shook his head. "It would be just as deadly in the moving sands as it was on the grasslands for the acorn gatherers. When spring arrives, then you may go to the black Land, but there is no sense in just the pair of you going. We need to send enough men to carry obsidian for all the camps. Besides, what would you do for dogs? Scorpion will not be available even then. Her pups will be too young. Centipede Man has not yet bred his dog, maybe he isn't planning on it, but there needs to be more organization than just the pair of you. I will meet with the other camp leaders and we will decide on a plan. I think, perhaps half a hand of men from each camp should go, with whatever dogs are available."

"We could search elsewhere in the meantime," Blue Coyote said, "Gray Wolf was saying just today that we should be looking nearer here. He hopes there will be a source of usable chert along the escarpment. Although I cannot imagine any place we have not already investigated. He has found tiny chips of stone, which is as good as what we found in the Black Lands. The only problem, he can't find the source."

"We should be looking everywhere, not only for a new source of stone, but for decent wood to make darts from as well. The trees growing in this area are entirely unsuitable for making darts. There is not a length of straight wood on any of them."

"Perhaps we need to make shorter darts then," Cougar said, "Or make them in pieces which fit together." He shook his head; "We cannot continue making trips all the way to the Black Land every time we need obsidian or straight wood. We need to be independent of that place and find solutions to our problems here."

"What do you suggest then, since you are knapper, where do we find decent stone?"

"I don't know," Cougar shook his head, "I just don't know."

"I have seen something which might be good stone," Star Woman stated, "But the pieces are so small, they are scraps from some other tool making."

"Where have you seen these?" Cougar questioned.

"All around the camp, wherever you walk, but as I say, they are such tiny pieces, they are of no use, but somewhere there is another source of stone."

"Unless it is large enough to make tools from, there is no reason to bother with little chips," he shrugged. "I have seen them as well, but they are worthless, probably of the same source as all the rest of the chert around here, all flawed and all too coarse to make anything of. We need obsidian."

"Well there is none here; I have not seen as much as a chip of obsidian in this entire land, beyond that which we brought with us." Fire Dancer replied, "So perhaps we will have to find a different solution to making tools."

"What do you mean?"

"Just an idea, it probably wouldn't work any way, but well, look at this," he handed Cougar something he dug from his pouch.

Cougar turned the piece over in his hand, frowned and handed it back to Fire Dancer. "I see what you are getting at, Fire Dancer," he shook his head. "I have already tried this stuff. I found it as well, when we pit roasted the meat upon our arrival. Sand got so hot it melted into this stone, but it is as flawed as the chert around here. I have tried making a fire hot enough to melt it, but my container always burns up first. This, however, looks far better than anything I have come up with. How did you do it?"

"I packed it into a mud ball and put the whole thing into the hottest part of the fire. Only the fire still isn't hot enough," he shrugged.

"Well we have all winter to find a solution." Fire Dancer tossed his experiment into the fire in disgust.

---

1. Megafauna refers to the species of extinct Pleistocene animals excavated at the LaBrea tar pits in California. Included in their

numbers are: mammoth, horse, camel, saber-toothed tiger, dire wolf, ground sloth and bison, mentioned in this book.

2. Younger dryas: a period of between 100 and 1,000 years of severe drought during which time the Pleistocene Megafauna died out somewhere between 12,000 and 11,000 years ago.

3. *Tyto alba: Barn* Owl: A pale owl with dark eyes and a heart-shaped face. Nests in cliffs and trees; typically have a raspy, hissing screech.

4. *Canus dirus:* Dire Wolf; much larger that today's wolves. Their head was broader, snout longer, legs longer and about a third again as large as modern day wolves. They died out at the end of the Pleistocene, circa 11,000 B.P. **Amann** 1998: 7.

CHAPTER 6

Wind whistled and screeched like a demented spirit beyond the hide closure of the unmated men's cave. The hearth was burned to coals, casting little light and throwing the walls into deep shadow. Only one youth remained awake, studying the shadows beyond his bed, his mind too active for sleep. *There must be a way!* He shifted, and noticed, for the first time, a shallow niche in the wall just beyond where he lay. Movement there had drawn his attention. A packrat hurriedly entered the cave and scurried to where the grain was stored. The youth watched the animal and then followed it with his eyes as it vanished into the wall.

That's odd! He crawled from his bed to the spot, *there's air coming in here! Must be an opening into another part of the cave!* He began scooping an accumulation of packrat debris and dirt away from the wall with his hands. It was easy digging, yet he searched out a deer scapula and soon had the hole big enough to squirm through. He collected a torch and stuck its lighted end through the hole. *Black! Must be big!* Quickly he squirmed through the opening.

It began in his toes, just barely a feeling, gradually building, and then thrumming up through his body, vibrating along his nerves into an all-encompassing feeling. *Power!* He could feel it in every nerve and sinew of his body. It cast an eerie blue light around him. *This is a spirit place! Get out!* His mind shouted and then ignored its own command. He held the torch up high and nearly forgot to breathe. *Indeed, a spirit place!* Quickly his eyes searched over the wall before him, it danced eerily in the flickering torchlight, the animals and human figures seemed to move with a life beyond that of stone and paint.

Dominating the wall to his left was a beast such as he had never seen. It stood well over the height of three men, its domed head nearly touching the roof of the cave. From its mouth descended a set of tusks, the like of which no animal living had ever carried. They swept nearly to the ground, then curved and crossed in the middle. The creature's nose was stretched out into a long thick leg-like projection reaching the ground. There was a huge hump on the creature's back and its legs were like the trunks of trees found in the Starving Mountains. Standing beside the creature was the form of a woman, a large dog at her side. Beyond were more animals. Some like the one, and others, still strange to his eye. There were antelope, but they had different prongs, more and longer. Then there were animals he could not identify. One had a long neck, big feet and a hump on its back. Another had long stiff hair along its neck and was shown running like the wind. There were terrifying catlike animals with huge long canine teeth, cats with a thick mane of hair about the head and yet more animals with thick hairy hides, humps, huge heads and long sharp horns.

They all lived within the stone of the cave wall, brought to brilliant life by a hand so artistic they seemed to be moving. The pictures told a

story, but this did not interest the youth. He drank in the shapes of the animals; he absorbed the power from the very air he breathed. Something caught his eye in the flickering light. It lay on a shallow shelf just at eye level; the light caught the edge of its stone face. He reached out to touch it, jerked his hand back as static lightning shot from the object. He took a deep breath and grasped the object.

Turning it over and over in his hands, he marveled at its beauty, its perfect symmetry, and its lethal size. The torchlight reflected the cream and red swirling texture mixed with brown and gray. The object was as long as his hand and expertly flaked on both surfaces. At the base long thin flakes had been removed from both faces to thin the base for hafting to a spear shaft. The basic triangular shape was reminiscent of nothing he had ever seen.[1] It wasn't a knife, or any other kind of tool with which he was familiar, but it was sharp, the point brought blood when he tested it with a finger. Carefully he wrapped it in a rotting piece of rabbit skin and tucked it into his waist pouch. Then he looked around the room. It was large; nearly double the size of the outer cave. The ceilings were high and water dripped into a small pool toward one side. But the walls! The walls were all covered with paintings and drawings. It was then that he realized they told a story. Yet other things drew his attention. There were baskets stacked against the far wall, moldering into dust, their contents spilling out onto the floor; hides, huge, heavy, thickly furred hides. He pulled one out and spread it flat, marveling at the size of it. The fur was so thick a man wouldn't need any grass beneath to make his bed soft, and it would be so warm the cold would hardly be noticed. Soon he was digging through other baskets. There were more hides, a number of them from the same kind of animal, probably the one with the sharp evil looking horns. There was even a basket of blanks and cores, all of the same unusual marbled material as the strange object in his pouch.

After investigating the contents of all the storage baskets, the youth turned his attention back to the walls of the cave. Starting next to the entrance, it unfolded. The first drawings were really, little more than scratching on the wall. It showed a child and the large dog, then a journey, people and a great dreamer. There was a valley, many, many people gathered there, and into their midst walked the figure of the girl and dog; then the strange tusked giants followed. The dreamer led his hunters against the giants and slew them. The object in his pouch was the tip attached to huge spears, spears used to kill the giants. Then there was a battle, between the girl and the dreamer. The dreamer exploded into tiny pieces, and the girl was laid out to walk the wind with her dog. Then all the animals were shown in various stages of dying. A dark cloud covered the land, and the people walked away to the west.

By the time he had finished the story, the youth had absorbed so much power from the room his head throbbed, he felt nauseous. Dizzily he crawled back through the opening and filled in the hole. Gratefully he rolled again into his sleeping fur and laid staring up at the roof of the cave. Someone shook his arm and he woke up.

"Come on man! It's time to get started. You'd better get some food inside you. It will be nightfall before we take time to stop for food. Blue Coyote is hoping to make the trip across the moving sand in a couple of hands of days." Stone Man urged the other youth. "We are meeting the rest of the journeyers at the pond beside the moving sand. They are probably already there."

"I am on my way." The youth answered, crawling from his sleeping furs and quickly bundling them into a backpack. He frowned, glanced toward the hidden opening, could detect nothing, and prepared to leave the cave. When they returned from the Starving Mountains, he would again visit the secret cave. Yet, before going, he went to the place of the opening and ran his hands down the wall. His hand met the rock floor, no indication of any disturbance at all, only the continuous wall, meeting the hard rock floor. There was no second cave entrance. He frowned and looked about for the scapula he had used to excavate, finding no such tool.

*   *   *

"Come on!" Stone Man shouted. "We are leaving now."

Agitated the youth turned and gathered up his backpack and left the cave.

"What is keeping you?" Blue Coyote called. "We are already late leaving. If we don't go now, we might as well wait until tomorrow."

The youth picked up his speed and soon all three were shadows in the darkness at the edge of the now deserted camp, the wind whistling through the mesquite their only farewell. The remainder of the group was waiting at the pond, without so much as a greeting, all fell into a line and hurried west into the moving sand, a double span of men, each leading a dog and travois, heavily loaded.

"I hope the storm holds off." Stone Man glanced uneasily at the sky. "We don't need to be holed up out here waiting for it to pass. Maybe we should have waited like Fire Dancer suggested."

"We have waited too long already." Blue Coyote replied. "I wanted to leave at the beginning of the new moon, but first one thing and then another came up and now it is nearly the full moon. We must get across before the starving moon is over. We can't wait until this storm passes. If we must wait it out in the moving sand, then we will, but we are moving as fast as possible, traveling day and night with only short rest stops along the way. The more time we save going across, the more food we will have on the return trip."

"There will not be any food in the Starving Mountains," remarked Grape Leaf of the Rabbit Camp. "Blue Coyote is right. We are all out of shape from too much good food and excess. Now we need to be strong and tough."

"Already I am out of breath and tiring," groaned Centipede Man. "And I am not the only one." He chuckled as his companions came to a panting stop beside him. "We probably had better rest for a short time here and catch our breath," he suggested. "There is no sense in killing ourselves the very first day!"

"It must be only a couple of finger's time until dark now, perhaps you are right," Blue Coyote agreed. "We will toughen up in a day or so, we have done well for our first day."

"Should I get a fire started?" Shallow Water of the Quail Camp asked.

"We might as well have some hot tea and a little food. We haven't had anything all day," reminded Black Rain of the Pine Camp.

"Just don't get too comfortable, this is only a short stop," cautioned Stone Man. "We still have a hand of time to travel before sleeping."

"I will prepare the tea," offered Bear Killer. "If someone else wants food cooked we will need more wood for the fire. I gathered all I could find."

"Tea will be enough. We can eat cold food this night, save the grain cakes for later when we need the strength they give." Centipede Man brought the conversation to an end. The men gratefully dropped to the ground beside their dogs and rested while Bear Killer started a minuscule fire and soon had a skin of water heating for tea.

Now that they were no longer moving the drop in temperature was more noticeable. It was much colder than when they left the caprock before dawn. The wind had picked up as well. It sifted a steady fall of sand onto them. No one seemed to take notice however; they wolfed their food down, drank the tea quickly and were soon urging the weary dogs forward. In a finger of time even their tracks had been wiped away by the wind. They rested and then walked again, night lightened into day and it in turn again turned into night. Still they walked, fighting the snow and wind for another pair of days.

"We had better stop now," Centipede surveyed the blowout they were paused in. "The wind is a little less noticeable here, and there is a lot of brush for a fire. Best as I can remember we should be near where the sand storm caught us on the first trip across."

"You are probably right," agreed Blue Coyote. "This does look like that place. What do you all say? Are you ready to call it far enough for the day?"

"I don't think I can go any farther, to be honest," CatTail groaned as he slumped to the ground. "How did we all get so out of shape? Nearly starved to death on the trip across I don't think I got this tired, at least not during the first few days."

"Too much good food and not enough hunting," exclaimed Badger.

"Well, whatever the cause, I hope we toughen up in the next hand of days, for the trip back will be much harder. We will not only have less food but will be loaded heavily with obsidian. The dogs will be forced to go slower, even with us carrying our share of the load," Bear Killer agreed. "The Rabbit Camp has completely used up any tool material and the stuff at the escarpment is nearly useless for anything but cutting the bottoms of our shoes as we walk on it."

"Well I am getting some rest," commented Red Eagle. "Someone wake me when it is time to go." He spread his sleeping fur from the backpack and gratefully rolled up inside it, shifted his pouch, tools, and knife into a more comfortable position and was soon fast asleep.

"Red Eagle has the right idea," Stone Man commented. "I am following his lead."

"Me also," Blue Coyote yawned. "It will be time to go soon enough." He spread out his sleeping fur, called to Wolf and gratefully curled up with the animal, welcoming the additional body heat. The rest of the travelers were quick to follow their lead and soon all were sleeping soundly.

Blue Coyote was shaken roughly awake. Centipede Man knelt above him. "We had better dig into the side of the dune and sit this storm out." He muttered. "It has gotten far worse than we expected." He breathed on his hands, "No way that the dogs can travel in this much snow. Some of the men have even suggested turning back."

"Not if we want any obsidian for tools!" Blue Coyote muttered. "We knew the storm was coming and we were taking a chance. All right, let's get dug in," he sighed. "I just hope it doesn't last long. We only brought enough food for a hand of extra days, and as you know, all of us are used to eating regularly. No one can go without food like we used to."

"Just don't start looking back fondly at the days in the Starving Mountains."

"No, I am not, but you must agree, in some ways we were in better health."

"We got out more, had to, to find enough food to keep the soul inside our bodies, but I still miss all those we left behind there to walk the wind. I hope this is my last trip there, I had hoped never to see the place again."

"Well actually we are going to Black Land, so we aren't really going back, but I know what you mean," Blue Coyote replied.

"You two going to talk or help," Stone Man shouted?

"We are coming!" Blue Coyote rose and Wolf shook a blanket of snow from his coat. It had drifted as deep as a man's knees during the time they had been asleep. "Reed Gatherer, you had better rouse the rest of the men, or they will freeze in their sleep."

Reed Gatherer hurried to wake the rest of the group and soon every man was busy digging hollows into the side of the sand dune. They drove their travois poles into the earth and shelter hides secured to them to block the worst of the wind and cold out. Then, men and dogs crowded inside and prepared to sit out the storm.

Luckily the blowout provided a ready supply of brush. If they used it carefully, and were not holed up for too long, there would be enough for each small excavation to have a fire for tea, food and warmth. The wind howled and sent icy bursts of air around the flimsy shelter provided by the hides. Men and dogs were crowded together for warmth, but as the temperature continued to drop they were dangerously close to freezing to death right inside the shelters. The snow piled up outside, affording them some additional protection from the cold, but reaching the supply of wood became increasingly difficult. Day after day the snow piled up . . .

"How long do you figure we have been here?" Stone Man shifted to stretch a cramped leg, causing the dog crowded against him to whine in concern.

"A hand of days at least," sighed Blue Coyote. "There is no way we can go on. Shallow Water is right. We must go back to the escarpment."

"What are we going to do for tool-stone then?"

"Do you have any other ideas?"

"No." Stone Man grunted as he shifted again. "And if I ever get out of this miserable hole in the ground, I don't even care."

"It is odd, you know. In the Starving Mountains we had all the obsidian we needed, and no food. At the escarpment we have all the food we want, and no obsidian," mumbled Blue Coyote.

"And if we discover a place with both stone and food, it probably won't have any water! There always seems to be at least one essential item, missing. Perhaps Pinyon is right! Maybe the 'spirits' have deserted The People."

"Maybe The People have deserted the 'Spirits'!" muttered Blue Coyote.

"What do you mean by that?"

"I'm not sure, just a feeling I get sometimes . . ."

"Well, for all the good it did us, we might just as well have stayed at the escarpment and saved ourselves the freezing and discomfort of this trip. We did not even get a span of days from the camp!" Muttered Stone Man. "And the only feeling I am getting is frostbite in my toes and fingers. Storms in this new land are certainly much worse than in the Starving Mountains."

"Probably because there is nothing to stop the wind; it just blows harder and harder."

"This is our first winter at this place, and already we have lost over a double hand of people in the acorn gathering and now nearly ourselves as well. There is no telling if any have died at the camps."

"Everyone has moved into the caves with plenty of food and wood, so unless someone was foolish, like us, they should be all right."

"Hey! You in there! The wind is dying down, do you hear it?" Centipede Man called cheerfully from outside. "Come out and stretch your legs. I think the sun is coming out."

Both youths scrambled over dog and wolf and tumbled out of their cramped cave. Red Eagle was already striding about through the snow. "No!" He protested, "I think we should go on! We still have enough food, particularly if we save on it. The dogs are well rested, and so are we. We brought enough to stretch for the extra days."

"What about the snow, man!" Badger kicked a foot and sent some flying into the air.

"What about it? If we go back, we still must travel through it. Last time it snowed, in a day it was all melted. Besides, I have been to the top of the dune. Most of the snow has settled in a few of the deeper places, such as this one. For the rest it is mostly clear."

The men gathered and discussed the choices. "We need the obsidian," reminded Grape Leaf. "That is why we were making this trip. That need has not gone away. The trip must be made if not now, then later. We are already well over a hand's journey on the way. I agree with Red Eagle. I would go on."

"As would I," Bob Cat added.

"And I," agreed Bear Killer.

Shallow Water shook his head, "I don't know . . ."

"I think we should return to the escarpment and forget about this trip," stated Black Rain.

"We have been gone for over a span of days, our families will be worried."

"I agree with Grape Leaf," Reed Gatherer spoke. "Regardless of the hardships upon us now, without tools we cannot hunt, gather, or carry on the ways of daily living. The obsidian is of the most importance."

"More of us choose to go on," Grape Leaf nodded. "Do those of you who wish to return choose to go with us, or turn back?"

"We all started out together, we all return together," Shallow Water sighed.

"Then let's get the travois loaded and on our way," shouted Centipede Man, literally leaping into the air. "The sun agrees!"

It took a while to locate the things quickly dumped during the storm, but after a short time, all the dogs were in harness and the group was once again headed west, into a new day with the sun shining, warming their backs. By mid day the snow began to melt and by evening it was easy traveling.

"I see them!" Stone Man shouted. "Look, just there!" He pointed.

"You are right!" Centipede Man agreed. "We pushed so hard we have made up at least a pair of days lost to the storm," he smiled. "That is most definitely the mountains!"

"We made better time because we are in better condition, and we are traveling without women and children as well," Shallow Water joined them. "I am glad I decided to continue. It was the right decision."

"One thing is certain," Black Rain stated. "I will be more careful with my tools from now on. Just think of all the ones left behind!"

"We never had trouble locating good stone here, who would have thought it would ever be a problem?" Bear Killer agreed.

"Perhaps if we had ever traveled much, these things would not be a problem; but how do you know what to take and what to leave behind?" Red Eagle asked.

"It would be a good idea to always travel with these essential things, food, water and tools," suggested Centipede Man. "But at least we learn from our mistakes."

"I would add shelter to the list," Blue Coyote replied.

That night they camped at the deserted Yucca Camp site and the next day hurried on to the Black Land. They located their camp at the far west lava bubble. There were no signs of any game in the area. They settled down to repair their gear and get ready to gather the obsidian in the morning. At least there was plenty of wood for a descent fire and everyone was in excellent spirits as they sat around that fire and relaxed for the first time since leaving the escarpment.

"I think we should take only prepared cores and blanks with us. Why should we carry extra weight?" Blue Coyote sat diligently paring off the outside layer of stone, leaving only the usable core to be loaded. "Look at all that I have discarded!"

"All right, I will bring it in and you trim it!" Stone Man stomped off,

"I told you to learn some basic knapping skills!" Blue Coyote shouted after him.

"And I told you I have no talent in that direction!" Stone Man hollered back.

"You could have tried harder."

"And perhaps you could have followed the track of that mule deer!"

Blue Coyote shook his head, "You win! Each of us is better at something, but I am not so poor a tracker as you are knapper."

"If you pair are through throwing insults at each other, perhaps we could get back to the purpose at hand!" Red Eagle staggered into the camp with a hide bulging with obsidian nodules. "I agree with Blue Coyote on one thing at least. This stuff is heavy."

"I have one of the travois already loaded," Blue Coyote nodded to where it rested. "And this lot should fill another. We are doing well and it is not yet midday."

"And we are not yet mid-way with our load," reminded Stone Man returning with another load. "You need to trim faster; knapper, we gatherers are far ahead of you!"

"Perhaps, but I can trim after dark, can you gather then?"

"I think another pair of hides full should be enough," Red Eagle squatted beside the fire and took a swig of water from the skin. "I am going to see if I can dig that spring free and get the water to flow again. We need to fill our skins and I for one do not wish to hike half a day farther to find water."

"Good idea. See if one of the other men can help you, I have enough stone to keep going for a while," Blue Coyote agreed.

Red Eagle and Shallow Water went off to clear the spring while Stone Man squatted next to Blue Coyote. "It still makes me mad, the way Red Eagle sneaked up here following us and claimed our spring as his own find."

"We have no proof that he followed us," Blue Coyote reminded his friend. "He could have found it on his own."

Stone Man shook his head, "He isn't smart enough to have found it on his own. Besides it wasn't the first time he did something like this. I will be glad when you join the unmated men's camp; then I won't have to spend so much time in his company. I think I must have said something to give him the idea to follow us, but I cannot think what it was."

"You know how upset Mother is going to be!"

"You promised!"

"I will keep the promise. It is long past time I moved to the unmated men's camp, and my mother both knows and agrees with it, but she is still going to be upset."

"You are lucky to have such a fine mother," Stone Man spoke wistfully. "I still miss my own family, even though it has been seasons since they walked the wind."

"Soon it will be time to start your own family," Blue Coyote reminded him. "Then we will have more important things to do than think about the past."

Stone Man snorted, "Why would I want to mate?"

"Sooner or later we all must."

"Then later, if you don't mind! Besides, who is there to mate with?"

"I have seen the girl Moth looking at you . . ." Blue Coyote remarked.

"Moth! You mean the daughter of Centipede Man? Why she is just a child! She couldn't be more than a span of seasons!"

"They are never too young to look," reminded Reed Gatherer as he dumped his burden beside his travois and settled to trim the stone.

"So, how do you know which one to pick?" Blue Coyote questioned. "It isn't as if we have a lot to choose from, you know!"

"There used to be spans of young mating age females," Reed Gatherer agreed. "Now there are pitiful few, so your choice should be easy. After all, it is not as if they have any better choices."

"But how do you choose?"

"Usually the parents do the choosing, or if you find one you like, make the offer yourself. All our girls are brought up to be proper women of The People. Any one of them would make an acceptable mate for any youth."

"At least we have seasons before we have to worry about it any way," Stone Man dumped his load. "I think I will go see how the spring cleaning is coming." He trotted off.

"Did your parents pick your mate for you?" Blue Coyote questioned Reed Gatherer.

"My first mate, they did. She was a good girl, but she died giving birth to our first child. The child died as well," Reed Gatherer leaned back against a rock. "It was a long time ago. I do not even think of them much now, but at the time it was as if my whole life had ended. A hand of seasons passed before I looked at another woman, then I saw Yellow Basket. She was tall and slim and moved like a willow in the breeze. We have had a good life, a pair of children that lived and now we grow old together."

"I think I will choose for myself," Blue Coyote concluded. He finished with the stash of cores and began loading them onto the travois set beside him. When it was loaded, he secured the netting over it and dragged it to lie beside the already ready one. "There, I have one more load to do, and our backpacks. I hope that Stone Man or Red Eagle returns soon. I am almost out of nodules."

"You need not fear; Stone Man is returning right now with another hide full" Reed Gatherer nodded toward the approaching youth.

"Did they get the spring running?" Blue Coyote asked.

"They had to dig a long way, but they found enough seep to fill the water skins. They are what I returned for." He began gathering up the empty skins stacked beside the packs. "I will be back shortly with more nodules." He grinned and hurried off toward the spring.

By sunset all the travois were loaded to capacity, the backpacks were bulging, and all the water skins were filled. Backs were sore and fingers blistered as well. Everyone slept soundly. Wolf nudged Blue Coyote, whining softly.

"What is it?" Blue Coyote whispered. Wolf whined and wagged his tail looking toward the lava bubble. Blue Coyote could just make out the moving form. Quickly, quietly he rose and picking up atlatl and darts followed the wolf upwind toward the bubble. He squatted behind a shrub and waited, listening for the sounds of approaching hoofs. With a single smooth cast his dart flew and struck its target. The deer went down and the wolf landed atop it. With a quick cut the jugular was severed and hunter and wolf drank together. Blue Coyote gave thanks to the deer 'spirit' and began dragging the animal back to camp.

"It is cold enough the meat will not spoil," Centipede Man helped load a quarter upon his travois; another went to Shallow Water and another to Black Rain. Stone man carried the last. The hunters ate a meal at dawn, enjoying the organ meat and then they all shrugged into their backpacks, hooked leads to the dogs and once again headed into the Starving Mountains. After a pair of days into the moving sand they stopped, roasted a quarter of the deer while they slept and ate the fresh meat over the next several days. Then they rested for an entire night, again eating a roasted quarter as they traveled. By the time they reached the place where they had cached the return supplies, they still had some of the deer left. Here they rested a day and an extra night, repairing harnesses and replacing worn shoes. Then they began the last part of the journey home. They had been gone an entire turning of the moon and were beginning another.

"I am glad we do not have many days to go." Centipede Man sighed. "My dog is starting to show the strain of the trip. She has sore spots on both shoulders, no matter how I try to redo the harness."

"She should not have come on this trip in the first place." Shallow Water commented. "It was silly to bring her as near as she is to whelping."

"Had it not been for the storm we would be back by now" Centipede Man justified his decision. "She will be all right. I think I will pull the travois tomorrow though, just to give her a break."

"I will pull with you," Shallow Water offered. "After all, you have promised me one of the pups; I want it to be born."

"It would be a good idea if we all take turns and the bitch runs free the rest of the way," suggested Black Rain. "We all seem to have an interest in these pups. Centipede has promised me one as well."

"Scorpion will have whelped by now," remarked Blue Coyote. "I wonder what her pups are like. There will be more wolf blood in them than dog."

"Well you also have promised at least one pup," reminded Stone Man.

"One is all I was given to promise," replied Blue Coyote. "Scorpion is my father's dog."

"But Wolf is yours," Red Eagle replied. "I would think you should get more than one pup."

"One is all I asked for," explained Blue Coyote.

"Why is that?"

"Because only Stone Man wanted a pup; why ask for more than I need?"

"Perhaps other 'friends' would have been interested, had you bothered asking," Red Eagle replied. "I for one would have liked to have a dog of my own, but none was offered, even though we have been hunt brothers on several occasions."

"Then why didn't you say so? I would have gladly given you one, had I known you were interested. But you have been very negative toward Wolf, why would I think you would want a pup of his?"

"Well I am no longer interested!" Red Eagle stomped off.

"That one will make a bad enemy one day if you are not careful Blue Coyote," Centipede Man stated, "He is filled with envy, most of which is directed at you."

"I had hoped we could work through that on this trip. I was wrong. Perhaps things will be better between us once I move into the unmated men's cave upon our return. Father has remarked several times that our survival can often depend on the absolute loyalty of hunting brothers. I will have to find a way."

Centipede Man shook his head, "You would be wasting your time. Red Eagle is too filled with anger to listen to anything you could say. Short of saving his life, look to your back, for danger will likely come from that direction. I have seen it before; men, eaten from the inside, ruining their lives and the lives of others in their single-minded determination to right some supposed wrong. Red Eagle's father was just such a man. Fire Dancer finally had to banish him from the camp. This is part of the reason for Red Eagle's hate and envy. He blames you for the loss of his own father, regardless that you had nothing to do with it; or the fact that he was much better off without such a father. His mother's next mate treated him far more kindly than his own father ever had. You have everything he has always wanted. That is the point to his envy."

"I had no say in whom my parents are!"

"You know that, and I know that. Red Eagle doesn't think that way. He sees only the favored son of the headman, pampered by a mother who has position."

*　　*　　*

"In the Starving Mountains, the only position I had was that of a starving person, no different from anyone else. Sons' of headmen get just as hungry and frequently have less to eat because the food has been given to those more in need. There is more responsibility being the son of a headman. You are expected to act in a certain way, never make stupid mistakes that bring ridicule down upon you! You must always be the best, run the fastest, go the farthest, bring in more and give more than anyone else. That is the position of headman's son."

"I was the headman's son, Blue Coyote, I know what you say. But only one who has walked in those shoes realizes that there is far more responsibility, than privilege. The rest only see the privilege," Centipede Man smiled. "I was lucky, for I was not First Son. I was able to move to Water Woman's camp and be just another hunter and man of the camp. My brother became Headman in my father's place and he died because as headman he had the most dangerous position on the hunt. He led the men to hunt a wounded bear. It killed him because he was the first one it could reach. There was no glory in his death. He suffered a long time and died slowly in great pain. Then when he could no longer lead, another stepped into his place and he was left to walk the wind, a broken worthless man."

"Your brother was killed by a bear? Was he Running Elk?" Centipede Man nodded. "But that means that your father was Singing Wind! My Father says he was the greatest headman to ever lead. He is always telling me to pattern myself after Singing Wind. You must be very proud to be able to claim such a father."

"Why? Does it make me more than I was a hand of time ago? If you are ever to lead, Blue Coyote, you must look into the soul of a man, for that is all that can be trusted. I have seen sons' of the poorest of men do great deeds, and the son's of the finest, fail dismally to accomplish anything at all."

"Running Elk was not a wise leader?"

Centipede Man shook his head. "Running Elk was a dreamer of dreams. He saw visions of a better way. He was as unsuited for leading as is my young daughter. But it was his destiny. He did what was expected of him, and he failed."

"But you would not, would you? Had you been born First Son, you would have been as glorious a leader as Singing Wind."

"But I was not born First Son. Running Elk was, so each of us lived the lives our feet were set to. That is all one can do."

"No! It isn't! You could have changed it! You could have stepped into . . ."

"No! I could not! No matter how much I wanted it, it was not my place!"

"So you felt yourself as bitter and filled with envy as Red Eagle. You ran away!" Blue Coyote accused the old man hotly.

Centipede Man shook his head. "No." Sadly, "I was asked to leave." He sighed, "I loved Running Elk more than any person in my life. He was the moon to me. When Singing Wind died, and Running Elk began to depend on me to guide him, his mate, White Fox, couldn't stand me. She made so much trouble between us that finally Running Elk asked me to leave the camp. A hand of days later he was injured by that bear and died before the moon changed. I have spent a lifetime realizing that I could not have saved Running Elk, nor could I have changed him. White Fox was right and I could no longer stand in his way. But for many seasons I carried the guilt of my brother's death. It has eaten at me until there is little left of the man I once was. Now I am old and tired, and I have no more dreams."

"I do not agree, Centipede Man. It took a man of greatness and courage to go back for the ones left stranded by the food thieves. You did not hesitate to offer."

"My mate and daughter were with them."

"Perhaps, but I think you would have offered any way. If ever I am in difficulties with enemies, I would stand easier with you at my side."

"And I would be honored to stand there," replied Centipede Man.

They traveled steadily toward the east, and late in the day, a hand of days later they arrived back at the camps. Everyone was glad they had returned safely, with the obsidian so desperately needed in every camp. It became an item of barter, and soon the most valued possession of anyone fortunate enough to have it. People began hoarding obsidian. But no more trips to the Black Lands

The bitch of Centipede Man suffered no harm due to the journey. She whelped a hand plus of big, fat, healthy pups.

Scorpion, likewise, was a mother. Her litter was earlier and the pups were the largest anyone could remember. They were all gray except one. She was black and almost twice the size of any of the other pups. Her feet were so outlandishly large it was obvious that she probably would not walk. Her bones were heavy, and she could barely move. While the other pups were squirming around and trying to get their feet under them, Scorpion was still aiding her to the nipple. When the other pups opened their eyes, she was just beginning to try to move. Fire Dancer almost decided to destroy her, but Scorpion dotted on that pup and he had not the heart for it. But the black pup did not look like a dog. Fire Dancer called her a throw back, and he wanted nothing more than to give her away, but no one wanted her.

* * *

"Have you been to see Scorpion's pups?" Basket questioned Butterfly.
"I saw them, why?"

"I just wondered. I suppose they are all spoken for," Basket sighed wistfully.

"Not all. There is still one left I think, but why do you ask?" Butterfly questioned.

"I just wondered, that's all."

"We have nothing to trade for a dog, even if Fire Dancer was willing to let one go to us. The men are in a great need for dogs, and Fire Dancer is keeping most of them himself any way. As far as I know Blue Coyote has asked for one to give to Stone Man, and Cougar is getting one."

"But you said there was one other that Fire Dancer was going to let go?"

"Only because it is deformed."

"Do you think I could . . .?"

"What do you want with a deformed dog? It would be just a lot of extra work and not worth anything anyway?"

"You don't know that! How is it deformed?"

"Go see for yourself. I don't understand why Fire Dancer even let it live; it would have been kinder to have killed it at birth."

"I am going to see . . ." Basket ran from the cave and up the trail to the storage cave. "I would like to see the puppies," she greeted Star Woman with a smile. "I have brought a small gift for Scorpion." She held out a bone still full of marrow, "She needs the extra energy feeding so many."

"They are at the back, I am surprised you did not come sooner, as anxious as you have been for their birth. Most of them have their eyes open and soon it will be time to wean them. But be careful not to touch the black one, Scorpion almost bit Turtle Woman yesterday for getting too close." I have just been telling Fire Dancer he must decide soon about that one. It will never walk right. There was no sense letting it live this long."

"I just could not stand the look in Scorpion's eyes every time I made that decision." Fire Dancer shook his head, "It seemed she knew what I was thinking. But sooner or later, I am afraid Star Woman is right. The pup will have to be destroyed."

Basket squatted down before Scorpion and her pups and then went to her knees. A hand of inquisitive little bodies squirmed onto her lap and tried to climb up and lick her face. Basket laughed delightedly at their antics. Scorpion watched serenely as her offspring played, the black pup snuggled up against her, asleep.

"That one with the white ear is mine," Cougar leaned over and tickled the pup on the tummy. It wiggled in ecstasy. "They are all fine pups though."

Basket gently returned the pups to their mother, carefully studying the black one without seeming to. True it was big, rawboned and ugly, and its feet were enormous for its size, but she could not see any real deformity, it was just big! Then it opened its eyes. They were as blue as the sky; as blue as her own eyes. Basket caught her breath. She had never even heard of a dog having blue eyes, much less ever seen one. As far as she knew, no one else had blue eyes; only her. She was fascinated, unable to look away. Scorpion rose and picking the black pup up by the nap of its neck carefully stepped over her remaining offspring and dropped the blue-eyed pup deliberately into Basket's lap. Then she reached up and licked Basket on the cheek; wagged her tail and returned to the rest of her brood.

Fire Dancer sat with his mouth open.

Star Woman sputtered . . . "Would you look at that? Yesterday she almost took Turtle Woman's hand off just for getting to close to that pup!"

"Please," Whispered Basket, digging into her pouch and withdrawing something which she handed toward Fire Dancer. "Would this be enough?"

In the palm of her hand carefully wrapped in a rabbit skin lay a hand of beautifully crafted blades, made of a swirling mixture of pink, cream, red and gray fine-grained chert[2].

Fire Dancer studied the offering, then the pup and shook his head. "It is a Throw Back to something that lived before there were dogs. I should kill it, but . . . If you are determined, then this much I think." He selected one of the blades, "And even that is too much."

"Scorpion has already given the pup as a gift. I think we can do no less," Star Woman said. "As you say, anything is too much to accept for a creature such as it is."

Fire Dancer returned the blade to Basket. "I agree with Star Woman. Scorpion has guarded that pup viciously ever since it was born. She has obviously been saving it for you. Why do you want the throw back though Basket? It will never amount to anything. Even if it does learn to walk, such creatures are seldom tamable and only come to grief in the end."

His words were wasted. All this times Basket sat staring raptly into the blue eyes which were just as intent on her. It was absolute devotion at first sight. When the pups were weaned, Throw Back went to live in the wolf cave with Butterfly and her new person, Basket. She was still clumsy, tripping over her oversized feet and knocking things askew. And she grew . . . and grew . . . and grew. She was slavishly devoted to Basket, who took her everywhere with her, carrying her to begin with and when she became too big, adjusting her speed to accommodate the pup. By the time she had reached her third moon, however, Throw Back surprised everyone. She was nearly double the size of her littermates, but she was just as agile and quick as they were, and she was beginning to grow into those feet!

All the other pups were the same brown now as their mother, the gray giving way as they grew. Their ears flopped over the side of their head and their long short haired tails curved up over their backs, they were camp dogs, just like camp dogs had always been. Throw Back however, did not turn brown. She gradually added a silver-gray wolf coloring to her coat, the black just tipping the fur. And her coat was thick, lush and long, her tail curved to the ground thick and full. Her ears began to stand erect and her legs grew long. People marveled at her strangeness, only one recognized her, one who had seen power drawings one dark night is a secret dream cave. Just such an animal had walked beside the strange woman who had walked with the great beasts. That same woman had worn the canine teeth of the great cat on a thong around her waist.

That one man began to watch Basket, secretly. He noticed that she also wore an owl feather at the end of her braided hair. One day, casually, without causing any attention, he removed the feather and destroyed it. Basket never knew. She searched for the feather, but never found it. Butterfly muttered it was for the best, the feather had made her uneasy. Butterfly suggested Basket should try again to fashion her hair into the traditional knot. Basket shrugged and went her way, she was busy training Throw Back, and her hair was convenient braided down her back.

Blue Coyote had kept his promise. Upon returning from the Black Mountain he moved into the unmated men's cave. Star Woman sighed and kept her silence. It was hard to lose a son. They grew up so fast. Stone Man was spending much of his time during the late winter, doing the same thing as Basket; training his dog. Blue Coyote went off on his own at these times with Wolf, realizing as he worked with him, that Wolf was a natural pack hunter. They became a smoothly working team. Red Eagle watched, and waited . . .

1. A Clovis Point. This type of spear point was used by the Clovis culture, circa 11,500 years ago to kill mammoth.
2. Alabates flint; a natural 'mine' located on the Alan Bates ranch north of Amarillo Texas, now beneath Lake Merdith.

CHAPTER 7

What have you found?" Basket dropped to her knees beside Throw Back and reached for the object the animal had just unearthed. She picked it up and brushed the dirt from its surface. The sun shimmered on the smooth texture, the finely-flaked triangular object felt first warm in her hand and then as it settled into her palm her amulet almost vibrated with heat, the spot on her shoulder, always carefully covered, gave a warm thrill of pleasure. Basket caught her breath. It was a tool of some sort that was obvious, but it was a tool she was not familiar with. It lay on her palm, as long as her hand and three fingers wide. The edges tapered to a sharp deadly tip. The base had long thin flakes removed from either face, and the basal sides had been ground dull. She turned it over and over, frowning. *What could it be?* It was made of the same material as the blanks and cores still secretly hidden in the wolf cave. She frowned and slipped it into her pouch, glancing about to see if anyone was about to have observed her. She saw no one.

*   *   *

He had been following and watching her almost daily; at first the young 'dog' had sensed his presence, but now seemed to accept it. He crouched behind a patch of brush and waited until she moved on down the trail, then he rose and padded silently after her. Basket was on her way to bury her monthly flow, at the base of the selected mesquite tree. To follow a woman on such a trek was not only rude in the extreme but was also extremely dangerous. A woman's 'blood power' could cause all kinds of disaster to any unfortunate male coming into contact with it.

It must be a coincidence! He mused; *either that or I am losing my mind!* He recognized it, in that blink of an eye when the sun glinted from its surface. He had placed it in his own pouch in the secret 'spirit' cave, but it was no more in evidence the next morning than the opening to the inner cave. Now, *she* had it. *I must get it back! Who cares what happens to her? It was mine first. She has no right to it. It is mine!* He was shaking now, so angry was he. Somewhere during his inner conflict, she had escaped him. Search as he might, he could not find her track among those of so many on the well-trod trail. Finally, with gritting of teeth he gave up and returned toward the camp. Another time would come. *She will suffer!*

*   *   *

Stone Man had spent all morning working with his pup. He watched with a critical eye as the animal dragged a miniature travois along the trail. The pup was quick to catch on, but it would never be any bigger than Scorpion and although she was the largest dog among the camps, just a little smaller than Wolf; the size of Basket's pup filled him with envy. *I could have had that black pup!* He shook his head with chagrin. *But like everyone else I failed to see the potential of those big bones and feet. No! It took a female, barely more than a girl to realize what the Throw Back would grow into.* He watched as Basket hurried toward him down the trail, Throw Back at her side, already double the height of his pup, moving with a speed and strength which was the envy of every dog owner among The People.

"Have you put Throw Back to harness yet?" He asked as Basket stopped to give greeting.

"No," she shook her head, "She is still growing so fast I am afraid to." She rubbed the huge head just beneath her hand, "There is plenty of time once she is grown."

"Already she is nearly as big as both parents and she is still just half a hand of moons old. However did you guess she would turn out the way she has?"

"I didn't even think about that," Basket admitted. "She just stole my heart with one glance of those blue eyes. I would have given anything for her."

"Yet Fire Dancer gave her to you," Stone Man murmured.

"Not exactly," corrected Basket. "Actually, it was Scorpion who gave her to me. Fire Dancer didn't think Throw Back worth letting live. He was going to kill her. I did offer him blades for her."

"You did? How did you get blades? No one I know traded any to you," Stone Man frowned.

"No one traded the blades to me. I found them"

"You found obsidian blades; where?"

"Not obsidian. They are of a different material, never seen in the Starving Mountains." Basket admitted, "But just as sharp and strong."

Stone Man frowned, "No material is as sharp and strong as obsidian; everyone knows that. If they are of the chert around here, no wonder Fire Dancer turned them down. The local chert is worthless, no matter how good a tool of it looks, they just don't hold up. The first time used, they break."

"They are not made of the stone around here either. I have not ever seen the place where it comes from, but I can show some of it to you," She dug into her pouch, stopped, frowned and reconsidered, "Come by the wolf cave later and I will show you the blades and you can judge for yourself. I have been using one of them for over a moon now, and it is still just as sharp as any obsidian blade I have ever used. Besides, Grandmother and I have no obsidian, we had nothing of value to trade for it and now people are putting such value on it, we are unlikely to ever have any again."

"You could probably trade the throw back for obsidian. I would gladly trade with you."

"Trade Throw Back!" Basket stared at him aghast. "I would never trade Throw Back, she is my friend. Her mother entrusted her to me. Besides Pinyon says she is a 'spirit animal', not really a dog at all." She grinned, "Would you be willing to share space with a 'spirit' animal?"

Stone Man stepped back, away from Throw Back, eyeing her with misgiving. The dog sat, her mouth open, panting, and he was not sure, but she could have been laughing at him. She gave him that strange blue stare and he stepped back yet another pace.

"Are you sure," he questioned? "Pinyon said that?"

"He did!" Basket stated with satisfaction. Many people of the camps were now angry that she possessed Throw Back. Telling them that Pinyon had declared her a 'spirit animal' tended to make them change their minds about wanting the animal. She still caught rude stares and a few overheard remarks, but no one had tried to take the animal from her. Basket did not understand why the throw back was so important to her, but something within, deep inside herself pulled strongly toward the dog, if indeed she was a dog; and Basket was not at all sure there was any 'dog' in her at all. The older she got the less like a dog Throw Back looked. Old Pinyon had indeed confessed to Basket that he was of the mind that the animal was indeed a throw back to some far distant ancestor, the likes of which had not walked in this world for a long, long time.

*　　*　　*

"The legend tells," He had stated recently. "That the Mother of The People had just such an animal as her 'spirit guide'. It was a wolf, but not one such as we have today. The legend tells that it walked waist-tall to a man, its tail swept the ground and its ears stood erect. It was the color of the moon with black ends to its fur. An apt description of the throw back, wouldn't you say?"

"Grandmother says that the Mother of The People was my ancestor." Basket had whispered, "My mother gave me . . ." She hesitated, "My mother told her so," She concluded.

"Your mother was Feather of the Owl Camp, was she not?" Basket nodded. "Legend claims that the Mother of The People was indeed of the Owl Camp, which is the name the camp used after it was no longer the Bison Camp."

"What really is a Bison, Pinyon?"

"It was an animal which lived on the vast plains above here during the time of the ancestors. It looked something like this . . ." he drew a figure in the sand with the end of his stick. "It had a big hump on its back, a coat of long shaggy fur and a huge head with long sharp horns."

"They no longer live there?" Basket asked hesitantly. "Not even a few?"

Old Pinyon had shrugged and wandered off at the call of one of the men, leaving Basket staring at his drawing and wondering yet more . . .

*　　*　　*

"Well if Pinyon declared that creature a 'spirit animal'," Stone Man stated, "I am sure he had a reason. Have you seen anything which would lead you to think . . .?"

"Certainly not!" stated Basket, "Throw Back is her name, that doesn't mean she has any magical powers or anything. She is just a dog, she is my friend, and I won't stand here and listen to you say mean things about her. If you are interested in the blanks, come by the cave later today, but say no more rude things about Throw Back!" Basket stiffened her back and marched past Stone Man toward the camp, the throw back at her side, every bit as intimidating as any 'spirit animal' he could imagine.

"What took you so long?" Butterfly greeted Basket as she entered the cave. "I was getting worried about you; you were gone so long. Off wandering into the breaks with that miserable creature again weren't you?"

"I went to bury my moon flow. You know that. It is a long way to where I chose to do that. On the way back I stopped to speak with Stone Man. And now I am right here," Basket flounced to her favorite spot and sat down.

"Stone Man, you say. What did that unmated man have to say to you? You have not been acting improperly again have you? I told you after the last time you were reported running around with your hair unbound . . .!" Butterfly began.

"I have not been behaving improperly. One time my braid became unbound because I lost the thong. You would think I had broken every rule of propriety of the camp, as much as it has been reported back to you. Have the people of this camp nothing better to do than spy on me? If you must know, he is coming by here later."

"What! Did he make an offer to you?" Butterfly all but leaped to her feet, "And you have not the sense to tell me the very moment you return here."

"No!" shouted Basket, "He did not, nor has he ever, nor is he or any other man ever, likely to make an offer to me. Look at me, Grandmother! I am just plain Basket! Being the decedent of The Mother of The People does not make me any more desirable! Stone man is coming by because he is interested in the blades, nothing more!"

"Blades? You have spoken of them? You have told the men about them?" Butterfly sputtered.

"I have told him of a single find of blades, the ones which I have been using all over the camp for the last moon. It is no secret and I have told all who have inquired that I found them up in the shinnery last fall, just like we agreed. Remember it was your idea to use one of them when we had no other choice. But, just look at what I found today!" Basket jumped up and dug into her pouch. "Actually, Throw Back dug it up. What do you think it might be?" She held the object out on her palm for Butterfly to see.

The old woman looked down at Basket's outstretched hand but made no move to take the object from her. "How can you again and again treat such 'power objects' with so little respect?" she whispered drawing back. "I have no idea what that is, but even from here I can feel its power. Quickly! Before anyone else sees it, hide it, whatever it is."

"You feel it too?" Basket asked awed, "I thought it was just my imagination. I mean it seems that everything I touch now is some kind of power object. I mean, I can actually feel the 'power' race up my arm and spread over my body. Ever since you gave me the canines . . ."

"I should have left that packet behind in the Starving Mountains!" Butterfly muttered. "I would have if I had known what it would do to you. Just look at you! You run wild, behaving rashly, not at all befitting a woman of The People! The whole camp is talking about you and that creature!" She pointed at Throw Back, who merely yawned hugely in response. "And now you are speaking to unmated men when you know that you shouldn't."

"Grandmother! I grew up with Stone Man and Blue Coyote! Just because I have passed blood, doesn't change that! What am I supposed to do? Act like I don't know them? They are like brothers to me!"

"But they are not your brothers," pointed out Butterfly. "They are unmated men, and you are an available unmated woman. It just isn't proper, and you know it. Either one of them could ask for you."

Basket actually snorted then, "Ask for me! It is as likely that Old Pinyon would ask for me! This is me, Basket, your talking about Grandmother, not some mysterious beauty from elsewhere, just old ordinary plain Basket."

"Well, since there are no mysterious beauties likely to be coming into the camp and since they are among the few unmated men and you are among the few unmated females, all of you must mate with someone. Just who do you think there is to choose from? Well I will tell you. There is Willow, Cottontail Girl, Moth, and you Basket. Since Blue Coyote is related to Willow, and Stone Man to Cottontail, they have not much to choose from; therefore, it is likely that one of them will choose you." Butterfly shook her head. "Of course they could go to one of the other camps, but why should they, if there is a proper mate for them right here?"

"We will talk about it later," Basket shushed her. "Stone Man is coming."

"Did you hide that thing?" Butterfly hissed.

"Yes, Of course I did," reassured Basket, "Now smile and be pleasant."

"Good Day Grandmother," Stone Man greeted Butterfly formerly as he took the old woman's hand, "You have been well?"

"As well as can be expected with all of this cold weather," Butterfly replied. "At least this little cave is easy to keep warm, and with all of the wood you young men have kept piled against the escarpment, it has been a very pleasant winter." She motioned for the youth to be seated and Stone Man squatted on a stone near the fire. "Basket tells me you are interested in her little bits of stone."

"I would like to see it," Stone Man replied. "Any stone is of interest if it could prove a source of workable chert. I would rather know its source, but even the fact that it exists is of some hope. You say you found it in the shinnery?" He questioned Basket.

She nodded; suddenly shy with him, after her recent conversation with her grandmother. Now she looked at Stone Man differently, then shook her head and went to get the blade. She handed it to him, accidentally touching him in the process, it was just Stone Man, not some new stranger; just Stone Man, the same boy she grew up with, and no amount of new insight or changed thinking was going to make that any different. She sighed in relief and sat beside her grandmother, a discrete distance from the unmated man.

Stone Man turned the blade over in his hand, squinted at it, ran a finger along the edge testing the sharpness, and held it up to the light. He ran his tongue over the surface and taped in on his palm. "Interesting," he commented, "You have no idea where it came from?"

Basket shook her head, it was after all, not a lie, she was sure that her stash was not the original source, any more than this blade was the original one she had used at the beginning of winter. It was not. No blade would last that long. Even the best rarely ever lasted over a moon. They had been forced to dig into the stash out of necessity, but they were careful not to be obvious. It would go badly for both of them if the camp found they had a quantity of tool stone when everyone was so desperately without. Butterfly had not really thought about that when she had decided to keep the stone a secret. Now they were committed.

"Perhaps up on the plain somewhere," Basket suggested. "I saw bits of the same material off and on while we were collecting acorns."

"You did?"

"Only very tiny pieces," she admitted. "But it is such pretty stone, I always noticed it."

He sighed and rose "Thank you for showing it to me, at least I now know there is another source of tool stone. Perhaps it would be an idea to make a trip along the shinnery and find where it leads. We have not reached the end of it in any of our trips on the plain. Probably that is because we are more comfortable hunting in this country that we are familiar with. That grassland is a strange place. There are fewer landmarks there than in the moving sand. One would be completely dependent upon the ancestor fires to guide one across such a place. Good day to you Grandmother, Basket." He backed politely from the cave and walked thoughtfully down the trail.

*   *   *

He watched, hidden behind a shelter as Stone Man left the cave. He frowned, *up to something! What have I missed?* He slipped behind a mesquite tree and blended into the shadows. *I must do something, can't lose control. Must remember the spirit cave, always remember the spirit cave. I must get the spear tip away from her. Already she has contaminated it with her touch. I must get it quickly, before she does more.*

*   *   *

"I am going to visit with Water Woman; we are grinding grain for the spring ceremony today." Butterfly gathered up her tools and stuffed them into a basket. "See that you behave yourself at the tuber gathering," She frowned at Basket.

"I will." Basket assured her. "What trouble can I get into with Star Woman and Turtle Woman? I will be fine, I promise."

"Keep that animal under control!" Butterfly ordered. "People are talking about taking it away from you if you cannot keep it under control!"

"What do you mean?" Basket went white.

"Men talk! All I do is listen." Butterfly replied. "Many are filled with envy, men who do not have dogs of their own, while you possess the largest animal in all the camps. One move out-of-line and they will take her from you, and no number of tears or pleading will make any difference. Just remember my words."

* * *

Basket gritted her teeth as she gathered up her own tools. Calling Throw Back to follow her she also left the cave. A shadow beyond the mesquite blended into another shadow, a bit closer, and then another. Before Basket had left the camp, the shadow had slipped into the wolf cave. *Where?* He looked over the cave, *where would she hide it? In her bed furs?* Quickly he shook them and tossed them away, *nothing there!* He paced to the rear of the cave, *in the storage baskets? No, too obvious! Somewhere clever, she is very clever, must think!* He turned and began tracing the shapes on the wall, looking . . . Feeling . . . *Yes!* His fingers located a loose stone, cleverly fitted into an opening. He wiggled it loose and reached inside, a smile crossing his face. He withdrew his hand, and a packet all tied up in his hand. *Clever, but not clever enough!* Quickly he undid the knots and the leather fell away. *By the spirits! What is this thing?* He almost dropped the contents, so shocked was he when the light entering the cave reflected softly from the surface of the old canine teeth. *How can this be?* He began to shake as the power radiated from the sacred relics. Quickly he wrapped them and crammed them back into the recess, taking little care to replace the stone as he found it. His hands were trembling, and the power running up his arms was painful, he was relieved when they were no longer communicating with him. He had to get out of this place and think. More was going on here than he understood. He left the cave with a lot less care than he had entered it, hurrying back to the unmated men's cave, relieved to find it empty. He paced back and forth along the wall, trying to make sense of his recent discovery. Of course; he recognized the canine teeth. He had seen them in the very same sacred cave as he had seen the spear tip and the 'spirit' animal which daily the Throw Back resembled more and more. Something was going on here, *something very powerful*; something to do with the woman Basket. He fetched a digging stick and began attacking the hard floor at the rear of the cave. The digging stick bounced harmlessly off the hard stone, just as it had timeless tries before. He got down on his hands and knees and began feeling for the opening; he traced the entire circumference of the cave and then did so again. *It has to be here! I know it has to be here! Why can't I find it?*

It's a spirit cave, a voice whispered in his head. *It isn't real! It was a dream. A dream you were given to guide you. Use the information, the answers are there, you must find them, in your mind . . . in your mind . . .*

"It has to be real," he muttered. "I don't believe it was a dream. That cave exists; maybe not here, but somewhere."

You must dream to find it . . .

"Of course; the dream powder, I must have accidentally eaten some of the ground dream powder that night" he rose and went to a stack of storage baskets, rummaging through their contents, scattering things all over the cave, until finally he found what he hunted. A packet of ground powder, brought from the Quail camp at the request of their dreamer for Acorn, yet never delivered. With a smile he stuffed it into a pouch and quickly gathered up enough supplies to last several days. Within a finger of time he had left the camp and headed out into the breaks north of the camp.

*   *   *

Butterfly returned to the cave about mid day. She looked at the mess. "That girl is getting worse by the day! Just look at this mess she has left for me to clean up!" She muttered frowning. "I can't understand her anymore; she just doesn't listen to anything I say to her. Well I am not going to clean up her mess! She can just do it herself when she returns from tuber digging. I have been far too lax with her over the seasons. I can see that!" The old woman tossed some mesquite wood on the fire and began her midday meal preparations. The camp was quiet. Everyone was out hunting or gathering on this first warm day of the season.

In less than a hand of days it would be time for the Spring Spirit Giving Thanks Ceremony. Men were out hunting deer and antelope for the meal, women were digging tubers while she and Water Woman had been grinding grain and seeds in preparation for making grain cakes for the ceremony as well. Against the wall of the cave, neatly stacked, were the new hearthstones. Basket had already made the new broom, and their lightweight clothing was ready to be donned as well. The whole camp was caught up in the spirit of excitement that always accompanied any major ceremony, but the spring ceremony was probably the one that generated the most excitement because everyone had been confined all winter. Soon the people would be moving out of the winter caves and into the summer shelters. There would be a lot more socializing then, for the caves were some distance from one another, spreading the camp up and down the escarpment. The summer camp was all in one place, just below the wolf cave and the storage cave where Fire Dancer's family lived.

*   *   *

At mid afternoon Basket returned, lugging a large basket of tubers, her contribution to the ceremonial meal. "What happened here?" She questioned Butterfly, "Why have you thrown my sleeping furs all about?"

"Me? I thought you left this mess!" Butterfly sputtered.

"No, why would I do such a thing just after I straightened up everything. If you did not do it, nor did I, then who?" Basket set the carrier down. Throw Back wandered through the cave, growling softly.

"Someone must have been in here looking for something then," Butterfly replied. "Have you said anything to anyone about that stone; maybe one of the men?"

"I have said nothing to anyone, besides we were the last to leave the camp. All the men were gone before light. But someone had certainly been in here," She began gathering up her sleeping furs.

"Did you hide that tool? I told you to do so."

"I did not have time to hide it. It is here," she patted her pouch. "I had it with me. Our hiding place has not been disturbed either, she checked the smooth ground where the blanks were buried." She gasped, "But someone has found my secret hiding place for the Ancestor Relic!" Hurriedly she removed the stone, wedged in the opening, and removed the packet. "It is still here, but someone has opened it. Look!" She carried it to Butterfly, "It wasn't even tied up again. Who could have done such a thing?"

The old woman leaned back, away from the power object and motioned Basket to put it away. Basket carefully wrapped the objects properly and replaced them in the hiding niche, fitting the stone back carefully.

"Is there anything missing?" Butterfly questioned. "I have nothing worth stealing, and as far as I know that relic and the stone is the only thing of any worth in the cave. If none of that is gone, why would anyone take the time to make such a mess, unless the children were just out making mischief?"

Throw Back settled beside Butterfly, rumbling deep in her throat, her big ears laid flat against her head, anger flaring in her blue eyes. She knew . . .

"I am going to speak to Fire Dancer about this," Butterfly stated, rising.

"He is still out with the rest of the hunters. I just parted from Star Woman," Basket commented. "Perhaps it would be best if we say nothing yet. If we listen, someone might say something that would tell us who did this thing."

* * *

Dusk was settling in when the hunters returned. They had a very successful day, although they had traveled many hands distant before reaching an area where game still abounded. Fire Dancer carried a buck mule deer across his shoulders, Cougar a doe, while Centipede Man had a pair of pigs. Blue Coyote had a container filled with quail and prairie chickens and Stone Man had a span of ducks, all in all, plenty of food for the Spring Ceremony. Other camps would be bringing a further supply of food to help provide for the entire 'People'. An area beyond the camp had been cleared of brush to provide space for other camps to set up temporary shelters for the several-day-long event. Dry wood was stacked in profusion ready to light the fires, stones were likewise provided, for the camp had been preparing for the better part of a moon to host the event.

Other men had gone up into the grassland for antelope. All the meat would be fresh. None left over from the winter. It was tradition that only fresh meats were used. The grain cakes and seed products were provided as extras to be nibbled upon but were not part of the actual meal. Tubers and spring green plants would round out the menu.

Ordinarily each camp would conduct its own Spring Ceremonies; however, since this was their first spring in this new land, the leaders had wanted the ceremony to be special. They had selected the most central place to hold it and after the major ceremonies each camp would return to its own area for the renewing of the fire and the new clothing portions. The new women and men would be presented at the main festivities. There was still a lot of work to be done in the short time left before the other camps began arriving.

The hunters all carried their food to where the central fire pits had already been dug. It was still cold at night so the meat would not spoil before morning. Then it would be placed in the pits, hides covering it, and the earth replaced, letting the meat age slowly until it was ready for cooking. Then it would be removed, a layer of wood placed in the pits and burned to ashes. After three layers of coals were laid down the meat would be coated with a thick layer of mud, already prepared and placed on the hot coals. Then more wood would be put on top and burned to coals. Once a thick layer of coals was deposited over the meat the dirt would be put back into the pits and the whole thing left to cook for a whole night and day. The result would be so tender that it would actually fall from the bone, and the seasonings would be cooked in as well as all of the juices, sealed inside a container of baked clay. The clay hardened first, before the meat began cooking, thus sealing it within a watertight container.

Now however, the meat was just deposited in the holes, covered and dirt replaced. The men were tired. They had traveled far and eaten nothing all day. "Your mother promised to have food for the three of us waiting," Fire Dancer slapped the two youths on the back, "We did well, men. This should be the best Spring Ceremony any of us can remember. Never has there been so much food."

"The others have not returned yet from the antelope hunt," Stone Man observed. "I hope they had as much success as we. I am worried though; the game near the camps is becoming nearly as scarce as in the starving mountains. We will soon be forced to move again."

"If so, this escarpment goes for many, many hands in both directions. We will simply move farther north, or south. Besides, game always moves away from people."

"But Father, the animals have not moved away, we have killed them all just as in the Starving Mountains. The plants are not renewing either.

There are very few cattails growing back at the edges of the ponds, because we have taken all of them, leaving none to reproduce," Blue Coyote began. "It is the same as with our dogs. We ate too many of them, we did not keep enough to reproduce. This camp is the only one with new pups of any size. The ones from the Quail Camp are not nearly as large as Scorpion's litter. It will take a hand of years before we have a dog pack equal to the one I remember as a child."

"The plants and animals were put on this land for us, Son, the 'spirits' have always renewed them. That is why we thank them for their gifts," stated Fire Dancer.

"When we lived in the Starving Mountains, every bite was needed, then I could understand, but here we are taking many more animals and plant products than we need. Look at us! The People are getting fat and lazy! There is a difference between taking what we need, and this!" He swept his hand around. "We have been forced to throw out baskets full of meat these last few days, because we put back more than we could possibly eat during the winter. I cannot think that the 'spirits will smile on such waste. Yet you have told me stories of the same things happening when you were a child and The People lived in the Starving Mountains. Then it also was a land of plenty."

"Perhaps we did put away more than needed for this last winter, Son, but remember, this is a new land. How were we to know how long or severe the winter would be? It was best to gather more than we needed, rather than not sufficient."

"Why? At any time we could have gone out and got fresh meat. There was no need to eat dried meat all winter, the same with the tubers. Where were they going? Yet I saw Mother and Turtle Woman dump a hand of containers full of rotted tubers. Had they been left in the ground, today they would have been as fresh as those they just dug; only no one would have had to go so far to find them."

"The starving seasons have been fresh in everyone's minds. People have gathered more to be sure they had enough."

"And do they eat at each meal as though it were their last, because they fear it will be? No! I have seen hunters go from the camp, vomit the meal just eaten, then return and eat as much again. How do you explain that?"

Fire Dancer frowned, scratching his head, "I do not have an answer for you, Blue Coyote. I will have to think about your words. It does seem to put a shame toward honoring the 'spirits' when you speak like you just have. Perhaps Acorn will have an answer. I will speak with him. Now let's go and get some food! You cannot say we have eaten too much this day."

The three made their way to the storage cave where Star Woman and Turtle Woman were just finishing preparations for the meal. Cougar was already seated; a deer scapula heaped high with food and a full water skin handy. Fire Dancer glanced at him; Blue Coyote's words still fresh in his mind. He frowned, really looking at each occupant of the cave. Cougar was developing a tendency toward thickening at the waist. Turtle Woman had added at least one chin and was also getting fat. Even Star Woman had put on weight. He ran his hand over his taunt stomach, dismayed to feel an extra layer of fat there as well. Blue Coyote was right. They were eating too much. He sat down and put a single quail on his scapula plate and added a single tuber to it.

"Are you feeling sick?" Star Woman asked.

"Not at all; why?"

"Is that all you are going to eat?"

"It is." He replied.

Blue Coyote followed his father's lead, placing only a single bird and tuber on his scapula. "What is going on here?" asked Star Woman. "Are you playing some sort of game with me?"

"Not at all," replied Fire Dancer. "I have just taken a good look at myself, and I do not like what I see. There has been too much indulgence since we arrived at this land. Stone Man and Blue Coyote are right. We have started doing the same thing here as our ancestors did at the Starving Mountains. Soon, this place will be as barren as that one if we do not change our ways. We have all over-eaten, gathered far more food than we can eat, even then, and we have wasted much of that. Look at what we have thrown out at the spring ceremony! We discarded enough food to have fed the entire camp for a pair of moons in the Starving Mountains. One thing we should all have realized by now is that there is not an unending supply of food. Already we have stripped the plants in this area of the escarpment. Soon we will have to move to a new area, then again, and again, unless we learn to take only what we need and leave the rest."

Star Woman frowned, looked at Turtle Woman and nodded. "We have both put on a lot of weight from the good living," she agreed. "But what is the harm, we starved for all our lives, now you suggest we starve more in a land of plenty. That does not make sense."

"I do not suggest we starve," Fire Dancer corrected, "Just that we no longer waste."

"All winter we ate dried meat, there was no need to do so, we could have had fresh meat nearly every day, but because we killed so much and dried it, we ate that. We gathered so many tubers that before spring we were eating nearly spoiled food, when we could just as well have gone out and dug fresh ones as we needed them. This is all that I am saying. The acorns must be collected once a season, as many of the seeds and grains must, but the rest of our food supply can easily be taken just as we need it."

"This is a new land; we were bound to make some mistakes," Cougar remarked. "How were we to know that there would be a constant supply of deer, antelope and plants here?"

"We could have paid attention," Fire Dancer replied. "But the damage has been done here, we are going to be moving to a new place shortly, and there we are going to do things differently. We are going to kill only what we need, gather only enough of the season-round plants as we need, collecting such things as amaranth and acorns because they are only available once during the season. That way we always have fresh food, the best food, and there is much less work involved."

"That certainly makes sense," agreed Star Woman, "And perhaps we will be encouraged to not eat as much as well."

"Perhaps if you prepared less, we would eat less as well. I would feel better if I did not eat so much," Turtle Woman agreed, "I am getting far too fat."

Star Woman sat on a stone near the fire, her own scapula well filled. She looked at it, at Turtle Woman and Fire Dancer and nodded in agreement. "I have enjoyed eating all that I can hold ever since moving to the escarpment. After a lifetime of living at the edge of starvation I just haven't been able to stop eating, but you are right. It is time we all get this overeating under control. Right after the spring ceremony we will do so."

Stone Man and Blue Coyote finished their portions and rose, "We will see you in the morning." Blue Coyote nodded and the youths left to return to the unmated men's cave.

"What has happened here?" Stone Man stumbled over something underfoot. "Get a fire started before you move about," he cautioned, "There are things all over the floor."

"Uh!" Blue Coyote grunted as he tripped and sprawled on the floor. "I have discovered that for myself." He scrambled back to his feet and cautiously searched for one of the torches they kept stored against the wall. A few breaths of time later it flared into life, illuminating the cave.

"Wow! Someone has really made a mess here! It looks like half the storage baskets have been ransacked," Stone Man blinked, "Who would do such a thing?"

"How should I know?" Blue Coyote replied, "I have been with you all day. The rest of the fellows left at the same time as we, and no one else is back yet, so it must have been one of the women, but why? What could they have wanted, and why leave such a mess any way?"

"We had better tell Fire Dancer, perhaps it is more serious than someone searching for something for the Spring Ceremony," Stone Man suggested.

"Good idea, I will go get him, you get the hearth fire started." Blue Coyote turned and quickly left the cave.

"Do you see any tracks belonging to anyone not living here?" questioned Fire Dancer, a short while later as he stood looking around the cave, "Can you tell if anything is missing?"

"It doesn't look like it." Blue Coyote confessed. "Everything seems to be here, except Red Eagle's bed furs and a few days food rations."

"Then it is likely that Red Eagle is the culprit!" Stone Man exclaimed, "But why!"

"We will ask him when he returns. I don't understand any of this! First Red Eagle was going with us, and then at the last minute he decided to go after the antelope instead, now it looks as if he did neither!" Blue Coyote muttered, "He has been acting strange lately, even for Red Eagle."

"There is nothing more we can do tonight," Fire Dancer said, "I will ask about and see if anyone else has had the same problem." He turned and left the unmated men's cave and returned to the storage cave.

* * *

In a tiny cave, farther north than the camp usually wandered, Red Eagle sat wrapped in a fur before a small fire. On the quickly constructed hearth sat a tortoise shell within which was steeping water and a portion of the dreamer's filched powder. Red Eagle watched the liquid bubble, waiting for it to pull the dream power from the powder. When he decided it was ready he removed the shell from the hot stone with a pair of sticks and set it aside to cool.

I will find the spirit cave again! The answers will be there. Then I will know what to do. He had set his bed furs aside and made a place to sit upon them, wrapping himself in a rabbit skin robe for warmth. Following the instructions given him by a dreamer long ago, he had already prepared his body. He had washed in a pond nearby, cleaning and purifying his body. All day he had eaten nothing, now he sat, naked but for the rabbit skin robe. He had blocked the cave entrance with a hide and built a large fire in the hearth to warm the small area, and once the fire burned to coals he was ready. The preparations had taken most of the time since arriving here, and now it was dark outside.

Time to make my spirit trip! He tested the liquid in the shell, and with a grunt of satisfaction drank it all in one gulp. He crawled onto the furs, crossed his legs just as he had been instructed, and waited . . .

*   *   *

One heartbeat, he was sitting calmly; the next, Red Eagle was violently spiraling through the air, garish colors whirling in his brain, lifting, lifting, higher and higher into the spiral. Just as suddenly he was thrown face down onto the floor of the cave. A voice cackled . . .

*   *   *

Welcome Dreamer . . . I have been waiting for you, waiting a long time . . . but I knew you would come to me, eventually you would come . . . someone who would help me destroy her . . . the voice! It was familiar, yet . . .

Red Eagle opened his eyes. He was face down, all the breath knocked from his body. He looked around, *the dream cave!* He recognized the paintings flickering in the light of a hearth fire in the middle of the cave.

Next to it sat the skeletal figure of a man so ancient it was impossible to believe he was still human. Then Red Eagle realized; *he is a spirit!*

Get up, boy! The apparition moved, ancient tattered eagle feather robe flapping grotesquely about his emaciated frame.

"Who are you?" Red Eagle scrambled to his feet, sweeping the dirt from his body.

Don't you remember me? I'm your spirit helper, came the reply, *called me to help you get rid of that accursed female, you did. Now I'm here. We have no time to lose. We must destroy her, steal her power before she realizes . . .*

"Before who realizes what?" Red Eagle cautiously edged a step away from the gyrating figure.

That female! That spawn of the accursed Feather! Must kill her and take her power, before she realizes! Before she begins to walk the path!

"Basket," Red Eagle questioned? "She has special power? I know she has the throw back animal, and I saw her steal the power tip, and she has some strange teeth as well." He focused on the figure, trying to see better.

She has more than that! She was sent by the spirits to destroy The People! Just as the one before her was! I stopped her! The figure whirled about, *but not before she delivered this one, but we will stop her, you will steal her power, take the sacred objects from her, and eliminate her before she realizes . . . should have done it seasons ago, but you did not call! I had to wait until you came to me. We have wasted much time, cannot waste any more, you must strike now!*

"I want to know about this place, tell me what the pictures mean," Red Eagle demanded?

It all began long ago . . . I was a great Dreamer. She tricked me, she lied and hid the truth from me, she took my power, she . . .

"Who are you, or should I ask who were you?"

She tricked me! You were there! You saw! The spirit screamed. *Do you want power? Would you be the greatest Dreamer to ever live? I can give it to you . . . I can make you . . .*

"Yes!" Red Eagle grated through his teeth, "Yes, I want power; I want The People to notice me! I want them to realize that I am not an ordinary man. My father was a great hunter, a great leader, but Fire Dancer drove him away. Fire Dancer must pay! Blue Coyote must pay!"

Yes! The tattered figure swept close, *I will give you power . . . I will make you . . .* diabolical laughter echoed through the cave and the spirit leaped and flitted here and there. *I will give you the power, they will pay . . . and the woman, she will pay as well. You will take her power, crush her . . . she is the true enemy, she is the one to fear . . . you must destroy her, bring me the power objects, destroy the spirit animal . . . destroy! Destroy! Destroy! And I will give you power, more power than you have ever dreamed of!*

"I want to destroy Fire Dancer, and Blue Coyote," protested Red Eagle. "Basket is just a girl; she can be crushed with one hand. I want . . ."

What you want doesn't matter! I tell you, it is the girl who is the enemy! Destroy her and you destroy the others as well! She has the power relics! She bears the mark! This isn't about petty control! This is about power! Not just power over people but power over Spirits as well! Control of Power! You can have that! Through me you can have such power! Do you want it, boy? Do you want such control?

"Yes!" exclaimed Red Eagle, "I want the power. I want the control of Power! Yes!" He shouted. *Give it to me! Give it all to me!*

The figure continued to gyrate about the cave, its laughter bouncing off the walls, filling Red Eagle's mind, filling . . . Filling. *Filling . . .*

Dawn was fading the ancestor fires. The figure in the small cave began to move, unwinding joints that seemed to have been frozen into position for eons. A smile flickered across his face, his eyes lighted up, he flexed fingers, felt face and body, assuring that it was still intact. He added wood to the hearth and rekindled the fire. Then he began pacing back and forth. *There is much to do!* The voice in his head shouted, *there isn't time to waste!* Red Eagle grunted and began gathering up his things. *Don't forget the spirit powder!*

He left the cave and turned south toward the camp. *No! Not that way! We have much to prepare. Go north. I will guide you. There are things you must find; things to be made . . .*

With a sigh Red Eagle turned north and followed the directions given by the voice in his head.

*   *   *

The next day he returned to the camp, stashed a bundle of things back beyond the storage containers and smiling, made his way to find Fire Dancer.

"You are sure this is what you want?" Fire Dancer questioned the youth's unexpected request.

"It is," Red Eagle assured him, "I wish you to make the offer for me. It would not be proper for me to make it."

Fire Dancer frowned but nodded, "I will speak to Butterfly as soon as the Spring Ceremony is over."

"No! Speak to her now," Red Eagle insisted, "I want this thing settled before the Spring Ceremony."

Fire Dancer shook his head, "No, it would not be proper. Not until after there has been a presentation to the entire 'People'. It cannot be done before then," he insisted.

"Oh, very well; but just as soon as the ceremony is over!"

Fire Dancer nodded and the youth left.

"Strange fellow," mused Fire Dancer, "I am not sure about this . . . but there is a chance she will refuse. If she had any sense she will refuse . . ." he muttered.

"The other camps are coming!" Star Woman shouted, "The ceremony has begun!"

Fire Dancer looked up and saw that indeed others were coming, laughing, shouting and in fine spirits. He went out to greet the first camp, and then another, and was soon too busy to think further about the youth, Red Eagle, and his odd request. Soon children were running and shouting, playing games with others whom they had not seen in moons. Drums were set up and a steady tum, tum, tum, began to sound through the gathering like a communal heart beat. More quarters of meat were coated with clay and lowered into pits. Containers of tubers were piled ready to bake, or roast, or boil. Groups of women hurried purposefully from the camp to gather the freshest seasonings for the stew pot.

Skins of fermented brew were brought forth as the men gathered around the great central hearth. Much laughter was shared as the skins were passed around. Dreamers gathered in Acorn's cave, making their own secret preparations.

More and more people arrived, until the camp seemed to be literally bulging with people. A special shelter had been set up for the 'new women' and another for the 'new men' in preparation for their becoming 'official' members of the tribe. Fathers and uncles deposited materials for their initiation. Mothers bustled their daughters importantly to this special shelter. As evening approached, all was ready . . .

PART II: CAST OF CHARACTERS

People of the Yucca Camp

BLUE COYOTE: Young hunter of the yucca camp.

STONE MAN: Young hunter of the yucca camp.

BASKET: Young woman of the yucca camp. Owner of Throw Back. Thought by most to be 'spirit touched'.

BUTTERFLY: Grandmother of Basket.

RED EAGLE: Young hunter of the yucca camp.

ACORN: Dreamer of the yucca camp.

FIRE DANCER: Headman of the yucca camp.

THROW BACK: Dire Wolf. Basket's protector. Female offspring of Scorpion & Wolf.

STAR WOMAN: Mate to Fire Dancer.

TURTLE WOMAN: Sister of Star Woman

PINYON: Story Teller

CENTIPEDE MAN: Hunter who joined the Yucca Camp

MOTH: Daughter of Centipede Man

GRAY WOLF: Youth of Yucca Camp

People from other camps

BLACK DEER: Hunter of the Quail Camp

GRAPE LEAF: Headman of the Rabbit Camp

ANGRY Man: Headman of the Quail Camp

PART II

DISCOVERY

CHAPTER 8

Tum . . . tum . . . tum . . . the drums picked up volume, calling The People together. Dusk was beginning to settle and the ancestor fires were brightening in the night sky. Soon the full moon would rise. Men were shoveling dirt from the cooking pits and women were scurrying about busily stirring pots and adding seasonings to them. Large rocks were set up for people to sit upon, and places were cleared for the men to place the meat. Hides were spread on the ground and piles of deer scapulas were ready for heaping piles of food. Camp leaders were arranging lineups and dreamers were sorting out duties. Then suddenly, the drums reached a crescendo and stopped.

*   *   *

The storyteller from the Quail Camp rose, the ceremony began. "Long ago, before any of our grandfather's, grandfather's walked this land, the Spirits honored The People. They came down and up from the 'spirit' places and walked among The People," he slowly walked around the hearth, speaking to different individuals as he walked. "While they lived with our ancestors, they gave them direction...., direction about honoring the seasons, the animals given to feed the people, and later, the plants as well. Each spring since, The People have gathered, in small or large groups to honor the beginning of each new season, and the spirits. They gather also, to remind everyone once again of their responsibilities to the spirits and to The People."

"First Mother and First Father were awakened by Sun Spirit from a very cold place. They were naked and freezing. They were thawed out by Sun Spirit and given warm clothing and shoes to wear. They were brought from the cold place into the land." He singled out men; "here the spirits of the animals greeted them. Each animal gave The First Mates its name and explained all of the wonderful ways it would serve if only First Father and First Mother would honor it." Now he spoke to the women. "First Father and First Mother agreed with all of the animals. They were careful to remember just how each animal wished to be honored, and all the uses each animal offered. It was very difficult, for there was much to remember."

The Pine Camp storyteller took over the tale, "Moon Spirit came then, and explained to First Father and First Mother about the fingers of the season. Spring came first. It was to be a time of birth and renewal, a time for new fires to be built to honor the beginning of the season. It was a time for honoring the beginning of The People. Moon Spirit foretold how First Mother and First Father would have many children; so many that they would spread over this new land. Many animal spirits would provide food, clothing and shelter for the children of First Mother and First Father. There would be much food, the children would not go hungry. First Father and First Mother were very careful to remember all of these things."

Now Pinyon rose and continued. "Summer would be the finger of ripening. Animals would grow and become fat. Plants would produce fruit. Each fruit and each plant was to be honored in its particular way. Moon Spirit explained the uses of each plant, the ones for food, the ones for healing, and the ones for 'spirit' medicine. They explained that some of the ripe seeds of each plant were to be cast onto the ground to honor the plants. Harvest would follow summer, as a time of gathering all the ripe grains, nuts and cones. A time for putting away meat in the special way which Sun Spirit showed them. Again the ripe seeds were to be cast onto the ground to honor the plant spirits. Winter was the time of rest, a time to repair broken and worn tools and clothing. It was the season to work hides and make new tools as well. The starving time would bring the season to a close." He bent to speak to a group of children, "if First Father and First Mother did not honor the animals, plants and seasons, Sun Spirit would take them to walk the wind during the starving time."

"First Father and First Mother were very careful," the Rabbit Camp Story Teller rose. "They lived through the first season. Then as the spirits had said, First Mother gave birth to The People for many seasons; and they spread over the land. First Parents taught their children very well, and for a long time The People multiplied and there was no starvation in the land. The Animal spirits were pleased with the way The People honored them. The People did not waste the bounty that was given to them. They always remembered to give thanks to the animal spirit. They used the animals in all the ways that honored their spirits. They honored the plants as well, casting their ripened seeds as they had been instructed. The animals renewed their kind, and the plants grew again each spring."

Pine Camp now took over the story. "For many generations The People were careful. There was no starvation in the land. There was no death. People were fat and strong and healthy. Then they began to forget. First, they forgot to scatter the ripe seeds. The plant spirits became angry and did not replenish the plants each spring. 'So'! The People shrugged and said, 'we do not need plants, we will eat meat instead'. Then they forgot to honor the animal spirits. They did not remember the uses for the animals. They did not remember to take only what they needed. They killed and killed, leaving rotting animal carcasses to decompose and be eaten by predators. So Predator Spirit was pleased. He multiplied the predators. The animal spirits became angry. First Horse Spirit removed her kind from the land. For The People no longer honored the animal. Its beautiful golden hide was no longer chosen to make clothing, its flesh was left to spoil and rot. It was killed in numbers far beyond that necessary to feed The People. We know this animal not!" He sighed, "next to be removed by its spirit was the camel. No longer would it provide food for the people in areas of little water. We know it not! The bison spread over the land in herds so large a man could walk all day and never walk around one. The people forgot to honor the bison. They drove large herds of them off cliffs and left their bodies to rot. Bison Spirit became so angry she took away the bison. No more was food so abundant for The People." He shook his head and sighed, "and still the people did not change their ways. So Great Mammoth Spirit, totem spirit to The People became very angry. She sent a special messenger to tell The People to change their ways. The People laughed and did not listen. So Mammoth Spirit took her kind away also, but not before The People began to kill their totem animal. Soon all of the 'spirits' deserted The People."

Pinyon again took up the tale, "First Mother returned to the land from the Ancestor Fires in the sky. She was very angry with her children, but again she taught them the way to honor the animals and plants. She explained how important it was. That is why, at this time, each season The People meet at the Spring Ceremony and are again instructed in the proper veneration of the 'spirits. No longer will The People forget . . ."

From beyond the fire came a snorting, scuffling 'spirit', children giggled then became silent as Mule Deer Spirit came into the light. The 'spirit' danced forward on its hind legs, hoof rattles tied to either wrist. Upon his head he proudly carried a beautiful set of antlers. He pranced and snorted about. "I bring The People meat to eat, hide to be made into shelter covers, robes and clothing. I provide rawhide for the making of a multitude of tools and weapons. My antler provides hammers, flakers, shaft straightners and a multitude of other uses for The People. Tendons from my body provide sinew to use in the construction of clothing. To honor me, use my children wisely, do not waste the wonderful hide and antler products I give to you. Do not kill my children and leave their bodies for predators. Do not waste the food they provide to The People. When a hunter kills one of my children, he must release the spirit of that animal to be born again or soon there will be no more Mule Deer." He pranced around and shook the rattles, raised and lowered his head and pawed the ground, and then he left.

Antelope followed, then Rabbit, then Pig and on and on until each of them had their say. Various Dreamers, each explaining the uses for the plants, and how to give thanks for them represented the plants. This ended the 'Reminding The People' part of the ceremony. It was getting late by the time this was completed. The meal was to follow; the first of the Spring Ceremony meals. It honored the animals provided for food.

*　　*　　*

The men lifted the clay-coated portions from the pits and lay them out on stones and hides. The Dreamers came and opened each clay container by breaking it with a ceremonial stone hammer. The rich aromas burst forth, and tender meat was dished out with scapula spoons onto the blade platters.

Scapulas heaping with meat were passed around, until everyone had one. Then the women brought the containers of tubers, roasted, baked and boiled, fresh yucca stalks, wrapped in their own leaves and steamed over hot coals. Tender shoots of cattail and pollen and young heads were served. The People ate until they could hold no more, yet each had managed to eat everything on their plate, for it was an insult to leave food at the ceremony.

Then fermented drink was passed around among the men, the drums began again and soon the men began to dance around the fire. As they danced each told a story, the tale of their greatest hunt or deed. On and on they danced, until finally the Ancestor Fires began to fade and Sun Spirit lightened the sky.

Children were long fast asleep, cuddled in robes brought for that purpose. More foods were eaten, now seedcakes as well, for the first fruits ceremony was over. Skins of fresh water were passed around for any that had a thirst. Then the dancers staggered off to their shelters and slept for the day.

Now the women took over. They cleaned up the mess left behind by the feasting. They loaded the dirty platters and eating utensils onto hides and lugged them off to ponds to be scrubbed clean. Others swept the area, cleaning away any food dropped into the dirt. Then taking empty spirit brew skins to a central location where their owners could later claim them. More wood was brought in for the evening fire. More pots of stew and containers of tea were set out to cook and steep. Mule deer, pig and antelope had been the honored food for the initial meal. This evening rabbit, quail, prairie chicken and a multitude of smaller creatures would make up the menu. The spirit of Black Bear had been honored, but its flesh had been left out of the ceremony, for there were no black bears in this land. Turkey would not be eaten at this evening meal either. But both spirits were honored anyway, for one day they might again be available as food.

At mid day the women took a break and sat a while and visited. This night's ceremony would honor the new men and women. Each camp had at least one of these. The Yucca Camp would be presenting Black Falcon, Squirrel, and Basket.

Black Falcon was in the cave fidgeting as his mother critically checked him over yet again. "Be sure that you face the Dreamer when you tell your 'spirit' and stand up straight!" she admonished yet again. "And keep your clothes clean! You had better not shame us with dirty clothes. Remember how last year that youth from . . ." He escaped from the cave and raced to the edge of the camp where the rest of the youths were having a dart-casting contest.

Squirrel was standing sedately before Turtle Woman, in the Headman's cave. He was uncomfortable because he felt Turtle Woman begrudged him the time and attention. His own mother had died during the crossing, so now he lived with the unmated men, although he was by far the youngest one in that cave. Only the kindness of Stone Man and Blue Coyote had made the move bearable. "You have a 'spirit gift' to present Acorn?" Turtle Woman questioned.

"I have the dried blue jay I found the day of my 'spirit' quest," he responded. "It called to me and I have kept it in a secret place of honor ever since. One feather is in my amulet bag."

"Excellent!" Turtle Woman tried her best to put the youth at ease. "I am sure that you will make me and the whole camp proud both as a hunter and as a man." She gave him a quick hug and he made his escape.

*   *   *

Basket was the one causing trouble. "What do you mean you cannot tell your 'spirit animal,' sputtered Butterfly, "You are going to be my death yet, girl! Of course you will tell it. Now I don't want to hear any more of this nonsense from you, now tell me so that I can decide the proper 'spirit gift' to present the Dreamer."

"I cannot tell you what I do not know!" gritted Basket, on the edge of tears, "I don't have a name for my 'spirit animal'; I only think I know what it is called. Look, perhaps you can tell me!" Basket lifted the sleeve of her tunic to expose her shoulder. There, like a birthmark, was the clear image of the same animal as the charm in her amulet.

Butterfly gasped, "It cannot be!" She shook her head, "I should have known, what with your mother, and all the 'power' objects you keep bringing to me, that you would not have an acceptable woman's 'spirit'."

"Then I am right?" Basket twisted her arm so that she could see the mark; "it is Bison!"

"Yes, it is Bison," Butterfly sighed, "but you cannot go into that ceremony and claim a 'spirit' stronger than any claimed by even the strongest hunter. You will set the whole ceremony in an uproar and the men will be so angry that you will be stoned to death. I have seen that happen before when a woman claimed the wrong 'spirit'. We have to do something!"

"Perhaps I should disappear until after the presentation. If I cannot be found, then I cannot be presented."

"You can hardly spend the rest of your life disappearing every season. You must be presented. We will just have to come up with a lesser 'spirit' for you to claim."

"Can we do that?"

Butterfly shrugged, "we must," she rose and paced the cave, "think of something; anything else you can claim. Surely some other 'spirit' also spoke to you, contacted you in some way. This thing," she nodded to the arm, "it must be a mistake."

Basket bit her lip; "it is no mistake Grandmother. I have other proof, in my amulet. It was just there when I woke from my vision quest."

"I do not want to know!" exclaimed Butterfly. "It is not done to tell what is in an amulet bag. It is secret!"

"I wasn't going to tell you what it was, Grandmother, only that there could be no mistake."

She slumped to her sleeping robe, and then smiled. "I have it! A 'spirit' which will be both acceptable and unquestioned! The Owl of my mother's camp; see! I still have a feather here in my waist pouch!"

Butterfly shuddered with relief. "Yes, of course, Owl. No one will question Owl and it is a perfectly acceptable 'spirit' for a woman."

"It is not even a lie, for Owl Spirit did help me. It guided me to my secret place when I had lost it. It gave me this sign," Basket grinned in relief, "So long as I keep my arm covered, no one will ever know!"

"Tomorrow I will begin a tattoo to cover that symbol," Butterfly stated. "By the time I have finished, only you, I and the 'spirit' will know!"

"Can you do that?" Questioned Basket hopefully, "I mean, Bison Spirit won't get mad or bring some dreadful catastrophe down upon me?"

"Believe me; no catastrophe a 'spirit' could think of would be worse than what would happen if the camp discovered . . ." She sighed, "I knew I should have stopped your father from mating with that woman. There has been nothing but one disaster after another . . . Or so it seems . . . but I did not know . . ."

"We can hardly blame every bad thing that has happened since that time on my mother!" protested Basket, "I may not have known her, but surely she wasn't . . ."

Butterfly frowned, "I am sure she is not to blame for everything, but she is surely to blame for our present predicament. Where do you think I got the idea of a tattoo? Your mother had one, in exactly the same place. I always thought it strange, and it was an ugly tattoo as well. She was obviously also chosen by 'Bison Spirit', and did her best to hide the fact."

"Are we doing any differently?"

"Do you want to be stoned to death?"

"No," Basket whispered, "but I cannot think this is right."

"Right or wrong, you go into that ceremony, and you be sure to claim Owl loud and clear, so there can be no doubt in any one's mind. If 'that' comes out later, we can always claim it happened after the 'Spirit Naming' Ceremony." She pointed toward the offending shoulder. "And keep that shoulder covered!"

"At least that will not be a problem," Basket muttered, "my sleeve comes clear to my mid-arm."

"I don't mean just this day! I mean always, every single day, until we can do something to disguise that mark. Don't you even as much as think of removing your tunic, no matter how hot and uncomfortable you may be."

"I understand," Basked nodded, "believe me, I have no desire to be stoned. It is a fate which will remind me."

"See that it does!" Butterfly reached for a particularly beautiful rabbit-skin robe she had informed Basket she had been making as a gift to Star Woman. She ran her hand over the soft, intricately woven material. "This is my gift to you, Granddaughter," she handed the robe to Basket.

"But . . . you have been making that for Star Woman, Grandmother. You have spent hand upon hands of time on it. It cannot be for me! It is the most beautiful robe you have ever made."

"And you are the most beautiful thing that has ever happened to me," admitted the old woman, wiping a tear from her eye. "You have been my reason for living, all these seasons, watching over you, watching you grow into a young woman, and now that you have, I could not be more proud of you."

Basket flew into the outstretched arms and the women hugged and wept together. "I will always love you, Grandmother," she sniffed, "I realize that raising me has not been easy for you. I have not always been obedient, but Oh! Grandmother! I do love you so!"

"And I love you, my child."

Butterfly released the girl and straightened her tunic, running her fingers over the pure white fringe that adorned it. "Now go and join the others and keep clean!" she admonished as Basket smiled and holding her head high walked sedately to where the 'new women' were gathering in preparation for their presenting. A number of matrons were on hand to assure things ran smoothly. Basket joined the other girls and they were ushered to the special shelter erected for them. There one of the dreamers had spread out paint and upon questioning each girl proceeded to paint the marks. Basket bit her lip nervously as her turn approached. She seated herself on the stone before the dreamer.

"Your Father's Camp?" he questioned.

"The Yucca Camp," she replied.

He frowned and then began painting the yucca leaf on her left cheek, "Your Mother's Camp?"

"Her mother was Feather of the Owl Camp!" stated one of the matrons loudly.

The dreamer's hand shook, then steadied and he began painting on Basket's right cheek. Then he dabbed a rabbit skin in water and washed the cheek, beginning again. This time he grunted and motioned her on. Basket rose and went to stand with the other girls already painted. Her place was taken by the last one to be done. The same matron stated loudly the parentage of this girl also and Basket realized she had not been singled out after all. She gave a sigh of relief and relaxed a little, wishing the whole affair was over.

"They say the dreamer had quite an eye for Feather when they were young," one matron whispered to another, "must be hard on him; some say the girl is the image of her mother. He never got over Feather, when she mated with Cottonwood, well, he became a dreamer." She walked away from the shelter, but not before another said, "lucky for him! I hear Feather was the cause of Cottonwood's death," she snickered, "I certainly wouldn't let my son mate with her daughter. Some say she was very powerful;

straight descent from The Mother herself, or so some say. Personally, I never saw any proof of that. But she was strange. Let us hope the daughter is different."

Finally, after what seemed like forever, the girls were led from the shelter to a place where they could watch the 'new men' initiation and presentation. It was nearly dark now, and not a single one of them had eaten a bite all day. Basket's stomach grumbled!

*   *   *

At dusk the drums started. The men of the tribe lined up beyond the camp and on cue came running and shouting into the camp, atlatl and darts held over their heads. Each of them was naked but for their breechclout and they had symbols painted on their arms, legs, abdomen and face. They raced around the fire and then with a great shout fell to their knees and were silent. From the other direction the 'new men' filed up to the fire. They also were naked but for the breechclout. They also were painted. But they carried no weapons. The dreamers greeted them and as their name was announced a hunter rose from the ranks and stepped forward. Someone handed him a brand-new tunic and he in turn presented it to the youth. Then an atlatl and darts where given, followed by a knife, blade, and scraper.

The youth then turned to face the camp. The dreamer called again the name, and presented the new man to the tribe, naming his Spirit Animal. The youth then made a short speech and gave the dreamer a symbolic 'gift', to symbolize the 'spirit' connection. With this he joined the tribe as an adult.

*   *   *

When it came to their time, the girls were treated much more sedately. Each was led before her dreamer, dressed in pure white, her hair worn in the style of women of The People. A female relative, usually the mother, but in Basket's case, Butterfly, presented her to the Camp. Her lineage was stated so that any unmated man could know if she was or was not related, and thus taboo as a mate. Each was asked their Spirit Animal and Basket calmly and clearly called on 'Owl'. There were nods of approval, for almost everyone would have said they expected 'Owl'. She gifted the feather and the ordeal was over. She was now officially a woman of the 'People'. Basket sighed in relief, and so did Butterfly. It had gone well.

Then it was time to eat. Basket was famished. Fasting all day had not really been difficult for there had been much to do, but now that it was over, she had no difficulty digging hungrily into a prairie chicken and yucca spears. The men again began dancing, and the new men joined in. The women, as on the previous night, retired to their shelters, the dancing was a 'man' thing. They could not be bothered with such nonsense.

*   *   *

"Ouch! That hurts!" Basket protested.

She had returned to the cave with Butterfly, and good to her word, Butterfly began concealing the mark on Basket's arm. She had mixed black ash into a paste with hot water, and with a sharp bone needle was trying to apply a tattoo. "Hold still! I cannot do anything with your squirming around like that!"

"It hurts!"

"Of course it hurts! Did you think it would be painless? Hand me that rabbit skin. It is bleeding so much the ash is being washed away." Basket handed her the requested skin; Butterfly dabbed and again rubbed the ash into the wound. Again blood seeped up and washed the ash away. Butterfly muttered under her breath and again dabbed. Much later she signed and squinted at the results. "No wonder your mother's tattoo looked so ugly, this one is not much better. It is almost as if that mark is purposefully refusing to be concealed." She began applying a soft skin soaked in a healing herbal concoction over the entire area, "hand me that wide thong; that will hold the bandage in place."

"Are you done?" an exhausted Basket inquired.

"For tonight at least," answered Butterfly, "It will do for now, but once this has had a chance to heal, I will probably need to do more." Basket groaned.

"Here, drink this, it will help deaden the pain and help you sleep as well."

"It feels better now that you have applied the herbs," Basket admitted, "but I am very tired, not only due to this but the excitement today as well.

I thank you, Grandmother, for being the very best of mother's to me all of these seasons. I may not say it often, but I do appreciate all that you have done for me."

"It was a labor of love, child," the old woman hugged Basket and they both went to bed.

Both slept late and it was the arrival of Star Woman, which aroused them. This was the final day of the Spring Ceremony. Today, children would be recognized and those old enough given names. Any mating over the last season would be recognized as well as any approaching matings. Then after one more meal, finishing off all of the food prepared, the other camps would go home and the Yucca Camp would complete the last day of the ceremony on its own.

*   *   *

"Come on you pair, the drums are already sounding," Star Woman called, "This is no time to be sleeping!"

"We were late going to bed," Butterfly Yawned, "all of the excitement must have kept us awake." She pulled her tunic over her head and called to Basket, who was still sound-asleep. Basket groaned and rolled over, yelping as she put pressure on her arm.

"I am all right," she assured a concerned Star Woman, "I just strained muscles and am a bit sore. She pulled her tunic over her head careful to keep the bandage away from Star Woman's sharp eyes. Then they joined her and hurried to where people were gathering to join in this morning meal. There were quail, dove, and prairie chicken eggs and grain cakes and hot tea, as well as thin strips of meat fried on hot stones. Around mid morning the child naming began. It did not take long, for there were very few children, and then the new matings were recognized. By mid day camps began packing up and heading back to their own section of the new land.

Now the people of the Yucca Camp began cleaning up the mess left behind, burying the trash in the fire pits and filling them back with the dirt removed in the first place. The summer shelters were assembled, hides stretched over bare frames and new fire hearths dug and lined with stones brought down from the caves or wherever people had stored them. New spits were cut from fresh wood and new sleeping furs were set into place. Then the women went to one pond and the men to another and all washed the dirt of winter and the starving time from their bodies with fresh soap-yucca root. New clothes were put on and the ceremony was over. The People had renewed their pledges to the spirits for another season.

Basket was worried about the washing. She made sure that she was among the very last to go to the pond, and Butterfly was with her to act as a shield. The bandage was removed and Basket could see that the spot on her arm. Although a mess, it could not be recognized as what is actually was. Still she had Butterfly apply a fresh bandage and she quickly donned her new set of clothes, and they returned to the camp.

Although the summer shelters were ready, it was still far too cold at night to sleep in them. So the caves had been cleaned as well, and new hearths dug and lined there as well. Sleeping furs were lugged up from the shelters and for at least one more moon everybody would still be at least sleeping in the caves. Days, however, were warm enough to spend outside.

Acorn was relieved. Finally he began having 'spirit dreams' again. They were no where near as powerful as those of his youth were, but at least he was having them. Wolf Spirit still hid from him, but at least he heard the voice. *There is a new dreamer coming . . .* It had said repeatedly, *he must be destroyed!* On another occasion *they must be reunited!* Of course none of this made any sense, but at least the 'spirits' were once again talking to him. Everything had gone well at the Spring Ceremony. He had spoken with the other dreamers, one on one, and although it bothered him, they also confessed that the spirits were fickle recently. None were having much more success than he in communicating with them. He knew something was wrong but he couldn't figure out what.

The hunters gave honor to the animal spirits just as they always had, at least during his lifetime. They certainly did not waste anything in the Starving Mountains; however he had seen signs of much waste in this land lately. A lot of food had been thrown away at the end of the starving time. Yet tradition dictated this must be done. Women were casting the ripened seeds, as they always had done, although in the Starving Mountains, they had been few, for most were eaten.

He could see signs in the new land already that The People had brought change. Hunters were traveling farther to find animals to hunt, and the women were digging tubers and gathering plants farther from the camps as well. He supposed this was to be expected. The supplies nearby were always taken first. Yet he wondered, and he worried . . .

Fire Dancer was also worried. Red Eagle was the cause of that worry. He had come to Fire Dancer with a request that worried the Headman, then disappeared and missed the entire Spring Ceremony. Not only was his absence disturbing, but for a time Fire Dancer had thought perhaps he had been in an accident, hurt or something, but Stone Man had seen him sneaking around north of the camp only the day previously.

Blue Coyote agreed with the other pair of men that it had been Red Eagle who had broken into the storage vessels and scattered the contents at the unmated men's cave, but this did not make any since, for he lived there and had free access to anything there. The tale that the wolf cave also had been vandalized caused him further worry.

Now he frowned as the subject of his thoughts suddenly appeared before him. Red Eagle looked awful. He was very dirty and unkept, a far cry from his usually meticulous self. His eyes were blood shot, and he was sweating profusely. Even his gait was rough and uneven.

"You have made a decision?" Red Eagle did not even bother with a greeting.

"Fire Dancer frowned, "I am still considering," he replied, "I see no need to hurry. The Spring Ceremony is barely over, and the camp has hardly had time to settle down again. I have had other things to occupy my mind."

"No taboos are involved!" Red Eagle stubbornly persisted, "I see no need to wait. She is officially a woman, she is available, and I have spoken for her. What is the problem?"

"There is no problem," Fire Dancer began, feeling his way, "I just do not see any necessity for such hurry. After all she has hardly been given time to get used to being a woman, now you would hurry her into the added responsibility of a mate and hearth of her own? Besides, what of Butterfly; she also becomes your responsibility then."

"I realize that. Now answer me, do I get Basket or not?"

"Why not settle for Willow, or Cottontail Girl? Either of them would be equally suitable, and they are older, they should be mated before Basket."

"I don't want Willow or Cottontail Girl!" Red Eagle answered angrily, "I have spoken for Basket."

"Very well," Fire Dancer sighed, "I will make the arrangements."

"Today!"

"I will speak with Butterfly," Fire Dancer hesitated.

"Today?"

"All right, today, but she must agree. You do realize that Butterfly has the final say? If she refuses you, then you must look elsewhere."

"She will not refuse!" Red Eagle tossed his head, "I will be back at sundown to finalize the details. You already have my 'gift'."

Fire Dancer nodded and Red Eagle turned and quickly left the camp. With a sigh the headman rose and made his way to the wolf cave. "Good day to you, Grandmother," he greeted Butterfly. Basket was not in the cave. He had seen her leave with the other unmated women some time earlier. "I would have a word with you," Fire Dancer requested formally.

Butterfly frowned at the tone of his voice but motioned him to be seated. "I have come to present to you an offer for Basket," Fire Dancer came directly to the point. "The 'gift' is substantial, and the youth of an age and ability to provide for both of you. He has agreed to you living with them as well."

"Which youth?" questioned Butterfly suddenly excited; Basket was barely officially a woman, and already there had been an offer made. Both of the other unmated girls had been so for more than a season and no offers had been made for either of them. It had to be Stone Man, regardless of what Basket said. Butterfly just knew it!

"Red Eagle," Fire Dancer replied.

Butterfly blinked, her mouth fell open, "Red Eagle?" she repeated, "but . . ."

"He is quite determined," Fire Dancer stated, "he came to me even before the Spring Ceremony with his request," the headman shifted uncomfortably. "Of course you have the right to refuse him," he reminded her.

"A substantial 'gift' you say?"

"A span of deer hides, and an equal number of obsidian nodules."

"That is indeed substantial!" Butterfly was flattered. Perhaps the youth was not the one she would have chosen, for Butterfly had always hoped that Stone Man . . . However such an offering was certainly one which would raise their status in the camp. And to have a man at their hearth, providing them with meat, helping with the heavy work: that was not to be shunned. "Do I have to give you my answer now?"

"He wants it settled today," Fire Dancer admitted.

"My! My! He is in a hurry to claim my Basket!" Butterfly exclaimed, greatly flattered.

"You can still refuse," replied Fire Dancer hopefully. He rather wanted Basket for Blue Coyote, but he could not say so now. The other youth had spoken first, and he was honor bound as headman to treat everyone with equal fairness. Still, he did not care for Red Eagle.

"Oh, I do not think so," Butterfly replied. "It is a good mating, he is young and strong, and you did say he would make me welcome?" she reaffirmed.

Fire Dancer nodded and rose. "I will tell him," he finalized the arrangement and left.

Butterfly was so excited she could not sit still. A mating for Basket! So soon after becoming a woman too; yes! This would definitely raise their status in the camp. There was plenty of room in the wolf cave for one more person, and soon they would be moving into the summer shelter any way. She spent the rest of the day scurrying around and rearranging the cave. Basket returned at dusk.

"My! You have been busy!" Immediately she saw the changes.

"I have news!" Butterfly fluttered about just like her namesake; "I had a visit from the headman today!" she stated importantly.

"Fire Dancer; what reason would he have to visit you?" Basket frowned.

"The very best of reasons; the most important reason of all," Butterfly answered excitedly.

"And that is?"

"A mating of course," Butterfly replied smugly. "A mating with a very substantial 'gift' as well, so substantial in fact that it is safe to say none other in this camp has ever had such an offer."

She grinned ear to ear, "and with a pair of older unmated women passed over as well!"

"And you have said yes?" Basket went pale, "without even consulting me?"

"I... I guess I got so caught up in such a wonderful offer that I ... well ... I guess I did give Fire Dancer my answer ... but ..." she floundered.

"So it is done," Basked said dully. "Might I inquire to whom you have 'sold' me for that substantial 'gift' or is that to be a surprise as well?"

"Well I would have preferred Stone Man; or Blue Coyote . . ."

"Who!" shouted Basket, "who is it?"

"Red Eagle," Butterfly admitted suddenly unsure, "He said I would be welcome . . ." she added.

Basket turned white as snow and looked at her grandmother with an expression of such distaste, Butterfly suddenly began to cry, and her wonderful day of pleasure turned suddenly to ashes. Basket dropped her gathering tools against the wall and went to her sleeping furs. She rolled up in them, turning her back to Butterfly, and refused to speak to her.

Butterfly had a bad night, sleep was long in coming, and she tossed and turned and could not rest. When she rose the next morning, Basket was already gone. Even though it was early, she scurried off to find Fire Dancer. "I have reconsidered the offer," she quickly blurted out.

"It is too late," he shook his head. "It is already done."

"But I was wrong not to consult Basket!" Butterfly sputtered, "she is very angry with me, and rightly so."

"That, unfortunately, is your problem. You gave your consent and Red Eagle was at my hearth before dusk for your answer. How was I to know that you would change your mind?" Fire Dancer replied angrily at the old woman, "if you were not sure then you should have said so. It was up to you, after all, to decide. You decided, and now it is done. The consent was given. The mating goes ahead."

"But Basket . . .!"

"Basket is your problem. She is your grandchild. It is up to you to make sure she cooperates. You know the problems involved . . ."

"Yes . . . I know," Butterfly sighed; "Oh Dear, how could I have made such a terrible mistake?"

"Perhaps it was not a mistake," he said hopefully, "perhaps she is what is needed to steady the boy, and perhaps he is what is needed to bring her to her full potential."

"And perhaps I can fly," grumbled Butterfly, "When?"

"Almost immediately," he replied. "Perhaps it is best to get it over quickly, before she has time to get any more upset."

"I don't think it is possible for her to get more upset!" mumbled Butterfly.

"She has to mate sooner or later," reminded Fire Dancer, "and Red Eagle is a handsome enough youth. It isn't as if we were mating her off to someone old enough to be her grandfather. These things work out. It might be a bit rough at first, but they will grow together through time. After all, you and almost every other woman have gone through similar situations, and you have all survived them and settled down to be quite happy. Once children begin coming things will be fine. You will see, in a few seasons she will wonder what all the fuss was about." Fire Dancer was reassuring himself as much as Butterfly.

"I suppose you are right," she sighed, "I did not handle telling her properly that is all," she tried to convince herself, but Baskets expression would not leave her mind.

Butterfly thanked the headman and returned to the wolf cave. She sat for hours staring into the fire, more and more a feeling of dread coming over her. Nothing good would come of this, of that she was now convinced. She had failed Basket dreadfully. Basket, the only thing she had worth living for, and she had let her down. Had destroyed the light of her life, snuffing that bright flame out in one swoop of selfish unthinking greed! "Oh Basket," she sobbed, "I am so very sorry . . ."

Star Woman frowned at Fire Dancer. "You did what?"

"I made a mess of things! I should have spoken to you about it! I should have made him wait for an answer, no matter how impatient he was, and I certainly should have spoken to Butterfly long before I did. Had I not waited until the last possible time, because I was too busy with other things, none of this would have happened. Now Basket is committed to a man she does not even like and Butterfly is miserable, and I feel like it is my fault."

"Well there is nothing which can be done about it now," Star Woman slumped onto a rock, "I had hoped . . ."

"So did I."

"Well, what is done is done," she sighed. "Everyone will just have to make the best of it, unless . . ."

"Unless what?" hopefully.

"You couldn't find some taboo . . .?" she questioned hopefully, "some reason why . . ."

"Other than the woman is not willing? He shook his head, "I don't think so, but I will consult Acorn right now," he rose and left the cave.

"Let me get this straight. You want me to find a reason . . .?"

"That's right." Fire Dancer paced angrily, "I don't care what kind of a reason, just so that there is one, any taboo, even if it is one no one has ever heard of."

Acorn shook his head, "I cannot do such a thing, Headman; you know that! If there is no taboo, I can't make one up."

"I'm not asking you to make one up! Well perhaps I am, but at least search your memory, see if there isn't something!"

Acorn scratched his head, "she is of the Owl Lineage, he of the Quail. There is no taboo. I am sorry Fire Dancer; I would help you if I could."

"It was just a chance," Fire Dancer sighed, "I thank you for your time any way."

"Short of kidnapping the girl and whisking her away in the dead of night, there is no way to get her out of this mating," Fire Dancer confessed to Star Woman.

"I don't suppose we could do away with Red Eagle," she said hopefully?

"I think that I have even considered that," admitted Fire Dancer. "This has certainly taught me a lesson, unfortunately at Basket's expense. I will never again be rushed into agreeing again to a mating without consulting both parties personally, before hand."

"Both parties have usually already consented beforehand, long beforehand," Star Woman sat beside him. "How were you to know that Red Eagle had not spoken to Basket and she agreed before he even asked?"

"It is my place to be sure of these things."

"Being Headman is not always an easy task," she reminded him.

"It certainly is not going to be easy dealing with Basket," he sighed. "Speaking of which, I haven't seen her all day."

"Butterfly says she left the cave before light with the Throw Back."

"You don't think she has run away?"

"She only took her atlatl and darts and digging stick. I am sure she intends to return."

Well out into the shinnery, Basket was not so sure. "How could she?" She drove her digging stick savagely into the ground for the uncounted time, "I thought she loved me, how could she do such a thing?" She was shaking with sobs, "my own flesh and blood and she traded me for a warm place beside my fire! I would never desert her! What could she have been thinking?"

Throw Back did her best to comfort her person. She licked Baskets tears away, leaned into her for comfort and whined and rubbed against her. Finally however, exhausted, her tears spent, Basket wearily returned to the camp, unaware of how many people had tried to change things for her.

CHAPTER 9

The drum beat began. Basket stood in the cave, her head down, her heart numb. She was dressed in her 'new woman' clothes, but they gave her no pleasure. The spot on her arm that had once been a bison ached, as it had ever since Butterfly tried to conceal it with a tattoo. That hadn't worked either. The bison was still there; for so much blood had seeped from the wounds it had washed all the ash away. However, quite a scar remained, rendering the animal nearly impossible to make out. She no longer cared! Butterfly had cried and cried and begged for forgiveness. There was none to give. Basket could no more hate her grandmother than she could get out of this mating. She had repeated told Butterfly so, but the old woman blamed herself so much there was no consoling her.

The arrangements had gone ahead with such speed Basket had not had time to do anything except prepare for the mating. She had found time to move certain things from the cave to a safer place. Both Basket and Butterfly were now positive that it had been Red Eagle who riffled the cave. If this was so, he was aware of the existence of the tooth relics, and after their discovery, Basket had moved them to a place of safety, not even telling Butterfly. The 'gifts' had been delivered, and already Red Eagle had moved his things into the cave. All that remained was the headman handing her over to him. Butterfly had moved her sleeping furs into the storage cave for a hand of days to give them some privacy. She had been so upset that Star Woman had been the one to explain to Basket what she should expect. Of course Basket more or less knew or had guessed much of it. The young girls had a habit of discussing and guessing at such things, particularly when someone they knew was about to be mated.

As all other silly young girls, Basket had visions of a wonderful brave hunter, one who always resembled Stone Man, who would win her heart, think her beautiful, and all the other nonsense which young girls dream of. She had never met any woman to whom this had happened, but that did not keep her from hoping, only now all hope was gone and she had only Red Eagle to anticipate. He had been a nasty, sneaky child and a mean youth. She had no illusions that he would be any different as a mate. As a small child he had taken pleasure in pulling the wings from butterflies and breaking the legs from grasshoppers. Later he had graduated to young birds and puppies. He had actually tossed one of the camp pups into a pond with a rock tied to it just to see how long it would take the poor creature to drown. What she could not understand was why he wanted her so badly that he was willing to offer so much that Butterfly would be unable to refuse. This he had done. It made her feel very uneasy. She knew Red Eagle well enough to realize he would never have done so rash a thing without a very good reason. Unfortunately, she was certain she would find that reason all too soon, and it would not be pleasant. The only thing she could think of was the ancient relic, but why would anyone go to such extremes? He had held it in his hand at one time, why not just take it then and be done with it? There was no need to go to the extreme of mating with her just to acquire the canines.

The drum became more insistent, so with reluctance she hugged Throw Back and instructed her to stay in the cave. The animal whined but obeyed. Basket dragged her feet down the trail noting with some satisfaction that she managed to get her leggings very dusty in the process. Red Eagle was waiting for her, taking away her last hope that he had changed his mind. Fire Dancer waited at the communal hearth. Beside him were the 'gifts' to be handed over to Butterfly upon finalization of the mating. She looked no happier than did Basket. Her eyes were red and swollen from copious weeping. Basket tried to give her a weak smile, but felt she had failed. Fire Dancer assured that all was in order, Acorn stepped forward and established the lines of descent and confirmed there were no taboo's broken by the union. Then it was over. Basket had ended her all-to-brief time as an unmated woman and was now a matron.

*　*　*

"Get that creature out of the cave!" he shouted almost immediately upon entering it and facing the bared teeth and growling of the three-moon-old puppy. Basket, shaken, both at his attitude and her pet's response to him, quickly ushered Throw Back from the cave. She hurried the animal to the summer shelter and instructed her to stay there. Then Basket returned to the cave. Already Red Eagle was kicking her things around and settling himself in her sleeping space. "Where is it?" he demanded, as soon as she entered the cave.

"What?" she stuttered, blinking at him in the firelight?

"The spear tip; where is it? I know you have it; for I saw you pick it up, so don't lie to me! Hand it over. It is mine. I had it first!"

"I have no idea what you are talking about!" Basket replied in confusion.

"I saw you, out in the breaks. That abomination you call a dog dug it up and you put it in your waist pouch!"

"Oh, you mean the power object? Is that why you forced this mating? Just to get the power object? Surely it would have been easier to just force me to hand it over!" She went to where her pouch hung and withdrew the object. "Is this what you want?" She held it out on the flat of her palm. He grabbed it and backhanded her across the face a number of times, taking great pleasure in her pain.

"You dirty little thief!" he hissed, "don't you ever steal anything of mine again!"

Basket backed against the wall of the cave trembling. She wiped the blood from her split lip with the sleeve of her snow-white tunic. The bright red blood quickly soaked in staining the soft hide permanently. Basket did not care. "Why have you done this to me? I know that you have no real desire for me! Why go to so much effort? Or does it please you to have me to shove around?"

Red Eagle sat cross-legged on his sleeping furs caressing the object tenderly, gently, crooning to it. He completely ignored Basket. She slumped to the floor against the wall and wrapped her trembling arms about her body, trying to stop the tremors there. Later Red Eagle rose and made himself a drink from some powders he carried in his pouch. Then he returned to his bed furs and spent the rest of the night sitting there in some sort of spirit trance. Basket did not sleep at all. With the dawn she crept from the cave and began preparations for an early morning meal. Then she sat with Throw Back until he left the cave.

Red Eagle seated himself on his sleeping furs . . . *yes!* the now familiar spiral began. He clutched the spear tip in his hands letting it lead him to the secret cave. The creature was there.

* * *

Do you have it? Red Eagle showed the object to the apparition, *Yes! That is it! Bring it to me!* He did. *A single magic point; one of them survived! I thought she had destroyed all of them!* The crazy creature stroked the smoothly flaked surface. *Once I had containers full of them! She killed them all: all but this one. Now her spawn has grown, but you will deal with her for me! You will destroy that spawn of evil spirits. You have done well, dreamer, for you have found the sacred point and returned it to me. You will be rewarded.* The spirit tucked the object away somewhere inside his tattered clothing and then turned back to Red Eagle. *You killed her?*

"Not yet, it isn't time yet. She has other things; I will make her tell me . . ."

Other things! What kind of things? Suddenly the creature swept close and Red Eagle could smell the feted sourness of his breath.

He fell back a step. "She has the teeth!" Red Eagle replied, "The ones in the painting."

The teeth of the long toothed cat! You are sure? I knew it! You will get them for me!

Red Eagle shook his head. "I have brought you what you asked, now. It is your turn to keep your promise. I want Fire Dancer and Blue Coyote dead."

I offer you Power! More power than you can imagine! What are the lives of a pair of puny men compared to that? Forget this petty desire for revenge! It will come! I promised you the lives of Fire Dancer and Blue Coyote, and so I will give them to you, but at the right time. You are not through with the woman yet. The teeth! You must bring me the teeth! I must have them! Then I will give you Power beyond your imagination! Once she is dead, then and only then . . .

* * *

Red Eagle woke with a splitting headache, like always. He struggled back to awareness. The day had begun and Basket was no where in the cave. He grunted and got the circulation going in his legs. Then he hurried to the secret hiding place and loosened the rock. He reached inside . . . empty!

"She moved them!" he muttered to himself, cursing not taking them when he found them, "She will pay! She will be more than glad to hand them over to me!" An evil smile lit his eyes, *yes!* The voice inside his head agreed. *Then we will kill her!*

By the time he finished looking the cave was in shambles, he had literally left no stone unturned, but he had not found the teeth; nor fortunately, the stone cores, or the staff. Basket had hidden them all very cleverly. Angrily Red Eagle left the cave and went to vent his anger elsewhere until evening. Basket watched him go and sighed in relief.

* * *

Butterfly also saw the man leave, and she lost no time finding Basket. When she saw the swollen black and blue face and the split lip however, she came to an abrupt stop, "What happened?"

"He wanted the power object," Basket answered as best she could.

"He beat you for that!" Butterfly was already digging in her supply of herbal remedies.

"He only hit me to make a point, I refused to give him what he wanted quickly enough," Basket admitted.

"I shudder to think what else he did to you!" She began crying again.

"That is all he did," Basket sighed, and now he has gone, at least for a while.

"You mean he did not . . .?"

Basket shook her head, "He took some kind of spirit powder and spent the rest of the night in a dream voyage or something. I don't know, only he sat on his furs for hands of time without moving so much as an eyelid. I finally fell asleep. When I woke this morning, he was still the same way. I left the cave and came here. I have been here ever since."

"You mean he is some kind of dreamer . . .?" Butterfly asked.

"I don't know what I mean . . . I am just glad that he is gone. I hope he never returns, now that he has that which he came after!"

"But Basket; if Red Eagle is a dreamer, it is wrong for him to have mated with you, don't you see?" Butterfly grasped her hands and turned Basket to herself, "Go to Fire Dancer! We will give back the gifts and Fire Dancer can declare the mating undone!"

"He never mated with me Grandmother! I have told you what happened."

"Then all the better; I am going to Fire Dancer right now," The old woman finished applying the salve to Basket's face and left.

Fire Dancer shook his head, "other than speaking to him about striking Basket, there is nothing more I can do. You have no proof that he is a dreamer, and even if he is, unless he declares himself one, there is no taboo against his mating. I am sorry, for you and for Basket, but there is nothing I can do."

Butterfly returned to their shelter and spent the rest of the day there pampering Basket in every way she could think of. At midday they went to the cave and stood speechless regarding the mess which greeted them.

"At least he did not find the teeth!" Basket tried to smile, but it hurt too much, "Nor anything else!"

"You moved the teeth?"

"Oh yes! After he found them the first time that place was no longer safe. He will never find them where I have hidden them now. No one will."

"You took them from the cave didn't you?" Butterfly asked.

"I did!" Basket replied.

"That is why he mated with you isn't it? He wanted those teeth."

Basket shook her head; "it wasn't the teeth. He didn't even mention them. It was the power object I found. He was watching me and saw it, probably has been snooping on me for ages and I just didn't know it. That is what he wanted, and he took it. But he will remember the teeth, and he will be back for them."

"You will give them to him?"

Basket shook her head, "they belong to me. They were my mother's; he has no right to them."

"But Basket, he will hurt you again," Butterfly reminded, "Please, reconsider. They are just teeth after all, not worth your life. That man could kill you. He is crazy."

"He will not kill me; at least not until he has the teeth. And I do not intend to stay around here for him to try."

"Where will you go?"

"Somewhere safe, somewhere I can hide and he will not find me. Somewhere he has no idea even exists."

"Where can you find such a place?" questioned Butterfly.

"Come, I will show you," Basket started off.

"No!" Butterfly stopped her; "I do not want to know. It is enough that I will know you are safe. I cannot be forced to tell what I do not know."

"I do not think you would tell," Basket smiled at her Grandmother.

"I do not trust myself. If you were in danger, I would tell just to save your life. We both know that. Already I have done unimaginable damage to you. Just assure me that you will be safe in this place and that Red Eagle will not find you there. That is enough for me to know, I have learned my lesson!"

I will be safe there, Grandmother, he will not find me. I promise you. I found the place myself, only because Throw Back led me there. But I will move the cores and blanks to this place as well as enough food and water to last me at least a moon if I must. For now the flint is safe. He would never be clever enough to dig below the cooking hearth, even if he knew to look for the flint. The sacred teeth I have already removed from the cave and hidden there. I promise you, he will never find the teeth, for I will never tell him, nor will I give them to him. The staff he is not even aware of, it is safest of all."

"When do you move to this safe place?" The old woman questioned worriedly, "He could return at any time."

"Not just yet," replied Basket. "It is possible that he will be satisfied with the power object, at least for a time. We will wait and see. I have no wish for him to come after you, Grandmother. Besides, I need to get food and water stored in the place before I 'disappear'. All of this must be done without calling attention to me as I do it. I can only go to the place when there is no one in the camp. Therefore, I must wait."

"I will arrange for the women to go on a gathering trip just as soon as possible, and I will encourage Fire Dancer to take the men on a far hunt as well."

"That will be fine, Grandmother, but until then I had better clean up this mess, or Red Eagle will have just cause for beating me."

"I will help!"

"No, Grandmother, you go on back to the storage cave and get the rest of the camp organized away from here. That will be the greatest help."

Butterfly left Basket to the task of cleaning up the cave. It took her most of the afternoon, even with Throw Back bringing things to her while she arranged them once more in the storage baskets. Some of the meat had too much dirt on it to eat, that she gave to the dog.

Then she made sure that there was no sign of any excavation in the area of the fire hearth. Finally she was satisfied. He had not returned to camp by dusk so she ate a lonely meal in the shelter, happy with Throw Back for company. She spent the remainder of the day stroking the animal and finding courage there, and then she took Throw Back to the summer shelter and ordered her to "stay."

She had returned to the cave and had lit the hearth there before he appeared, apparently in no better humor that he left.

*　　*　　*

He looked around, then immediately went to the storage baskets, "if I had wanted them here, I would have left them that way!" he screamed at her, throwing the contents from the basket and kicking them about the cave. "I did not tell you to move things!" Again he slapped Basket. She staggered back, he followed, balled his fist and struck her with his full weight behind the fist, driving it into her stomach and knocking the breath from her. Basket gave a soft moan and doubled over. He followed with a fist to her chin, driving her teeth through her tongue, and knocking her into unconsciousness. He kicked her limp body a couple of times, then returned to his sleeping fur and ate the meal that she had prepared.

Basket moaned. "Where are they?" he questioned. She shook her head, "I know you have them for I saw them in your little hidden hole. But they are not there now, and I want them."

"They do not belong to you," she whispered as best she could.

"You belong to me," he stated, "so anything that you had, now belongs to me. I want those teeth, now you can get them for me now, or later, but I promise you, later is not a good idea. Now again, where are they?"

Again she shook her head. He merely shrugged and returned to his eating. When through once again he prepared the spirit drink and sat like a stone for the remainder of the night. Basket was far too sore and sick to move, or care what he did. When she woke in the morning, he was gone. So was Butterfly. Star Woman said she had seen the old woman going up the trail to the plain above just after the morning meal. By nightfall, Butterfly had not returned.

* * *

The old woman dug her walking stick into the ground as she stomped up the trail. Butterfly was mad. She needed to get away from the camp for a short while and think. Once on the plain she caught her breath then made for the shinnery. A couple of fat prairie chickens might make Basket feel better. She followed a well-worn path through the tough little trees; headed for a spot she had seen chickens earlier in the moon. Muttering to herself, she began to wear down the anger and resentment within. She did not see him rise from the brush behind her.

He was careful to make no sound. Silently, deadly as a rattlesnake he struck. The old woman crumpled to the ground without a sound. She never knew what struck her.

He drove the end of the hand ax so hard into her brain it nearly exploded. Barely breathing hard, he lifted her limp body and carried it a distance from the camp. There he casually tossed it over the edge of the escarpment to the rubble below. When they found her, the camp would assume she had fallen to her death accidentally. The strange light glistened in his eyes as he smiled. *I told you that you would be sorry, Basket! This is but the beginning!*

That evening Basket again had a meal ready. She had not cleaned up the cave; it would have been impossible for her, even had she dared. Besides she was worried about Butterfly. Star Woman and Turtle Woman had gone up onto the plain and called her again and again. They had made the trip to Water Woman's cave, but she was not there either. Night came. Butterfly did not return.

"Where are the teeth?" Again he questioned her. Again she refused. He shrugged and ate his meal. As on the other nights he drank the spirit drink and sat the entire night. Basket would have struck him down while he sat there, but she couldn't move without hurting. She had an idea that he had broken her ribs, they did not feel right. It had taken all her strength to even move. Star Woman had brought the food; she was horrified at the condition Basket was in, but helpless to do any thing about it. There were strict rules about interfering between a man and his mate; if he beat her that was his right. That is just the way life was.

*   *   *

Butterfly had not returned the next morning. Fire Dancer took a party of men out to look for her. They found her broken body and brought it back. None, however, could explain the head wound, for she was laying face down when they found her. Nothing could be proved so nothing was said to Basket. She was hardly in any condition to attend the lying out. Butterfly was set out to walk the wind at her favorite spot up in the shinnery, and life in the Yucca Camp returned to normal. Or as normal as it could, with every member of the camp aware that Red Eagle was mistreating Basket.

*   *   *

A hand of days went by, then another. Basket began to heal. "Are you ready to tell me where the teeth are?" he asked casually as he ate.

She shook her head in silence. "I see," he replied, "perhaps another 'accident' will convince you," he smiled evilly.

"You killed her," Basket said dully, affirming what she already suspected. "She was just an old woman. She did you no harm."

"She would still be alive and well, had you given me the teeth," he replied sinking strong teeth into the tender flesh of a quail. "It is your fault she is dead. You killed her."

"I will die before I ever tell you!" she screamed at him, throwing her deer scapula at him. He ducked then lunged at her with deadly intent. Basket screamed. He knocked her over and began pummeling her in the face with his balled fists, enjoying every punishing blow. He straddled her, intent on his punishment one heartbeat, but then suddenly he was sprawled beyond Basket, a mass of snarling snapping, furious, more wolf than dog, animal doing her best to rip his throat out.

Throw Back had him by the scalp, then let go and tried for the throat, but missed. Her teeth ripped open the side of his face, and one canine punctured his left eyeball. Red Eagle screamed in agony, and with great strength managed to break free. Blood soaked his face and tunic, he could see with but one eye. He rolled away from the animal, already scrambling to her feet to renew the attack. Into the hearth Red Eagle rolled and screamed again as his hair and clothing caught fire, even then however, with a powerful swing, he struck the animal with a rock. With a yelp she crumpled, a pool of blood forming from her skull. *That takes care of you, you abomination! Now for Basket!*

"I told you!" he hissed as he kicked and beat the body of Basket until he was sure there was no life left in it, and then sobbing in pain he gathered up his things and staggered from the cave, to vanish into the wild land beyond.

* * *

Idiot! You failed! You didn't get them! The teeth! The teeth! I want the teeth! You didn't keep your word! Now I will never have them!

* * *

He finally staggered into the little cave far to the north. Red Eagle was under no illusion about returning to the Yucca Camp. Beating one's mate was one thing, murdering her was another matter. The death of Butterfly could not be proven against him but losing his temper and going too far with Basket could cost him his life. He had crossed the thin line, and now he could never return to The People.

The burns to his head and body were mostly superficial, but they scared horribly. He had also lost an eye, the tooth of the dog rupturing it.

* * *

"You hear that?" Star Woman shook Fire Dancer.

"What?" Fire Dancer shook himself awake.

"Listen, there it is again, I'm going to investigate," she scrambled from her sleeping furs and quickly donned her tunic, "sounds like the Throw Back, howling in the wolf cave. Basket may be in trouble." She only just beat Fire Dancer to the trail, "he probably beat her again. All that shouting and screaming earlier."

Throw back sat beside Basket's unmoving body, her head thrown back howling mournfully. Blood covered the side of her head, and there was further blood pooled on the floor of the cave, but head wounds bleed profusely, even those caused by a glancing blow. Basket, however, was another case. A runner was sent to the Quail Camp to bring their healer. Acorn, meanwhile, applied what talent he had to keeping Basket alive until the healer got there.

A hand of days passed before anyone was certain that Basket would live at all. Her skull was probably cracked; her arm and one leg were broken, as were several ribs. However there had not been extensive bleeding, grimly, she hung onto life. Slowly she began to win. At least her body looked to recover; the damage to her spirit was yet to be discovered.

Basket lay inside the shelter for over a moon, tended gently by the matrons of the Yucca Camp. Nothing like this had happened to a member of their camp for farther back than anyone could remember. They got her to take liquid; water: a little broth, but gradually she lost weight and began to fade away from them. She did not speak, and she did not seem to recognize anyone. If her spirit remained, it was locked inside. Throw Back was tied outside the shelter, she would not leave her person, but the women did not think it safe to let her get close to Basket, she was in such a fragile state, and the pup was so big and clumsy.

* * *

Summer arrived; Basket still clung stubbornly to life. Little by little she began to eat solid food, and slowly she obeyed when told to move. Her broken bones healed and the women were able to get her to sit up, and then with help walk a few steps. Slowly she was able to feed herself, then dress herself, and then care for herself. She began wandering aimlessly around the camp, staring vacantly at nothing in particular. She limped, leaning heavily on a staff, but she could walk. Throw Back, freed from her tether, never left Basket's side. By midsummer the body had healed. Basket looked and moved much like her old self. Still she had not spoken a word, nor indicted she even understood anything but the simplest commands. The animal guarded her, never leaving her side, always watchful, her blue eyes reminding all of the sharp teeth just below.

People became used to her wandering about the camp. She was harmless, most felt sorry for her. The men had made an attempt to find Red Eagle and bring him back for punishment, but he had vanished without a trace. Throw Back began leading Basket on longer and longer excursions, as she became stronger. One day, at midsummer, the entire camp had gone one place or another: leaving Throw Back and Basket alone.

The wolf, for everyone agreed, she was no dog, led the woman up a trail which was so hard to see that no one would know it was a trail at all. Slowly they moved, the woman clutching the animal by the ruff. Then they vanished, right into the escarpment. It was cool inside. Cool and quiet. Basket sat on a handy rock and watched without much interest as Throw Back began digging at the rear of the cave. Soon the animal returned with something in her mouth. Gently she laid the packet on Basket's lap. Basket smiled at her friend, aimlessly running her fingers through the thick fur. Throw Back nudged her hand. The wrappings gave way and the packet opened, and her hand slid onto the contents. Basket ran her finger along the smooth ivory colored object. It felt good against her fingertip. She began to absently stroke it. Then the tingling began; it ran up her fingers and into her hand, up her arm and spread through her entire body. It felt good, it felt familiar, and it felt right. Basket sighed and closed her eyes. Gradually her body became encased in a soft pulsating blue light. Still, she stroked the objects. Slowly, ever so slowly, the thing that had gripped her brain crumbled and gave way. The confusion, the pain, the blankness, all dissolved into the blue light. When finally she opened her eyes again, Basket had returned.

*   *   *

We are with you, softly the spirits in her head assure her, *and we will guide you and lead you. Trust the watcher, she is of an ancient lineage, she will protect you, you will be safe! It is time Basket, time for you to lead The People to the Sacred Spring, time to lead them to the place of the stone, time to return The People to the life they were born to live! You have the stone showing the way, take it, use it, and follow the path of your ancestors. The pair must be united!*

*   *   *

Tears began running down her face and she knelt and wrapped her arms about the wolf, burying her face in the rich deep fur. She cried, and cried, hugging the creature and taking comfort in the communion of their souls, with the soul of the wolf, which had brought her back! It all came crashing back, the beatings, Butterfly's murder, and the last awful night when she knew Throw Back had been taken from her as well. Finally, her mind had healed. Basket was again whole. The girl, however was gone, the young woman as well. What remained was strong, tempered by pain and loss. What remained was what the spirits had chosen!

"Some day we will find him," she promised, whether to the spirit of Butterfly, herself, or Throw Back, or perhaps all three. "Someday . . . and he will pay . . ." With shaking fingers she lifted the relics and rubbed them against her cheek, absorbing the healing 'power' they offered. Her amulet throbbed gently at her throat, soothing, softening the ragged edges of her mind. The spot on her shoulder tingled with a pleasurable surge of feeling. The leather thong had all but rotted away. Basket tucked the teeth into her waist pouch and smiled at Throw Back. "Come on, girl!" She spoke softly, "we have a lot to do!"

They left the secret cave and returned to the camp. The cave had been cleaned up. There was no sign left of the mess created by Red Eagle, or of the last dreadful night there. Basket rummaged through storage containers finally finding what she wanted. She sat on a stone beside the dead hearth and threaded a length of leather through the holes drilled into the base of the ancient canines. She held her handiwork up, tilted her head to one side, "There, I think that looks right," she looked at Throw Back, "what do you think?" Throw Back whined and wagged her tail, "you agree?"

"Woof!"

"Right!" Basket slipped the thong round her slim waist and knotted the end. Then she found a deer scapula and began digging. The ash had been cleared from the hearth; she tossed the stones lining it to one side and soon had an arm's depth of dirt scooped from the growing hole and piled upon a deer hide. "This has been kept a secret for long enough," she muttered. "It is time to share with the rest of the camp." Soon she had a container rapidly filling with cores and blanks of the beautifully striated flint. The ancient tough staff was carefully removed from its burial place as well. Then she returned the dirt to the hole, and finally replaced the stones lining the hearth.

"We are never returning to live here Throw Back!" She whispered, still unable to speak with much strength, "this camp is our home only for the present. I do not feel safe in the shelter, he could come back." Throw Back growled, her size already truly menacing. "Yes. I know, you will watch, but I still do not feel safer here, besides there are memories of Grandmother here, and I do miss her so." Throw Back whined and washed her face, "You miss her also, I know."

*   *   *

That evening Fire Dancer returned with his hunters and the women from their gathering. Basket sat waiting at the central hearth, her polished, ancient walking staff at her side, the canine teeth dangling from a thong at her waist. She had gone to the pond and washed her hair and body with soap yucca root. She had braided her long hair again down her back, and the owl feather fluttered there once again. Sometime during the day the scaring on her face and body had disappeared. The mark upon her shoulder was clear for all to see. Around her pulsed an aura of 'power'. Beside her rested the containers of flint, brought from the cave to await the headman.

Fire Dancer stopped abruptly. He frowned, studying the quiet figure seated beside the hearth. There was something different about Basket. Then he realized she had bathed and cleaned her hair and looked so much like the old Basket it tore at his heartstrings.

She raised her head and he caught his breath. "Good evening, Headman," she greeted him softly.

"Basket?" He questioned, really looking at her, noticing the changes, the teeth, the feather, and the staff.

"Yes Fire Dancer, it is really me. I have returned from whatever place I have been. I am ready to live again, and I have much to share with you, with The People. Where I have been, few have traveled, but now I have returned with a message and with a gift," she motioned to the container beside her. "I will lead The People to the place where this can be found."

Fire Dancer dropped his hunting tools and approached Basket. Before looking into the container, however, he embraced the young woman, tears of joy running freely down his face, "Thank the spirits! You are returned to us. Star Woman, Turtle Woman, Acorn!" He shouted, "Basket has returned!"

Members of the camp came running at his shouts.

"I didn't know she had left the camp," Star Woman came running, "where did she go?"

Then the matron gasped, "Basket!" She ran to the younger woman and hugged her, eyes watering in joy, "you are back with us! It has been so long. I have almost given up hope . . . Oh Basket!"

Soon every member of the camp had gathered at the central hearth, all overjoyed to welcome the spirit of Basket, back into her body. "This certainly means a celebration!" shouted Fire Dancer.

"I have prayed to the spirits for so long . . ." sighed Acorn; "perhaps they heard me after all."

"They heard you," Basket assured him, "they heard you and they have answered your prayers. Another dreamer, a powerful, bad dreamer has been at work here, but he has lost some of his power, and now the spirits can speak with you again. They have sent me from that place where my spirit has been, to bring a message to The People, a message of great importance! And a gift," she motioned to the containers beside her, "a gift for The People!"

Now everyone crowded around Basket and peered into the containers. There were exclamations of wonder and of delight. Fire Dancer reached into a container and withdrew several of the blanks and cores, handing them around. "This material, it comes from near here?" asked Cougar.

"Not from near here, but the spirits have given a map stone, showing the way," Basket replied, "A way to a new life for The People as well. The stone comes from a place far out on the grasslands, a place where there is a river, shelter, much tool material, and many animals to hunt, not deer and antelope, but bison!"

"Bison?" questioned Blue Coyote, "I thought they were all gone! Are you sure? I mean, I have only heard of bison in legends. No one has ever seen one."

"You will," promised Basket, "you will see bison in numbers so great no one could ever count them. They are there, just waiting for us." She rose, "tonight I have brought you material to make tools; material given by the spirit of our ancestors; the same ancestors that want The People to return to the ancient way of life. I have been with these very same Ancestors all the time I have not been with you. Now they have sent me back with a message for the people, we are to hunt the bison again, as they did long in the past."

Acorn nodded, turning to Fire Dancer, "she is indeed 'spirit touched',", he remarked, "can you not feel the 'power' she is giving off? It is so strong I can almost see it!"

"Indeed, I can almost see it myself," Fire Dancer agreed, "how can this have happened? This woman has grown up with the Yucca Camp. There has never been any sign of 'power' associated with her."

"Acorn shook his head, "I have seen such signs, for many seasons, do not forget, she is the daughter of Feather, and she claimed The Great Mother of The People herself, as an ancestor. Basket is in the direct line. There were 'little things' when she was a child, an ability to know when something bad was going to happen, and an ability to locate things that were lost. As she grew older, the power has gotten stronger. When she became a woman, remember that she was given that feather directly by 'Owl Spirit'. When she presented it as her ceremony, I could feel it very strongly."

"Why have you not said anything about this?"

"I was not sure," Acorn sighed, "I have been having so much trouble communing with the spirits myself, that I could not get any message from them regarding this woman. But Butterfly was concerned. She came to me a number of times regarding Basket. When your dog gifted her Throw Back as her protector; then I was sure. But things happened so fast that I have not had time to sit down with you and discuss these things. After Red Eagle beat her so badly, the spirit power left her, so there was no reason to speak to you about it," he spoke with regret. "Now, she is back, and I have never seen a person with so much power. Perhaps this power is resulting from her losing her spirit for so long. I have heard of persons being granted special vision after a head accident, perhaps Basket is one of those, but I do not think so. I think she was sent by the spirits, sent with a message, and a purpose. The thing with Red Eagle, this was to test and strengthen her, temper her power and bring it forth."

Basket rose and the old dreamer saw the thong at her waist for the first time. He drew in his breath, "look! The teeth! She has the teeth of the long toothed cat! Where did they come from?" he gasped, "How did she get them; and the staff? She carries that as well!" He began to shake, "Indeed she is powerful," he whispered, "she is The Mother of The People returned. I should have recognized the signs! The Feather, the wolf! But she grew up with this camp, and I have been blind. Red Eagle knew! That is why he was willing to give so much to mate with her! He wanted to steal her power and use it for his own ends. Red Eagle is the dreamer I did not recognize!" Acorn was white with shock, "and he nearly succeeded. Because of my blindness he almost killed Basket and took her power. Have you any idea the damage those power objects could cause, in the wrong hands?"

Fire Dancer shook his head, "I am not . . . I have no knowledge of 'power'. I am just an ordinary man, and I leave dealing with such things to you, Dreamer. It is dangerous to get in the way of 'power'." He shook his head, "indeed I do not even recognize the staff as a power object, but I do remember legends of the teeth. I wonder how Basket came to have them?"

"Power probably led her to them. They have probably been waiting here all these generations. Pinyon was certain this was the very area that The Mother brought The People."

"How could he possible know that?"

"Said Basket told him," replied the dreamer.

"We must talk, tomorrow, not a heartbeat later!" Fire Dancer was drawn away from Acorn, who went in search of the storyteller.

"You say Basket was interested in hearing the legend of the teeth?" He questioned Pinyon, a short time later.

"Interested; I would say almost obsessed!" Pinyon replied, "After they lived through the acorn incident Basket couldn't get enough of the legends. She asked to hear them again and again. Even had the audacity to tell me that this was the very place that The Mother brought The People to learn the new way of life."

Acorn nodded, "she became a woman on that trip. She went on her vision quest right after returning. That is about the time that 'Owl' gifted her that first feather. Remember she wore it in her hair until Butterfly made her knot her hair in the traditional manner. That feather almost vibrated with power. But where did she get the teeth of the long toothed cat, and the staff of The Mother?"

"She has those things?" questioned Pinyon, "I cannot believe that! They have been lost for generations; no one knows where they went!"

"Perhaps they were hidden around here somewhere? Maybe the spirits led Basket to them, who can know about such things? I only know that Basket has them now."

"I must see," Pinyon hurried away.

But Basket had left the hearth and retreated to her cave. The group around the hearth had begun to drift away to their shelters as well. The stone had been carried to Fire Dancer's cave for safekeeping and the sleeping time was settling over the camp. Soon all was quiet, but some were not able to sleep. Acorn hurried to his own shelter and went to seek the spirits.

She has returned! Wolf Spirit whispered softly, but at least he spoke.

Pinyon sat staring into his fire; his mind going back over the legends again and again, searching for some clue; he found none. If Basket was indeed some messenger of the spirits, there were no indications to be found in the legends There were no hints there that 'the chosen' would return. Indeed, after The People moved to the Starving Mountains, there were no legends at all. It was most puzzling, and the strangest piece of all, was Basket. How had a girl, born and raised in the Yucca Camp, suddenly, without warning on any sort, come to possess the most powerful relics of The People? Unless of course, it was some sort of elaborate trick! The only way he would ever get the answers to his questions was of course to speak with Basket. This he promised he would do at the very first opportunity.

The next morning, however, the entire camp was in fervor of preparations. They were going to welcome Basket's spirit back with a celebration. Already Fire Dancer had led a party out to kill deer, and the women, Basket included, were all out gathering plants in preparation. Acorn was still in camp, however, and he and Pinyon sat talking for hands of time. Acorn was convinced that Basket was The Mother Returned. Pinyon, on the other hand, was inclined to think trickery was afoot. After all, Basket had shown an inordinate amount of interest in the legends long before she even hinted at possessing power. She had wanted every single detail, no matter how minute, about her supposed ancestor and he had been only too happy to delve into his own memory of the legends to feed her interest. Truth to be known, he had been flattered that she was so interested in his stories.

Maybe she hadn't been 'wrong' in the head all these moons, maybe she had been tricking them all while secretly creating the staff. And she probably made the teeth, hoping they would be convincing enough to fool the people of the camp. Why she would do such a thing, eluded him, but he was sure that she had a reason, and he, Pinyon, intended to find out just what that reason was. Then he would expose her, and perhaps gather a bit of status in his own stead.

Basket, was not, however, gathering with the women. They had insisted she could not make the preparations for her own celebration. She was, instead, again, in the secret cave with Throw Back, drawing strength from the place, and finding peace there. Pinyon, agitated after his talk with Acorn, had gone off on his own to think. He found a quiet place at the edge of the escarpment to sit and think. This he was doing, when a slight sound behind him alerted him that he was not along. It shook the old man considerably to find the focus of his thoughts, suddenly materialize right beside him! It startled Basket as well, to step from her secret cave and nearly stumble over the old man. Pinyon gave out with a yelp and ran back to the camp, considerably shaken.

"Woof!" voiced Throw Back.

"I tell you, she just appeared!" Pinyon protested to Acorn. "I was completely alone. There was no way she could have gotten where she stood without me seeing her! I had a perfectly clear view of the path in both directions. She wasn't there and then, poof! There she was!"

"Power!" was Acorn's answer.

*   *   *

"Do you think she is right?" asked Blue Coyote.

He and Stone Man were following the trail of a small herd of deer, "I mean, do you think there could really still be bison? Just think of it!"

"I am thinking of it," replied Stone Man. "I have thought of little else since last night. You see, now you even have me caught up in the excitement! But where are they? We have been all over the breaks and even out onto the plain for a hand of days, and we have seen no sign of them."

"We thought the moving sand could be crossed in a span of days, and we were very wrong about that. We could be equally wrong about the plain. If what she said is true, there is no way a herd of animals that large could survive on an area even as immense as the moving sand. Maybe we are thinking too small. What if the Starving Mountains and the Moving Sand areas are small in comparison to the plain? What if it stretches, not for a span of days, or even a span of moons, but a span of seasons?"

"Could any place be that large?" Stone Man asked in amazement.

"I have no idea, but I suppose it could be possible, and if that is so, why, we have not even explored a tiny edge of it. There could be huge herds such as Basket described, and we would not have come anywhere close to finding them."

"I did get a quick glance at the 'map stone' rock. It shows the shinnery as a mere dot," Stone Man nodded.

"We know how large the shinnery is, and this Sacred Spring, it is but a dot as well, both on the very edge of this plain. I do not know what a 'map stone' is, but it seems to be some kind of picture legend showing places-of-importance. It shows a place and then how many moons traveling to get to the next place, and the direction to go. It told of pair of moons to reach the place of the stone. Does that not make you think perhaps this plain is much bigger than we ever imagined?"

"We could spend an entire lifetime traveling on such a place, and never see all of it!" Stone Man said in wonder. "There is no telling how many wondrous things we could see. Perhaps the great beasts even walk out there somewhere!"

"This is the kind of adventure I have always dreamed of. Could it be that we will actually get the chance to live it?" Blue Coyote asked

"Quick, there are the deer!" Stone Man whispered, diving into the brush.

"That was close!" he admitted a short while later as they removed their darts from the carcasses of the pair of deer they had just brought down. "Perhaps it would be best if we paid attention to the task at hand and left our 'thinking' for evenings beside the hearth."

"But I just can't let it go," Blue Coyote admitted. "Even at night, I lay awake thinking. . ."

Stone Man sighed, "I know what you mean. It makes my head spin, just imagining what might be out there, just waiting for us to find it. As you say, there could be herds of bison, numbers beyond comprehending. Why it could mean a whole new way of life for The People. A life such as our ancestors lived. A life such as we used to imagine as boys back in the Starving Mountains."

"We had the courage to dream then," admitted Stone Man, "Your visions brought us across the moving sand to this place. Perhaps this is just the beginning of another dream; one far bigger than we ever imagined."

"And we are here to live it!" Blue Coyote grinned, "I can hardly wait!"

They returned to the camp and preparations went forward with the celebration. By evening there was a bounty of food, and everyone enjoyed eating and welcoming Basket back from the 'spirit place' where she had lived for the past moons. Everyone agreed Basket was her old self again, yet . . . there was something . . . different.

Fire Dancer, Cougar, Acorn and Pinyon spent hands of time studying the 'map stone' stone. It fascinated them. Headmen from the other camps came by and they also studied the rock with amazement. For a moon people talked . . .

Then Fire Dancer began to prepare. Night after night he lay awake planning...

CHAPTER 10

Fire Dancer had called a meeting of the Camp, everyone knew something was going to happen. For the last span of days Fire Dancer had been to all the camps, other headmen had been to the Yucca Camp as well, but no one knew, although some hoped . . . Finally, they would find out.

"I want to make a trip out onto the plain," Fire Dancer stated to the group, particularly to the small number of men he had assembled to study the stone. "We have all studied the 'map stone' and there is plenty of time to travel at least a moon onto the plain in search of the bison. The pups are old enough to pull the travois, and the bitches with pups can stay behind in the camp with the women. I have in mind a hard-traveling group of men, able to cover a lot of ground in a day. What do you say? Are any of you interested?"

"Yes!" Was the answer? Everyone wanted to go!

"Only those who are really fit," Fire Dancer added, "we need to have some men left in the camp, for we will be gone the rest of the spring, summer and into the fall moon and well beyond. It would be impossible for the entire camp to make such a journey. It would slow us down too much."

"How will you choose who is to go then?" asked Gray Wolf, knowing in his heart that he was too young to be selected. "Not many need remain behind, for there is plenty of food and we already know that other than the acorn harvest, and the grain, we can hunt season-through for meat. The women can gather those things."

"What of protection for the camp?" reminded Fire Dancer, "would you leave the women unprotected?"

"What is there to protect against? There are no raiders in this land. We have seen signs of no others beyond ourselves. Will the Quail Camp attack us?" He could see his chances dwindling away like smoke on a breezy day.

"I had thought a select few men from this and the other camps," admitted Fire Dancer, "perhaps a hand or so, and your name is among them Gray Wolf," he replied.

"You mean it? I am to go?" Gray Wolf was nearly beside himself with anticipation.

"You have earned the right. I had selected in my mind the following others, Porcupine, Chipmunk, Stone Man and Blue Coyote. We have just enough dogs for each to tend one. Are there any objections to this group?"

"I would go," Cougar admitted.

"I need you to be responsible for the camp," Fire Dancer replied, "there will be other trips, and everyone will get a chance. But for this first journey, I do not wish to take the chance with every man capable of leading, should we not return. This is why, other than me, I have only selected unmated men." Other men sighed and agreed with the logic of his thinking. Still, they were disappointed. "I have suggested a similar choice to the other headmen. In fact other than myself, only unmated men are going. The other camps have decided it too hazardous a journey to risk their headmen. If something happens to me, Cougar, you are able to take my place."

"What dreamer is to accompany us, Not Acorn, surely?"

Fire Dancer shook his head, "we are taking the woman Basket as our dreamer," he admitted, "she sees clearly into the 'spirit' realm, and it is her vision we follow. We need her to interpret the things we find and guide our path." He did not admit that this was Acorn's idea and he himself was not comfortable with it, but Acorn had convinced him of the logic.

"Basket" Stone Man frowned, and then nodded, "that makes good sense, and she has the throw back to draw her travois?" a point that Fire Dancer had missed.

"When do we leave?" asked Blue Coyote.

"The other camps are already assembling, and we leave in a pair of days. Pack plenty of water bags, for we do not know what the water supply is like on the plain. We have not found any in the traveling we have done so far, and only the one source is on the stone. It is best to assume there are no other sources. We have enough dried meat to provide an ample supply for the time we plan to be gone, and there is, of course, an excellent chance we will find animals to hunt on the plain as well."

"Do the other camps agree to our taking an untried dreamer? A woman at that?" asked Pinyon.

"I have not told, nor asked them," replied Fire Dancer. "This trip I have organized, if they do not like the way I have done so, they are free to stay behind. That goes for any of you!" He looked from man to man. None stepped back. "Then it is settled. Each of you has much to do, in the morning, come by and I will assign you one of the dogs." The youths nodded, and grinning headed to the unmated men's cave to begin sorting through the things they would take.

"Basket knew she was going all along," Stone Man told Blue Coyote.

"How do you know that?"

"She has been training Throw Back to pull the travois for the past span of days."

"It could be coincidence," suggested Blue Coyote, "or my father instructed her to do so."

"Or, perhaps her 'spirits' told her."

"Do you really think she is a dreamer," Blue Coyote asked, "I mean, have you ever heard of a female being a dreamer?"

Stone Man shrugged, "I don't see why not; just because there are none that we know of?"

"But Basket? I mean I know she has been through something awful, and her 'spirit' was certainly somewhere else for a time, but I find it hard to believe that Basket, the girl we grew up with, is suddenly some kind of 'power' holder. I certainly haven't seen any evidence that she has any more ability to speak with 'spirit's than I do."

"She brought the 'map stone' to us didn't she, and the stone?"

"Yes, but she explained about how she found them. There is nothing special about cutting your finger while leveling a floor, and although that staff she carries is certainly unusual, it is just a mesquite root after all, and birds lose feathers all of the time, it just happened to be an owl she saw."

"And the teeth, do you have a perfectly ordinary explanation for her having them?"

"They were a gift to her from her mother, and she told me that Butterfly had saved them for her all these seasons, to be given at her time of becoming a woman."

"I suppose the 'gifting' of Throw Back was just a quirk as well? If you look at each of these things individually, then yes, there seems to be a logical explanation for each of them, but taken all together, there is just too much coincidence. I do believe that Basket has a 'spirit link', a person could not go through what she did and live, I mean she was just too badly hurt, everyone says it is amazing that she survived at all."

"She doesn't seem any different. She doesn't act any different."

"It is not uncommon for someone with a head injury to be 'spirit connected' afterward. Remember the man who was attacked by that bear a few seasons back. He was always having 'visions' after that bear made him fall over the cliff."

"I also remember that his visions never came true," pointed out Blue Coyote.

"We don't know that! Some say he predicted The People leaving the Starving Mountains."

"So have a span of other people, look at how many times it has been suggested. It was just a matter of time before someone found the way; it is just coincidence that it was you and I."

"Exactly when he said so?" Reminded Stone Man.

"All right, so maybe he got one thing right. But if he was so filled with visions, why did he not see the cougar which killed him?"

"Who knows? Maybe dreamers can't always see particularly when their own death is involved. Have you spent any time with Basket since her return? Have you seen anything which leads you to believe that she isn't a dreamer?"

Blue Coyote admitted that he had not so much as spoken to Basket since her 'return'. "But it is hard for me to accept one of my childhood playmates taking such an unusual path in life, I mean we know Basket! She grew up with us. Doesn't the idea make you feel uncomfortable?"

"I do not question every single thing the way you do Blue Coyote. You would take a thing apart just to see how it was put together. I am quite content just to accept that the thing works. Perhaps that is why you lead and I follow. One day you will be the leader of the Yucca Camp, so it makes sense that you always need to know the answers, nearly before the questions are asked. Me, I am happy waiting for the answers."

"You could be a leader, Stone Man, you are an excellent thinker, and seldom are your decisions wrong."

"Yet constantly you are going against my decisions, and every time, you have been right."

"That doesn't mean you were wrong though, just that the outcome was different."

"Well I haven't the time to spend on one of your endless 'what if' challenges. I have a harness to repair and reinforce and you have just time to get Wolf used to pulling a travois if he is going to be of any use to us at all. I told you moon's ago that you needed to train him. My Deer Killer is already well trained. Even Basket has the sense to know Throw Back needs some time to get used to pulling. Have you even measured Wolf for a harness?"

Blue Coyote shook his head, "I have not yet spoken to Father, but I am taking Digger to pull my travois."

Stone Man came to an abrupt stop; "you are leaving Wolf behind?"

"Never! But he isn't going to spend his life pulling the travois like an ordinary camp dog; he is after all, a wolf! He will run free with me, just as he always has."

Stone man stared at his best friend, his mouth hanging a bit open, "that is the most ridiculous thing I have ever heard! Good grief man! Even Throw Back will be working, and if there is a true wolf among the animals, she is every bit as much one as that pampered creature of yours! I can't believe Fire Dancer actually . . ."

"Father doesn't know, but we need a hunting dog, and Wolf is the best one we have, it only makes good sense."

"I think you had better teach him to pull, just the same," recommended Stone Man.

Fortunately, for once Blue Coyote listened and followed his friend's advice, for when it came time to leave, Fire Dancer claimed Digger, as his own, surprising everyone by leaving the faithful Scorpion behind... or so he thought!

"Be sure that you have enough water bags and be sure they do not leak." Fire Dancer was giving last minute instructions to his party. They were leaving at dawn. "I am sure that we will find water, but just in case . . ."

"There must be ponds or rivers or something, how would the animals get water if there were not?"

"So far, the only animals we have found are the antelope, and they all come to the springs below the escarpment. We must, therefore, assume there are no other animals for a great distance, or that they have found ways of getting water we do not know about. Perhaps they can get it from the food they eat. We do not know that any more than we know the kinds of animals we will come across. All we can do is be prepared the best we can and hope we all return."

At dawn they assembled at the top of the trail, on the plain, to await the rest of the camps. First to join them was the Quail Camp, for they were the closest. When the men saw the woman and her throw back wolf, they came to an abrupt halt. "What is she doing with you?" questioned Black Deer, their self-appointed leader, "nothing was said about a woman."

"Basket is our dreamer," replied Fire Dancer, "she leads the way."

"No one said anything about a woman. Much less that she was leading this expedition. I am not following any woman; particularly one we all know is wrong in the head! Come on men, we are going back!" He turned and headed south along the escarpment. Not one of his group followed him, they stood uncomfortably, looking at his retreating figure and at Basket, standing quietly beside Throw Back, a small figure, but one which for some reason gave them confidence. Black Deer looked back and realized none of his group had followed. He stopped, looked forward, looked back at them uncertainly, and then deciding to reconsider, slowly returned. "I would speak with you Headman," he requested of Fire Dancer. They walked a few paces from the group, "you follow this woman?" He frowned, "knowing that she is not right in the head?"

"Basket is fine, she returned to us some span of days ago, all of the camps have heard that. She has shown us the 'map stone' and has explained the path. She knows where we are going. I cannot explain how, but I trust her. Look, our first stop is the place she calls the Sacred Spring. It is but little more than a hand of days from here. Go with us that far, and if by then you still lack confidence in her ability to lead, you are free to return."

"Very well, I will go that far, and if she does not lead us to this spring, then I will leave with my men, and I will encourage the rest of the camps to do likewise. It is bad luck to bring women on a trip such as this! They always cause trouble among the men. I do not want her along, but this is not my decision, as you say, you are the leader of this expedition. I will say no more against her, but I will stand that I do not favor this! That is fair, for you have not been completely honest with us."

Fire Dancer nodded, admitting that he had purposefully omitted including Basket in the expedition. "She does not really lead," he explained, "but her 'spirit helpers' guide us upon the trail. She has become as-one with the 'spirit's, as you know, not uncommon with head injuries."

"Not uncommon, I agree, but those I have had experience with, have not been in touch with reality either. They made no sense, all they said was gibberish."

"Basket makes very good sense. She is completely in this world, but the door to that other place has remained open for her. She has told us of many things she saw from there. It was she who told us the bison are out there yet, when we all believed they had perished generations ago. If you believe they are still there, then believe also that Basket knows the way. You will see. She will change your mind."

"We all respect you as a wise leader Fire Dancer. For this reason, I will keep my doubts to myself, but I go only that hand of days, if she does not lead us to this spring you speak of, then I return with my men."

"I understand, and that is the right of any group. If others feel the same as you, I will not try to stop anyone, even though it is my right as leader of the expedition. But I believe so strongly in Basket that I am sure you will be convinced. Now others approach, I am glad you are with us Black Deer, for I value your opinion."

The Rabbit Camp had no problem with Basket going along as a dreamer, the Pine Camp, however, had decided to bring along their own dreamer, and they were against Basket completely to a man. They absolutely refused to accept her as dreamer. The group stood at the head of the trail at an impasse. The Pine Camp refused to move until this was settled. Their dreamer quickly made the trip down to talk with Acorn. He returned shortly and informed the group that he was returning to the camp, for there was no need for more than one dreamer and Basket was the one. The Pine

Camp hunters frowned, but they stayed as their dreamer returned to the camp. So, the journey got a late start.

Each night for the first hand of days, Basket was shunned by the other camps, their way of showing Fire Dancer that they were unhappy with her presence. For one thing, it was bad luck to take any woman on a hunting trip because their 'spirit's interfered. This was a trip of moons in length, what of her blood flow time? How did Fire Dancer intend to protect them from her 'spirits' at that time?

Since Basket set up her shelter a short distance beyond the rest of the camp, as a dreamer usually did; and she had Throw Back with her, instead of placing her within a common area, as the other animals were, Fire Dancer did not see there was a problem. She also kept to herself on the trail, never approaching any hunter without invitation. She was, after all, a woman of The People, and she knew the proper way to behave. Also, Acorn had advised her completely regarding some of these very problems, so they did not occur.

"How much farther?" questioned Fire Dancer as he strode along beside Basket.

"I think this day, or tomorrow at the latest," she replied. "The stone shows a hand plus a pair of fingers as the distance. If we understand it correctly, we are near. This day is the last of the fingers. Therefore, we should reach this Sacred Spring very soon.[1] We have followed the direction set down on the stone, if we understand the escarpment and the guiding Ancestor Fires correctly, but the only way we will be sure is to reach the spring when and where we think it should be. Our trips gathering acorns have not brought us this far out onto the plain. It is hard to judge the speed of the one who created the stone also, perhaps that person moved faster, or slower than we do."

"Your 'spirits' do not tell you how close we are?"

"They do not indicate that we are going wrongly," she replied, "my feelings are that we are going just as we should."

"Woof!" Said Throw Back and began moving rapidly forward, "Woof!" She repeated. Basket and Fire Dancer picked up their pace following her and suddenly they found themselves at the edge of a slight swayle. Just below them, not a finger's distance away laid a pond.[2]

"We are here!" Basket exclaimed. "This must be the Sacred Spring. Look. There is something rising from the water. Let's go see!" She ran down the incline, the rest of the group following more slowly.

"What do you think it is?" asked Blue Coyote, "I have never seen anything like it."

"Nor have any of us," replied Stone Man. "It is clearly the skeleton of some kind of animal, but not one which I would choose to meet in the flesh. Look at those horns! It would take a huge animal to carry them. I hope they do not belong to bison."

Basket had unharnessed Throw Back, and both had waded out into the pond to investigate the skeleton. She now stood beside the remains running her hands over the protruding skull and the 'horns' of which Stone Man spoke. Power ran up her arm. This was indeed a sacred place. The men set up their camp on the rise above the pond, leaving Basket to her own devices. One did not interfere with power. One respected it.

"What is it Throw Back," Basket asked, "do you think it is a bison, or perhaps the giant beast which guided our ancestor?" She tilted her head, studying the skeleton. "I think it is the great beast."

"Woof!" Throw Back agreed.

"I want to get a closer look at that skeleton," Blue Coyote told Stone Man, "are you coming?"

"Do you think we should disturb Basket?"

"She looks to stay there all day, and I want to see for myself. Why would she mind?"

"How would I know; if you are going, however, I am going with you. Perhaps we could drag the skull from the pond and have a better look at it."

"I don't know about that," Stone Man protested, "if it is a 'power object', we had better leave it a lone, but there should be no harm in just looking."

He was as good as his word for Blue Coyote trotted down to the spring and stood on the bank; Stone Man followed.

"May we look also?" Blue Coyote called to Basket from the edge of the pond, just a short distance from where she stood.

Basket glanced over her shoulder at the pair of anxious youths, "certainly, if you are not nervous coming so close," she grinned.

"I knew it!" Stone Man muttered, "I told you it was a power object."

"This is a Sacred Place, Stone Man, everything here holds power, even the very water, but it will not hurt you. It is merely a place greatly valued by our Ancestors. There are, however, strong feelings here, much must have happened in this place. It must have been very important to the Old Ones, perhaps because of the remains of the great beast."

"Is that what this is?" asked Blue Coyote as he ran his hand over the glistening ivory tusk, the only evidence remaining that the great Mammoth, Mother Spirit of The People, had ever walked the land. "It truly must have been huge. If this animal were standing, why Stone Man could stand on my shoulders, and I on my father's and still we would not reach the top of its head."

"Look. It is the same shape as the top of my staff!" Basket said, "only the long nose has rotted away, see?"

"Well, it does sort of look like that, or at least it would if there were still flesh upon it. Do you think that staff is so ancient? Or is it just an accident of nature?"

Basket shrugged, "who knows! It was buried in the cave along with the stone and the map stone. It could be that old; Acorn claims it is just like the staff carried by The Mother of The People. But I cannot believe that an object of wood could remain so long. It was probably found by someone much later and saved because it was so unusual, perhaps by a descendant of The Mother. Maybe it was left there purposefully when The People moved to the Starving Mountains. I have asked Acorn and Pinyon, neither could say."

"Do you feel the presence of bison near here?" Stone Man questioned from the bank; he found that he was close enough to the skeleton. "Do you feel such things at all?"

Basket shook her head. "I do not feel them, or at least I don't think so. My 'spirit' doesn't tell me that much, only that they are out there. We will find them, but I think we will have to travel farther than this. I do not 'feel' that they are this close."

"What is it like? Talking to 'spirits', I mean, is it frightening or painful or anything like that?" Blue Coyote wanted to know, "I mean, do you really 'talk' to them?"

"Mostly they come in dreams while I sleep. Sometimes I remember when I wake up, and sometimes I don't."

"Then they don't talk to you, like we are doing right now?" Blue Coyote was disappointed. It didn't seem like such a big deal. He had dreams as well, sometimes of the future and what great deeds he would perform. Was 'spirit dreaming' no more than that?

"I certainly hope they do not!" Basket exclaimed, "it is bad enough that they invade my dreams, I much prefer they stay out of my waking hours. At least then I have some semblance of a normal life, it you could call what I live normal! As it is, everyone avoids me like I have some disease they might catch. It can be very lonely, having no friends. Grandmother is dead, and no one wants to have anything to do with me. Willow and Cottontail Girl will not even talk to me, and other than your mother and Turtle Woman, the women also avoid me. But then I don't really belong to any group anymore. I am no longer an unmated woman, yet I am not a matron either. Perhaps I just don't belong anywhere." She sighed, wading from the pond. "I don't even belong to the Yucca Camp. The only one who accepts me unconditionally is Throw Back, and she doesn't belong either. Perhaps we make a good team because we are both outcasts."

"That is nonsense Basket, of course you belong! You grew up in the Yucca Camp, why you are almost like a sister to Stone Man and me." Blue Coyote replied. "That is why it is so hard to accept that you suddenly have all this power. You are just plain Basket, no one special, just my friend."

Basket smiled, "thank you, Blue Coyote, I am glad that I can still count someone as 'friend', although Stone Man has not said that he considers me as such," she looked questioningly at Stone Man.

"Of course I am your friend," he hurried to assure her, "it is just that, well, we were set apart from you once you became an unmated woman, and then after Red Eagle, well, you know . . . and then . . . well, how are we to regard you? Are you a matron, and do we regard you as such, or will you return to being an unmated woman, although how that can happen I don't know?" He sighed, "Things were much less complicated when we were children and none of this mattered."

"I am just as confused, in addition, I do not know if Red Eagle is still alive and I am still mated to him, or if he is dead and I am again unmated." She grinned, "I hope the latter, and I really don't care one way or the other, for after that experience I am not anxious to be mated again. Once was enough?"

"Father has declared you free of that mating," Blue Coyote replied, "has no one told you that?" Basket shook her head, "Well he did, right after we found you and Red Eagle ran off, but I guess you don't know anything about all of that, do you?" She shook her head again, "well, Mother heard Throw Back howling and ran to see if you were in trouble. She found . . ." he told Basket the story . . . "and no sign of Red Eagle was ever found. We just assumed that he was beating you again and Throw Back attacked him. There was evidence that he had rolled into the fire, and the cave smelled of burning hair and flesh, yet neither you nor Throw Back had signs of such. There was a lot of blood leading from the cave, so we know he was injured, He ran off to the north, but once the blood stopped leaving a trail, we lost it. To be honest, once it was understood that you were still alive, there was no reason to follow him, I mean, he didn't kill you, so he had committed no crime." Blue Coyote was uncomfortable with this revelation, for he had been in favor of following the other man and killing him, regardless of whether Basket lived or died. Fire Dancer had stopped him and Stone Man from doing just that.

"If he ever shows his face again, we will kill him!" Stone Man muttered.

Basket shuddered, "I hope that he is dead! But we cannot know, I may never know, but I will always be afraid that he is just out there, waiting . . . only Throw Back gives me any confidence that he is not nearby, for she would surely smell him, and I know she would like to rip his throat out."

"She is not alone in that?" Blue Coyote shook his fist in the air.

Basket went to where she had unhitched Throw Back, took up the traces of the travois and they walked together to where the camp was set up. Blue Coyote and Stone Man helped her set up her shelter and even though Fire Dancer frowned at them, they also ate their midday meal with her. Fire Dancer started to call the pair away from her and give both a lecture on proper behavior, but he realized that there were no guidelines regarding the present status of Basket. His heart ached so for her that he decided that for the present at least, there was no harm in the three who had grown up together, once more spending time together.

"What did Pinyon say about this place?" Blue Coyote questioned Basket.

They were sitting around the campfire well after dark, still catching up. "He said legend called it a scared place because it was here that The

Mother fought the crazy dreamer and they both lost their lives. That is probably why there are so many 'feelings' here. It is also the place where The Mother made offerings of tools to the 'spirit's to bring rain."

"Nothing else… nothing about bison?"

Basket shook her head, "there was only a single mention of bison in the legends, and that was that the 'spirit's became angry with The People and took them away; but Pinyon did not say where they were taken. My dreams say they are returning, however, as such things go, they do not say where, nor even when for that matter."

They retired to their shelters for the night, and late, long after the ancestor fires had brightened the sky, Throw Back lifted her head, thumped her tail on the ground and said, "woof!"

An answer came from just beyond, and guiltily, Scorpion sneaked into Basket's shelter. She hugged the animal, laughed to herself and hoped that Fire Dancer would not be too angry. Evidently Scorpion had decided she was not going to be excluded from their 'great adventure' after all.

He was not. In fact Fire Dancer was delighted to see his loyal dog, for he had in fact sorely missed her.

The men, and Basket, had all filled their water bags with fresh water and were planning on heading still farther out on the plain in the morning. Now that the stone had led them correctly to the Sacred Spring, the other men had gained confidence. They now believed that it would lead them to the 'place of the stone' as well, and the bison if they did in fact still exist. Black Deer still glowered at her, and he had spoken to several of the other men against her, but she had led them directly to the spring, and he had given his word to Fire Dancer. Basket had been tolerated, if not accepted by the other men, although no one had seen her show any sign of 'power' or indeed signs of her being a dreamer at all.

They walked for another hand of days, always directly where the stone told them, following the pattern of the moons.

"What do you make of this?" Fire Dancer questioned a group of men he had called to where he squatted, "it is some kind of dung, but I have never seen any like it before."

"It is old," replied Black Deer.

"There are no tracks of any animals about, and we have seen no signs of any animals other than antelope," another added.

"It is a grass eater," Stone Man crumbled the dung, "maybe it is bison dung," he added hopefully.

"Here is more of that dung!" exclaimed Blue Coyote much later and some distance ahead, "and it is fresh, and there are tracks!"

Everyone swarmed to his find, exclaiming excitedly.

"Woof!" voiced Throw Back, looking to the east and wagging her tail. The hunters rose and stared that way.

"I see something!" Stone Man exclaimed, "over there!" he pointed, "see, just on the horizon."

"Yes! I see!" exclaimed one hunter.

"I see it also!" exclaimed another.

"Woof!" Barked Throw Back and started dragging her travois as rapidly as possible in that direction, Wolf at her side. Everyone was quick to follow.

* * *

"Do you think they are bison?[3]" whispered Blue Coyote. All the party was crouched down in the grass peering through it at a small herd of animals grazing without concern a short distance before them.

"They are like the animal on my arm," whispered Basket in reply, "Acorn said it was a bison."

"Let me see!" Blue Coyote squirmed around, "where did you get that? It didn't used to be there!" He frowned at the spot; "it looks like those animals."

"It just showed up," Basket replied, "about the same time as everything else which has gone wrong with my life. Grandmother said it was a bison also, my mother had the same mark, and she told Grandmother that it was a bison."

"Huh!" was Blue Coyote's reply.

"What should we do?" Stone Man wanted to know.

"I think we should dart one of them," answered Black Deer, "we came hunting, they are meat. Whatever kind of animal, we can eat them."

"Do you think a dart will kill one? They are a lot bigger than a deer!" asked another hunter, "in fact they are the largest animal I have ever seen. A dart seems kind of puny.".

"I intend to find out!" Black Deer started to rise. Fire Dancer griped his arm and motioned him back down.

"We need a plan first. You frighten them and we might never get another chance."

"They are not paying us the least bit of attention. I say we rush them. As many of us as there are, we are bound to hit at least one of them!" Black Deer glared at Fire Dancer.

"We could sneak closer, stay down wind and wait until dark. They are eating during the daytime, perhaps, like antelope, they lie down and sleep at night," another hunter suggested.

"Just how do you plan to see them at night?" Another hunter asked, "There is no moon."

"Well I am going to smear some of their fresh dung over myself and see how close I can get," said Stone Man. "It worked in the Starving Mountains, why not here."

"That is the best idea offered so far," all agreed.

"The woman stays here!" Black Deer stated, glaring at Basket.

"Basket stays here," agreed Fire Dancer, "she is no hunter."

"Gladly!" replied Basket. "I am as close to those animals as I wish to be so long as they are alive. Has it escaped all of your observations that they have very sharp horns?"

"Just get ready to butcher one," Blue Coyote muttered, "I am going to get me a bison!" Already he was vigorously rubbing fresh dung over his body. Others fell to following suit and soon the men were ready. Slowly, so as not to spook the creatures, they crawled nearer and nearer, until they were almost close enough to reach out and touch those at the outer edge of the herd. Then silently, in unison they rose and cast their darts. A hand on animals bellowed and collapsed to the ground. The rest of the herd galloped away, tails in the air, shaking the ground with the pounding of their hoofs.

The group of hunters quickly dispatched the still-living animals, and grinning ear to ear they yelped and danced around the carcasses. Honor was given to the spirits of the slain creatures and the hunters quickly dug out the eyeballs and savored them, then began dressing the carcasses. Now Basket was welcomed, she and Fire Dancer began dressing his animal,

Blue Coyote and Stone Man another, and the rest were claimed by the men who had darted them.

"What do we use for wood to cook the meat?" Basket sat back on her heels, admiring the huge pile of fresh meat they were accumulating. "It is going to spoil in this heat if we do not dry it, and we have no wood."

"There is plenty of grass!"

She shook her head, "not enough, it burns too quickly, and it would take forever to gather enough of it any way." She frowned, then reached down and picked up some of the dried dung, crumbling it in her hands, "perhaps this?"

"There is plenty of it," admitted Stone Man, "let's see if it burns." He began gathering up several of the dung objects while Basket started a small fire with grass, then added bits of the crumbled fecal matter. Indeed it did burn. The smell was not particularly pleasant, but fuel was fuel!

They crossed and secured two sets of travois poles together and used another as a spit to suspend the hump steaks over their fire, careful to turn the spit so the meat did not burn. It smelled delicious to those who had been living on dried meat for nearly a moon. Soon others had followed suit and there were a number of fires set up.

"It is delicious!" Blue Coyote mumbled indistinctly around a mouth full of meat. Juice dripped freely from his chin; "I always new there was nothing like bison meat!" He grinned once he had swallowed.

"It tastes nothing like venison," said Stone Man.

"We certainly have a lot of it," replied Basket.

"This is an excellent source of meat," added Fire Dancer.

"I would eat it for the rest of my life!" stated Gray Wolf.

"Crunch!" offered Throw Back as she broke the bone she was gnawing upon.

"Have any of you any ideas how we are going to dry all of this meat?" Fire Dancer stood looking at the huge pile of meat and then at the people surrounding it.

"We didn't think of that," admitted one of the hunters. "It would be a shame to let it rot, but we certainly have no way to dry it, even if we needed it. Even the hides are too heavy to take along, which is a shame, for they would make an excellent shelter hide."

"We cannot just leave this meat to rot!" Fire Dancer stated, "it would be an insult to the animals, the 'spirits' would be angry, and perhaps take away this new source of meat. Legend says they did it before. We killed the animals. We are taking the meat with us, and at least trying to use it up."

"There is little more than a double span of us, and even a pair of those animals is more meat than we can eat!" protested a hunter.

"We should have thought about that before we killed so many," Fire Dancer pointed out.

"We can cook some of the meat and mix it with the dried berries and nuts we have with us, and then we could stuff the intestine tubes and make trail food," one hunter suggested.

"We can dry some of it and eat a lot more," another said.

"We can use our extra travois poles and the hides and make more travois, then pull them ourselves. But even then, there is no way we can eat all this meat before it rots," another admitted.

"Then let us hope the 'spirits' understand that we made a mistake; and are sorry for it!" Fire Dancer finally concluded. "Do all of the things you have suggested. Then we must be on our way. It is a long way yet to the place of the stone. From now on, however, we take no more meat than we can carry."

With regret they left most of the bison meat behind. They carried what they could and ate as much as they could, still much more began to rot and was discarded. Then the hunters got tired of dragging the travois and the hides were discarded as well. Still, they pushed on, following the directions on the stone. They began to see more and more of the bison, and soon the animals became so common a sight they didn't even notice them. They had been gone from the escarpment a pair of full moons and part of another. According to the stone, they should soon be at the place of the stone. They had killed no more bison, afraid that the waste they had made would anger the 'spirits' if they killed more. Fire Dancer explained that the 'spirits' might believe that they were sorry one time, but if they did it again, no longer would the 'spirits' be convinced. Black Deer angrily protested that he saw no reason to eat dried meat when fresh was but a dart cast away! He grumbled but Fire Dancer held firm. They would kill no more bison on this trip, but they did study them. They learned a lot about the animals. For one thing they were nearsighted; they seemed to see only a short distance. They had little fear of other animals, human or otherwise. They roamed in herds grazing during the day and sleeping at night. They were not prone to attack; but fled when startled. All in all the long vicious horns were of little danger. In fact, bison proved a disappointing challenge to hunt. What they were, however, was a ready supply of fresh meat, on the hoof. A camp of people could live very well near the bison; they would provide almost everything a camp would need. Except stone!

"It should not be much farther according to the map stone," Fire Dancer sat studying the thing again. "We have been gone from the spring this long," he pointed to the pair of moons depicted on the stone, "and we have traveled in this direction," he traced the route, "so we should be very close."

"Another day perhaps one more after that" suggested Blue Coyote.

Fire Dancer nodded. "At least we have discovered where the animals get water," he smiled. They had watched countless animals dig but a short distance into the ground and find water. The frequent thunderstorms which they had endured the entire time they traveled, had provided them with an abundant supply of water, captured in their shelter hides spread upon the grass. They simply poured the captured rain into their water skins and continued on. By now everyone could recognize the places where they could dig down and find water. But the stone was correct; there were no rivers nor streams, and no ponds of fresh water; although they did come across a few alkaline ones, unfit to drink from.

"Look at Throw Back!" Blue Coyote nudged Stone Man, "we are not far from water, watch her ears, her head. She knows that we are nearing something, and I bet it will be the river."

"Animals can smell things long before we can," Stone Man agreed, "you are probably right. Hey! Basket! Wait up!" They hurried forward, "we are approaching the river."

"How do you know that?"

"Woof!" Came the answer. The unrepentant men just grinned at her.

"Throw Back! I should have known, she always knows long before I do, let's go tell Fire Dancer!"

"Tell me what?" Fire Dancer asked just behind them.

"I think we are nearly at the place of the stone,⁴" Blue Coyote stated, "There is a river just ahead."

"Really! And just how do you know that? Do you also have 'spirits' which talk to you and tell you secret things," he grinned at the youths.

"We just use our noses, and our eyes," Blue Coyote replied, "Throw Back smells water, we have been watching her."

"Now that reasoning, I will accept," he stroked the head of the huge animal, sorry that he had ever let her go, but glad just the same that Basket had such a dependable friend. "Come on men!" he shouted behind, "we are almost there!"

A short time later they began the slow descent into the river valley. Cottonwood trees lined the river on both sides and brushy breaks extended beyond them. They followed a wide game trail down to water and looked back the way they had come.

"Look at those bluffs just there!" exclaimed Black Deer; "they are made of the same stone as you showed us! We have found the place of the stone!"

"There is a trail leading up to the bluffs," a hunter called, "I am going to follow it!"

"Wait for me!" called another.

Soon all had drunk their fill and were following the trail up to the stone bluffs. The quarry spread wide, a broad area having been cleared by countless people coming here to gather the rare and precious commodity. There was even a shelter cut into the bluff, perfect to set up camp and keep the rain off.

"I am going to kill another bison," Black Deer whispered to another hunter, "I plan on taking at least another partial load of stone back to trade. We have only room enough on the travois that the dogs pull, to take back what the camp has been promised. I want some of this for myself."

"You know what Fire Dancer said about killing the bison," the other hunter cautioned, "I think I will be satisfied with what I can carry in my backpack. Besides, we can come back next spring with a whole string of dogs and take back enough to trade for many seasons to come."

"As could any man among us, then the stone would have no value. What value is there in something which is available in plenty?" He shook his head, "now is the time, not later."

"All right, but a deer, that will give a large enough hide to stretch for a travois. Stone is heavy, it does not require a large hide, and Fire Dancer is not as likely to get angry over a deer, particularly if he doesn't know about it. What is one more deer hide, more or less? A bison hide he would surely notice."

"I am not afraid of Fire Dancer," Black Deer replied, "but you are probably right, a deer hide is plenty big enough, and a deer is much easier to dress. There is still time today to get one and return before dark," he picked up his atlatl and darts and slipped away.

"We will be here a hand of days, there is time to cure the meat we do not eat fresh," explained Black Deer, as he brazenly walked into the camp with his deer, "I am tired of dried meat, how about the rest of you?" All agreed.

Fire Dancer frowned, but let it go, he had other things on his mind, but never again would he accept Black Deer as a member of a hunting party he led. The man was insolent and a troublemaker as well.

"I think if we start on that back wall," Stone Man suggested.

"I think we are best served starting at the side," Blue Coyote argued, "and what do you know of stone knapping for that matter, you always sneak off when it comes to working stone. You are badly named!" Blue Coyote chuckled at his joke.

"Fine, we will start on the side, and when you find that the rock face is all exposed and covered with patina, and then perhaps you will realize that for once I am right!" Stone man replied stubbornly.

"What plans have you decided upon," Fire Dancer joined them.

"They haven't decided on anything but to disagree with each other," Basket replied. "How these two can be best friends is beyond me, all they have ever done, their entire lives, is disagree on every single thing the other one suggests; and one is just as bad as the other. If Stone Man says right, Blue Coyote insists on left, and if Blue Coyote says north, Stone Man says south!"

Fire Dancer grinned, "one day they will grow up and realize that both are right some of the time and neither the rest of the time. So, Basket; where do you suggest we dig?"

"There is a smaller quarry just up the canyon, the stone there is finer than here, this place has already given the best it had to offer. I would go to the other place," she grinned at the men who looked one at the other and then grinned back.

"Leave it to Basket, she always comes up with the right answer," they both replied together.

They did, however, honor her suggestion by going to the smaller quarry, and both agreed that she had been right; the stone there was of better quality. All the other men had already gathered their supply of stone, taking the easiest pickings during the first day at the quarry. Blue Coyote and Stone Man along with Fire Dancer had been busy repairing harnesses and seeing that their dogs were cared for and any sore spots treated. The animals were well fed and settled in a cool protected place to rest. Basket had spent her time exploring the side canyon with Throw Back, making a point of staying out of the way. Now the other members of the party were off exploring the river or just resting before the long trek back to the escarpment.

The members of the Yucca Camp were just beginning to collect their selection of stone. Gray Wolf had been learning the knapping techniques from Cougar for so long that he was nearly as expert as the older man was. He marveled over the fine texture of the stone; and was impressed with how it broke and chipped. Before the day was out, they had an impressive supply quarried and ready for packing onto the travois. "One more day and we will have an ample supply," agreed Fire Dancer, "one day beyond that to rest and then we head back."

"We should reach the escarpment well ahead of the first winter storm," Blue Coyote remarked, "I would not like to get caught out on this plain with a blizzard. There is nowhere to shelter, not even a sand dune to dig into, and the ground is too hard to cut into."

"Yet our ancestors lived season-around on the plain," reminded Stone Man, "they must truly have been hardy."

"We do not know that they actually spent the winters out in the open, but I can see that a shelter made of bison-hide would provide a lot of protection. I would say they spent a lot of winters inside caves, just as we have whenever we could find them," replied Basket, "besides, this place would provide everything a camp could possible want for winter. There are a number of caves up that canyon there, and that overhang faces south. Winter storms tend to come from the north; at least they did last winter. They would blow right over the top, and the sun would warm the shelter during the day. There is water nearby, plenty of kinds of plants to gather, and lots of bison within easy hunting distance."

"And plenty of good stone!" Gray Wolf added.

"Actually, I have been thinking along those same lines," admitted Fire Dancer, "what do you think of the idea of bringing The People to live along this river?"

"Here?" exclaimed Blue Coyote.

"Why not? As Basket has just explained, it has everything to offer."

"But this place is out in the middle of the plain? There are no mountains even in sight!"

"There are no mountains in sight at the escarpment," Fire Dancer pointed out, "and there is as much game around here for hunting. Although I admit I have become partial to acorns, there are some here, and for the rest, I would suggest that the availability of a ready supply of stone and the bison, are enough to offset the loss of the acorn crop."

"Maybe, someday, but we are happy at the escarpment. Why do we have to move again, we just got there?" Blue Coyote protested.

"We do not have to move right away. It is just that I like this place."

"I cannot see the other headmen agreeing to move," Gray Wolf agreed with Blue Coyote, "not even for an easy supply of stone, after all one trip every pair of seasons and that objection is overcome. The acorn crop is just too crucial to our way of life. No one will want to give that up easily. It means so much less work for everyone."

Fire Dancer considered his words and nodded, "you are probably right," he agreed.

Basket had set her shelter up a bit beyond the rest of the camp, as she had done the entire trip. They planned on leaving the next morning. The camp had settled down early, for they would rise well before Sun Spirit. She lay on her sleeping fur studying the Ancestor Fires in the sky. Throw Back raised her head and became quiet, her blue eyes watching . . . Something, or rather someone was approaching the shelter; sneaking quietly, carefully, so as not to alert the camp.

"Who is there?" Basket called, suddenly frightened. Throw Back growled, softly, low in her throat. A form appeared, and Basket found the hunter Black Deer standing before her shelter.

"What do you want?" She asked; her hand on the wolf, "it is late, and you have no reason to be here!"

He smiled, his eyes going over her in a way which Basket certainly did not like, "a little pleasant company," he replied, rubbing his hand suggestively over his crotch.

"Leave my shelter!" She told him, "I do not invite you in!" Basket replied in the exact manner that Acorn had advised her, should such a situation arise.

The hunter shook his head, "I do not think so," he replied, inching closer, "a woman on a hunting trip; she comes to be of service to the men. You have been servicing the ones of your camp, now I want my share," he began to undo his breechclout.

"I said NO!" Basket stated.

He kept coming.

Throw Back laid back her lips and growled louder, her blue eyes flashing.

Black Deer kicked at the animal, "git out of here!" He ordered.

In a flash the wolf had him by the leg, the force of her attack toppling him backward. The hunter kicked with his free leg and began to scream. Fire Dancer was the nearest, he was there in a flash, his dart at the hunter's throat.

"That animal attacked me!" Black Deer shouted; "kill it!"

"I think not!" Fire Dancer replied, "If there is a varmint here, it is not Throw Back! Go back to your place, and do not again come near this woman. If you do, I will personally turn the wolf free on you!"

Basket sat crouched behind the furious form of Throw Back, clutching the animal in terror.

Black Deer glared at her, at Fire Dancer and particularly at Throw Back, but he limped away into the dark.

"Are you all right?" Fire Dancer asked. Blue Coyote and Stone Man standing behind him concerned expressions on their faces as well.

Basket nodded, "Throw Back did not let him harm me," she said shakily.

"What did he want?" Blue Coyote asked. Stone Man kicked him and muttered. "Oh!" Was all Blue Coyote could find to say, as his face flamed red with embarrassment. He quickly ducked back and vanished.

"Would you prefer I move my shelter closer?" Fire Dancer frowned, "or will you be all right?"

"I will be all right" she replied shakily, "Throw Back is with me. I do not think he will be back." Fire Dancer nodded and returned to his shelter.

They left on schedule. All but the Yucca Camp was loaded heavily and all were traveling much more slowly. The stone they had added to their loads far outweighed the supplies it replaced. So much so that before the first day had come to an end, the loads pulled by the dogs had to be lightened. "I say we discard the food and some of the water skins!" Black Deer shouted. His hand and one leg were wrapped in bandages, and he glared angrily toward Basket once and then ignored her. Throw Back watched him, her eyes never wavering. He stayed far from the pair of them.

"And I say we have far more stone than we need," Fire Dancer replied, "some of that stone will be left behind. What good does it do us to leave the food and water behind and carry only the stone? We cannot eat it, nor can we drink it!"

"There are plenty of bison out there to eat," challenged Black Deer, "and we can collect the rainwater just like we have been doing all summer."

"And if it stops raining, then what?"

"We can dig for water, just like the animals do!"

"And how many animals did you see before we sighted the bison? How many days did we travel between that time and when we left the Sacred Spring? How many places of water did we see there?" Fire Dancer growled "none! That is how many. Is all of this extra stone worth taking a chance with our lives?"

"You have status among the camps! Some of us do not, but this stone will give us status! That is important to us!"

"You leave the stone behind!" Fire Dancer would not budge.

"I no longer recognize you as leader!" challenged Black Deer, "I and my camp will make our own way back to the escarpment. Who will go with us?" He strode away from the group to make his stand.

The men of the Quail Camp followed Black Deer a short distance away, men of the Pine Camp looked at each other, nodded and slowly went to join the Quail Camp. Two of the Rabbit Camp men started to join them. "Get back here!" shouted Grape Leaf, "Have you forgotten that it was Blue

Coyote who led us through the moving; sand and Fire Dancer who led us to this place? Black Deer is a status hungry fool. What good is status when you are hungry, or thirst or are dead?"

The men sheepishly fell back into place.

---

1. Blackwater Draw Local #1. The Clovis type-site. Located between Portales and Clovis, N. M., Blackwater Draw in one of the major early man sites in North America. The Paleo-Indian people throughout their habitation of the area used it. It was used as a kill-site and as a campsite. They killed the animals as they came in for water. They set their camps a short distance away and processed the meat. The Folsom layer lies adjacent to and just above the Clovis level stratigraphically. In 1962, the Eastern New Mexico University archaeological excavations uncovered a spring which had been active during the Clovis, Folsom and more recent Paleo-Indian cultures. It is this spring to which the story refers.

2. *Bison antiquus:* the species of bison present during the Folsom Period. These animals had been present during the Clovis era as well, and were one of the species that did not become extinct at the close of the Pleistocene. They were larger than present day buffalo by about 1/3 the size and had straight horns as opposed to the curved horns on *Bison bison.*

3. Alabates Flint Quarry: located north of Amarillo, Texas, on the Canadian River. This source of workable stone was one of only three sources on the Great Plains. The second, located at the Edwards Plateau, in southern Texas is the other source mentioned in this novel.

CHAPTER 11

That, and that!" Instructed Fire Dancer, "and you do not need the extra hides either. We can share shelters and save weight as well. There, does that seem easier for your dog to pull? Fine, if you feel you can add any of the discarded things to the pack on your back that is fine, for you are carrying that, not the dog." The hunter nodded. So it went, until the members of the Rabbit Camp were about evenly loaded as were the Yucca Camp.

Beyond, the other groups were already arguing and discarding the food and most of their water containers as well. Fire Dancer did not look back as their group moved forward. They were still more heavily laden than on the trip to the place of the stone, but they stopped earlier as well. When the dogs tired, they stopped to rest them. "Without the dogs, we are lost," reminded Fire Dancer, "they are more important than we are. Take care of your dog, and he will take care of you."

Throw Back strode out strongly, she was by far the largest animal, and loaded heavier than the rest, for Basket carried a few things for others. A couple span of cores, and an extra hide or so, but Throw Back didn't even seem to be aware of the extra weight.

Wolf also pulled his load easily, but then Blue Coyote made sure his load was easier to pull, for Blue Coyote carried by far the heaviest backpack. No dog, or for that matter, man was allowed to struggle beneath their burden, they had a great distance to go, and all would need their strength to get there.

"We should be about here," Fire Dancer put his finger on a point on the stone. They sat at their evening fire a span of days after leaving the place of the stone.

"Woof!" Barked Throw Back

"Woof!" Barked Wolf.

"Someone is coming!" Gray Wolf rose.

"A pair of men from the other group," Fire Dancer replied, "They have been trying to catch up with us. I saw them previously, before we stopped. That is why we halted earlier this night. Let them join us."

"But they chose to go with Black Deer!" A hunter protested "they threw away their food and water."

"I doubt that," Fire Dancer replied, "they are not so stupid. No they merely waited until they had an opportunity and then slipped away from the other camp. It will be Horned Toad and Bear Man. They did not wish to go with Black Deer in the first place, I could see it in their faces, but they felt obliged to stay with the Quail Camp."

"And now," questioned Stone Man.

"Now they join us," replied Fire Dancer, "and they will return to the escarpment alive, and they will remember and in the future The People will be stronger because they remembered."

"Hello, the camp!" Came the shout from the dark,

"Come on in Horned Toad," shouted Fire Dancer, "and you as well Bear Man! You are both welcome in this camp."

"How did you know it was us?" questioned Horned Toad a short while later. He had seen to his dog, set up their shelter and now came to join the others at the fire, Bear Man at his side.

"You have too much sense to follow Black Deer," was he reply, "I have been expecting you for a hand of days."

"Well if you were not traveling so fast, we would have caught up days ago!" admitted Bear Man. "As it is, we discarded half our stone in order to catch up with you."

"What is a load of stone compared with your life," Horned Toad muttered, "we should have dumped the whole lot?"

"We do have an obligation to the Camp," Bear Man reminded, "even if that idiot Black Deer gets back to the escarpment alive, do not forget, the camp does need the stone. We dare not throw away more than we did. As it is, they will not be pleased with what we carry, but they will get through the winter with it. Besides, if Black Deer does manage to return, we will be leaving the Quail Camp any way. He is crazy to become leader, and Angry Man is old. Black Deer is very popular."

"He is also very ambitious, and he would not be a good leader, for he puts himself before his people. If Angry Man still lives when we return, it would be best if we established another in his place, someone capable of combating Black Deer," suggested Horned Toad.

"I would invite Centipede Man back and request him to be Headman," Bear Man suggested.

"He has shown no interest in leading," reminded Horned Toad.

"Still, he is the son of Singing Star, and before his brother died, he was certainly the force behind him. I think, if we asked, if the entire camp asked, he would come back. He cares too much not to return. Remember the camp was the family of his wife."

"Water Woman seems to be happy with the Yucca Camp," reminded Fire Dancer, "but I know she misses her family and friends. I wish you luck with Centipede Man, he is a fine person and would make an excellent leader, if he can overcome the guilt he feels for the death of his brother."

"What chances do you give for Black Deer and his group?" Stone Man asked.

Horned Toad shook his head; "they have discarded all of their food, and kept but a single water skin for each man. So far they had killed a bison each day before we left. They are arguing among themselves, have been since the beginning. Others beside us were in a mind to leave, but they stayed, for they did not figure you would take them in without food and water. We did not discard either."

"I am glad that I did not under-estimate you," Fire Dancer laughed. "Our years as hunt brothers were not lost."

Soon the men retired and the camp settled into sleep.

"I tell you. They won't take us in!" The thin man hissed at his portly companion. "Why should they? We were idiots to follow Black Deer!"

"We cannot be far behind Horned Toad and Bear Man. Besides, we have the water skins from the bison and more than enough of the meat. I would rather trail behind Fire Dancer than walk with Black Deer. If we catch up to Horned Toad they will take us in, Horned Toad is close to Fire Dancer."

They struggled through the dark, almost missing the faint fire of the camp.

Throw Back growled and nudged Basket. "What is it?" She asked, the animal growled again and wagged her tail. Basket crawled from her shelter and they went into the camp. "Fire Dancer, Throw Back senses something, or someone is out beyond the camp."

"Go back to your shelter, Basket, I will see to this," Fire Dancer rose and motioned Blue Coyote to join him. Quietly they left the camp and slipped silently into the night. They circled around, Wolf silent before Blue Coyote, leading the way. They came up behind the arguing men and stopped their conversation with darts tapping them in the back.

"We come in peace!" Squeaked Rat, his skinny frame shaking visibly even in the faint light, "we seek to be known!" He gave the traditional request. "We have food, and we have water, and we can provide for ourselves," quickly he added.

"Shut up Rat!" His companion said regretfully, "don't you understand, they plan to kill us."

"No such thing," replied Fire Dancer, "but sneaking up on a sleeping camp could not be good for you, had I not been alerted of your arrival. Just come into the camp quietly and get settled down. Tell me, is there likely to be any more of you?"

"No, we are the only ones, at least the only ones we know of," replied the plump man.

They followed Fire Dancer into the camp and quietly set up their shelter. Neither complained that they had not eaten all day. Fire Dancer, however handed them food and again the camp settled to sleep. If in the morning some were surprised that their numbers had increased no one complained. These men had become hunting brothers, and as such would be mourned if they had been lost.

"We should be at the Sacred Spring in a hand of days," Fire Dancer said as he again studied the stone. "How is the water holding out?"

"We have enough, just barely," admitted Stone Man after a careful check. "Who would have imagined that there would be no more rain after we had so much all summer?"

Fire Dancer merely grunted.

"It has been nearly a span of days since we left the bison herds behind as well," added Gray Wolf. "At least we have enough food. There should be some animals around the Sacred Spring, even if only antelope. I was glad to go on this trek, and I will be just as glad to get back to the camp. It has been a long hard trip."

"You mean you wish you hadn't come?" Fire Dancer teased.

"Oh No! I would have died, had you left me behind! I would not trade this experience for anything!

"Well we will see to it that we get you back in one piece." Fire Dancer laughed, "Now everyone, to bed, we still leave just as early in the morning."

Basket lay in her sleeping fur watching the Ancestor Fires in the sky, wondering if one of them was Butterfly. She sighed and tried to sleep. The low growl from Throw Back alerted her to wakefulness. The animal growled again and slipped from the shelter. Basket frowned, for Throw Back had never left her like this before. She pulled her tunic over her head and crawled from the shelter. She squinted around the camp. Throw Back was nowhere to be seen. Basket crawled to Fire Dancer's shelter, only a hand from her own. "Fire Dancer," she whispered, "Blue Coyote," she frowned, for neither was in the shelter. Now she became concerned, and did not know what to do. A hand on her arm made her jump and yelp in fright.

"Sh.!" Stone Man quieted her. "Someone is moving around beyond the camp. Fire Dancer, Blue Coyote and the dogs have gone to investigate. Throw Back woke me and then came and got the others. We are to wait here. They will be back." Basket nodded, grateful for the company.

"Who do you think . . .?" She began. Stone Man tightened his hold on her arm and Basket became silent.

Throw Back bounded into the camp and proceeded to wash Baskets face and make sure she was all right. Fire Dancer and Blue Coyote followed with Wolf. "Whoever it was, we scared them off," Blue Coyote said quietly.

"Are you sure someone was out there?" Stone Man questioned, "We haven't come across signs of anyone else in over a season of being at the escarpment."

"We heard someone running away. It was definitely a person," Fire Dancer said quietly, "someone with whom Throw Back is familiar and . . ."

"Red Eagle," whispered Basket going deathly white and beginning to shake.

"We can't be sure," Blue Coyote shook his head, "it could have been someone else."

"Who?" She was sobbing now, "Who else would Throw Back consider an enemy or a threat?"

"We are days out on the plain well beyond the Sacred Spring, how on earth would Red Eagle be looking for you here? How would he even know to look for you at all? Remember, he thought he killed you."

"He could have discovered that he didn't, he could have returned to the camp; he could have forced them to tell him, killed everyone and come after me!" She sobbed.

"Perhaps it was Red Eagle," Fire Dancer agreed, "for who else would upset Throw Back in such a way? But even if it were he, I doubt he was after you Basket, he would just be checking us out to discover who we were. That is all."

"It doesn't matter," she sobbed, "he will find out, and then he will come back and take them from me and kill me and Throw Back."

"He will do no such thing!" Blue Coyote shook her, "we are here Basket, you aren't alone anymore. You don't have to face him by yourself, not now, not ever."

"You don't know him! He will wait, just like before, he will watch and follow, and no matter how hard you try, he will find a time when I am alone, and he will strike, just like a rattlesnake."

"What will he take, Basket?" Fire Dancer asked quietly, "what did he want so badly that he was willing to kill for it?"

"The teeth!" She sobbed, "He is obsessed with the relic teeth. He nearly killed me before because I refused to give them to him. He tore the cave apart looking for them."

"I don't understand; how did he even know you had them? None of us did until after you came back." Fire Dancer was frowning now.

"He found them," she sobbed, "when we were all out of the camp, he came snooping in the wolf cave and found where I had them hidden, but he didn't take them, he stuffed them back into the hiding place, I knew someone had found them, but not who. I moved them to a safer place. And then Grandmother said not to say anything to anyone, and we didn't, and then he went to you and made me mate with him and he killed Grandmother and . . ."

"Butterfly fell, Basket, no one killed her. She was an old woman; she got to close to the edge and lost her balance . . ."

"He killed her!" Basket insisted, "He even admitted to it. He hit her from behind with his ax and threw her over the escarpment so you would all think it was an accident."

Fire Dancer remembered the wound, he nodded, "I admit, what you say fits; I always wondered how she could have such an injury on the back of her head when we found her face down."

He sighed, "That means murder. When we return, we will hunt him down. I promise you Basket. We will find Red Eagle and make sure that he never hurts anyone again."

"If we get back! If he doesn't kill us all in our sleep!"

"Don't forget Throw Back!" Recommended Blue Coyote, "she will be watching, just like she always does. I have thought she was over protective, but now I understand, she has known all along that he would return, she has been waiting."

"And now we all know, and now we will all be waiting," Stone Man added.

"Well he is far away by now, any way, and it is unlikely that he will return this night. You go back to sleep, Basket, one or the other of us will be on watch for the rest of the night."

"You really think I can sleep knowing . . . that he is . . . out there somewhere, watching?" She sobbed.

"Look, Basket, I will be outside, just beyond your reach, and Wolf will be watching and Throw Back will be watching. I think you can sleep safely, at least tonight," Blue Coyote assured her, "and remember; it might just have been a stranger that Throw Back was nervous about, it might not have been Red Eagle at all. I cannot see her letting him escape. I think she would follow him, no mater where, no matter how long it took her. She was content just to run the intruder off."

This did make sense to Basket, she nodded and went off to her bed furs, but she slept little more than did Throw Back. Fire Dancer did not tell her that there had been more than one person, or that he and Blue Coyote had nearly been killed. Only the quick action of Throw Back, knocking him down had saved him from ending up darted through. He was absolutely sure that he recognized Red Eagle, but he was no longer alone. Fire Dancer also recognized one other man, one Hairy Bear, formerly of the Rabbit Camp, one of the thieves of water and food crossing the moving sands. He had no reason to suspect the others were not the rest of the thieves. He just hoped they reached the escarpment before there was trouble there. Cougar was dependable, but he was not necessarily a leader in time of difficulty. *Centipede Man is in the camp* he sighed and got what sleep he could before it was his turn to keep watch.

Quietly, the word was spread the next morning; careful to do so out of Basket's hearing. Stone Man was assigned to keep her occupied and allow Fire Dancer and Blue Coyote make their preparations. From now on they traveled as a fully armed camp, day and night. They reached the Sacred Spring without further incident. There were signs that someone had been there, the ancient skull had been pulled from the pond and someone had tried to break free the great tusks, but they had not been able to do so. Blue Coyote and Stone Man returned the skull to its position in the pond once again and as soon as water bags were filled they pushed on.

Fire Dancer knew they were out there, just by watching the wolves, both of which were uneasy and watchful. Wolf now paced near Basket as well as Throw Back. It was as though his daughter had communicated her concern to him, so now they both watched. The closer they got to the escarpment, the more anxious the animals became. It was almost anticlimactic when they filed down into a quiet peaceful camp, greeted only with welcoming smiles and happy faces.

*   *   *

"There has been nothing!" Centipede Man replied, "It has been very peaceful, it has not even rained since mid summer."

Fire Dancer related their experience. "They are not far away, even now. There is going to be trouble. I can almost guarantee it."

Yet fall passed peacefully, with no sign of Red Eagle, or anyone else for that matter, Basket began to relax. When it came time to move into the caves, however, she refused to return to the wolf cave, nor would she move into the storage cave. Instead she insisted that she had a safe place to hide. While everyone was gone from the camp one day, she moved an entire winter's supply of food and a number of water skins into the secret cave. She planned on staying inside the cave, perhaps for the entire winter, just in case Red Eagle was nearby watching. But she planned without Wolf. He led Blue Coyote straight to her while she was setting up her new home. He nodded and agreed it was an excellent place; he in turn informed her that he and Stone Man were moving into the wolf cave since she wasn't going to use it. They would be but a stone throw from her. Winter arrived, the group led by Black Deer had not returned to the escarpment. It was unknown if they had perished crossing the plain, turned back and settled in at the river, or perhaps been attacked by the outlaw band. The stone brought back by Fire Dancer was distributed evenly to all the camps, there was not an abundance; but there was enough. Still, it did not rain.

"Tell us again about the bison!" pleaded the child, Mouse. He just could not get enough of the stories of the bison. Blue Coyote had told the tale almost every night. "Do you think that one day they might come here and I could actually see one? Why didn't you bring back a bison skin? We would have all liked to see one," he pestered with endless questions.

It was a dry cold winter along the escarpment. There was little or no snow, although the wind was bitterly cold. Spring arrived, and with it at least, warmer weather, but the wind did not lessen, instead it moaned and whipped up the sand; out in the moving dunes it rolled in huge clouds. Above, on the escarpment, the grass came up and quickly withered. The antelope moved away. The game below the escarpment also moved, the hunters had to go farther and farther, the plants suffered as well. Soon all of the cattail within more than a day's walk had been gathered. The quail and prairie chickens just seemed to have vanished. Even the acorn crop failed. As spring progressed, the situation became worse. All of the stored food had been disposed of at the Spring Ceremony, now there was no food. The last of the acorn flour was used.

"We have to do something!" Fire Dancer had called a meeting of the Headmen. "Either we move along the escarpment, or we go elsewhere," he said.

"How far are the bison?" inquired one headman.

"Too far!" Fire Dancer assured him. "We could not make a hunting trip that far and return with any food."

"Perhaps not, but we could move the camps, follow the bison, perhaps even move to this place of the stone, you have continued to speak of," he suggested.

"It is a long way. It took us over a pair of moons and a double span of days beside to reach the place of the stone."

"But you reached the bison before that?" The hunter questioned.

"That is true; the bison were nearly a double span of days beyond the Sacred Spring, out on the plain. But with no rain since last summer, there is no knowing if they are still there or not." Can we take the chance with our families?" questioned Grape Leaf, now headman of the Rabbit Camp.

"What other choices do we have? We stay here and starve, we move up or down the escarpment, and starve, or we find the bison." The headman of the Pine Camp spoke, "I would find the bison."

Angry Man of the Quail Camp nodded in agreement. Grape Leaf and Fire Dancer studied them and then nodded, "we find the bison," it was decided. Within a hand of days the camps had been disassembled, the new litters of pups were old enough to pull travois, and luckily there were enough of them, it seemed that every bitch among the camps had mated with Wolf. They were large and sturdy dogs, more wolf-like than ever. They all filed up onto the escarpment and the camps stretched out nearly as far as the eye could see into the distance, a long thin line, slowly moving across the plain. The wind was constantly sending biting bits of dust into their eyes, and it blew night as well as day. Everyone was exhausted by the time they reached the Sacred Spring.[1] There they rested and replenished their water bags, but the ancient skeleton was now on dry land. The spring and pond were very small, completely surrounded by stagnant, evil smelling muck. Still, they camped there.

Star Woman waded out through the muck to the water and Turtle Woman waded part way as well. They made a relay, empty water bags passing one way and full ones the other, until all were filled. Then the women waded from the goo and did their best to remove the smelly, sticky muck from their legs.

"Tell us the story of the Sacred Spring!" Jackrabbit requested of Pinyon. "I would hear it on the very place where it is said to have happened."

".... And The Mother of The People brought her camp to this place, to serve the spirits." He stated, "And it was here that she made offerings to the spirits, and the rain came, and the grass grew, and the animals returned."

"Would the rain return if we gave gifts to the spring?" asked Mouse.

Pinyon stared at him, suddenly speechless, then he nodded, "it might. At least it couldn't hurt, but who would make the offering?"

"What about Basket?" Mouse frowned, "she speaks to 'spirits'."

"I will speak to Acorn," Pinyon promised.

"Why not just ask Basket?"

"Why not just ask Basket, what?" She questioned, just behind the child.

"Pinyon says that The Mother gave gifts to the 'spirits' at this place and brought the rain, I asked him why you could not do the same," he replied. "You could do it couldn't you Basket? Everyone says you are 'spirit touched', they would listen to you. If it rained, the grass would grow and the bison would come, and I so want to see a bison. Please, please say you will do it Basket, please!" He pleaded.

"It could do no harm," offered Pinyon.

"What kind of gifts do you offer a 'spirit'; and how? I have no knowledge of such things!" Basket protested.

"You could do it! I just know you could," Mouse pleaded.

*   *   *

Acorn was drawn into the discussion, and soon others as well. Before Basket knew it, she was chosen to make a 'spirit offering' to the spring. "Tools; that is what the legend says were offered," Pinyon supplied, "each camp could give up a few."

Soon Star Woman came forward with a tunic she had just finished. Basket dug out her feather, braided her hair down her back, donned the sacred teeth, and carried the ancient staff. With Throw Back at her side she went to a slight rise just above the spring, the closest approach. There she stood, feeling ridiculous as she made up a prayer. Yet the words came easily. She thanked the directions for guiding them; she thanked the spirits of the animals that had provided food for them thanked the spirits of the plants as well. She promised that The People would walk with the spirits and honor their ways. She asked for rain; rain for the grass, rain for the animals; rain for the people. With each request she carefully broke a precious tool, wrapping it in a rabbit skin and rapping it with an antler baton.[2] Then she tossed the pieces into the spring. Around her spread an aura, a blue light that enfolded her and the throw back at her side. When is was over, The People realized that they had just seen something special, something so ancient that they could almost convince themselves that she was the living return of The Mother of The People, herself. The spot on Basket's arm sent thrills of pleasure through her body, her amulet throbbed at her throat, and she felt more at peace than she had since her childhood. That night the clouds assembled, the thunder roared, and the rain came. The people stood on the rise and watched as the muck and slime which had formed around the pond was washed away in a sudden quick river of water. When it passed, the pond was once again clear and the spring brought forth fresh cool water. The ancient skeleton glistened from its place in the pond.

Basket now wore the teeth of the long toothed cat openly, where she had carried them secretly in her waist pouch. She walked with confidence, the owl feather fluttering at the end of her braid; the ancient staff supporting her weak leg as it had for the last season. By her side walked a creature so like the ancient dire wolf, no one would be able to tell the difference. She did not remember a 'spirit trip' that she had taken upon becoming a woman, nor did she remember the animals with which she had spoken, but she walked confidently upon the path they had set for her. The people of the camps were convinced that her prayers had brought the rain.

*   *   *

She lives! You idiot! You said that you killed her! The voice in his head ranted. Red Eagle lay in the grass watching the camp. He had almost gotten caught the previous summer. He and his group had sneaked up on the camp trying to find out who they were, he had recognized Fire Dancer and Blue Coyote, had almost darted Fire Dancer through, but for the sudden appearance of Throw Back, which he had also thought dead. Now he could clearly see the figure of Basket as she made her offerings to the spring. Rage filled him. *She has the teeth! See she wears them just as that other cursed female did! You promised them to me! You get those teeth!* The voice always seemed to be in his head any more, always demanding something. Red Eagle sighed and slipped quietly away.

"What do you think they are up too?" Hairy Bear questioned the leader; "Do you think they have left the escarpment for good? Where do you think they are going?"

"How should I know?" Red Eagle snarled, "Do you think Fire Dancer sends me messages informing me of what they plan?" He glared at the other man.

"We should have attacked the camps last summer when Fire Dancer was gone!" muttered Antelope, "We could have attacked them and taken all of their food and obsidian. We wouldn't have ended up starving all winter then."

"We will strike, but at my time and my place. *No! We will strike at my time! And in my place!* The voice reminded him. *Then I will give you Fire Dancer and Blue Coyote, but only when you bring me the teeth, and the staff, I must have the staff! When you bring me those and proof that she is dead, then I will give you Fire Dancer and Blue Coyote!* The laughter echoed within Red Eagle's brain.

*   *   *

"They just left the bison meat and hides to rot on the plain," related Fire Dancer to the other headmen, "and that is the last time it rained. I am convinced the 'spirits' caused this drought because of that waste. Now that Basket has renewed the promise that no more waste will take place, the rains have returned."

"But we always discard the left over food at the Spring Ceremony!" Angry Man protested.

"We did not do so in the Starving Mountains," reminded Acorn.

"We had no surplus to throw away in the Starving Mountains," reminded Fire Dancer. "When we first reached the escarpment, there was so much game and plants we became wasteful. The first spring we discarded many containers of food, think back, it was then the game became scarce, and the plants began to disappear."

"The women gathered every tuber and root within walking distance." Acorn said, "They did not leave any for the following season, even though they did not need so many, still they gathered them. We killed all of the game nearby as well, even though we already had more than enough. I think that is why the 'spirits' took the rain. We must be careful now, in this new land. We dare not take more than we need, or the 'spirits' may become so angry with us that they desert us forever. They heard Basket, and they answered her prayers. But for how long?"

The camps had left the Sacred Spring a pair of days before. It had rained on both days from mid day until evening. The rain made travel slower, but no one complained. They were laughing and catching drops on their tongues; they washed the dirt from the exposed parts of their bodies, and enjoyed the cooler weather that the rain brought. The mornings were bright and clear. Now they were camping, relaxing after a hard day of travel. There were no fires, for there was no fuel for them, had they had food to prepare on them. Once again The People were gaunt, the fat accumulated over the past pair of seasons melted away during the starving time and the lean spring. Once again children went to bed on empty stomachs. A baby, born to the Rabbit Camp was set to walk the wind, as was an old woman of the Pine Camp.

"Keep the people here," Fire Dancer ordered, "We will return with meat."

They had found signs of bison. The dried dung was scattered about, "and have Basket explain to the women how to tell when the dung chips are dry enough to serve as fuel. They can be gathering them for the fires, setting up the travois poles for supports and spits. We will not be long." He led a group of a double hand of hunters away from the camps.

"If it will crumble easily in your hands it will burn," Basket instructed. "Take your travois and travel in groups this way and that until the travois are full, then return to the camp. We will need at least a hand of travois filled for each fire. Go now, and do not get lost," she led one group to the north of the camps and soon all had their travois filled with dry bison chips. They returned to the camp and as other groups came in, the chips were stacked in a central location. Again they went out until Basket was convinced they now had sufficient fuel to cook and dry the bison meat the men would soon be bringing in.

*   *   *

You fool! You could have had her! There is a span of you, and only one of her! Still, you let her get away!

"Why don't we kill the woman?" Questioned Antelope, "you said that was what you planned!"

"Not yet!" Red Eagle muttered, "Not until I say! We follow the camps and find out where they are going. When I know that, then I will kill Basket, with pleasure! I will enjoy watching her plead for mercy, but I will give her none. No, but I will use her, and when I have finished, then each of you may use her as well. We might even keep her for a while, but I will kill her, I will beat her and whip her, and when I am through then I will slit her throat and watch her life blood flow from her body, I may even drink her blood." *Yes! Drink her blood* the voice cackled inside his head.

* * *

"Here they come!" shouted Mouse. He had been anxiously watching, hardly able to wait to see a bison, even if a dead one. He was obsessed with the animal. He ran out to meet the hunters and was smiling from ear to ear with he walked into the camp with them. The headmen had decided that three of the animals would provide enough meat for the camps for a couple of days, and then they would hunt again. Fresh meat was the proposed idea, it took less time to prepare than drying did, and there was less weight. They would roast the animals, parcel out the cooked meat, just enough for the evening meal, one in the morning, and something to eat at midday as they walked. This was preferable to taking several days to dry the meat and then carrying it with them, and eating dried meat. Why not just kill a day's ration and hunt every day? Bison would be plentiful the rest of the way to the place of the stone.

"It is a wonderful animal!" Mouse sat surrounded by the few younger children, he was telling them all about the bison, for he had finally seen one alive. He felt really important. "They really are not very smart though. They let the hunters sneak right up to them, and then only go a short distance when they realize we are going to kill and eat them. But they are hard to kill; it takes a really strong hunter to drive a dart directly into a bison's heart. Some day I will be such a hunter!"

"What is the matter, Throw Back?" Basket was trying to sleep, but the animal was restless and wouldn't settle down. Throw Back whined and once again went from the shelter. She did not growl, a sure sign of danger, but something was bothering her. By morning Basket had rested little. The camp got underway smoothly. They had fallen into a routine, and now were underway much more quickly than they had at first.

"We are going out now for meat," Angry Man announced to the camp and went to where the next camp walked to deliver his message. This was the signal for the camp to stop and get ready to prepare the meat the hunters brought in. Several travois had been designated to carry the bison chips, and people loaded them as the camp moved. Usually by stopping time they had gathered sufficient for their cooking. Basket frowned at the travois of the Yucca Camp. The children had been responsible for collecting the bison chips, but had gotten sidetracked and had been playing 'bison hunters' for hands of time. Now they did not have enough bison chips to cook the evening meal.

Throw Back was still behaving strangely. Now she circled, whined and began circling a large group of people and herding them protestingly toward a large outcropping of rocks a short distance from where they were setting up camp.

"What is the matter with that animal?" Turtle Woman questioned, "She has never acted this way before."

"She has been acting unsettled ever since we camped last night," Basket confessed, "but she has a reason for what she does. I think we had better go along with her. Throw Back never does things without a reason. Perhaps she wants the camp to be set up behind that outcropping of rocks; if so, we had better do it."

"Move the camp; just because of a dog?" One of the men from the Quail Camp shook his head; "I have never heard anything so foolish before!" He stomped off, but the Yucca Camp started loading unpacked things back on travois and they moved to where the outcropping stood, setting up their camp at its base.

"Star Woman, Turtle Woman, let's get more bison chips. I am going to head toward that rise over there and circle back, why don't you come in the same general direction?" The other women nodded and they set out with the dogs pulling the travois while others of the Yucca Camp set up the shelters and cooking spits. Throw Back had settled down but now she became agitated again, she whined and skewed the travois, "what is the matter girl?" Basket frowned, for she was beginning to feel uneasy as well. The spot on her shoulder was actually becoming painful. Then she felt it. The ground beneath her feet began to tremble and then a cloud appeared and began to get bigger and bigger. Suddenly she understood. "Star Woman, Turtle Woman, head for those rocks, just as fast as you can. Hurry!" She began running, the bison chips bouncing off the travois as Throw Back dragged it over the rough ground, headed toward the rock outcropping just ahead. "Hurry!" She shouted to the other women who were watching the horizon with a puzzled expression. "The herd has turned toward the camp. We are all in danger!" She dropped to her knees and released Throw Back, "Go make the camps run for safety, go!" The animal streaked toward the camp and began leaping and barking. People looked at the approaching dust cloud, and then understood, people began running in every direction, seeking shelter of any kind. Many followed Throw Back as she ran for the rock outcropping.

Thunder shook the ground. The cloud engulfed the people hunkered down behind the rock outcropping. They huddled, hoping that it would give them some kind of protection. Now they could see the animals, a solid undulating mass of animals spreading across the horizon. They would not be safe, already those crouched there could see, but there was nowhere else to go. People were still running most away from the approaching herd, some at angles away from it, but the herd was too big, no one could outrun it.

Basket gripped Throw Back, hugging the animal as close as possible, terrified that she would panic and run. Even an animal as fast as Throw Back could not outrun the bison; she would be trampled in no time. Already the first of the animals were galloping past them, tongues hanging out, wild eyes rolling in their heads, vicious horns glistening even in the dust. Now the ground undulated, the sound of the herd making it impossible to hear anything, not even someone shouting directly into the ear. It rolled over them; engulfed them and time seemed to stand still.

A bison came over the top of the rise, charging directly into the lone tree, which eked out a survival on the rocky outcropping. The animal tumbled over the heads of those crouched there, and another followed, but the people remained unharmed. Most of the herd went around the outcropping. Breathing was almost impossible; everyone was choking on the dust. Some had covered their noses and mouths with their tunics, but even the filtered air was filled with dust. Then it was over.

The sound gradually abated as the herd slowed then stopped somewhere beyond their sight. The ground surrounding them was trampled into raw dirt, the new-grown grass, so fragile, mangled into the earth. They stood in a sea of destruction. Where the camp had been, remained one lone shelter. Scattered bits of travois and shelter hides were nearly unrecognizable, as were the trampled remains of people, lying where they were over-ran by the stampeding bison. A baby cried in the lone shelter, miraculously still alive. Throw Back and the other pair of dogs seemed unharmed, as were most of the people who had sheltered behind the outcropping, but compared to the numbers who had shortly before been enjoying life, they were pitiful few.

On shaking feet they cautiously made their way to what had been the camp. Four women of the Quail Camp sat clutching each other in the only remaining shelter, a baby crying lustily in the grasp of one. Feather, unmated woman, Tortoise and her infant son, Sage Girl and Song Bird were frightened, but unharmed. They brought the total number of survivors so far, up to a double span. Spotted here and there were dead bison, their bodies providing a minute barrier, but sufficient. Several men had darted the animals and took refuge behind them, a few more lucky individuals staggered into the camp. The hunters were now returning, some helping others and the injured limping along. A few people had found refuge in a tiny arroyo, so small that the bison had ran right over the top. The dogs were gone, either run off or trampled by the bison.

The hunters limped into the remains of the camp. Cougar had a broken leg, Stone Man, a deep gash in his upper arm, Blue Coyote had blood running freely from a head wound, Centipede Man seemed unharmed, but of Fire Dancer there was no sign. Star Woman looked at her son and began to wail.

"I tried to reach him, but there was no way," Blue Coyote explained. "He knew it and motioned me to stay where I was," He sobbed, "I watched as the bison . . ."

"There was nothing you could do, there was nothing anyone could do," stated Centipede Man. "We were lucky that we had killed a pair of bison plus one, we had stacked them together, or we would have been trampled as well. Taking shelter behind their bodies is all that saved us. By the time we understood what was happening it was too late, if in fact we ever had a chance, any of us."

"What spooked them?" asked a man who had sheltered similarly and was now standing shakily within the small group.

"Something far away, I think," explained Stone Man. "We heard them long before we saw them and realized what was happening. The small herd we were hunting bolted before them, and we had only time to drag our kill and pile it together to provide a barrier against the oncoming herd. I think they had been running for a long time. Some of them just dropped dead."

"We had better see if we can find any more survivors before it gets too dark to see," sighed Centipede Man. "There could still be a few."

Everyone spread out and called and looked, but only a hand more survivors were found. Mouse lay in a crumpled, mangled mound along with the playmates with whom he had been playing 'bison hunters'. His life tragically taken by the animal he had so come to love. Some of the dog's bodies were recognizable, but most people were just a mangled mass of flesh, not enough left of them to even put a name to.

"Help me cape out some of these animals," Blue Coyote staggered to the nearest bison, "we can make shelters from the hides. Collect anything you can find which we can use, someone see if you can find any travois poles."

"You need that head wound tended," Turtle Woman said over the head of her weeping sister, "Star Woman does not need to lose her only son as well as her mate this day." She sighed, "There is time tomorrow to do these things. Just now we can erect shelters for those hurt the worst. We need to look for survivors."

Throw Back leaped into the air and with a woof streaked out toward the east, Stone Man frowned and then barely able to see in the faint evening light remaining, began to run after her. Blue Coyote reeled and collapsed, to the ground, holding his aching head. Scorpion broke lose of the hold which Star Woman had on her and followed the other pair of dogs barking joyfully.

"Fire Dancer!" Basket leaped to her feet and went to help Stone Man bring the badly injured man into the camp. Star Woman staggered after her, laughing and weeping at the same time. Fire Dancer was cut and bruised over his entire body, but he looked far worse than he was.

"I guess I was lucky," he explained later, "I was sure that I was dead, but the bison fell dead on top of me and the others mostly went around.

The body kept me from getting trampled, but I fear I have broken ribs. By the time I returned to consciousness and was able to crawl from beneath the bison, you had all left. It took me a while to make it back, because I had to stop so many times."

"We are in bad shape," Centipede Man sighed, "what you see is all that are left of The People. For every finger of persons here, a pair died this day. It will take us all of tomorrow just to find them and lay them out to walk the wind. There are a number of us, who are injured as well, and we have only the hand of dogs and Wolf, and two of them are injured as well. We will need to stay in this camp for several days before moving on, and then we will be going slowly."

"We are in no hurry," Stone Man sat beside the fire feeding bits of cooked meat to the injured lying about. "We have plenty of meat, and at least some water. I know there is a seep hole just where we were hunting, we can fill the water skins there, and at least in the shelter of this out cropping we are safe from another stampede."

They huddled together at the base of the outcropping, a few, like Basket, Star Woman, and Turtle Woman, unharmed, but others were badly injured. By morning a pair more had passed to the star fires. Those who were able scoured the plain for the remains of family and friend, to complete the sad task of sending them to join the ancestors. The children were the saddest. By evening most individuals had been accounted for, yet a few were still missing. During the day several dogs came into the camp, having somehow miraculously escaped mangling by the bison herd. But a long list of friends and loved ones had been set out to walk the wind.

Horned Toad, hunting brother and loyal fried to Fire Dancer, Mouse, the child who loved the bison, Angry Man, headman of the Quail camp, Bear Man, stalwart hunter, Rat, little provider, and Grape Leaf, friend and valued advisor. Little Deer, girl of only a span of years, on the brink of life, Tender Antelope, and Spring Maid, ripe for mating, Feather Robe and Wandering Spirit, old matrons were laid out; and many more.

Fire Dancer and Centipede man set cougar's leg, and wounds were cleaned and dressed with healing herbs. Acorn, the dreamer of the Yucca Camp was still among the missing, as was the storyteller, Pinyon. Throw Back was lying at Basket's feet beside the evening fire. She lifted her head, listened, sniffed, and leaped to her feet, tail wagging happily as she streaked from the camp woofing. Stone Man followed and soon led the missing men into the camp.

"We were hunting way north of here," Acorn admitted, "I needed some herbs and we were out looking for them. When the bison stampeded by, we took shelter in some trees beside a dried up pond. They passed us, but I twisted my ankle getting down from the tree. We ended up staying at that place until I could walk on it again."

"We will move a short distance today," Fire Dancer announced a double hand of days later. "Cougar, you will ride on a travois for the time being, as will the other injured men. Women, see if you can discard anything more. We will replace what we can as we can." Scorpion sat patiently at Star Woman's side, already harnessed and her travois waiting.

"I can carry more," Basket offered, "Throw Back is strong, she should be pulling one of the injured men," she frowned, "but since she is not, her load can be heavier as can mine."

Fire Dancer shook his head; "we are not taking any chances with what we have. Things are not so important that they cannot be replaced. Already Throw Back carries the water supply, it is heavy and she is doing her share. If I see you take one more thing into your pack, Basket, I will come over there and go through it myself!"

"But . . . !"

"No! You are carrying enough!" He shook his head; "we travel until midday. Then we rest and go again in the morning. If tomorrow goes well we will travel longer, but there is no hurry. We have food and water, and all summer to reach the place of the stone." He went along the line of waiting people and checked each travois, and every injured person. Fire Dancer was the only surviving headman of The People. He now took his position very seriously. He felt that due to his leadership so far, clearly the majority of his people were dead; it was a feeling that did not sit well on his broad shoulders.

"I think we should combine what is left of these camps into one," suggested Pinyon, "one camp with a new name."

"What do you suggest?" Stone Man questioned.

"I thought perhaps that since we are now hunters of bison, perhaps the Bison Camp," he smiled, "once there was such a camp among us, why not again?"

"There is one among us who can claim that camp," Acorn rose, "perhaps you should be asking her, after all she would be adopting each and every one of us as a relative."

Fire Dancer shook his head, "if we all combine into one camp; how would anyone find a mate? We would all be related, which makes everyone taboo for mating. This is not an acceptable idea, but we can class ourselves as the bison camps, keeping each separate." Everyone nodded. So they became the bison camps right there on the open plain.

"Tell us about bison hunting, Pinyon. What do the legends say about how the ancestors hunted?"

"Well . . . let me see, yes, the bison hunters had a number of traditions. Before each hunt the dreamer made a special ceremony, asking the spirit of bison to bless the hunt. The hunters participating ate meat prepared only by men, special meat, not touched by any women. There were those among the men who had the responsibility of making sure that there was always 'sacred meat' removed and prepared only by them. This extra reverence was very important to the ancestors, for they were closer to the spirits than we are. Any woman, of course, never touched the hunting tools. The night before hunting men did not have relationships with a woman."

"They also had special hides, called hunting capes. These were the tanned hides of young bison. When a boy reached the age of his vision quest, he and his father, or another man responsible for him went out into the herd and selected a young bison. The boy had to kill the animal himself, cape it out and eat the liver raw as an honoring to the spirit of this special animal. He had to prepare the hide in a very special way. The head skin and the leg skin were kept with the hide. Once it was tanned, the legs were stitched part way up and the legs and arms were inserted into these. The head skin was pulled over the head, like a hood, and when on hands and knees, crawling, the legend says that a man could enter right into the herd. Bison cannot see well, and they regard this individual as one of the herd. These bison capes were very important, for the spirit of that particular bison was thought to protect the hunter. Its spirit remained with the hide. Therefore a hunter took special care of his hunting cape, for he had only one to last a lifetime."

"We should think on this idea, perhaps we should also have hunting capes," Stone Man suggested.

"I will consult the spirits about this," Acorn said, nodding.

* * *

Attack! What are you waiting for? They are almost wiped out from the bison stampede you caused, now is the perfect time! "I will say when it is the time," Red Eagle mumbled. He sat crossed-legged within a small shelter set apart from those of his group. They now numbered a double span of individuals; him, the thieves, and later a group of nearly dead hunters led by one Black Deer. They all had one thing in common. They hated Fire Dancer and Blue Coyote. They had spent the wintertime north of the camps, working the vast store of stone brought by Black Deer and his group. Sometimes Red Eagle regretted not killing the hunters and simply taking the stone, but Black Deer knew the secret of its location, so for now at least, Red Eagle tolerated the older man. He knew however, that in time he would be challenged for leadership, provided he allowed Black Deer to live. Once he knew the secret location of the stone, there would no longer be a reason for Black Deer to live. Now however, that man assured him they were daily drawing nearer the quarry. He waited . . .

---

1. In 1962 the Eastern New Mexico University archaeological excavation uncovered a spring. It had been active during the Clovis and Folsom times as well as during later Paleo Indian times. The spring was filled with pure white sand and literally hundreds of artifacts. All, sand and artifacts had been highly polished by the action of the sand and water. Among the artifacts was a predominance of tools and points, all broken, yet both pieces present. The author was part of the team that excavated this spring. The story tells a possible explanation for the presence of the many tools, which were broken, yet both parts were located within the spring sand.

CHAPTER 12

We need more shelters, and more travois poles, and more stone," protested Blue Coyote, "and I need another pair of shoes, these are worn through!" He and Stone Man sat beside the hole they had recently dug and were waiting for the water to seep deep enough to fill the stack of water skins waiting beside them.

"We also need more dogs to pull the travois," agreed Stone Man. "I hope that we do not end up dragging them ourselves all the way to the place of the stone. How much farther do you think we have to go?"

Blue Coyote shrugged, "what does it matter? We still have plenty of time. The injured are just now beginning to walk. Cougar plans on making the effort tomorrow, now that Fire Dancer found a walking stick stout enough to support his weight." Blue Coyote squinted down into the hole, "I think we can start," he reached for a water skin, "do you still find signs that we are followed?"

"They are still there," admitted Stone Man, "nearly as many as are we, why they do not either attack or join us I do not know. What do you think they are up to?"

"I would say that Red Eagle leads the group, whether he is waiting for us to drop our guard so that he can capture Basket, or if he has some other plan is hard to say, but I would wager that he is up to no good."

"What do you say to the idea of a little night trip tonight?"

"Count me in, who else do we take?"

"No one else, just us; Fire Dancer would never approve, besides who is to say, we might meet them sneaking up on us as we are sneaking up on them," Stone Man grinned.

"Hand me another skin," Blue Coyote lay on the ground, the upper portion of his body down in the hole, he handed the full skin to Stone Man and placed the new one in its place. "How do we explain our absence? Father is sure to notice that we are missing."

"Be sure to settle your sleeping furs on the opposite side of the camp from him. There is less chance he will notice."

"I will try, lately he has been preoccupied any way, something is bothering him, he probably won't even notice we are gone."

"When do you want to leave the camp?" Centipede Man questioned Fire Dancer.

"Just s soon as everyone has settled and you are sure they are asleep," Fire Dancer replied. "Blue Coyote would certainly insist on coming along if he knew what we were up to, and of course then Stone Man would as well. A pair gone from camp will not jeopardize the safety of the camp, but any more than that, well . . ."

*   *   *

"What are your plans Red Eagle?" Antelope questioned.

"We get as close to their camp as we can, I know which shelter she sleeps in, when I give the signal, you and the rest attack the camp from the other direction, that will give me an opening to slip inside her shelter and grab her. I will dart that cursed animal of hers at the same time."

"We will use the fire darts just like you showed us."

"That's right; shoot them into the shelters at the far end of the camp. That will keep everyone busy there."

"What if Basket goes to help?"

"She won't have a chance. As soon as you attack I will grab her. We meet back at the camp afterwards."

"Black Deer assures us that the place of the stone is easily defended. Even if they do decide to follow us, they will find that we have vanished into air, just as before," Antelope grinned.

"We should be well on our way before they even realize that she is gone."

*   *   *

"Come on Stone Man, I think we can leave now. Everyone else is asleep." Blue Coyote whispered.

"I am coming," replied Stone Man, "But do you think it was a good idea sending Wolf to Basket? She was awfully suspicious?"

"I didn't want her to be left with only Throw Back to protect her. Usually we sleep close by. Remember why we are taking this trip? If we are to protect Basket, we need to know what we are up against."

Quietly the two men slipped from the camp.

*   *   *

"I think everyone is asleep," whispered Centipede Man. "There was some movement from the other side of the camp just a bit ago, but I think it was just one of the dogs," he handed Fire Dancer atlatl and darts, and the men quietly left the camp.

*   *   *

"What is it girl?" Basket whispered as Throw Back nuzzled and licked her face, "is something wrong?" Throw Back wagged her tail, looked away from the camp and whined. "Blue Coyote and Stone Man are up to something, aren't they?" Throw Back whined again and nudged her, "all right, I'm coming, just let me find my bolas, all right, let's go," she tiptoed quietly from the camp following Throw Back. "Which way did they go?" Throw Back snuffled about, picked up the trail and led the way. Wolf followed quietly, a discrete distance behind. Throw Back led Basket well away from the camp, carefully testing the air, then leading yet farther, well to the east.

*   *   *

Blue Coyote and Stone Man were sneaking through the grass headed northward. Fire Dancer and Centipede man were a hand distant from the other pair, also headed north. Between them were Red Eagle and his cutthroats, sneaking through the grass, headed into the camp. When Red Eagle's group attacked, Basket jerked around and began running back toward the camp. Throw Back leaped, knocked her to the ground and held her there, assisted by Wolf.

"Let me up!" she hissed, "get off me you big lug!" Throw Back merely whined and licked her face. Wolf lay on her legs. "I will get you for this!" Basket threatened; "come on Throw Back, people are in trouble!" Her pleading made no difference.

"Blue Coyote, Stone Man, Fire Dancer and Centipede Man all jerked about and began running swiftly and silently toward the camp. They met the attackers head on, and by surprise. Antelope went down with a dart, and Black Deer limped away with another in his leg. Red Eagle had no time to reach Basket's shelter. He was brought to the ground by Scorpion and bitten savagely on the leg. He kicked the dog loose and limped quickly away from the camp. Blue Coyote and Stone Man saw the moving shadow and cast darts. One penetrated his shoulder, but he kept going.

The camp was in turmoil, Cougar and another hunter finally got the fire out, but it burned most of their bedding and shelter hide, others were milling about peering out into the darkness. No one saw any attackers, and all were nervous. Fire Dancer and Centipede rushed into the camp. "Where is Basket?" Fire Dancer quickly noticed her absence. "I have not seen her, perhaps she is still asleep," Turtle Woman answered. Fire Dancer shook his head, "she would be one of the first out, has anyone seen Basket?"

"We got one of them, and wounded another," Centipede Man answered Cougar's question, "but the second one got away."

"We also darted one of the raiders," Blue Coyote ran into the camp. "Where is Basket, and Throw Back and Wolf?"

"Get off of me!" they all heard her shout in frustration, a good distance from the camp. The four men clutched atlatl and dart and left the camp at a run. They found her. At their approach the wolves stepped daintily away and allowed her up. Basket was spitting mad. "What do you think you were doing?" She accused the animals, "do you think it was funny to lead me astray like that? Someone may be hurt back at the camp!" she scrambled to her feet and found herself facing the armed men.

"What are you doing out here?" questioned Fire Dancer.

"She did it!" Basket pointed at her best friend. Throw Back merely smiled and wagged her tail, very pleased with herself. "And when there was trouble, she knocked me down and sat on me!" an indignant Basket sputtered, "and he helped!" pointing to Wolf.

"Thank the spirits!" Centipede Man chuckled, "we clever hunters couldn't work together, and it was left to the animals, but they did a fine job of protecting her," he slapped Fire Dancer on the back.

* * *

"I think we have all learned a lesson this night." Stone Man began to chuckle, "With all the sneaking about in the dark, at least Throw Back did her job." He sobered, "I have also realized that we have endangered the entire camp. It was foolish of Blue Coyote and me to think we could do anything alone. We only made things worse, and Basket could have been in more danger than we can imagine. I will never again do anything so foolish."

"Nor will I," agreed Blue Coyote, "we should have consulted your Father, and followed your advice. I guess I still have not grown to be an adult," he sighed, feeling very small.

"I should have shared my concerns with each of you and we should have made the decision together, with full knowledge of the camp. Had we done so this night, the camp would have been prepared, perhaps even been able to capture some of the raiders. We have had no right to keep the camp in the dark about this."

"All because of me," sniffed Basket, "you should just let him have me and be done with it. My presence with the camp serves only to endanger everyone else. I should go."

"Do not be ridiculous!" Snapped Stone Man, "Do you think you are the only one he is after? You are not that important! He wants Fire Dancer and Blue Coyote just as much as he does you, and he wants all of you dead! Go on, leave the camp, go on your own, and give him the satisfaction of doing the job for him!"

"You needn't be so nasty about it!" Basket gasped, "I only want what will help everyone, and since it seems to be me that Red Eagle wants, perhaps you should just give me to him!" She stuck her nose up in the air and marched past him. Stone Man merely grinned at Blue Coyote and fell in step behind her.

The camp was awake, so it made sense to tell everyone what had happened. Fire Dancer began the tale. "We became aware of another group of people trailing us, nearly a moon ago. Since that time we have kept watch, and track of them. They number nearly as many as we, although now they are one less and have at least a pair of wounded. They are following us; just far enough away to believe we did not know of their presence. We are almost certain that they are Red Eagle, the food thieves, and now I have reason to believe that Black Deer and his group have also joined them."

"That they are a danger to the camp goes without saying, but we have not been fair to you keeping this knowledge from you. We only wanted to save you worry, but this night has shown us that this was wrong. Now we will all be prepared."

"What do they want?" asked a woman of the former Rabbit Camp.

"First and foremost, Red Eagle wants Basket. She was his mate for a short period of time and during that time he did his best to kill her, because he wants the sacred Ancestor Relics which she carries. They are powerful 'spirit objects', and I think Red Eagle has become a dreamer and wants those 'spirit objects'. Also he hates me because I ran his father out of the Yucca Camp before Red Eagle was even able to walk. Always he has resented that. He hates Blue Coyote, because he feels that he should be in such a relationship with a leader. Whatever his reasons, they make sense only to Red Eagle. But he is a danger, a danger to all of us. If as I now believe, he caused the bison stampede, you can understand just how dangerous he is."

"What can we do?" asked one woman, "we have children and babies, are you saying that they are no longer safe?"

"She endangers us all! Force her to leave the camp!" demanded another.

"No one is safe, not until we are able to find Red Eagle and kill him! He is a murderer even not counting those trampled by the bison, for we now are convinced that he murdered Butterfly, Basket's grandmother."

"What do you plan to do about this situation?" demanded another.

"That is a good question. For the time I have no answer, but I am willing to consider any suggestions."

Centipede Man rose, "we decided to find out about their camp tonight. Evidently so did Blue Coyote and Stone Man. While we were sneaking out to spy on them, they attacked the camp. This is what we know. I darted one, Antelope, one of the food thieves, and Fire Dancer wounded another as did Blue Coyote. If by chance either of the wounded is Red Eagle it will slow him down, but unfortunately it will also feed his hatred and push him even closer to going over to the 'spirit' side. This hopefully gives us time, but not much. Now everyone; back to bed. We have done as much as we can this night. Guards will be posted around the camp, tonight and every night from now on. And we will be alert during the day as well. They will not catch us unaware again. Now go to bed, and we will talk again in the morning."

Basket went to her shelter. There she discovered Scorpion. "Fire Dancer, your dog has been hurt," she called. Fire Dancer came quickly checked Scorpion and found the place where Red Eagle had kicked her but could locate no wound to account for the blood.

"Evidently it is not her blood," he finally deduced, "she must have attacked one of the raiders."

"But she was here in my shelter!" Basket now began to tremble, "if Throw Back had not led me from the camp . . ." she sobbed, "Oh Scorpion! I am so sorry that you were hurt. You gave me your daughter, and now give me your protection as well, how can I ever thank you?" She hugged the dog who wiggled and squirmed with pleasure.

"It seems the animals have banded together to see to your safety Basket, just as well, since we humans seem to have failed you this night. Try to sleep, we will be here, and we will be alert," Fire Dancer moved the few paces to where he had now moved his shelter. Scorpion went with him, her job complete.

"I think it would be a good idea if we sent scouts out before the camp, at least then we would know what lies ahead." One of the hunters suggested the next morning.

"We traveled farther north of the path we follow now," Stone Man agreed, "But we did not discover anything special about the plain. It is big, far bigger than any of us can imagine, but it is flat and featureless as well. Scouts could get lost, and we already know that there is nothing between us and the place of the stone."

They moved the camp a short distance that day, stopping before midday. Throw Back and Wolf were soon discovered to be missing. They had been spotted leaving the camp together by one of the women, just after they stopped. By dark they had not returned. Scorpion spent the night with Basket, keeping a faithful watch. The men of the camp took turns watching as well. By morning the pair had not returned. Now both Basket and Blue Coyote were concerned.

"Throw Back has never left me before," Basket sighed, "Perhaps I was too severe scolding her. You don't think she has run off do you?"

"Wolf is gone as well," Blue Coyote reminded her, "he also has never left me. They are up to something! You will see! They know something which we do not."

Late in the day the two animals returned, both exhausted. They stayed with the camp for a hand of days, then Wolf, barking and leading, drew Blue Coyote away from the camp, and back along the trail they had already traveled. He led him for nearly a day, and then suddenly vanished right before Blue Coyote's eyes. Only his bark kept the man following, and suddenly he understood. Quickly he returned to the camp. They were set up and it was decided that the camp would stay in that place for a pair of days. Fire Dancer disappeared with Blue Coyote and returned in the morning. He called Stone Man and Centipede Man together and they went a short distance from the camp.

"I think we could do it!" Centipede man nodded, "If this place is a cleverly concealed as you say Blue Coyote, and it is at least a day behind us, it could work!"

"If we are clever, it will work. They are camping to the north of our location, they cannot see the camp, so there is no way they would be able to watch us. By using the dogs carrying packs, leaving after dark, we could transport most of the things in one trip. Then have the camp travel another pair of days farther to the east. They will never think to look behind for us. We will have just vanished!"

"I think we should begin this very night. And make sure that Basket is with the first group and leave her there! Stone Man said, "And it would be a good idea if Turtle Woman went as well."

"That is a good idea, we can take several of the women, and that will save us time when it is time to vanish!"

* * *

"We are going to a place which Blue Coyote has found. You all know that he was gone for a day and a night. During that time he located a place where we can all live for a while at least, without fear of detection. We are going to begin moving to this place this very night, but it will take some trickery on our part, for we plan to simply vanish!"

"How can we do that? The followers will find our track?"

"Where is there to disappear on this plain? It goes on and on just as flat here as it was where we left the escarpment?" another questioned.

"You will see," Fire Dancer promised. Now however, what we need to happen is for the camp to travel at least another few days as though we are all together. Centipede Man will lead you to where we will all meet and go to our new home. I can promise that you will like it. For now however I want the following persons to wait until dark and prepare to travel, Water Woman and Moth, Turtle Woman, Cougar, Stone Man, Basket, Acorn, Feather, Tortoise and her infant, and Sage Girl. The remainder of the camp will be led by Centipede Man and I will be joining you again some time tomorrow."

"What is going on?" questioned Turtle Woman of Basket.

"I have no more idea than you, but if it gets the raiders away from us I am all for it."

"This has been particularly hard on you Basket, we all feel bad about the way Red Eagle treated you, and now it seems you may never be rid of him. If it is possible however, Fire Dancer will do it."

"I know that! And I thank you for your concern. It makes me feel less alone knowing that at least there is someone who doesn't blame me for everything bad that has happened. People cannot like me when it is my fault, and their loved ones and friends now walk the wind."

"That wasn't your fault!"

"Tell that to Cottontail Woman or Sage. They have openly said hurtful things in my hearing. They blame me for the bison stampede. They say that Red Eagle was behind it and so it is my fault. They have said it would be best if I left this camp."

"They have, have they; well we will see about that!" Turtle Woman stomped off as mad as Basket had ever seen her.

They sat around the fire, just as on every other night, except that Stone Man was absent from the camp. He came in well after the ancestor fires burned brightly and nodded. Quietly, like ghosts a group of people leading pack dogs melted into the darkness. The rest of the camp slept peacefully. They traveled well into the night and then rested. Fire Dancer went to Basket. "Throw Back will lead you to the place. She and wolf found it when they were gone from the camp. Stone Man will help as well. He has been told what to expect. Now I go and erase your trail. Once the camp has arrived, we will make sure that no trace of our track will ever be found. The place we go to will be safe for seasons if we decide to stay there. Now go safely."

Basket nodded, now understanding why Throw Back carried no pack. Basket went to the head of the column of people and knelt before her friend, "take us to the hidden place," she told the animal. Throw Back wagged her tail and said "woof!" then she raised her head, scented the breeze and started out, cutting away from the trail they had made. For the rest of the night the people followed, barely able to see, the ancestor fires giving off little light. Eventually, however they dimmed and Sun Spirit brought Dawn Woman to grace their day. Now even though they were tired, they picked up speed. They stopped to rest about mid morning and then traveled again until nearly dusk. Suddenly Throw Back vanished.

Basket stopped, called, and heard the reassuring bark, and then cautiously she went forward. Suddenly the plain ended, just dropped into a canyon, yet beyond the plain simply continued unbroken for as far as one could see. Unless one happened upon this place, so small in the vastness of the plain, it would never be discovered. Yet it was not a small canyon.[1] Quickly she called to the others and they followed a well-worn animal trail and like the wolf, vanished.

"There is a large cave close to the bottom of the trail," Stone Man said, "we will make our camp there, and wait for the rest of the camp. They will be here in a double hand of days. In the meantime, we can explore the canyon and get settled in."

"This place is wonderful!" Turtle Woman said, standing at the mouth of the cave and looking down the valley, "I can hardly wait until morning to really see it."

"I can!" Sage moaned. "My shoes developed holes early in the night. I fear that I have worn off the bottom of my feet."

"Why did you not say something?" Basket exclaimed, "I have an extra pair of shoes, and you are welcome to them!"

"You would give me your shoes, after the things I said to you?" Sage blushed in shame.

"You had just cause for your words," Basket admitted, "I bear you no grudge, but I would be pleased if you could forgive me for causing you so much pain."

"I don't really believe that you were responsible for the bison stampede, I only said that so that Cottontail would be my friend. I think perhaps, I would rather have you for a friend instead. Cottontail is vain and selfish."

"I would like to have you as a fiend," Basket smiled. "I have no friends. People are afraid of me, or think I am strange, and my grandmother always kept me close to her so that I made no friends, also there were no other girls in our camp my age. I will get the shoes," she went to her pack and withdrew a pair of shoes that she had made during the evenings on the trail when there was little else to do. It had helped her concentrate on something except worry.

"I think I am going to like this place," Sage smiled.

The next morning, as Basket looked out, she smiled; *I think I'm going to like this place also!* She stood at the mouth of the cave and looked down. Just below, lying in the middle of the stream lay the remains of another Great Beast, just like the one at the Sacred Spring. Already, she could feel the gentle 'tug' of its 'spirit' calling to her. She hadn't noticed it the previous night because it was hidden by thick brush from the view down the trail. It had been nearly dark when they arrived, and she hadn't been near the mouth of the cave after that.

*　*　*

Fire Dancer joined the camp again at light. He strode out before them, a target for any watcher to see. All day they walked then another and another, and another. The camp was set up as usual, and everyone was glad to crawl in his or her furs to rest. "Wake the camp, quietly. No fires are to be made. Pack just as quickly as you can," he instructed Star Woman, "I will be back. Be sure that nothing is left, and no travois. The dog must carry packs, as must you. Leave the heaviest things for me. I must see to the others."

"Be sure that you do not leave anything behind," Centipede Man said to one and then another, "work quietly, and quickly." Finally all were ready.

The dogs were carrying packs now and the travois poles were sticking from backpacks. Everyone made sure that nothing was left behind. Then they followed Fire Dancer and Centipede Man back the way they had just traveled. Blue Coyote stayed behind. He had sage, covered with fresh bison dung and a pungent odor of skunk. No dog would be able to detect their scent. He was careful to obliterate every single sign of their presence. All night he followed, removing their scent from the trail. As dawn approached it began to rain. All day it rained. Their tracks were washed away almost as soon as they lifted their feet. The range of sight was greatly lessened, another favor from the spirits. They traveled for a hand of days, and it rained each day, again washing away their trail. Then suddenly they were at the canyon and were being greeted by those who had gone ahead.

"What do you think?" Fire Dancer questioned; "will they be able to track us?"

"I could not track us!" Cougar replied "and I am the best tracker among The People. You have done it Fire Dancer! You have made the entire camp vanish!"

"For a time at least I want lookouts posted, and no one is to go onto the plain until I have been convinced it is safe!"

"If this rain keeps up no one is going to want to leave the cave," Stone Man protested. "You all look to be half drowned."

"I am soaked to the skin!" Admitted Star Woman, "and I have been that way for days. I just want to dry out and warm up. Who could believe one could be so cold during the summer?"

"I have dry clothes for you," Turtle Woman called, "And there is hot food for everyone. Come now and get dry and rest. Believe it or not we have fresh venison to eat!"

"Venison! I cannot believe how much I have missed fresh venison!" One hunter smacked his lips in anticipation.

"Well eat your fill!" Turtle Woman called, "we have plenty for all!"

The wet and bedraggled travelers were more than happy to dry out, get warm around the hearths and eat the first real meal they had in days. There were tubers and green plants and all the venison they could eat. Afterwards everyone settled down to sleep. Stone Man stood watch at the top of the trail. Later another relieved him.

"We have been in this canyon a double hand of days now. Do you think we should make a trip to the plain for bison?" A hunter asked.

"Soon," Fire Dancer replied, "soon, but when we do, the entire animal must be packed back to the canyon. We cannot leave any signs of our presence, not for a while at least."

"I would make a trip to the place of the stone," Stone Man said to Blue Coyote. "It cannot be many days from here, and we are desperately in need of stone. Do you think that the pair of us and a hand of dogs could make the trip and be back before Red Eagle reaches the place of the stone?"

"I will ask Father, but I think it an excellent idea, also we can find out what that group is up to, and where they are, and if they search for us."

Blue Coyote found Fire Dancer discussing a possible bison hunt with a group of men. He waited until they were through and then approached. "Stone Man and I would make a trip to the place of stone and bring back tool stone. We also seek to understand what Red Eagle and his band is doing and where they are."

Fire Dancer nodded, "I have been considering the same thing. If you take a string of pack dogs rather than travois you can move fast on the trip to the place of stone, get your supplies and get back. If you find Red Eagle, see what he is up too, and if he is already at the place of stone, look elsewhere for stone. Do nothing to endanger yourselves."

"We will be careful, Father," Blue Coyote promised, "and we will return with stone, fear not."

"When do you leave?"

"We thought as soon as we are prepared, if we are to reach the place of stone before Red Eagle we cannot go too soon." Fire Dancer nodded.

*　　*　　*

"I want you to take her" Basked stubbornly insisted.

Stone Man searched for a reason not to include Throw Back in the pack string. Finally he smiled, "she would be an announcement that it is us!" he exclaimed, "Those feet would leave footprints which could be made by no other animal. Red Eagle would know for certain that it was us. As it is all he can know is that someone had been there, and there is no reason to suspect that those individuals were of The People; for there will not be travois markings." He finally convinced Basket that Throw Back should not be included on the trip.

"With a sigh of relief, Blue Coyote and he left the canyon. They were dressed differently, not in the traditional clothes of The People. The dogs they took all looked like wolves; chosen from the meager selection left. Scorpion was left behind as well. Only Wolf would be an animal easily recognized by Red Eagle, and he also was now different. His thick bushy tail had been carefully sheared so he now had a thin rather scraggily tail. He was not concerned, however, if Blue Coyote wanted his tail thus, so be it!"

They traveled all day and set up a dry camp late. "Do you think either of us will ever mate?" questioned Stone Man. "I mean, we are certainly past the seasons when most men are mated and have set up their own shelter. Yet even though I have given it some thought, there has always been something else to do, first the trip for obsidian, then the trip to the place of stone, now this movement of the camp to the spirit canyon."

"I have thought about it," admitted Blue Coyote. "The unmated woman, Sage, she is not bad to look at."

"You thinking . . .?"

"Have you?" Stone Man shook his head, "Me neither," Blue Coyote sighed, "last winter I almost . . . but then something came up and I . . ."

"Yeh, me too," Stone Man grinned, "Wind Song, from the Rabbit Camp."

"Oh! Did she indicate to you also?"

"You?"

"I almost did, only . . ."

"There was Pond Girl," Stone Man smiled, "now there was a woman to warm a man's furs!"

"Yeh, any man's furs" Blue Coyote snorted.

"Moth will be a woman before spring, and she is a kindly creature."

"I suppose so . . . but don't you ever?"

"Haven't you dreamed . . .?"

Both sighed and sat staring into the fire.

"There is Basket," Stone Man said casually, "I suppose . . ."

"Basket!" snorted Blue Coyote, "that would be like mating with our sister!"

"But she is not our sister," Stone Man pointed out, "and she is certainly very kind and we have been friends with her all of our lives."

"Exactly! Don't you want something . . .? Oh I don't know!" Blue Coyote tossed his stick into the grass and rolled over in his furs.

Long into the night both men thought, those nebulous dreams of . . . they could not quite put a name to . . .

*   *   *

"Do you see anything?" questioned Stone Man.

They lay crouched above the river across from the place of stone.

"Nothing has moved in a hand of time, if there is anyone there, they are not showing themselves. Do you think it is safe?"

"I think one of us should go and if all is clear wave back."

"If time is running short, we are wasting a lot of it!" Blue Coyote reminded.

"We saw no trace of anyone the whole way to this place! I wonder why? Do you think we are wrong and they were not headed here?"

"I am sure they are headed here. It is the only reasonable place! But they should have gotten here nearly a moon ago, something is wrong, either Red Eagle is no longer leading, or they have found somewhere else."

"Hopefully not our secret canyon" Stone Man frowned, "I am going down there, I am tired of sweating in this blazing sun for no reason. If they are there, then I am a fool and deserve to be captured, if not then I will get the stone and we will be gone from here."

"All right, I will give you a hand head start. If you reach the quarry and all is clear, whistle like a quail and I will join you, otherwise I will watch out of sight. If you are captured then I will be able to rescue you."

"I am on my way!" Stone Man grinned; "meet Stagnant Muck, at you service!" he made a sweeping gesture and both men laughed. It would take someone who knew them well to recognize either of them. Stone Man had requested that Star Woman shear his hair all a length even with his chin. He wore a twisted headband to hold it from his face. Acorn juice had dyed his skin several shades darker than natural and he wore a bison hide vest hanging to just below the buttocks, his breechclout hanging to the knee. His shoes came to the ankle and beyond that he was bare. Blue Coyote was similarly dressed but his hair had been twisted into a knot at the back of his head and he wore a pair of eagle feathers from it.

"On with it Stagnant Muck; Green Slime will keep watch!"

Both men grinned at the nicknames they had chosen. If anyone captured them, they had a fantastic tale of traveling from the south, of unbelievable herds of bison and trees and rivers and strange, never before seen animals.

Stone man hurried down the narrow trail from their outlook post to where they had left the dogs, resting in a well-concealed spot. Blue Coyote remained where he was. Not long after he could hear Stone Man whistling casually as he noisily led the string of dogs up the wide trail to the quarry. He came into view and followed their plan. Stone Man wandered about, as if looking for bits of stone, rather like he had stumbled upon this place accidentally. His sharp eyes were scanning for any signs of human occupancy, or even presence in the area. Then he casually led the dogs toward the small canyon, which contained the quarry they had used the previous season. There were no signs of anyone having been in the area since they themselves had been there. He settled the dogs and went to the canyon entrance and gave the quail call.

Stone Man began setting up a minute camp and settling the dogs to rest in the shade. They had been watered well at the river and now he fed them as well. Soon Blue Coyote joined him.

"I cannot understand where the others are, but they obviously haven't been here. Still I would get the stone and get out of here as fast as we can. They cannot be far away."

"I agree. Unless Red Eagle was one I wounded, and his wounds were fatal, I just don't understand! Let's just get our stone and get out of here!"

They quickly set to mining the stone that they came after. Before dark they had half of the dog packs loaded, and before Sun Spirit sank in the west on the next day they would be away from the quarry.

"I am going up top and see if I can locate their fires," Blue Coyote said after they had eaten. "The night sky is dark so I should be able to see a long way."

"We" Stone Man corrected him; "I am going with you."

They followed a narrow twisting path to the plain above, but try as they could they did not see any fire. "They could be dry camping, and of course unless they have learned to use bison chips, they would not have a fire at all."

"Antelope was with them, which means Black Deer's entire group is probably as well. So they do know about bison chip fire."

"Well I see nothing!" Blue Coyote stated, "Which doesn't mean a thing. I have an idea," he whistled and soon Wolf joined them. "Sniff the air boy, human! Do you smell any humans?"

Wolf sniffed, and sniffed, and turned and sniffed some more, then he whined and rubbed against Blue Coyote, "What does that mean?" Questioned Stone Man.

"Blue Coyote shrugged, "probably that he smells nothing. He is not concerned so at least we can be certain that there are no people upwind."

"Let's just get out of here. I think we could set up torches and fill at least another pack yet tonight. I don't like this!"

"Nor do I. Come on, we might as well get back to the canyon. I think we are safe at least for tonight."

As soon as the sky lightened, the next morning they were back at work and mid-afternoon saw all the packs filled. "Let's get out of here!" Blue Coyote suggested, "I would suggest we follow the river downstream for the rest of today, camp there and wait until tomorrow to go up on the plain."

They did so and were a good distance east of the quarry before climbing up to the flat where they could be seen for a long distance.

* * *

You failed again! The voice screamed at Red Eagle. He no longer had to take the 'spirit powder' to travel to the secret cave, but merely close his eyes. The wound in his shoulder throbbed and no matter how many times it was cut open and drained, the poison persisted. The entire area was swollen and putrid smelling.

"You! Cripple! My shoulder needs attention, why is the herb packing not drawing out the evil spirits?" His head was swimming with pain and fever, "you get some fresh herbs and tend to my wound!"

The man, Cripple, grunted and frowned, but did at he was bid. Black Deer had recovered from the wound in his leg days ago, but both the dog bites and the shoulder wound acquired in the raid on the Yucca Camp were taking their toll on Red Eagle. He could barely walk, so the raiders were now camping in a bison wallow until he was able to travel. Then the rain came, and he got thoroughly soaked for days on end. Now gradually, however, he was recovering. Black Deer smiled to himself, as long as Cripple was attending Red Eagle he would not recover. Cripple was Black Deer's man, and he was secretly adding a bit of fresh bison dung to the herb poultices making sure the spirits remained in Red Eagle's wounds. Soon, very soon, he, Black Deer, would take control of the raider band.

But Red Eagle was tougher than he thought. In spite of Cripple's ministrations, he did slowly recover. Then he was ready to go in search of the Yucca Camp once again. They spent a span of days searching but found no trace of them.

"They are probably already at this place of stone!" Shouted Red Eagle; "You are a stupid man, Black Deer! Now lead us to this place!"

Black Deer did lead them, far west of the place of stone, but eventually they did reach the river, and then had only to follow it east. Black Deer realized he was no longer essential to Red Eagle, and it was only a matter of time . . . either he challenged for leadership, or he was dead, or perhaps both.

I should have killed him while he was weak Black Deer thought, *now he is recovering, I cannot wait any longer! Tonight, just as we planned!* He nodded to Bear and a pair of other hunters as he retired, sending to them the agreed upon signal. He rolled in his sleeping fur and waited until the Ancestor Fires were bright in the sky. He heard a slight sound and began to rise and join his cohorts. Someone grabbed his hair and jerked back his head, a slight pain at his throat and he was thrown to the ground. Black Deer blinked; hot red blood gurgling and choking him as the jugular veins pumped it vigorously from his body. The world went black and he sighed in death.

Red Eagle stood over his body, smiling evilly. He had bribed one of the pair of hunters and was waiting, and now they were all dead. Red Eagle did not trust even one who could be bribed. "We will follow this river to the place of stone!" He said the next morning. The bodies of the four slain men were left to rot where they lay, but their possessions were taken.

"The Yucca Camp is probably already there, so we will be very careful approaching the place. We will follow the river and stay out of sight. Now let's go!" He led the way.

A pair of days later they entered the place of stone. There was no sign that anyone was there, or even had been there for a long time. Of the Yucca Camp there were no signs.

"Where could they be?" He questioned, "Have you searched everywhere? Are you sure there are no signs of them?"

"There are fresh quarry marks, but there is no way to tell how long ago they were made?" One of the men replied, "They could be from last season, I don't know, but there is no one here now."

Well to the south, Blue Coyote and Stone Man had made their way up to the plain from the river bottom.

"We will set up our camp here!" Red Eagle stated, "Then we will go looking for them! They must be around here somewhere!"

*   *   *

"I feel more at ease," Blue Coyote sighed. They were a hand of days from the place of stone. Yet they were completely unaware of the near encounter. "I just had a feeling that they were near, nothing that I can explain, but it is gone now."

"Wolf would have smelled them, wouldn't he?"

"Perhaps, and then again, I don't know. They could have been camping where the wind did not bring their smell. I am just glad that we have stone enough to last the camp seasons, and that we need not go back to that place for a long time. By then maybe Red Eagle will have gotten tired of hunting us and gone away!"

"I hope so," Stone Man sighed, "who would have thought he would turn out to be so much trouble? We should have left him behind in the Starving Mountains!" Just then Wolf raised his head, sniffed the wind, and began to growl softly. "What is it, boy?" Blue Coyote hurried to look in the direction the wolf stared. Way out, just barely visible, he saw a campfire. "There they are!" He quickly doused their minute fire. "Come on, I want to get a closer look!"

"Let's just get out of here," recommended Stone Man, "if they are hunting us we had better go now!"

"We have covered our trail, and they have come nowhere near it anyway," Blue Coyote shook his head, "I want to know how many of them there are, and what they are up to. I am going to sneak up close enough to their camp to hear what they say. You stay here with the dogs, but be ready to go as soon as I return. I won't be long!" He left the camp, signaling Wolf to stay behind. Quietly, quickly he made his way to just down wind of the camp.

* * *

"I cannot understand," a hunter was saying, "they couldn't just vanish! They have to be here somewhere! We have come south for a hand of days and found no signs of them, perhaps they went North and we passed them when we followed the river?"

Red Eagle shook his head; "They should have reached the place of stone before we did."

"Maybe they were not even headed there!" suggested another hunter, "maybe they crossed the river and just kept going! They could by anywhere on the plain! If it were me, I would go north and cross the river. Somewhere there should be mountains and that is where I would go!"

"You know Fire Dancer," Red Eagle turned to another hunter, "is that the sort of thing he is likely to do?" The hunter nodded, "it is exactly the kind of thing he would do."

"Then in the morning we will head north and follow the edge above the plain until we find their trail!" Red Eagle said. The camp nodded, and they began retiring to their sleeping furs. Blue Coyote slipped quietly away from their camp smiling happily. Fire Dancer had come very close to doing exactly as the hunter had predicted. Only the discovery of the canyon had changed his mind. Red Eagle would never think of looking for them in a direction they had already passed.

* * *

"Let's go! I will tell you as we travel," Blue Coyote said to Stone Man. "We must be beyond their sight by morning." They snapped leads to the dogs and headed south toward the hidden canyon. "They are going to search north for us for they think we have crossed the river and followed the plain north looking for a mountain home."

"Which is exactly what Fire Dancer intended to do" Stone Man nodded, then laughed. Now Red Eagle chases ghosts! I don't suppose there could possibly be other people out there somewhere and he could end up following them forever?"

"We must hurry to the canyon and give The People the good news," Blue Coyote said, "soon we can hunt and live without fear of Red Eagle. He will never find us, and eventually he must give up!"

---

1. Palo Duro Canyon, south of Amarillo, Texas. Palo Duro is 120 miles long and 20 miles wide. It has been occupied more or less for the last 13,000 years.

PART III: ADDITIONAL CHARACTERS

STAR CHILD: VERY YOUNG WOMAN OF THE EAGLE CAMP
BISON MAN: HEADMAN OF THE EAGLE CAMP
RED EAGLE: RAIDER- WHITE FALCON
MAKES A ROBE: WOMAN OF THE EAGLE CAMP
RAIN WOMAN: STAR CHILD'S 'MOTHER'
MOON: DREAMER OF THE EAGLE CAMP
SOFT WIND: MATURE LONE WOMAN

SINGING SERPENT: CRIPPLE, GOOD MAN CAPTURED BY RED EAGLE'S RAIDERS
MOURNING DOVE: WOMAN DISCOVERED AND SAVED BY THE CAMP
JOURNEY'S FAR: HUNTER IN LOVE WITH MOURNING DOVE

WIND WALKER: HEADMAN OF THE RIVER PEOPLE SAVED FROM SAVAGES
SAND CATCHER: HUNTER OF THE RIVER PEOPLE
LAUGHING WATER: WOMAN OF RIVER PEOPLE
CHERT BOY: SON OF MOURNING STAR, RAISED BY BASKET
BADGER: HUNTER
RAVEN: WOMAN OF THE RIVER PEOPLE
SPIRIT WOLF: REPLACEMENT FOR THROW BACK
OWL: HUNTER OF THE RIVER PEOPLE

DREAM CATCHER: DREAMER OF THE RIVER PEOPLE

WHITE FALCON: RAIDER-DREAMER
HAIRY BEAR: MAN OF THE RAIDERS
SPREADS HER LEGS: WOMAN OF THE RAIDERS
SAND CRAWLER: MAN OF THE RAIDERS
GROUND SQUIRREL: MAN OF THE RAIDERS
HOT WIND: MAN OF THE RAIDERS
SPIDER: MAN OF THE RAIDERS
ELSEWHERE: WOMAN OF THE RAIDERS

SUN SPIRIT: BASKET'S DAUGHTER
WINTER RAIN: SUN CHILD'S DAUGHTER

PART III

THE TRAIL OF TEARS

CHAPTER 13

What do you think about the Sacred Beast lying in the stream?" Blue Coyote asked Basket. Do you think it is a good sign?"

The Sacred Beast protected the Ancient Ones. I do not feel any anger from it. Only peace; actually I feel that its presence here is a good sign."

Blue Coyote nodded, "I thought as much. But when I saw you down there actually touching it, I could see a faint bluish glow all around you. I knew you were communicating with it, just as you did with the one at the Sacred Spring."

"I felt it 'pulling' me, just as the one at the Sacred Spring did, but as there, the feelings I got were only good. I think the 'spirit' of the ancient totem feels kindly toward us. I think it is glad that we are here."

* * *

"I think it is time we made a bison hunt!" announced Fire Dancer. The People had been in the sacred canyon for a pair of moons now and there had been no sign of Red Eagle. Hopefully he was far to the north. The summer season was gone, as was most of the fall. Winter would soon be settling in. They had been living off the deer abundant in the canyon. The women had gone up to the plain and garnered many containers full of grain seeds, they had dug tubers and dried many plant products, but there were few acorns in the canyon, for there was not an abundance of oak trees.

"I will prepare the ancient ceremony for the hunters!" Acorn smiled, "just as dreamers did for our ancestors!"

"We will also make it a hunt for hunting capes!" Fire Dancer declared; "for each of the established hunters, and for the new man who joins us!" He grinned at Badger, the newest adult among The People, and Badger grinned back. "You go and consult with Pinyon and Acorn to be sure that you understand the taboo's connected with this hunt." Badger willingly obliged.

"I have not seen any bison the last several times that I went to the plain," Star Woman said, "Perhaps they have moved somewhere else."

"You did not think to mention this?" Fire Dancer frowned.

"No, why would I? You said that we would not be hunting bison for some time, so it did not seem important."

"Perhaps it isn't, there is a chance that the animals are just not in the immediate vicinity. I will send runners to seek them out."

Soon Porcupine and Gray Wolf were headed away from the canyon to locate the bison. They returned late in the day, exhausted and with bad news. "We found signs, but it was at least a double span of days old. All the bison tracks head south. Is it possible that they leave this area during the winter?"

"Pinyon," Fire Dancer questioned? "What do the legends say? Do they mention the bison leaving this area?"

Pinyon thought, "The legends say that The People followed the bison," he frowned, "that would indicate that the animals moved constantly, but we have not seen signs of that! They were here all summer."

"But is it possible?"

"According to the legends The People followed the bison north during the spring and summer and at midsummer gathered in a place far to the north, where they held ceremonies and gathered chert, then traveled south during the fall and wintered in a more southern area. That could mean they are no longer here, for we do not know where in the north-south area this canyon is located."

"Acorn, would you consult the spirits? Perhaps they can enlighten you."

The dreamer nodded and went to where he had set up a spirit shelter, a short distance from the cave. Here he made the preparations, thankful that once again Wolf Spirit was talking to him.

*   *   *

The spiral began and soon Acorn felt himself flying high above the earth. The scene below him was amazing; the plain was vast, far greater than he had imagined. People followed a scattering of bison herds, slowly north. It was spring, the grass just greening, he wheeled in a circle and found himself moving north rapidly. Here, in a valley at the edge of a great mountain range, the people were gathered to celebrate the midsummer ceremony, he wheeled again and the people were headed south, once again following the herds; herds that traveled every winter far to the south of the place of flint. Wolf Spirit had given him his answer. Slowly he returned from his journey. In the morning he would tell Fire Dancer.

*　　*　　*

"Then we are dependant upon the animals within this canyon for our survival during this winter," Fire Dancer frowned, "it is a very large canyon, but we are three spans of people."

"IF we do not waste, there should be enough game to support the number we are, for at least the winter and starving times, but by spring, the animals will have been hunted out," Centipede Man stated.

"Do you think it advisable to gather the camp and follow the bison south?"

"How far; Star Woman says they were not there a double span of days ago. Can we catch up with them, do we have enough food to carry us that far, and what do we do for dogs to pull our travois if we must carry not only food but winter shelters as well?" Centipede Man questioned.

"Let Blue Coyote and me go out in search of bison!" Suggested Stone Man, "We can make a quick run to the south and if we come across a herd be back here in a short time, if not, we will not have wasted everyone's time."

Fire Dancer nodded. "Take Gray Wolf and Badger with you. If you find only a few bison, kill them and wait for us to come to you. It is cold enough that the meat will not spoil quickly. You can take branches to make drying racks and be doing that while you wait. Go now and prepare."

At dawn the four men hurried up the trail and headed south and east of the canyon, moving fast. They traveled for the entire day, noticing that always the tracks were old and they were headed south. They dry camped that night, eating little and dropping quickly to sleep, at dawn they rose and were again headed south. "I see fresh tracks here!" Gray Wolf shouted to his companions, spread out to cover a wider area. "No more than a day old!" All gathered. "It looks to be a very small herd," Gray Wolf sighed, "But better than no herd. Do we send Badger back for the others?"

Stone Man squatted and studied the tracks, "Only a double hand of animals, but that will be enough if we can bring down all of them, I think we can bring the men and dogs."

"I will hurry," Badger promised.

"No need to push to the limit," Blue Coyote replied studying the sky, "Unless a storm shows up we will be all right. Are you sure that you can get back to the canyon all right? I will send Wolf with you if you are not sure."

Badger sighed and asked, "Would you? I am sure, well almost sure that I can make it all right, but I would feel much more so if Wolf were with me. I would also feel safer and less lonely." Blue Coyote nodded, and Wolf was soon trotting beside Badger.

"I am glad you suggested Wolf," Gray Wolf sighed, "Badger was really afraid he was going to get lost, but he wouldn't have said anything to either of you. I know that Wolf can find his way back to the canyon and also follow our scent back."

"We were young and unsure hunters not so long ago," Stone Man reminded him, "And there are very few marks to show the way on this plain. Remember we learned to chart the way in the moving sand." He grinned, "Badger will be fine with Wolf to help him, and he will grow to have confidence in his own judgement. This is the sign of a good hunter. Remember, you learned on the trip to the place of stone. The more young hunters we have with experience, the less we are dependent on the seasoned hunters, but each must learn. Come on now, we probably have a way yet to go to find these bison!"

They headed again southward at a fast pace, now the three of them tracking the small herd. At mid-afternoon a pair of days later they spotted their prey and were soon smearing fresh dung on their bodies. Stone Man suggested they get as close as possible to the animals and take out the lead bull first. This left several cows, a pair of immature males and a pair of half-grown calves to be darted after the lead bull. They eased carefully, keeping down wind and were able to come almost within touching distance of the herd. Stone Man would take the lead bull; Blue Coyote and Gray

Wolf each a mature cow. In unison they rose and drove their darts into the breast of the chosen animal. All three went down without a sound, quickly, before they scattered, they attacked the remaining adult cows, bringing down the pair. The remainder of the herd disappeared over the horizon, leaving one half-grown calf behind, bawling for its mother, lying dead; and soon it joined her.

"Do you think we should follow them and try for more?" Gray Wolf asked.

"They are not going far," Blue Coyote shook his head. "Let's get these cooling, and then a pair of us will go after the rest." Quickly they set to work, and before night came had the carcasses caped out and quartered to cool. "In the morning, while you two begin processing this meat, I will see where the rest of the herd is, they will not have gone far, but they will be more alert."

"Even if these are all the bison we manage to get, this kill is going to be enough to supplement the deer from the canyon, so we will not die of starvation this winter," Stone Man said, "But I would feel better if we managed to bring down several more."

"So would I," agreed Gray Wolf.

"Look!" Gray Wolf pointed to the east, "Another herd! Lets go!" they grabbed atlatl and darts and quickly made their way to where another straggling herd was munching their way southward, they took another hand of animals from this group, thus assuring an ample supply of winter food. They caped these animals and quartered them. Night fell, and they rested, the next day again they worked at butchering the bison. The next morning, they heard the dogs barking in the distance. The camp had arrived.

Travois were lined up and loaded. Hunters began stripping large chunks of meat from the bones, and the later they tossed into a pile,[1] then the girls tended to these; breaking the bones open and scooping the marrow out into containers. Skulls were broken open and the brains removed, tongues were cut free, and horn sheaths were removed. Already the eyes had been eaten. Women rolled up the hides and stacked them to one side, while everyone worked to get the meat loaded. Far to the north, high piled clouds appeared, and a cold wind began to blow. Everyone worked more quickly. Not all had come on the hunt. Tortoise had remained behind with her infant son, and Song Bird had been ill. A pair of old women also had stayed at the cave.

They worked all day and far into the night, but dawn brought icy air and overcast skies. "We have to leave!" Centipede Man glanced at the sky. "That storm will be here before we get back to the canyon if we don't leave now and travel well into the nights as well."

"Start back with the loaded travois," Fire Dancer ordered, "Basket, you and Throw Back lead the way. Take those who are ready, the rest of us will follow just as soon as we are loaded."

Basket nodded and began hitching Throw Back to the travois. A double hand of travois was soon ready, and that used every dog they had. The hunters would have to pull their own loads. She and the women and children all headed for the canyon and safety. They kept going well into the night, resting only for short periods of time and then pushing on again. The wind was getting colder and colder.

By morning the snow began to fall, at first as a biting sleet which cut through their lightweight winter clothing. No one had thought to bring anything heavier because no one had anything heavier. The younger children were either now carried by their mothers or were tucked as warmly as possible atop a travois. But as the morning grew the light stayed dim and the snow fell harder and harder. The wind was cutting, and the snow blew almost horizontally, freezing on eyelashes, and flying up noses with every breath. Star Woman could no longer feel her feet, and there was so much snow on the ground they couldn't find any fuel to build a fire with. They had to keep moving. Turtle Woman began to flounder and she fell to her knees. Basket and Willow raised her and helped her. Soon the weaker ones were relegated to following while the stronger broke trail. They moved slower and ever slower. By midday everyone was exhausted. Star Woman began sweeping snow from an area of the ground. Here they erected a shelter and managed to get a small fire going. They brewed hot tea and passed it around while everyone rested. It helped. Fingers were thawed over the fire as well, and even a few feet thawed back to feeling. But all knew they could not stay any longer. The wind let up slightly and the sky became brighter well after sun-high, they pushed faster then. They walked long into the night, depending on Throw Back to lead the way, for the ancestor fires were nowhere to be seen. Finally, they were forced to halt, from exhaustion, and when they nearly lost the rear travois in the dark, Star Woman decided it was too dangerous to keep going.

Behind them the men were already following, their burdens pulled by hunters and packs on their backs carrying the hides. Each was heavily weighed down, but they were determined to leave no meat behind. This group rested for a hand of time just before dawn and then pushed on again. It was late afternoon the next day before the men caught up and they were still a long way from the canyon. Now however, going was getting very slow. The snow was blowing directly into their faces again, cutting cold and freezing. They could not see where they were going, depending entirely upon Throw Back to know the way. Some had repeatedly stumbled to their knees in the drifting snow, and most were deadly tired. This is how the men found them. Fire Dancer struggled to lead the way and finally three days later they staggered down the path into the canyon.

The snow was very deep here, but the wind no longer cut through them. "You all rest here and some of us will break a trail to the cave. We are almost there."

"Why not leave the travois here for tonight and take them the rest of the way in the morning?" Basket suggested.   Fire Dancer considered this and nodded. "The meat is in no danger of spoiling in this cold weather. We can unload it here. Star Woman, you get those who are in the poorest shape onto travois, those who can make it follow me to the home cave.

The few people who had not gone on the trek were worried and more than glad to see them

Had it not been for you, Basket, and you, Willow, I would be walking the wind now."

"Had we not helped you, other would have," Willow replied, "We are all lucky that we made it this far. I have not much experience with snow storms, but this is the worst one I have ever seen!"

"It is as bad as the one which killed the acorn gatherers," Star Woman replied, "And that was by far the nastiest storm I ever saw!"

"There were others, last season as well. I think that every season this plain has killer storms. It is not the place to be at this time of season that is for sure. No wonder our ancestors traveled after the bison! No wonder the bison themselves leave this place!"

"Were we not in this canyon, we would not survive this winter time either. It is only by going south that our ancestors lived through the winter, or they also spent it in caves just like this one. In fact, it was probably our ancestors, who lived in the home cave."

"I miss the mountains!" Willow said with a sigh, "The winters there were not so severe, and we had plenty of water. I do not like this plain where everything is so flat and the wind always blows," she rose and walked to the cave entrance, "Here come the hunters."

"...There, that is the last bison hide!" Star Woman rubbed the small of her back, "I am sure we will find a use for them, but they are far too heavy to make clothing. Shoes, maybe, but they are too heavy to be used as travois hides, and why use them anyway when there is perfectly good cordage available? I suppose they would work as shelter hides, but again they weigh so much it takes a pair of people to handle one. Perhaps the hair could be used as cordage for nets? That would be a use for it," she sighed.

"I think I will try one as a sleeping fur," remarked Willow as she studied a hide, "It would be soft with such thick fur. The hide of the calf would be perfect for many things. It is the same size as a small deer and the fur is much thicker and far less scratchy. I think I will ask for the hide of a calf," she decided.

"We will find some use for them," Sage Girl said, her head tilted to one side, eyeing the hides with a thoughtful expression.

"I am going out and dig up another load of the bison meat," remarked Turtle Woman, "We have processed most of the last load. I will start a stew when I return," she wrapped her rabbit skin robe about her and eased out of the cave opening. It had been a hand of days since they had all returned to the home cave. The bison meat was still buried in snow at the base of the trail down into the canyon. She hitched one of the dogs to an empty travois and headed down the faint path. The snow was still deep, and more was coming down on a regular basis. She was half way to base of the trail when she heard a movement behind her, she turned, "Wolf! It is not nice to scare a person like that!" she exclaimed as the animal stood above her on a ledge. 'Wolf' leaped directly at her, snarling and growling. Turtle Woman screamed and floundered backward in the snow. Her awkward fall saved her from the full force of the wolf's attack, for it landed to one side of her and by the time it twisted and locked its jaws around her arm, Turtle

Woman had screamed again and now hunters were running toward her, Wolf in their lead. He leaped on the intruder and they rolled away from the frightened woman. Blue Coyote helped Turtle Woman to her feet and sent her back to the cave with an escort of armed men. The hunters watched as the wolves fought. Soon the snow was red with blood and with a yelp one animal went limp, its throat torn open and its lifeblood spraying the snow. Blue Coyote glared at the surviving animal, dart raised. It also was injured, and when it whined and thumped a still not fully refurred tail, he realized that it was Wolf. He and Cougar lifted the animal onto the travois and carried the traumatized wolf back to the cave.

"I will take some hunters and back-track this animal," Cougar said.

"There have been wolves up on the plain recently. I have heard them howling!" remarked Stone Man, "But they are afraid of the smoke and smell of The People. They have never come into this end of the canyon before. Perhaps the storm has forced them here."

"Someone had better check on the bison meat." Pinyon stated, "I will go, but not alone. If there is one wolf in this canyon, there are probably more. Who will come with me?"

"I will come with you, "Stone Man volunteered. "Somebody locate Fire Dancer and tell him what has happened." The two men headed up the canyon toward the trail. "Look here! There are fresh wolf tracks everywhere! There must be at least a span of them," he looked about, suddenly the hair on the back of his neck creeping chills, "We had better be careful, and we had better go back and get help. A pair of us is not enough to fight off that many wolves."

They turned and stopped. Silently, stalking on feet of death, a double hand of wolves had cut off their way. "Shout for help!" Stone Man began hollering at the top of his voice, "help! Help! Help," Cougar joined in. One wolf tipped back his head and gave out a mournful howl. "Help," they shouted with renewed vigor as they backed away. Shouts from a distance told them help was coming. Stone Man turned to find a spot of safety. Coming silently from the other direction was another hand of wolves. Now the hunters stood back to back, atlatl held in one hand and a dart in the other. They were prepared to either bash the wolves on the head with the heavy end of the atlatl or let them impale themselves of the sharp darts, either way dangerous for the hunters. Shouts were coming nearer, again the wolf howled, and close by others answered. Help was far away! Then the wolves broke as a larger animal crashed into them and scattered them in all directions. She grabbed one by the throat and with a quick twist broke its neck quickly she dropped the carcass and drove into another, ripping its throat wide open. She had only time to attack a third before a full hand of the animal jumped her. Throw Back fought with every bit of cunning and instinct she possessed. Another wolf yelped and fell limp. Then darts sailed through the air and the wolves beyond the hunters yelped and ran. The last pair of wolves on Throw Back suddenly quit the fight and fled. One of them was darted before it made a pair of jumps. The other escaped.

Stone Man went to his knees beside Throw Back. She was covered with blood and panting heavily. He ran his hands over her, found numerous tears and bites, but nothing life threatening. The blood had probably come from the dead wolves. "Good girl!" he hugged her. Throw Back whined and nuzzled him to see that he was unharmed as well.

"What happened?" Fire Dancer arrived, out of breath, "We heard you from where we were hunting, and we got here as soon as we could."

"Wolves!" stated Centipede Man, "We were closer and were able to drive them away." He shook his head, "Throw Back came streaking past us and we followed. Got here just as she did in those over there, that animal sure can fight!" He said in admiration.

"Turtle Woman was attacked!" Stone Man said "We heard her screaming and got here just as a wolf had her by the arm. Wolf killed it and Blue Coyote took them back to the cave. We decided to check things out and got ourselves cut off. That's when we started hollering for help!"

"There was at least a span of them that we saw, and more that answered from farther down the canyon." Pinyon added. "We had better get back to the cave before they decide to come back!"

"We had better take out a hunting party and scout this canyon end, Fire Dancer added, "With a well-armed force of men."

"The meat," Stone Man slapped his leg; "They are probably, after the bison! We had better hurry!" They headed back to the home cave and were soon gathering up extra darts. "We will pick up the carcasses on our way back, the hides will make soft tunics for our winter clothes," he grinned. "I for one will enjoy wearing the hide of one of those wolves, and the dogs will enjoy the flesh!"

"Look over there, where we left the meat!" directed Fire Dancer, "I thought I saw movement there." He moved carefully, checking every possible place a wolf could hide and pounce. The men were moving slowly, but carefully toward the trail down into the canyon. They had spotted shadows, a fleck or so of blood, but beyond those only footprints. Lots and lots of foot prints. A finger of time later they were at the spot where they had left the bison. A few pieces of scattered flesh were all that remained.

"We risked our lives for that meat!" muttered Cougar, "All for nothing!" He stamped his foot, "Now the wolves get fat and The People starve!"

"They didn't get all of it," reminded Fire Dancer. "We had already carried most of the hump meat and organ meat back to the cave and there have been at least a pair of travois full as well."

"They got enough! There was the better part of a hand of animals left to bring in. Turtle was coming for a load for the women to process today. That's what she was doing when she was attacked." Cougar explained. "I didn't even get a chance to see how badly she was hurt."

"There is nothing more we can do here," Fire Dancer tossed the frozen bit of flesh down, "Let's get back to the cave. I want the hides of those animals we did manage to kill."

"Turtle deserves at least a tunic from them," Cougar stated.

"She will get it, as will Basket, for Throw Back can claim at least half a hand of them. We will sort that out later. Right now let's just get back in one piece. I saw movement ahead! Keep together men, and someone, watch our backside!"

They moved forward in close formation, but the wolves had lost enough blood for one day, they melted into the shadows as the men approached and there was no more trouble.

"I am going to refill this water skin," Willow stated. "She and Basket were working on the wolf hides, tanning them for tunics. "We really need one more hide," she rolled back on her heels, "But first we need some tea. I will be back shortly." She wrapped in a robe, picked up a stout pointed walking stick, to break the ice on the edge of the stream, and left the cave. A few breaths later she screamed.

Basket lunged for her bolas and Throw Back leaped through the opening. Willow lay on the bank, half in, half out of the water; there was blood everywhere. Basket gasped, Throw Back did not even slow down as she passed Willow. There were a snarling and shaking in the brush beyond, a yelp of pain and then silence. Basket pulled Willow's limp body from the stream. She rolled her over and slapped her on the back. Willow moaned, vomited up water, choked and coughed. Blood still oozed from a long cut on her scalp.

"My head!" she whimpered, "Something hit me!"

"You broke the ice with your head," Basked replied, "Are you hurt any where else?" Basket was already running her hands over Willow,

"I don't think so, other than swallowing half the water in the stream and freezing to death from the cold." Hands lifted her and people thrashed through the brush and Basket called Throw Back, she answered and dragged the carcass of yet another wolf from the brush, wagging her tail.

"When I said I wanted another wolf hide, I didn't quite have this in mind!" scolded Willow a short while later as she hugged Throw Back. "I will be careful of what I wish for in the future."

"From now on, no one leaves the cave alone!" Centipede Man stated. "When the rest of the hunters return from the deer hunt, we will start hunting these wolves. No one is safe with them in the canyon." He bent to the stream and filled the water skin as other assisted Willow back to the cave. They all returned together.

A hand of days later, the women had all the wolf pelts they wanted. Soon every member of the camp had a warm tunic of wolf-hide. After that they made pants which reached to mid calf and were attached with shoulder straps to hold them up, under the tunics. It was warm clothing. Yet, no matter how many wolves they killed, more took their place. The heavy snow stayed on the plain, making travel there all but impossible. In the canyon a few well-trod trails were easy traveling, but for the most part, it was little easier than above. The condition lasted through the entire moon. The wolves had done much more than steal the bison meat however; they had taken many deer as well. At night they could be heard howling out in the canyon and up on the plain. Wolf now wore a wide harness, so people would not mistake him for one of the wild ones.

Turtle Woman had suffered severe damage to her forearm. It was healing, but she had limited use of the hand. Cougar rubbed salve into the scars and healing wound to make the pain less, but the hand would never be completely healed, for too many ligaments had been chewed apart.

The wolf meat had been fed to the dogs, for unless they were starving, The People did not eat the flesh of predators. Now it was the coldest part of winter. People stayed close to the fire and listened as Pinyon told stories.

"Tell us the story of the wolf like our Throw Back," one of the children requested. Pinyon sat back and put on a thoughtful expression. He slowly leaned forward.

"She was only a girl!" he whispered, "Alone and lonely, all through the winter time. It is said that she lived in one of the very caves that we called home at the escarpment. In her loneliness she went searching for something which would make her feel less sad. She found an old wolf, lame and as alone as she, but the girl could tell that the wolf had pups. She followed the wolf, an ancient one, such as Throw Back, much bigger and more fierce than the wolves which live today," he made shadow figures against the wall of the cave with his hands, illustrating his story.

"This girl did a very brave or very foolish thing! She stole one of the wolf's pups and took it to live with her in the cave. It grew and grew, until it was the largest wolf ever! The wolf became her best friend, and the girl was no longer alone. But this was a special wolf, for it was sent by the spirits to watch over and protect the girl."

"Just like Throw Back protects Basket?" asked a child.

"Exactly that way!" replied the old storyteller.

"When it came time for the girl to rejoin The People, they traveled together and found the Bison Camp. It was led by a strong and intelligent Headman, but the dreamer was bad, and he was the dreamer of the whole 'People'."

"And the girl was The Mother of The People?"

"That is who the legend says she was, and Basket can claim her as an ancestor!"

"And she fought with the bad dreamer?"

"What happened?"

"Ah! That is another story!" Pinyon closed the tale and everyone went off to their sleeping furs. Outside the mournful howl of the wolves sent shivers down the spines of the listeners...

"What are we going to do?" asked Centipede Man.

"I wish that I knew," replied Fire Dancer, "This canyon seemed the perfect place to live. I would never have guessed that the wolves move from the plain and live off the deer in the canyon during the winter. Now that I think about it though that does make sense from the wolf's point of view. But there are not enough deer for both The People and the wolves. No matter how many we kill, more just take their place. Now the deer are gone, and it is still the middle of winter."

"How much meat do we have?" Blue Coyote questioned.

"Not enough!" Centipede Man answered, "There is enough for perhaps another moon but that is all."

"We must leave the canyon then or find another source of food."

"Where," questioned Gray Wolf.

The other men shook their heads.

"The weather is far too cold to try to trek to the place of stone, even if we had dogs to make the trip. And the wolves would rip us to pieces long before we got there" Fire Dancer replied, "That is not the solution."

"How far is that river from here?" Centipede Man asked.

"We traveled south and east for a double hand of days to reach the canyon. The dogs were heavily packed, as were we, and we were wiping away our trail as well. Traveling in snow, even carrying only the necessary equipment for survival, it would take at least that long, or longer," Stone Man replied.

"There is only one thing to do," Blue Coyote grimaced, "We will have to eat the wolves."

"Then what do we feed the dogs?"

"We will have to eat them as well," Sighed Centipede Man.

"We need the dogs to leave this place. There are few any way, for the wolves have killed several already. We need another solution."

"What about the tree bark?" Suggested Stone Man. "In the Starving Mountains we were able to utilize some of that to extend our food supply."

"That is a thought!" Fire Dancer nodded, "Anyone else have any ideas?"

"I am going up on the plain and see if there is anything there we can hunt!" Blue Coyote rose, "Anyone want to come along?"

"I will!" Gray Wolf nodded, "maybe we can locate some antelope."

"I will go as well." Badger claimed.

"So will I," Stone Man added.

"We will speak to the women and then we will all go." Fire Dancer and Centipede rose and followed the path back to the cave, leaving the ravaged deer skeleton where they had found it.

"What do you think we will find?" asked Badger.

Blue Coyote shrugged, "We will not know until we look."

They gathered up atlatl and darts and making sure that someone carried extra, the double hand of men filed up the trail to the plain above. The desolate expanse greeted them with a biting cold wind. They scouted for the better part of the day, traveling in ever widening circles. Wolf pounced on several mice, gulping them down hungrily. Then he routed a rabbit. Stone Man brought it down with his bolas, and soon another pair was added to their waist thongs. But there were wolf tracks everywhere. "I think we should try farther from the trail. With the wolves coming and going in this area constantly, they will have already taken most of the small game here. Tomorrow I think we should go directly east and see what we find," recommended Blue Coyote.

"You are probably right. There should be plenty of rabbits! They were abundant during the summer, and they do not go south!" Gray Wolf replied, "We might as well give up for this day; it will be nearly dark before we get back to the cave, and I don't like the idea of being up here with so many wolves around." All agreed and quickly they returned to the cave.

"These rabbits will not go far, but they are better than no food," Star Woman accepted the offering, "And we can use their skins to repair warn places in our robes. I often wondered why there were no rabbits in this canyon, now I know. The wolves ate them all."

The next day a double hand of hunters again spread out from the canyon to the east. They returned with enough rabbits and other small rodents to feed the camp for at least a day. Each day after that the men went to the plain, they hunted to the west as well, and over the next moon were able to provide enough food to keep The People from starving to death, just barely.

"Badger, look out!" shouted Gray Wolf, as he cast his dart. It struck soundly, and the attacking wolf yelped and dropped dead.

"I didn't see it!" exclaimed Badger, "I was trailing this rabbit that I wounded."

"So was the wolf, and he got there first," replied Gray Wolf.

"I have lost at least a hand of rabbits that way," admitted Badger, "It seems half the time all we do is help the wolves by slowing down their dinner," he attached the rabbit to the others cast over his shoulder, "I think this is the last one for today. I don't like the looks of that sky!"

"Hey! Wait a minute!" Gray Wolf went down to his knees in the snow, "look, antelope tracks; at least a double hand of them!"

"It is getting late," reminded Fire Dancer, "We can go after them tomorrow."

"They could be far away by then!"

Fire Dancer shook his head, "They lay down at night; you know that! They will be little farther tomorrow than they are now, but we will be wolf-bait if we don't get back to the protection of the cave. These rabbits are just an invitation!"

"Storm coming in," Badger remarked. Centipede Man studied the sky, shrugged and followed Fire Dancer back toward the canyon. Gray Wolf nodded, Badger was right, and it was stupid to take chances. Badger was becoming a fine hunter. He was pleased with his friend and hunting brother. Over the last few moons the pair of them had become as close as were Blue Coyote and Stone Man.

"We will all go after the antelope!" Fire Dancer stated. "If there are as many as you think, and if we are clever hunters, we should bring in enough meat to keep this camp from starving through the next moon. The pair of you are to be commended!" he smiled at the young men.

"Here are their tracks!" Centipede Man squatted in the snow, "They are headed that way, "he pointed, "Let's go!"

They had left the cave before the sun spirit had risen and were now at the spot where the tracks had been discovered. A double hand of hunters silently followed Centipede Man. They found the herd just at mid day. There was a triple span of animals, the largest group they had seen. "Probably banded together for protection against the wolves," Fire Dancer nodded, "So they will be nervous and alert. It will not be an easy hunt."

"What if we circle around down-wind? Then the pair of you ease them toward us?" Stone Man suggested, "That worked well at the escarpment."

"Keep an eye out for wolves," cautioned Badger; his experience of the previous day still fresh on his mind. Gray Wolf and he remained behind, and the rest of the hunters circled to await the antelope. "At least let's try for a couple," Badger suggested, "All we will do is send them right where we want them any way."

"I doubt we can sneak close enough to get within dart range," replied Gray Wolf, "And it would make for a more successful hunt if we do not have them at a full run when they approach the hunters."

Badger sighed but agreed. They worked their way upwind and the alert nervous antelope trotted away, toward the rest of the hunters, keeping an ever-watchful eye on them. Each hunter could possibly dart a pair of animals, provided they did not go after the same one. Suddenly the herd flashed their white rump patched and whirled about. Darts flashed and animals fell, the herd now coming directly toward the pair. Quickly they ducked and as the frightened antelope approached close rose and darted one each. The herd whirled around and fled again toward the other hunters who; seeing what was happening quickly ducked out of sight. More antelope fell as the remainder fled past the hunters and out of sight.

Blue Coyote Whooped! "We did it!" He leaped into the air and danced about in a circle, "Yes! We brought down a double hand of them! We eat!" Quickly the hunters loaded the carcasses onto their shoulders and headed back to the canyon at a fast trot. Already the wolves were howling in the distance, calling their kind to hunt, to hunt the hunters! The antelope headed to join another herd before they also became food for the predators.

"Keep close men," Centipede cautioned, "I can protect from this side, but only if someone else carries my antelope. I can't do both!"

"I can carry it!" Stone Man took the antelope. "Badger, can you carry another? Fire Dancer needs to have his hands free!" A wolf yelped!

"Got him" Centipede grinned, "Come on you rotten carnivores!" He muttered, "I have more darts!" He and Fire Dancer darted several wolves as the hunters eased toward the top of the trail. They were completely surrounded by the silent killers. Already those darted were being ravaged by the pack. The wolves were starving as well as the people. They were not so fussy! Yet more and more of the predators were drawn by the blood smell of the antelope. They eased closer and closer, hunger driving caution away. Another was darted, then another. The rest dropped away to feast on their companions, the hunters disappeared down into the canyon.

The starving time was coming to an end. Already most of the snow on the Plain had melted, a faint tinge of green grass taking its place. In the canyon spring flowers were pushing their way up through the thinning layer of white. The wolves had vanished as quickly as they had moved into the canyon, now only an occasional far away howl could be heard. The people sighed in relief. They were always hungry. A pair of old ones and Tortoise's infant had gone to walk the wind. They had indeed been lucky!

*　　*　　*

"Are you sure?" the child asked,

"Yes," the other answered.

"All right, this better work, or we will both be ripped to shreds."

"I have watched. She leaves every day at the same time. She won't return until nearly dark."

"She is alone? You have not seen a male at all?" The other child shook his head. "You are smaller, you go; I would get stuck."

"But . . . oh all right," she got down on hands and knees and peered into the dark, "I had better take off my clothes, I don't want to get them dirty," she began wiggling out of her tunic, "here, you hand me that robe when I tell you, all right? He nodded, and she began to crawl. First her head and shoulders disappeared, then only her feet were sticking out, then she was gone. He waited and waited.

"Sunflower, are you all right?" He called into the hole.

"I'm fine," her feet reappeared then the rest of her, "here, hold on to it! Don't let it chew out of that robe!" In she went again, "Hand me another robe!" her muffled voice called. Again time passed, then her feet emerged, "Here, there is one more that is all." He handed her another robe and once more she vanished. When she reappeared, she had dirt, grime and other things unmentionable in her hair and on her body. She shook and wiped away as much as possible then quickly donned her clothes, for it was still cold. They gathered their gear, dumped it as well as the tied robes and their contents onto the travois and both began pulling it back toward the cave, grinning from ear to ear.

"They are going to think we are so clever!" he chuckled, "I know where we can get at least a double hand more. I have been watching for half a moon. They are all here, in the canyon. I don't suppose you could tell how old they are?"

She shook her head, "It was dark in there, if we do this again you go in next time! And remember I get one for my very own!"

"If Fire Dancer says you can," he replied.

"That wasn't the deal! You said you asked Fire Dancer and he said it was all right! Did you lie to me?"

"Not exactly," he admitted, "I was going to ask Fire Dancer, but well . . . he was busy, and I didn't want to bother him."

"So, in fact, he could not only be less than pleased, he could be really mad at us! Honestly, Dog Boy, I don't know why I let you involve me in these hair-brained ideas of yours!" Sunflower stomped.

"It was a good idea! Just wait and see, they will all agree that we are clever and soon everyone will think so."

"Huh!" replied Sunflower, "I will probably get scolded by my mother, and I hope she refuses to let me play with you anymore, and you're a liar!"

They trudged back to the cave, keeping an eye on their cargo. Once there each took one tied robe and they carried the other between them, into the cave.

"What have you got there?" Turtle Woman spotted them.

"Uh . . . Just some old robes," Dog Boy said.

"And what have you got in 'just' some old robes?" Turtle questioned. "The last time the two of you brought something back to this cave we all smelled like a skunk for nearly a full moon, now what have you got?" She blocked their way, "You don't come into this cave until I know what you got tied in those robes!"

"Oh all right," Dog Boy sighed and settling one on the floor he carefully untied the other making sure to keep a good hold on the contents. The robe fell back, and two flipped forward ears and a pair of frightened brown eyes stared out.

"Pups! You found where one of the bitches had her pups?" Turtle Woman squeaked, "Fire Dancer will thrash you for sure!"

"Not pups!" Dog Boy corrected her, "Wolves!" He grinned, "I have been watching, and today we stole the litter! Now we will have more dogs to pull travois when we leave here," he grinned at Turtle Woman.

"Wolves! You bring wolves into the home cave! Their mother will come after them and kill us all!"

"No, she won't! She is afraid to come to this end of the canyon."

"What is going on here?" Fire Dancer tried to enter the cave.

"Wolves! These two have gone out and stolen pups from a wolf's den that is what has happened here!" Turtle Woman sputtered, "Children! What in the spirits are they going to do next?"

"Let's see what you have here," Fire Dancer knelt before the bundle, and carefully undid it. He lifted the small growling creature by the scruff and looked it over. "I see, very clever, they are old enough to eat solid food, yet still young enough to tame. How many?"

"Only these this time, but I know where there's at least a hand more dens," Dog Boy grinned. "There must be nearly a double span of pups in dens scattered through this end of the canyon. I know where at least a hand or more are."

"I see," Fire Dancer thought for a moment, "I think you had better put these in that deep storage pit at the rear of the cave. It is dark there and they will adjust quickly, before they are old enough to crawl out. Tomorrow you will take me to these other dens."

"You mean to encourage this boy?" Turtle Woman questioned.

"I have been wondering what on earth we were going to do for dogs when it is time to leave this canyon. We have less than a hand now, since the wolves killed those during the winter. Dog Boy had just supplied the solution!" He grinned at the child, "And a just solution it is. The wolves killed our dogs, and we steal their pups!"

Turtle Woman thought about it "You really think these wolf pups will tame into camp dogs?"

"Wolf did, and he was considerably older when Blue Coyote trapped him."

"It would certainly solve a big problem. Perhaps I was too hard on these children, and they are thinking of the good of the camp and not themselves. In fact now that I think of it, this was a very clever thing," she rumpled the hair of Dog Boy, "You are a scamp at times, Boy, but one day you will grow to be a good headman, like your father was."

"Now take these pups back to the storage pit and make sure they have food and water. They are your responsibility now, and when we get more, I am putting the pair of you in charge of making sure they stay where they should, get used to being handled, and are fed and watered. Can you handle such a responsible task?"

"We can do it!" Dog Boy nodded, "And I will find more dens if you want more pups, I know there is at least a pair more near here in the canyon."

Fire Dancer nodded, "we will see how many pups we are able to steal tomorrow. If everyone thinks we need more, then by all means, find the dens."

The children carried their captives, still tied in the robes, back to the storage pit. Dog Boy jumped down into the pit and Sunflower handed him first one and then another of the bundles. He untied the first and its contents leaped to the back of the pit and huddled growling and bearing teeth, shaking in fear. The next one joined it and then the last. Sunflower handed Dog Boy a large tortoise shell of water and they found some scraps of rabbit and a few bones that he gave the pups. They immediately forgot to be afraid as they snarled and fought each other over the food. "These wolves are nearly as starved as The People," Sunflower sighed, "Now we have the responsibility of feeding them as well. I hope the hunters are successful on their next antelope hunt. I am tired of going to bed hungry."

"We will go without and feed these pups if we have too. Without dogs to pull the travois, we will never get away from this canyon."

"I liked it here when first we came. The sacred beast head made me feel safe, but it did not keep us safe from the wolves attacking or from hunger."

"We are still alive; perhaps it did look after us, we have always found enough food to keep from starving. You were too young to remember the Starving Mountains . . ."

"I was not!" Sunflower protested, "You always treat me like a baby, Dog Boy, and I am only a season less than you. I can remember the Starving Mountains just as well as do you, I was nearly a hand of seasons at the time!"

"Well we had better find more food for these hungry pups, you heard Fire Dancer; they are our responsibility."

"What are we going to find to feed them?"

"There are some bones and a rabbit head over by the entrance if someone has not already fed them to the dogs. Go see," he motioned her. Sunflower ran to the entrance and pounced upon the scraps.

"Where you going with that," Turtle Woman grabbed her; "I saved those for old Scorpion! She is nursing pups!"

"We need them!" protested Sunflower, "You heard Fire Dancer; we are to feed these pups!"

"Well go find your own food!"

Sunflower sighed and returned to the storage pit and shook her head, "Turtle wouldn't let me have it; she claimed those scraps for Scorpion."

Dog Boy nodded, "She is right. It is our responsibility to provide food for these, not hers. Come on let's see what we can find." He climbed out of the pit. The wolf pups watched him and stayed as far away as possible.

"Get you bolas and a rabbit stick, I know where we might get a prairie dog or so, come on!" He led the way.

"There, see it? Just beside that sage, you are in a better position than I."

"I see it!" She took careful aim and sent her rabbit stick spinning through the air. Thunk! The prairie dog leaped, flipped onto its side, kicked a couple of times and lay still. "Got it" She started to go retrieve her kill. Dog Boy stopped her, "What?" she whispered. He pointed, "Oh, I see it," again a rabbit stick flew and again another prairie dog died.

"These should be enough for three pups!" She retrieved their kill and their weapons. "We will come back to this spot. There are lots of prairie dogs here."

They hurried back to the cave and tossed the food to their pups. They immediately began fighting over them. Two ate, and one went hungry. Sunflower sighed, "I guess we need one more prairie dog!" She turned and left the cave. Dog Boy followed more slowly. "We will soon run out of prairie dogs if we have to feed every pup one every day."

"Next time we only give each half a prairie dog," Dog Boy answered.

*   *   *

"How do you plan to get the pups out of the den?" Blue Coyote asked. A group of hunters stood around the opening to the wolf den.

"How did you get them out?" Fire Dancer questioned Dog Boy.

"Sunflower crawled in and got them," he admitted.

"Perhaps them we should have brought her rather than you," Stone Man frowned. "We are all too big to crawl into that den."

"I will go get Sunflower," Dog Boy offered.

Fire Dancer shook his head; "I have a better idea, bring Scorpion instead. Let Sunflower tend her pups while she is gone." Dog Boy grinned and ran back to the cave. Centipede Man had managed to dart the bitch wolf, so she would not be a danger to the raid on her den. He was busy skinning the carcass as they waited. They rolled the hide up and set the carcass aside for food for the dogs. Soon Dog Boy returned with Scorpion. Fire Dancer squatted down and talked to the dog. She licked his face and crawled into the den, in no time at all she returned with a pup, then another and more than a hand of them later, yet another. Then she wagged her tail and let him know that was all there were.

"We will take these back to the cave, and be sure to toss the hide into the pit with them. It will comfort them to have something with their mother's smell upon it." They all trouped back to the cave. "Now, where is the next den?" Dog Boy led them to one after another, and before dark they had a double span of wolf pups in the storage pit.

Everyone was interested in the wolf pups and soon they were scrambling all over the cave, into everything, chewing up shoes and baskets and anything they could get their sharp little teeth into. Before long everyone had their own particular choice; and the pups bonded to the people who gave them care and food. It would be a lifelong attachment on the part of the wolf, and soon there was also a ranking among the pups.

"Quick!" Stone Man shouted, "The Bison are back!" He ran into the cave and grabbed extra darts and soon he and a hand of hunters were racing up the trail to the plain. That night everyone, human and animal alike ate their fill. The hunters had darted a pair plus of bison. Already women were setting up drying racks. The wolves on the plain would no longer bother them this season, for they had a surplus of bison calves to feed upon. Soon The People would be ready to leave this starving canyon. Over the next few days another pair of bison was brought down and then Fire Dancer and Centipede Man said, enough! They had preformed the Spring Ceremony earlier in the moon. Now they began preparing to move. More deer moved into the canyon, but they did not hunt them. Every member of the camp beyond the age of eight seasons now had the responsibility of caring for and training a pup. With all the food they could eat, soon the animals grew like weeds. They were big boned and strong, and loved to pull on anything. Before spring was over, the men felt that they were old enough to begin the trek to the place of stone. The camp would travel slowly, only a short distance each day, giving the pups experience, yet not putting strain on their still growing bodies. The pups ran free and the people pulled the travois.

"Is everyone ready?" questioned Centipede Man, "make sure that you have not left behind anything that you wanted, for we cannot return for it if you do," he cautioned. "All right," everyone nodded, "Let's go!" He led the way up the trail and onto the plain.

---

1. Paleo Indian butchering techniques are known from several sites. Perhaps the clearest evidence for the technique described here is the Olsen-Chubbock site in Nebraska. The process is described as follows.

    1. Skin split, probably along backbone.

    2. Front legs, with scapula removed.

    3. Rear legs, removed at socket.

    4. Backbone severed just in front of rib cage.

    5. Backbone severed just behind rib cage.

    6 .Lower leg, actually the foot, removed, probably to be used as a hatchet for breaking ribs just below their articulation or further down.

    7. Backbone sometimes severed just in front of sacrum, sometimes not.

    8. Cervical vertebra may or may not be removed from skulls. Evidence of vertebrae laid forward across face of animal suggests neck meat removed.

    9. Mandibles often removed from skull and broken as symphysis, presumably to get at tongue.

    10. Skulls not usually, if at all, broken into for brains.

    11. Horn cores sometimes broken off as if to remove horn.

    12. Ribs and vertebrae sometimes cut into segments 3 to 5 in number.

13. After each leg was removed, there seems to have been a dissemble line. Evidence for this is as follows. Piles of pelvises, sometimes broken in half. Nearby, a pile of femora, often broken; then a pile of tibiae, usually with everything lower down gone. Tibiae sometimes broken. Likewise, piles of scapulae, then humeri, then radii, often with the ulna part missing. The humerus was often broken, the radius less often. Also piles of skulls with piles of mandibles nearby, and vertebrae and rib units concentrated, but not so much as were the other types of units. Sometimes in place of hind legs being removed at socket, the whole hind half of the animal aft the rib cage would be cut free and butchered. **WENDORF** 1962:167.

Palo Duro Canyon is 120 miles long and 20 miles wide. The People utilized only a small portion of the north end at this time.

CHAPTER 14

I would make a suggestion!" Cougar rose, the camp had been traveling for several days, now they were seated around campfires resting after a meal of bison meat, "I have been studying on a problem we have mulled over for more than a season now. This is what I have seen. We have left the old ways behind. Now we travel from place to place and call no spot home. We wear the hides of wolves for clothing, we have tamed wolves and they serve us. I would suggest that we call ourselves the Wolf Camp."

People thought about this, talked to one another and finally nodded. "I like this Wolf Camp idea," one hunter stood, then another. "It is a fitting name. We no longer gather yucca and use it for food and cordage, for we no longer live where it grows. We are wolves of the plain now! We are proud and strong!'"

"What of those of us who did not belong to the Yucca Camp," questioned another hunter? "We have always traced our lineage through the woman's camp. If we are all that is left of The People, then we must mate with members of this group to continue the line. How do we trace our relationship if we all are of the Wolf Camp?"

"We know how we are related one to another, but for those who follow us it must be stated and kept track of. We can't allow taboos to be broken. There must by a rule to follow."

"In ancient times," Pinyon rose, "descent was traced through the father, when The People moved to the Starving Mountains this was changed. There, descent was traced through the mother. If we return to the old ways, then relationships will be changed within the camp. We must have a way to remember."

"We could trace relationships by the spirit bond?" someone suggested, "Our spirit animals have powerful influence over us. It is a very strong bond."

"We are not the same people that our ancestors were, not even the same as we were when we left the Starving Mountains, but it would be very confusing if those we have called brother or sister was suddenly not related any longer. I would suggest that perhaps we could combine all these ideas. Trace the line of descent through both mother and father and make spirit ties taboo as well. That way we take no chance of angering the spirits."

"I suggest that we have Acorn confer with Wolf Spirit on this matter and report back to all their answers," suggested Fire Dancer. "What you have said is good. We do not know what faces us this season, or the next, but we are few and we must work in a relationship one with another. This last season we did well under tough conditions, but when things are not so bad, then people tend to quarrel and not get along. We must be aware of this, and we need to develop relationships that are strong within the band, yet realizing that we are all that there is, and we must also mate within the band. We will hear what Acorn has to say and decide then."

Acorn nodded and went to his shelter.

* * *

The spiral began, vividly colored, swirling warm and pulsating. Spirit Wolf came to him.

The People honor me! I am pleased! They use the fur of my children and wear it proudly. They take the offspring of my children to serve in a useful manner, this pleases me, and they did not dishonor my children by leaving their bodies to be food for other carnivores but used them to aid and sustain the people in an acceptable manner. To be also honored by The People by their claiming me openly as their guiding totem pleases me greatly.

I will guide these people and watch over them. Trace your descent through the spirit relations, as well as through both male and female lines. This is acceptable by all the spirits. Have the storyteller relate the relationships as such. Keep the lines pure, in the people and in the animals which serve you. Hold the same rules of relationship for your animals; do not allow brother and sister to mate. The circle has opened. The people have been given another chance. The woman has shown the way to honor the spirits! Soon the pair will unite and power will come to The People. See that you do not forget!

* * *

Acorn relaxed and fell into a deep sleep. On the morning he related his dream to the others, and so The People became the Wolf Camp. The storyteller related the lines of decent through the woman, and as best as he could through the man as well. Spirit relationships were also established. Many were pleased to add a spirit brother or sister to their lineage. In the end, only one remained alone, with no relatives at all; Basket.

Her mother had been of the Owl Camp, once the Bison Camp, but she had been the last member of it. Through Butterfly she was of the Yucca Camp, but then not, because Butterfly mated into the Yucca Camp but had been the last of her line as well. No one beside Basket could claim bison as their spirit guide. It made her feel very lonely.

The new relationships strengthened the ties among members of the camp. Men went out to hunt in spirit brother groups, now called hunting brothers. This traced a relationship that went back to the very beginning of the ancestors, when the spirit relations were the most important of all.

Slowly they moved toward the place of stone, keeping a vigilant eye out for raiders, danger and the chance encounter with other people.

They sat around the campfire another night. "Tell us the legend of the hunting capes," requested Stone Man, "we need to have hunting capes, and we need to initiate new men."

* * *

Pinyon told the legend. The hunters nodded and discussed ways and strategies. It was decided that the camp would rest a few days. Acorn was called upon to prepare a ceremony to cleanse the hunters selected to procure the hunting capes. Women were relegated to the far end of the camp to be sure that no female spirits drew upon the power of this ancient ceremony. He sat in his shelter and waited; Wolf Spirit came and instructed him in the ancient ways.

Acorn came to the fire. He carried his dreamer's staff and was robed in a cape, which he had made himself during the winter, preparing for the time when men must purify. He called to the ancestor spirits, made an offering of meat and plant food to the spirits of fire, sky, earth, sun and moon. He had prepared a drink earlier, made from fermented bison blood, collected by Centipede Man and Fire Dancer. The hunters had scrubbed their bodies with grass and none had touched a woman since. Atlatl, dart and bolas had been purified by passage through smoke, to drive any female spirit away which might have invaded them. This night the hunters would sleep near the fire, away from the women. The fermented drink was passed around, and each hunter drank from the horn. Then the remainder was cast into the fire.

Pinyon rose, "remember that each hunter must kill the calf himself. None other may help in any way with the preparation of the hunting cape. It must be offered to his 'totem spirit' and a prayer must be made requesting for that 'spirit' to bless the cape and aid the hunter each time he wears it. This is very important."

"The meat of the calf must also be treated in a special manner. The hunter must eat of the liver raw as soon as the animal is killed. He must also share it with his hunting brothers. Any not consumed must be given as an offering to the spirits, an offering made by fire. No part of the liver must be wasted on the ground. This is the spirit life of the animal, if it is not treated exactly as I have instructed, the hunting cape will be violated and the spirit will not aid the hunter."

He looked to his listeners; "this is very serious! The eyes may be eaten by the hunter who kills the animal and by no other. The other organ meats are to be distributed thus. The heart will be prepared only by men and eaten only by spirit brothers. The other organ meats and the tongue are to be shared equally among all hunters of the camp. The meat of the calf is to be dried, and stored separate from all other meat. This is to serve as food for the hunters before a hunt. Never may a woman touch this meat."

"The hide is to be removed with the head skin and leg skin intact. It is to be tanned only by the hunter, using the brains of the animal and his own urine and ash from the men's hearth to process the hide. A special container of wolf skin is to be made to store the hunting cape. It is to be made only from the hide of a male wolf, one killed by the hunter and the hide must be prepared by the hunter. Are there any questions?" There were none, so the gathering retired each man to his robes about the fire.

"This hunting cape ceremony must be very important!" Turtle Woman said as she stirred the stew. "I have never heard so many rules relating to one thing."

"It certainly seems that way," Willow agreed. "I was actually made to go around when I wished to pass through the other end of the camp."

"We are instructed to be careful of the weapon taboos as well," Sage added. "One would think we are unclean, the way these new rules treat us."

"They are not new rules," Star Woman reminded, "but rules far older than we, rules we have become sloppy in observing. Perhaps that is why the spirits repeatedly let us starve, maybe they are trying to remind us," she handed around bowls of stew.

"Perhaps we should consult the dreamer and storyteller regarding women's ceremonies. Maybe there are rules we have forgotten as well." Willow said.

"We should do this, just as soon as we are allowed near enough to approach them," agreed Star Woman.

"There is no need," Basket spoke, "I will tell you these ceremonies, for I have heard them from Butterfly, who heard them from Feather, who carried them from her mother on and on, right back to The Mother of The People."

"Why have you not spoken of this before?" Turtle Woman questioned.

"It has not been the time, until now," Basket replied.

*   *   *

"Tell us now!" Cottontail Girl requested.

"Very well, gather round," Basket requested. When all were seated and waiting, she began. "Women do not hunt bison!" stated Basket. "Bison are taboo for women to hunt. We are to hunt deer, antelope, and other smaller animals. Only bison are taboo for women to hunt," she rose and continued. "We are to make our atlatl of hardwood, but not of oak. Oak is for men! We are to make our darts of fruitwood, but never of oak. The flight feathers of our darts are to be from birds that are eaten, never of the eagle, nor the hawk, nor the owl. The raven is also taboo. Our bolas is to be made of rabbit hide and deer leather, never of bison. We are to respect male hunting tools and never touch them, even by accident. If we do so, by accident, the hunter must immediately destroy the weapon, so that no bison is killed with it."

"Are there also taboos regarding tools other than hunting tools?" Willow asked.

"A man's knife, blade, and scraper are to be considered hunting tools. A hunter must not use a woman's tool. They are taboo to him. We must also remove ourselves from the men during our time of blood. This has been impossible this last winter, but at this time of new beginning, the spirits request that this come back into being. We are to reestablish the blood shelter, and it may not be made of any bison product, not even sinew"

"This is a lot to remember," Sage protested. "I am not sure that I can keep it all straight."

"We will help each other to remember."

"Are we prohibited to use any part of the bison?" questioned Sage.

"We may use the hide of female bison for sleeping furs. We may eat freely of any bison meat, except the ones taken for sacred hunting capes. Our shelters may be constructed on hides of either male or female bison, only the blood shelter may not be made of bison."

"Personally, I am just as glad that we can't hunt the bison, I would be afraid if I had to try to kill one," admitted Star Woman.

"The taboo is partially to protect the women," Basket replied, "they are dangerous and unpredictable, their horns and hoofs sharp. The taboo is meant to keep the men from requiring us to help hunt bison, thus exposing us to danger. Women carry the children of The People in their womb. They are not to be exposed to such danger. Pregnant women and women nursing are prohibited from hunting altogether, until the child can walk alone. This protects both mother and child; and secures the future of The People. There are powerful spirits which protect women, these spirits can pull the strength from a hunter and expose him to danger. That is why we are all responsible, women as well as men, to observe these taboos."

"If the bison is such a male spirit, why does it claim you?" asked Sage.

Basket shook her head, "I can only guess at the answer. Perhaps because I trace descent from The Mother, or perhaps the spirits have chosen me to represent the women, I do not really know. I have frequently asked this same question and have yet to receive an answer."

"Do the spirits talk to you?"

"Talk to me? Not that I am aware of, yet sometimes . . . I get the feeling when I wake up . . ." Basket shrugged, "I just do not know!"

"You spoke to the spirits at the Sacred Pond and they sent the rain," reminded Turtle.

"That was not my idea," reminded Basket. "I just did the best that I could. But no spirit directed me, none spoke to me, none told me what to do, I just did as the legend said The Mother did, and the rain would more than likely have come any way. It was probably just a coincidence."

Star Woman shook her head, "we all saw you. You were 'spirit touched' during that ceremony, whether or not you were aware of it. So was Throw Back. She has protected you since the beginning, a special animal, and I believe that she was given for a special purpose, one we are not yet aware of. You, Basket, are not like the rest of us, you are also special."

"At times I certainly feel 'especially' alone," Basket replied. "Every one of you including the men can claim family relationships, 'totem spirit' relationships! I alone have none, and it makes me feel very lonely and outcast at times."

"Nonsense! You were born and raised in this camp! You are like my own child!" protested Star Woman, "I could not feel closer to you had I carried you within my body! It is just that you are special to the women, sort of our very own dreamer, and this sets you apart, but it also ties you to each of us in a very personal way. You alone are of the ancient line; in a way you are our 'Mother' showing us the ancient paths that women are to follow. You are important to each and every one of us in a way no other can be."

Basket hugged Star Woman and tears ran down her face, "it is just that sometimes I feel so very alone," she sighed.

"I think that each of us has those times," Turtle Woman replied, "I know that I have. When I was young . . ." she started to say something, then changed her mind, "when my first mate died, I felt cast loose. Cougar has given me new ties, but for a long time I felt that I was merely a burden upon the camp and particularly upon my family who was obliged to provide for me during the starving times. In a way this was worst of all, for I was causing stress for those whom I loved the most, and other than making the choice to walk the wind, there was nothing I could do about it."

"You did a great deal!" protested Star Woman, "you gathered and grubbed right along with the rest of us, doing your share, and at times more than that."

"I hope that someday we will be able to put the time in the Starving Mountains behind us," Star Woman stated, "we need to look ahead, not behind!"

* * *

At dawn the men quietly left the camp. They went in groups, each in a different direction, each a group of hunting brothers. Their goal was one hunting cape for each group. The oldest hunter in each group was to take the first calf. Once it was properly processed, they would hunt again. Pinyon, Cougar and Centipede Man were those men.

Red Tail Hawk had claimed Pinyon, Gray Wolf, Chipmunk and Jackrabbit on their spirit quests as youths. Until now, this spirit relationship had been more or less ignored. Wolf claimed Blue Coyote very closely, but also Stone Man, Centipede Man and Badger. While, Eagle claimed Fire Dancer, Porcupine, Squirrel, and the Wolf Spirit of all dreamers also claimed Acorn, the dreamer, he being the only member of the camp with two spirits. Acorn would not hunt bison, however, so he had no need for a hunting cape. This left the others to accomplish the task.

Jackrabbit and Pinyon led the way, Gray Wolf and Chipmunk followed. They headed north where bison had been seen some distance from the camp. Try as they might, however, they could not find the herd. Finally they gave up and returned to camp.

The Wolf Pack had better luck. Before noon, Centipede Man had secured his kill. Eagle led Cougar to his calf at sun high. Both groups were careful to follow the rules very carefully, and both returned to camp long before the Red Tail Hawks. While they began the ritual processing of the two calves, the last group garnered its calf and joined in, Pinyon now able to grin and joke as well. The camp spent a hand of days in that location before moving on. They traveled another hand of days and hunted again. Jackrabbit, Stone Man and Porcupine then had hunting capes. Just before reaching the place of stone they again hunted, leaving Chipmunk, Badger, Fire Dancer, and Squirrel still without.

"I think we should camp here and scout the river valley before moving to the quarry," Fire Dancer peered down into the arroyo. "I see no signs of people, but Red Eagle could still be around somewhere. I would rather not take that chance."

"Red Eagle is probably far away from here!" Blue Coyote replied, "If he was ever here, remember when I overheard them talking, they decided to go north along the plain."

"They still needed stone, and this is where they would come to get it." Fire Dance was firm.

"The Wolf Pack will scout the canyons then," Stone Man replied, "just to be sure."

The camp settled for a time while the men scouted the arroyo, reported it empty of humans and they filed down the trail and into the quarry campsite. They settled into three caves, located side by side in a small canyon just beyond the quarry. Each hunting pack took possession of a cave, and the women settled with their mates, or relatives. Star Woman, Turtle Woman, Antelope Woman and her daughter Sunflower shared the cave with the Eagle pack. Water Woman and her daughter Moth as well as Sage, her young brother, Dog Boy, and Cottontail Girl settled with the Wolf Pack. Willow and Basket settled with the Red Tail Hawks. Right away people could see this wouldn't work.

The farthest cave was brought into use, moving the Red Tails into it, moving the Wolf next and placing the unmated females in the cave vacated by the Wolf Pack. This placed Willow, Cottontail Girl, Feather Woman, Tortoise, Sage and Basket together, and Dog Boy with them for he was the responsibility of his sister, Sage. He howled and complained and refused! In the end he was sent to the Wolf Pack because there, Centipede Man could keep an eye on him. This arrangement worked, and it was decided that it would be maintained even after leaving the place of stone, which they planned on doing just as soon as they had an ample supply of material.

*　　*　　*

Basket gathered up her atlatl and darts and her bolas and called to Throw Back. She had been uneasy ever since they arrived at the place of stone. The men were busy, the women had their tasks and she was, as usual, feeling somewhat outside of it all. There were activities for the women regarding their spirit helpers. They were preparing for a special, 'women's feast. Basket had no one to prepare with, and so she was going hunting.

"Throw Back let's go!" She called.

"Woof!" Throw Back answered, her blue eyes sparkling in anticipation. This was the first time since leaving the escarpment that they had been free to go out by their selves. It felt good just to get away from the camp for a while and be free! She led the way up the river for a hand of time, just enjoying the quiet and the companionship of the wolf.

Basket, however, was almost feeling nervous. Something was, well not exactly wrong, but she couldn't explain the restlessness she was feeling. They ate their midday meal a hand's distance away from the camp. This was a wide river valley full of game, but they were not in any hurry. Several fine deer jumped up at their approach, but Basket did not even reach for her atlatl, she just enjoyed watching the graceful animals leap away and disappear from sight.

Fire Dancer would not approve of her going out like this on her own, with just Throw Back so she had not told him. Finally she had just enough time to dart a deer and return to the camp before it got really dark. Regretfully she did so, dressing the animal and giving thanks for its gift. Then she loaded it onto the travois, assembled from parts she carried, and they started back down the valley headed toward the quarry. The birds were singing and the sun was warm and absolutely everything was right, so! Why did she feel so restless?

*   *   *

"People are coming!" Dog Boy leaped from rock to rock, announcing as he sped into camp from his favorite perch atop the highest point on the bluff. "They are on the other side of the river, and they don't look much like us!"

"Quickly, everyone, Pinyon, Jackrabbit, take the women and children and dogs up the canyon and stay there, out of sight until someone comes for you, Dog Boy, you go with them!"

"I saw them first! I want to know who they are!" he protested.

"Go!" Fire Dancer had no time to argue, "You endanger us all with this arguing!"

He went, not happily, but obediently.

"Smother all of the fires and find places to hide and observe. Perhaps they will not stop."

"They will need stone," reminded Centipede Man, "they will stop. Hopefully they will not come into this canyon, and we have not been here long enough to have left many signs of our presence."

"Maybe we could scare them away! I wish we had asked how many there are!" Stone Man said.

"We will soon know. I can hear them approaching." whispered Fire Dancer.

"I hope it isn't Red Eagle!" Blue Coyote added.

"No, they are strangers. I do not recognize any of them. They dress differently as well. Can anyone hear what they say?" Centipede Man asked.

"I can hear, but I do not understand them. They speak differently than we," Stone Man said.

The strangers numbered almost as many as the Wolf Band, and they traveled in family units. Their dogs were small, brown, flop-eared creatures, much like the Starving Mountain dogs of The People. They had no wolf blood in them.

Pinyon scrambled up to join them, "Is Basket with you?" he questioned,

"No, of course not. Isn't she with the women?"

"No, Willow said she went out early with Throw Back after a deer."

Fire Dancer started to rise; Blue Coyote pulled him back down, "she is with Throw Back, Father she will be all right."

"I hope so I don't know what we would do if they captured her, for they certainly would not let her go freely."

"I just hope they get their stone and leave quickly!" muttered Centipede Man.

"They look to be settling in," Stone Man observed.

The strangers were unharnessing their dogs, laughing and unpacking their shelter hides. A pair of women took water skins and followed the path to the river. Obviously these people had visited here before, for they were relaxed and knowledgeable about the layout of the quarry.

"What do we do?"

"Stay where we are and wait!"

"What about the women and children?" Pinyon questioned. "Someone gather sleeping furs and food and take it to them. It will not hurt if they spend the night up the canyon," Fire Dancer replied.

"What about Basket?" Stone Man questioned.

"She will just have to see to herself," Fire Dancer replied, "I cannot jeopardize the entire camp for one person, not even Basket! Besides, as Blue Coyote pointed out, she has Throw Back with her."

All afternoon they sat hidden in the rocks, the sun beating down on them. Fire Dancer was uneasy, wondering where Basket could be; should he have sent one of the men back up the canyon and over into the valley to find her. He might have told Stone Man that she was on her own, but he was far more conscientious regarding his camp. He was mulling over the idea of sending Blue Coyote after her. Still, he did not do so.

They waited, night settled in, still they waited. The people camped below looked weary and travel-warn. They were unkept and several showed sighs of wounds. They now sat around their campfire, listening to an old man talk. "I think I can understand what he is saying," Pinyon whispered, "he talks funnily, but the more I listen, the more I can understand him."

"What is he saying?"

*   *   *

"He is telling the story of the ancient ones, those who once lived here and hunted the great beast. He is telling the story of someone called The Chosen. This is the ancient name for The Mother of The People. They may look strange, and talk strangely, but they are of The People."

*   *   *

Basket lay concealed a short distance beyond the camp of the strangers. She had Throw Back held to her, hushing her, and she also was listening. At first she also had a hard time understanding what these strange people were saying. At least she now understood why she had been so restless. She must have sensed that there were others nearby. As soon as she saw them, all her fears settled. She had scrambled quickly into concealing brush before the women making their way to the river for water caught a glimpse of her and Throw Back; her deer lay on the travois just below, where she had unhooked Throw Back and eased up in the brush.

Do it! Now! She sighed. This was no time for voices in her head! For a hand of time now she had been advised to walk boldly into the camp. She eased back, drawing Throw Back with her, and quickly attached the harness. She would just have to go back up the river to another trail and come down the canyon to the caves. It was a long way to drag a deer. Throw back however, had other ideas, before Basket could stop her she trotted up the trail and into the camp of the strangers. She stopped just beyond the light of the campfire. Basket could not leave her friend, nor ignore the voices in her head. She stepped out into the light beside Throw Back.

Absolute silence descended on the camp. The storyteller stuttered to a halt, right in the midst of his tale mouth-hanging open in surprise. The headman frowned, and a number of hunters made moves toward their weapons. He raised a hand and halted them. The camp seemed to freeze into stillness. Then a girl gasped, "Chosen", and the camp watched in awe as Basket and Throw Back walked completely into their presence. Basket, feeling almost as if a stranger was moving her arms and legs, pulled the deer from the travois and dragged it to the edge of their camp. She laid it there, bowing and backing gracefully back, as was the custom of a well-behaved woman of the people when presenting a gift. Then she waited.

So did the hunters above, poised to descend and do harm to anyone who made an unfriendly move toward her. "What is she doing?" Whispered Blue Coyote, "has she completely lost her mind? I am going in there!"

Fire Dancer pulled him back, "wait! No one has made any move to harm her. Do not do anything that might endanger her! Throw Back would never allow her to come to harm!"

Within the newcomer's camp, the old storyteller quaked like a leaf in a strong breeze, opening and closing his mouth. He had been so wrapped up in his tale he had not seen the woman until she and the animal beside her had stepped into the light, almost as if he had called them from the spirit land to join the camp. The first to move was the girl who had named this apparition; she rose and went to stand before Basket, completely unafraid. "Are you the Chosen One?" she asked in an awed voice, then; "may I touch you?"

"Star Child!" wailed the mother, "Come away!"

The girl glanced at her mother, then reached out and actually touched Basket, almost as though she could not help herself. When she did so, a faint humming began, deep inside, and her arm throbbed with pleasure, her amulet pulsed like a second heart beat. She felt an unbelievable sense of peace and well being. The feeling was absolutely right!

Basket had nodded, and the girl reached out and touched her. A soft blue aura enveloped the pair of them, causing all that watched to gasp. Basket felt her amulet throb and the spot on her arm give a leap of joy. Inside, she became calm and peaceful. The girl reached out and traced the mark on Baskets arm; a glittering of almost unbelievable joy in her blue eyes. The girl smiled and turned to her mother, "the Chosen One is our friend," she announced. "See she has the same mark on her shoulder as I have on mine. We are spirit sisters!"

"I come in peace," stated Basked in a clear voice, "I would be recognized."

The headman of the camp rose then and stepped forward. "I am Bison Man, Headman of the Eagle Camp. Who asks to be recognized?"

"I am called Basket! I am a woman of The People! I wear the teeth of the Long Toothed Cat, I carry the ancient staff of the Mother of The People; I walk with the ancient wolf and wear the owl feather. I am sent from The Mother to unite The People." Basket had no idea what she was saying, for she was as scared as were the people she faced. Had it not been for Throw Back she would be long away from here going farther. The words were just coming from her mouth unaided by her.

"You bring a gift of peace. This is recognized, you would be made welcome, but where are your people?"

"I am of The People," she replied, obviously having no difficulty understanding their way of speaking.

"This small band is all that remain of The People," the headman shook his head. "We were caught in a stampede and attacked by raiders and many of our number were killed. Now we seek a place where we can live peacefully, harming no man and seeking harm from none."

"That place does not exist," Basket stepped forward, clearly into the light. They could see her clearly now, a small girl-woman standing beside the largest wolf any had ever seen. She was as she had claimed, of The People. But she was dressed more strangely than any had ever seen, for although her clothing was of a style similar to their own, it was made entirely of wolf pelts. And the animal beside her was certainly a wolf. She was powerful indeed to have control over such an animal.

Then from out of the shadows stepped another creature, one nearly as terrifying. Wolf walked to join Throw Back. Again silence. Fire Dancer stepped forward, as did Centipede Man, Blue Coyote and Stone Man. The rest stayed hidden in the rocks, ready to attack should it be necessary.

*   *   *

"I am Fire Dancer, Headman of the Wolf Camp," he stepped forward, "Basket is of my camp, she was out hunting when you arrived and was cut off from entry into our camp. We are of The People, and we live in peace, offering harm to none, asking the same in return."

"I have not heard of a Wolf Camp among The People."

"Once, long ago we were called the Bison Camp," Basket replied.

The headman nodded, "We know of that camp, can you really be the 'Chosen One' returned to guide us in the ancient paths?"

"So some say," Fire Dancer replied. "You have been offered a gift, do you accept and invite us in, or do we remain outside?"

The headman was backed into a corner and he knew it. Tradition insisted that he invite them in because he had already accepted the gift. "You are welcome," he said with a sigh.

Fire Dancer nodded and waved to the men in the rocks, "Pinyon, go and get the camp, tell them it is safe to return," he turned back to Bison Man, "we will talk."

Star Child still stood before Basket, eyeing the animal standing patiently with her. "She will not harm you," Basket said, reading the other girl's thoughts, and the girl stepped cautiously forward and reached out and touched the throw back. Throw Back licked her hand and thrust her head beneath it to be petted. Star Child laughed delightedly.

"Why, you are little older than am I," Star Child said, getting a good look at Basket finally, "I lack but a season of being three hands."

"I am just the same," admitted Basket.

"And you are chosen!"

"Chosen?"

"By Bison, you bear the mark of Bison," nodding to Basket's shoulder.

"Bison is my spirit guide, is that what you mean?"

"Oh, it is more than that! Prairie Dog says this mark means that we were chosen to be spirit leaders of The People, 'spirit guides'. Do the 'spirits' not speak to you?"

"Sometimes," admitted Basket, "Just now they made Throw Back disobey and come into your camp, they wanted me to let myself be known, and when I chose instead to slip away, they had Throw Back decide for me."

"Throw Back, is that her name?"

"Fire Dancer said that she was a throw back to an ancient kind of wolf when she was born, so everyone just called her that. Now it is her name."

"And this other wolf, does he live with you as well?"

"We have many wolves which live with us, which is why we call ourselves the Wolf Camp."

"And do all of you dress in wolf skins as well?"

Basket nodded, "It was a hard year in the Secret Canyon and there were many wolves and not much food. We killed the wolves before they killed us. They stole the bison meat and they killed our dogs. So we killed them in return, fed their flesh to what remained of our dogs, and now wear their hides, we stole their pups and made them into friends and companions. Thus, we honor Wolf, our spirit leader."

"You live here, in these canyons?"

Basket shook her head; "we are here for the same reason as you, to get stone. Had you been a hand of days earlier, or later, we would not have met."

Star Child shook her head, "we would have met. I could feel you, the closer we came to this place, the stronger the feeling. That is why I was not so surprised when you stepped into the campfire light. I was calling you"

"Then it was your voice I heard just now, and not that of some 'spirit'!" Basket sighed, "You say that you had been drawing me to you? Is that what I have been feeling lately, your approach?"

"Probably, if it was an uneasy feeling, like someone was going to jump out and scare you, but you didn't know when or where."

"That sort of describes it. I went hunting today on my own, just to get away and think, Fire Dancer frowns upon anyone going out alone. Red Eagle is out there somewhere, just waiting," she shivered.

"Red Eagle? Is he horribly scared with only one eye, and leader of the raiders?"

"I don't know what he looks like now, once he was very pleasant to look at, but that is all. He was nasty as a boy, nasty as a youth, and much more than that as a mate."

"You were mated to the raider?"

"He wasn't a raider then, merely a youth with his eye on things not belonging to him. He killed my grandmother, which is why he is an outcast. If he is horribly scared, that probably happened the night he nearly killed me and Throw Back knocked him into the fire. He had both eyes last time I saw him."

"If Red Eagle is the raider, he is badly scared, fire burns down one side of his face and badly healed wounds down the other, the one without an eye." Basket shuddered. "The rest of his band is almost as bad. They captured me and would have killed me but for my father. He gave them the sacred spear point, which has been with this camp since ancient times. He should have let them kill me," she said bitterly, "Nothing has gone well with this camp since the relic was taken. The bison stampeded and trampled our camp and most of our dogs as well, and then we had no tools with which to hunt. We have walked hard and far to reach this place."

"That sounds like Red Eagle. I also had a sacred object, pointed at one end, as long as my hand," Star Child nodded, "Red Eagle forced me to give it to him. Then he demanded the teeth of the Long Toothed Cat as well. He would have demanded the staff also, but he did not know of it!"

"I have heard of the teeth, but we all thought them lost generations ago. They just vanished with the 'keeper' and no one ever saw either of them again."

"My mother was called Feather, she had them, when she died she made my grandmother save them to give to me upon the time of first blood. I have no idea how she came by them, but all say that she was a descendant of The Mother, and she had the same sign on her arm."

"Really! My mother does not have it. No one I know has ever been so marked, until now!"

"Star Child, you are to go to your mother," an elderly woman called.

"Yes, Makes a Robe, I will, soon."

"Now," insisted Makes a Robe.

Star Child sighed, "We will talk again tomorrow," she bid Basket good night.

Basket left the camp and led Throw Back to the cave where she unharnessed the animal and gratefully crawled into her furs.

Far into the night the men of the two camps talked. They had much to say. With each hand of time more and more they were glad that the camps had come together.

The next morning the Eagle Camp moved into the canyon and erected their shelters below the caves. The women first eyed each other with caution and then gradually began to talk. By evening there was only one camp.

"Wolf Spirit has demanded we have a celebration!" announced Acorn, "To welcome our spirit brothers and to become one with them!" Moon, Dreamer of the Eagle Camp agreed.

"We have as a Relic, one of the ancient bison capes," admitted Bison Man, "I will show it to you if you wish."

Fire Dancer nodded, "I would like to see it. We are trying to follow the legends which Pinyon relates, but I have never seen what one actually looks like." Bison Man led the way to his shelter and rummaged through the contents of his travois until he uncovered a ratty looking hide carrier at the very bottom.

"It has not always looked so poor," he apologized, but this hide is so old it is falling to pieces. Perhaps we should make a new carrier such as you have," he unrolled the hide and exposed the hunting cape. The head and tail had indeed been kept intact, but the hide had been removed from the legs without splitting it. They had split theirs. There were lacings to hold it in place, and intricate design along the edge. Fire Dancer fingered the hide; it had been wonderfully tanned and was indeed very ancient. He offered the holder he had made for his own hunting cape to protect it. Bison Man accepted gladly, admiring the deep wonderful fur and the clever way the container was constructed, the head of the wolf folding down to close the opening, feet crossed and the tail hanging free.

The women of the two camps found they also had much to talk about. It was wonderful, for both to have new people to converse with, to share ideas and experiences with. To hear new experiences was always a treat, particularly when one seldom saw a new face.

*　　*　　*

"We are going down to the stream to wash," Basket called to Star Woman, who merely nodded in return. Basket had given Star Child her extra tunic, and Star Child was anxious to change into it. Star Woman and Rain Woman, Star Child's mother, were in the process of making a new tunic for Rain Woman. The women of the Eagle Camp were thrilled to be invited to dress in the same manner as those of the Wolf Camp. Star Child and Basket had been nearly inseparable since meeting. Star Child had begged and pleaded until finally her parents had consented and she had moved into the unmated woman's cave as well. The pair and Throw Back made their way to the stream in the side canyon, where with the aid of soap made of ashes and bison fat. They washed their bodies and their hair. It was the first opportunity for bathing that Basket had since leaving the spirit canyon, and it had been just as long for Star Child.

"Do you think we could braid my hair like you wear yours" asked Star Child.

"I see no reason why not," replied Basket, "It is the way many of us wear our hair while traveling, and now that we travel constantly, most of the women are doing so." Star Child slipped her new wolf-hide tunic over her shoulders and Basket combed her hair and expertly braided it. Then she pulled on her own tunic and did her own hair. The two grinned at each other and headed back to camp.

*　　*　　*

Rain Woman stopped in mid-sentence. Star Woman stared, open-mouthed. Basket and Star Child stopped, looked at them in some confusion, "By the spirits!" yelped Star Woman; "they could be twins!"

"I cannot tell which is which!" admitted Rain Woman.

"We look alike?" questioned Star Child.

"As much so that you could be one person," nodded Star Woman. I had not noticed more than a superficial resemblance before, I mean they are of a size, but Star Child was so scruffy . . ."

"And Basket so unkept," added Rain Woman.

The young women looked at each other; "You are what I look like?" questioned Basket,

"If you are what I look like," answered Star Child,

"How can this be?"

"She lied to me," whispered Rain Woman.

"Who lied to you?" Star Child questioned.

"That creature that brought you to me," Rain Woman stated, "She never said there was another one."

"Mother, what are you talking about?" Star Child whispered.

"I never told you. It was for your own safety. I tried, several times, but I just couldn't. You are my child. I raised you from an infant, gave you my own dead child's place in my life, and in my heart," she pleaded.

"You are not my mother?" Star Child went white.

Rain Woman shook her head, wiping the tears from her eyes. "I did not give birth to you, but I most certainly am your mother, in every way which counts," she sobbed. "My child, my beautiful baby girl, she died. The men were out hunting, far from camp. They had been away nearly a moon. This woman came into the camp. She was old, sick, and nearly dead. She had you wrapped in a robe, clutched to her chest. She was frightened, claimed men were trying to kill her, to kill you. She died right there in my arms. And you, you were the same age as my dead child. No one knew, for only I knew that she was dead. I switched places with the pair of you. When the men came, I led them to where we had laid out the old woman. I put my child with her, and the men went away satisfied. You have been mine ever since, not even Bison Man knows. To a man, all babies look alike. He had been gone for a moon, during that length of time babies grow and change. He never knew. No one did."

"Who was this woman?" questioned Star Woman.

Rain Woman shook her head, "she did not give me a name, the only thing she said was that the child was special and must be saved at all costs. She gave me the sacred Ancient Relic and said that Feather would come for the child. No one by that name ever came, no one ever claimed her."

"Feather, was my mother's name," Basket said, "She died before I could walk."

"Do you think?"

"Could it be possible?"

"We are sisters, twins?" They said in a single voice.

"That is why I could feel you as we came to this place!" Star Child nodded, "We shared the same womb, were born of the same body!"

*   *   *

"That is impossible!" Star Woman stated mouth agape. "Feather died in the Starving Mountains!"

"If that is the name you give to the mountains beyond the moving sand, this is also where we lived at the time. But we left there and traveled far south and then east and have been living on these plains for many seasons, following the bison herds."

"But how could she have given birth to twins and no one know?"

"She was certainly large enough," Turtle Woman had been silently listening to the conversation. "And that crazy mother of hers delivered Basket. She disappeared right after that and was never seen or heard of again."

"And you think that Feather. . . no that is not possible; she was certainly odd but split up twins! That would be bad luck indeed," Star Woman shook her head.

"And what have we had ever since?" asked Turtle Woman.

It makes for a good tale, but who would want to kill babies, especially twins?" Rain Woman asked.

"The dreamer! That's who!" Star Woman sat up, "White Falcon! You remember him?" She looked to Turtle Woman; "He raped you when you were barely a woman."

Turtle Woman shuddered, "It would be something he would do. He was obsessed with 'power', and twins born to Feather, they would be very powerful. It does make sense, strange as it is. And it all fits. He hated Basket from her birth. Butterfly was always afraid of him."

"Who is White Falcon," Basket questioned, "I have never heard the name mentioned?"

"No one speaks it," Admitted Star Woman, "nor should you. He was evil, gone over to bad 'spirits'. You were still a baby when they sealed him in that cave . . ."

"Alive?"

"Oh yes, he was very much alive. Screaming like a demented thing, his scrawny body barely more substantial than the tattered eagle feather robe he wore. I can still hear his screams some nights," Turtle Woman shuddered.

"Why would the men of the Yucca Camp do so terrible a thing?"

"Because he raped me," cried Turtle Woman, "He was a dreamer, and he raped me." She sat rocking back and forth sobbing.

Star Woman went to her, taking her into her arms, "It is all right Turtle; it was long ago, far away, best forgotten!" She rocked her sister back and forth. "His spirit was locked in that cave forever. It cannot escape. You are safe Turtle, safe and far away."

"Hey Basket!" Willow came running up, "We are going to call wolves, want to come?" She spoke directly to Star Child.

"I might, if you asked Me!" Basket replied, smiling widely.

Willow looked at one, then the other, her mouth fell open, her eyes grew round, and whispered, "Spirits help us!"

"I want to go call wolves," Star Child stated, "I have never been to a wolf calling!" She glanced at Rain Woman and the others; not easy about leaving them after all they had heard, yet wanting to get away where she could think. Rain Woman nodded with understanding.

"Well I think we have both been invited," Basket stated, "And you have no idea how to call a wolf, so come along, and learn!"

"Are the others ever going to be surprised" Willow exclaimed, "How did this happen?"

"We went to the stream to wash, used the same water, the same soap, and came out the same," Basket grinned at her reflection, which grinned back. *This could be fun!*

*   *   *

"I will be back before dark!" Turtle called to her mother, "When Star returns tell her that I am sorry that I didn't meet her, but this message is important." The girl hurried off to meet with the dreamer. He had promised her a special ceremony to bring her first blood. All of the other girls had begun and become women a season ago. Only Turtle, at double hands plus a pair was still a girl. The dreamer had promised to help. He was waiting at the spirit cave. Turtle dared not be late or he might change his mind.

She ran down the trail and a hand of time later arrived at the dreamer's cave. Few had ever been inside, but they had claimed that the cave was really special. Turtle was feeling very special for she had been invited in for this ceremony. She arrived out of breath but stopped short of the cave and settled her pulse and got her breathing under control. The dreamer was waiting.

Turtle hesitated at the entrance and called out, "Dreamer, White Falcon!" A voice invited her in. Her eyes adjusted to the subdued light. People were right! The cave had the most wonderful pictures painted upon the walls.

"Come here child," called the dreamer, "I am ready to begin."

Turtle came further into the cave and saw the dreamer, seated beside a pile of furs.

"You must drink all of it," he handed her a tortoise shell of liquid. Turtle did as she had been bid, swallowing the drink. It tasted awful, strong and bitter. She grimaced. "Now lay back and wait until the potion takes affect," instructed the dreamer. Turtle did so, and soon the room began to get fuzzy, then it seemed to move. Her eyes drifted closed.

Pain shot through her body, jerking her to wakefulness. The dreamer was on top of her, lying on her stomach, and he must be inserting something inside her, in her woman's place! It hurt dreadfully! Turtle screamed. White Falcon jerked up his head. His face was contorted, and he was panting hard. He grunted again and again as he continued to shove inside her. Turtle tried to push him off, but he was too heavy. On and on he kept stabbing into her. Finally, with a groan, he jerked and collapsed onto her. Turtle was extremely frightened, she was still very groggy from the drink, and she hurt, and she was being squashed, and suffocated as well. When finally he rolled off her, Turtle could see that his exposed man member was all bloody and she could feel blood on her inner thigh as well.

Sobbing she tried to get up, but she was still groggy from the spirit drink and her insides felt on fire with pain. The dreamer grabbed her by the shoulders and shoved her back into the furs. "You tell anyone of this, and I will send evil spirits to shrivel your soul!" He hissed, "You wanted to be a woman, to bleed, well see! You bleed!" He jerked her by the hair and showed her the blood. "Go now and have you 'woman's ceremony'," he commanded, "But remember, keep your mouth shut or . . ."

Turtle staggered, still sobbing from the cave. She was distraught and paid little attention as she hurried back to the camp. She kept wiping the blood away, but it kept coming. She crawled into her furs back at the camp and rolled into a small ball of misery. Her whole insides hurt. She lay sobbing quietly into the furs. This is where and how her mother found her. Her mother could draw nothing from her that made any sense. She discovered the blood. Star arrived but Turtle was so upset even she could not make sense of her blubbering. The healer was called, and he gave her a drink that took away the pain. The headman, Fire Dancer was called, and he and her mother questioned Turtle again and again, and finally Turtle broke down and told them what had happened.

*   *   *

"I make a promise to you," Star Child said solemnly. She and Basket were seated beneath a huge oak tree far up the canyon. "I will never be parted from you again. We are of a single soul, a single mind, and a single body, one parted into a pair. Legend demands we remain together. For the sake of The People!" She passed her hand dramatically upward; "Our destiny is one!" She bowed her head and gave a deep sigh.

Basket tilted her head. "Well, that was certainly dramatic enough!" She replied.

Star Child grinned, "I did that well, didn't I?"

Basket nodded, "But seriously, what do you think this all means? If it is really true that Feather was your mother as well as mine, and it certainly seems irrefutable that this is so, where does that leave us?"

"Well, if bad luck has followed your camp ever since your birth as it certainly has mine, then maybe the legend is right, and separating us had brought this upon The People. If this is so, logically, as long as we remain together, good luck should come to the camp!"

"The legend doesn't say that," reminded Basket, "Only that bad luck follows the separation of twins."

"All right," Star Child frowned, "But there must be something special about us! Bison chose you, and me, and no one else can claim that! I have voices in my head," she admitted, "At least from time to time, and I did feel you!"

"You spoke to me very clearly the first night here at the quarry." Basket replied.

"Really! I wonder if we can do that; I mean, speak to each other without talking? That would be really something! Let's see if it works! You go down the canyon, and I will call to you."

"That is silly!" Basket protested! "I can talk to you right here."

"Come on, at least try!" Star Child pleaded. "It could be all kinds of useful!"

"Oh, all right!" Basket sighed "But I still think it's kind of silly!" She rose and ambled a way down the canyon, Throw Back at her side.

That's far enough! Basket halted in mid-stride, her eyes open in surprise.

Did you do that, she questioned?

Sure did; came the reply.

Tell me something else. Something that I couldn't possibly know. I don't trust that I'm not just thinking this! Basket was not convinced.

When I was a child of a hand of season's I had a favorite toy. It was a hide in the shape of a dog. I named it Puppy! Star Child replied.

That wasn't a very original name!

No worse than Throw Back!

I didn't name her that! Fire Dancer did.

Wolf isn't a very clever name either! Your camp has no imagination!

And yours does?

Well, perhaps not.

Basket stepped beneath the oak again. Both girls grinned at each other.

"I can't believe we just did that!" Basket shook her head.

"It was really something, wasn't it?" Star Child grinned.

They began practicing on their 'calling' all of the time. They even went into separate canyons and practices. Loud and clear, they spoke with their minds, it worked every time. If the people found them a little confusing, they were polite enough not to say so. If at times one or both broke out into a fit of giggles, Rain Woman might frown, but everyone soon just ignored such things. They were, after all, twins, and that made them different.

Soon the camps got used to the Basket-Star Child pair. There was little problem figuring out which was which, because they were always together. After spending so many seasons separated, they could not get enough of being together, of belonging. For the first time in her life, both felt complete. Basket finally had family, she belonged, and she was part of something very special- she was a twin! Her immediate world blossomed! Never had she felt so complete, never had she felt so much a part of someone else.

Star Child had always felt a pull at her soul. Now that pull was gone, she had Basket! Throw Back went everywhere with the pair. She was a bit more reserved with other people, Basket had always been her 'special person' and now Star Child came very close to entering in that association, but not quite. Throw Back would not go with Star Child unless Basket told her to, no matter how much Star Child called and enticed. Throw back would finally just yawn, close her blue eyes, cuddle next to Basket and ignore Star Child.

Star Child wanted a wolf of her own so badly she could almost taste it, yet she did not say a word. That would be very impolite, and there were so many hunters without dogs, she could hardly justify her want. Basket, of course, sensed this, but she was nearly as helpless as Star Child.

It will be spring before we can raid the wolf dens; you will just have to wait!

But why; sometimes wolves mate late and, we could go up the canyon and at least look, couldn't we . . . ?

None of the females we have called in are still nursing. I am sorry, but you will just have to wait until spring.

I will find a way . . .

Don't do something foolish!

Blue Coyote told me that he trapped his wolf and tamed it!

Well that was Blue Coyote, and a really stupid thing to do any way, even if it did work. But we are not trapping a wolf! We leave here in a few days any way, no time . . . And we will be traveling all of the time. There won't be time to hunt for a den, even if we did come across a female still nursing. But don't worry! When the spirits want you to have a wolf, you will have one. That is the way they work

But I want a wolf now! I can't wait!

You can't do anything about it. The spirits decide such things.

Both girls sighed. But Star Child waited, impatiently, but she waited....

CHAPTER 15

I trusted you! You promised me those teeth! You want Power, yet you continually fail to bring me what I ask for. I will not give you anything! No Fire Dancer! No Blue Coyote! Nothing! Not power, not control, nothing!

*   *   *

"I don't need your power!" Red Eagle shouted back at the creature dancing before him. He was getting tired of the 'spirit' and his continuing demands. He, Red Eagle had handled Black Deer without any help from 'spirits'. He would handle Fire Dance the same way. He ran his finger over the smooth surface of the power object; it would give him 'power' far more than the spirit in his head.

"Get out of my head!" he muttered, "leave me!"

You owe me! Screeched the voice, *you can't just walk away and ignore me!* Red Eagle closed his mind and turned it to other things. The voice was silenced. He sighed. Always his head ached, ever since that animal of Basket's had knocked him into the fire and he had cracked his head on a stone. Ever since that creature had taken out his eye, and scared him for life, twisting his face into a grotesque parody of the once handsome continence. It always came back to Basket!

He rubbed the power object again smiling; the voice didn't know he had it. Finally, late into the night he slept . . .

*   *   *

"What are you doing, Father?" The child Red Eagle questioned, trotting along beside his father.

"Go back to the camp, boy, this is nothing for you, go stay with your mother."

"But where are you and the hunters going and what are you doing?"

"Men's work, Son," was his answer. The man he called Father, watched as the boy trudged back toward the camp, then turned to rejoin the group of grim-faced men, led by Fire Dancer, new headman of the Yucca Camp. The men filed silently to the west. Long into the evening they dragged, hauled, and carried the largest boulders and rocks they could, until the light was gone and they could no longer see. Behind them, hidden and watching silently was the child. When the men headed back to the camp, he scampered quickly ahead of them. For a pair of days he followed and watched them, curious, but unable to get close enough to see what they were doing. Then they did not go to the place. Red Eagle slipped quietly from the camp and ran all the way there. He slipped inside. It was a wondrous place. The walls were covered with pictures; pictures of strange animals and people so alive they seemed to move. He ran his fingers over the walls, absorbing the essence of the place, there were huge beasts, each with an extra leg and teeth that reached the ground and curved back again. He saw animals with sharp horns and huge hairy bodies and people just as magical. There was a dreamer, magnificent in his eagle feather robe, and a woman, a small woman with a huge nasty wolf at her side. And she killed the dreamer. She blew him into little pieces! And the cave told their story.

Outside he could hear the hunters returning so quickly he scampered to cover and peeped over a ledge. They had someone with them, a thin scrawny figure of a man. The dreamer, White Falcon! They were dragging him; all trussed with thongs, all tied up so he could not escape. The dreamer was screaming and cursing at the hunters, jerking and trying to free himself. To no avail! They all ignored him, dragging him through the dirt, dirtying his beautiful eagle feather robe. Tears ran down the boy's face, but he made not a sound.

The hunters dragged White Falcon into the beautiful cave. They threw him to the floor and then they defecated on him, kicked him and left his broken body lying in the filth. They filed from the cave and began blocking the entrance with the largest boulders they could handle, more and more, until there was no longer an opening, no more beautiful cave. Before they finished, it was deeply buried. Only faintly could the dreamer's curses be heard. Then the hunters left. Red Eagle crept to the pile of stones, he called to White Falcon but he could not move a single rock. Day after day he returned to where the dreamer had been entombed. After a while there was no sound. The boy stopped going to the place.

*   *   *

The man had no memory, *but I do*, the sprit had waited in that rock pile, waited and been rewarded. Silently, carefully it had slipped into the child, nestling deep inside, taking away the memory, hiding, waiting . . .

The child had grown. Still, the spirit waited . . . The child became a youth and then a man, still the spirit waited, waited until it was time to strike!

I know where they are! Red Eagle bolted wide-awake. He shivered and shook his head. *I have seen them! They are all alive, alive and well. You thought the woman dead. Well, she isn't! Not only that but she is no longer alone. The other one has found her!* "You talk gibberish!" Red Eagle muttered, glaring at the man sitting beside the fire and glancing curiously at him. *They are even stronger now that they are together, so strong no one will be able to defeat them, not without the power objects.*

"So where are they?"

Why should I tell you? "You don't know!" Red Eagle hissed. *The place in the secret cave, that's where they are! See!* Suddenly a blinding flash of pain seared through his head, and Red Eagle found himself once again in the cave. *Here!* The spirit flitted to the wall, *here, at this place. I have seen them there. I feel them there. Forces have called them there!* "Place of stone!" muttered Red Eagle, "should have known they would go there sooner or later," he rolled onto his sleeping fur clutching his head in agony. The man at the hearth shook his head and tossing the last of his tea into the fire went to his own fur.

"Crazy!" he muttered to himself, "must find a way to escape this miserable camp."

*   *   *

"Now you try," Basket ordered.

Star Child lifted her head, tilted it back as Basket had and let forth with a long-drawn-out mournful howl. "Better!" Now again, but more feeling this time, make it sound as though you were the loneliest thing you can think of. Again Star Child tried. "That's it!" Across the plain she got an answer.

"I did it!"

"Finally," sighed Blue Coyote, "are you pair about through! We have more than enough wolf hides for everyone, and still you call more wolves."

"We are through, but you promised to take us to the cave you discovered," reminded Basket.

"No time today," Blue Coyote rose, "we are going on a cape hunt tomorrow, I have to purify, and already I am going to be late."

"Then just tell us where it is, we will find it ourselves!" Star Child pleaded.

"One of you was bad enough!" muttered Blue Coyote as he led the way down a faint trail. He stopped and pointed. "See that brush over there, just below the top of the wall?"

"Where that huge boulder is?" Star Child squinted.

"Yes, just beside it."

"I don't see any cave entrance!" Basket complained "are you sure?"

"Of course I'm sure. I was in it just yesterday. It goes way back inside the earth, probably opens into a different canyon at the other end."

"How do you know that?"

"I don't know, I'm just guessing," he rose and started away from them at a run, "and now I'm leaving. You pair, check it out yourselves if you can't believe me."

"I think he is making fun of us!" Star Child stated, biting her lip.

"Let's go see, come on Throw Back, you can find the cave for us!" The twins headed down into the canyon and up the other side. They were panting by the time they had scrambled up to the boulder. "Not a route I would choose to take every day," panted Basket.

"Woof!" Throw Back's voice echoed funnily.

"She found it!" exclaimed Star Child. Both climbed with renewed vigor.

"There are some old torches here against the wall," Basket whispered as they stood in the faint light within the cave, "let's light one and look around." She struck her firestones and soon they each held a brightly burning torch. "Blue Coyote's right, this is a wonderful cave!"

"Too bad we are leaving the place of stone so soon. This would make a great 'secret place' for just the pair of us," Star Child sighed.

"Not very secret if Blue Coyote knows about it. If he knows, then so does Stone Man and probably half the camp beside," reminded Basket.

"Well it can be our 'secret place' while we are here any way," Star Child said. "Blue Coyote, Stone Man and the rest will have no time for anything except the 'cape hunt' for several days, and then we leave here any way." She ran a finger down the wall, "look, we can draw pictures in the soot!"

Basket tilted her head, "why would we want to draw pictures and of what?"

"I see things in my dreams," replied Star Child, "things like this!" She quickly drew the outline of an animal, which Basket recognized, only because she had seen its skeleton at the Sacred Pond and in the sacred canyon.

"The Mother Beast" Basket said.

"Is that what you call it? I have heard it called mammoth!"

"Mammoth!" Basket rolled the word around on her tongue, "I like that; mammoth, move over, I want to try!" Star Child moved and soon both of them were drawing in the soot on the wall.

"Woof!" Throw Back barked, bringing them back to the present.

"We had better go. It is getting very late! We are going to be caught in the dark before we get back to camp!" Basket wiped her fingers on her tunic and snuffed the torch. "We will come back again tomorrow!"

They scrambled from the cave, all but fell to the floor of the canyon and took off toward the camp on a run. "Where have you been?" questioned Rain Woman, "I have been calling you for some time."

"We were out hunting," replied Star Child.

"Well it was getting late and I was becoming worried," Rain Woman replied.

"Are the hunters finished with their ceremony yet?" asked Star Child.

"Some time ago, which you would know had you been here. It is rude of you not to be interested in the ceremonies of the new camp. They are different from ours, and you should be here to learn them."

"Basket can tell me all about them; I called a wolf today, mother," Star Child hugged Rain Woman.

"And this should make me happy? That you called a dangerous predator to you?" Rain Woman shook her head. "I would wish that you would spend more time with the rest of the camp. She shook her head, "ever since you discovered each other, always you are together, you girls."

"Basket is not a girl, Mother, she has been mated and she has the same freedom that you enjoy."

"But you have not, and you do not!"

"Yes mother," Star Child sighed, "I am sorry. I will remember."

"Also remember that you should not be going about with unmated men as well."

"But Basket serves as . . ."

"Not! That is my last word." Rain Woman stomped back to the fire.

"You are lucky, Basket, you do not have anyone watching your every move all of the time."

"My grandmother was just as bad, and I would give just about anything to have her scold me again," Basket said wistfully. "Be glad that you have parents and they care for you. Until you came into this camp I had no one, and it was dreadfully lonely at times. I would not have stood it but for Throw Back."

"Now you have me, and you will never be alone again. We are connected, special! We have a closer relationship that anyone else in either of our camps, for we came from the same mother, at the same time. Twins are considered to be very good luck by my people."

"By mine as well but only as long as they are together; separate them and you will be punished by the spirits!" Basked admitted and Star Child nodded.

"What was it like? Being mated?" Star Child questioned later after they were rolled in their sleeping furs and the hearth had burned to embers.

"If you are asking what I think, I have no idea," Basket replied, "I was mated to Red Eagle, that doesn't mean that I 'knew' him. He wasn't interested it that at all, he only wanted my 'power objects'. We only shared the cave as mates a few nights, and all those nights he spent in a dreamer's trance."

"Dreamers are allowed to mate in you camp?" Star Child questioned in surprise.

"No. Of course not! A dreamer would lose his 'spirit power' if he lived that close to a woman. Red Eagle was no dreamer, at least he never admitted to it if he was. It was a pair of seasons ago, I have no idea what he has become since then, other than dangerous, for he is determined that I die, and now probably you as well, for we share the power he fears."

"I met him once, not long ago, and I don't care to do so again. He captured me while I was gathering acorns and he thought I was someone else, now I know whom. Still he held me captive until my father gave him the 'spirit point' for my return."

"Which means that he now has a pair of 'spirit objects', so we must be very careful that he does not get more, for he will turn their 'power' against us."

"But those you carry must have much more power than the 'spirit' points! I could feel something when I held it, but nothing as strong as when I have touched the teeth! Now they have real 'power'. As does your staff, but all that I had was the point and he took that," Star Child sighed.

Basket said nothing, merely smiled, but her amulet throbbed gently and the spot on her arm felt pleasant. She knew she had made the right decision.

"Do you think he is still after you?"

"Fire Dancer does, and Blue Coyote does, and Turtle Woman and Star Woman do, and I also do. Red Eagle wants power, and he has convinced himself that the teeth will give it to him. I do not think he will give up until he has the teeth and I am dead, or he is."

"Then it is up to us to see that he never gets them!"

"At least he does not know where we are, and soon we will have left this place and there will be even less danger, for we will be continually moving. He would not recognize the camp now unless he got close enough to identify individuals. We have changed the way we dress, we walk with wolves, and now that your camp has joined with us, we are also many more than he would expect."

"Are the pair of you going to talk all night, again?" Willow called out; "some of us would appreciate getting some sleep!"

"Sorry!" they replied in unison.

I told you this would come in handy!

"We are going just up the canyon," explained Star Child, the next morning, "I promise we are not doing anything that you would not approve of. No wolves, no leaving the canyon." Star Child was doing her best to escape, while Throw Back whined and ran to the trail, anxious to be on the way, Basket waited little less-patiently. Finally, Star Child joined them.

"See that you also return before dark," Rain Woman admonished, "I worry when you are late returning to camp. It happened once before, and we almost lost you to those raiders."

"I will be careful Mother, we both will. We will be safe as well. Throw Back is with us. She will protect us."

"Yes, I suppose that is right, it is just that . . ."

"I promise. We will return long before dark."

The pair along with Throw Back filed up the trail toward the head of the canyon. "Did you think to bring food?" asked Basket.

Star Child nodded, "so did I. At least we should not go hungry like yesterday. I brought some water as well," she lifted the water skin.

Star Child grinned and lifted a similar one.

"Woof!" called Throw Back.

"You are in a hurry!" Laughed Basket, "all right we are coming." Throw Back set a fast pace to the cave, leaving both women breathless even before they began the climb to the boulder.

They set up the torches, discovering a substantial supply of them a bit farther from the entrance. Star Child was quickly involved in the drawing she had abandoned the day before. Basket sat, back against the wall some distance away, her hand busy in her lap. "There!" She said a while later, critically evaluating here work.

"I thought you wanted to draw?" Star Child finally noticed that Basket was not finishing her own picture.

"I had something to finish first," Basket replied, "and now I have done so, here," she handed Star Child her gift.

Star Child stared down at the offering and her lip began to shake and she shook her head, "you cannot mean this! It is too much! It belongs to you!"

"Now only one belongs to me. It is right, sister. My amulet tells me so. They were meant one for each of us, I am sure only our mother did not have time." Basket smiled, "here let me help you." She encircled Star Child's waist with the thong and attached the ends. "There, now we are even more alike! I would share the staff as well, but it cannot be separated."

"But will this not lessen the 'power', to separate the teeth?"

"We are always together, so are the teeth, they merely do not share the same thong," Basket answered.

"If for any reason, we go separate paths in the future, I will return it to you," Star Child stated, "I am sure that their 'power' would be lessened by distance. Do not argue with me on this, for I am determined."

"Very well," Basket conceded, "But only if our paths separate," she grinned, "for now I think there is little danger of that!"

They set about their drawings laughing and making silly stick figures in the soot. The day passed. They ate at mid day and then returned to their endeavors. "It is too bad we did not think of bringing pigment and adding color to these," Basket stood back and admired their handiwork, "You draw quite well. Mine are not nearly so lifelike."

"I have been drawing pictures in the dirt all of my life. You have just started. Give yourself some time, and it will come, just as I learned to call the wolves. There is much we have to share and teach each other."

"There is much that we have lost as well," Basket sighed, "I would that we had never been separated."

"Me as well," Star Child sighed, "and now it is well after mid day and I promised Mother that we would return before dark. We had better go now;" she began gathering up their water bags and food containers. When they were ready to leave, Throw Back stood blocking the entrance to the cave and whined, refusing to let them out.

"What is it, girl?" Basket went to her knees beside the animal; "Don't you want to leave?" Throw Back whined again and Basket frowned. "Something is wrong! She was in a big hurry to get us here, and now she doesn't want us to leave. The camp! Something is wrong at the camp! Come on, we must hurry!" She tried to push past Throw Back. Throw Back refused to move. She whined and licked Basket's face, but she would not let them leave the cave.

"Perhaps we should do as she wants," suggested Star Child.

Basket shoved again, and then sighed and slumped back against the wall. "She has no intention of letting us out of this cave. Come on Throw Back, people in the camp may need us! They could be hurt, or in danger, and we could help!"

Throw Back merely whined and lay down blocking the entrance, a sad look in her eyes. Then Basket knew. Dread filled her and she began to cry. "They are all dead! Here we have spent the day drawing stupid pictures and enjoying ourselves while those we love lie in their own blood, dying, and you knew!" She accused the wolf.

Throw Back lifted her head and gave forth with a mournful howl that echoed back at them. Then she rose and stepped aside, allowing them to leave. They did so as quickly as they could, stumbling and sliding down the steep path. They ran as fast as they could back to the camp.

*　　*　　*

See! I told you they were here! But did you believe me? Did you trust me? No! Red Eagle lay on the bluff; his men hunkered down beside him, watching the peaceful camp below. He had been watching for nearly half the day and had not seen any he searched for. Yet he recognized Turtle Woman and Star Woman and the dreamer Acorn. There were many he did not recognize. But of Fire Dancer, Blue Coyote or Basket he had found no trace. Then he realized that most of the men were gone from the camp. *They are out hunting!* He eased back from the edge. "We will circle away from the camp and pick up their trail," he led the way from the spot and the scruffy band that followed him, fell into place behind. They moved quickly and soon had located the trail that the hunters took out onto the plain. They followed. Behind them, hidden from their view, a ragged figure rose, and staggered to the spot they had been.

*　　*　　*

A short time later Basket and Star Child tumbled into the peaceful camp.

"I was so sure!" Basket exclaimed. "Throw Back must have had a reason for keeping us . . . where she did," she ended lamely.

Star Woman nodded, "she must have had a reason, that animal has always protected you, and I am sure that this is no exception."

"Someone coming into the camp," Dog Boy scampered down the rocks, "one man."

The camp turned and silently waited as a man hobbled into the camp. "I come in peace," he called, "I would be recognized. I bring news, and I seek refuge!" He staggered to a rock and sank down.

"Who are you," questioned Jackrabbit, presently in charge of the camp?

"I am called Cripple," the man replied, catching his breath. "I have been with Red Eagle for the last pair of seasons, but I am through with him and those killers of his. I hold no anger toward this camp, or any other. So far I have managed to avoid joining in the raids, for I am crippled. But I followed them and I have been watching them while they were watching this camp."

"That's why . . .!" Basket shivered and began to shake. She dropped to her knees and hugged Throw Back; "you always keep me from danger," she whispered, "and I so seldom thank you." Throw Back licked her face, whined and leaned into Basket.

"Where are they?" Jackrabbit looked around nervously, "did they just let you walk in?"

"They have gone by now," Basket answered, "or Throw Back would not have let me return to the camp."

The man swiveled his head and looked at her. "She the one?" he questioned.

"Where is Red Eagle now?" Jackrabbit repeated.

"Gone, they went west, following a trail I'd guess."

"The cape hunters," Jackrabbit leaped to his feet, "quickly, there is no time to lose! Every man who can walk, get your weapons and follow me!" He ran to his shelter and scooped up his own atlatl and darts and was soon joined by a double hand of men, some young, some not hunters at all such as Acorn and Moon, dreamer of the Eagle Camp.

"Why do you betray Red Eagle and come to us?" questioned Turtle Woman.

"I have looked for a while to escape him. He would kill me if he knew. He is obsessed with revenge against a man called Fire Dancer. He seeks that man's life. The other one he particularly wants dead is the woman, Basket. He is 'spirit touched' when it comes to that woman. He wants her dead even more than the man. It is all that he lives for!" The man shook his head; "I have nothing against any man. I will not take a life. My misfortune was hunting alone. Red Eagle captured me, and I was given a choice, join or die. I chose to join," the man looked at his feet in shame, "I wish rather that I had chosen to die. My life has since been a shame," he struck his leg with a fist, "were it not for this leg. . ."

"We waste time," Jackrabbit cut in. "Star Woman, get the camp to a place of safety and wait there. We will return with the hunters if possible, but however this turns out do not expose the camp to danger."

Star Woman nodded and even before the men had left, the camp was scurrying to gather up necessary items and prepare to flee. Already people were threading their way up the canyon. Star Child and Basket ran to where Star Woman was organizing the rest. "Pack the wolves," Basket called, "put food and water in the packs and we will lead you to a place where no one can find us."

"What of the men when they return?"

"Blue Coyote will know where to look," Basket smiled, "or Wolf will lead him. But the camp will be safe."

Star Woman nodded, and Star Child hurried to lead the people, while Basket remained behind to help Star Woman and the ones remaining.

"I will remain here," the man said, "I do not deserve . . ."

"You will come as well," Basket said, "you have information that will be valuable to the leaders, you know more about Red Eagle and his group than anyone. This information will keep you still breathing if you are lucky!" The man nodded and rose and went with them.

"Do you think we should tie him up?" questioned Star Woman, "can he be trusted?"

Basket shrugged, "where we go it little matters. He could not add any danger to our position. You will see; I haven't time to explain now." They ushered the crippled man and the stragglers from the camp and up the canyon. Sun Spirit was taking the light and they hurried to catch up with the others. Star Child led the women, arriving at the boulder while she could just see.

"Wait here, I will light the way," she scrambled up the steep path and vanished. Almost immediately a light appeared, and she called the first of the women to climb the trail. By the time Star Woman arrived with Basket there was no one in sight. Basket led her and between them they helped the crippled man up the steep trail, Basket going back and carefully brushing their trail clear, as she had for some distance back. Throw Back glanced over her shoulder, wagged her tail once and went up into the cave before Basket.

*   *   *

Stone Man lay flat on his stomach in the grass; waiting, Blue Coyote, Fire Dancer and Bison Man had circled around to approach the bison from the other side. Porcupine and Squirrel lay with him, just beyond the bison herd. They heard the quail call and started to rise. A blinding pain knocked Stone Man to the ground, burning hot agony, drove through his shoulder, and try though he might he could not force his body to move. He forced his eyes to focus on Squirrel beside him. The other man had a surprised expression on his face, his eyes already fading in death. Stone Man tried again, his vision blurred, blackness descended and then nothing.

He did not see the raiders run forward, did not feel the shaft being jerked then broken just beyond where it entered his body. The bison herd turned as one and thundered away, directly toward the other hunters. Fire Dancer rose and turned just as the lead bison lowered its head and drove a horn into his leg, just above the knee. The animal jerked its head up, ripping a deep gash up Fire Dancer's leg. Just beyond him Badger screamed as a bison horn drove deep into his belly. Cougar leaped to escape sharp hoofs and horns but went down, the bison trampling over him. Behind, where the others should have been, Fire Dancer could hear screams and shouting. A blinding swirling of color descended, he struggled to keep aware, but darkness followed.

Badger could feel little after the bison threw him and he landed on his back. The rest of the animals ran past him. He clutched his gut; blood oozing from between his fingers, yet there was little pain. Cougar spit dirt from his mouth and managed to regain his feet. Fire Dancer lay a short distance from him, lifeless.

* * *

People were seated silently round inside the cave, their animals held beside them, those prone to barking muzzled with a thong. Someone had found a pack rat nest and started a fire with it. Others were spreading out sleeping robes and settling the few children to sleep. It was going to be a long night. Most of the adults sat quietly and waited. Morning arrived, but it made little difference to those in the cave. They waited all day and through another night. Near mid day Throw Back lifted her head and her tail gave a single thump on the floor. Outside there was scratching and Wolf crawled in, followed closely by Blue Coyote. He was dirty, there was blood on his face and on his clothing and his face was grim. He was alone.

"I guessed that this is where I would find you," he nodded. "I will bring the others, they wait just below, those of us left," he disappeared and was soon replaced by Bison Man, helping Fire Dancer. Others were also helped inside. Then Blue Coyote and a hand of others returned to the camp. A hand of time later they returned with sleeping furs, food and whatever else they could carry. Throughout the night they worked, and by morning, everything had been transported to the secret cave and their path completely erased. Once again the camp had simply vanished.

Bison Man settled Fire Dancer against the wall, then again tightened the thong around his thigh. Blood oozed from a vicious wound that extended from the hip nearly to the knee. Jackrabbit had a deep cut on one shoulder and another on his arm. Stone Man was also wounded. He was pale, and weak from loss of blood. The broken shaft of a dart projected from his back. Cougar carried a head wound, and Badger was tightly bound around the middle, blood oozing from the spaces between the bindings. Chipmunk was not with them, nor Pinyon, nor Centipede Man, Porcupine and a hand of men from the Eagle Camp. Gray Wolf, the dreamers and Bison Man were the only one's unhurt.

Water Woman sat at the rear of the cave weeping silently and holding Moth to her. Moth cried and threatened vengeance against Red Eagle. Then she threw herself back into her mother's arms and wept heartbrokenly.

"We were just getting into position for the cape hunt," Bison Man began the tale. "They struck from out of nowhere. There were many of them and only a few of us. We were lucky however, for Jackrabbit appeared almost immediately and saved us from sure death. As it is, our losses were heavy. Those who bore the first attack did not have a chance. We were farther into the herd, as it is and the bison seemed to be on the side of the raiders. One gored Fire Dancer in the leg and another Badger, in the gut. Some of our numbers were trampled, but most of them were darted by the raiders."

"They lost a hand as well," added Fire Dancer, "at least the bison were not partial. Unfortunately, Red Eagle escaped with a number of his camp, and we were unable to follow him." The headman leaned back and closed his eyes. Acorn approached him with a collection of skins and herbs. "See to the boy first," Firs Dancer nodded to where Badger lay. Acorn looked his expression was sad and shook his head.

"There is nothing to be done for him. I have given him a drink to ease the pain. I need to treat your wound and then remove the shaft from Stone Man. The others will wait until I have tended you." Fire Dancer bit his lip and nodded. He sat stoically as the dreamer washed his wound with a solution of healing herbs purified in boiling water, then pulling the edges of the wound together he made small holes in the skin on either side and ran sinew through them tying the sinew. When he finished with this, he again washed the leg with the solution and covered the wound with a powder. Then Bison Man expertly wrapped the leg with a bandage of rabbit skin.

Stone Man was next. While several people held torches over head, Acorn took hold of the end of the shaft and pulled. It did not come out, but Stone Man groaned and writhed in pain. Bright red blood again flowed freely from around the shaft. "Why does it not come out?" asked Acorn.

"You will have to cut it out," a voice from the shadows answered. Red Eagle has a new weapon. There is a stone point attached to the shaft. Every time you move it that point cuts deeper and wider." Acorn stopped and wiped the blood away; he nodded to the other man, "how wide need I cut?"

"At least a finger wider than the shaft, then someone will have to pull back the flesh while you remove the weapon. It will bleed a lot."

"He has already bled a lot. He cannot lose much more blood or we will lose him," Acorn stated. "If you know so much, come and help me!"

"You would trust me to help?" The man sounded surprised.

"You saved many lives this day, I, at least, trust you," was his answer. There were a scraping and a thumping, and the stranger eased down beside Stone Man.

"If you will allow me, I was once a healer, before I. . . some other time. Hand me that blade," he quickly and expertly cut a deep, but narrow gash beside the shaft and expertly pulled the flesh away. Acorn easily removed the shaft and point from the wound. With it came a fresh gush of blood, which Acorn quickly wiped away and then again stitched and tied with sinew. Already the stranger was kneeling beside Jackrabbit and with swift precise moves he soon had his wounds treated. Blue Coyote was given a drink for headache and his scalp stitched again into place. There were a number of other minor scratches, which were tended to. The stranger went to where Badger lay and with a sharp blade cut through the bandage. The wound was bad. The bison had gored him directly in the stomach. He bent over and sniffed the wound, opened it a bit and sniffed again. He nodded, "bring me some of that herbal powder and a poultice from that bag," he instructed. "This looks a lot worse than it is. The wound is not putrefied. I don't think the guts were punctured. There is a chance he will live." Quickly Acorn handed him the things he asked for and the stranger treated Badger. The man was in intense pain. "Do you have any of that pain killing drink left?"

"There is some, and I can prepare more."

The stranger nodded, "It will be necessary to provide it frequently for the next several days. If he is to live, we will know by morning. If there is enough, you might give those other hunters some as well. The headman and the man with the dart will be much more comfortable with the aid of the drink." Then the stranger melted back into the shadows.

"How safe is this cave?" questioned Bison Man, "is it likely that Red Eagle can trap us in here?"

"He will never find us," Blue Coyote replied, "we left no trail for him to follow, even if he does return. We are quite safe in this cave, and since we have everything from the camp, we can stay here for many days without need to expose ourselves outside," he pointed. "If you watch the direction that the smoke takes, there is probably another entrance one which it would be to our advantage to find. Now however, I would know the name of the man who saved our lives at considerable risk to his own!"

The stranger spoke from the shadows. "I have been called Cripple for many seasons, but before that I was known as Singing Serpent," he sighed, "once I was proud to be called by that name, now I shame the memory of that man."

"I would take the hand of Singing Serpent in friendship!" stated Bison Man.

"And I," added Blue Coyote, "but for the timely arrival of Jackrabbit and his men, I would be mourning my best friend, or lying beside him to walk the wind," Blue Coyote walked to where Singing Serpent sat and offered his hand. The other man took it and was pulled to his feet. The pair walked to where Bison Man sat beside Fire Dancer, the latter extended his hand and welcomed Singing Serpent.

"Thank you for coming to our aid. Without the help of your timely warning, I fear we would all be walking the wind. Your unselfish act has assured you a place of honor and status within this camp if you should choose to join us, if not we will do what we can, to aide you in reaching your own people. You will remain deeply in our gratitude either way. I would be honored to name you friend."

"Singing Serpent accepts your generous offer with a glad heart," the man replied, "I would be honored to name you friend. I have no camp any longer; they cast me aside when I could no longer hunt and provide my share of the food for the camp. There was no one who would carry my burden until my leg recovered. I was left to walk the wind, only to be captured by Red Eagle and enslaved by his band of raiders while attempting to provide myself with food."

"How long were you with him?" questioned Blue Coyote.

"I was with him for the better part of a pair of seasons. He had been injured just before my capture. My ability to care for his wounds is all that kept them from killing me. I am quite familiar with each member of his camp and can provide useful information regarding them, information that could prove beneficial to the safety of this camp. For your generous offer of inclusion in this group I will share not only this knowledge, but that of healing which I possess."

"Then he must have captured you just after he attacked us on the plain. What were his injuries?"

"He had a dart wound in the shoulder and a leg badly mangled by, he claimed, a wolf."

Fire Dancer laughed, "That 'wolf' was my dog, Scorpion. She has always taken a dislike to Red Eagle," he laid his hand on the old dog's head for she lay beside him.

The next morning Blue Coyote and Bison Man took torches and with Wolf to accompany them, they went in search of another opening to the cave. Jackrabbit was feverish and there were signs of evil spirits in his wound. Acorn cleaned it again and replaced the poultice. Badger was still alive but also feverish. Stone Man slept the day through, but his was a healing sleep free of fever. Fire Dancer was in considerable pain, but his wound was also free of evil spirits. Late in the day Throw Back, who lay guarding the entrance of the cave, growled softly. Everyone became silent and held their breath. Through the brush concealing the entrance to the cave they could see Red Eagle and a hand of men far down the canyon, searching for signs of the camp. They found none and came no closer, finally turning and leaving. All sighed in relief for they felt safe, for now.

Blue Coyote and Bison Man returned late, long after dark and reported that indeed there was another entrance to the cave at a considerable distance from this one in a different canyon to the north and west. The other entrance cave was both larger and provided better lighting. It was suggested that perhaps a move to the other end of the cave be in order. This underground passage had clearly been used before. There were marks indicating that people had followed at least the main path on more than one occasion. The signs of habitation were also more pronounced at the other end.

"I will lead the first group through," Blue Coyote agreed, "they can get settled there and another group join them in a day or so. This will also give more room for those of us remaining here to watch. Once the injured are able to be moved we will all relocate to that entrance, except for a pair to remain here and watch." Jackrabbit was recovering now, his fever gone and the arm and shoulder healing. Badger was still alive, but his fever was greater. Stone Man had wakened; he was very weak and could not stand to be moved, even slightly. Fire Dancer could not stand. The others were able to make the trip to the other end. Over the next hand of days most of the camp moved, leaving the wounded hunters and a pair of watchers behind.

Bison Man took charge of the main group. Cougar and he made sure that no smoke escaped to alert anyone that they were there. They took several trips to the lip of the plain but saw no signs of the raiders. Hopefully they had not discovered this canyon. Unfortunately, Red Eagle had decided to set up camp, at least temporarily, at the place of stone. He had moved his entire camp there, so they were in considerable danger at all times. Time passed slowly. The moon went from full to a thin crescent. Fire Dancer could now move well enough to make the trip to the far end of the cave, but he did it in segments, resting along the way. Jackrabbit had made the move a pair of days after the main camp. Badger and Stone Man however, were still unable to be moved. Badger was slowly winning the battle with the evil spirits, but it would be a long time before he would be able to travel at all. Stone Man was able to walk around for short periods, but he was still weak, and his arm and shoulder useless. The food supplies were running low, and each trip to the stream in the canyon was dangerous.

Still Red Eagle camped in the quarry.

"We spotted a small herd of bison just beyond the lip of the canyon," Bison Man stated, "I think we could dart a pair of them and safely bring them into the cave without leaving any trace."

"We haven't found any signs of Red Eagle's men this far north. They are probably hunting deer in the river breaks for food," Cougar added.

"We need to be preparing to travel, and travel fast," Fire Dancer said, "and to do so we must have equipment repaired, we will not be able to use the travois for a while at least, if we are to move without leaving any trail. We have nothing else to do while trapped here, so we might just as well get everything in perfect order so that when the time comes we can go and do so quickly, silently, and without signs of our presence."

All agreed. Star Woman and Turtle Woman and Water Woman got things organized. Soon people had tasks to do, time went faster, and everyone was less strained. Carriers were made for every animal, even Scorpion, who had been relieved of work duties, but still tried to do her part. The wolves were strong, sturdy animals and they loved being part of a pack including humans. Now nearly full grown, they could carry a heavy load. Hides were cut, sinew snipped, and carriers began to take shape. Each animal was fitted with a harness attached to a pair of carriers, one on either side. These would be filled, and then a sleeping fur or shelter hide rolled and lay atop, attached at both sides with straps. Each person also carried a pack. Those of the Wolf Camp already had such things, but the Eagle Camp had depended upon their dogs and travois, only the men carrying packs. Now each person would be fitted. Luckily there were enough deer hides to do the job. Blue Coyote and Bison Man slipped out early one morning and darted a pair of young bison, small enough that they could carry them back to the camp upon their shoulders. The next day they repeated this operation, thus supplying not only food but also hides that could be used for the carriers as well.

Neither camp had been able to gather their full supply of stone, but both had enough to last them until Bison Man led them to another supply far to the south. Since Red Eagle was convinced that Fire Dancer would go north, they would be safe going south. They would leave at night and pass the quarry in the dark some distance away. Then descend into the river valley and follow it for a time before cutting again south.

"Who is carrying the food for the first night?" asked Star Woman.

"I have charge of that!" Willow replied, "All is as it should be."

"The healer's supplies?"

"I carry them myself," Singing Serpent answered, "they add little in the way of burden to my pack, and although I am less than graceful, my leg did heal strong. I can keep up and do my share as well."

"Who begins the journey supporting the bed for Badger?" Fire Dancer questioned. The young hunter was shamed and upset because he was becoming a burden to others, but since no one desired to leave him behind, nor put his life to an end, the only solution was to carry him until such time as he was able to walk again. All of the wounded except Badger were now able to stand the punishment of the long hard trip. He could walk a few steps but was then doubled over in pain. The wound had to be opened regularly and the evil smelling pus drained, but it was healing. In another moon Badger would have an interesting scar and a tale to go with it, but he would still be alive to tell the tale.

All afternoon the people packed, made sure nothing had been forgotten and got in line for the trip. Darkness fell and the Ancestor Fires burned brightly in the sky. Bison Man led the silent string of people and wolves and dogs from the cave, up the trail and to the south until he was sure they were safe from detection. Blue Coyote and Gray Wolf followed behind, erasing even the faintest sign of their passage. Then they hurried over the open plain and just before Sun Spirit began to bring day they cut back east and down into the river valley. Here they skirted the water, following game trails and crossing streams carefully, just in case . . . Always Blue Coyote and Gray Wolf came behind, making sure.

At dusk they were well east of the quarry and were able to rest for the night. Everyone was exhausted and willing to stop. They made a start the next day well after the sun was up and traveled south on the open plain. A hand of days later, Bison Man and Fire Dancer gave the word and the travois were assembled and life was much easier for all. They traveled steadily for the remainder of that moon and all of the next, slowly following the southward migration of the bison. Fall found them in an area of plateaus; an area where they found working stone,[1] and were able to replenish their supply. Still they went farther finally locating in a deep wide canyon[2] through which a river ran. It had ample game and they would be sheltered from the fierceness of the wintertime. Badger was now fully recovered, and Stone Man was getting more and more use of his arm, although his shoulder still stiffened if not worked constantly.

The women gathered tubers and grain and acorns in the canyon. The men hunted deer and bison. They had a ceremony uniting the two camps into one, and plans were made to mate the wolves to increase their pack. Throw Back chose to take a mate and by deep winter she was heavy with pup. Secretly, Star Child hoped there would be one like her, one for her very own.

Moth had become a woman, and the lifelong friendship between her and Badger deepened into something more, so they mated.

To everyone's surprise Jackrabbit decided to take a mate, he chose Makes A Robe, and they settled down quite happily.

---

1. The Edwards Plateau region of Texas.
2. Big Bend, south Texas, along the Big Bend River.

CHAPTER 16

What are you doing?" Stone Man sat watching Blue Coyote busy with cords and rocks and the branch of an oak tree a short distance from their shelter.

"You will see very shortly."

"If it is anything involving one of your schemes, leave me out of it!" Stone Man stated, "I have no time for such things. I must get this shoulder to work, or I will be a cripple the rest of my life." He was again trying to raise his arm, but the muscles had tightened and would not allow for such freedom.

"There!" pronounced Blue Coyote, "I think that will do it! Come here," he motioned to Stone Man.

The other man went more out of curiosity than obedience. "What is it?" He questioned.

"A means to help with your arm," Blue Coyote explained. "You have trouble raising your arm. I have made a sleeve here for you to put your arm in, these thongs attach at the wrist and go through the hole I drilled through that antler, which I have wedged above the branch and then they are attached to those bags holding rocks. It works like this!" Blue Coyote slid his arm into the sleeve and with his free hand released the thong, letting the weight of the rocks raise his arm. "It will need a bit of adjustment now and then later, but I think it is about right. You try it!"

Stone Man put his arm into the sleeve and took the thong from Blue Coyote, "Not too much the first time, you don't want to rip the tendons from the bone!" Stone Man cautiously let out a bit of cord. His arm raised, his face went white with pain, and he gritted his teeth and released a bit more cord. The arm raised a little more. "That is enough to be starting with," Blue Coyote recommended, "see how long you can stand the pulling. It will be there for you any time you want to use it."

Stone Man pulled the thong and tied it and removed his arm from the sling. Looking very remorseful, said, "Just when I accuse you of involving me in another of your schemes, you do something both considerate and unselfish for me. It makes me realize why I have always ended up going along with you. You are the best friend I could ever have!"

"Have to get you fit again!" Blue Coyote grinned, "I have many terrific ideas to share with you." Blue Coyote sobered, "When I thought you were dead, it was the worst experience of my life. I can understand the way the twins feel about one another. I feel the same way about you. You are not just my best friend and hunting brother, Stone Man, to me you are like a brother who shares the same blood. We are a team, parts of a whole, I can't find the words to explain it, but I care about you, no matter how much we joke, our friendship is very important to me."

Stone Man nodded silently and returned to the tree and the stone mechanism, vowing to show his appreciation by using it at least several times a day. He was not as good with words as Blue Coyote, but his feelings were close to the same.

*　　*　　*

A small group of hunters entered the camp a few days later from up the canyon with an inert body piled upon their travois. Singing Serpent saw them arrive and hurried as fast as his awkward gait could carry him to meet them, sweeping up his medicine bag on the way.

"What happened?" Star Woman also saw the hunters' arrival. She saw a body on the travois, but everyone was accounted for.

"Don't know, found her in the river!" Cougar explained.

Singing Serpent removed the robe and studied the pallid face of the unconscious woman. "I don't recognize her!" he said in some surprise, "She is not of the camp!"

"We left the others to investigate while we brought her in. I don't even know if she is still alive. There was a lot of blood once we pulled her out of the river. She could have been swept from far upriver. I have no idea how long she was in the water, but she was still alive when we pulled her out."

"Still is," replied Singing Serpent, "Has a head wound, can't tell if she got it by accident or not, but other than that, she doesn't seem to be hurt. Heads always bleed a lot."

He recovered the form and suggested she be taken to a nearby shelter where he could get her settled in and try to treat her. "Someone get her out of those wet things and wrapped in a robe. First, she needs to be gotten warm. The water has taken the heat from her body. If she is not warmed up soon, I fear the spirit will leave her body."

"I can put heated rocks around her," suggested Turtle Woman, "That will help warm the air and even seep through the furs."

"Not so hot that they burn, she cannot tell you."

Turtle Woman nodded and soon was devising a method of her own. She dug a shallow depression in the ground with a deer scapula and transferred the hot rocks to it. Then she filled the depression with sand and placed a hide over it.[1] With help she had the girl lifted and laid upon the fur, then covered her with another. Turtle Woman frequently checked to make sure that no spot got too hot. When she was satisfied, she lifted a robe from a rack over the fire and making sure that it would not burn, replaced the top fur with the warm one and replaced the cold wrap on the rack to warm. Each time the robe cooled, she replaced it with the warm one. Slowly the blue began to leave the body and after a time there was again a healthy, rosy hue to it. The woman began to breathe more evenly and more deeply. Still, she did not move.

Singing Serpent had checked several times to see how she was doing, commending Turtle Woman on her clever method of warming the woman. He checked her breathing, her eyes and nodded, "She will wake up soon."

Star Woman brought her and Turtle's food and they sat beside the woman as they ate. A number of people wandered by curious about their strange guest. The rest of the hunting party returned. "We found the place where she went into the river," Fire Dancer said, "Some distance above the camp. She seems to have been alone, but how and why I cannot say. We found the trail she made to the river, evidently she was trying to cross on the rocks and slipped and struck her head. We backtracked for a distance but found only her tracks."

"What would a lone woman be doing? Where are her people? How did she get here?" Many questions, the answers to which it seemed only the woman could give. Night came. Still she did not waken, but Singing Serpent assured the watchers that her sleep was now a healing one. He had managed to get her to swallow a few mouthfuls of one of his potions. She lay in the shelter belonging to Basket and Star Child, so they were elected to keep watch over her during the night. They sat beside their hearth fire and drank tea and wondered about the woman.

"She does not look to be much older than we," observed Star Child.

"She is certainly striking to look at, even asleep," Basket replied, "It will be interesting to see what she is like awake."

"Just think how frightened she must have been, out here all alone!"

"I would not be too sure that she is alone!" Basket shook her head; "It doesn't make any sense. She must have people. The hunters must just have missed them somehow! Perhaps she was just returning to her camp and they are waiting there worried about her!"

"Blue Coyote and Wolf went up the river on one side and down on the other. They did not find any trail and Wolf would have found one had it been there. She must have had a camp, but where? So far there is no trace," she sighed, "It is most puzzling. I would be worried but Throw Back doesn't seem to be concerned."

"That animal is only concerned with the growing puppies inside her." Star Child remarked. "She is not even interested in going on short trips with us anymore."

* * *

"She will whelp any time now," Basket replied, "She has no need to move about much, I provide her every need. It is the least I can do, for she will provide us with any number of big healthy pups; maybe even one such as she; one which I can give to you."

"You would do that?" Star Child questioned. "That would be a very valuable animal. There will be many wanting it."

"But it is yours!" Basket was firm. "If she has another such as she; it will be a watcher sent from the spirits. Her mother gave Throw Back to me. Scorpion protected her from birth. Fire Dancer was intending to kill her, fearing she was deformed. Scorpion protected her and gave her to me.

As she will protect any special pup and give it to whomever it was meant to go, which will be to you, wait and see. We will know soon."

"Sooner than you think," Star Child leaped up; "She just gave birth to one!" Both women were soon leaning over the big animal. Throw Back licked and licked and then finely sighed and lay back on her side as the pup began nursing lustily. Soon it was joined by another and another, each a perfectly normal wolf. Finally, there was a hand plus a pair, all identical. Throw Back collected her brood and settled happily to motherhood. The birthing complete, the women checked once again on their patient and Basket remained awake while Star Child slept.

A time later Throw Back groaned once, and Basket smiled broadly. The last born pup would be Star Child's. She spoke quietly to the animal stroking her huge head as it lay on her lap. Throw Back closed her blue eyes blissfully and slipped into a much-needed sleep. Basket watched. She did not waken Star Child to take her turn. Just before Sun Spirit brought light to the sky, Singing Serpent came to once more check on his patient. She was sleeping peacefully and naturally. Singing Serpent admired the pups, remarking on the last.

"No, it is not deformed," assured Basket, "That is just how Throw Back looked at that age. Many thought she would never walk or be normal. It just took her longer because of her size. So it will also be with this one."

"You will be giving it to Star Child?" he asked wistfully. Basket merely nodded. "You will soon have a wolf of your own," she assured him, "But this one is special." He nodded and left. Basket sighed, the pup was still wet from birth, and already the desire to own this unique creature was beginning. Basket had already spoken to Fire Dancer, and in the event, she had been assured, the pup would go the Star Child. If a hunter so desired, the wants of a woman would usually be overlooked. Basket had explained that Throw Back had been a spirit-sent watcher. This pup would be so as well. Fire Dancer agreed that if Throw Back did, as had her mother, her decision would be honored. This was the best assurance Basket could get, but then she intended to make sure that Throw Back bestowed that pup on Star Child.

She had little to fear. Sun Spirit had brought light to the sky long before the strange woman began to move. Star Child still slept as well. Basket went to the woman and pushed her hair from her brow. Her skin was cool to the touch. Slowly the woman opened her eyes. A frightened look crossed them. "You are safe here in the Wolf Camp," Basket reassured her.

The woman tried to rise, Basket reassured her again and then the woman began to speak, rapidly and totally incomprehensibly to Basket. Basket sat back on her heels, thought and pointed to herself, "Basket!" She said.

The woman frowned then nodded, "Mourning Dove," she pointed to herself; at least that was as close as Basket could come to the name. She tried to get up and realized that beneath the robe she lay naked. Basket pointed to where she had hung the woman's clothes to dry out. They were immodestly brief for a woman of The People, but they were the clothes the woman had on. She went and got them. Mourning Dove smiled a 'thanks' and quickly pulled them on. Still Basket motioned her to stay on the bed furs. Basket brought her a horn of hot tea and set one for Star Child who had began to groan.

"Time to wake up Sister and greet our guest," Basket called. Star Child sat bolt upright and looked at the bright sunlight.

"I thought you were going to wake me to take my turn!" She scrambled from her furs.

"I was not sleepy," Basket replied. "We have something of a problem here. Our guest cannot understand us; nor we her."

Star Child came to stand beside Basket. Mourning Dove looked from one to the other and scooted away from them in fear, crying out something in her own language. Star Child reached out a hand and replied, calmly, in that same language.

"You understand her?" Basket squeaked.

"Of course, she is of a tribe which lived to the south of us beyond the river. I do not speak it well, but I should be able to get the idea across."

"What did she say?"

"She said we were spirits! I think she was under the impression that she had died and gone to walk the wind and thought we were her greeters."

"Oh!"

"I explained that we are members of the tribe she knows as The People, that we are twins and told her it was our hunters that pulled her from the river."

"Ask her where her people are."

Star Child did so and replied, "Her people are all dead. The great tribes to the south raided the camp and took everyone that they did not kill as slaves. She escaped because she was out gathering acorns. When she reached the camp she found it empty; she ran and has been running ever since. She thought to find a place to hide in this canyon, a place where she could spend the cold season and decide what to do next."

"I had better get Fire Dancer, you on the other hand had better check on Throw Back." Basket had left the shelter when she heard Star Child squeal in pleasure. She smiled and hurried to find Fire Dancer.

* * *

"That creature has been nothing but trouble since they pulled her from the river!" Star Woman muttered, as she slapped grain cakes onto hot stones to cook.

"She has only been in the camp a hand of days!" protested Turtle Woman.

"She has upset Throw Back and Basket. And Blue Coyote and Stone Man as well as almost every other man in the camp, are falling all over themselves to do her every bidding. She has Singing Spirit run ragged, and I even heard Moth and Badger quarreling over her." She stomped to the storage container and started to pour more grain into her bowl.

"Don't you think that you have enough grain cakes?" asked Turtle Woman. Star Woman frowned at the hearth, realizing that already she had made double her usual number. She sighed and returned the grain to the storage container.

"See what I mean? She even has me upset!"

"How did she upset Basket?"

"She was snooping in Basket's things and Throw Back growled at her. She claims 'the horrid beast attacked her', which is nonsense, for everyone knows that Throw Back is the gentlest of creatures!"

"Throw Back also has pups. Perhaps Mourning Dove got too close and the wolf took it as a threat, after all this is her first litter and she is probably over anxious. It is all a simple mix up, I am sure."

"Mix up or not, she has now insisted on moving to a shelter of her own, very close to that of Blue Coyote and Stone Man!"

"And Fire Dancer has allowed this?" Turtle Woman questioned in surprise.

"He has not said no, probably for the sake of Basket and Throw Back, but giving that creature her own shelter will be trouble. No one else lives alone. We all share in this camp! There should be no exceptions. If she is uncomfortable with Basket and Star Child, then let her live with the unmated women!"

"I am sure she would be more comfortable with the unmated men!" Turtle Woman joked, more than half seriously. "Look, Sister, if you are this upset over the situation, perhaps you should speak to the woman yourself, after all you are the headman's mate. You have a say in these matters."

"You are right! This has always been such a peaceful camp that I forget! I will speak to her this very day; not that it will do any good, she will just pretend that she doesn't understand what I say."

"Have Star Child there; she understands very well the language that Mourning Dove speaks." Star Woman nodded and the pair finally settled down to completing the meal preparations.

"Put her in with the unmated women!" Fire Dancer said in frustration, "Or better yet, throw her back into the river! Never has one person caused so many headaches! The unmated women are upset about the way she is dressed. They insist that she conform! She has, however, refused to accept any of the garments that they have offered. Singing Serpent is upset because, she has accused him of trying to poison her with his potions. The men of the camp seem all to have lost their heads. I assign them a task and they cannot do it for they have promised to do such and such for Mourning Dove. I begin to wonder if her story is true, or if she was just so much trouble that her camp chucked her out! I promise you this; if she continues to cause trouble, I will not tolerate her in this camp.

A shadow slipped away behind the shelter.

* * *

Basket sat beside Throw Back on one side, Star Child on the other, puppies between them. Each woman had a lap full of puppies. Throw Back had one. Not even Basket had chosen to try to touch the big black pup. Throw Back; like her mother before her, was extremely protective of the special pup. Mourning Dove had pronounced them all ugly and flounced from the shelter. The twins gritted their teeth to remain civil, but it was hard. "I hope that Fire Dancer makes a decision soon! I do not know how much longer I can be polite to that . . . that!"

*   *   *

Blue Coyote sat beside Mourning Dove, his eyes feasting on her beautiful face, his heart beating rapidly. They had walked far enough up the canyon to insure privacy. He could not believe that he had her all to himself. She ran her tongue across her lower lip, driving him even more frantic. He had been an adult for a hand of seasons, but never before had a woman affected him so. He squirmed in his furs at night, groaning in frustration, his need actually painful. When he slept his mind created fantasies, which were simply unbelievable! When he woke, he could not get them out of his mind.

The way she looked at him! The invitation in her eyes, in every move of her body, they all told him what he could not believe. She wanted him! She had fabricated this trip and from the message he was receiving, soon, very soon, he would be moving out of the unmated men's shelter into one of his very own; his and Mourning Dove's.

He hardly dared to breathe, angry with himself for acting like an untried youth. He was quaking inside; hoping her message was true, but afraid of being too eager. She looked at him again, deeply into his eyes, he was drowning in that look, then she ran her fingers along his thigh and Blue Coyote came very close to exploding.

"I am so glad that you took pity on me and came walking with me," she said in that wonderful way she had of speaking, slurring her words softly. "I get so lonely sometimes, for although I know they mean to be kind, Basket and Star Child are so . . . so . . . ."

"I know, they can be intimidating at times, but I have known Basket all my life and she is really very kind," he tried to make excuses. "But if you are unhappy there . . ."

"Oh I just knew you would understand. I realize how busy your father is and I do so hate to bother him, but . . ." she sighed softly, her finger tips causing waves of heat, which made concentration on conversation very hard. "Perhaps you could suggest, well, it just would be better if I moved out of their shelter and well... I would rather have my own privacy, you do understand, don't you?"

Blue Coyote was getting a message all right, but he was having more and more difficulty understanding what Mourning Dove was saying. His hands began to wander, softly, gently, and she did not protest. He was encouraged. He began to caress her in earnest, his hand sliding beneath the short tunic she wore, up the smooth soft skin of her belly and finally cupping her exquisite breast, hard tipped with desire. He groaned and began to breathe hard. Mourning Dove was panting; her mouth slightly open, making little moaning sounds. It was driving him crazy! He didn't want to rush her, but . . . she rose and pulled her tunic over her head, carefully laying it on the ground, her rounded globes glistening with the sweat of passion.

When she lay back and smiled so sweetly at him, Blue Coyote waited no longer. He pulled his breechclout aside and slid between the soft inviting legs that opened for him. Mourning Dove opened wide and rose to meet him. He plunged deep inside her wet inviting warmth and almost before she could wrap her legs around him he exploded, groaned and collapsed upon her. They lay so for a short time, them Mourning Dove began to tighten and release her muscles. Beyond any ability to think, or even consciously control his movements Blue Coyote felt his member respond, quickly growing. This time he was able to give her pleasure as well. He ran his tongue around her hard nipples and gently suckled on them. She groaned and pushed harder. He increased the tempore of his actions and she kept pace with him. Again and again he drove into her, harder and harder, picking up speed as well. She writhed beneath him, moaning and digging her fingers into his back. She arched to meet him with each thrust and finally in exploding passion they both found release.

Blue Coyote lay upon her, awareness slowly returning he rolled away and lay on his back, still unable to think of anything but the experience that he had just had. If this was what mating was all about, no wonder . . .

Mourning Dove rose and shook the dirt and grass from her tunic. Adjusting her short apron back into place, she smiled at Blue Coyote and began removing the grass from her long hair. He watched her, enjoying the intimacy of the moment. Then he rose and donned his own clothing; the air was cold now that he became aware of his exposed nature.

Blue Coyote decided to speak with Fire Dancer this very day. He would begin immediately building their very own shelter and he knew the perfect spot. There was a secluded place just at the edge of the camp. The trees were a thick grove, but at its' very center, was a clear area just large enough for a shelter. It would be ideal. Plans were going through his head one after another. All blissful, passion filled and Mourning Dove the center of each.

They returned to the camp. Stone Man was working on his arm stretcher. He frowned when he saw Blue Coyote alone with the unmated Mourning Dove, but then he returned to his exercise. The muscles were beginning to respond. The afternoon sun was warm on his shoulder and he was able to move the area more and more as the days went by.

*   *   *

"Have you seen Fire Dancer?" Star Woman questioned Basket; "He went out early this morning to check for bison signs. He should have been back before mid day. It is nearly dark now and I am getting worried."

"Who went with him?"

"Blue Coyote," answered Star Woman.

"Blue Coyote has been around the camp most of the day. If they went together, they returned long ago," Basket replied, "I will go and ask around."

"Would you? I would appreciate that, I will see if Bison Man has any knowledge of Fire Dancer's plans."

Basket nodded and headed toward the more male end of the camp. She questioned Singing Serpent, Acorn, Jackrabbit, Cougar and Stone Man. None had seen Fire Dancer the entire day, though several did mention that he had been going out with Blue Coyote. "Then where is he?" She questioned, not seeing him anywhere in the camp either.

"Over in the grove," replied Stone Man, "He is building a shelter there for Mourning Dove."

Basket frowned and sighed, making her way through the thick brush. Mourning Dove was sitting prettily on a stone watching while Blue Coyote was down on his knees excavating a hole with a sharp digging stick. Beside him was a freshly prepared structure support. "I have been told that you went out early this morning with your father," she began.

Blue Coyote shook his head, "we were supposed to go out after bison sign, Father didn't meet me so I guess he forgot or something else came up, because we didn't go." Basket glanced at Mourning Dove, catching a quick satisfied expression of victory as it crossed her face. Then it was gone. He was now settling the support in the hole and tamping rocks and dirt around it for an anchor. Blue Coyote seemed more interested in the task involving him, than the disappearance of his father.

"Well he in not in the camp and your mother is worried. It would be appropriate if you would join the search!" She stomped off back through the brush, irritated at the smug expression that she saw on Mourning Dove's face.

The camp assembled, including Blue Coyote, but not Mourning Dove and a search was initiated. The area adjacent to the camp was searched, but dark descended and they could do no more without torches. It was decided to wait until morning. If Fire Dancer had not returned by then, a further search would be conducted. This bothered Basket, what if the man was out there somewhere, hurt and in need of help. She couldn't wait until morning. She found Singing Serpent and he agreed to accompany her. Throw Back was reluctant to leave her new family, but Star Child assured her that she would take care of them. Basket gave the command to Throw Back to find Fire Dancer. The pair took lighted torches and followed the big wolf. Throw Back went beyond the camp toward the trail to the plain above. Once there she circled a few times then wagged her tail and headed up the trail. They followed.

At the top, the trail turned to follow the edge of the canyon, this puzzled them both and then Throw Back whined, looked over the edge and whined again, her tail tucked between her legs. "What is it, girl?" Basket held the torch down, "Look, there are fresh marks here at the edge; it looks as if a section of the edge gave way, Oh no! We must go back, what if he fell?" Already she was hurrying back to the trail, Throw Back leading the way and Singing Serpent following.

"I think about here," Basket began pushing her way through the thick brush at the base of the cliff, her torch not giving enough light to illuminate the lip. "Go back to the camp and get some of the men, we cannot search this area alone!"

"I think I see something," Singing Serpent pushed past her and Throw Back woofed and shot past him. They found blood on the rocks but the wolf was some distance beyond them now barking urgently. They struggled to her and found what they feared. Fire Dancer's broken body lay in a grotesque mockery of the fine man he had been. Already scavengers had been at him. His eyes had been plucked from their sockets and parts of the flesh from his face as well. Larger predators had also been at the corpse. The abdominal area was ripped open and most of the entrails eaten. He had landed on his back. His skull must have exploded on impact.

"I will go get some men to bring him back to the camp," Basket said woodenly, "if you would stay here and keep further predation from him." She led Throw Back away and they returned to the camp. Star Woman saw her expression and began to weep. Stone Man, Blue Coyote, Gray Eagle and Bison Man accompanied Basket back to where Singing Star waited. Silently they lifted the lifeless body of their friend and leader and carried him back to the camp.

"What happened?" sobbed Star Woman.

"I cannot say for certain, but it looks as if the ground gave way beneath him and he fell into the canyon. We will have to wait until tomorrow to be certain." Singing Serpent answered.

"I don't understand," wailed Star Woman, "He was going out with Blue Coyote," she turned to her son, "Where were you? Why weren't you with him? I heard the pair of you discussing it last night!"

Blue Coyote shook his head; "We were to meet at the central hearth just after the morning meal. I waited and waited, Father never joined me, so I went about other things!" He flushed uncomfortably, remembering just what 'other things' he had been occupied with, while his father lay dead or dying at the base of the cliff.

"We will look in the morning," Bison Man said. "There must be an explanation. Fire Dancer was far too seasoned a hunter to fall from a cliff."

Turtle Woman stayed with her sister and the remainder of the camp went to their respective shelters and to their sleeping furs. Basket returned to the shelter and found Star Child desperately holding Throw Back as Mourning Dove cowered against the far side of the shelter. Throw Back had her lips curled back and was growling and glaring hatred at the woman. "What is going on here?" Basket questioned.

"That horrid creature!" screeched Mourning Dove, "She tried to attack me again! I will not spend another night in this shelter!" She grabbed up her sleeping furs and few possessions and fled.

"Well that settles that!" Star Child said with some satisfaction as she released the wolf, "Personally I agree with Throw Back, good by to that problem!"

"But; why? I mean Throw Back always has a reason! She doesn't just take a dislike to a person!"

"Why not? I certainly have!" Star Child answered. Throw Back settled and gathered her brood to nurse. The black pup had not yet opened its eyes, but the others had. Throw Back nuzzled the large one to her and began licking it.

"I cannot believe that Fire Dancer is gone!" Basket sat on her furs; "I will certainly miss him! We all will!" She wiped away a tear, "Poor Star Woman!"

It was a somber group of people who trouped up the trail. Selected men carried the wrapped remains of Fire Dancer. They carried him to a place he had especially liked. It was some distance from the camp but those men bearing the burden did not mind. They lay his atlatl and darts beside him, placed his bolas and hunting tools upon his chest and Acorn, the dreamer sent a special prayer to the spirits to carry the soul of this beloved man to the ancestor fires in the sky. Then it was done and they all trouped back to the camp. Star Woman had Scorpion on a lead, for she cried and tried to return to Fire Dancer. Mourning Dove was careful to stay inconspicuously to the back of the group, her expression carefully veiled. After all, she was not really a member of this camp and she had hardly known the man.

Later that same day Bison Man, Blue Coyote and Cougar went to the place where Fire Dancer had obviously gone over the cliff. They were able to discover nothing. There were no tracks, not even Fire Dancer's. This was a puzzle. The death was a puzzle. Why had Fire Dancer even come to this spot? Why had he failed to meet Blue Coyote as arranged? Had he seen something and gone to investigate? So many questions; no one had any answers.

Blue Coyote returned to his task of building a shelter for himself and Mourning Dove, saying nothing to anyone about this project, yet many know what he was doing. Star Woman frowned at him, he was not acting at all normally, but then the death of his father was probably the cause of this. She went about her own duties in a fog, hardly noticing anything, nothing that is except the chewed through lead. Stone Man made the lone trek to where they had laid out Fire Dancer. He had tears in his eyes as he related that Scorpion lay beside her beloved master and refused to leave him. He shook his head, proclaiming that by morning she also would have gone to walk the wind. It was decided that this was fitting. The loyal old dog remained with Fire Dancer and a pair of days later she grieved herself to death.

A few days later Bison Man called Blue Coyote, Gray Wolf and Cougar to accompany him to seek signs of bison. They would be gone at least a pair of days. Jackrabbit remained behind to guide the camp in case of an emergency. Stone Man was not yet able to throw an atlatl, so he stayed behind as well, more intent than ever to get his arm working. Most of the women were gathered in the main hearth area, working hides, making winter clothes and repairing things that were in need of such.

* * *

Stone Man was working at his arm exercises. This is where Mourning Dove found him. She seated herself prettily on a rock within his line of view and watched the bulging muscles move beneath his tunic. She ran her tongue over her lip, a move that got his attention. She squirmed on the rock and tossed her long loose hair behind her shoulder, exposing a length of smooth neck and breast. Stone Man frowned; he had been so obsessed with working the stiffness from his shoulder that most things had passed him. He had not realized that Blue Coyote, for example, had been spending time with Mourning Dove. He had been concentrating on only one thing, his arm and shoulder.

It surprised him that Mourning Dove was here watching him work, but it did not displease him. He smiled at her and purposefully made movements which showed to advantage his fine-muscled body. Stone Man was taller and broader than Blue Coyote, and his muscles bulged from constant use. He found that he liked the attention of this strikingly beautiful woman. Finally he finished and tied up the cord, released his arm and wiped the sweat from his brow with a rabbit skin.

"You are certainly a powerful man." Mourning Dove murmured, "I have been watching you, you are nearly recovered now. Soon you will be back hunting with the others."

"Do you think so?" He asked, "I still have some stiffness in this shoulder and it does not have the strength that it used to."

"Have you tried to throw yet?"

Stone Man shook his head, "Soon though," he replied.

"Why not now? I would accompany you. We could find a place to practice; I will help you and then think how surprised the others will be when you are suddenly your old self again!" She clapped her hands and bounced excitedly.

He considered this, "I don't know . . ." He glanced about, "I had thought that Blue Coyote and I . . ."

"Oh why wait? He is off hunting and won't be back for a pair of days! You could get that much practice in before he returns. Of course if you don't want my help . . ."

"I would enjoy that!" Stone Man quickly stated, "I just, well you know, after all you are an unmated woman, and there are rules . . ."

"Not from my people," she assured him, "my people have no such rules. After all how are men and women to get to know each other, to discover if they are drawn to someone," she arched her neck, throwing her breasts into relief against her tunic and giving him a very tempting glance.

"You are sure . . .?"

"Of course, would I suggest such a thing if it were not proper?" She rose and again tossed her head, "I know the very place! It is secluded, private and far enough from the camp that no one will even know."

Stone Man looked at the woman, gathered his atlatl and darts and followed her from the camp. "See! Just ahead! That dead stump will make a perfect target and I will retrieve your darts for you!" She smiled warmly at Stone Man. He grinned back in return. This day was turning out better than he had expected. Finally he felt confident that his shoulder was nearly back to normal. He had wanted to surprise Blue Coyote with his complete recovery. Now he had just been offered the opportunity to do so and with the help of the most beautiful woman he had ever laid eyes on and she was obviously finding him just as attractive!

For a time he practiced, the darts not always hitting the target, but the woman cooed sympathetically and hurried to retrieve his dart when he missed and she bounced excitedly and praised him when it struck the target. Progressively however, his mind was straying from the target and landing on her. She was so very beautiful, her long shapely legs bare beneath the short apron she wore beneath an abbreviated tunic.

Most women would feel the chill with so much exposed flesh, but it did not seem to bother Mourning Dove and Stone Man certainly was not about to complain. He had not realized how much pleasure there could be found in watching a beautiful woman. And Mourning Dove flitted back and forth, her bare rounded buttocks flashing occasionally and her breasts bouncing attractively. And those eyes, they promised . . . they invited . . . and Stone Man willingly followed.

She was driving him crazy, the way she ran her tongue over her lower lip, the way her breasts pushed against the soft skin of her tunic, the hard nipples pertly standing out. Stone Man found himself responding no matter how hard he tried to concentrate on the atlatl and darts and target. He managed to make a dead on shot at the stump. Mourning Dove threw her arms about him in excitement, rubbing her soft body against his. With a groan, Stone Man dropped his hunting tools and encircled her lithe body with his arms. Mourning Dove pressed even harder against him, inviting . . .

She stepped from his embrace and looking deeply into his eyes slowly reached down and pulled her tunic over her head, lifting her long black hair up and behind her shoulders, presenting him with an unbelievable sight of her ripe breasts and taunt stomach. With a groan he laid her on the soft grass beneath a tree and began to caress that wonderful body. Mourning Dove writhed and moaned softly, each movement, exciting him further. He stroked her breasts; gently bit the nipples, sending her into even greater passion. Then he spread her inviting thighs and pushing his breechclout to one side he gently pushed into her, commanding his every control to be gentle.

Mourning Dove wrapped her legs around him and arched her back slowly receiving and adjusting to his size. Then she sighed and began the age-old move of the mating. She pulled him deeply inside and then released the pressure, again and again, until Stone Man was pumping wildly into the thrashing moaning body. His mind spun and he lost control releasing into her just as she made a final arch and cried out in her own release.

They sank panting to the ground, he upon her, yet careful not to crush her with his greater weight. He started to roll free, but she tightened her muscles and smiled at him and Stone Man found his body responding with a mind of its own. The second time was even better, if that was possible. They had both sweat profusely and now had grass and dirt all over their bodies. Mourning Dove rose to her feet and walked the few steps to the stream and began washing the dirt and grime from her body. She had undone the tie of her apron and now stood completely naked in the ankle-deep water.

Stone Man dropped his breechclout and went to join her. They washed each other, caressing and mouthing sensitive areas. She dropped to her knees and Stone Man felt the earth move as she took his member into her mouth. He groaned and squirmed as she pleasured him. Then he carried her wet body from the stream and again they mated, this time quickly and almost violently. His passion spent, Stone Man washed quickly in the stream and pulled his clothing onto his chilled body. Mourning Dove was not in so much of a hurry and treated him to a wonderful scene as she bathed and donned her own clothing.

So this was what mating was all about! No wonder it is so popular! How could I be so lucky that such a wonderful, passionate, beautiful woman has chosen me? Visions of a blissful future were running through his mind.

"Let's keep the practicing a secret, just between you and me," Mourning Dove purred softly once they stopped on the trip back to the camp. "After all, there is no real hurry!" She arched her body to his and smiled deeply into his eyes, "and of course it would be my pleasure to help you with the practice . . ." again she smiled.

Stone Man nodded, promising himself that he would work on the muscle mechanism even harder, if just to please this wonderful woman. There was no hurry to announce their mating. It was proper to respect the dead for a period and Fire Dancer had held a high position in the camp. There would be a prolonged period of mourning. There could be no hurt in waiting.

*   *   *

The runner returned and the camp went to the place of the bison kill. Basket stayed behind, as did Acorn and several of the older members of the camp. Throw Back was still nursing her pups, there were enough women without Basket and she was loath to leave the animal. She was thankful that Mourning Dove did go with the camp.

At the bison kill, Mourning Dove was absolutely the proper young woman. She did not so much as look at a man, old or young. She worked with the women, stayed with the women and if she did not work as hard, or as long, at least she behaved herself. There was no trouble. Moth glared at her and although the other women did not have friendly feelings toward her they did not treat her any differently than any other. The meat was processed and the people returned to the camp.

Blue Coyote resumed work on the shelter, completed it and Mourning Dove moved in, alone. There could be no announcement of their mating until the mourning period for Fire Dancer had been observed. This did not, however, mean that they could not sneak off occasionally to their secret place, watched over by a dead stump. Meanwhile, Blue Coyote assumed more and more of the leadership duties of the camp. He was young, but it was understood by all that he would step into the place of the headman, soon.

Stone Man concentrated harder on his recovery. Since Blue Coyote was increasingly taken up with affairs of the camp, they spent little time together. Stone Man found opportunity to slip off and practice, Mourning Dove always with him. They could not announce their mating until the mourning period was observed, but that didn't mean they could not slip off secretly and . . .

All through the harvest moon and into the next . . .

Even though it was now deep winter, both men found that at the end of each day they were glad to simply roll into their sleeping furs and quickly fall asleep. There was not even time to talk and neither wanted to chance revealing the secret each held dear to his heart. It would not show proper respect for their beloved fallen leader. Both missed Fire Dancer and his wise leadership.

* * *

The black pup opened its eyes and they were just the same blue color as the eyes of her mother. Throw Back duly presented the pup to Star Child and Basket presented the rest to others in the camp. There was one pup, larger than the rest, one with one blue eye and one yellow eye, this one she gave to Singing Serpent, for it showed signs of being a 'spirit animal'. One she gave to Star Woman, not to replace Scorpion, but as her very own dog. The remainder went to hunters, selected by Bison Man. The winter passed mildly in this southern canyon. The weather was not nearly as severe here and it was not even necessary to locate caves to shelter in. There was much game in the canyon and bison, although not numerous, did winter on the plain above. Occasionally the women went out to gather a few tubers or acorns far up the canyon. Seldom did Mourning Dove refuse to accompany them if asked. She seemed to be fitting into the camp life far better than Star Woman had first expected. The elders frowned upon her having a shelter to herself, particularly so far removed from the camp, but she assured them that this was customary among her people, so it was allowed. The women disapproved of the way she dressed, but this also was the custom of her people, so again, it was tolerated.

All were busy with their daily lives. There was much to do and every day was filled to the brim. If occasionally a hunter disappeared from the camp for an afternoon, no one was aware of it. If Mourning Dove spent part of a day secluded in her shelter, no one bothered seeking her out. Yet more and more frequently this happened.

Gray Wolf took to wandering off alone up the canyon. He always returned refreshed and smiling. Evidently a brisk walk alone revitalized him. If Journey's Far, a young brawny hunter of Bison Man's old camp disappeared, no one noticed. He was shy and kept much to himself any way, yet these excursions seemed to do him good.

Even Running Man, a mature hunter of the same group took to going on lone trips up the canyon. None, however, were gone from the camp at the same time. Mourning Dove, on the other hand, also kept much to herself, seldom leaving her shelter, having little to do with the women of the camp unless invited. However, any time she was invited she always accepted and was a perfect well-behaved female.

Bison Man and Jackrabbit had not given up investigating Fire Dancer's death. Methodically they questioned every member of the camp. Bison

Man had pieced together some information. They had scoured the area for a distance in every direction from the area; there was absolutely no sign of anyone, not strangers, or a member of the camp who had left a trace above. The only person missing from the camp on the day of Fire Dancer's death had been Mourning Dove, yet she claimed to have remained within the confines of the camp all day. No one had questioned Blue Coyote about his whereabouts. Bison Man had suspicions, but they made no sense.

What possible reason could she have for wanting him dead? How could a small woman manage to push so large a man over the cliff?

* * *

Mourning Dove had slipped like a shadow from where she crouched behind the headman's shelter. She scurried up the path to a place where she had nearly fallen to the rocks below. The ground here was unstable. Carefully she withdrew an article of clothing, which she had actually constructed herself. With a long stick she placed the article just where she wanted it, eased back and returned to the camp. It wasn't a good plan, but it was the only one she had. Fire Dancer was not going to throw her out of this camp. She was not going to sit quietly by and be ousted again to walk the wind! This time she had been lucky, who could say it would happen again.

She slipped into the camp and barely had time to place herself in a strategic spot before Fire Dancer came by on his way to meet Blue Coyote. She stepped out, "Headman, I am worried about something," she said docilely, assuming a worried attitude. "I was gathering grain above the canyon last evening. I do not know if it is important, but I saw an article of clothing up there. I don't recognize it as belonging to this camp. As you know men from the south raided my home camp, it looks like something they wore and I am very worried. Would you have time to look into it? It is not far and would take little time."

Fire Dancer frowned; sighed and nodded. It was early for meeting Blue Coyote, so he followed the woman from the camp and up the trail. He had many concerns on his mind. They needed to locate bison for a hunt and this woman weighed heavily as a major problem. He followed her to the plain above the canyon and a short distance along the brim. He could see the object from a distance. Someone had laid and watched the camp from a high vantage spot. He went toward the object and was about to bend over and pick it up when something struck him solidly in the back, propelling him forward. Suddenly the ground gave way beneath him, his feet found no purchase and he somersaulted through the air; there was an unbelieving flash of disbelief, a searing pain a blinding flash of light, then nothing.

Mourning Dove eased cautiously to the edge and glanced down. She smiled. Below on the rocks lay the broken body of Fire Dancer. She studied it for several breaths, making sure he was dead. Then, ever so carefully, she inched backwards to safety. She looked around; reassuring herself that no one else was about. Then she went about the task of covering her trail, already wiping the memory of the grisly remains below.

Mourning Dove retrieved her stick; snagged the object and using the selfsame twig to carefully erase her footprints and slipped back into the camp, every trace carefully removed. There would be so many prints that no one would be able to discern to whom they belonged. She returned to the hated shelter she had shared with Basket and Star Child and the ugly deformed creature which Basket was so fond of growled at her. She backed from the shelter and entered the main part of the camp. She smiled and went about the camp as normal. Blue Coyote she noticed was waiting irritably at the central hearth and after a time wandered aimlessly off on his own. Later she went to find him.

---

1. This method of keeping warm was used by many historic Indian tribes, and adapted by Europeans as well during the 'Mountain Man' days of settling the west.

CHAPTER 17

Bison Man stood staring at the place where Fire Dancer had fallen to his death. He had visited this place over and over again, trying to piece together what had happened. Mourning Dove watched him from the shelter of brush below. She had been following Bison Man secretly for some time and was almost sure that he had pieced together the events leading up to Fire Dancer's death. *He can't prove anything!* Again and again she had reminded herself. *There is no way he can connect me with Fire Dancer.* No one had seen her leave the camp, of that she made certain. No on had cause to suspect her, except maybe Star Woman, and she was too filled with grief to be suspicious. Besides as far as anyone knew, it was an accident. Fire Dancer merely stepped to close to the edge and fell. *I left no evidence.* She had been extremely careful. Yet she worried. She still had the distinctive object, tucked away in her shelter. Once Gray Wolf had almost found it, so she had hidden it more carefully, actually burying it under dirt beneath her storage containers, a place no one was likely to look. It was becoming increasingly difficult to keep the various men from being suspicious of each other. Once Grass had shown up unexpectedly and almost met Gray Wolf leaving. Since then she had impressed each man with the need for secrecy. Since all revered Fire Dancer, it had not been hard. Soon however the time of mourning would be over, and as once before, her insatiable need for men had brought her to trouble.

At the moment Bison Man was becoming the greatest risk however. She had devised a plan, but it would take careful maneuvering to bring it about. She had searched the canyon for a place that would serve, finally locating one. It was all set up, but the problem of getting Bison Man there still had to be solved. She watched him thoughtfully, then smiled, *yes, it just might work! Why be complicated if simple does the job?* Quietly she eased from her crouching place and slipped through the brush beyond the camp to her shelter. She smiled and was soon headed up the canyon at a fast trot. She shinnied up the tree with an agility and quickness more in line with the antics of a boy than a mature woman, but she snagged an object from its position high up in the tree, scraping her leg on the bark as she climbed down. Back at her shelter she whimpered as she rinsed the inner thigh with herbal solution, after picking several splinters from the tender skin.

Later in the day, while everyone was occupied with camp chores, Mourning Dove made her way up a dangerous, barely discernable path to the plateau. She had located this path one day watching a bobcat use it. Curiously she followed, discovering an interesting feature as yet unnoticed by the people of the camp. She edged to the spot she was seeking, not far from where Fire Dancer had met his end, and again placed the strange object near the lip. Easing back, she removed all traces of her presence and made her precarious way back down into the canyon. Then she returned to her shelter and waited. The chances that anyone else would discover the object before morning were remote, and since Bison Man went to the spot every day, there was always the chance that he would solve her problem for her. Besides, Gray Wolf was expected at any moment.

"What happened?" he ran a finger along the raw flesh then ran his tongue along it as well, causing Mourning Dove to moan and forget to answer him. Later, he returned to the subject.

"Oh that!" she laughed. "Basket dared me to climb a tree for pine nuts. I slipped coming down, but I got the pine nuts!" she laughed. Gray Wolf loved her laugh. It was like water tumbling over wet stones.

* * *

Bison Man sat at his fire late into the night. He just could not convince himself that so small a woman could have pushed Fire Dancer to his death. It made no sense! What reason could she have? She had been taken in by his camp, she had been made welcome, was being protected and becoming a contributing member of the camp. She was well behaved and proper. He felt ashamed to even consider her. There had to have been something or someone else responsible. With a sigh he retired, *I am missing something here . . .*

*   *   *

The next morning, he again went to the *place. There has to be a clue!* It was then that he noticed something farther down the edge. It had not been there previously, of that he was certain. Was it possible that strangers were involved in Fire Dancer's death after all? They had found no evidence of anyone, particularly strangers during the whole time they had been at the canyon. Still if others were spying on the camp, they would hardly be likely to leave evidence behind. Yes! Strangers, men, big, strong men! They could have cast Fire Dancer over the cliff! This made more sense than suspecting the poor innocent young woman! He felt ashamed of himself! Yet he also felt relief. He walked to the object, leaned over to pick it up and in a flash understood exactly what had brought Fire Dancer to his death. The earth crumbled beneath him, and Bison Man had only time for a surprised grunt before his body crashed onto the boulders far below, and with a blinding flash of excruciating pain, he knew no more. A small figure smiled and quietly slipped from her hiding place and returned to the camp.

It would be tomorrow before the hunters would go out to look for Bison Man. By then it was even possible that predators would have drug his body to a place where he would never be found. She would suggest, perhaps Strangers, the same mythical strangers who had supposedly attacked her camp. Mourning Dove returned to her shelter, remembering that attack.

It was not Strangers, however, who had attacked her and brought her to her lonely state when the Wolf Camp found her. It was in fact her own camp and her own father who had been responsible. He had caught Mourning Dove coupling with Sagebrush, her own brother. It had so infuriated him that he had gathered the men of the camp and driven the pair of them from the camp, naked and with no tools. Sagebrush had been a creative youth; he had made a dart of a straight branch, crafted crude stone knives and scrapers, made an atlatl and killed the deer from which they were able to construct their clothing. They had lived like wild people for several moons, then they had been following the big river to the south, but Sagebrush had decided they would go up this smaller stream, basically because he did come across signs of other people. They had fled to this canyon and lived in a cave far upriver. Then a javalina gored Sagebrush, 'spirits' invaded his leg and he had died.

Mourning Dove had stayed in that cave, with his moldering corpse, for nearly a moon longer, eating the last of the food. She had seen these people move into the canyon and set up camp. Had spied upon them for some time before the hunters surprised her and she had slipped and fallen into the water, hitting her head on a rock in the process. But, in the long run, all had worked out.

Mourning Dove joined the women of the camp at their daily chores that morning and spent the day with them, going about whatever task she was assigned quietly and with absolutely perfect composure. People were beginning to change their opinions of her. Women were actually being civil to her, not that she cared. These people served only one purpose as far as Mourning Dove was concerned. They would care for her until something better came along. Only now she had gone a long way to creating that something better.

*   *   *

Star Woman remembered the rough start the young woman had made, but she was beginning to meld nicely into the daily life of the camp. Perhaps the women should make more of an effort to include her. She had, after all, not been used to the traditions of The People, and those of her own group might have been vastly different, which would explain why she had such outlandish ideas to begin with. Perhaps they had judged too harshly!

By mid day Bison Man had been missed. No one was unduly alarmed for Bison Man frequently went off by himself to think. At dusk, however, the camp became uneasy. By dark they were alarmed. Bison Man was never this late returning.

"Did he say where he was going?" Jackrabbit questioned. Hunters shook their heads or shrugged. Bison Man kept much to himself of late. Something had been bothering him, but no one knew what. He had made long walks along the upper edge of the canyon, particularly the place where Fire Dancer had fallen. He had not given up finding the answer to Fire Dancer's death.

"If he has not returned by morning, we will go looking for him," Stone Man said, "it is too late tonight."

Morning arrived, Bison Man had not yet returned. Rain Woman had spent an uneasy night along, waiting . . . The men gathered their weapons and followed Blue Coyote and Stone Man up the trail up to the plateau. They looked about, found his trail and followed it... until it ended abruptly at the raw edge of the cliff.

"Do you think . . .?" Jackrabbit questioned.

Cougar started toward the edge, Blue Coyote held him back, shaking his head. "It is too dangerous! We do not know what the ground is like there."

"There is but one way to find out! Hold onto my ankles, I am going to look over the edge," Gray Wolf instructed. Stone Man and Blue Coyote each took hold of an ankle and Gray Wolf edged to the precipice. Earth crumpled beneath his shaking fingers, rocks dug into his gut, yet he edged closer, until he could look down. "He is down there! Pull me back, before I join him!" The edge began to crumble farther, and the men quickly pulled him to safety.

"Is he alive?"

Gray Wolf shook his head, "I don't think so, he is a long way down, and he is wedged into a crevasse at the bottom. The only way to reach him would be with a heavy rope, unless there is a way into that fissure from the canyon itself."

"I will go for rope," offered Jackrabbit, "The rest of you stay away from that edge, it is dangerous!" He loped off toward the camp.

"There is a lot of rope near the main hearth!" Blue Coyote shouted after him. Jackrabbit nodded and kept going.

They waited silently for his return. "I will go down," offered Blue Coyote, "you can pull him up and send the rope back for me." They agreed, and he was lowered over the edge, taking a good bit of it with him. The upper edge of the fissure was unstable, looking up he could see that it was mainly composed of broken rock, held in place by the roots of the trees lining the edge, but the ground itself was giving way. He reached the body and undid the rope, securing it to the corpse. Bison Man was certainly dead, his back had most likely been broken by the fall, and his head was busted open. "All right pull him up he shouted and ducked out of the way as still more of the unsound edge gave way. The body swung grotesquely back and forth, bumping into the side of the wall time and time again, raining more rubble down on him, but was finally hoisted over the edge. Blue Coyote slipped on the loose rock and searched for safer footing. It was then that he saw the object. It was a little lower among the boulders; he eased to his belly and reached down, just able to grasp it. Carefully he retrieved the thing, turning it over in his hands, frowning. He had never seen such a garment before, if that was what it was. It was a funnel-shaped piece of leather attached to a wide strap or band. It had been stained with a bright red dye for one thing, something which The People did not do, and for another, he could find no logical use for it. Then the rope came down and he was pulled to safety, the object clutched in his hand.

"What do you think it is?" Jackrabbit turned the object over and over in his hand.

"I have no idea, but it must have been what Bison Man spotted. It was beneath him." Blue Coyote replied.

The men stood, looking down into the canyon. The narrow fissure did not obstruct the view of the camp. Anyone could creep to this spot and watch the comings and goings below completely undetected through the screen of brush. This could explain a lot; the lack of any evidence when Fire Dancer died, and now again with the death of Bison Man. Both incidents were similar, no evidence of footprints. Strangers had been spying on the camp, completely unknown to them! Even with the tragedy of Bison Man's death, they could not hesitate. They were in danger and leaving the camp for the safety of the open plain was the only logical solution readily available to them. On the open plain it would be impossible for anyone to sneak up on them, here they could be trapped and darted from above, their every move seen clearly.

The men stood expectantly watching him, and Blue Coyote finally realized that they were waiting for him to make a decision. Suddenly the safety and direction of all these people had just settled heavily onto his shoulders. He swept the dirt and debris from his clothing and stood to face the others. "We will make the arrangements to leave this place immediately!"

He led the way back to the camp, "This evening we will lay Bison Man out in the canyon, he was a mountain dweller first and foremost. This is fitting for him . . . I will tell Rain Woman," he stated woodenly, "Perhaps she and my mother will find comfort with each other."

The People listened to what he had to say stoically, and then began swiftly to prepare to leave the canyon. "It would be best if there were watchers set until we leave," he had called the camp together. "Jackrabbit, Stone Man, you deal with protecting the camp, set up a watch, and make sure there is always someone watching. The rest of you men help strike the shelters and replace travois poles and whatever else needs to be done. Women, you make needed repairs and pack supplies and food."

"What of the Spring Ceremony?" Questioned Turtle Woman; "It was to be in a pair of days."

Blue Coyote thought, "If the watchers discover no one, it will go on as planned," Blue Coyote decided. "Do not pack things you plan to discard. Keep out your Spring Ceremony change of clothing, and we will leave the following day. The ceremony will be brief and in honor of Bison Man there will be no celebrating. Even though we will be moving, the period of mourning will be observed," he stated. "We owe it to Bison Man, just as we did and do to my Father," he sighed, "There will be no new people named, no matings, no naming of children until the mourning period is over," he turned and left the gathering with a heavy heart. He had hoped to announce his mating with Mourning Dove at the Spring Ceremony. He had planned on telling her tonight, now it would be midsummer before he could claim her. Added to that, there would be no opportunity for them to slip away on any more of the magical trips up the canyon. It looked to be a long time until mid summer.

A sad and mournful camp followed the carriers and Bison Man's body was taken to the far end of the canyon. He was laid out beneath a large oak tree to walk the wind. His atlatl and darts were laid beside him and his other tools set upon his chest. The camp bid him a final farewell; Moon sent a prayer to the spirits for his soul and they all filed quietly back to the camp, Rain Woman weeping quietly beside Star Woman.

* * *

Mourning Dove was not entirely pleased with the results of her plot. She had looked forward to at least another moon in this canyon. She hated being on the move! There was no privacy, little opportunity and no time for coupling, and now with Blue Coyote assuming leadership of the camp, no way to slip off with Stone Man, whom she greatly preferred. Stone Man was a lusty man, more inventive and endowed with far greater 'stamina' than Blue Coyote, yet given the choice, she knew she would choose Blue Coyote, for he was now Headman. Now was the time to begin breaking off her relations with the other men. Mourning Dove reluctantly made the decision.

The opportunity arrived sooner than she anticipated. Gray Wolf appeared at her shelter shortly after dark, "I told you not to come here again," she greeted Gray Wolf, "It is too dangerous! What if someone saw you! Could you not have waited until I contacted you? Already he was nuzzling her and helping her from her clothing. Mourning Dove reluctantly let him. After they had coupled, she returned to the topic of his unexpected visit.

"It matters little! Although now we must postpone our mating, what difference does it make if we let it be known?" Gray Wolf said reasonably.

"It matters to me! It was bad enough sneaking around dishonoring Fire Dancer, but now, Bison Man as well!" she protested, "I cannot so dishonor a pair of such worthy leaders. It was wrong of us to break the taboo! It was wrong of us to give in tonight. I know that you care, just as I care, but I asked you not to come to my shelter uninvited any more. You endanger both of us! If a man cannot be depended upon to abide by a simple request, perhaps I should not find him suitable for mating! I had asked you not to come to my shelter again, yet here you are! I am afraid I must insist that you go now. I can see that I allowed my heart to direct when my brain demands that I be through with you! You shame the trust that I put in you! All you think of is your lust!" She sobbed prettily; "I cannot trust you, no matter how much I may wish it otherwise!" Now she sobbed openly, "I thought you were perfect . . . now I see that I was blinded by desire!" She wiped away a tear, "Please go now," she whispered.

"But . . ." Gray Wolf protested.

"Go!" She almost shrieked. He left, so upset that he did not see another man slip silently behind the shelter, nor another duck into the brush and allow him to pass. The latter stepped into the trail and made his way to Mourning Dove's shelter.

She lay in his arms a time later, "We will have to stop this relationship after tonight," she sighed, "it is becoming too dangerous!"

"We can just let it be known that we are mating!" Protested Grass, "Who is to care, really?"

"I cannot betray the trust put in me by these, my new people! She sighed. "I realize now that the ways of my people are different. What we have done would not be frowned upon by my tribe, but I will no longer dishonor these good people." She grabbed her tunic and slipped it over her head,

"We will just say we cannot wait any longer, they will understand!" pleaded Grass.

"How can you even suggest such a thing?" She looked down at him soulfully. "Perhaps I was too quick to trust my heart, I had no idea that your only interest was to take me to your furs, I thought," she began to sob, "obviously wrongly, that you cared for me, but now I see it was only selfish lust! How could I have been so blind?" She pointed to the door, "Leave! I can see that you are not the man I thought you to be. We are ended!" She again pointed. Grass tried to reason with her, but she only became more hysterical, he pulled on his clothes and left.

The figure behind the shelter melted away, he had much to think about, and much was becoming increasingly clearer. He had been just as much a fool as the other pair, and he knew not how many more beside. For moons now he had thought of little else but the pleasure he found between her legs. She had been the most perfect, most purely beautiful thing he had ever found. All the beauty he had seen in her vanished as he watched and listened. He saw clearly now. Oh, she was clever, that he would give her, and talented. He would truly miss the times spent coupling with her supple body, but any caring he had for the woman quickly vanished with his discovery of her faithlessness. She would be given no opportunity to send him on his way.

The camp began the process of breaking down the next morning. Stone Man was dismantling his muscle stretcher when Mourning Dove sauntered by. She looked speculatively at him, but he was busy dismantling and he had so much on his mind that he did not even seem to notice her. Disgruntled she went on to join the women and help with the packing of carry-bags and travois. There was no more time to speak with Stone Man. Their paths went in different directions. She frowned yet accepted that Stone Man would have to wait.

Blue Coyote was just as unrewarding. He had no time for her, barely able to even find a moment to speak with her. When she approached him, he merely whispered, "Not now!" and then totally ignored her. Mourning Dove frowned and bit her lip. She returned to the women and stayed there the rest of the day. This was the last night they would spend in the shelters. In the morning the hides would be pulled from the frames and separated to make them into traveling shelters. There would not be another opportunity to see either man. She paced restlessly, hoping that at least one of them would realize this and come to her. They could hurry into the canyon and have a quick coupling without notice. Neither came. Finally, Mourning Dove went alone to her furs, flouncing on her side and finally sleeping.

*   *   *

Stone Man sat beside the fire, mending the harness for his wolf. Friend lay beside him as Wolf lay beside Blue Coyote opposite. Both men were making repairs, and both were thinking private thoughts. Stone Man completed his task and rose. Blue Coyote sighed and tossed his to the ground. His heart was heavy, and he had much on his mind, much he needed to express to Stone Man. Much he needed to clear from his conscience.

"I would walk a distance from the camp and speak with you," he said. Stone Man raised an eyebrow and nodded consent. The men followed a well-trod path up the canyon and found a place to sit.

"It seems that suddenly we are being thrust into adulthood," Blue Coyote said breaking a stick into small pieces and tossing each to the ground. "It seems only yesterday that we were carefree boys playing at being adults in the Starving Mountains. Now suddenly I realize that I have the responsibility of the entire camp as my care and burden. We have drifted from one another these last few moons my friend. Even sharing the same shelter, we seem not to talk any more. Perhaps that is my fault. I have had much on my mind of late, yet even with the death of Father; I had not begun to realize that leadership is being thrust upon my shoulders. It was not so bad until the loss of Bison Man. He would have helped and advised me, even shared the leadership. But now, there is no one that I can trust, no one that I would want to trust other than you, Stone Man. We always knew this day would arrive, I suppose. I just didn't think it would be for seasons yet"

"I have always been by your side," Stone Man replied, feeling guilty, for the last moons, here in this canyon, he had been far more interested in coupling with Mourning Dove than his friendship with Blue Coyote. "I will be here if you need me," he offered with a tinge of guilt.

"I will try to be a leader such as my father was, but suddenly I realize that I am young, far too young for such responsibility, yet it is mine and I must assume it. I guess I just needed to hear that you are still there for me," he concluded lamely. *You idiot! It is your own fault if Stone Man refuses to be second to you. He could go his own way and be a very successful leader on his own. Why should he follow you? You have been able to think of nothing but Mourning Dove all winter! Who could blame him if Stone Man had refused?*

"Would you help me decide the division of people into shelters? I am having trouble placing some. For example, Mother has always shared with Father and Turtle Woman and Cougar, now I feel that perhaps Rain Woman would benefit from being with her."

"Why not just ask them?" Stone Man advised, "It would be simpler, and they would appreciate being consulted."

Blue Coyote nodded, "And what of Mourning Dove? A young unmated woman cannot be allowed to shelter alone, yet I hesitate to put her with the others. Willow and the other unmated women make a full shelter. Star Child and Basket tend to shut others out of their special bond, and they are so 'power' filled, I do not think it fair to put her with them either. And she has a genuine fear of Throw Back!" he added.

"Then put her with the old ones!" Stone Man was irritated suddenly, "What difference does it make where she sleeps at night?"

"Blue Coyote suddenly grinned, "You are right, it makes no difference, none at all!" *You won't get the opportunity any way!* "That solved the immediate problems. Do you really think there are strangers spying upon us?"

Stone Man shrugged, *how would I know? I have paid attention to nothing but a woman for moons now, the safety of this camp has been far from my mind!* "So it seems," he replied lamely.

"Tomorrow is the Spring Ceremony." *I had planned on announcing my mating then!*

"Yes." *I had so many plans for tomorrow . . .*

"We leave the day after."

"I know," they both sighed.

"Well I guess we might as well return to the camp," Blue Coyote said. *Idiot! Why can't you just tell him about Mourning Dove? He is your best friend! He would understand! He might even suggest a way out of this mess!*

Stone Man rose to follow Blue Coyote. *Coward!* He accused himself. *Why couldn't you just tell him what happened? He would understand! Any man can make a fool of himself over a woman! There was a time you shared everything. But not this! That's the problem! Had I, from the very beginning . . . But now it is too late.* He kicked a rock and followed his friend. It was time to put the woman from his mind and take his place beside Blue Coyote and lead The People. Women! Who needed them? He had no time for such complications just now.

Blue Coyote was thinking on amazingly different lines. He could think of nothing but how he was going to find time to spend alone with Mourning Dove, even though he knew that there would be none. However, they went to their furs in a far better frame of mind than either had in some time.

*   *   *

The Spring Ceremony was a much-abbreviated affair. The usual hand of days ceremony was cut too but one. The ceremonial discarding of the starving and wintertime was completed without much enthusiasm by anyone. The old things were thrown away, and since they were leaving the canyon, there was no need for the symbolic new hearths. People were more concerned with making sure they had everything they wanted packed on their travois or in backpacks. Blue Coyote consulted his mother and Rain Woman and they offered a ready solution, they would share with Star Child and Basket and let Jackrabbit and Makes a Robe share with Cougar and Turtle Woman. This solved another problem for it left no where to put Mourning Dove except with the old women. Blue Coyote almost smiled when he told her. It was a pleasure to see her beautify face and watch her fight with herself and quietly agree. She was such a passionate little thing! The shelters were struck and before nightfall the camp had been arranged into the groups they would be with until the following winter. Mourning Dove was furious.

How could he? Those old hags will drive me insane within a moon! There is no way now to slip away and meet him, nor anyone else! Not with those old busybodies always curious about one's comings and goings, always snooping . . . She assumed her place in the line of the camp, behind Little Antelope Woman's broad behind.

Blue Coyote led his camp up out of the canyon and onto the plain, in the wake of the first bison herds to head north. The People were on the move again, following the path that their ancestors had followed. They swung by the southern place of stone, gathered what they needed, and then headed north. They were watchful, and the camp was protected at night. A pair of hunters took the beginning of the night, and another pair finished it. Each night different men watched; one at each end of the camp, just as Fire Dancer had done.

"I found this among Father's things," Blue Coyote set the stone beside the fire. "Remember how we used to sit at night and discuss where we were and which way we should go the next day?"

"It led us to the place of stone, but we had always planned on going beyond that," he ran his finger over a path of moons scratched onto the stone, "We never followed the trail north."

"We always planned to. First Red Eagle attacked, and then we sheltered in the secret canyon. By the time we got to the place of stone, well Red Eagle attacked again and we went south instead." Stone Man mused. "I wonder what lies north...?"

"Let's find out!" Jackrabbit suggested. "I know Fire Dancer always intended to go north. Perhaps there are mountains there, filled with deer and bear and turkeys!" he added wistfully.

"I also would like to find out!" added Cougar.

"We have no need to stop at the place of stone," reminded Gray Wolf, "We have an ample supply for now. Look at this line here," he pointed at the faint moons, "It goes north a long way. I bet there are mountains there, just as there are west of the moving sand. I would like to find out!"

"What of the rest of you?" questioned Blue Coyote, "Would you like to see what lies north?"

"Yes!" was the resounding answer.

"Then we go north!" There was a cheer through the camp; people seemed to be more relaxed than since Fire Dancer's death. The death of

Bison Man had cast the whole camp into a grim silence. Now they had a definite destination, a purpose! Blue Coyote felt satisfied as he returned the stone to its place on his travois and retired to his sleeping furs. Gladly he closed his eyes and yielded to the bittersweet dreams . . . of Mourning Dove.

She came to him in his dreams, as she could not in reality. He held her, caressed her, and possessed her again and again, waking, as frequently he had, under circumstances where the rabbit fur he had recently been tucking unobtrusively into his sleeping furs, was needed. He sighed, rolled over and again slept.

Fire Dancer stood a short distance away, beaconing him; Blue Coyote frowned, then rose and went toward his father. But Fire Dancer, a soulful expression on his face and in his sad eyes, receded. Each step Blue Coyote took toward him, he went farther away. He called, "Father, why are you here?" Fire Dancer tried to answer, but Blue Coyote could not hear him. His form was fading away, thinning and disappearing. The rising wind took his voice away; a wind that moaned and shrieked around him, a wind that seemed to be made up of the voices of all the angry spirits. The harder Blue Coyote struggled to reach Fire Dancer, the farther away he faded, until finally, Blue Coyote was alone in the thrashing swirling storm. The wind tore at him and tried to sweep him from his feet. Cold fingers reached inside his clothing, chilling his body, the air seemed determined to lift him right off the ground. He clutched at the branches that whipped him and held to the ground. Fire Dancer had joined the host of spirits howling and plucking at him, attempting to steal his very soul!

Blue Coyote sat bolt upright, his body covered in a cold sweat and shaking violently. His heart was pounding and he was breathing hard! He found sleep impossible after that. Until the Ancestor Fires faded and Sun Spirit began to claim the sky he puzzled over the dream. What message was Fire Dancer trying to send to him? He thought over the events of the last few days; *perhaps the trip to the north was a wrong choice!* Or was it an expression of sorrow over the loss of Bison Man? He determined to speak with the dreamer at his first opportunity. Acorn might shed light on the dream.

As the morning arrived, thunder rumbled far to the north and high dark clouds began amassing on the horizon. The people ate their morning meal hurriedly and quickly packed and loaded the few things back onto travois.

Wolves were set into the traces and the camp filed slowly northward. By mid morning the storm was much closer. The wind began to rise and whip hair into faces. It made the going progressively more difficult, but it was nothing that they were not used to. By mid day the rain began. At first it was a slow steady downpour, but then it gathered strength. Soon all were soaked to the skin, their wolf skin tunics heavy and uncomfortable against their bodies. Then the wind died down and the weather changed.

The air became so unseasonably hot and so heavy that breathing was labored. People began to shed their clothing. The children stripped to the most abbreviated of cover, Dog Boy wore only his breechclout, and Sunflower but a short apron. The rain dripped from their hair and finally adults took the time to draw it back and braid it. Other children were also tended to. Their shoes were a sloppy, wet mass of stretched-out-of-shape pieces of saturated hide. Women shook their heads and removed these as well, leaving the children free to romp bare footed through the wet prairie grass. Others were equally uncomfortable. The young girls also braided their long hair into the single braid down the back which Basket had always chosen, now Star Child as well, it was a style increasingly more practical and comfortable. Soon they also shed their tunics leaving them in their aprons. They looked longingly at the children, but regretfully, kept their soggy foot-coverings in place. They were, after all, proper, well-behaved girls.

Men, young and old stripped to their breechclouts, much relieved at the lessening weight they were carrying now, and they were certainly warm enough. Women eyed them frowning. They could not in all propriety shed to their aprons. The heavy wet tunics were, however, very uncomfortable. Star Woman stopped her wolf and rummaged through her belongings, smiling as she found an abbreviated, sleeveless vest she had made for later in the season. With help she shed her tunic and donned this in its place. She grinned at Turtle Woman and Rain Woman, who grimaced and began digging in their belongings as well. Soon all of the women had located their summer vests and shed the soaked and uncomfortably hot tunics. Just as rapidly the traditional knotted hair was forsaken for a simple braid.

Much more comfortable they took up the trail once again, the wet tunics draped across travois to dry once the rain stopped. Clumsily they stumbled through the long grass, their wet, heavy, moccasins tangling at every step.

Willow frowned down at her feet, "I don't care if it is proper or not!" She exclaimed, "I cannot make one more step in these misshapen and soggy shoes." She untied the thongs and discarded her shoes, tossing them with her tunic on top the travois. "There!" she exclaimed, "Now that is much better!" Everyone else smiled and followed suit, and sadly abused footwear bounced dejectedly upon travois loads.

While the shoes had become saturated and the upper leather began to stretch; blisters had formed on heels making walking increasingly more painful. Now walking was easier, the blisters no longer were so painful, but the bottoms of their feet, softened from the wet leather began to pain. By late day the sky was a sullen purplish black, the clouds swarming and moving in a curious circular fashion. The air however was still hot and heavy. There had been not a single breeze for hands of time.

The camp came to a stumbling halt, Blue Coyote studying the sky with increasing concern. The suffocating stillness was eerily unnatural. Shivers of distress ran along his nerves. There was nothing he could put a name to. But this was an experience far beyond his ken. The Dreamer was studying the sky as well. Stone Man surveyed the prairie.

A bison herd in the distance had been ambling along, parallel to them, grazing nervously. Suddenly they began to move, scattering in every direction. The People watched in amazement as a low black cloud sent down a long swirling tongue toward the ground. The sudden silence was eerie, and then the roar of the wind and the moving cloud was so intense they covered their ears. The bison herd began to run, wildly, first one way then another. The cloud swept hungrily along the ground now. Bison in its path were picked up and The People watched in amazement as they saw them lifted into the sky, their heads jerking and their feet still running.

The people watched dumfounded! Never had any seen such a sight. Bison carried through the sky, like huge birds, and then one dropped from the cloud and landed on the ground a short distance away, no one moved. The funnel twisted and turned, tearing the grass and sod as it ate across the ground, closer and closer.

"Run!" Someone shouted, "Run for your lives!" People scattered, just as had the bison; wolves and travois bouncing and scattering possessions as they skittered across the ground. Stone Man grabbed Antelope Woman by the arm and hurried her sideways. Basket followed with Throw Back, and Star Child dragged her puppy, Dire Wolf after them. Water Woman, Turtle Woman and a number of other adults went to the east, away from the direction of the funnel. Blue Coyote tried to reach Mourning Dove, but she was being swept along with the old ones back the way they had come.

People were screaming in terror, yet no one could hear anything but the shrieking of the wind. They fell to the ground, cowering in abject terror as the wind tore at them, greedily trying to pull them into the swirling vortex. The storm screamed like a demented spirit, grabbing at their very souls. The cloud rose suddenly, still carrying the bison and swept over the people, just as suddenly discarding its load of animals and trash, directly down upon them; and then is pulled back up into the cloud and the storm swept past.

People, animals, and possessions lay scattered across the ground, as unmoving as the sudden silence. Tentatively at first, they began to rise. Many checked to make sure they were unharmed. Some of the wolves, those unhampered with travois had fled in terror. Hunters went out calling them and most were recovered. Travois and possessions however, were scattered over a wide area, finding them made more difficult by the quantity of debris dumped by the cloud. A hand of bison lay among their things, a gift of the storm. By the time the camp had regrouped, it was far too late to go any farther. They camped on the spot. Hunters dressed the bison and soon there were hunks of meat added to travois. It was too wet to start a fire, had there been anything to do so with, so people made do with food they carried. Hopefully by morning things would have dried out.

Amazingly, no one had been harmed. A few travois poles were broken, and about a hand of the animals were yet not recovered, beyond that, though frightened, none were hurt. Basket, Star Child, Star Woman and Rain Women set up their shelter and sat on their bed furs. Tunics were laid out on the travois to dry. "I have never seen such a storm!" Star Woman said, "I was certain it was to be our death!"

"We saw one like it last season, not nearly so near, though!" Rain Woman replied. "But it did not pick up whole animals and throw them at us!"

"This is the first time that a cloud has gifted us with food." Basket said in an awed voice, "It was the most amazing thing! Did you see how that Bison was carried? I felt that I could almost hear it call to me."

"Really?" Star Child questioned, "Now that is odd, I felt the same thing. It was almost as if it wanted us to follow it up into the cloud!"

"It was just a trick of the wind!" Star Woman assured them, "I felt the very same tug."

"As did I," Rain Woman nodded, "It was the wind."

Blue Coyote had gathered a hand of hunters together. They sat huddled before a shelter talking. "What do you make of this day's happenings?" Blue Coyote asked of Acorn and Moon, the dreamers.

"I have seen such a storm before," Moon admitted. "It is something which happens on these plains. It only happens during the hottest part of the season, and the storms are usually brief."

"Then you do not see a message from the spirits in it?"

He shook his head; "All that I saw was a lot of easy food!" the dreamer grinned.

"I had a dream last night," Blue Coyote said, "Fire Dancer came to me, but when I started to go out and meet him a storm swept him away. Do you think it was a foretelling of what happened today? Do you think Father was trying to tell me?"

The dreamers sat thoughtfully for a time, first one then the other shrugged, "I just do not know," admitted Acorn, "Did he actually say anything?"

Blue Coyote shook his head, "He just looked very sad," he admitted, "But my heart was racing, and I was breathing hard when I woke. Perhaps I do not remember the entire dream."

"That is possible, if you do so, let me know immediately. I will see if Wolf Spirit will shed light on this in the mean time," he rose and left.

"Have you anything more to suggest?" Blue Coyote turned to Moon.

"I will also ask guidance," that man replied, "What you have given us is not much to go on."

Stone Man sighed and rubbed the back of his neck, "This has been the strangest of days!" he muttered. I had better get the watchers some food. He rose and prepared a scapula of food and carried it to where Journey's

Far was stationed at one end of the camp. Then he prepared another for Jackrabbit positioned at the far end.

"It will be a long night, Jackrabbit said as Stone Man joined him. "I still do not like the look of that sky. You don't suppose that storm could come back during the night do you?"

Stone Man shrugged, "I hope not! Would you like me to stay with you for a while? I am not really all that sleepy."

"I would enjoy that," Jackrabbit nodded.

Stone Man found a place to sit and they watched the quieting camp silently for a while. "That storm, it sort of makes you realize that we are really insignificant when all things are taken into consideration, doesn't it?"

Jackrabbit thought for a time, "I suppose so. You have not lived long enough to realize that the things which you see as great tragedies in your life tend to pass into less significance as you grow older. When I was a young man, I mated and we had a child. My mate was such a beautiful, gentle person, and I cared deeply for her. She died bringing our son into the world, and then took him with her to walk the wind. At the time I felt that my world had ended. I would never forget her, never be able to go on. Now I can barely remember her face."

"I felt the same when my parents died," Stone Man admitted, "but as time passes, the loss is getting less. Now I find that I miss Fire Dancer and Bison Man much more deeply."

"That is because the loss is still fresh, that also will pass."

"Are there pains, losses which do not lessen with time?"

"There probably are some. Things seem to take on different degrees of importance as life changes. In the Starving Mountains, food was much more important than anything else, then we moved to the escarpment and food was plentiful, then stone became the important thing. I think that the situations of life decide what and who are important to one. For example, take you and Blue Coyote. All your lives you have been the closest of friends. You think little about that friendship, because it has always been there. But, what if suddenly it was gone, if Blue Coyote was gone, then you would realize and understand how important it and he really were to you. You only seem to understand the importance of people and things when they are taken from you."

Stone Man thought about his words, he nodded, realizing that what Jackrabbit said was true. The situation of life dictates what you value. The friendship between him and Blue Coyote was a perfect example of that. They had always been best friends, yet during the moons he had been infatuated with Mourning Dove, that friendship had faded into insignificance beside the passions he felt for her. Now, however, he did realize that in reality, the passion was a passing thing and the friendship the lasting quality. They talked well into the night.

* * *

The night was very dark. No fires had been lighted in the camp and the clouds still hid the Ancestor Fires. A slight shadow flitted to the far end of the camp. "What are you doing here?" Journey's Far whispered, "You should be asleep in your furs!"

"I am not sleepy," Mourning Dove smiled, "I thought to take a short walk."

"It is dark out there. You can't be serious! You would get lost in no time. There are not even any fires to lead you back to the camp!"

"I would not get lost if you were with me," she ran her tongue over her lip and looked longingly into his eyes.

"I am on watch!" Journey's Far stuttered, "I cannot leave my post to go walking with you!"

"We need not go far," she pleaded, "And we need not stay long," she swept her long free hair behind a naked shoulder, leaning forward to give him a view of her round breasts. "Besides, what is there to guard against? The camp is safe enough."

Journey's Far looking at her, licked his lips and felt the desire rise in him. It had been many nights since he had coupled with her. She was like a disease in his blood, one he was incapable of escaping. With a sigh he set aside his atlatl and darts and followed her into the darkened prairie. She was right. They did not go far, nor stay long. Quickly they coupled, frantically they mated, their explosive releases almost too soon. Then they returned to the camp. He to his watch and she to the shelter shared with the old ones.

One old eye had watched her leave, it watched her return as well, and the old nose recognized the odor of coupling.

*   *   *

Morning brought a return to blue skies. The breeze soon had tunics dry and shoes were reshaped and set atop travois to dry and the soles harden again. Meanwhile, all remained barefooted. As they moved, they collected bison chips and by mid day had enough to cook the bison roasts they carried. Repairs were made, and the meat was set to cook. Tunics and upper shoes were worked and softened so they could be worn again. Other things as well were aired and dried. The camp lay about lazily and enjoyed the bright sun. Hunters went out and called, finally locating the missing wolves. A hearty meal was prepared, and the remainder of the bison meat taken from the storm offering was cooked. People sat late around their fires, talking and just relaxing. It was quite late when all retired. Blue Coyote and Stone Man had the first watch shift. They settled at either end of the camp and prepared for the long wait until their relief came and took over.

The old one faked sleep and watched. Mourning Dove again left the shelter. She slipped silently to the edge of the camp and joined Blue Coyote. They sat for a while and talked, then slipped silently from the camp. Some time later they returned. and the woman slipped undetected back into her furs. The old nose smelled, detecting again the odor of mating. *No wonder she wanted her shelter apart from the rest of us all winter!* She smiled sourly.

The next night the old one watched for nothing. Mourning Dove remained in her furs. But the watcher was determined to find out what was going on. She kept her vigil and the next time Mourning Dove left the shelter, she followed. She had not far to go, nor long to wait. Journey's Far had little hesitation leaving his post and following the woman into the night. They were gone a considerable time, the camp left unprotected, while they were out enjoying their illicit coupling. The old one returned to her furs and waited for Mourning Dove's return. She had much to consider.

In the nights that followed, Mourning Dove regularly slipped out and joined with one or another of the watchers. The old one realized that there was not just one man, but a number of them, always the watcher. She kept this to herself. She watched carefully; but was hesitant to speak.

Then another of their shelter noticed, she also followed, and she also discovered . . . and she also kept silent.

*　　*　　*

Acorn settled in his spirit shelter, apart from the camp. They had stopped early, and it was an opportune time for a 'spirit journey'. He had fresh spirit powder and prepared a healthy dose of it. He sat upon his furs and waited. Wolf Spirit came quickly! *The spirits are pleased! A new ceremony is to be initiated among The People! Bison are to be greatly honored. I will tell you more, as the time is right. For now, however, the hunters and stone knappers are to go to the place of stone. The material that they gather is to be free from the taint of females. None may touch it. It is to be gathered by men who are cleansed. Enough will be gathered so that a special tool can be made for each hunter, a hand of them for each. Tell the men, tell the hunters, tell the stone knappers, and tell the women!* Acorn returned to awareness just as quickly as he had gone into the journey. He quickly called the camp together.

*　　*　　*

"The spirit of Wolf has contacted me," he stated, "We are to prepare for a special ceremony. I have been instructed to direct the camp to the place of stone. There we will gather supplies for this ceremony."

"We have plenty of material from the southern place!" Cougar protested, "Why endanger ourselves going to the place of stone?"

"Because Wolf Spirit has instructed us to go there," answered Acorn.

"The material to be gathered must be gathered in a specific manner," Moon added, "There are cleansings and taboos to be observed. These tools are for a sacred ceremony!"

"The instructions are very specific!" Acorn added.

"We will go there," Blue Coyote nodded, "It is on our way to where we are headed."

"How long before we reach it?" questioned Moon.

"A span of days, I would estimate," Stone Man replied.

The dreamers both nodded, "Once at the place of stone, the men must purify in a cleansing ceremony. They must keep themselves from women, and there are strict taboos about women touching this stone. It is to be collected only by and touched only by cleansed men. The spirit was most clear about this. Remember this is for ceremony! Not just any stone will do." Acorn reminded.

Cougar nodded and went back to his chore. He understood about ceremony, about cleansing and about the seriousness of such things. They would go to the place of stone.

CHAPTER 18

That night Mourning dove again left the shelter. Blue Coyote was watcher at the north end of the camp. She had made sure of this earlier. She had tossed and turned in her furs it seemed forever before the steady snoring of her shelter companions told her it was safe. Silently she stepped over the bulging form of Little Antelope Woman, a sour smile on her face, for nothing of a graceful Antelope reflected on the old woman's person.

She crept silently through the camp, picking her way past travois and belongings careful not to trip over anything and make noise. The wolves were used to her and merely yawned as she passed or paid her no attention what so ever. A larger, less graceful shadow followed safely at a distance. The wolves wagged their tails as this one passed.

Mourning Dove ran her hands down the arm of Blue Coyote, and she nibbled at his ear, blowing hot air gently. He groaned and tried half-heartedly to pull free. "I have been waiting until it was safe to come to you," she whispered, "It seems like forever before those old windbags finally began to snore."

"I told you last time that we should not be doing this!" Blue Coyote protested weakly, "It is not safe!"

"Who is to know, or for that matter care?" she shrugged, "It is really none of their concern."

"If the safety of the camp is jeopardized it is their concern; what if someone attacks us?"

"What if the sky should fall? It is just as likely to happen! All this fear of raiders; I have told you before; the raiders do not come this far north. They seldom cross the big river, and we are spans of days beyond that! There is nothing to worry about. You have said that your friend Red Eagle does not come this way, so what is there to fear?"

"Red Eagle is no friend!" Blue Coyote replied, already setting down his atlatl and darts to follow her into the darkness.

They hurried a discrete distance from the camp. Already Mourning Dove was pulling her tunic over her head, her perfect breasts glowing in the soft moonlight. With a groan Blue Coyote bore her to the ground, panting softly. She squirmed beneath him, sending his already failing control over the edge, he spread her incredibly soft, perfect thighs and releasing himself from his breechclout united himself with her pulsing ready body. As always coupling with Mourning Dove was perfect; he caressed her perfect round breasts, licked and suckled on the hard nubs, sending her into spasms of response. She groaned softly and urged him on, tightening and releasing the muscles and bringing him closer and closer to release. As always just when he could stand it no longer, she magically found release and they reached perfect unity together.

The old one grunted and stayed hidden behind a shelter far enough away not to be detected, yet near enough to watch for their return. *If the headman were so woman-caught that he could not do the job assigned by himself then she would watch in his place.* Finally, much later, they returned, and she slipped back to her now cold bed. She was 'snoring' lustily when Mourning Dove returned.

* * *

The camp meandered slowly north and came to the river which one day would be named Canadian. They followed it north and west toward the place of stone, located along its bluffs. Little Antelope Woman hurried to walk beside her nephew; she had made a habit of this over the last span of days so that no one would be suspicious. Mourning Dove had frowned the first time she did so, and had mentioned it to her, but Little Antelope Woman merely said that if she wished to walk with the son of her sister, that was her right. Nothing more had been said, but the younger woman seemed suspicious any way. Little Antelope Woman was sure that she spoke of family things and nothing important and she was careful that Mourning Dove was within listening distance. If Stone Man thought this sudden interest and attention from his aunt unusual, he did not in any way indicate such.

"Basket is growing into a very nice woman do you not think?" Little Antelope Woman questioned.

"Basket has always been nice," Stone Man replied, "Why should she not grow into a nice woman? Star Child is becoming a reflection of her though, and she also is growing into a very nice woman. One day she will make some lucky man an excellent mate."

"Is that the way of your inclination?" Little Antelope Woman was suddenly interested, "You find Star Child to be a suitable mate?"

"For some lucky man, yes, for myself, no, I have no desire to mate Aunt, so put away your ideas in that direction. There are many things for a man to do besides mating," he replied somewhat bitterly. Mourning Dove smiled secretly, deciding that perhaps the next night Stone Man was on watch . . . then she sighed, no, he and Blue Coyote always shared the watch. It would be too dangerous to arouse Blue Coyote's suspicion. Why could not Stone Man have been Headman?

Mourning Dove listened for a time further, then realizing that she was wasting her time she went to walk elsewhere, leaving Little Antelope Woman to chatter inanely to Stone Man. Little Antelope Woman was paying far more attention than Mourning Dove realized. "I must talk with you, nephew," she whispered.

"I thought we were doing that?" he replied, "However I have realized that you have something on your mind, and eventually you would come to it. Something is bothering you, Aunt?"

Little Antelope Woman nodded. "It is the woman, Mourning Dove," she admitted. "She leaves the shelter, long after everyone is asleep, and I became curious and have followed her . . ."

"That is dangerous!" Stone Man quickly replied "Do not do so again."

"I can take care of myself!" Little Antelope Woman sputtered!

"So could Fire Dancer and Bison Man, and you know what happened to them!"

Little Antelope Woman stopped dead. Stone Man took her arm and forced her to continue walking. "Are you saying . . .?"

"I am not saying anything!" Stone Man whispered "But I certainly have my suspicions. Now do not follow that creature again, for your own safety and for my peace of mind. I have a very good idea what she is up to."

"You know? I mean about her and the watchers?" He nodded, "And you do nothing?"

"What would you have me do Aunt? I cannot come out and accuse her before the entire camp. Blue Coyote is so smitten; he would refuse to listen. And the others! I have no idea how many there are!"

"At least a pair more," Little Antelope Woman said. "But how do you know?"

Stone Man had the grace to blush. "Not you as well!" she sputtered.

He frowned, "No longer," he admitted. "For a time I was drawn into her web just as were the others. She played with a hand of us all winter. But when I discovered that I was one of a string, and that she had no interest in mating with any who did not further her ambition, I saw her for what she is and have had nothing to do with her since. But Blue Coyote is deeply ensnared. I did not realize that until just recently," he shook his head. "I cannot criticize him for falling into the very same trap, and I cannot think of a way to open his eyes."

"That is simple; just get him to follow her when she sneaks off with one of the other men!"

Stone Man shook his head, "He is too unsure of his decision making. It would seriously undermine the safety of the entire camp if his confidence was so shaken. He must be a strong leader, and if it takes letting that woman lead him for a time yet, then so be it. I have thought about this Aunt, and I know that I am right. Blue Coyote has all he can handle just now. He has not yet recovered from the loss of Fire Dancer, and he is very unsure of his own ability to lead."

"But what of the safety of the camp" Little Antelope Woman sputtered, "While she is out coupling with the watchers the camp is vulnerable!"

"I know this as well. I have been watching, Aunt. I have an idea which men she is coupling with, and when it is their watch, I do so in their stead, except for Blue Coyote, for I am watcher then also."

"There is not another in whom you could confide?"

Stone Man shook his head, "Had not Bison Man . . ."

"You think she was involved in their deaths?"

"I do not know. I have thought and thought about this. Bison Man was on to something! I think he was getting close to figuring the cause of Fire Dancer's death, and I think he was purposefully led to suffer a similar fate."

"By Mourning Dove; then you don't think there were raiders at all? You think she planted that object? But why?"

"This is what doesn't make any sense. What reason could she have for wanting Fire Dancer dead?"

"I will speak to Star Woman; perhaps she will be able to shed light on a reason!"

"No! You will not speak to Star Woman, or to anyone else! Please Aunt, if this woman is in some way responsible for their deaths, you would be in much danger."

"But she must be stopped! How many more . . . ?"

Stone Man again shook his head. "Keep out of it Aunt, I mean this, you promise me, right now that you will let this thing drop," he waited, "Your promise . . ."

Little Antelope Woman frowned, sighed and grudgingly gave the promise. "Now go back and stay with your group. Do not do anything more which might draw suspicion to you," he advised, and regretfully Little Antelope Woman agreed, dropping back to walk with Kind Heart.

That night, when Mourning Dove left the shelter, Little Antelope Woman did not follow; she rolled over and forced herself to sleep. Another how ever did follow, and she was not so careful, nor so agile. She made a sound, tripping over a travois pole, and although she scurried back to her furs in fear, Mourning Dove was alerted that she was being watched . . .

For several nights, Mourning Dove remained in her furs. Then the perfect opportunity yielded itself. Little Antelope Woman went, late in the night just beyond the darkened camp to pass water. She was brutally struck down from behind and her throat slit with a sharp blade, before she could utter a sound. A strange dart was buried deep in her back. There were no footprints at the scene, and no one had seen, nor heard anything. Stone Man was filled with guilt and remorse, for he was sure now that had he allowed Little Antelope Woman to share her fears and concerns, she would still be alive. As it was all he could do was lay his beloved Aunt to walk the wind and keep his own council.

The hunters scoured the area all around the camp. The watchers were questioned, Stone Man and Blue Coyote; they had neither seen nor heard anything. Blue Coyote was relieved that for some reason Mourning Dove had chosen not to come to him that particular night. And he made the decision that no more would he be led away from the camp during his watch, no matter how much his desire for her drove him to weakness. He could not endanger the camp and more than that he could not take the chance of endangering his beloved Mourning Dove. They were but a hand of days away from the place of stone any way, and with the added danger of Red Eagle, the watchers were doubled, and the chance for Mourning Dove to meet with any of the men was eliminated. This was Blue Coyote's way of insuring that he did not give in to desire. With another man beside him on watch, there was no danger of Mourning Dove coming to him.

During the day, a pair of hunters went out ahead of the camp and they scouted for signs of anyone else in the area, following the paths and trail along the river and beyond. For all the signs they found this camp could be the only humans on Earth! They did, however, come across the occasional deer, and so the camp ate well of fresh venison. They reached the place of stone without further problems.

"Gray Wolf, Stone Man, Jackrabbit, go ahead and scout the quarry, we will remain here until you return," Blue Coyote instructed his most trusted hunters.

"We will return in a hand of time," Jackrabbit assured him. Blue Coyote nodded, and the hunters left the camp.

"No fires!" Blue Coyote called as he noticed one of the women preparing to make tea. She nodded and stopped. So the camp waited. "Do you think it advisable to move into the secret cave?" asked Star Woman. Blue Coyote had come to wait with her, keeping Mourning Dove a safe and discrete distance away.

"We will wait and see what Stone Man has to say. If there is no recent sign of occupation, I do not see that we need take such precaution. We will wait for their recommendation before deciding. I would keep the cave a secret as long as possible, for we must visit this place again and again. I would that Red Eagle never knows of it."

*   *   *

"Do you think we might have time to visit the secret cave," whispered Star Child, "I would just like to get away by ourselves for a while. We have been unable to leave the camp for so long I would just enjoy doing so for a while."

"We can try," Basket answered, "I am feeling the same," she sighed, "It has been a long hard journey, and I am not convinced that there is a lone killer out there somewhere. Do you believe in these invisible 'raiders' who seem to be carefully killing our number?"

Star Child shook her head, "It is not the way of any raiders that I have ever heard of, they attack; they murder and rape, then leave. They do not follow silently along for spans of time, killing only helpless old women for no reason. There is more here than meets the eye. What do you say to trying to contact the spirits ourselves and see if we can answer some questions?"

"Us!" Basked exclaimed, "I have never tried to contact a spirit, I wouldn't know how; have you?"

"Once," Star Child admitted, "When I could feel the pull to you."

"Did it work?"

Star Child shook her head, "Not that I am aware, but the feeling became stronger, of course that could be because we were getting closer and the attachment was getting stronger. But I would like to try again."

"It could be dangerous!"

Star Child shrugged, "And it could prove successful. Are you afraid to try?"

Basket nodded, "But I will if you will, the only spirit trip I have ever taken was on my becoming-a-woman- quest. I don't remember any of it, just that I woke up with a headache and a sick stomach." Star Child nodded and grinned.

"Have you any morning glory seed?" Star Child again nodded and grinned. "Then we will try, at the secret cave, just as soon as we can." Yet again Star Child nodded and grinned. Basket grinned back.

* * *

The hunters returned with the news that no one had been in the quarry for a long time. The people cheerfully and noisily made their way to the caves and settled in. They were planning on staying at this place at least a span of days, perhaps even a moon. There was much to be done to prepare for the new ceremony.

Acorn and Moon set their shelter up a short distance from the camp, beneath the spreading branches of a huge oak tree. They had much to prepare. First, they needed fresh spirit powder. They settled their shelter and then made their way together up the river canyon seeking the Thorn Apple plant. They found a good supply some distance from the camp. Nodding they went to the river and washed thoroughly, both cleaning and scouring their bodies and hair. Even their clothes were scrubbed and spread over bushes to dry. They had new blades, just struck from fresh stone, absolutely untouched by female hands. These they used to collect the plant parts needed. They were put in special pouches, made from the hide of a young bison, taken for a hunting cape, which unfortunately there was no longer a hunter to wear. It was pure. They then returned to the camp and proceeded to further prepare the plants for the ceremony.

Star Woman and Rain Woman set their, and the twin's shelter up at the base of the canyon below the caves. Star Woman still found herself looking for Fire Dancer and Scorpion among the people of the camp. There were many memories of them in this place. She sighed and went about her work. The girls had slipped off to the secret cave, this time with permission and instructions to return well before dark. There would be things for them to prepare as well. The dreamers had already informed the women that there were strict taboos, and Basket and Star Child had gone to ask their 'spirit helper' to assist the women in knowing what they were to avoid, and what they were to do to help during the ceremony.

*　　*　　*

Throw Back led the way, followed by Basket, Star Child and Dire Wolf. The pup was now as large as her mother and the group consisted of a pair of identical people and wolves, but for Basket's staff and slight limp. They scrambled up the steep trail and into the cave. It was exactly as they had left it. "Do you have it?" Basket questioned. Star Child nodded, "I will start the fire while you prepare the water in the bowls." They set about their preparations. "Throw Back, you are responsible for making sure that we are safe and do not harm ourselves." The wolf wagged her tail and licked Basket's face. Basket hugged her back, ruffling her fur.

"I think it is ready," Star Child said a short time later. "I hope that I didn't mix it too strong."

"How old is this powder?" Basket questioned.

"I collected the seeds when first we came down into the river valley. There was a lot of morning glory growing up the bushes there."

Basket nodded, "I remember seeing it but I didn't think to collect any."

"You were still upset over old Antelope," Star Child replied.

"I still find it hard to believe that she is gone," Basket admitted, "She had been part of this camp all of my life, she was nearly as much my aunt as Stone Man's."

"You are partial to Stone Man, aren't you?" Star Child asked casually.

"In what way?"

"I just thought . . ." Star Child shrugged, "It doesn't matter."

"We grew up together," Basket reminded her, "Stone Man and Blue Coyote are like brothers to me. I am sure that you see them far differently than I do. For me to regard either of them as . . . well, it would almost be incest!"

"Still, Blue Coyote is a handsome man," Star Child said.

Basket shrugged, "I am not interested in men, which is just as well, for none are interested in me. After Red Eagle, everyone thinks that I am 'spirit touched' any way."

"Well after today, perhaps you will be! Perhaps we both will!" Star Child grinned, "Let's find out!"

They spread wolf pelts which they had brought along for the purpose and settled themselves cross-legged. "Do you think we should hold hands?" questioned Star Child.

"Sure, why not," Basket replied. And so they did. They swallowed the spirit drink and clasped hands and waited . . .

The spiral began . . .

*   *   *

Who calls? The voice came to them from a thick white fog, they could not even see each other, and but for their clasped hands would not have known that they were not alone.

It is I, Basket.

And I, Star Child, cane the answer. Then the fog shifted, and they found themselves facing the spirit of a female wolf, a wolf much like those who watched.

I am Dire Wolf. The spirit you seek. I have sent the watchers to protect you and have called you to me. The People are on the brink of a new way. The circle has opened and The One has given another chance. It is up to the pair of you to make sure that the people, both men and women, adhere to the proper veneration of the spirits and do not break the taboos. For many generations The People have become lax. You were sent by the spirits, a powerful pair to lead the way. But the very first thing that The People did was to separate you. It took many spirits a long time to bring you together again. This must not happen again! There is a dreamer, he seeks your life, but he cannot overcome the pair of you. You must seek him out and destroy him, or the circle will close, and The People will walk no more. There is danger from the dreamer if you are separated; alone, his power is greater! You are the power of the people. You are the link to the spirits. So long as you are together, The People will flourish, but if you are separated, then again will death and starvation will be brought down upon the people. Women interfere with the power of men. They have become casual even to the point of drawing power from the men by touching their tools. This must stop! If The People are to have power over the bison, then they must adhere to the rules laid down by the spirits. Your dreamers only know the things which men must do. You will tell the women the things that they must do as well.

I will guide you, my children will protect you, as long as there is danger, you will walk with one or another of my children. You each carry the sacred tooth of your ancestor. They have much power, but only if kept together. You have much power, but only if kept together. If the people are to flourish, the power must remain united. Dire wolf instructed them. Basket looked at Star Child and Star Child looked at Basket. Both nodded. This then was their destiny, to be the luck of the people.

Basket called to the wolf spirit, "how will we know?"

The same way that you have always known! Your amulet will tell you, look inside yourself, and you will find the answer. It is there. You need not search farther. The answers were given to you at birth.

"What of our birth? Can you tell us why we were separated, why no one even knew?"

Look to the evil dreamer, the one no one will name. He is the secret; he is the evil that you battle. It is his power that will seek to overcome you.

"The Dreamer, White Falcon?" Star Child questioned.

He is the one. Dire Wolf nodded.

"But he is dead? Fire Dancer walled him alive in his cave many seasons ago!" Basket protested.

His spirit lives! His spirit left the cave and took shelter in a child. That child has grown to a man. Now the dreamer seeks to live again, he seeks you lives; he must have your power objects to live again. He is a source of danger!

Basket thought, "The child, it was Red Eagle!" she stated.

"You say a source of danger," questioned Star Child, "Are there others?"

There lives an evil among you; an evil which must be plucked out and driven away. This evil sucks the life from your people!

* * *

"What kind of evil?"

Dire Wolf did not answer. She faded back into the fog.

Slowly Basket and Star Child returned to awareness. They looked at each other and both were somber for a time, taken up with their private thoughts.

"Do you remember anything of the journey?" questioned Star Child.

Basket shook her head, "if we took one," she replied.

"I do not know how we can be expected to be of any help to The People if we cannot know what to do!" *You will know!* The thought popped into her head. Star Child had a surprised look flash over her face. It was mirrored in Baskets.

"We did it!" Basket grinned, "I don't know how, but we did it. It has happened to me, when the camp wanted the ceremony at the sacred spring. I did not know what I was going to do, but it all came to me, like someone else was guiding my hands and putting the words into my mouth. All I did was clear my mind and pray for guidance. It came."

"Really; that must have been exciting! I have not had such an experience!" Star Child replied.

"But you just did!" Basket informed her. "That is how it works! You ask yourself a question and the answer just pops into your mind. I never realized that I even did it, but I have. When the acorn gatherers died, I knew not to go, but I didn't listen to the voice, and they died."

"But, what kinds of questions am I to ask?"

Basket shrugged, "They will probably come as well, without thinking."

"All right, let's think of a question and see if we get an answer."

"I don't think that is a good idea," Basket replied, "It would be better if we just cleared our minds and asked for guidance. We want to know the role of the women for this ceremony, perhaps we should try concentrating on that."

"Very well, that makes sense. Let's try that!"

They again sat on the pelts and both cleared their minds and concentrated on the ceremony, posing the question, 'what roles do the women play'. *They must be cleansed! They must be chaste, refrain from stealing power from men! They must help the men remember, be aware of the power in male hunting tools and do not draw it away. Do not let the blood power go near a man!* They looked at one another and smiled. No words were necessary. Both had felt the answer. They quietly gathered up their pelts and followed the wolves back to the camp.

*   *   *

Star Woman and Rain Woman were waiting at their shelter, full of questions, but one look at the twins answered them without a word. "We will prepare the women for a cleansing ceremony of our own," Basket stated.

"There must be a woman's shelter erected, quickly, and Moth must go there immediately, with you, Willow. Both are unclean and a danger to the men," Star Child stated.

"How can you know this?" Willow exclaimed, "I only just became aware that I was starting my woman's flow on my way here!"

"We must erect the shelter immediately then," Star Woman stated, "we have been very lax about such things over the seasons. There used to be many rules that we have ignored. I can remember a time when to touch a man's hunting tools meant that he must immediately destroy them. But in the starving mountains these things did not seem so important, and so we forgot them."

The women quickly sent a pair out to cut saplings and others gathered deer hides and began assembling the blood shelter. "Do not use any part of a bison!" the words came unbidden from Star Child. Rain Woman nodded and cast aside the sinew she was about to use, selecting instead that from a deer. Sage Girl and Willow returned with the saplings and Cottontail Girl and Water Woman dug holes with sharp sticks and they secured the saplings and covered the shelter with the hides. With many hands the work went quickly. When it was completed, Moth and Willow reluctantly took their place inside. The blood shelter was not a popular tradition among the younger women. They had not grown up with its restrictions. The older ones could remember it as a time when they were relieved of chores and were allowed to rest and even be pampered a bit by the other women. Their food was brought to them and they had time to relax and visit.

Basket and Star Child went out into the valley and gathered soapberries. They gathered a container full, careful to go down-river, for the men were collecting their things upriver, where no woman had trod. They returned to the camp just as Sun Spirit was darkening the sky.

"Each of us must wash our entire body, wash our hair, and then make sure that we do not touch any thing which is related to male hunting. The washing will remove any manpower that we have stolen. It will be released to return to them." Basket instructed the women gathered with her and Star Child the next morning. They had led the group, minus Willow and Moth, to the river, a way downstream.

"If the men are cleansing upstream, do we not risk their discarded power finding us?" questioned Cottontail Girl.

"It no longer has power once discarded. It has become harmless. It is our power that we must be careful of. Woman's power is very strong, and it lasts much longer. Particularly at the time of blood we are very powerful. That is why the blood shelter is so important! We dare not go near the place where the men's ceremony is being held. Even at a distance we could weaken them."

"My people do not do these foolish things!" Mourning Dove stated sullenly, "I see no reason that we should be so careful. For seasons we hunted bison and there was no taboo against women having relations with the men at any time it pleased the pair. We suffered no ill effects! I frequently used my brother's atlatl hunting deer. It never caused him any harm!"

"I did not know you even had a brother!"

Mourning Dove shrugged, "He is dead."

The women looked one to the other, nodded and resumed their preparations.

"I have never met people who are so intimidated by 'spirits'!" she sneered, "You are afraid of your own shadows! This camp does not do anything without first consulting some spirit or other!"

"If this does not please you, or you do not choose to comply, then perhaps you should find another camp!" Cottontail Girl answered suddenly tired of the other woman's constant harping and criticizing.

Mourning Dove gave her a dirty look and began washing.

Afterwards they returned to the camp together and the women went about their chores, carefully separated from the men. Mourning Dove muttered something under her breath, grabbed her bolas and rabbit stick and headed down the canyon. The remainder of the women merely smiled and sighed in relief. "She did seem to be fitting in for a time," Star Woman said, "Now suddenly she has become difficult again." she began shaking out her sleeping furs, "I hope that this is short-lived and she settles in again. It can be so unpleasant when one person is disruptive. It upsets everyone."

*   *   *

Mourning Dove was smoldering. She ground her teeth together as she attacked the path with her mocassined feet. First Blue Coyote doubled the guard, just because she had disposed of that fat old snoop Little Antelope Woman! Now she was being forced to participate in their stupid cleansing ceremonies and abstain from men altogether for who knows how long! The men were like children, heaping glory and attention upon themselves. They followed the dreamers without question, and the women follow those weird twins that everyone was so fond of. What could be so special about a pair of identically plain women, particularly ones so fond of those obscenely ugly animals?

She looked about for something upon which to vent her anger. The only thing she could find was a raven perched upon a branch just before her. She brought back the rabbit stick and with a vicious cast knocked the unfortunate bird from the tree. It fell to the ground, a mass of gently floating feathers following it. She went to the body and picking it up jerked the remaining feathers from the carcass and cast them into the brush, then tossed the body to the ground, kicked through the feathers lying in the path and continued on, her anger unquenched. She shoved through brush and emerged on the plain. Here, at least, she could move unhampered. She did not return to the camp until nearly dark, resenting the fact that circumstances forced her into such and untenable position. All of her life Mourning Dove had fought against the restrictions forced upon her by her society. Her own camp, much like the one she presently walked with, were preoccupied with spirits and taboos. This is why they had cast her out.

It did not occur to her that any group of people would frown on coupling with a sibling. But Mourning Dove was too upset to think rationally about this or any thing. She had been forced to go without any relationship with any man for a span of days. This situation had been tenable while she was isolated from contact with men, but now she had become accustomed to relieving her sexual frustrations on a regular basis. Without this release she was prone to losing her temper and acting rashly. Her explosion earlier was a result of these frustrations. As before in her life she had brought trouble down upon herself by acting before think about the consequences of her actions.

She was still too angry to go into the camp, so she skirted it and found a stump to sit upon.

The ancestor fires were bright in the sky; Journey's Far had finished the cleansing and had much to think about. He wandered from the camp to find a quiet place to think. Instead, he found Mourning Dove. He came to an abrupt stop almost, but luckily, not touching her. "What are you doing out here?" he questioned.

"The same as you," she replied. Quickly taking advantage of the situation, she pouted softly, "Looking for a place which is private and quite. Now we can find it together."

"I have just completed the cleansing!" he explained, "I dare not even touch you until after the ceremony."

Mourning Dove laughed low and softly, "Who would know!" she smiled into the darkness; "Unless you plan to say something!" she reached out and ran her fingers down his arm.

"Don't!" he jerked back shaking, "You touched me! I have been cleansed and now you made me unclean," he nearly sobbed.

"Oh! I am so sorry, I didn't realize . . ." she sighed, "But now the damage is done, what difference does it make? Can you have it undone?"

He shook his head, "The cleansing took all day, and the ceremony is in a pair more. There is much to be completed meanwhile, but now I will not be able participate in the ceremony. I will be cast out of the celebration!"

"I am so sorry," she pleaded softly, "I did not know! Your beliefs are strange to me. I did not mean to cause harm. It is just that, I have been missing you and the companionship we have shared. I have just been sitting here thinking about you, longing for you and then suddenly you appear, almost as an answer to my prayers to the spirits. I did not think! In my joy, I just did not think!" she sobbed softly.

Journey's Far was at a loss. She was so very Beautiful, and she was his, but for the claiming. The damage was already done, so he saw no harm in taking her into his arms and comforting her. Mourning Dove responded so tenderly, so lovingly that Journey's Far could do no more than lead her farther from the camp for her own safety and his. Was anyone to find them both would be in great trouble. The taboo was explicit, for both men and women. He settled her beneath a tree and sat beside her.

"What do we do now?" he questioned. "Should I seek out the dreamer and ask his council?"

Mourning Dove smiled and shook her head, "In a while, if you must. But now that you are here, at least let me have a short time for the pleasure of being with you, before you must go and leave me alone and needing your comfort." She slipped a tiny distance away from him, "You need not touch me if you would rather not, but please I beg of you, do not leave me just yet."

"I must!" he protested, "Being together, even without touching, it is against the taboo!"

"But you said the taboo was already broken, what further damage can there be in just talking?"

"Do you not understand? I cannot sit here beside you and just talk, not when I burn inside for wanting you. The torture of being so close, yet unable to hold you, to touch your wonderful body, to make it sing in unison with mine! I cannot bear it!" he began to shake.

"Oh!" she sobbed, "I feel exactly the same! It is a punishment for me daily, to see you only from afar, to know that I cannot come to you, cannot mold my body to yours and find the perfect bliss, the perfect match to my own soul!"

Journey's Far groaned and reached out for her, drawing her exquisite perfectly matched body against his own. The burning pleasure of her gentle fingers upon his bare thigh was nearly a pain, and he drew her beneath him, pulling aside his breechclout and uniting with her in perfect soul-blending harmony. Mourning Dove wrapped her legs about him and their coupling was almost frantic. Journey's Far held himself back, fighting his own body's need for release, controlling with every bit of strength he still had, to give her the greater pleasure, the joy of each thrust driving him closer and closer, until finally, with a last powerful thrust he and the world around him exploded into numberless fragments as he joined her in a perfect joined release. They sank to the ground in peace and perfect harmony.

Mourning Dove smiled and let the man lay for a few breaths, then began the age-old dance of bringing him again to full male power. For a youth, she was pleasantly surprised at Journey's Far's ability to pleasure her. Beside Stone Man, he was by far the most gifted of the men she had coupled with. She sighed and lay a time in his arms. "There is no reason to tell anyone about this," she whispered, "Let it be our little secret."

He pulled away from her, "The spirits . . ." he began.

"Will do nothing!" she assured him. "Do not your people and mine pray to the same spirits? Does not Wolf Spirit direct your people just as he does mine?" Journey's Far nodded, "Yet in my camp there are no such taboo's, in my camp the spirits encourage coupling, encourage the mating of a man and a woman, to bring children into the camp and to thus glorify the spirit. Can we say which is right or wrong?"

He did not know how to answer. "I tell you, the dreamer makes up these taboos just to give himself importance! Did you have them before, in the Starving Mountains?" He shook his head, "And did the spirits destroy you?" again he shook his head. "Do you not ask yourself why? Why now and not then?" He thought and then again shook his head, "I will tell you why! These Dreamers, they seek to elevate themselves above the rest. They make up these ceremonies and taboos just to give themselves more status, more importance within the camp! I have seen it before, only my camp saw through them and cast the dreamer out!" she ran her hands over his body, "Can anything which gives the pleasure that you find in this be wrong? Does it feel wrong to you when our bodies join? When together they sing a prayer of joy to the spirits?"

"No, of course not, you know that you are the most beautiful, most perfect thing that has ever entered my life. The joining of our bodies is the most perfect prayer a man could imagine."

"Then how could it be wrong?" she pleaded with him. "The rest of the camp need not know, the spirits will turn a blind eye, you will see!"

"You mean, go on with the ceremony? Participate as if this night did not happen?" he looked dumbfounded.

"That is exactly what I mean." she answered, "Go early in the morning, back to the place where you cleansed. Again wash your body, again clear your thoughts, and then return to the camp. The spirits will find you acceptable. Trust me; they care about the soul, the attitude of mind, not the physical body."

"I don't know . . ." he hesitated.

"Then go from me, go to your dreamer and shame my affection and lay me before him as the blame!" she sobbed. Journey's Far could not stand the tears clouding her beautiful eyes. He gave in and promised to go early in the morning and do as she had bid. Then she rewarded him, yielding her perfect body once again to his. Late in the night both returned to the camp, she smiling; he thinking only of the joy found in her arms.

*   *   *

Down beside the river the next morning, the men began to clear an area large enough to erect a sweat lodge. It was a structure made of saplings and the inner bark stripped from trees and held together with bison sinew. It took them the entire day to construct it, and if Journey's Far was a little late joining them, no one noticed. He worked as hard as anyone did with the construction, giving a helping hand wherever it was needed. No spirit struck Journey's Far down, no man, hunter or dreamer, pointed a finger at him. He sighed, realizing that Mourning Dove had been right. It was the state of mind and soul that were important, and his mind and soul were as perfect as he was able to make them. That night the hunters striped and sat around the sweat lodge fire, listening to the chanting prayers of the dreamers and breathing in the pungent pine filled air as they poured water over the hot rocks releasing their purifying steam. Far into the night they stayed, until the dreamers were certain that they had followed the instruction of the spirits to a word. Then and only then, did the dreamers claim the hunters ready!

The women had completed their own preparations and cleansing. They were gathered at the far end of the camp, seated around their 'woman's hearth' drinking tea and relaxing. Basket and Star Child were telling them how the woman's hearth had come into being, drawing on their spirit to guide their words.

"In the very beginning, The People walked with the spirits. Then there were no taboos against women hunting with men, sharing the same tools and facing the same dangers. The female 'spirits' saw this danger and they were concerned. They approached the most powerful spirit of all and asked for the women to be taken out of danger's way. The most powerful spirit considered their request and granted it, but only on the condition that the women protect the men from their female power. So it was that the taboo's came into being." Basket began.

"The women of The People were grateful that they no longer had to face the hunting dangers beside the men. They were glad to keep these taboos. But the men saw this as a way to gain power over the women. Soon they forbade the women from more and more of the communal camp life. Until, finally, the women were little better than slaves to the men. They were at their beck and call always, and yet they were forbidden to share in the bounty of the hunt. The men claimed it for themselves. Women were left with only those scraps that the men gave them. They were no longer allowed to have any weapons but their woman's bolas and the rabbit stick. If the men were away from the camp and a wild predator attacked, they had no protection."

"This greatly angered the spirits!" Basket took up the tale again, "So they sent a special woman to The People. She led the women back to sharing with the men. Once again they hunted beside the men, but not again with the dangerous animals. The people once again venerated the spirits. But, once again they forgot, and again the women suffered. Now they had not even the 'woman's hearth'. They had nothing! The spirits went again to The One, and pleaded. Again they were given another chance. This time they chose the one we call The Mother of The People. She came among The People. She reestablished the 'woman's hearth', and the women were again allowed to hunt. The spirits were once more respected and honored. But, again The People forgot! The spirits brought down a great drought! They took the animals away and sent The People to live in the Starving Mountains."

"There," Star Child picked up the tale, "The people continued to forget. Now, however, we are being given another chance. This is why our dreamers are telling of the ancient taboos. This is why, for the first time in many generations, The People are celebrating the Sacred Ceremony. Now the spirits have given us a special tool, the sacred point, to continually remind us; So that we do not forget them!"

"The spirits have brought back the bison. They have given this animal to The People. It is up to us to be sure that we do not anger the spirits by dishonoring the bison. Men are forgetful! It is the responsibility of the women to remember, and to remind them so that they do not forget!"

"We have become lax about the 'blood shelter' as well. In the Starving Mountains there were no special animals to hunt. The blood shelter was not so important. This is why it was allowed to fall into disuse. But now we have left the Starving Mountains. Now again, The People hunt the special animal given by the spirits, so now again, the blood shelter must be used, and again the special taboos for the sacred animal must be observed."

"If these taboos are broken, the hunters will not have the spirit's protection. They will be open to the dangers of stampede, or even of starvation."

"How do you know these things?" Cottontail questioned, "You grew up in the Yucca Camp the same as I and the others, yet we have no such knowledge."

"I cannot exactly answer you," Basket admitted, "For I do not know how I have this knowledge. Perhaps the spirits have put it into my head because I have the mark of bison, because Star Child and I have been chosen to know this and share this knowledge with you. Spirits do not always tell one everything that one would like to know, only what they feel they want to tell. Perhaps it is because we are twins!"

CHAPTER 19

Acorn and Moon sat in their shelter waiting. They had taken the spirit powder and now the spiral began. *Where are you?* Acorn called, *Wolf Spirit!* Moon called. The spiral continued black and silent. They waited, and waited, but no spirit answered. Finally, well after the ancestor fires twinkled in the sky, they returned.

"Did you contact the Wolf Spirit?" questioned Acorn.

Moon sadly shook his head, "I searched and searched, but I could not find him"

"What could we have done wrong?" Acorn frowned, concentrating on the instructions they had been give. "I am sure that I did not forget anything! We followed the cleansing instructions perfectly. The sweat lodge and the chants! I cannot see where we could have gone wrong!"

"Perhaps we misunderstood Wolf Spirit! Perhaps we are to continue following his instructions, have the men prepare the stone and strike the sacred point.'"

"I am sure that he said he would give us further instructions at this point. But perhaps you are correct. After all we have the exact directions for creating the hunting tool and carrying out the ceremony. Perhaps I did misunderstand."

"Then you agree, we should go ahead with the ceremony?"

Acorn thought for a time, "I cannot think of any reason why we should not, unless you think we should go once again over the cleansing with the hunters, making sure that no one forgot a step, that no one has, even accidentally been contaminated by a woman?"

"We have been over it already, very clearly. I cannot think that any have been so careless as to break a taboo. And the women have all stayed to the far end of the camp, and non have come near the ceremonial spot. I saw the twins take them down to cleanse, so the spirits must have spoken to them as well. Do you think I should ask?"

"Do we dare intrude upon women's 'spirit' powers?" Moon questioned; "They are very powerful, what if they took anger at us? What if merely inquiring breaks one of their taboos? We do not know what the female spirits have requested. Would it be safe?"

Acorn did not know. "I will inquire of Star Woman, at a discrete distance. If there are things which we should know, she will be able to tell us."

*   *   *

That good woman stated that all was well with the women for they had done as the spirits requested. They had cleansed, set up the blood shelter and isolated the dangerous women there. All was as it should be as far as the dreamers could tell. So, they decided to continue with the ceremony. First, the cape hunt. There was still a pair of hunters without capes. This must be completed on this day and the hides prepared over the next pair of days.

The men were waiting for them. Running Man and Journey's Far still had not taken their cape animals. The hunters went out in a pair of groups, half with Running Man and the rest with Journey's Far. They had not far to go and both men were successful. The meat was prepared, as they had learned the last season at this place, when the cape hunting ceremony had last taken place. Each step and all the rules were followed.

*   *   *

"What do you make of it?" Blue Coyote stood looking over Stone Man's shoulder.

"It is certainly a bad sign. Look, whatever killed the raven pulled out bunches of feathers, no animal did that! See how the neck is broken? This bird has been here at least a pair of days, yet no predator has bothered it! What do you make of that?"

"Perhaps there has been no predator by," suggested Blue Coyote.

"There are tracks over the tope of human tracks. Coyote were last down this trail, yet he did not take the bird for food, this is a bad omen. A spirit bird was killed."

"We should inform the dreamers immediately! They will know what to do."

Stone Man rose, "Be sure to warn all to avoid this trail!"

"Where are you going?"

"I am going to look around, see what I can see," was the ambiguous answer given to Blue Coyote as Stone Man disappeared into the brush beside the trail. Blue Coyote hurried to tell the dreamers of their discovery. "What can it mean?" he asked.

"It is certainly a bad sign," both agreed.

"A sign bad enough to halt the ceremony?" They hesitated, "Then we go on with it, unless Stone Man comes in with information indicating otherwise."

"Are you sure that none of the men broke a taboo?" Questioned Moon, "Unintentionally, I mean."

"I will ask. Why? Have you had other signs?"

The dreamers hesitated and then shook their heads.

"Then I see no reason not to go ahead. We have gone to a lot of trouble so far, I would be most unhappy if we had to do it all over again due to carelessness on the part of one man. We will see what Stone Man finds."

Stone Man searched, but he did not find any evidence around the dead bird. He returned to camp and joined the other hunters. The ceremony went on as planned. Each man went to a particular spot along the wall of the quarry, a place recently cleared so there was no woman' spirits there. Each mined a nodule of stone, struck blanks, some more expertly than others, and each fashioned the dart point as the dreamers had instructed. Stone Man was muttering under his breath before he finished, and he had a bloody finger as well, but the point he crafted, although not as perfect as Blue Coyote's was symmetrical and the flutes were within acceptable standards. *I really must learn to Knapp more expertly!* He decided.

They went out in groups and selected hardwood shafts and returned to the camp. Here they straightened them, tied them into bundles and dried them evenly over a slow, low fire. The ends were notched, and the points fitted into the slots. Pine pitch was added to hold the point more firmly and the base was hafted to the dart shaft. Then the feathers were added. New atlatls had already been constructed.

Journey's Far had set out upon the cape hunt feeling that surely the spirits would strike him down, or at the very least allow a bison stampede to trample him. When this did not happen, he sighed in relief, accepting Mourning Dove's suggestion that it was the soul and mind, which were important. He knapped his points and made his shafts and hafted and feathered them.

They sat around the ceremonial hearth waiting. The dreamers appeared, and the ceremony began. Acorn, resplendent in his cape of rabbit fur and eagle feathers danced into the circle, followed by Moon. They sent up prayers and chanted as they danced. Then when the drum stopped, they turned and lifting high sacred packets they then cast them into the fire. The fire gave off a slight burst of flame and they went on to the next step.

Each hunter as his name was called stood and declared that he was pure, had abstained from all the forbidden things, and had made his own tool. Then the dreamers passed around the fermented spirit drink, all drank again and again as it passed from hand to hand, until all was consumed. Then the hunters were told the steps of the hunt.

No woman may at any time touch the bison hunting tools!

Before every hunt the hunters must cleanse, purify and abstain from women.

The first bison each hunter killed, on each hunt, must be taken with the sacred darts. Others after that may be taken with darts having fire hardened tips. The sacred darts were to be used on male animals only. The hides of these animals were to be used by men only. Women could work the remaining hides, they could process the meat and they could eat of it. Only those animals from which hunting capes were made were restricted only to males.

Atlatl and darts used for hunting other animals were freed from the taboos and could be used at any time, by anyone.

The eyes of a bison were the property of the hunter whose dart claimed it. It was his choice to whom the organ meats go, but it was reserved only for men. Each hunter was responsible for distributing the animals he killed.

The following exceptions were; portions of a second animal were to be set-aside for the dreamers, for they did not hunt. It was the responsibility of the camp as a whole to make sure that every member was provided for. Women who had no man to hunt for them were to take their share out of the general camp supply, if a hunter did not specify for them a part of his kill.

These then, were the rules.

The women were seated a distance away, clearly in view and hearing of the entire ceremony. They also understood the rules.

Each hunter had made a double layered pouch, the inner one of hide untouched by women, the outer of wolf hide. Within these pouches each hunter stored his supply of stone from which to craft the sacred points. These were tucked safely away.

All retired to their ceremonial sleeping arrangements, and upon the next sunrise the camp merged once again. Women moved back into their shelters and were at first nervous about touching something they should not, but they were reassured that the bison darts and atlatl were safely protected within a double layer of hide, so they need not worry. The camp settled down to relax once the ceremony was over and life proceeding again as usual. The men hunted deer in the river valley and the women gathered grains and tubers along the river. A span of days passed, and it was time to leave on the journey north.

"Let's make a last trip to the secret cave!" Star Child suggested, as she and Basket were setting out to gather tubers up the canyon.

"All right, but we cannot spend the whole day there, we have much to do before leaving tomorrow. Remember that your mother wants you back at the camp well before dark."

"We need not stay long, I just want to make a quick spirit trip, there is something bothering me, and I can't quite put my finger on it, maybe Wolf Spirit can help."

"I know what you mean, something is not just right, and I too have been uneasy. Agreed, we make a quick spirit trip." They hurried to the cave and quickly set up their hides and steeped the morning glory seed powder. Then they waited . . .

*   *   *

Evil is loose in the camp! Wolf Spirit hissed; *you must stop this evil! No man may know! The spirits have forsaken the men of the Wolf Camp, for evil has contaminated one of them. He has participated in the sacred ceremony with unclean body. He has associated with a woman after the cleansing ceremony! He has angered the spirits! But the evil is from a woman, and it is powerful evil. A sacred raven was killed, purposefully, savagely! The spirit of the one killing is now very powerful, but it is evil, it contaminated the man, he contaminated the ceremony, and thus every man in the camp! The dreamers are helpless! A woman caused this problem. A woman must cleanse the problem.*

Seek out the bad seed and cast it from the camp! Then and only then will the spirits return to the Wolf Camp. I will not again speak with you until this is done. Cast forth the evil one and cleanse the whole camp, to the last individual cleanse it! The sacred hunting points, darts, and atlatl must be destroyed in a cleansing fire, new ones made by cleansed hunters. The women must scour the touch of the evil one from their midst as well. Any item that she has touched must be burned. She must be cast away. I have spoken for the last time until this has been done.

*   *   *

Basket and Star Child looked at each other, frightened and sober. "What do we do?" questioned Star Child, "Who is the evil one? What do we tell the dreamers and the hunters, for we must tell them?"

"We cannot!" Basket replied, "You heard the spirit as well as I, the hunters and dreamers must not know. We must find this evil one and cast her out! We must do so quickly, for the spirits have deserted the men, and the dreamers have no guidance!"

"But who, I mean, where do we begin, how do we find the evil one?"

"We must question each of the women, someone must know about the raven! Who could have done such a thing? Everyone knows that to kill the sacred raven is to bring suffering upon the camp. I cannot imagine anyone doing such a thing!"

"Maybe that is why Antelope Woman was killed!"

"You think Antelope . . .? No! She could never do such a thing! Besides the spirit said this woman had contaminated a man after the cleansing ceremony, Antelope was killed before."

"You are right," Star Child sighed, "We must go about this very carefully. If whoever killed, Antelope Woman is responsible for killing the raven, she would not hesitate to kill one or both of us as well."

"We must be very careful how we question the women also. If we bring suspicion upon ourselves, it could be dangerous! And we dare not speak to the dreamers either; nor to any of the men!"

"Not even Stone Man?"

"Not even Stone Man or Blue Coyote! Only after the evil has been cast from the camp may we consult with the dreamers, and then we must tell them about the hunting tools! This means that Running Man and Journey's Far are not protected by the 'spirits' of their hunting capes either; this could be very dangerous for them!"

"Does this also mean that any sacred hunts for bison will be evil as well?"

"I don't know, but we must somehow, someway, make sure that neither man participates in the bison hunt!"

"How do we do that?" Star Child questioned.

"I don't know, but Wolf Spirit was very clear about one thing, she will not speak to either of us again until we accomplish this task!"

They eventually left the cave and gathered their tubers, returning to camp much sobered. They kept their own council and spent many hours together trying to work out a plan. They were very much on their own, and this was a huge task for a pair of untried female 'spirit leaders'.

* * *

"What do you think? Should we strike off across country, or follow the river?" Blue Coyote questioned the group crowded around the stone.

"In the Starving Mountains, streams always started in the mountains. Perhaps if we follow the river, it will lead us to mountains!" Jackrabbit suggested.

"This is true, but we know already that this river wanders from here to there across this plain. Would it not be shorter to cut in a straight line toward our goal?" Gray Wolf offered.

"What is our hurry?" a hunter questioned, "I like the hunting along the valley, it is easy traveling and we can move to lower ground at night so that our camp fires cannot be seen from any distance."

Others agreed, so it was decided to follow the river. They ambled slowly along, hunting deer and the occasional bison along the way. The bison hunts were made strictly according to the rules set down by the dreamers, and one or another of the spirit brother groups made the hunt. Basket and Star Child were able to keep both Running Man and Journey's Far from participating in the hunts, but Running Man was becoming suspicious. They could but hint that perhaps, due to nothing on his part that he might not have the full protection of his 'hunting spirit'. Running Man was superstitious enough to take the hint! Journey's Far gave them a frightened look the very first time they hinted, and he made sure not to participate in the hunting from then on. This was a puzzle!

"Have you kept trying?" Moon questioned.

Acorn nodded, "Nearly every night! Something is wrong! It must be tied into the killing of that raven! Wolf Spirit has refused to speak to me ever since!"

Moon nodded, "The same with me. I even spoke with Star Child, but she only confirmed that Wolf Spirit hasn't spoken to either of them for the same length of time. I got the feeling that there was more to it than that; that perhaps she was not telling me everything, but if Wolf Spirit told them something they are not sharing, or have been forbidden to share with us!"

"How can we know what to do if Wolf Spirit refuses to help us?"

"Perhaps it was a female taboo which was broken! Then it would make sense that the women take care of it," Acorn mused, "Perhaps our hunters are not to blame at all!"

"Then why has Wolf Spirit forsaken us?"

"We must keep trying. These spirits! Wolf refused to speak to me for many years and then suddenly he began to talk to me, now just as suddenly, he refuses again."

"Did you ever figure why he left you the first time?"

"It had to do with the separation of Basket and Star Child. But how I was to know that is beyond me, for I was not even aware that Feather had given birth to twins. That is the way of spirits though! They expect you to accomplish things even without knowing what it is you are to do."

"At least this time we know it has to do with the death of that raven!" Moon stated.

"Did Stone Man or Blue Coyote ever discover anything further about that?"

"Not that they have told me."

"I think we should discourage any more sacred bison hunts until this is cleared up. It might anger Wolf Spirit, and it could be unsafe for the hunters. We will soon be in the mountains. It would be advisable to encourage the hunters along a different path there."

"This is logical, and besides, there is much game in mountains, most of which carries no taboo with it. Deer, bear, elk and turkey are all safe to hunt. Perhaps we should encourage the camp to remain in the mountains until this puzzle is cleared up," Moon suggested. Acorn nodded in agreement.

Blue Coyote sat beside his hearth fire, staring into the flames. The dreamers had just left him, adding to the burden he carried with their suspicions. The raven had been killed before the Ceremony. It would make sense that therefore the Ceremony was worthless. Their sacred tools carried no spirit protection, and the capes of the last pair of hunters would not protect them as well. The suggestion that they remain in the mountains and hunt safe game also made sense, once they reached mountains.

So far they had meandered north, west, southwest, and now again west following the river. At least there had been no sign of Red Eagle. Now there was a hint that mountains lay to the north and west. They would know tomorrow. Blue Coyote was worried. Summer was beginning, and in another moon they would be celebrating Midsummer Ceremony. He certainly hoped that this time they could have a real ceremony. He was eager and anxious to claim Mourning Dove. They did manage to sneak off a pair of times, but he was tired of sneaking. He wanted to claim her proudly, before the entire camp.

There was also the worry of that raven! Stone Man had been able to discover nothing more about its death. He had spoken to every hunter, and even to some of the women, but no one claimed any knowledge of its death. Blue Coyote had shared his concerns with the only person he could trust completely. Mourning Dove was anxious for him, supportive, but she also had been unable to shed any light on the subject, although she assured him that she had spoken to a number of the women and no one had any knowledge. The death of that raven hung over the camp like a black cloud!

"I cannot figure it!" Basket grumbled, "We have spoken to every single woman in this camp, and no one has any knowledge to shed light on what we need to know."

"Then someone is lying!" Star Woman stated wisely.

"But how do we know who that is?"

"We could claim that whoever killed that raven will suffer something awful, and then watch to see who worries about the symptoms," suggest Star Child.

"That would work ordinarily, but whoever killed that raven isn't going to believe in some 'spirit' disease. They would not have done the deed to begin with!" Rain Woman replied. "I wish it would work! I do not at all like the idea of sharing a camp with anyone who would kill a sacred messenger."

"Do you think that the raven could have a link to Antelope's death?" questioned Basket.

"In what way," Star Woman frowned?

"I don't know! That is the problem. I have thought and thought, but I cannot find any answers. When Stone Man first told me about the raven I thought it could be a message, but if it is there has been no follow-up."

"You just do not accept that strangers killed her, do you?" Rain Woman asked.

"Do either of you accept the idea that strangers killed your mates?" questioned Basket

Both women looked at each other and then at Basket, both shook their heads. "I am not convinced," Star Woman admitted, "But why anyone of this camp would wish either of them dead makes no sense. Fire Dancer and Bison were both good fair headmen. Now the camp is in the hands of Blue Coyote, who, although I love him dearly, even I admit is very young and inexperienced."

"It almost seems that over the last season some evil has been making sure that the Wolf Camp is without seasoned leaders, first Centipede Man, then Fire Dancer and Bison Man, all dead. Cougar makes an excellent and dependable support, but he is too old to lead, and Jackrabbit has not the head for it. It is lucky that both Blue Coyote and Stone Man are level headed, even if inexperienced," Rain Woman added.

"I wish Stone Man had thought to seek me out when he found that raven. Throw Back could have picked up the scent of the raven killer and led us directly to her," Basket grumbled. "Well I am going to bed. All this thinking has given me a headache." They all wandered off to their furs, but the four women lay awake long into the night puzzling . . .

"You are right, there are mountains up ahead," Jackrabbit grinned at Blue Coyote. "I am certainly looking forward to hunting in mountains again. Just thinking of a roasted turkey makes me hungry!"

"Thinking about any food makes you hungry," shouted Cougar.

"Well, turkey, bear and elk will make a nice break from bison and venison!" Jackrabbit admitted. "Besides there should be pine trees, and we have all missed acorns and pinyon nuts. It will be good to have more plants in our diet. This dependence so heavily on meat is hard on the digestion. Besides, it will be good to settle again for a while in one place."

"We must be on the move again after the Midsummer Ceremony," reminded Blue Coyote, "We do not want to be this far north by winter. That season is severe enough at the escarpment so there is no way to tell how bad it could be in these mountains ahead," he sighed. "Besides, I have a funny feeling that Red Eagle is about somewhere, nothing I can put my finger on, just that every time we begin to relax he has a habit of showing up and sending some of us to walk the wind. I just want everyone to keep prepared that is all."

"We have watchers every night," reminded Jackrabbit, "And we have not seen signs of any others in moons."

"What about Antelope Woman?" Asked Stone Man; "It was a dart of 'others' which killed her."

The men looked uneasily, one to the other, for no one really believed the tale of 'others'. Not in the death of Antelope Woman, nor those of Fire Dancer and Bison Man, but there had not been a single scrap of evidence otherwise. No one replied. Stone Man looked about the group, "That is what I thought!" he stated.

"We were both on watch that night," reminded Blue Coyote, "And I just don't think the camp would just sleep with a stranger nearby. For one thing, Wolf, or Throw Back would alert the camp to intruders."

"But if one of us killed her then who?" Cougar questioned, "I mean, who would want to kill old Antelope? She never harmed a soul."

Stone Man didn't speak but the lines about his mouth tightened. He had suspicions . . . but no way of proving them. There was one who had cause to want Antelope shut up, but Blue Coyote would not listen to such accusations, this Stone Man knew. The raven could also be blamed on the same source. It would not be something she would consider important, the killing of a 'spirit' bird, unless the raven was considered sacred by her people as well, and since he was very careful to avoid Mourning Dove, there was no way he could question her about such things. He feared alerting anyone else to the possibility because he had a suspicion that those who suspected Mourning Dove ended up dead. So he did not speak of his suspicions to anyone, nor did he follow up on them himself, for the same reason. He did not care to anticipate a dart in the back when he was least expecting it. He did however give serious consideration to the thought of an accident. One that Mourning Dove would not survive, but it was not in his nature to do such a thing, something he could live to regret . . .

"Have you given my idea any more thought?" Moon questioned.

Acorn nodded, "I think it might work. At least it might scare the culprit into confessing! But we must be very careful when we do this, for it will leave the entire camp exposed to danger. We can only do it where all are safe."

"Then we will wait for that time," Acorn nodded, satisfied.

They reached the foothills that day and the women spread out and gathered enough tubers so that everyone could enjoy them with the evening meal. Then they entered the mountains proper.

"Look at all the pine cones!" Willow exclaimed. "I have not seen so many since leaving the Starving Mountains, come to think of it, not even there! I think I will gather some for the evening meal, Cottontail, will you help me?"

Cottontail Girl nodded, and they hurried the short distance to where the trees stood.

"Do not get separated from the camp!" called Star Woman.

"We will hurry!" Willow assured her. They did, catching up with a robe filled with cones.

"There were so many that it did not take long to gather these," she informed Star Woman.

As they walked, the women began prying the nuts from the cones and saving them in their pouches, which they had tied to their waist thongs for this specific purpose. When the robe-full of cones was depleted, Willow and Cottontail gathered another. The twins and Sage gathered yet another thereby providing ample to make pine nut cakes for the evening meal for everyone.

"Turkey tracks!" exclaimed Jackrabbit.

Blue Coyote called a halt. "All right," he conceded, "Jackrabbit you and Cougar go after the turkeys but keep track for we will be camped up ahead, see where that big rock juts out?" The hunters nodded, "We will be camping just below it," they grinned and hurried off.

"Sh! I think I hear them!" whispered Jackrabbit, motioning Cougar behind him, "Just beyond this brush!"

The hunters crouched and waited. Shortly the birds came into the open, gobbling, and darting hungrily at anything and everything that caught their eyes, clucking and calling to each other. They waited until the animals had just passed them, then rose and cast first rabbit sticks, taking a pair quietly, then with bolas taking a further pair that squawked and flopped noisily, alerting the flock, which vanished. They collected their birds, "Let's cut over these hills and see if there are more tracks in the next valley," suggested Cougar, "These birds will not go far in feeding the whole camp."

Jackrabbit agreed and the men quickly worked their way across the ridge. "Look here," Jackrabbit called, "More tracks!" They followed and soon added another pair to their collection, they headed along a ridge, and back in the direction in which Blue Coyote had said the camp would be. "It is good to be hunting again in mountains," he sighed, "I have missed this! The plains are a fine place and bison is good meat, but I do miss the choices that we had in the mountains."

"We are mountain people, Jackrabbit, we grew up in the mountains, and it will always be where we feel most at home. The younger ones, they adjust better than we do. Like you, I miss the variety of food we found in the mountains," Cougar agreed.

They cut back across the ridge and below them lay the camp. They hurried down and relinquished their turkeys to the eager hands of the women. "A turkey feather robe could be made from these," suggested Willow, "It would make a fine gift to Moon; I have noticed that the robe he wears it getting tattered. Dare we suggest such a thing?" she spoke to Rain Woman.

"I think that is an excellent idea, but, no, we do not ask him, for then it would not be a gift! We will make it and find a time to present it to him."

"The Midsummer Ceremony is not far off. That would certainly be a good time," Star Woman said. "Our times of mourning will be over and it will be a joyful celebration," she sighed, "At least for some."

The women plucked the birds carefully, saving the feathers for their project. "We will have to ask the hunters for more turkeys," Willow said, "These are not enough."

"There will be more turkeys," Star Woman replied, "Jackrabbit is ever-so fond of turkey."

"How much further do you think we will go into these mountains?" questioned Cottontail.

"Probably not much farther, the hunters will want a sacred bison hunt just before the Midsummer Ceremony, and the bison do not come far into the mountains," replied Rain Woman. "I have heard the hunters discussing settling down for a while in one place. This is probably what is planned. I will not mind, it has been a long journey, and after the ceremony we will turn around and repeat it."

"When we lived in the Starving Mountains, we did not move at all, but stayed in the same camp season after season," Basket said, "Now all we do is travel."

"I like the traveling!" Cottontail replied "It seems that every time we settle in any one place for any length we end up starving! I prefer to keep moving and eating as well," she glanced around the camp, "And we certainly have enough animals to pull our travois!" She scratched the head of her own wolf, "Who would have thought that the secret canyon would give us such a gift after nearly starving us to death?"

"Dog Boy and I had something to do with that!" reminded Sunflower, stuffing pine nuts and grains inside a turkey.

"That you did!" Agreed Turtle Woman, "I still remember the day you came into the home cave with that rascal!" She nodded to the wolf by Sunflower's side. They both grinned recalling the shared memory. "These wolves were something good which came from that canyon, as was the clothing we wear. Perhaps it was not so bad a place after all. We tend to only remember the bad things."

"What bad things?" laughed Basket, "You can't mean nearly freezing to death in that blizzard and nearly being eaten by their relatives can you?" They all laughed.

"One day I would like to see that place," remarked Rain Woman.

"And I," added Star Child. "Particularly, I would like to see the bones of the great beast," she added wistfully.

They scooped out places within the hot coals and packing the birds in mud they settled them to cook, piling hot coals over the top and keeping the fire burning. Then while there was still plenty of light, for they had stopped early, they went out looking for other things to add to the meal.

Their first meal in the mountains was a treat for all. It had been several seasons since any had enjoyed the gifts of the mountains. "Tomorrow the women might as well rest and enjoy their day," Blue Coyote announced as most sat around fully satisfied and full. "The men on the other hand, have a job to do. I want you to break up into your 'spirit brother' groups and scour this area for a suitable place to camp for at least a moon, perhaps longer. We are settling for a while!" A cheer went up and the men broke into their spirit groups. It was decided that the Red Tail Hawks would go north, the Wolf Pack west and the Eagle somewhere in between. It was decided also that Badger and Dog Boy would remain in the camp.

* * *

"Are you sure?"

"There are only a few men in the camp! All the rest left early to scout ahead. It looks like they plan to spend some time here."

"And you saw the woman I described?"

"I know Basket! I have seen her on a number of occasions. I told you she is in the camp. You said she had a huge wolf that never leaves her side. I saw her, and I recognized her. She has an oddly shaped staff . . ."

That is it! The staff! I want it! The voice demanded.

"If we cause a commotion at the other end of the camp, do you think you could get in, grab the staff and get out again without getting caught?"

"What about that pack of wolves which share their camp? They could rip a man to pieces!"

"The only one you have to worry about is the big one."

The man shook his head, "It would be easier to wait and catch her by herself or out with a few of the women. We could attack, kill her, take the staff and no one would know the difference. It would also be a lot safer for us!"

"We will wait. Just keep out of sight and keep track of them. An opportunity will present itself. So long as they do not pull another vanishing trick! You say that you did not see Fire Dancer?"

"Blue Coyote seems to be leader. I saw no sign of Fire Dancer, but Star Woman is with them. A number of people I do not recognize as well, but one which I do, Cripple is also with them."

"That rat faced little traitor! I knew he was responsible for alerting them when we attacked the bison hunt! But I will get mine back at him as well!" Red Eagle snarled, "We will wait and watch. This time I will not fail. I was too quick before, but I have learned to be patient these last seasons. I will not fail again!"

The small group of men carefully erased their tracks and hurried back down into the river valley. They had been watching and waiting and following for a pair of moons, always far enough back and down wind. The Yucca Camp had no idea they followed. "They certainly have some strange habits since leaving the starving mountains," Hairy Bear said. "I wonder where they got all those wolves, and how they got them to live and hunt with them?"

"Blue Coyote captured one while I still lived with them. Perhaps these are all his offspring? Or perhaps they have been capturing them and taming them. But the wolf pelts they now wear, they are truly impressive! I think the idea is one that would make us more frightening. And perhaps people would think that we are they when we attack! This is even a better idea." Red Eagle laughed "Blame our attacks on them, leave some sort of clue!"

"So far the only people we have found were the ones who joined them. We can hardly blame the Yucca Camp for attacks on the Yucca Camp!" Hairy Bear remarked.

"There must be others out there as well, Stupid! When we find them, we will make sure that any survivors blame Blue Coyote for the attack!"

Hairy Bear scratched his head, puzzled, but not smart enough to follow this train of thought.

* * *

The Wolf Pack found the place to camp. They located a small wide valley with a good-sized stream running through it. There were numerous large trees to erect shelters beneath, and sufficient wood for fires. The surrounding area would yield an abundance of easily gathered plants. The vertical cliffs on either side would give them protection from attack but were far enough away that they could not be attacked from on top. The valley was wide enough that no one could sneak up on them or pin them down either. It was almost as easy to protect as the canyon, without the hazards involved.

The camp moved in and within a hand of days had the shelters erected and people settled in.

"I want my own shelter!" Mourning Dove pleaded. "I don't like living with the old ones! And they don't like me! Soft Wind and Kind Heart are sharp tongued, and they want me to do things for them all of the time. It is always 'Mourning Dove, save my old bones and fetch me this, or Mourning Dove, we need more wood on the fire, these old bones need to rest' and of course I always do as they ask, but I do get tired. They do not realize just how much they do ask of me!" She pouted prettily "Besides I had my own shelter in the canyon, so no one will be surprised."

"Well, I don't suppose it will hurt," Blue Coyote gave in, "I will have it erected immediately, there is space right beside my mother's."

"Not there!" Mourning Dove said sharply, then forced herself to soften, "I mean, how could... you visit me . . . if I were there?"

"But you would not be safe outside the protection of the camp!"

"Of course I would, if your shelter were near by."

"I share a shelter with three other men, as you know. There is no way I can visit you, no matter where your shelter is. We will just have to wait until the Midsummer Celebration and then you will share my shelter every night," he nibbled at her bare breast. "Until then, we will just have to be satisfied with these stolen times," he sighed, "And now I had better get back to my watch. You must not be missed either," he rose and she began pulling on her tunic.

Mourning Dove got her shelter, but it was next to that of Star Woman, Rain Woman and the twins. She did not like it but she settled, at least she did not have to share with Kind Heart and Soft Wind. She also had been forced to give up her relationship with Journey's Far, for it also was too dangerous. The youth however, took it well. She wept and made promises, none of which she had any intention of keeping, for if the opportunity should happen to present itself, she certainly would take it. Journey's Far might be young, but he did well satisfying her needs. Blue Coyote seldom had time, was always in a hurry and had too many other things on him mind, but he was Headman. Mate to a headman was a position well worth the struggle of maintaining the appearance of being the perfect woman. If Mourning Dove had to spend days working pleasantly with the other women, then she would. It she had to fetch and carry, offer, or even give up, to keep the illusion; then she did.

Star Woman welcomed her with a friendly smile, and if the twins were less than friendly, at least they were no longer hostile; the same could not be said for Throw Back and her equally ugly offspring.

"Leave it!" Mourning Dove waited for Basket and Star Child to help her lug the bison hides to the open area where they could peg them for working. Basket could not carry the hides and her staff as well. With a sigh she left the staff beside the hearth and took up her end of the hide. The wolves were both off with Star Woman and Rain Woman bringing the remainder of the bison hides in from the plain. They would be back directly and then there was more work for all. Willow and Cottontail Girl, Sage and Song Bird were working the hides either side of Mourning Dove and the twins. The camp was quiet.

*   *   *

"Now!" The man whispered, "I can sneak in now!"

"Then do it!" Red Eagle muttered. The man slipped like a shadow from one spot to the next. Slipped around the shelter and reached the hearth. It took him but a second to grab the staff and vanish as quickly as he came. The pair of men then slipped quickly from sight and erased their trail.

You have them! "No, but I have this!" *What is that? Bring it closer! No! It can't be! You have done well, very well! Yes! The staff, this is strong power indeed!* "Then you will give me the life of Blue Coyote?" *I have given you Fire Dancer!* "But you promised! I have kept my word! I brought you the spirit points, the old hunting cape, and now this staff, and all you have given in return is Fire Dancer! These things are worth more than just one life!" *You are right! They are worth more than one life, and they give me the power to take that life! Yours!* The spirit cackled and danced, slowly forcing the spirit that was Red Eagle from his body. "Ah, this is much better," White Falcon breathed deeply for the first time in more than three hands of seasons, running his hands over the tunic and testing the tastes and textures of the world again. "It isn't perhaps the body I would have chosen, but then I was in rather a fix at the time," he muttered to himself.

"We have what we came for!" He explained to the raider band "There is no reason to stay here any longer, besides when they realize this staff is gone, they will be looking for us. We will be elsewhere by then. We go to the place of stone; there will be people coming by there for stone, and we will take many prisoners," he instructed, still feeling the full pleasure of living once again. There was time to do battle with Basket later.

*   *   *

Back at the camp, things were going along smoothly. Star Woman and her group came in from the plain, both travois heavily loaded, but not really a problem for Throw Back and Dire Wolf. They were dragged right up to where the women were working. More bison hides were spread out and soon all the women were hard at work stretching, pegging and scraping them. Makes A Robe brought stew and kept it hot so that the women could take a break, rest a bit and eat. They worked until it was too dark to see.

Basket missed the staff immediately. "I am sure that I left it right here beside the hearth," she said. "You were with me Mourning Dove, is that not where I left it?"

"Yes! That is where you left it, what difference does it make! It is just a root after all! There is no need to make such a fuss, surely?"

"Just a root," Basket was shocked, "Is that how your people treat Sacred Objects?"

Mourning Dove thought quickly, "I had no idea that there was any significance to the staff," she admitted, "You always carry it, but I just thought that is because you are crippled!" *there! You miserable pain-in-the-side! See how you like it!* "I had no idea, honestly!"

"Well there is nothing we can do about it until morning," Star Child said, "So we might as well get some sleep. We have another long day working those hides before us." The women retired, exhausted after the backbreaking work on the hides. Morning brought no answer to the puzzle of the missing staff. Stone Man went out and cut another to make Basket feel better, but it didn't help. The staff was gone, and with it 'power'. Basket looked everywhere for her staff, but she knew it was lost to her, another in a long line of unexplained things that had happened to this camp. They stayed at the mountain camp for a full moon and then began to prepare for the Midsummer Celebration. The bison hides were all prepared, for they would serve as their new shelter hides. The dreamers were busy with their own preparations and men and women alike had much to do.

"We are no closer to knowing who killed that raven!" Stone Man sat hafting a point to a bison dart. "I have gone over it again and again in my head but come up with no new answers."

"It is a puzzle," admitted Blue Coyote, "And now we must go on a sacred bison hunt, and I do not feel confident with this mystery still hanging over us. Have the dreamers nothing more to contribute?"

"They say not, but then who can tell with a dreamer?" Stone Man finished the dart, "Anything more on Basket's staff?"

"Again nothing, we have searched the camp from one end to the other and the surrounding area as well. I fear that my conclusion was the right one, she left it beside the fire and somehow it fell in and was burned. That is the only answer which makes any sense," Blue Coyote stated, "And I am going to rule on that! It is at an end! We have spent enough time and effort on the search. Basket will just have to realize that it was her own carelessness which brought the Relic to its end."

Stone Man frowned at the tone of his friend but said nothing. Blue Coyote was under considerable strain. There was a lot of extra work placed upon his shoulders with the ceremony. He just hoped that everything went of smoothly, although he had a feeling of dread that he just could not manage to shake.

*　*　*

Star Child and Basket were out gathering tubers the next day. "Basket! Come here, quickly!" Star Child called.

Basket straightened from where she was digging and laid aside her carrier. She joined Star Child, "What is it?"

"Look!" Star Child rocked back on her heels. "I was digging these tubers and my amulet began thumping. What do you think? Will it do?"

Basket squatted beside her twin and ran her fingers up the tree root, *power*, she knelt beside it and began digging with her fingers and then with her digging stick, undermining the root. It took them considerable time to chop through above the nodule, but finally they had their prize. Basket held it up and turned it over in her hands; "do you think Stone Man could smooth this area for me?" she ran her hand down the length of the root and tested it for strength, "What do you think?"

"It has power, I can feel it," Star Child admitted.

"So can I, but you found it, so it should belong to you!" Basket handed the staff over.

Star Child took it, turned it over in her hands and returned it to Basket. "No, my amulet tells me that it is for you! Perhaps one day I will have a staff, but this one is for you," she handed it back to Basket, "But I think we had better do the smoothing ourselves. A man might get hurt dealing with women's power."

"You are right. I should have thought of that myself. This does look like the head of a bison doesn't it?" she turned the root over again.

"It certainly does, Star Child grinned, "And that sandstone over there will probably do the job of smoothing the rough end, come on, let's see!" she led the way, Basket followed, her new staff clutched in her hand, Throw Back at her side. They worked for some time, carefully rubbing the end of the root-staff over the sandstone until it was smooth and shaped to fit the hand. The other end was cut through at the proper length and Basket had a new staff.

"Do you really think the other one burned in the hearth?" Basket questioned.

"Only if Mourning Dove tossed it there," Star Child muttered in response.

"She was with me the whole time, "Basket admitted, "Or I would probably agree with you. I don't know, I suppose when I laid it down I could have been careless, it is possible that it rolled into the fire . . ."

"You don't believe that any more than I do! Someday we might know the answer, but until then, the spirits have provided you with a new staff!"

"I wish you had one as well. It is hardly fair that I get a pair of them and you none!"

"It held no power for me, only for you. One day there will be one for me if the spirits desire, but for now, at least one of us has one," Star Child replied.

Dire Wolf woofed! Both women stopped and watched while the animal began to dig furiously, on the same tree, just opposite of where they cut Basket's staff. "What is it girl?" Star Child questioned.

"Woof!"

She went down on her knees beside the wolf, and a cloud of dirt rose around them.

"Here let me help you!" Basket exclaimed as the wolf and Star Child were sending dirt flying in all directions,

"I think I have all the help I can deal with!" Star Child laughed as she brushed dirt from her tunic and face; "Dire Wolf is up to something, what I can't tell, for she is sending dirt in all directions."

The animal stopped and wagged her tail, "Woof!"

Basket knelt before the gash and swept away the loose dirt, "look!" she squealed!

Star Child looked and began to laugh, "I can't believe it; a pair of identical roots from the same tree!"

"Just as we are a pair of identical persons from the same mother," Basket whispered in awe.

"Here, let me help you cut it free," they both now knelt beside the tree root. Basket chopped as Star Child held the root steady. Then they went back to the sandstone and ground the raw edge smooth. When they finished, they lay the pair of staffs side by side. They were as identical as the women who would carry them! "Just in time for the Midsummer Ceremony," Basket murmured. "I can feel the power in these," she laid a hand on each.

"We need to say a prayer of thanks to that tree, and bring it a gift as well, but first we need fill in the wounds which we made," Star Child suggested. Basket nodded and they carefully refilled the gouges where the roots had been, they gave a prayer of thanks to the tree and picking up their new staffs and their containers and headed back to the camp.

"Perhaps the spirit took away your old staff and led us to these new ones," suggested Star Child as they walked.

"I suppose that is possible," agreed Basket. "It is so puzzling; Wolf Spirit refuses to speak with us, yet obviously has not deserted us. It is so difficult to know what to do! We have thought and thought, and questioned every woman in the camp, yet we are no closer to knowing the identity of the raven killer. I just cannot imagine any woman of The People killing the sacred messenger!" she sighed.

"Perhaps it wasn't a woman of The People," replied Star Child, biting her lip, "Perhaps it was one who merely walks with The People!"

"You mean Mourning Dove?" Basket frowned, "I have thought of that as well, but we cannot always blame everything on Mourning Dove! Besides I have questioned her and she has no more knowledge than we regarding the death of the raven. She was shocked that anyone would do such a thing! It seems that her people hold Raven in even higher regard than do The People."

"Well someone in this camp is lying! You know the members of your own camp better than I do. Are any of them capable of such a deed?" Basket shook her head. "Well neither are any of my camp! So where does that leave us? Right back to Mourning Dove, that's where!"

"Well she was with me the entire time while my staff disappeared, so she could not be responsible for that. I realize that we always first jump to suspecting her, regardless, and perhaps this makes me blind to the possibility that she could, in fact, be the one we seek. Without Wolf Spirit to lead us, how can we ever find the truth?" Basket sighed.

---

1. The Folsom Point. Named for the Folsom Type-Site near the town of Folsom, in northern N.M.

CHAPTER 20

I just do not understand!" Mourning Dove sobbed broken-heartedly against Journey's Far's chest; "I had no idea!"

"I will go and talk to him! Surely he will change his mind once he understands how it is between us!"

"No!" Mourning Dove shouted and then got herself under control. "It is too late, he has already made the decision, and . . . and . . . I accepted." She cried all the harder, "He gave me no time to think, I didn't know what else to do. I couldn't tell him about us, he was already angry that I didn't jump at the opportunity, that would have angered him even more, so . . . I . . . didn't say. . ." she finished lamely. "Now it is done. But I will always . . ." she sobbed, "Always carry you in my heart," she ended on a soft whimpering whisper.

Journey's Far was white and shaking, but he knew that once a mating was sealed there was nothing to undo it. He had just, by some cruel shift of fate, lost the only thing in his life that mattered, his beloved Mourning Dove. And now he was faced with the additional burden of having to live with seeing her every day, mated to the Headman, forever beyond his reach. *Perhaps this is my punishment!* He returned to the camp, resolved to face it like a man.

Mourning Dove sighed as she sank onto the log *that was close!* She bit her lip contemplating the seasons ahead, mated to the Headman. *Mustn't look too pleased! It wouldn't be proper!* Blue Coyote had come to her that morning and confirmed that he intended to announce their mating at the Midsummer Ceremony. It was up to her to make sure that Journey's Far heard it first from her lips, before he did anything rash and spoiled all her plans. Now that was done! She saw something move and glanced up just in time to see a raven fly off, it lost a feather, which floated down to land just at her feet. She smiled, remembering another raven, and on a whim picked up the feather and tucked it into her amulet bag. It was definitely a sign! Suddenly her stomach flared again, and she was sick behind the log. That was the third time in as many days. *I hope I'm not coming down with something!* She returned to the camp and found a grain cake to nibble on as she began her day.

* * *

"They are amazing!" Star Woman and Rain Woman admired the matched staffs, "What did you have in mind as a gift to the tree?"

"We thought perhaps you might have an idea what would be proper," Star Child admitted.

"Well, let me think . . . we gather the pine nuts, so we thank the pine trees with a prayer offering of seeds," she began, "And the fruit trees the same way, but I have no idea what a proper offering would be for roots,"

"Tubers and cat tails are roots," suggested Rain Woman, "We offer pollen for them."

"Perhaps if we planted some seeds of the same kind of tree . . ." Star Child suggested.

"I think a gift of water would be appropriate," Star Woman decided. "The root brings water into the tree, and this would provide what the root removal took from the tree."

"I agree!" Basket nodded, "We will give the tree a gift of water every day while we are here!" the twins grinned at each other, it was settled!

* * *

"It gets harder daily to tell them apart," Star Woman sighed, "Now with matched staffs it will be nearly impossible." She laughed, "It is as well that we know them so well that we are likely never be so confused!"

"I could not believe that I caught Star Child affecting Basket's slight limp!" Rain Woman shook her head. "It is as well they are grown, for if they had been together as children, I have an idea we would have many more gray hairs."

"Sometimes they worry me," Star Woman admitted, "They have a purpose, and together they are so very powerful!"

"Power always has a purpose," agreed Rain Woman. "I am glad the 'staff' problem has been solved. It bothered me that Basket's staff disappeared, but now I begin to think it was done by 'power' just so that they could be provided with matched staffs. Beside the new staffs have a bison, the old one had the great beast; bison holds more power!"

"I still would like to know what became of the other!" Star Woman stated.

True to their word, Basket and Star Child went to the stream and brought water to the tree. In doing so they discovered a small pond, secluded by trees, wherein lay another Great Beast skeleton. Star Child was fascinated by it, and spent hands of time running her hands over the tusks, gaining power from it. They also planted a hand of seeds, evenly spaced around the old tree. Satisfied, they went their way.

*   *   *

"I want to try contacting Wolf Spirit again," Star Child stated. "We have done everything we were able to find the evil one in the camp. We have not succeeded, but Wolf Spirit must not be mad at us, she provided the staffs!"

"We can try, but do not be upset if all you get is a headache and an upset stomach!" Basket advised, "Where do you wish to do this thing?"

"I was sort of thinking . . . well. It sounds silly when I think about it, but well . . . under the tree?" She suggested lamely. Basket merely nodded.

"When?"

"The sooner the better!"

"Then we had better get back to the camp, gather our equipment and make sure the wolves know they are on watch duty, however, if someone should decide to do us harm, I am not sure how much help either of them would be. They would be easily darted if an enemy really intended us harm."

"If that was said to reassure me, it didn't!" Star Child frowned.

"I am only stating facts. It seems to me that everyone has strangers or raiders on the brain of late. As usual, we have seen nothing of either. There have been no more incidents of violence since Antelope Woman's death, and if, in fact, my staff fell into the fire, there is nothing to fear, right?"

"Yes, I suppose so," Star Child agreed, "So let's do it!"

The sun was fleeing night spirit when they finished their spirit search, "I told you all we would get from this was a headache and an upset stomach!" Basket reminded Star Child.

"So, you were right as usual!" Star Child admitted just after she finished emptying her stomach onto the ground. "We had better get back to the camp before my mother and Star Woman start to worry; and next time I will listen to you!"

Basket merely looked skeptically at her and led the way.

*   *   *

"How are the plans for the ceremony progressing?" Blue Coyote questioned the dreamers. "Are there things which you need? Do you need help?"

"Things are going fine. Stone Man just left after asking the very same questions. We have everything that we need. The cleansing is complete, and the hunters are blessed for the sacred bison hunt. You have only to give them direction and the hunt begins as Sun Spirit lightens the sky. The wood has been gathered for the ceremonial fire, we have all the 'spirit' preparations complete and as far as I know the new people have been prepared, the only naming is organized, and the matings arranged. I do worry about Basket and Star Child, however, for I can but think something special should be asked of them. They are our 'power' in this camp. They should make an offering of some kind. Something from the women I should think, but neither has said anything to me about such a thing. Have they spoken to either of you?" Acorn concluded.

"No, but I will go and inquire," he nodded, "I will let you know."

Blue Coyote made his way to where the women were gathered around their hearth but stopped a distance away. He almost forgot his errand so beautiful did Mourning Dove look, sitting in the reflected fire light, which made deep mysterious pools of her marvelous eyes. He called to Star Woman, "Mother, a word with you, please."

Star Woman rose and came forward, stopping a safe distance away, "what is it son?"

"I would know if Basket and Star Child plan an offering at the Midsummer Ceremony?"

"I will ask them," Star Woman returned to the fire, spoke to the twins and then returned, "Yes, they plan an offering similar to the one made at the Sacred Spring." Blue Coyote nodded, bade her good night and returned to the dreamer with the information.

Mourning Dove watched with narrowing eyes. She hated being left out of Blue Coyote's life like this. She should be the one to answer his questions, the one to be consulted about camp matters for the women! Soon! Very soon she would be. Then Star Woman and the others would have to ask her permission! *Yes!* She liked that!

*　　*　　*

That night the hunters gathered to partake of the 'spirit drink'. Each swallowed his ration and went to his assigned place. This was the very first time that hunters were included in a 'spirit trip' such as the dreamers made regularly. Many were nervous. Some actually frightened, with good reason. Blue Coyote felt the tingling, saw the spiral and was lifted over the plain. He could see the mountains where they were camping, and the bison herd they planned to hunt, beyond that he looked out over the plain. He saw herd after herd of bison, spreading as far as the eye could see; more bison that could be numbered! Then he was back at the camp, but the camp was not as he had left it! Those in the camp walked about with hideous open gaping wounds. Acorn had a dart driven through his belly, Star Woman held her hands to her throat, from which ran the red blood of her life, yet she reached out to him pleading, he could not hear her words, but her face was filled with sorrow. Mourning Dove had a cord around her soft tender throat, and her breasts were uncovered, exposed, slashed open with brutal intent, blood running freely from the wounds, her beautiful face was gashed and horribly disfigured. Basket and Star Child had been torn apart, they reached out to each other, but were taken farther and farther away, crying out, pleading, to no avail. Others were also separated, into files; Stone Man led one away. Rain Woman and Star Child were with him, Basket remained behind.

Stone Man could hear the wailing long before he saw them. Basket and Star Child, torn apart, separated, each forced to go a different direction. The people cried and pleaded, to no avail. He saw himself leading a group of people away, he could hear the sobbing of one of the twins, which one he could not say, but he suspected it was Star Child, for Rain Woman walked beside her. They he saw season after season of death and unhappiness for The People.

Singing Serpent followed in the wake of Stone Man's dream. Each hunter found a role to play in the overall group dream. Each saw the future from his point of view, but none saw it as happy.

Journey's Far saw his beloved Mourning Dove, first grossly misshapen, then giving birth to a many-headed monster, her face twisting into that of a hideous hag. She followed after him, laughing and dragging her abominable offspring. He ran and ran, into a herd of bison. A long sharp horn pierced his belly and he could feel the lifeblood leaking from him. The animal tossed his body over its head and others came and he could feel them, goring him and trampling him, but he did not die, on and on they mangled him, yet he lived. The hunters returned from their 'spirit journey', yet none shared with any other. Each man kept his own council.

*   *   *

At dawn the hunters, except for Journey's Far and Running Man, left for the sacred bison hunt. They were left to protect the camp, run errands for the dreamers, and keep things running smoothly. The bison hunt should take no more than a pair of days. Meanwhile, the women were busy with their preparations. The eagle feather robe had been finished, and Acorn had accepted on Moon's behalf, blessed it and presented it to Moon, who, unfortunately, due to the taboos, was unable to properly thank those who had done him such an honor. He had to be satisfied with shouting it across the space between the parts of the camp.

The Wolf Pack led the way down to the plain. The bison herd had been spotted and kept track of over the days of preparation. Now they were ready. Blue Coyote led the way, followed by Stone Man, Singing Serpent, and Badger. They were to take the first bison, choosing the leader of the herd. The next group was led by Gray Wolf, followed by Jackrabbit and Grass. They were taking a large bull with a bent horn. Only Cougar represented the other group, the Eagle hunters. He had selected a prime bull as his target.

Blue Coyote could feel Wolf Spirit walking at his shoulder. The feeling was so strong that the man felt that if he but turned his head he would actually see the spirit. His footsteps were guided to the chosen animal and he squatted on hands and feet within touching distance of the target when he gave the final prayer and pleading still with the spirit of the animal to do him honor drove the sacred point home, into the very heart of the great beast. As the animal gave up it spirit, Blue Coyote looked into his eyes and felt the spirit go gladly, and with honor. Badger and Stone Man came to kneel beside him. They also thanked the spirit of the animal. Then Blue Coyote removed the sacred dart and broke it, taking the rabbit skin from his pouch he wrapped the still bloody point and broke it as well. This magic insured that the sacred point would never be used again.

Gray Wolf followed a very similar pattern. Cougar, however, did not manage to kill his bison. It ran with the remainder of the herd and he held the broken shaft in his hand. He also lost his sacred point[1]. However, a pair of bison was enough for the ceremony. Taking three had merely been a safeguard. The hunters opened the pair of bison and removed the liver. This organ, the dreamers had instructed them was to be eaten, raw, on the spot, shared equally by all hunters participating in the hunt. The remainder of the liver was returned to the spot of the kill and offered in fire to the spirit of the animal. Then the pair of bison was taken back to the camp. It was the evening of the second day when they arrived. The hides of the bison were given to the dreamers for further purification and preparation. The meat was removed from the bones. It was carefully cut into pieces and cooked, each piece encased in a ball of mud and buried in the coals of the great hearth. Here it would slowly cook all day, the juices sealed inside. The remainder of the bison, organ meat, bones and hide would be burned on the sacred fire after the ceremony, burned until nothing remained but ash. If the people were to receive the blessing of the season, this part of the ceremony was of the utmost importance.

The women had been busy for the past pair of days as well. They had erected a special shelter for the new women. Inside this each, resplendent in their pure white tunics and leggings, was being prepared by a mother or older patron. Their hair was worked into the traditional knot. The new amulet tied about their neck lay against the pure white of the tunic. Most were nervous, they told their spirit animal, and the symbols were painted on their faces. Then they waited.

Boys wore their new clothing, and they donned their hunting capes for the first time. They had instructions to follow. When the drum began to beat, it was time. The adult hunters gathered around the great hearth. They began to dance around and around the fire. Acorn led them in and then retired for the next part of the ceremony. Moon led in the boys. They came into the circle tossing their heads and pretending to be bison. The hunters played out a mock hunt and lifted each new man onto a pair of shoulders and danced him around the hearth. Then each new man was given his first fermented drink. A great shout went up and they all danced together around the hearth. The dreamers came out and asked the spirits to bless the camp, to make the new hunters brave and strong, and offered parts of the bison to the fire, the heart of each was cast into the very center of the fire.

Basket and Star Child stepped forward. They had brought gifts as well. Each of the women's societies had given their finest tools to be offered. Each twin; accompanied by her wolf stepped forward. They were surrounded by the soft blue aura as they carefully wrapped each tool in the rabbit skin, clunk! They broke it with the bison head of their staff, and then tossed the pieces into the fire. Now was the time for presenting the new women. They filed into the ceremonial area. The women allowed for the first time to join in. Each new woman, beginning with Moth was presented and her sacred spirit named. Gifts were brought to each by every member of the camp. Badger brought a very special gift, one presented not to Moth but to Water Woman, her mother. Water Woman smiled her consent and Moth went happily on with the ceremony. In a few days' time she would move from her mother's shelter into one shared by Badger. She was the first to mate at this gathering of the people.

Gray Wolf watched Willow as she moved among the women. He was determined to ask Blue Coyote for her just as soon as possible. He had watched her, and she had smiled back on many occasions. He was sure that she would be willing. Running Man planned to ask for Mourning Dove, for although she had spurned him moons ago in the canyon, he was certain that she still held feelings for him and had forgiven him in her heart for his selfishness. He had not had an opening to speak with her however.

Now the women and children joined in with the drinking of the fermented brew. Everyone danced and laughed and finally all sat down. and the dreamers passed out the bison meat still wrapped in its clay case the grain cakes and tubers were passed as well and soon each held a scapula heaping with food. Together they all broke open the clay and everyone began eating. Even the drums were silent now, for the drummers were also eating. Soon, however, they would resume and the matings would be announced. The camp was pleasantly silent; merely an occasional voicing of satisfaction could be heard as the meal was leisurely consumed.

Blue Coyote and Stone Man were deep in conversation at the far end of the fire. Then Stone Man shook his head, said something and both men rose in anger. Blue Coyote swung his fist and struck Stone Man on the chin. Stone Man staggered back, shouted something and again Blue Coyote struck. Now the men were fighting in earnest. Blue Coyote drew his knife and Slashed Stone Man on the arm, cutting through the hide of his tunic and drawing blood. The stunned onlookers stood silently by watching with increasing concern.

*   *   *

"I think that we should announce our matings with Basket and Star Child," Stone Man had said. "We have discussed this before, and now is as good a time as any. I will go and speak to Rain Woman and you can speak to Basket," he rose to follow suit.

"You announce your mating with whomever you wish!" Blue Coyote replied, "I intend to mate to Mourning Dove. It is all arranged between us!" he stopped Stone Man dead in his tracks!

"You cannot be serious!" Stone Man wheeled around. "We have spoken of this on a number of occasions! You agreed! You have never said anything about this before. You know that we agreed to mate with the twins, to strengthen the bond between us! To make us truly brothers in every way! For the good of the whole camp! You cannot just throw this all away for the sake of the empty promises of Mourning Dove's spread legs! Man, she has serviced half the men of this camp! She is not worthy of you! I knew that you were coupling with her in the canyon, half the camp was, even me! But sooner or later we all saw her for what she is! I had thought . . . evidently, I was wrong. If you must, get her out of your system, then wait before mating with Star Child, couple with her until your brain fries, but you cannot set that whore up over even your own mother!"

"How Dare you! I always knew that you were angry because Mourning Dove chose me over you, but I never thought that you would go to this extent!" ground Blue Coyote, "You go too far!"

"She didn't choose you over me!" Stone Man ground out. "I rutted with her the entire winter at the canyon, me and at least a pair of others that I know of for certain. She had me all tied up in the guts, just as she does you, but I got lucky. I came upon her rutting just as lustily with another man. I saw her for what she is! She is not worthy of you! She only wants the position you offer!"

"I have chosen, and if you do not like the choice, then get out of this camp!" Blue Coyote struck Stone Man with his fist. Stone Man fell back and rubbed his jaw, but Blue Coyote was not finished. He again attacked, "How dare you dirty Mourning Dove's pure reputation with you foul remarks. Yes she has slipped away on accession and we have been together, that is true, but she is as pure and true and loyal to me as Sun Spirit is in warming the sky!"

"All of my life I have named you friend! Now my eyes are open! I see now that I have held a poison serpent to my breast! No More! You are no longer welcome in this camp!" He took out his knife and tried to stab Stone Man. Stone Man brought his arm forward to protect his stomach and was cut across the arm. He staggered back, kicked the knife from Blue Coyote's hand and the men went down, kicking and punching, rolling in the dirt and shouting curses at one another. Stone Man finally broke free and rose. Dirty blood ran freely from the cut on his arm and from a split lip as well. His left eye was swelling closed and he was breathing hard.

Blue Coyote had a number of bruises, his eyes were both swelling, and he was holding his ribs where a lucky kick had probably cracked at least a pair of them. His right knee was bleeding where he landed on a sharp rock and his hair was singed from the fire. "Get out of this camp!" He shouted. "From this day forward, the name of Stone Man will not be spoken in the Wolf Camp! He and any who follow him are dead to this camp!"

Blue Coyote shouted, "I have spoken!" He turned and walked from the ceremony, Mourning Dove flying after him.

Stone Man wiped the blood from his mouth and looked around the stunned gathering. "Any who would go with me are welcome. I choose not to live in a camp where the headman is mated to a whore who serves any man who looks her way. You are all free to choose. Follow Blue Coyote and Mourning Dove or follow me. I will wait on the hill for any that chose to accompany me," he left the camp and went to the place he indicated.

*   *   *

"I am not staying in a camp where the headman cannot see the truth of a whore!" Running Man rose, "I go with Stone Man!"

Cougar went to Turtle Woman, "What is your choice woman?"

"I would follow Stone Man," Turtle Woman answered, "But I care not for leaving my sister and she will stay with Blue Coyote."

"I go with Stone Man," Cougar stated.

Turtle Woman began to sob as she made her way to their shelter and began loading their things on the travois. Star Woman went to her and pleaded, "You cannot mean to do this?" She cried, "We have spent our whole lives in this camp! You are my sister! Blue Coyote is your nephew! How can you leave us? How can you just walk away and throw it all to the wind?"

"I cannot live in a camp headed over by that tart!" Turtle Woman said, "What Stone Man says about her is true, and I am sure much more beyond just the rutting and coupling. That creature is truly evil! I know that you must stay with Blue Coyote, for he is your son, but I go with my mate."

Sobbing the sisters clung together one last time and then Turtle Woman trudged toward the hill where Cougar already waited with Stone Man.

Gray Wolf looked toward where Willow stood and sighed. He also could not continue to live in a camp where Mourning Dove ruled. She had tricked him as well as Blue Coyote, and as Stone Man has said; how many others? His visions of mating with Mourning Dove had turned to ashes as he finally saw her for what she was, a woman obsessed with her own pleasures and her own climb to power. It amazed him that it had taken him so long to see the light! He went to where Willow stood, spoke to her, she shook her head sobbing and pleading and so he packed his things and joined Stone Man.

Grass also went; a bitter taste in his mouth as he remembered the times between Mourning Dove's legs; as did Running Man.

"Get your things together!" instructed Rain Woman, turning back toward their shelter, "We go with Stone Man!"

"Basket! You heard Mother. We must pack!"

"I cannot!" replied Basket woodenly.

"But you must!" Star Child wept, "We cannot be separated! You are my other half!"

"Then you stay as well!" pleaded Basket!"

"I cannot! I must go with my mother; I am not free to choose like you are. Please Basket; do not do this thing to me, to us!"

"I must stay." Basket whispered. "My amulet so instructs," Tears ran down her face, "But until the day when we will again be united, keep the Sacred Tooth to remember me by. Walk proudly, wear the owl feather and display the power staff. Go with Stone Man and serve him loyally. That is your destiny. I must stay with Blue Coyote, for he will need me."

Star Child followed her mother to the hill, spoke to Stone Man and he came to the shelter, "Come with me!" he pleaded, "Be my mate and help me to be a strong leader," he beseeched. "You know that I have always intended for us to mate, I need you, Basket, I need you to be strong!"

Basket shook her head silently, "Star Child is meant for you Stone Man" she said dully, "I have known this for some time. She cares very deeply for Blue Coyote, just as I care for you, but it is not to be, my amulet tells me that I must remain, and Star Child must go. Treat her well. She will stand loyally beside you. Go now and give my sister the love you would have given me. I send my heart with both of you."

Star Child ran back and pleaded again with Basket, They sobbed and clung together, until Star Woman held Basket while Rain Woman led the whimpering Star Child away. The dreamer Moon went with Stone Man, as did Kind Heart, Song Bird, Soft Wind and Prairie Dog and a double hand of others. The rest remained with Blue Coyote.

* * *

Basket sat in the shelter, along except for Star Woman, and both wept for their loss. Both wept for a sister now decreed dead by Blue Coyote. They would not be able to even speak the name, except in the privacy of their shelter. Basket wanted desperately to go with Stone Man, who truly carried her heart with him. She had not spoken to Star Child, but she had known, since the matched staffs that they were to be separated. She had felt it much stronger than any dread she had felt before. The spirit trip which Star Child had not taken had shown her the path she was to follow. Silently she had tried to prepare.

Throw Back lifted her head and gave forth with a mournful howl, echoed from the hilltop. Then Stone Man and the rest walked from their lives to follow a path of their own.

Blue Coyote called the camp together in the morning. He announced his mating with Mourning Dove and he had already moved into the shelter that he had built for them, but she had occupied alone. "We will be leaving this place and going further up into the mountains for the remainder of this moon," he stated, "Then we return to the escarpment for the winter."

A silent stunned camp nodded.

Water Woman moved in with Basket and Star Woman, while Badger and Moth joined the shelter of Jackrabbit and Makes A Robe. It did not take long before Mourning Dove began to make her position known. Star Woman was her first target, "You will lead the woman with the hide tanning," she directed, giving the former head-woman the lowest, most unpopular of tasks. "Basket and Willow will work with you!" She flounced off to instruct others to begin gathering pine nuts and tubers, as if anyone needed any instructions!

Star Woman clamped her mouth shut and led the way to the hides. They worked on them all day, and the next, and the next, realizing that the pattern of shifting tasks had just been broken. For some reason, known only to herself; Mourning Dove had taken the same dislike to Willow that she had always reserved for Basket.

Blue Coyote frowned, he had walked past where the women did the hides daily, and on each occasion, he had discovered both his mother and Basket at this backbreaking task. He decided that he would speak with Mourning Dove on the very next occasion he came across her, obviously she had forgotten to rotate the tasks of the women. He smiled, remembering the wonderful nights of mating that he had enjoyed with his beloved. She was proving a bit sharp tongues of a morning, but this he attributed to the fact that already she had started a child. He was very proud of his 'Dove', already proving to be an exemplary woman of The People.

Mourning Dove was less than pleased but had guessed that she was pregnant some days before they were mated. She shrugged; nothing anyone could do about it now! But she was sick, every single morning, and already her waist was beginning to thicken. She considered taking something to rid herself of the unwanted burden, but since the healer had chosen to go with Stone Man, she was stuck with carrying this child, unless she could find a way to rid herself of it. She considered this. It had worked one time before, when she found herself with child by her brother. Then she had repeatedly jumped from a big rock, jarring the fetus until it aborted.

Blue Coyote however was deliriously happy about the prospect of approaching fatherhood. She had waited too long any way. So she took her frustration out on others. She smiled as she considered the three women assigned to the hide scraping. She hated Basket with a special passion. For a time she had thought that Blue Coyote had a leaning toward the plain woman, but she was certainly confident in her control over him now. Willow had looked, however briefly at Gray Wolf, whom Mourning Dove had long considered her own. Thus, Willow also came to feel her wrath. Star Woman merely needed to understand that she no longer ruled.

"I do not agree!" Mourning Dove replied, "The women work more efficiently if they do the same task day after day. No one else has complained!"

"No one else has been relegated to working the hides day after day!" Blue Coyote pointed out.

"How am I to establish any control over the women if you continually undermine me?" Mourning Dove sobbed, dabbing her eyes with a shaking finger. "Just because Basket has come whining to you!"

"Basket has not spoken to me," Blue Coyote corrected her, "Nor has anyone else. I have seen these things for myself, and I do not think now is the time to be changing the way we have always worked together, that is all," he ended lamely.

"I am bound to make mistakes!" Mourning Dove sobbed "But if I start changing my decisions, soon no one will regard me with respect!"

"Then let it go for a while," he gave in, "But remember, fairness is the mark of a good leader."

So the three women continued to work the hides. Other chores were rotated among the remainder but those three remained . . .

It soon became obvious to everyone that Mourning Dove was pregnant. Some hoped that motherhood would sweeten her, or at least give her other occupation than the unilateral attention she gave to making sure that their lives were as unpleasant as possible.

The camp moved farther up into the mountains. They spent the last moon of the summer there and then began meandering south toward the caprock. They joined with the escarpment and followed it back to the caves. Here they settled for the winter. The men made a trip to the Sacred Spring and hunted bison. The women gathered the acorns and pigweed and stored them in containers in the cave.

Blue Coyote moved into the large storage cave, once the place of his parents. Against Mourning Doves wants he installed Star Woman with them. Mourning Dove was now well into her pregnancy, and she did not feel well. Star Woman bit her words back frequently and did her best to help her. Basket and Willow had moved into the secret cave and were well away from the harping and complaining that they knew Star Woman was getting.

Journey's Far had consented to mating with Cottontail Girl, now Cotton Tail Woman. She was also pregnant; but blooming with excellent health. Moth also was with child. This was certainly an excellent start for the camp.

Where are you, sister? Basket tightly closed her eyes and concentrated. The feeling of bonding was becoming ever weaker. She could no longer feel Star Child. *Why do you not answer?*

Finally she gave up and went to sleep.

The first blizzard struck with a fury remarkable even for this place of bad storms. People were stranded inside the caves for days on end while the elements raged outside. "I am going to spend a few days with Cotton Tail," Willow packed her robe and an extra fur. "She is nervous with this weather. Will you be all right alone?"

"I will be fine," Basket assured her, "And I will not be alone, for I do have Throw Back."

"You are sure?"

"I am sure, go ahead and help Cotton Tail, there are things which I need to do any way, and 'spirit things' always make you nervous."

Willow nodded and went to where Cotton Tail lived only a stone throw away, in the wolf cave. Basket sighed, it was good to be alone. Now she could really concentrate. She quickly prepared the morning glory seed drink and setting Throw Back to guard she settled on the wolf hide. "Come to me Wolf Spirit!" She pleaded, "I have discovered the evil! It lives in the woman Mourning Dove! She has separated me from my other half, has split soul brothers apart and broken this camp into a pair."

*　*　*

Yes, replied Wolf Spirit, *what do you do to correct this? The power of The People has been weakened. The power must be reunited! The evil cast out! There is greater evil waiting. The power must be reunited or that evil will destroy The People!*

"Red Eagle?" Basket questioned.

He is no more! The power is now with White Falcon. He lives where once Red Eagle dwelt! "White Falcon?" the dreamer no one speaks of? How can this be?"

He dwells within! He has the power to defeat either of you! He cannot defeat the power united! You were sent to defeat him! This is your destiny, but only united. You were sent together and together you must be, or the power will go to the dreamer!

"What of Mourning Dove? What do I do about her?"

She has served his purpose! Was her only answer, with this Basket had to be satisfied. At least she now knew whom; the only problem was how!

*　*　*

"You might as well move into the unmated men's cave for the next while," Star Woman advised Blue Coyote, "This is woman's business and it is not for a man to interfere. Someone will come for you when it is over."

"But she will want me here!" he protested.

"It matters not what Mourning Dove wants at this time. The baby will be coming shortly, and I need help with this. I cannot move other women into this cave while you still occupy it, so please just do as I ask and move for a few days," she asked.

"Very well, but do not blame me if she becomes difficult! Mourning Dove does not like to be parted from me." Blue Coyote replied.

She could not possibly be more difficult; thought Star Woman. *How can a son of mine be so blind?*

Blue Coyote moved out and Water Woman moved in.

An ear-shattering scream rent the air. Star Woman and Water Woman both bolted upright.

"It is time," Star Woman said, "Her labor is started."

"I will get the fire going in the hearth and brew some of the painkilling tea." Water Woman crawled from her furs and pulled her tunic on.

* * *

Mourning Dove lay whimpering in her furs, her bulging belly quivering with each sob.

"Come on, you must sit up now," instructed Star Woman.

"It huts!" wailed Mourning Dove. "It rips me apart! This child seeks to kill me!"

"Nonsense! That is just the way of birthing; we have all gone through it. Once you hold the babe in your arms, the pain will be forgotten. Now come, let me help you into a sitting position, Water Woman is brewing you some tea which will help with the pain."

"No! It hurts when I move!"

"You must move, but first I will check on the babe, lay back and open your legs. I will be able to tell more accurately how long this birthing will take."

Mourning Dove moaned but did as she was asked; Star Woman checked the progress of the labor and sighed. It was going to be a long night, and probably a longer day. The birth canal was barely beginning to open. This would not be an easy labor. Water Woman arrived with the tea and they coaxed Mourning Dove to drink it. With a sigh she settled back on her furs and the older women sat beside the fire until she began to snore soundly. With gladness they returned to their interrupted sleep. Morning came. An additional examination supported Star Woman's first estimate. All day they waited on Mourning Dove, providing her with numerous cups of the painkilling tea. For the time at least the labor had stopped.

By evening the birth canal had opened more. Still, it was not time. All night one or the other of them stayed awake and encouraged and soothed Mourning Dove. From time to time she screamed and sobbed or moaned as the labor pains contracted her. By morning the baby had turned and positioned itself for birth. By midday the canal had enlarged enough that the head was just visible. They had already positioned the supports, prepared the receiving skin, and had copious volumes of water to heat. A large container was kept constantly ready.

By dark the labor had finally started in earnest. Mourning Dove cursed, ranted and raved, shouting at them, throwing things at them and threatening them with every sort of dire consequence. Star Woman and Water Woman stoically took the abuse.

"It is time for you to move into position for the birth," Water Woman was trying to get the uncooperative Mourning Dove to move to the birthing supports. Finally the pair of women forced her to the place where the supports were set up and they straightened the furs beneath her which she viciously kicked away.

"Let this child drop onto the bare stone!" she screamed, "It rips me apart!"

They replaced the furs, "Push!" ordered Star Woman.

"What do you think I am doing?" screamed Mourning Dove, "Just get it out of me!" She thrashed side to side and then became rigid again as another labor pain tore through her.

"I can see the head. It is through!" Water Woman encouraged, "One more push and it will be born!"

Mourning Dove arched her back and with an almighty final contraction expelled the unwanted burden from her body. She slumped exhausted against the supports as Water Woman tied and cut the umbilical cord, carried the baby to the hearth, washed it, cleared the breathing passage and sighed as it began to cry weakly. Star Woman kneaded Mourning Dove's abdomen, avoiding the occasional kick, until the after birth was also expelled. Then she helped the now exhausted woman back to her furs. Water Woman carried the baby to her to suckle. "It is a boy!" she remarked.

Mourning Dove exposed her breast and the small mouth latched on hungrily. "Ouch!" she jerked back, "It bit me!" she shoved the infant away, it began to cry again and Star Woman put it back to feed. "It will be a bit painful for a short time, but you will soon get used to it," she said. The baby again began to feed, this time Mourning Dove bit her lip and let it.

The women cleaned up the birth mess, setting aside the section of umbilical cord to save for the child's amulet. The remainder they packaged up and placed at the mouth of the cave to be taken out and buried in the morning. With this done, and Mourning Dove again sleeping, exhausted from the travail, the infant to her breast. They gratefully crawled into their furs and slept.

The next morning Star Woman took the afterbirth and birthing skins far out into the brush and buried it. On her way back she swung by and informed Blue Coyote that he had a son.

* * *

"I will go to her right now!" he exclaimed "Has she been asking for me?"

Star Woman raised an eyebrow at him, "She has been busy giving you a son there hasn't been time for her to miss you!" she said dryly.

Blue Coyote was oblivious to her scold as he hurried off to meet his son.

"A bit early isn't it?" Remarked one of the women seated at the central hearth, "Must be a very small child."

"No smaller than most!" remarked Star Woman, "Just started earlier than it should have been."

"There are those who even question that Blue Coyote fathered it," another remarked.

"I have heard rumors that . . . well it isn't for me to say . . ."

"Then don't!" Star Woman stomped off to her own cave, relieved that Water Woman had offered to stay until Blue Coyote moved back.

Basket woke with a start, *danger!* She looked around the cave, Throw Back was sleeping peacefully, and Willow was rolled into her usual ball, breathing evenly.   The feeling wouldn't go away. Then she realized it wasn't a feeling it was a message. Quickly she sat, crossed her legs, closed her eyes and concentrated.

* * *

Where is the danger?

Attacked! Horrid, Savages, brightly painted! Took Soft Wind, we follow south!

Don't go! Basket pleaded.

Must get Soft Wind back! Think of me!

Basket tried again and again but the link was broken. She finally made some tea and sat too upset to sleep and thought back over the experience.

Several nights later, it happened again *Terrible! I can't speak of it! We watched it! We flee! Danger in this place! Death in this place! Flee! Flee!*

*   *   *

Mourning Dove was an indifferent mother, habitually ignoring her child and letting it cry until she could no longer stand the sound before she tended to it. Frequently it suffered from diarrhea and its bottom was red and sore most of the time, for she also neglected to keep it changed regularly as well, it did not thrive, but it did live.

"There is no way that I can organize the women and take care of that squalling infant at the same time" protested Mourning Dove.

"What do you suggest I do about that?" Blue Coyote was becoming more and more disillusioned with mated life. Mourning Dove constantly harped on one thing or another that she didn't like. He was sick and tired of trying to appease her. He had hoped that motherhood would finally settle her down, but it seemed to be having the opposite affect. She was increasingly irate and impossible to live with. The child was sickly, requiring a lot of attention. Finally Blue Coyote gave in and consulted his mother.

Star Woman hid a satisfied smile, and suggested he ask one of the younger women to help with the care of the baby. Moth, now half way through her own pregnancy offered to take over the care of the infant part time, more from the desire to have experience for her own, than any desire to help Mourning Dove. The baby responded to her care and finally began to thrive. For a time, things settled down. Winter was over, the starving time past and spring on the verge. Now however, Moth approached her own time of delivery.

"I realize that it is asking a lot, but I would appreciate your helping my mother when it is my time," she approached Star Woman.

"Not at all," replied Star Woman, "It is just that I help, for without your mother, I would never have gotten through the ordeal with Mourning Dove."

"I hope not to be as great a burden," Moth smiled, "I can hardly wait! I so want this babe!"

Water Woman came for her at midday. The ordeal was long, Moth quiet and cooperative, after a difficult birth, delivered a daughter. Now however, Mourning Dove was once again on her own.

Again, the infant, now a pair of months old, began to fail. Mourning Dove again approached Blue Coyote who promised to find someone to take care of the child. "Let Basket take care of him!" Ordered Mourning Dove, "She does little enough around here! He can go and live in her cave!"

"That is a bit impractical isn't it?" He replied. "She can hardly suckle him!"

"Moth can! She has enough milk for both of them!" I am drying up any way! That is why he cries so much! With all the strain I have been under, my milk is not strong enough!"

So Blue Coyote approached Moth. She agreed that she probably could suckle both infants, and so Basket became responsible for the boy, while Moth provided for him. He thrived!

"My bleeding has again resumed!" Mourning Dove announced, "I have my figure back, and I feel better than I have since conceiving. I really think we can resume mating."

"The proper time has not passed!" Blue Coyote replied.

"That didn't bother you before?" She reminded him.

*　　*　　*

"A lot of things didn't bother me before; Things which should have!" He replied, "Things like how you became pregnant when we had no relations for a moon either side of the date you conceived!"

"What are you suggesting?" She hissed! "The brat was a long time coming. He took longer than he should have; even you surely can see that he was big when he was born. This is why it was so terribly painful for me! He was a full moon over time for birth!"

"He was no larger or smaller than any other baby at birth!" Blue Coyote replied. "I would know who his father is, for it is not I!" He grabbed her by the hair and twisted. "Stone Man was not lying, was he? You played me the fool; right from the beginning, didn't you? And like a lovesick puppy I fell all over myself cooperating! You are in fact, exactly what he labeled you!"

"You break your own rule!" She jerked free; "Stone Man is dead to us! You yourself declared it!"

"I asked you a question! Who fathered that child, for it was most certainly not I?"

Mourning Dove cowered like a wild animal against the cave wall, Blue Coyote had never before shown her violence, and she had been certain that he never would. Now she was not so confident. "You were the father," she whimpered, letting her pouting mouth work its magic once again.

"I repeat," Blue Coyote stepped up to her, "Who is the father?"

Mourning Dove glared at him, losing her temper, "How should I know!" She hissed "As you say, Stone Man was right; I coupled with half the men of the camp! Why do you think so many went with him? Why? Because they could not bare to see me mated to one such as you!" she spit at him.

Blue Coyote saw a blinding flash of rage and he struck her solidly across the face.

Mourning Dove dodged away from him, wiping blood from her split lip, "You think you are so great in the furs!" She taunted "You are nothing! Do you hear me, nothing? Even Journey's Far is a better man than you! Yes, Stone Man was right! I have coupled with many men, even after your precious cleansing! And the hunter went right on with the ceremony, because he wanted me so badly, he couldn't resist!"

She laughed hysterically, "So what can you do about it? You are mated to me, and that is the fact. You can beat me, sure, but that will get you nowhere!" She laughed again; "You have truly made your furs Blue Coyote! Now you may sleep in them alone, for I will not share them again with you! From now on I sleep alone in this cave. I take no more chances on getting pregnant again."

---

1. At the Folsom Type Site 26 Folsom Points were excavated with Bison antiquuis bones. **Metlzer.** 2006

CHAPTER 21

Stone Man is more of a man than you will ever be!" Mourning Dove hissed, "He gave me pleasure you cannot even begin to imagine! To think that I could have had him instead of you!" She threw at Blue Coyote; "You are a joke! even Journey's Far is more of a man than you!"

He brought back his arm and struck her soundly across the face. "You will tell me all of the truth before I am through with you," he promised. "How many?" Again and again he struck her, sending her reeling around the cave. She wiped the blood from her split lip and eyed him warily. Again, he started forward.

She scrambled across the cave from him, hate spewing from her eyes. "Before or after you found me?" She laughed at him. "You are more of a fool than you think!" She hissed, "You believed everything I told you. All that drivel about Strangers, there were no strangers, my camp drove us out and left us to die!"

"Us? There were more of you?"

"Only me and my brother; you see my father caught us coupling. That was the last chance he had for me, he had warned me frequently enough. I had been caught before with other men, but then he found out that I carried Sagebrush's child, so like a loving parent he threw us out to die! Well I didn't die. I got rid of the brat, just like I tried to get rid of this one, only it worked that time!" She laughed hysterically. "You all fell all over yourselves to make me welcome, and I made you welcome, you and every other man who looked my way. That winter in the canyon I coupled with all the stupid hunters who lusted after me. It was one long glorious winter of rutting, one after another, each of you thinking you were the only one, the special one. Mated and unmated alike, I serviced them all, and you were the least. The only reason I coupled with you more than once was because you were the headman's son, and you would be headman after him!"

"Fire Dancer!" Blue Coyote said quietly, "If there were no Strangers, how did he die?"

"Exactly as Bison Man suspected! I pushed him over the cliff! He was going to throw me out of the camp! I needed the camp to survive! I couldn't let him!"

"And you killed Bison Man exactly the same way," he nodded, "It all begins to make sense! And poor old Antelope, what did she do to you?"

"That stupid old snoop! She followed me, she found out I was sneaking from the camp with the watchers, and she told Stone Man."

"Even then you were spreading yourself for all of us?" Blue Coyote was amazed at her audacity. And Antelope discovered you sneaking off. So you drove a dart into her back then slit her throat, so she couldn't tell anyone else, and I like a fool, wouldn't have believed him had Stone Man come to me with his suspicions."

Slowly he advanced upon her, and reached out to grab her, only Mourning Dove was quick, and he was left with her amulet while she escaped from the cave. In anger he shredded the amulet, staring in fascination as the raven feather floated to the floor.

His soul filled with black dread as he stared at the feather. He began to shake and all the pain and anguish this beautiful woman had put him through came to a head. Fire Dancer, murdered so uselessly, for the vanity of a woman. Bison Man, so honorable a leader, murdered, just because he had figured it out; Little Antelope Woman, like a second mother to him for most of his life, and Stone Man, the other half of his soul. He could some day accept the guilt of the deaths, but he could never forgive her the loss of Stone Man!

The feather lay there, accusing him, reminding him. The messenger had tried to communicate, even in death, but he had not listened. For so long his mind had been closed. He had not listened to anyone, to anything except his raging hormones. Even those had, in the end, deserted him. At last he saw Mourning Dove for the unbelievably ugly person she was inside.

But now, the camp was split, those honorable people gone, and it was his fault! His lusting, non-listening fault!

Suddenly, Blue Coyote was no longer out of control; he was in fact very much in control, deadly control, as he walked from the cave. "Has anyone seen Mourning Dove?" He questioned, "She must have come through here only a breath or so ago."

"She went to the Wolf Cave," Makes A Robe replied without much interest.

Blue Coyote made his way there and shortly all heard Mourning Dove scream. He dragged her, by the hair from the cave and into the middle of the camp. "Get everyone out here," Blue Coyote ordered, "I have a great deal to share with you," he twisted her hair cruelly and Mourning Dove first hurled obscenities at him, then tried to bite, and kick, and when none of this had an effect, finally began to whimper.

"It has been an interesting morning," he began casually once the camp had assembled, "A morning of truth, finally. We will go back, more than a season now, back to the canyon far to the south, back to the fateful day that we fished this creature," he jerked, "From the river, unfortunately for us."

"We took her in, offered her shelter, friendship, even love, and in return she has betrayed us at every turn. She began by murdering Fire Dancer," several gasped, and Star Woman groaned, "And Bison Man as well, not to mention Antelope Woman. She is a murderer, yes, and worse! She led me, and any number of other men, to break the rules of the camp! I admit, she took me in, far longer than any other, I suspect. I followed like a dog on the scent of a bitch in heat, coupling with her, not once but repeatedly, endangering the camp, leaving my post as watcher to follow her into the grass for rutting. I have no excuse for myself," he said quietly, "Nor will I point fingers at others also taken in by her. That is past. She has broken even worse taboos, by her own admonition. She coupled with her own brother; incest!" He stated, twisting the hair again cruelly. "She killed not only people however, but also the sacred Raven, messenger from the spirits!" He raised her onto the tips of her toes, "She admittedly coupled with a hunter after the cleansing ceremony at the place of stone, bringing bad luck and danger to all. The evil that she had brought into this camp must be cleansed, and she must be punished! Death is the traditional punishment for any one of these deeds. The damage she has brought to The People goes deep, far deeper than I probably know."

"She coupled with me after the cleansing ceremony," admitted Journey's Far. "She told me that it would be all right, that it was the mind and soul which must be pure not the body!" He stuttered, "I believed her."

Blue Coyote held up the damming feather, "She killed the sacred raven!"

Acorn sighed, now the spirit would speak to him again.

He drew his knife from its sheath, "And for her punishment," he slashed the knife across her right cheek, laying it open, Mourning Dove screamed and calmly he cut the left. He slashed down through her eyelash and across her nose, again and again, until her face was a field of blood, then he ripped open her tunic, "No man will every look upon you again with desire," he said through gritted teeth. "Death is too easy a punishment!" He nodded for a pair of hunters to come and hold her, and he continued the mutilation, not deep enough to kill, but to scar horribly. All the while Mourning Dove screamed shrilly and fought to be free.

"You led me to drive away the best friend I ever had!" He said; "You led me to separate the 'power' of The People, endangering us all," he worked his way down her legs and then had her turned around. 'You even tricked me into believing that I fathered another man's son." Her back became a bloodbath, but now she hung quietly between the hunters, her head lolling to one side.

"Death would be too quick a release for you, no, for the damage which you have done to these good people you will remain an outcast for the remainder of your days. No person of this camp will lift a hand to help you. You will share no shelter with any! None will provide you with food! You may eat the leavings of the wolves, until you become food for them as well!"

He turned from the still bloody mass hanging limply between the hunters.

"I cannot ask the forgiveness from the camp for the wrong which I have done, but at least I can give you the justice which until now I have been too blind to see." Again he turned to Mourning Dove. He took her by the hair and ruthlessly sawed that last vanity off close to the head. When he finished there was nothing beautiful left of Mourning Dove. He nodded, and the hunters released her lifeless body letting it drop carelessly to the ground. No one moved to help her.

"Go now to your shelters and think on my words. Later I will again call the camp together, to choose a new headman." He nodded to Acorn, "Please come to my cave, we have much to discuss."

Acorn nodded and followed him. Others looked as the pitiful creature, the one that had once been so beautiful a woman, on the outside. Many felt anger, a few hate, but the entire camp, they felt no pity. Quietly they went back to their own affairs.

Soon the central fire was deserted, but for the whimpering form slowly crawling away. Shortly however, gentle hands lifted her, lay her carefully on soft furs, upon a travois and swiftly carried far from her enemies. No one even saw her go.

"What do you suggest we do?" Blue Coyote questioned Acorn.

"All of the tools, the sacred points, all must be destroyed by fire. The hunting capes made after that ceremony, the sacred meat; it must be burned as well. Everything, which that woman has touched, must be purified. I would recommend that the entire camp pass through a cleansing ceremony. It is nearly time for the Spring Ceremony, I would suggest we move it up and remove every trace of that female from this camp, before her evil is allowed to spread farther!"

"Perhaps now the spirits will again speak with me!" He sighed, "I will try, this very night, but it would be as well if you also requested it of Basket, perhaps she will have more success. Wolf Spirit has refused to speak with me since before the ceremony at the place of stone."

"Yet you said nothing?"

"I had nothing to say, nothing which would make any sense!" The dreamer shrugged, "Spirits are fickle, sometimes they come, other times it may be seasons before they decide to answer prayers. One can but keep trying! Again, and again I questioned the hunters! None admitted to breaking any taboo, certainly not Journey's Far! There was nothing more I knew to do!"

"Where do we go from here?" again questioned Blue Coyote.

"Perhaps that is for the next headman to decide," answered the dreamer.

"My mother waits outside; would you ask her to come in as you leave?"

Blue Coyote sat staring dismally at the wall of the cave, his whole life a pile of ashes about him. Star Woman entered and seated herself, "Can you ever bring yourself to forgive me, Mother?"

"There is nothing to forgive, Blue Coyote," she replied softly. "I will always miss your father, but you did not kill him, that evil creature and his own suspicions did that. Besides, I knew his feelings regarding that female, and I did not speak up, even after his death. I also feel guilt, but neither of us is to blame. We must put this behind us and go forward. You could be a good leader, if not a great leader, but you were forced into leadership far too young. Now the fire has tempered you. Like a dart point, you are stronger for it."

"I don't feel strong. I don't even feel capable of making a decision on my own."

"That is a natural reaction, one which will pass. What you need now is to go forward with decisive action."

"The next move is to allow the camp to select a new headman," he replied.

She shook her head, "There is no one else, they will select you," she stated.

"If they do, will you return to share this cave with me and take up once again the role which you handled for so long?"

Star Woman shook her head. "I will return to the cave, if that is your wish. But lead the women, no, that role is for another, and the time has come for you to realize that as well. Your father tried to tell you again and again, but always you have refused to listen Stone Man tried to tell you,"

"Basket!" he sighed.

"Basket," she agreed.

He nodded, "If she will come, please ask her to do so immediately," he rose and began gathering up Mourning Dove's things.

"No! It is time for you to go to her, I will do that," she took the furs from his hand, "Take your time, when you return, this place will have no trace of that creature." Already Star Woman was casting things out of the cave, calling others to cast them into the central hearth.

Blue Coyote left the cave, unwillingly glancing at the place where so recently his mate lay bleeding. There was no sign, not of her, not of the blood, hair or any other trace. Members of the camp moved around, going about their daily routine, as though nothing had happened. This then was their answer; he nodded to them and made his way to Basket's cave.

She met him at the entrance and looked deeply into his troubled eyes. Stepping aside, she allowed him to enter. Willow had gone to spend time with Cotton Tail, taking the infant with her to deliver him to Moth. They were alone.

"You know why I am here?" He asked evenly. Basket nodded, "You have always understood these things better than me. Why didn't you say something?"

"What words could I say to which you would listen? You would not have listened to any words of mine, no more than you did to those of the man who loved you like a brother."

"I have ruined all of our lives, haven't I? You care for Stone Man do you not? And I drove him from you."

"Stone Man was never for me," Basket replied, "He was for Star Child."

"And I?" He shook his head, "Have I been so blind all these seasons?"

Basket sighed, "Our paths were torn asunder before we could even walk," she replied.

"How is that?" He questioned, "I can see where things have gone badly since we grew up, but when we were but babies? Even I could not have gone wrong that far back!"

"White Falcon," Basket answered, "It all began to go wrong as Feather was giving birth. White Falcon was determined to make sure the infant, or infants as the case was, did not survive. It was White Falcon who brought my grandmother to such desperate measures that she took Star Child and fled, hoping that by her actions at least one of us would survive. You see, Star Child and I posed a threat to the dreamer, for if legend was correct, we would grow to be very powerful. He is obsessed with power."

"Was," corrected Blue Coyote, "White Falcon is dead."

Basket shook her head.

"Of course he is dead. My father had him walled up in his spirit cave. No one speaks of it, but the whispers get around."

"But he escaped," Basket replied, "Escaped inside the child, Red Eagle, where he took refuge until the time was right."

"And Red Eagle made an offer for you too grand to turn down," she nodded, "That is why he tried to kill you!"

"He didn't want me dead, at least not then, he wanted the Power Relics . . . If Red Eagle could collect enough power and give it to White Falcon . . . only Red Eagle lost his temper and he thought he killed me, so he fled. Now White Falcon is trapped and cannot take control unless he can persuade Red Eagle to bring him 'power' objects."

"How do you know all of this?"

"I have thought about little else, most of it I have pieced together, a bit here another there, until the pattern emerges. Also, Wolf Spirit has hinted."

"What does Red Eagle get?"

"Probably us dead. I know that he hated Fire Dancer and me and he envied you. White Falcon more than likely struck a deal with him. Power objects for our lives."

"But if what you say is true, would not White Falcon have to kill Red Eagle in order to take over his body?"

"Probably."

"Then why would Red Eagle . . ."

"White Falcon would not tell him that!"

"It does make a sort of sense," Blue Coyote shook his head, "But where does that put us, you and me, right now?"

"You have a camp to lead and a son to raise," she reminded him.

"He isn't my son."

"Maybe, maybe not, but he is your responsibility."

"He isn't my son, believe me, he isn't, and I don't want him!"

"He is an infant, Blue Coyote; he isn't responsible for his mother's actions. Do we just forget him, allow him to grow into another Red Eagle, filled with hate and envy, or do we guide his steps and raise him to be a leader?"

"We?"

"The camp, you, me, everyone; each of us is responsible for all the rest that is why a camp survives."

"Let's go back to the 'we'."

"That is why you are here, of course," Basket rose and went to stand in the opening of the cave. "Looking out over the camp it is hard to believe that such an act of violence was so recently carried out there. You have been through a stressful time of late, and it has been only this day that you have . . . Are you sure that you don't want more time to. . ."

"I have had most of my life to come to this decision," he replied, "Do you really think I need more?"

"But . . ."

"I have had moons to become disillusioned, trust me, I have wished for a long time that I had chosen you to begin with, as I should have!"

"And the child?"

"He is, as you say, my responsibility. I will see to him, but I would rather he did not live with us. He will always be a constant reminder of . . . my foolishness."

"Very well, but I would ask the remainder of this moon before . . . and if you should change your mind!"

"I won't, but the remainder of this moon it shall be," he nodded and left.

Basket returned to her quiet contemplation, stirring the now cold spirit drink and replacing it on the fire. She waited until it was ready and then swallowed it in one gulp. "Am I doing right?" She questioned.

* * *

The evil has been driven from the camp! You must reunite the power! He is free, and he seeks to destroy, only the united power can defeat him! If he is the victor, the circle will close, and The People will die!

* * *

With a headache and a sick stomach to pay for it, this was the only answer she received.

Acorn had a similar response to his questions.

Willow returned from visiting Cotton Tail with the news that Journey's Far had fled with Mourning Dove, leaving his very pregnant mate to face not only life alone, but the birth of their child as well. "I begin to be glad that I said 'no' to Running Man," Willow settled the infant back into his furs where he gurgled happily and soon slept.

"There is more to life than we expect." Basket agreed.

"What is the news of the camp? Are we to select a new headman; and if so; who?" Basket shook her head; "At least that is a relief! Blue Coyote may have had his thinking mixed up, but he is still the most qualified to lead, now if he would only realize . . ."

"He has asked me to mate with him," Basket interrupted.

"Well it is about time!" Willow hugged her, "And you of course said 'no'!"

"I asked for the remainder of the moon," she admitted.

"What is it about people? A blind man could see that you are the perfect match for Blue Coyote, but both of you continually drag your feet in the dirt!"

"It probably comes from growing up together. Blue Coyote has been like a brother to me, and you need not remind me that he is not my brother, for others have done so repeatedly! I will mate with him, and I will do my best to lead the women of this camp. But do not ask me to be filled with blushes and excitement at the prospect!"

"Willow looked thoughtfully at Basket, "But if it were Stone Man?" She guessed.

Basket blushed and quickly turned away.

Willow sighed and added; "Life can be so complicated at times!"

The camp pitched in with a thorough cleansing! All signs of Mourning Dove were cast into the fire, the caves were purified with smoke and the Spring Ceremony went under way at the same time. Everyone was busy with the preparations. It gave them time to get things into perspective. Then the camp settled for a brief time into peaceful quiet.

The moon gradually thinned and finally was gone. The mating of Blue Coyote and Basket arrived. The entire camp was in a festive mood, all, perhaps but the woman, who went quietly to her fate, laying away the last shred of hope, finally accepting the part which fate had drawn for her.

*   *   *

Oh Sister, I would I were you and you me! Silently she wept.

*   *   *

Far to the south, hidden away in a tiny cave, Mourning Dove gradually recovered. Her wounds were really only superficial, but they became infected and Journey's Far labored long and diligently to drive out the evil spirits. He made poultices and bound them to her wounds. He hunted and prepared the tastiest broth, and later the prime bits of meat. But Mourning Dove gave him no thanks. But she clung tenaciously to life. The devastation of her body was complete. No man would ever look at her again with desire. The knife blade had done a thorough job. One side of her mouth was drawn up in a permanent sneer, and one eyebrow was quirked upward. Her breasts and her back and belly were a game-trail of puckering scars. Still, she was alive, and Journey's Far has been a lusty lover. His devotion would be heart touching, had she possessed a heart. Now whatever had been at her center, only hate remained. She drew Journey's Far repeatedly to her furs, coupling lustily with him. He even went so far as to perform a simple ceremony declaring them mated. Mourning Dove sneered at this but held her silence. He had proven useful, and she was not yet recovered. Besides, for now at least, he was the only man available, and running her fingers over her face, she was convinced that he probably was the only man alive who would not run screaming from the sight of her.

"We should have brought our son with us!" He exclaimed again and again. "I am probably a father again, and yet I have no children to show for it!" he whined.

"We are better off without him!" Mourning Dove dismissed the child. "And whatever that bison cow you were mated to dropped. You are better off free of it as well!"

"Do you not want children?" he asked.

"Never again!" She shuddered, "I will never go through that pain again!"

"How do you expect to prevent getting pregnant?" he questioned "You certainly enjoy the mating!"

"I did not say I could prevent it, merely that I would not go through with it," she replied, "I was able to dislodge more than one baby; others will not be more difficult!"

"You would do this to our child?" he was definitely hurt by her attitude.

"I told you; I will not go through such pain again."

"The first is the worst, or so they say," he assured her, "Perhaps another would not be nearly so hard."

"I do not intend to find out!" she shoved him from her furs; "If children are what you want, perhaps you should return to the mother of the one you left behind! I do not need you. I didn't ask you to rescue me, so don't expect me to be grateful to you, certainly not to the extent of having any more children."

Journey's Far sighed. The time mated to Blue Coyote had certainly affected Mourning Dove; she was as sour as a green plum anymore. There were times that he completely lost patience with her; yet he stayed. Cotton Tail would never consider taking him back, and the mating had not been that successful any way. Cottontail Girl had, so it seems, set her sights on Stone Man. When he was banished from the camp, and it looked as though she would end up without a mate at all, she had finally consented to being mated with him. This was the idea of one of the elders, of that he was certain, for Cotton Tail had little enthusiasm for it. She accepted him, did her part as a well brought up woman of The People, but there was certainly none of the explosive passions he had become used to with Mourning Dove.

Escape with his beloved had seemed such a good idea at the time, but now he really wondered if perhaps he had not been a bit too hasty. As the days drew on and Mourning Dove recovered completely, Journey's Far finally became convinced he had made a bad choice.

*　　*　　*

The celebration was drawing to a close. Basket retired to the storage cave, where she would now live, alone for the first hand of days, with Blue Coyote, then with Star Woman as well, and with the infant son of someone. For now the child was staying with Moth and Badger, with help from Star Woman and Water Woman. Once he was weaned, he would move into the storage cave permanently. Not yet a mate, Basket was already a mother.

She waited for Blue Coyote with some hesitation. She had not yet found the moment to explain to him that although she had been mated to Red Eagle, he had never claimed that privilege. She was still untouched by a man, and she could only hope that Blue Coyote would treat her gently. Then time ran out. He was there, shedding his clothing and sliding naked into the furs beside her. Basket shivered and tensed.

Blue Coyote hesitated, "Is everything all right with you?" he asked. She nodded tensely, he ran his hand down her naked body beneath the robe and she could not help herself, Basket began to shake. "Look, if you would rather not, I will understand," he frowned.

She could feel his desire as it pressed against her; it was frightening, yet she was curious as well. "It is all right," she replied shakily, "It is just that I . . ." she didn't know how to finish.

"Remember how it was with Red Eagle, and you are afraid that I will be brutal to you as well?" he concluded.

Basket shook her head, "He wasn't brutal, he wasn't anything," she said lamely.

"You mean you didn't . . .?"

"No, I mean yes, we, I mean he didn't . . ."

Blue Coyote began to chuckle, "Trust the pair of us to muck up! Why on earth did you not just come out and say you had no relationship with him? Did you think I would not understand?"

Basket became flustered. He continued to chuckle at her confusion, "No!" She sputtered, "I just didn't know how to say it! What was I supposed to do? Just casually remark, 'oh, by the way, I know nothing about coupling beyond what I have seen in the animals!'"

"That would have done," he admitted, "But I must admit that I rather like your freshness, your shy lack of forwardness." He ran a finger down her arm, "I promise, I will be gentle, Basket. I have no desire to overwhelm you. Relax, and we will do this at your rate, all right?"

"All right," she sighed, "I still think we should have just been friends though!"

"We can be friends, we are friends," he replied, "You are my best friend. This mating, it just means that we will be even closer friends, for we will share more of ourselves with each other. Now come, let me lead the way," he began and slowly Basket understood. There was a brief heartbeat of pain, then they were joined, and she found it not an unpleasant experience. Afterwards she did feel closer to Blue Coyote.

Later still he explained the things which brought him pleasure and together they explored and discovered what pleased Basket as well. By the time Star Woman moved into the cave they had established a very comfortable relationship.

Cotton Tail gave birth to a boy. With no mate to provide and help her it was decided that she would join the little family in the wolf cave. Moth was pleased with the company and the pair of them managed the three infants quite well. Badger spent a lot of time with the men. The camp remained at the escarpment until late spring, when it was decided the babies were old enough to travel.

"What do you want to do?" Blue Coyote took up the tradition of his father, asking the camp.

Hunters looked one to the other, Women shifted uncomfortably, and finally Jackrabbit spoke out, "Find Stone Man, and the rest of the camp!"

Blue Coyote smiled, "That also is what I would choose to do! Anyone! Where do we start?"

"Ask Basket! Ask the dreamer; make your best guess!" Were solutions various members of the camp offered.

"What do you say to beginning at the Sacred Spring, making an offering there, and going on to check the secret canyon? If there are no signs of him there, we go to the place of stone, the far canyon for the winter and if we haven't located them by then, let someone else make suggestions!"

All agreed that this sounded like a logical plan. So they headed for the Sacred Spring. There they rested for a hand of days. Basket was to give the offering, but her woman's time came on her and everyone had to wait until it passed. She made the offering, again with Throw Back at her side and the eerie blue aura surrounding them. Then they headed east toward the bison and the secret canyon.

* * *

"Do you feel her at all?" Blue Coyote questioned.

Basket shook her head, "Nothing; I have not felt her since we left the mountains," she shook her hair behind her, "I think they are very far away."

"Could you ask Wolf Spirit?"

"I could ask, but there would be no answer, no more than there has been the number of times I have already asked," she admitted.

"Try to think back, the first time you felt Star Child, can you remember when that was?" Star Woman questioned.

Basked nibbled her lip, "When we left the secret canyon, I think, but I didn't know at the time what I was feeling, so I can't be sure."

"But there was something?" Blue Coyote asked.

Basket nodded, "But there is nothing now."

"Maybe as we get closer," offered Star Woman.

* * *

Late that night as she lay wide awake beside Blue Coyote, Basket cried out *where are you? Why do you not answer?*
I hear you! The time is not yet! There is still too much hurt.
When?
Not yet!

* * *

She sighed and shifted to a more comfortable position. The secret canyon might yield a clue, but she knew they would not find Stone Man and the remainder of the camp there.

Midsummer found them at the secret canyon. Now Basket knew that she was pregnant, yet she hesitated to say. The naming ceremony gave the infants welcome into the camp. Moth named her daughter Laughing Water, Cotton Tail her son Lone Boy, and Basket gave Mourning Dove's child the name of Chert Boy, for he was forever picking up pieces of the stuff. There were signs that someone had been in the canyon; but who?

Basket wandered down to the stream and sat beside the ancient skeleton of the Great Beast. This was a favorite place for her; she had sat here a number of times since they had come down into the canyon, yet now she noticed something that had escaped her before. She kicked off her shoes and waded out to the skeleton. Tucked carefully, under the water, where the massive tusk joined the head, was a small tool. The sun struck at just the right angle, she pried it free and stood with it in her hand; she smiled. They had been here, probably right after leaving the mountains. The end scraper she held in her had was one which she herself had made and given to Star Child shortly before the breakup of the camp.

She had described the Giant Beast to Star Child countless times, relating how she liked to sit here, on this very stone and think about the ancestors. Star Child had remembered and left a message for her. Basket tucked it into her pouch, deciding to keep this to herself, just as she had kept the messages to herself. There was no sense in telling anyone, particularly Blue Coyote, that her only message was 'leave us alone!'

They stayed at the secret canyon for a span of days and then headed for the place of stone. The hunters scouted vigilantly for signs, friend or foe, and found nothing fresh. They settled in the caves and men set about mining stone and preparing cores. It was a pair of days before Basket and Throw Back could slip off to the cave. The feeling was strong there. *I miss you, Sister!* She held the torch up to the wall and grinned. There was a stick figure of a woman with big tears falling from her eyes standing beside a large wolf. From her waist hung a single tooth. Below that was a series of carefully made wolf tracks going down the wall and below them the unmistakable outline of the canyon. Basket knew where Stone Man had led his people for the winter. Tears streaming down her face as she carefully erased the message; *I miss you too!*

She returned to the camp without anyone but Star Woman even missing her, "Were there any feelings?"

"Only those of loneliness, mine!" she wiped away a tear.

"They must have gone south then, to the canyon,"

"Why? They could have gone to the Starving Mountains for all we know! Blue Coyote drove them out! Why would they go where he might find them?" she said bitterly and then began to cry.

Star Woman took her in her arms and soothed her as best she could, "I miss them too," she whispered, "I miss Turtle! We spent our entire lives together in this camp, and now she is gone; not dead, but she might as well be!" She rocked Basket back and forth, "I can only imagine how much more so it is with you and Star Child, for you are connected. That is why I keep asking if you get messages."

"Well I do!" Basket, wailed, "Go Away! Don't find us! It isn't time! Those are the kinds of messages I get!" She sobbed, "How do you think it makes me feel, when my own sister, my twin sister, tells me not to follow?"

Star Woman continued to rock her, finally she sighed; "How far are you?" she gently brushed the hair from Basket's face. Basket looked puzzled. "With your pregnancy?" she explained.

"How did you know?" Basket sniffed, wiping the tears away with the back of her hand.

"I cried buckets every time anything upset me. Fire Dancer said I kept the furs damp the whole time. Does Blue Coyote know?" Basket shook her head. "We seem to be making up for all the lost years at once; soon there will be more babies in this camp than adults!"

"I don't know how to tell him!" Basket began to sniffle again, "He doesn't like Chert Boy at all, and now I..." she began to wail again. "Soon I will be large as a Great Beast! I have always been plain! Surely he will turn away from me!" Star Woman quieted her and then made them both a cup of tea. "He is going to be mad. . ." she hiccuped.

"He is going to be delighted!" Star Woman corrected her. "Don't you see, Chert Boy is a constant reminder that he was made a fool, no man likes such a reminder, and it makes no difference how many times we point out that it was hardly the child's fault? There will be no doubt that this child is his, he was excited when Mourning Dove first became pregnant, but the moons which followed turned him bitter."

Basket sipped her tea, "I don't want to tell him about the messages," she said, "I don't know where they are any more than anyone else does. She doesn't tell me that!"

Star Woman nodded, "Even if they did go to the canyon for the winter, they would not still be there. Star Child is probably right; it will take time for the hurt to lessen."

"Something happened to them."

"What do you mean?"

"Star Child did contact me. She was terrified, cried out about danger, attackers and death, she said Soft Wind was dead, they fled. Since then all I get are the 'don't follow' messages."

"When was this message?"

"The night that Chert Boy was born," Basket admitted, "That is why I said nothing about it. There were too many other things going on and after that it just never seemed like the right time. I don't know what to do! If they were attacked at the canyon, we certainly should not go there, yet how can I explain that they were attacked unless I admit that Star Child and I are in contact; and I don't want to do that! I promised!" she began to sniffle again.

"Have some more tea," Star Woman refilled her horn. "How do you feel, other than tearful?" Star Woman asked.

"I was sick in the morning at first, but that has passed."

"When was your last blood flow?"

Basket thought back, "at the Sacred Spring," she finally answered.

"That makes you a little less than a hand of moons. The babe will be born during deep winter. We must be sure to select a place where there is plenty of food. You also should take things a little easier, at least toward the end."

"Will I continue to feel as if the least thing is overwhelming?" Basket questioned, "I do not wish to be a 'wet sister'!"

Star Woman shrugged, "Who can say, each of us is different! I was as you say a 'wet sister', the entire time. I will do my best, however, to keep you cheerful and free of tears."

Blue Coyote found them sitting in companionable silence sipping their tea. "Is there any left?" he inquired, "Work on stone is harder than it used to be, or I am less fit, or both!" He settled beside Basket, stretching out his long legs and groaning. "I have muscles which I never knew existed!"

"You say that every time we come here," reminded Star Woman.

"Well it is true, every time we come here," he admitted. "We have all the stone we need for the trip south. I think we can safely leave in a pair of days."

"Are you sure that they went to the canyon?" Star Woman questioned, "It is a long way."

"No farther than it was the last time we went there," he sipped the tea, "Besides I wish to visit the places where . . ." he shook his head, "I just wish to return there."

"It could be dangerous!"

"What makes you think that? We only thought that the camp was attacked, it didn't really happen. The canyon is probably one of the safest places we have spent the winter. It is certainly safer than living with hungry wolves, or constantly watching our backs for Red Eagle!"

"I do not have a good feeling about that place," Star Woman stated.

"Why would you, Fire Dancer met his death there? If there is a reason for not returning, that is it, not some fear of strangers!"

"I would suggest that we return to the escarpment and start again in spring for the canyon," said Star Woman.

"Why? Give me an acceptable reason and I will consider it, otherwise I see no reason not to continue with the plan already set into action."

"I'm pregnant!" Basket stated suddenly.

Blue Coyote stopped, mouth open and turned to her.

"What did you say?" he asked with a strange expression on his face.

"I'm pregnant! Star Woman feels the trip would be too much of a strain on me, since we have no idea how this will affect me, she is just trying to protect your child."

"Pregnant?" A silly grin began to spread across his face, "Pregnant!" He swept her into a bear hug and let out with a boyish yell, "Pregnant!"

They all began to laugh and hug one-another and the decision of their immediate future was forgotten in the excitement of the moment.

Late in the night, after Blue Coyote finally fell asleep Basket reached out with her mind.

*   *   *

Sister?

I am here.

I have news.

So do I, wonderful news.

What?

I am pregnant! Stone Man is so happy! I am happy. The fear has passed, we are following a new river and the strangers did not follow.

I also am pregnant! Blue Coyote is happy.

Blue Coyote?

Yes! Mourning Dove . . . well it is a long story, she is gone, Blue Coyote and I are now mated, and I am also happy. But I miss you! Star Woman misses Turtle.

Turtle misses Star Woman.

Where are you?

I am not sure, but we are in a place I have never been before, Stone Man has not been here either. It is a good place.

Blue Coyote is sorry. He seeks Stone Man. He misses his brother and needs to say that he is sorry.

No! Stone Man is still too hurt; his wounds are not healed.

You won't tell me where you go?

I cannot! I promised.

We go to the canyon.

No! Do not go to that place! There is danger! There is death! Horrible death there!

I have no way of stopping Blue Coyote unless I give him a reason.
Do not go there! Find a reason; any reason!
I found you messages!
I am glad.
You are safe, and happy?
As happy as I can be parted from you. Safe? Are any of us safe? Good
night Sister . . .

*   *   *

Basket sighed and finally slept.

The next morning, again they argued. Star Woman put forth all the reasons that she felt were valid. Basket offered that she felt it too far for her; she would prefer to return to the escarpment. Blue Coyote would not be moved.

Basket lay late into the night watching the Ancestor Fires bright in the sky. Finally, she closed her eyes and slept.

Throw Back raised her head, curling her lip in a silent snarl. Quietly she left the shelter and slipped like a shadow from the camp, Wolf at her side. She raised her head, sniffed the air and trotted to the north. A hand of time later she lay on her belly in the grass, watching. Then they returned to the camp. When Basket woke up Throw Back was in her usual place.

Wolf nudged his head under Blue Coyote's hand.

"What is it, boy?"

Wolf looked to the north, whined and washed his friend's face.

"Something out there?"

Again, he whined and nudged. Looking to the south and wagging his tail.

Blue Coyote squatted beside the wolf, hugged him and ruffled his fur, "All right, boy, we will leave, just as soon as I can get everyone loaded. The wolf wagged his tail and again looked to the north. It was then that Blue Coyote noticed that Throw Back was also watching that direction anxiously.

He called the camp to hurry their preparations. There were grumbles, particularly from his mother. He chose to ignore them. Finally, all were ready and lined up to leave.

Blue Coyote checked the quarry. There were no signs that they had ever been there. Satisfied, he led the people from the place of stone, south,

Jackrabbit and Badger erasing their trail. Wolf and Throw Back glanced to the north, silently communicated and picked up pace. They communicated their anxiety to the other wolves and all moved faster. By night they were far south of the place of stone.

"I think it would be best if we made do with a dry camp tonight," Blue Coyote suggested as women were collecting wood for fires. "Smoke can carry a long way, especially up a valley."

"You suspect we are followed?" questioned Jackrabbit.

"I would be cautious," Blue Coyote replied. "I did not wish to upset the women, but the wolves have sensed that there are others near, to the north of the quarry. This is why I decided to leave so abruptly. We left no sign that we were there, so they should have no reason to follow this valley, but I would feel better . . ."

Jackrabbit nodded, "You figure to find Stone Man in the far canyon?"

Blue Coyote shrugged, "I have no idea where he could be, but he was not at the secret canyon, and if he has been at the place of stone, he left no clues."

"We just left there, and we left no clues. He might have done the same."

"He might have returned to the northern mountains."

Jackrabbit considered this, "I don't think so, that would be a painful . . ." he faltered.

"A painful place? Yes, I know; which is why I did not consider it. Logically he must have gone to the southern canyon. If he is not still there, we should meet him returning to the escarpment."

"Unless he has gone somewhere entirely new" Jackrabbit replied.

"Acorn, have you been able to find out anything helpful from your spirits?"

"Wolf Spirit speaks freely to me again, but on the subject of Stone Man and the remainder of the camp, he will not say," the dreamer replied.

"So, we go to the far canyon to see," Blue Coyote sighed.

"Are we going to stop at the secret canyon again on the way?"

"We might as well, it is in our path.

The men finished their conversation and their tea and went to their furs.

Behind them, a ragged band of men, led by a man with but one good eye, poured like ravaging predators into the quarry; they found nothing.

CHAPTER 22

Stone Man looked one last time down into the camp where his heart remained. To the man whom he had hoped to call Brother, in fact and to the woman he had given his heart to, *oh Basket!* Then he led his people to the east. Star Child wept for hours, soothed by her mother, but too little avail. Cougar helped an equally distraught Turtle Woman. All the hunters wore grim expressions and were silent. Singing Serpent walked beside Stone Man, doing more of the leading than he . . . Without Blue Coyote at his side, Stone Man felt as if part of himself was missing. Without the hope of Basket, his heart would never be whole.

Why? Why didn't I say something in the beginning? Had I spoken to him! Had I admitted my actions with Mourning Dove, all of this would have been prevented! What happened; to me as well as he? I cannot understand, for seasons I have yearned for Basket, yet I followed that bitch like a dog in heat! All thoughts of anything but rutting with her was driven from my mind, even though I knew what was happening to me. "Why didn't I see what was happening with him?" he muttered to himself.

"You were not looking," answered Singing Serpent. "Do not blame yourself! There was Fire Dancer's death, then Bison Man's. We were so wrapped up in trying to solve those mysteries . . ."

"I wasn't thinking about Fire Dancer, or Bison Man," Stone Man admitted, "I was as much at fault as Blue Coyote! All winter the only thing I could think of was that Bitch, Mourning Dove! I was so wrapped up with rutting with her that everything else was wiped from my mind! I was blind to what was going on around me."

"Youth!" sighed Singing Serpent, "That is the way of it; it is as natural as breathing."

"Basket should have come with us," Stone Man muttered, "Basket and Star Child were my plan all along, but he couldn't see it."

"Basket had to stay."

"It was wrong to separate them! The People will suffer."

"Basket would not come, and Star Child could not stay." What could be done?"

"I don't know if anything could be done, but I should have insisted that Basket come with us! I should have demanded to be mated to her before all this happened; then she would have been forced to come with us!"

Singing Serpent shook his head; "The ways of 'power' are not for us to understand. She would not have come, even then."

Stone Man shrugged and pushed hard headed to the secret canyon, shutting his painful thoughts out. There they could regroup and decide where to go.

"We will need to go to the place of stone," Cougar joined him; "We have little or no supply of stone." Stone Man nodded and altered their path, only slightly. A hand of days later they filtered down into the canyon. Star Child was still red of eyes and silent. Dire Wolf at her side whined and tried to comfort, but too little avail. While the men collected stone, Star Child and Dire Wolf slipped off to the secret cave. Stone man hoped this would help ease some of her grief. When she returned, she did seem better. Gray Wolf and Grass darted a deer and the next morning the little party left the place of stone and headed to the secret canyon. It had been decided that they would spend the winter in the canyon far to the south. The secret canyon was but a stop along the way. There they settled for a while in the home cave. Star Child spent many hours sitting on the stone where Basket had always sat, seeming to draw comfort from the skeleton of the Great Beast.

"Why!" She whispered, "Why did this happen? What evil invades our lives and turns them upside down. Blue Coyote! I will never see you again, my heart!" *Perhaps it is just as well! It would be painful to have to see him every day, mated with that bitch!* "Will you ever return to this canyon? I will leave a message," she dug into her pouch and found the blade which Basket had given her, she would recognize it, smiling wistfully Star Child removed her shoes and waded out into the stream. She wedged the blade at the base of the tusk and ran her fingers over its smooth hard surface, drawing some comfort from the process. "I should not have separated the teeth," she muttered, "I should have insisted Basket take it back!"

*　*　*

Oh Sister! Will I ever see you again?
We will find a way! Basket answered.
Star Child smiled, *I miss you! Take care of yourself! Take care of Blue Coyote!*
I miss you! You take care of yourself as well! Take care of Stone Man for me!
I will!

*　*　*

"It is necessary that we have a cape hunting ceremony before we leave this canyon," Stone Man announced, "Running Man, you will destroy your hunting cape with fire, and we will get a new one. We also need the meat for the hunting ceremonies. While the women are repairing equipment and resting, we will get this thing done. Are there any other taboos that this group broke? If so, now is the time to correct them." No one answered. He nodded his head and Moon took his place. This time when we cleanse, there will be no chance of interference by woman's power. The men will move their shelters beside the stream, and the women will remain in the cave.

All nodded in agreement and the cleansing was accomplished and the men went out on the cape hunt. A hand of days later, Running Man had a hunting cape that he could rely upon, the equipment had been repaired and they filed down the canyon and out the path at the southern end.

A pair of moons later they entered the southern canyon. The trip had been uneventful.

"I think it would be a good idea if we set our camp farther up the canyon," suggested Gray Wolf, "It is less visible, and we would be more protected there."

"I would agree," Cougar added. "If we are careful and do not leave obvious signs of our presence, we should be safe farther up the canyon. It would be difficult for anyone to spy on us for one thing, and virtually impossible for them to sneak up on us."

"Then this is what we will do," Stone Man nodded, "The pair of you, scout and find a good location. While you are doing that, more of us will scout above for any signs of people as well." Stone Man was somewhat nervous, for they were a small group of people and were vulnerable for that reason.

"Perhaps there are caves at the upper end of one of the side canyons where we could shelter; I seem to remember seeing several while we were hunting, scout there as well."

"Hey! Look up there," directed Gray Wolf, "What do you think? Does that cave look promising?"

"Let's check it out," Cougar suggested, "The path is a little steep for my liking, but if the cave itself proves exceptional, it could be what we are looking for."

They climbed the narrow steep trail leading up to the cave, "Wow! I don't think I would care to make that trip on a regular basis!" Gray Wolf panted as he reached the entrance, "Still it does give a really great view of the canyon and it would be hard for anyone to sneak up on us here!"

"Look!" Cougar pointed inside the cave, stopping his forward movement.

"What?" Gray Wolf came up behind him.

"We are not the first to climb this trail!"

"I wonder what killed him?" Gray Wolf edged toward the desiccated body lying upon moldering furs at the back of the small cave.

"I wonder when he died!" Cougar added, "Come on let's get out of here, this cave is too small any way."

"Do we leave him here? What if he was alone, no one to set his spirit to walk the wind? Do you think we should do something . . .?"

"Leave it to the dreamer. Come on let's get out of here! Bodies, particularly long dead ones, give me cold chills. I do not like this place; let's check another canyon."

They slipped and slid hurriedly down the steep path and quickly left the small side canyon, marking it in their mind to tell the dreamer. Late in the day, far up the main canyon they found a smaller side canyon, and within it, a cave, similar in size to the Home Cave and with an easy access. Both agreed that this would do for their winter home.

"It would be easy to defend," murmured Stone Man, "There is an ample supply of wood for fires, and the big canyon is close by and filled with game, and there is easy access to the plain above. If all are in agreement, I think we have found the very place."

Rain Woman stood hands on her hips, surveying the back of the cave. "We will dig our storage pits along that wall over there, I think," she nodded her head toward the spot. "The digging is easier there, for the pack rats have already softened the ground. We can put the woman's hearth and the blood shelter toward the back, the shelter just over there, and the hearth about here," she went and stood where she thought the hearth should be. "What do you think?"

"It would be warmer at the back of the cave," agreed Soft Wind, "And the hunters need not come into the area. They can put their storage pit closer to the front. Besides, if strangers attack us, they will be closer to the front and more able to protect the cave. It makes sense!"

"Well, since Turtle Woman and Cougar are the only mated pair in this camp, it does seem logical that all the women share one hearth, the pair in the middle, and the men have their hearth toward the front!" Kind Heart said, glancing thoughtfully toward Running Man, "and if any more decided to mate, they also could move to the middle."

"Poor Running Man!" laughed Rain Woman, "Does he know that his days of freedom are about to end?"

Kind Heart grinned, "He has some idea," she admitted.

"Well if we are all in agreement, let's get started!" Rain Woman directed.

Star Child chose the spot farthest back for her sleeping furs. She settled them there and showed Dire Wolf where she was to sleep. Soft Wind settled beside them and Rain Woman just beyond. Kind Heart chose the spot nearest to where Turtle Woman and Cougar would place their hearth, hoping soon to share it with Running Man.

The men placed their hearth toward the front of the cave and the camp settled in for the winter. There were tubers to collect, acorns to gather, and pigweed to harvest as well as grain from above. The men followed the trails and familiarized themselves with the area in general.

Gray Wolf led Moon to the mouth of the canyon and pointed out the cave, "It is right below the top of the cliff, see?"

Moon nodded, "You say there is only one person?"

"That is all we found, but to be honest, once we saw that body we did not look more, we just got out of there."

"All right, I will go and set his spirit free, just to make sure. If he died alone, then the ceremony will be necessary, if not, it still is better to be safe. We do not need any restless spirits causing problems. You go on about your tasks, I will be all right. I can find my way back to the camp all right."

Gray Wolf nodded and left.

Moon took the steep path slowly, stopping to rest frequently. As he climbed, he looked out over the canyon. This was certainly a good place to be protected, he decided. He had brought everything he needed to perform the ceremony. He made a small fire and burned the cedar branch, waving the smoke toward where the grim bundle lay. He chanted to the spirits, and laid a pair of hunting tools, a knife and blade, carefully on the body. Then he gave prayers to the spirits and asked them to take the soul of this unfortunate man to the ancestor fires in the sky. He finished, put out the fire and left the cave. The spirit of Sagebrush sighed and finally was freed to find his peace in the world of the spirits.

Stone Man had a mission of his own. He put a portion of the sacred bison calf meat into his pouch, found the offering which he had made of raven feathers and bison hide and left the shelter. On his way he found a cedar tree and cut several small branches from it.

Beneath the spreading branches of the oak tree he started a small fire, looking sadly at the scattered remains which lay beyond. The skull was exposed now, and the wide crack was plainly visible where it had struck a rock. He sighed and seated himself beside the fire. Slowly feeding the cedar, bits at a time, to it and watching as the smoke drifted over the bundle.

"It has all gone crazy," he spoke, "I could use your sound advice. There are times I wonder if I am doing the right thing. My heart is so raw, and I constantly long for the closeness which is no longer there."

"Rain Woman and Star Child are with me, but Basket stayed behind with the rest." He fed more cedar to the fire, "I just don't understand!" he shredded the bark in his fisted hand, "Why did it happen? How did we all come to this sad end? What is there about that woman that she blinded so many of us for so long?"

"You discovered something! I wish you could tell me! What happened to you? How did you come to fall? I know that Fire Dancer must have discovered something as well, but what? How does it all fit together? There has to be a pattern, but I cannot discover it."

"So many questions and no answers; how I wish you could speak with me, old friend! Perhaps you know who killed the raven, what happened to curse the Midsummer Ceremony? The dreamers no longer have visions, the twins have been separated, their 'power' lessened. The camp has been split into parts, and life long friendships broken asunder. It seems the whole world is falling to pieces and I have no idea how to put it back together again."

"The brother of my heart has declared me dead! The woman I care for forever lost! Now I lead this ragged, sad handful of people, but where, to what purpose?" He sighed and tossed the remainder of the cedar into the fire.

The soft wind gently sighed and lifted the hair on his forehead, but he discovered no answers. Still, he felt better for it. For a further time he spoke softly, hoping the spirit of Bison Man was nearby and heard his words. Then he finally ground out the fire, bid the silent bundle farewell and returned to the camp.

Winter set in. From time to time Stone Man returned to the old oak tree and talked, but Bison Man did not answer. Stone Man made a trek to where they had laid out Fire Dancer. Nothing remained of the man, or his faithful companion Scorpion, who had chosen to die with him. It saddened the hunter's heart.

* * *

I miss you! Where are you? Why do you not answer?

I am here! You have just not heard me. I have called, and you did not answer. Are you well?

As well as can be expected! We returned to the escarpment. I am back in my old cave. Willow shares it with me. Why do you not tell me where you are?

I promised.

Mourning Dove is pregnant!

How is Blue Coyote?

He no longer smiles. How is Stone Man?

He does not smile either.

*   *   *

Star Child sighed, released her hold on the tooth and cuddled up to Dire Wolf. The animal whined and did her best to comfort. The cold wind whistled outside the cave. Star Child shivered.

The hunters were out in the main canyon, after deer. The cold had increased, and the women were huddled around their hearth, feeling the chill even at the back of the cave. Suddenly Dire Wolf leaped to the front of the cave and began growling and barking savagely, but it was too late. A rabbit stick struck her on the head and she crumpled silently to the floor. Women screamed and tried to evade the hideous creatures that leaped into the cave. Soft Wind was closest to the entrance. The attackers grabbed her and dragged her screaming from the cave, leaving the remainder of the woman weeping and frightened. Star Child sat huddled over the still form of Dire Wolf, her tears wetting the soft fur as she tried to stench the flow of blood. Rain Woman grabbed a digging stick and holding it before her made her way to the entrance of the cave. She watched helplessly as the strangers carted the now silent form of Soft Wind up the faint trail and out of view.

"Someone must go after the hunters!" She stated.

"We don't know where they are!" whimpered Kind Heart. "What if they return for the rest of us?" she began to cry "Poor Soft Wind!"

"Crying isn't going to help! If they were interested in the rest of us, they would have us now!" Rain Woman frowned, "We have to do something about going after her!"

"We?"

"The camp! As soon as the men return, we will find their trail and follow them. The hunters will be able to follow their trail, and if not, then Dire Wolf will."

"Dire Wolf is dead!" Kind Heart blubbered.

"No!" Star Child suddenly called, "She lives! She has a head wound, but she is still alive." With a sigh her strained face eased a little, "But she has lost so much blood!" Her hands were covered with it, as was her tunic, but grimly she sat cradling her precious friend in her lap.

"Well, head wounds are generally not as bad as they look, she is lucky, all she will have from this attack is a headache!" Rain Woman ran her fingers over the wound on the side of the wolf's head. Dire Wolf whined and gave her hand a feeble lick. "You will feel better soon, girl!" She organized the women, settling Kind Heart near the entrance of the cave to watch, and made a poultice for the wolf and some tea for all of them, adding a pain killer to a portion and feeding it to the wolf. Dire Wolf sighed and laid her head down to sleep. They waited, and waited...

*   *   *

"The hunters are returning!" shouted Kind Heart.

Rain Woman nodded. Already she and the remainder of the women had begun to pack the camp's goods into backpacks, for the animals as well as themselves. She knew they would have to travel fast and leave no trail.

Star Child fretted beside the sleeping form of Dire Wolf.

*   *   *

"You say they grabbed Soft Wind and made no attempt for the rest of you?"

"She was closest to the entrance," admitted Rain Woman, "It all happened so fast! One heartbeat everything was peaceful and then Dire Wolf must have caught their scent, for she went crazy, barking and growling. Then they were inside the cave, and before we could do anything one of them had struck Dire Wolf and they grabbed Soft Wind. I saw them carry her up the trail."

"How long ago?"

"About midday."

"Then they have considerable head start on us," Stone Man frowned. Already the men were swiftly packing their things. In less than a finger of time the camp was following Friend, and Dire Wolf, still a bit shaky on her feet, the poultice strapped rakishly to her head. Stone Man followed hard on the heels of the wolves, on the trail after the abductors.

"What did they look like?" Gray Wolf questioned Star Child as they hurried along.

"It happened so fast!" she shook her head. "They were truly horrible! I think they were men, but it was hard to be sure. They had paint all over their bodies, not the kind we use, but bright blue and red and yellow, in swirling patterns. And on their heads their hair stood straight up and was also brightly colored or they had something on their heads. I cannot say!"

"Their weapons?"

She shook her head, "Perhaps Mother could tell you more. She watched them leave, I was concerned with Dire Wolf," Star Child confessed.

They pushed hard, far into the night, by which time exhaustion forced them to stop. Yet the wolves led them steadily south. With the morning again, they followed; for a hand of days, finally crossing a big river[1] late in the day. Yet the wolves were still on the scent they followed, always just far enough behind that they could not catch the fast traveling band.

Those they followed did not fear pursuit. They made no effort to conceal their trail. Even without the wolves to guide them, they would have been able to follow. For a further hand of days, they followed. Then, late in the day, Dire Wolf stopped, and growling dropped to her belly. Friend followed suit. The camp hesitated, and Stone Man motioned them to find cover and hide. They did.

He crawled on his belly to lie beside Dire Wolf, and Friend

Below them spread a large valley. This then was the camp of the Strangers. Stone Man paled. There was easily a span of spans of them; as many as had once been the camps of The People. They spread far out over the valley; hearths and shelters set up everywhere. Gray Wolf joined him, then Cougar and Singing Serpent.

"No wonder they didn't worry if we followed," whispered Cougar.

"It is some kind of celebration," Moon wiggled between a pair of hunters.

"Who are they?"

No one answered.

"That big hearth, about a hand down, that seems to be the main focus," Stone Man said.

"What is that structure at the edge of the camp?" Cougar squinted, "It seems to be some kind of a cage, and there is something in it."

Stone Man slid a bit to the left. "It is a cage, made of poles and hafted together with rawhide or cord of some kind. There are people inside it."

"Can you see Soft Wind anywhere?"

"If she is in the camp, she is probably in that cage with the others," Stone Man muttered.

Dire Wolf yelped softly and dived for the cover of bushes.

"Someone is coming!" Stone Man dived as well. The rest of the hunters followed suit, just in time. A group of men was coming into the camp from behind them. No one dared even breathe until the procession passed.

A hand of men, tall, strong, well muscled, their entire bodies covered with brightly colored markings of serpents and swirling patterns, wearing little else, beyond fantastic head coverings of feathers, feathers of every color imaginable, strode by. They carried a pole between them, the still form of yet another woman. Her long hair hung limply from her still body, gently wafting in the breeze. She was tied, hands and feet and strapped to the pole like a pig being brought into camp for dinner. They could not determine if she breathed.

"I think we should work our way around to those bushes over there!" Gray Wolf suggested, "We would have a better view of that cage, perhaps we can discover if Soft Wind is inside with the others."

Stone Man nodded, and the camp slowly worked its way around to the bushes indicated. "This is better any way," Stone Man whispered, "We are no longer upwind of the camp. I do not see any dogs, but if there are any, they will not be able to alert the camp to our presence."

"At least we are no longer in the middle of a major route into the camp!" Cougar sighed.

"Can you make out anything?"

"I have a clear view of the cage. There is perhaps, a double hand of people inside. They seem to be prisoners, for there are guards as well, but I do not see Soft Wind, or the woman we watched them bring in. They must be being held somewhere else," Stone Man remarked.

"Can you make out anything which will help us?"

"We must study the camp; each of us becoming familiar with as much of it as possible. We will have only one chance, after dark, to make any rescue."

"What about the people in the cage? Do you think we could release them as well? Perhaps they know where Soft Wind is likely to be. If we free them, they might help us rescue her," Star Child wiggled beside Stone Man.

"Get back with the women!" He whispered, "You are in danger here!"

"As we all are! If we are to make a rescue, we must all know the layout of this camp. We may not be able to help you with the rescue, but we certainly need to know which way to run!"

"Back to the big river, if anything should happen to us, stay out of sight and return to the big river[2]. Follow it upriver," Stone Man whispered, "Now please go back to the other women."

Star Child sighed and wiggled back from the edge.

"What did you see?" questioned Rain Woman.

"It is a big camp, there are many people spread far down the valley. Just below where we hide, is a cage, there is a double hand of people being held prisoners there. There are guards, but Soft Wind is not with them."

"What do we do now?" asked Kind Heart.

"We wait, at least until dark. Stone Man plans on releasing the prisoners and hopes someone among them know where Soft Wind is being held. Then we run!"

"That is the plan?" Turtle Woman squeaked! "That is no plan, it is walking into death!"

"Well it is the best we have so just be ready to run back to the big river. If you get separated follow it up-stream."

The day was well past sun-high. Singing Serpent nodded to Stone Man and wiggled back. He crawled to where the women were huddled. "I am taking you farther away from the camp, back toward the big river. Stone Man feels you will be safer there!"

"No!"

"We can help!"

"Soft Wind is our friend also!"

Soon the women also had wiggled to a point where they could see the camp. Night Spirit would soon chase Sun Spirit from the sky. "We will wait, until all but the guards sleep. Then we will sneak into the camp. Cougar and Gray Wolf will dart the guards, I will release the prisoners and we will try to locate Soft Wind. Then we get out of here! I have seen no dogs, but that does not mean there are none, so be alert! Are there any questions?"

"What if we get separated?"

"Go to the big river. Follow it a day to the upriver direction and then wait!"

In the camp the drums began.

Danger! Horrible men, they stole Soft Wind, we follow. Star Child had called out.

People began to gather around the huge central hearth. Beside it rested an enormous stone, one which had steps cut into it so that a man could walk to the top of the stone. There was a festive air about the camp. Men dressed in the same gaudy feathers as those who had passed them followed the call of the drums. Many people, most without the elaborate coloring began to amble forward. The women also were painted, but they had fewer feathers. Children ran naked, laughing and calling to each other. They saw no dogs. They could hear the people talking, but the language was strange to them.

Someone passed around a skin of something, probably fermented drink, from which the men imbibed freely. As the night wore on, these became increasingly drunk. Fine! This could only help the watchers. Eventually all the people had left their shelters to surround the main attraction.

"Come on, I think we can get closer!" Stone Man whispered. "There doesn't seem to be anyone left at this side of the camp. Keep together; and stay behind me!" He eased over the edge, and the rest carefully followed. They gathered behind the outermost shelter, Dire Wolf scenting the air nervously. "Let's slip behind that shelter over there," Stone Man whispered and led the way, quietly slipping from one hiding place to another. Cougar followed, and Gray Wolf was next. Star Child and Dire Wolf duly went as did each member of the camp, until all were gathered, just a stone throw from the cage.

The guards stood before the cage. They had their darts safely secured in the dart holders on their backs. They held only clubs, but these were certainly sufficient to control the frightened prisoners.

A double hand or so of people clung nervously to the bars of the cage. Most were able-bodied men, less than half were women. There were no children among them. Several looked to be in excellent health, but a pair had obviously been wounded during their capture. One carried a broken arm, and yet another needed help walking.

Wind Walker stood beside Black Cloud as they peered through the bars of their cage. They had been here for over a moon now. This was the second ceremony to take place and they knew with dread how it would go. Angry Mountain cowered behind them, shaking in fear. Gentle Breeze was as usual castigating him in hissing whispers. Shifting Stand came to stand on Wind Walker's other side.

"Do you think they will do it again?" He questioned.

"Looks like it! I saw them bring in a pair of women, just like last time. They have them in that shelter beside the stone, also just like last time."

"Did anyone have any luck with the cordage holding this cage together?"

"I cut nearly through one spot in the rear of the cage before my sliver of blade broke into such a small piece it would no longer cut," Shifting Sand admitted.

"We will be next to mount that stone!" mumbled Black Cloud, "Just you wait and see!"

"Not this time," Wind Walker disagreed, "They have others. But I agree with Black Cloud, if we cannot escape this infernal cage, our time will come, probably at the next full moon. These people seem to do things at that time. And I am sure they plan us all to suffer the same fate. It just isn't our time yet!"

"I am getting better," offered the limping man, "My leg is nearly healed."

"Do not worry, Sand Catcher, we will not leave you behind!" Wind Walker assured him.

"My arm is nearly healed as well," commented Traveler.

"Fine! Now we are all healed and ready to flee! There is just one problem! It may have escaped your notice, but we are still prisoners in this cage!" Black Cloud muttered to those around him.

"Perhaps we could call upon you to furnish us with a plan;" suggested Shifting Sand.

"Beyond chewing our way out, I see no escape!" sighed Laughing Water.

"What is happening now?" Traveler questioned, "I can't see over the heads of the crowd."

"So far, nothing, but if it is like last moon, they will be a long time yet."

Silently they waited. A hand of time passed, then another. Now the drums began to pick up speed. The people crowded about the central hearth became increasingly noisier.

The guard to the left of the cage jerked and then slid to the ground silently. The people inside froze in stunned silence; the right guard turned toward his fallen companion, and with a surprised look on his face followed the same path. A lone man slipped from behind the closest shelter. He made a motion for silence. They gladly complied. Then there were a number of people at the cage. Silent, desperate people, their leader swiftly cutting the cord holding the cage shut. It was jerked open and with a burst the people inside were free.

"Who are you?" Wind Walker questioned as he reached his rescuer.

"We followed a hand of men to this place. They kidnapped one of our women. We come to rescue her." Star Child managed to answer. Stone Man understood not a single word.

Wind Walker shook his head, pointing toward the camp. As in a dream the camp watched. Soft Wind dressed in a beautiful white tunic and her hair wound and decorated with feathers of all colors was led up the steps cut into the stone. Her face shone softly in the firelight, there was a peaceful expression in her eyes.

"Soft Wind," whispered Gray Wolf.

"They must have given her some kind of drug," Singing Serpent remarked, "Look at her eyes!"

"What are they going to do to her?" Star Child questioned in a frightened whisper.

"It is too late, if that is the one you seek to save," Wind Walker replied, "The best thing we can do is get out of here while we can. There is no sense in risking your own lives. You can do nothing for her!"

The crowd roared, then in mass fell to their knees. Now the scene was easy for them all to see. From the other direction a procession of men arrived at the stone, led by a tall thin man dressed in a feather cloak so beautiful that Star Child caught her breath. The man matched the cloak. His face was cleaved in perfect planes. His eyes were dark pools of mystery, his well-muscled torso naked but for the feather cloak. It gleamed with a coating of some sort of oil. His powerful legs brought him smoothly to the top of the stone.

Gently the night breeze lifted his long hair, fluttering the eagle feather that was secured there. Mesmerized, Star Child found herself unable to look away. The crowd parted and another woman, a little younger than Soft Wind was also led to the stone. She climbed, escorted by a pair of gaudily dressed men, to stand beside Soft Wind. Now a pair of men mounted the stone from behind the beautiful one. They came to stand on either side of him.

Stone Man recognized the other woman. He had last seen her being carried into the camp like a pig on its way to the roasting pit. He felt a cold chill race up his back and it settled at the base of his neck. He took a step forward, stopped by the hand of Wind Walker. "You can do nothing to stop it!" the man said quietly, a strange soulful tone to his voice. "We must go! there is no need for you to watch this!" He tried to turn Stone Man away, "At least send you women away!" he whispered.

No one moved.

The beautiful man came farther out onto the stone. He lifted his arms up to the night sky and intoned strange words, turning he did so again, and then again. Then he lowered his head, bringing his thick mane of hair cascading down either side of his face, throwing it into shadow. He closed his eyes and began a slow incantation, swaying gently side to side in rhythm with the drum.

Soft Wind stood calmly, a smile on her face, radiance in her eyes. The other woman knelt at the feet of the beautiful one. He said something to her and she gracefully rose and went to Soft Wind. Carefully she undid the lancing down the front of Soft Wind's tunic, and then slipped it from her shoulders. The crowd caught their collective breaths and became silent. Now only the sound of the drum broke the night stillness.

Soft Wind stood now naked but for a decorated cord around her waist. Her body had also been covered in some kind of oil her skin glowed softly, her breasts gently rounded in the light cast by the fire. The other woman led her to a shelf raised from the top of the stone. Here she lay as directed. The other woman lifted her hair and spread it behind her head like a robe. Then she bowed and stepped back.

The beautiful man came to stand before Soft Wind. He reached to his waist and brought forth a blade, kept is a hidden sheath. It was a blade such as the camp had never seen; at least a pair of hands in length and all along either edge were serrations flaked by a master craftsman. He raised it over his head and turned to show it to the gathering. The fire flickers and cast light from its perfect surface.

Again he raised the knife. "Come on man!" Wind Walker urgently pulled at Stone Man.

Then with the speed of lightning he brought the knife down and in one smooth motion reached and lifted the still beating heart of Soft Wind. He raised it to the sky and tipping it poured her hot blood into his mouth and drank[3].[1]

The crowd went wild. Stone Man could not move. Star Child could not believe her eyes.

The pair of men lifted the body of Soft Wind and dancing around they circled the stone and then cast her viciously directly into the fire. The crowd roared and Stone Man shifted into action.

"Let's get out of here!" he grabbed Star Child and all but dragged her whimpering out of the camp.

Once they were moving, the spell seemed to break and the small band of people flowed from the camp and into the darkness. They moved then, just as fast as their legs would carry them, just as far from the horror they had just seen as they could go. The pack wolves were where they had left them and led by Dire Wolf they traveled far into the night, into the dawn of another day and yet again into the night. If they were followed, they did not look back to see. They left an almost unintelligible trail, impossible to follow but with the aid of dogs.

They reached the big river days later and stepping into it they walked upstream. Finally, exhaustion forced them to stop. Sand Catcher was having trouble keeping up because his weak leg no longer able to support him. Turtle Woman was being helped by Kind Heart and Star Child.

"We will rest here," Stone man said tonelessly.

The people dragged themselves from the shallow water and staggered to where they could collapse.

"I will watch!" Stone Man drew himself up and found a stump to sit on.

Wind Walker made his way to join him.

They sat for a time in silence, "What I saw, it was real?" he questioned, "It truly happened?" Star Child slipped beside Stone Man. Quietly she translated.

Wind Walker nodded, "We have seen it before on the last full moon."

"Why?" Stone Man shook his name, "Why would anyone do such a thing?"

"I think it has to do with their dreaming," Wind Walker replied. "We could not understand them, and even had we been able to it is unlikely that anyone would tell us any way."

"How did you come to be there?"

"Wind Walker sighed, "Many generations ago my people came from a place to the north of here. The stories tell of following a mythical animal to where the salt waters meet the land. We chose to return to the home of our ancestors and seek to find that land and The People. We were captured a pair of moons ago as we followed this very river from the salt waters."

"Well you are at least partially successful!" Stone Man replied, "For you have found us."

Slowly, Stone Man began to understand the words of Wind Walker. It wasn't so much another way of speaking, just a different way. He finally turned to Star Child, "I can understand his words; you do not need to stay." Gratefully she nodded and left.

Star Child took the time to release Dire Wolf from her pack and then curled into a ball on the sand and slept. The wolf settled beside her for a time and then rose and went to Stone Man, laying her head on his knee. She whined.

"I have never seen people such as you, nor animals such at this one!" Wind Walker stated, "I was not sure if you came to rescue us or carry us off into an even more hazardous existence."

"Perhaps we have," Stone Man replied, "But at least you are free."

"Free, yes, and I would know something of those who have freed us!"

They spoke for some time, then Gray Wolf and Running Man came, and the pair retired to sleep for a time.

Danger! I cannot think of it! Poor Soft Wind! I cannot remember! We flee! We flee!

A hand of days later they realized that no one followed. They were still camping beside the big river. But where were they?

"We followed the men far south of the canyon," Stone Man stated, "If we continue to follow this river it will lead us away to the west of there."

"I never want to go back to that place again!" Turtle Woman shuddered, "There are only sad memories there!"

"We should go north, follow the bison." Gray Wolf suggested.

"The bison do not move north for at least another moon, perhaps more."

"We need a place to hide, where we can wait out the winter," Cougar stated.

"Perhaps there is another river which joins thins one," suggested Wind Walker. "We have come across several."

"Surely there is no way those savages could still be following us?" Star Child questioned.

"Unlikely," Stone Man said, "But we dare not take the chance that they are seeking victims throughout the area. We are not familiar with this land. It would be best if we left it."

"I will agree with that?" Angry Mountain added.

"I think Wind Walker has a sound idea," Stone Man said, "We will follow this river for a while yet and see. I hope that we are beyond the territory of the savages, but I would feel more comfortable farther north. So tomorrow we move on. That leaves the job of erasing our presence from this place. See to it, men!"

"She is very devoted to you," stated Laughing Water, nodding at Dire Wolf.

"She is the watcher," Star Child replied, packing sleeping robes into a carrier.

"Why do you call her that? As far as I can tell everyone in your camp, animals as well as people are constantly watching."

Star Child stopped her work and rolled back onto her heels. "Dire Wolf is one of only a pair like her. For example, Singing Serpent's dog, Spirit Wolf, is her brother, yet they are nothing alike. Dire Wolf is like Throw Back, her mother. They are said to be of the ancient kind of wolf which no longer walks but in legend."

"But you called her watcher?"

"Yes, she is my protector. She was sent by the spirits to keep me safe."

"Why you; I mean, why just you; are you special among your people?"

Star Child nodded. "I am half of a pair. I have a sister, identical to me. Basket stayed with the other part of the camp when the camp split. I came with my mother. This tooth I carry is half of a pair, my staff has an identical other, and Dire Wolf is just like her mother Throw Back, who walks with my sister."

"Twins are said to be very powerful among my people." Laughing Water nodded.

"Of course they are. We are of the same people! Do you not have stories about the Chosen One, the Mother of The People?"

Laughing Water thought, 'No, she shook her head, "We have stories about a terrible fight at a place where The People met each season. It is said that the dreamer and a woman threw lightning bolts at one another. It was then that our ancestors fled. They could not follow a woman, and they would not follow the dreamer. So they traveled across a great plain to the woodland and across the woodland to the sea. We have followed the sea to the big river and the big river to where we were captured."

Star Child nodded, "The woman who threw the lightning bolts, she was the Chosen One; she is also my ancestor. I carry the mark on my shoulder, as does Basket."

"You have spoken to 'spirits'?"

Star Child nodded, "We did, but the 'spirits' do not talk to us anymore," she sighed and resumed her packing.

"Do you think that some day I could have a wolf?"

"Ask Stone Man. There are a number of pups due in less than a moon, perhaps he will say yes, if your people decide to stay with us."

"Wind Walker is happy walking with this camp. I think that we all are. I would like it if we stayed together. Perhaps someday I will even meet your sister!"

Star Child shook her head. "We are dead to them! Basket and I used to talk, but I have been afraid since the savages attacked, for fear there is one among them who can hear us."

"You talk to Basket? How can this be?"

"We are connected. We share thoughts. It isn't really talking."

"Maybe she could tell us where we are!"

"She keeps asking, but I do not answer. Stone Man is not ready to meet again with Blue Coyote. His heart still hurts. Perhaps someday we will find them again, when the hurt has lessened but not now."

"Star Child fetch those furs to me, I have room for them in this last pack," Rain Woman called. Star Child gathered up the furs and carried them to her mother. "Do you think the captives will stay with us?"

"I think so, if for no other reason, it makes sense. We are stronger and so are they. They have skills we lack, and we have some that they have never developed. Do you know, for example, they have never seen a bison?"

"Really, Laughing Water, you never told me that!"

Laughing Water smiled and shrugged, "Why talk of things which make us look ignorant and stupid!"

"But you showed me how to net a fish! I never even thought of eating fish! So that makes me equally stupid and foolish! Yet I did not stop the learning"

"Nor will we once we have met the bison, we also will become hunters of them. We will wear the hides of wolves and become wolves of the plains!"

"Wolves of the plains; is that how you see us?" Star Child was amazed.

"That is what Shifting Sand calls you."

"Perhaps then, we are, perhaps you will soon be one of us as well. I have seen the way that at least one wolf of this camp looks at you!"

Laughing Water blushed to her roots and became extremely busy with her packing. Star Child smiled. It was about time that someone within their group has some luck. Gray Wolf was certainly going to have it.

"I would speak with you." Stone Man walked beside Star Child.

"I am here," she reminded him.

"Not here, later, alone," he stuttered, hurrying away.

"Now what was that all about?" Star Child mused to herself.

"I see what looks like a river cutting to the north up ahead!" Gray Wolf called back, "I'm going to investigate!"

"Wait for me!" shouted Traveler, "I will go with you!" He ran to catch up.

"The camps are merging into one very nicely, don't you think?" Wind Walker asked Stone Man as they watched the men go off on their investigation.

Stone Man nodded, "In more ways than one! Gray Wolf has asked me to speak to you regarding Laughing Water. It seems that he wished to ask for a mating with her."

Wind Walker nodded, "And what of you? Do you find any of the women of my camp acceptable for yourself?"

Stone Man shook his head, "I have already chosen, I have but to tell her, and tonight is probably the best chance I will have."

"Since the woman Kind Heart has obviously selected Running Man that leaves only Star Child, the plain one. She is your choice?" Wind Walker seemed surprised.

"Why is it that whenever anyone speaks of them, they are always called the plain ones?"

"Them? I see only one." Wind Walker frowned. "And I did not mean any insult. It is just that there are much more comely women in the camp."

"None with a more beautiful heart though; none more suited to walk beside me." Stone Man sighed, *but the wrong one!* "She is one of a pair of twins. The sister Basket, remained with the main camp when we parted."

"Why is that? I would have thought that a woman as strong and protective as Rain Woman would have insisted that both of her daughters go with her!"

"Oh! Do I detect an interest here?"

"Most definitely!" Wind Walker nodded, "And I am not afraid to come out and say so!"

"Star Child and Basket are sisters, but Rain Woman is not Star Child's real mother. Although she raised her from a baby, Feather was her real mother. And Star Child did not grow up with the camp. Basket did, and her choice was to stay with the camp."

Wind Walker looked silently at Stone Man for a time, then nodded. "Perhaps it would be good to find a spot, call a halt and get some mating organized with this camp!" He grinned.

* * *

"Will you walk with me to beyond the trees," Stone Man requested.

Star Child put aside the strap she was about to mend and rose, at a loss to know what was so secret that Stone Man could not speak before her mother. Rain Woman smiled to herself as she watched Star Child go. *Be happy, my daughter!* She sent a blessing.

Stone Man stopped beyond the trees, Star Child waited, and waited . . .

"I. . . that is we . . . I mean . . ."

"What on earth is the matter?" Star Child finally lost patience. "If you have something to say do so, before morning catches us and you are still not finished!" She laughed.

"Mate with me!" He almost shouted and then clamped his mouth tightly shut.

"What?" Star Child stared at him open mouthed. "What did you say?" She said weakly.

"You heard me!"

"I think I heard you," she nodded, "But ask again, please, so that I can be sure?"

He sighed, "Mate with me Star Child," he smiled, "I am not good with words, but I do most sincerely care for you, and I would most sincerely like for you to share my fire, and my life," he finished all in a single breath.

"Yes!" She answered quickly, holding her breath, fearful he would take back his words. "Yes!" She whispered again softly, a tender light filling her eyes, and spreading over her face, for once making it almost beautiful.

"Yes?" Stone Man was taken back by her quick answer. "You don't want time to think about it?"

"Why? Are you regretting already that you have asked?" Her face clouded quickly with disappointment.

"No!" He shook his head, "It is just that.... well....I have wanted to speak to you for so long. But there just hasn't been time.... I mean. All Right! So I was afraid!" He admitted frowning.

Slowly Star Child began to smile again. "I can't believe it!" She actually chuckled; "Big Strong Stone Man! Shy of a mere woman." Her smile slowly faded. "However, I fear you have not asked your first choice." She sighed. "I saw how you watched Basket."

Stone Man shook his head. "No!" He quickly denied. "Once perhaps, but that was before I got to know you. That was when there was only Basket. And she has always been intended for Blue Coyote. He was just too caught up with Mourning Dove to realize it. That is what the fight was really over. I wanted us to speak to the pair of you together....." He shrugged, remembering that it had been Blue Coyote he had urged to speak to Star Child. "It hardly matters now. He has gone his way and mated with his Mourning Dove. But that is no reason why we cannot fulfil at least part of the plan." There was still a great deal of hurt and anger in his voice.

Star Child sighed and nodded. "I will be very happy to mate with you." Again the soft light filled her face. This time however, it remained.

---

1. The Rio Grand
2. the Pecos river
3. Even before the Aztecs made blood sacrifice common, there were a few instances of it depicted from other groups. This part of the story has no basis in the archaeological record. It is just good story telling.

CHAPTER 23

It is time to leave," Blue Coyote called together the people. Quietly they shouldered packs and led their wolves to follow him and Basket, Throw Back and Wolf, south, through the lower valley and onto the plain. Chert Boy bounced happily atop the travois. Behind, watching them go, were Badger and Jackrabbit. They would catch up later. It was their task to make sure there were no traces of their occupation, as in the quarry and now again in the secret canyon. They had traveled fast from the place of stone, back to the secret canyon. Here they had rested a hand of days. Now Blue Coyote decided it was time to push on, to the southern canyon. Badger and Jackrabbit spent a hand of time at the job, finally certain that no trace remained, then, sweeping away their trail behind them they hurried to catch up to the camp.

*　　*　　*

The raiders stumbled to a halt, almost falling into the canyon. They found the trail and flowed down inside to explore. There was no sign of any recent habitation. The remains of a dead Great Beast calmly ruled the canyon. "This is a good place to spend the winter!" Red Eagle-White Falcon declared. *So this is where they disappeared to! Well they will be back! And we will be waiting for them!*

*　　*　　*

"What on earth makes you think they will be at this canyon?" demanded Mourning Dove. "We have been dragging these travois for over a pair of moons and we have seen signs of nothing but bison dung! And that is what you are, Bison Dung! Do you hear me Bison Dung?" she shoved her hair out of her face. It was growing, but was still far too short to tie back, so always it was in her face, blocking her eyes and just generally bothering her.

Journey's Far tried to ignore her. For the last several moons he had begun to wish that he had stayed safely mated to Cotton Tail. By now he would be a father again and would have been able to watch his son grow up as well, but no! He had to be ruled by a head lower that the one on his shoulders. It was his own fault, so now he bit his lip and kept walking.

"How much farther?" she questioned for the uncountable time.

"Another day at the most," he answered.

"That is what you said a hand of days ago! Yet here we are, still walking! I don't think you know where you are going; I don't think you know where we are! For all I know we have been walking in circles!"

"Then go by yourself! No one is forcing you to come with me!" he lashed back.

Mourning Dove worked her mouth silently, then shouldered her travois and stomped off, "Are you coming?" she shouted over her shoulder; "A day at the most, you promised!"

Journey's Far mumbled under his breath and yanked the lead on his wolf. The animal showed teeth at him and reluctantly followed.

"We will camp here," she dumped her load to the ground, "I will gather bison chips while you dress the rabbits!" She meandered off across the plain picking up dry bison chips and tossing them into the robe bag she dragged behind her. Journey's Far sighed, unshouldered his pack and unhitched the wolf. He took out his knife and gutted the rabbits, tossing the entrails to the animal. The wolf was true to his name and swallowed the offering without chewing it, then he sank tiredly to the ground.

Mourning Dove skewered the rabbits and set them over the fire to cook. Then she spread their robes and made some tea. Finally, Journey's Far sat and rested, there was not much to say so after eating they crawled into their furs and slept. Far across the plain a wolf howled, a shadow raised its head, listened, and then quietly left the camp and loped away.

"I told you that you should tie that animal at night!" Mourning Dove was furious, for it was her day to lead the wolf and his day to pull the travois; now they would both have to pull.

"He has never run off before. That must mean we are close. That is it; he has gone to join the rest at the canyon! I thought I heard a wolf call last night!" Journey's Far began to load his travois faster.

"What if we find this canyon, and what if it isn't Stone Man there, what if it is Blue Coyote instead? He will kill me and you likely as well! Did you think of that?" she stomped off.

"I wouldn't even care!" Journey's Far muttered beneath his breath, "Even that would be better than your constant complaining!" He sighed and picked up his backpack and took hold of the travois leathers, falling into step behind her.

"There is a path ahead," Mourning Dove stopped. "you go find out where it leads!"

Journey's Far dropped his travois leathers and backpack and trotted down the trail. It stopped abruptly and dropped down into the canyon. He sighed is relief. They had found it! He hunkered behind brush and surveyed the canyon below. There were people there all right, but none that he recognized. It was not Blue Coyote's camp, nor unfortunately Stone Man's.

He returned to Mourning Dove, "I have no idea who they are!"

"What difference does it make? We are travelers, we ask to be made welcome, we travel with them or stay with them for a while and if we like it we stay, if not," she shrugged.

"I don't know . . ." he hesitated.

"Fine! You stay here! I am going down into the camp," she flounced off dragging her travois behind her. Journey's Far crouched where he was, biting his lip and hesitating. A nudge at his arm caught him unaware, and he turned to come eye to eye with his wolf. The animal wagged his tail and whined, heading toward the east. He stopped, whined again and took a few more steps.

Journey's Far grinned, for the first time in many moons and hoisted his backpack and grabbed the traces to the travois. He followed the wolf.

Mourning Dove dragged her travois down the trail, calling to the men below. They stopped whatever they were doing and watched her approach,

"I have traveled far," she called, "I come to this camp in peace, and I wish to be made welcome!'"

"Oh you will be made welcome!" Hairy Bear grinned "You will be made very welcome!"

Mourning Dove smiled back, "You alone?"

*   *   *

She nodded, *let him make his own way!* and followed the hunter to the Home Cave.

Journey's Far dumped part of his load for it was Mourning Dove's stuff any way and picked up speed. The wolf, now back in the traces, almost ran, bouncing the stuff on the travois as he went. Journey's Far had all he could do to keep up. At evening he stopped, just beyond the camp and stood waiting.

Blue Coyote came out from the camp. "What do you want?" He almost shouted.

"I .... I want to come back . . ." he said lamely. "I was wrong and believe me I am sorry! Could I at least speak to Cotton Tail?"

"I will ask her," Blue Coyote replied. "But she is a fool if she says yes!"

Cotton Tail came out from the camp. "You are looking good!" He twisted the travois leathers in his hands.

"What do you want, Journey's Far? Haven't you brought enough pain and shame down onto me? Must you now flaunt your relationship with that 'woman' before me as well?"

"I deserve all of the blame you could ever heap on my head, believe me, I have been heaping it on for moons, but I am finished with her. I really was finished with her before I even began; I was just too stupid to know it. All I have been able to think of these last moons were you and our baby, and . . ." he stopped lamely, "All I can say Cotton Tail, is that I am sorry, I just want to come back to you and be the best mate I am capable of being. Please say that you will give me another chance!"

Cotton Tail began to cry, and he reached out to her. With a sob she ran back to the camp. He waited, finally Blue Coyote returned. "All right," he relented, "She wants you back, the spirits alone know why! But you can come in." With a relieved sigh he led the wolf into the camp.

Throw Back greeted her son. Cotton Tail brought forth his son, and Journey's Far knew that he had finally come home.

Later, after the welcomes and something less than welcome's he sat beside Blue Coyote, late into the night. "There were people in the secret canyon. I watched them from behind the bushes. I did not recognize anyone, well actually there was one I thought I recognized, but I couldn't be sure. He was a long way away, and it has been a long time, but maybe just the impression, for a moment I thought it was Hairy Bear."

"We only left that canyon yesterday," Jackrabbit exclaimed. "Did it look like they were searching for us?"

"No, it looked like they were moving in. They were cutting poles and erecting a shelter across the mouth of the Home Cave."

"Thank You for sharing this information with us."

Journey's Far nodded and left the fire. He was on trial with Cotton Tail, so he went to sleep with his wolf, his place in the camp until she decided he had been punished enough. He was satisfied.

"What do you think?" Jackrabbit questioned "Can we trust him?"

Blue Coyote sat thinking for a time, "The wolf came in alone. Obviously he had run off, yet his loyalty took him back. He is a son of Throw Back, yet he brought the man to this camp. Perhaps the information he brings was the reason. I do not know, but I do believe that Journey's Far has been through several moons of one of the hardest learning experiences a man can go through. He has returned, this alone took courage, and he is sorry. I do think he can be trusted, yes."

"What about . . . ?"

"Mourning Dove? You can say her name. I won't flinch! At a guess I would say he was correct in assuming that she joined up with the men in the canyon. Will she wonder what happened to Journey's Far, that depends on how many men there are in that camp, and how hard up are they for a woman. Either way, she has no knowledge of us, and will probably assume that Journey's Far either was attacked and eaten by predators, or more than likely, returned to the escarpment alone. Either way we are not involved."

"There are no means by which they could trail us and it is highly unlikely they will bother with a lone man. Besides, even scarred, if it is dark enough, and a man is desperate enough!" Blue Coyote actually grinned. "I can think of nothing more deserving of that group of throat cutters, than they are gifted Mourning Dove! Now let's get some sleep!"

Later as he lay beside Basket, Blue Coyote was discussing Cotton Tail. He shook his head "I can't believe she was actually willing to take him back!"

"He is the father of her child," Basket reminded, "Besides, looking at the practical side of it, what chance does Cotton Tail have of finding another mate? She has a child, and there are already more unmated women than men."

"Would you take him back, in her place?"

"I took you," she reminded him.

"Do you ever regret it?" He nuzzled her heck.

"No," she replied, "I have found that men who have badly burned their fingers, rarely put their hand in the fire a second time."

They traveled for another hand of days plus a pair, before Cotton Tail finally took Journey's Far back. In the days that followed, he did his best to make up for the hurt he had caused. He even offered to take the responsibility of Chert Boy, who he admitted was probably his. So it was decided, Chert Boy now rode on Journey's Far's travois, and Blue Coyote found that another ravaged bit of his soul had healed.

"I am still worried about going to the canyon!" Star Woman walked beside Basket, now quite obviously pregnant, but blooming.

"There is nothing more I can do about it, he has decided. I think it has something to do with healing," she sighed.

"Healing?" Star Woman shook her head, "What are you talking about?"

"Inside, I think he has to return, return to Fire Dancer, return to Bison Man. He needs to. I know this will sound foolish, but I think he needs to talk to them, to explain. Then the healing will be nearly compete."

"Nearly? What else?"

"Stone Man," Basket sighed, "Then we must find Stone Man."

"Do you still 'speak' to Star Child?"

Basket sighed, "Sometimes! She also is pregnant! But something terrible happened, something she refuses to share. Every time I say anything about the canyon, she gets very upset, she keeps repeating that there is danger there, that Soft Wind died there horrible. Then she flees and will not talk to me for days on end."

"Have you any idea where they are?"

"She says they follow a river," Basket Sighed.

"That is hardly helpful!"

"Oh!" Basket stopped, then took a shallow breath.

"You all right? What happened?" Star Woman was white with concern.

"She kicked me!" Basket laughed, running her hand over her swollen stomach.

Star Woman sighed in relief, "Will you quit calling that baby 'she', it could be bad luck."

"But it is a 'she', Basket replied, "I carry a daughter, one of the line. I thought you had realized that! Star Child carries the other. She will be called Sun Spirit."

"You stop that right now, Basket!" Star Woman stopped angrily, "Don't you dare say again what this child will be, and I never want to hear you give it a name! Do you wish to call all of the bad spirits down upon yourself and the child? No child is ever given a name until it has passed its third moon!" She began to cry, "Not even yours!"

Basket sighed, feeling very guilty "Very well," she gave in, "I will not say."

*　　*　　*

Where are you?

Getting nearer, nearly there.

Don't go there!

How are you doing? How is Winter Rain?

We are fine. You? And Sun Spirit?

Very well. Are you still following the river?

Yes.

Blue Coyote must go there, he needs to heal I think, he needs to speak with Fire Dancer and Bison Man.

Yes, Stone Man did that. Perhaps you are right but be careful. Make sure that Throw Back is always on the alert. Dire Wolf got fooled!

I will be careful! Are the others well?

Mother has mated with the hunter Wind Walker. She is happier.

And Gray Wolf? He fares well?

Yes, Laughing Water has been good for him. We are all happy. The wounds are healing.

Not here. Blue Coyote still has not healed. Mourning Dove has joined the raiders! Did you know?

It fits in with what the spirits say. I must go now, remember be careful!

*   *   *

Acorn went to walk beside Basket. "I spoke to Wolf Spirit last night," he opened the conversation.

"And . . . ?"

"You are in contact; that is what he says."

"And?"

"It could be dangerous, for all of you."

"Did the Wolf Spirit say that, or is it Acorn, the dreamer speaking?"

"Basket, you endanger the child inside you, you endanger us all!"

"I don't go to her. She comes to me! I do not take the spirit powders, yet she visits my dreams! What am I to do? I cannot refuse to sleep!"

"I just hope that you know what you are doing!" The dreamer kicked the ground with his toe.

"So do I! How else do you suggest that we get them back together?"

"We? Meaning members of this camp, or you and Star Child, or you and the Spirits?"

"Maybe I mean all of those!" She whispered.

"Does Blue Coyote know that you are in contact with Star Child?" She shook her head, "Or the Wolf Spirit?" Again she shook her head.

"You do not think all of this will harm the child you carry? It could do him irreparable harm!"

"I carry a girl!"

"You cannot know that!" The dreamer was shocked.

"Of course I can know that! I knew from the moment of her beginning! Star Woman has forbid me to speak of it!" Basket sobbed "And everyone merely criticizes me at every turn, when all I try to do is keep the spiral moving in the right direction. How can I keep the circle from closing if I am to be cut off from Star Child? We are stronger than ever with the children we carry, cannot you see, they are spirit children, just such as we. And the evil dreamer, he will soon know, and he will come searching for us! He has the power! I do not know where he got it, but he is in control now, Red Eagle is no more. These are the things that I know, but what I am to do? This, nothing tells me!"

"Stay out of it! Let me handle power," he was shaking, "You could be hurt Basket! Power is not something to play with!"

"I was born to power! Even you can feel it, can't you?"

He nodded, "I have always known that there was something . . ." he admitted.

* * *

Star Woman had been going on and on about Blue Coyote as a child.

"How much longer until we reach the canyon," Basket changed the subject, "I seem to tire earlier each day."

"A pair of days and your child will be born at the canyon. You will be able to rest the last moon and let it grow in peace."

"If there is peace to be found in the canyon," She tightened her mouth.

* * *

"We will stop here for a while, "Blue Coyote halted the camp. Star Woman sighed and went with Basket. They sat together on a rock. The camp set up and Blue Coyote made his way to the place where they had laid out Fire Dancer and Scorpion.

"If you are correct, then this stop should help him heal, but I cannot for the sake of it see how talking to a place will help! Fire Dancer is no longer. His spirit would dwell in the place where he died, not where we laid him out. Besides, Acorn released his spirit."

"If it helps Blue Coyote, what does it matter?" Basket rubbed her lower back. "I am just glad we are here. I do not think I could go another hand of days. It is hard to believe that I was so excited the first time this child kicked. It seems to have done nothing else ever since! I just want to lie down until it is born! It takes all of my strength just to keep from screaming each time it kicks, and it does so with more and more frequency"

"We will be in the canyon before dark. I am sure that Blue Coyote will have your shelter erected right away. Then you can lie down."

"Only until I need to pass water again," Basket groaned.

"When you lie down, the pressure is shifted and that feeling will be less. You will be able to rest!"

"That is what you say; you are not being kicked to bits from the inside!"

"The child is active because you have been constantly moving. Once you are settled in the camp, this will let up."

They rested until Blue Coyote returned and led them on into the canyon. True to Star Woman's prediction, Blue Coyote ordered the setting up of their shelter first, and he and Star Woman got Basket settled in.

"Mother will be by with you meal shortly," he handed her a horn of tea. "She sent this, said it would help with the back pain. Are you in much pain? You have not said anything."

"There is nothing to say. Star Woman assures me that every woman has pain in the back. It comes from carrying the load in the front. I am better now, and if I can just stay in one place until it is born, perhaps this child will stop kicking in protest!"

"Maybe there is a pair; after all you are a twin!"

"No, Star Woman could discover only one heart beating, and I only feel a single set of feet kicking. Do you think we could settle the camp farther up the canyon, where it is a bit more hidden? This place makes me nervous!"

Blue Coyote sighed, "Mother has already made the same suggestion. Honestly Basket, why are you worried? We all know there were no strangers here. No strangers attacked Father, or Bison Man. We all know the cause of their deaths. We are perfectly safe here."

"No, we are not!" Basket protested, "We did not want to come to this place, but I know you had a reason, so we came here, I know that you do not know how I know, and I will not tell you. The danger, however, is real!"

He shook his head stubbornly, "Soft Wind died here! She shouted at him!"

"How would you know that?" Se shook his head, "Soft Wind went with Stone Man!"

"I just know!" She said equally stubbornly.

"Well I hope you are embarrassed when you see her again and have to explain how you knew of her death!"

Basket began struggling to get to her feet.

"What are you doing?"

"Getting up!"

"You just got laid down, where are you going!" He called after her as she awkwardly gathered up her sleeping furs and waddled from the shelter.

"To find a place where I feel safe!" she shouted at him.

"Basket!" He followed her, "Be reasonable! Come back to the shelter and lie down."

"Will you move the camp to a safer place tomorrow?" She stopped.

"Very well," He shook his head, "If it is that important to you, we will move the camp to wherever you want it! Now will you please return to the shelter and lie down?"

She sagged, "I can't" she whimpered, "I think my water just broke!"

"Mother!" he shouted, "Water Woman! Help me get her back to the shelter! She is having the baby! Now!"

The whole camp came running. They finally got Basket back to the shelter and settled on her furs. "Go be with the men!" Star Woman shooed Blue Coyote from the shelter, "Water Woman, get those skins ready, and get the water heating!"

"Come on Basket, Lie back and let me look! Spirit's alive," she muttered, "No wonder you were hurting. How long have you been having labor pains?"

"Labor pains? I haven't had any labor pains! It is just this constant kicking!"

"Basket, you are having this baby, Now!" Star Woman hurried about, "I can see the head, she is fully open. How on earth have you been able to walk?"

"It hurt!" Basket admitted "But I thought of other things and it wasn't so bad." Now she grabbed Star Woman's hand, "That was a labor pain," she hissed through gritted teeth, as her body rolled in contraction.

"Here, try to drink some of this!" Star Woman put the horn to Basket's lips.

"Not now!" She groaned and doubled over.

"The head is out," called Water Woman, "Quick I have it!" She called as the baby slid into her waiting hands. Even before they tied and cut the umbilical cord, the infant began howling in protest.

"Nothing wrong with her temper!" she handed the squirming bundle to Star Woman.

Water Woman finished cleaning up, removed the after birth and got Basket settled with her new daughter. The babe hushed immediately when she was placed to Basket's breast. She grabbed the nipple and began pulling noisily at it. "Will you look at that?" Basket laughed weakly.

* * *

I have a daughter! Basket called out!

So have I! Came the tired response . . .

Later . . .

Yes, later . . .

She lay cuddling her beautiful, perfect daughter, and drifted off to sleep.

You are pleased? Wolf Spirit questioned, *she is as I promised.*

"She is perfect!" murmured Basket.

* * *

Now you must leave the canyon! I gave her to you early, the birth was easy, and she is strong. Evil comes from the south. In a pair of days the camp must leave the canyon. Go north to the river near where the flint is; follow it for a moon, then rest.

"Yes," murmured Basket. She sighed and slept.

* * *

Acorn waited for Blue Coyote to return to the camp. He had left early and went to where Bison Man had been laid out. There were fragments of the bundle, part of a skull, nothing more. He said the things he came to say and felt better for it afterwards. Another bit of his soul healed.

"What is it Acorn?" Blue Coyote questioned "You seem upset!"

"I had a vision last night!" The dreamer began, "Death comes to us, from the south, we must leave this place tomorrow, or it will be too late!"

"That is impossible!" Blue Coyote shook his head. "Basket just gave birth last night. She will be in no shape to travel for at least a hand of days!"

"We must leave tomorrow! Put her on a travois if necessary but get out of this canyon or we will all die here!" Acorn was white and shaking. "You have no idea the horror which comes from the south! I have seen it! They rip the still beating hearts from their victim and while the heart still pumps drink the blood! Then the body is cast into the fire, its soul trapped forever in the burning flames! Is this what you want for your family, friends, and new child?"

"You say you saw this in a vision? Tell me of it?" Blue Coyote drew him to the hearth and sat him down.

"I saw it! A large stone, people gathered all around it. They led her there and a tall man, he took a knife, shaped like none I have ever seen and he cut her heart from her body, and drank her blood while the heart still beat."

"Who? Whom did you see?"

"Soft Wind," whispered the dreamer, "I saw her death!" He began to shake again, "They are near here now. They seek new sacrifices to feed their hungry spirits! They know that we are here, and they come for us! Please, Blue Coyote! If you never again believe anything I tell you, believe this!"

"I believe that you saw something, Acorn, and if you insist I will believe that you truly mean well, but it is out of the question. Basket needs to rest. We have seen no one, and if it will make you feel better, I will post watchers around the camp, but we are not leaving!" He rose and went to the shelter where amazingly Basket was up, fully dressed and busily packing.

"What is this?" He questioned "Have you lost your mind?" He began angrily pulling things out that she had just packed. "I am really losing patience with this, Basket! It is bad enough that you try to scare me, but to frighten old Acorn like that, really! How did you do it? Have someone give him something?"

"What are you talking about Blue Coyote? Give that to me?" She grabbed the hides from his hand and shoved them back into the pack. "I haven't seen the dreamer since we came into the valley, unless it escapes you, I was rather busy last night, bringing your daughter into the world, and now if you won't help, then at least don't get in the way."

"What do you think you are doing?"

"Packing! What does it look like?" She brushed her hair from her face, "And believe me, if Acorn had a vision anything like the one I had, he is packing as well!" She brushed angrily by him, "Stay here if you insist, but your daughter and I, we are leaving this place."

"Don't I have anything to say about that?"

"Only if it is 'how can I help'," she answered.

"All right! All right! I can fight one of you, but not both! How can I help?" He gave in.

"Get the people up and moving just as quickly as you can. Don't bother packing everything, hopefully, little has been unpacked, but we must be away from this place before midday today."

"I don't suppose you were told where we are to go?"

"North, to the river by the flint, follow it for a moon, there we will be safe."

"Basket, you are in no condition to travel like that!"

"I can ride the travois if necessary. Throw Back can pull us."

"Where is Mother?"

"She said something about Water Woman, I don't know, I wasn't paying much attention." Basket admitted, "I think they were going somewhere, I don't know!"

"I will find someone to help you, sit down and rest," he led her to a log and made her sit. "I will get us out of the canyon before midday, I promise."

He went through the camp, advising everyone to pack up again, they were leaving immediately, he called and asked, but no one seemed to know where Star Woman and Water Woman had gone, but one of the women suggested to bury the afterbirth. He had their things packed directly on the wolves and the travois poles loaded into backpacks, and with a sigh of relief finally saw them returning to the camp from up the canyon. He rushed to them and hurried them back to the camp. They were out of the canyon just before midday.

"Stay behind us and keep a sharp eye out," he advised Badger and Jackrabbit. "I have never seen Basket so upset, or Acorn."

"Will she be all right?" questioned Badger.

"For now she seems fine, and if later she needs to be carried, we will support her between hunters, as we have injured before. The most important thing just now seems to be away from this place. We go, and quickly!" He led the way.

They traveled for a hand of time. Badger and Jackrabbit joined them, their faces white and pinched. "We escaped just in time!" They reported. "You were no more than out of sight before they came! More than I could count and they swarmed down into the canyon like vultures to a kill."

"Do they follow?"

"Not yet, I think they found something in the canyon," admitted Badger, "I heard screaming!"

"Who is not here?" Blue Coyote shouted, "Who is not accounted for!"

"Journey's Far," Cotton Tail wailed, "He took Chert Boy out for a walk. I thought he was with the wolves, but he isn't" she began sobbing.

"Acorn, Mother, Water Woman, help Basket. Lead the camp north to the river, we will catch up, go now!" He ordered, "Come on Badger, Jackrabbit," he headed back toward the canyon.

Acorn called the camp forward and they kept going, Blue Coyote led the pair of hunters back to the canyon. They approached carefully, easing to the brink of the edge. Their camp was alive with activity. Hideously painted men were laughing as they jerked and pulled at the lifeless body of Journey's Far. Beyond sat a string of people, tied together and led by a huge man, a man who held the largest club Blue Coyote had ever seen in his hand as casually as though it were a twig.

Already the place where so recently Basket had given birth had been cleared and a huge hearth prepared. Hunters were putting together a cage, beyond the hearth. Others were setting up shelters and all were laughing and shouting.

Finally the men tired of tossing the dead flesh and cast the body aside. One of the women tied in the line held onto Chert Boy. They watched for a hand of time and when the cage was completed the people were herded into it and it was secured. A large drum was set up and soon the steady beat could be heard all up and down the canyon.

"What can we do?" Whispered Badger, "We are only three against . . ." he gulped.

"I don't know, but so long as Chert Boy lives, we have to try to save him. And we might as well get those other people out as well."

"I know of a trail down into the canyon beyond their camp. Maybe we could sneak in after dark and get the boy. He could be passed through the bars of the cage!" Jackrabbit offered.

"And just leave those people!"

"Surely if we can get the child, we can get the others as well!" Blue Coyote was already easing back from the edge, "Show us this trail," he whispered to Jackrabbit.

"Why?" Badger whispered.

"There are at least a span of men being held prisoner by these savages. Perhaps you have not noticed, but except for the dreamer, there are dangerously few men in the camp. We could use them!"

"Here is the trail, be careful, it is steep!" Jackrabbit led the way.

Hand by hand they eased down the treacherous steep and narrow trail.

They reached the canyon floor without detection. Now the people of this camp were mostly gathered around the hearth. The shelters were empty, the cage unguarded. The beat of the drum increased as they slipped ever closer. It was dark now, Blue Coyote slipped like a shadow to the cage. There was no one about, quickly he sliced the cords holding it closed and motioning those inside to be silent, he led them from the camp. With difficulty they made it to the top of the canyon, where Wolf waited and before the revelers below realized it they vanished into thin air.

They kept going, at a punishing speed, helping the weaker, supporting those in need, until they felt certain they were safe. As long as they could hear, and that was for a great distance, the celebrants had not noticed that their prisoners were gone. Now behind them all was silence. Going became more difficult once the moon set, but they kept going. Near dawn they reached the camp and roused it. The tired and ill were loaded onto travois and the camp pushed on. No one spoke, not the recent prisoners or any member of the frightened camp. They just ran!

"Get on the travois!" Blue Coyote supported the exhausted Basket.

"There are others . . ." she began, but got no farther. He lifted her and placed her on the travois, "Mother, stay with her and make sure that she stays there. I do not want to look back again and find her walking!" Star Woman nodded.

"How many days have we been traveling?" Basket questioned in a weak voice "It seems like forever!"

"We left the canyon a span of days ago, according to Acorn we must keep going for a full moon before we are safe. Here is Moth with your daughter." Star Woman took the baby and tucked her next to Basket. "If you do not stay on that travois, you are going to bleed to death! Blue Coyote is right, you know. It will serve no purpose if you drive yourself to exhaustion."

"I know, but poor Throw Back, it is not fair to her, she is stumbling herself."

"I think we will stop and rest for a day. We have been pushing so hard I am sure that we are no longer followed. Everyone needs to rest!" Blue Coyote walked beside Basket's travois.

Basket shook her head, "Keep going, the spirit said not to stop until a full moon had passed. Maybe they follow, or maybe another group that we know nothing about will be in this area, I do not know, but we cannot stoop until the full moon has passed."

"But we have made excellent time! There are some that just cannot go farther, and I do not know if I can either. I am so tired. I have not slept in nearly a span of days." Star Woman admitted.

* * *

"Ask your Wolf Spirit and perhaps she will give you an answer."

"I will ask!" Basket slipped into sleep.

I am so tired, need to rest, she muttered in her sleep.

* * *

There is a cave just ahead, high up the cliff. It looks to be only a small opening, but inside it is large, and there is water there. Take the people to this cave and send the hunters out for a hand of deer. Destroy any sign of presence. Stay in the cave for a span of days. Do not leave the cave for any reason! Those you fear will pass you by and then it will be safe to continue on.

* * *

"I must talk with Blue Coyote. The Wolf Spirit has sent a message," she woke and immediately called to Star Woman.

"There is a cave such as you described just there," he pointed. "I will send Badger to investigate. Everyone, wait here, we rest for a short while!" He called and had the message passed down the line. People merely sat where they stood.

"She is right!" Badger reported back, "The cave is very large inside, there is plenty of room for us and the wolves, and there is even water in there."

"Start getting the people inside, have someone help you with Basket, I do not want her trying to climb up there alone. I will get hunters after the deer in the meantime." Blue Coyote went to where Jackrabbit stood. "Have you been able to talk to these people at all?"

"Not really, but I think we are communicating. I will try to get a message across."

"We need several hunters to go with us after deer, can you tell him that?"

"I will try." Jackrabbit taped himself and Blue Coyote on the chest and then pointed to three of the new people. He made a sweeping move with his hand pointing up and down the canyon, then took atlatl and dart out and moved like he was hunting. Then he made antlers of his hands and looked at the man. The man grinned and nodded, calling something to a pair of others and they came to join Jackrabbit and Blue Coyote. The men quietly headed up the canyon, atlatl and dart ready. Badger meanwhile did his best getting the remainder of their three span in number up and into the cave.

Basket had to have help. In the end, a man on either side all but lifted and carried her up and into the cave. Star Woman carried the baby, and an exhausted Throw Back crawled behind them, too tired to stand upright. Basket was settled on furs against the wall and the wolf dropped beside her and was instantly sound asleep. Basket followed very shortly. When she woke, all was quiet in the cave. Someone had lighted torches and there was a small fire farther back, its smoke drifting yet farther back into the cave.

Throw Back opened one eye as Blue Coyote led his hunters in, each carrying a deer, then they went back out and carried in another load. In all they had killed a span of deer. Yet they could not stop. Now they went back out to the trail and removed any sign of their passing, for a distance far down the river. It was nearly dark when they returned.

"Set up a guard at the mouth of the cave," he instructed. "Tomorrow I am moving the people even farther back into the cave. Even if they should discover this place and come to investigate, they will find no sign that we are here."

Badger nodded and he and one of the new people took up watch at the mouth of the cave. Below them nothing moved but a few night animals. Far up the valley, however, the savages began sounding on the drum.

"Can you tell where they are?" Blue Coyote squatted beside Badger late in the night.

"Still a long way away, I think. Sound travels far in a valley. But they will be here tomorrow. It is a good thing that Basket's Wolf Spirit has warned us, or we would have been caught. We would have walked right into them."

"I just hope this cave proves to be safe, or we have trapped ourselves."

"Unless they are searching, no one would think to look here, the entrance is so small that a large man barely fits through. You had to hand the deer in because it was too small for you to carry them in. I would not bother searching this place if I were looking for even a single person. Besides, it is hidden from that direction. The brush conceals it."

"That's it! Come on!"

"Where are you going?"

"You just gave me an idea. We are going to make the entrance to this cave vanish!"

"I am coming!" Badger grinned, instantly catching on. The other man scratched his head and then grinned as well. They scrambled down the trail and quickly dug up a pair of small bushes, taking care to smooth the ground afterwards. Within a finger of time, the entrance to the cave was no more than a shadow behind the brush. Then Blue Coyote sighed in relief.

The next day the savages swarmed down the valley. They made no effort to be quiet, but laughed and shouted as they went. They were not looking for anyone; that was obvious. They seemed to be heading for a special goal. Blue Coyote guessed the canyon, to join with the others. They also had a string of prisoners. They camped just beyond the bend.

"What do you think? Dare we try to free them?"

"We could be endangering the whole camp?"

"We also could be adding greatly to our number! Call their leader over here!" He nodded to the silent group watching. Badger went to the man who seemed to be the leader and motioned him to join them. The man nodded and did so. Blue Coyote drew the river in the dirt. He marked the cave and the camp of the strangers. Then he raised both hands and then one more, holding his hand together like he was being led. The man nodded. Slowly, using the drawing and hand motions Blue Coyote got his message across. Would they help he and Badger see if they could rescue these prisoners? The man grinned and nodded, pointing to a pair other of his group. Blue Coyote agreed and as soon as it was good and dark the hand of men slipped beyond the brush and down into the valley.

The savages were not expecting any trouble. They had gathered noisily around their central hearth and were dancing and passing around bladders of what looked to be fermented drink. The prisoners were as before, being held in a cage. They had but a single guard and he was watching the celebration at the central hearth. One dart and he crumpled to the ground. Blue Coyote cut the binding and motioning the people inside to silence he led them back up the canyon. Badger motioned one of the other men to carry the body of the dead guard and he brushed away their trail. One more group of prisoners simply vanished.

The new group of people was as easily communicated with as the first. Not only did they not understand the language of The People, it seemed they did not understand the others either. But they easily had a span of days to get to know each other. First, however, they were settled down to sleep and Blue Coyote and Badger carried the body of the slain guard down one of the side paths inside the cave and dumped him there. Jackrabbit stayed on guard at the entrance.

The camp was far back in the cave now. Morning brought the savages swarming back up the canyon, searching for their escaped prisoners. They did not even give the brush near the top of the cliff a second glance. They searched and searched, finally giving up. Blue Coyote and the leader of the new group both gave a sigh of relief as they watched the last of the savages disappear around the bend. A pair of days later, he decided the danger was past. Still, a guard was kept posted.

Basket was feeling much better. The bleeding had stopped and she was regaining her strength. She lay comfortably on her furs against the wall of the cave. A hearth fire was burning in the middle of the large room and a number of torches were lighted as well. Over a hand of spans of people now occupied the camp. She watched them going about their daily chores and smiled as the difficulties of communication began to be solved.

Blue Coyote called the headman of the first group to him. Now they had time to get acquainted. He pointed to himself and said "Blue Coyote!" Then to where Basket lay, "Basket!" He continued on, naming each member of the camp.

The man grinned and pointed to himself, "Gatherer", then to each of his people, "Raccoon, Carp, Possum, Shell Fish, Black Tail, Diver, Sand Digger," and to the women, "Wind Song, Whispering Breeze, and Sun Woman." Each nodded as their name was called.

The new group of people had gathered together to watch this. They began to smile and nod among themselves. Then one stepped forward and bowed to Blue Coyote. Blue Coyote nodded and the man pointed to himself, "Nighthawk," he said, and then introduced his group. "Whippoorwill, Owl, Swamp Cat, Palm Leaf, Shark's Tooth, Wolf Caller, Thunder, Dream Catcher, Sparrow," and to the women, "Fawn, Blossom, Heron, Raven, Swift Fox." Now everyone had a name, known to all.

Acorn stepped forward and held up his Sacred Bundle and looked at the new people questioning. Dream Catcher nodded and stepped forward, the pair drifted away learning . . .

Blue Coyote called out for a healer, no one understood. Then he brought out herbs and made the motions of fever and stomach ache. Owl of the new group stepped forward and nodded, he was a healer. Blue Coyote grinned and gave him a special welcome.

Star Woman was called forward and she gathered together the women and led them to the woman's side of the cave. The men began to try to make each other understood. The days passed.

Basket regained her strength, rest helped, and the powders of the healer Owl did even more.

It was finally learned that the first group of people they had rescued came from a big river far to the east of the plains, the second, from the shores of a great salt sea an equal distance to the south. Soon both groups had learned a few words of the language and as the days passed even more. The woman Raven took an immediate liking to Basket and her baby. Once she had a few words, she was able to explain that she also had a small child, but that the savages had killed it, a boy of but a season.

Moth carried Chert Boy, now able to take steps on his own to Basket. The child entertained himself by crawling all over the ever-patient Throw Back who even let him hold on to her fur and led him a few steps. He tottered to Basket and laughed, "Mama!" He said.

"You have a son as well?" Raven managed to communicate.

Basket shook her head, unable to explain that his mother was dead, and she and the other women of the camp took turns caring for the child. Something must have gotten through for she could see a yearning and pain in the other woman's eyes. Basket determined to speak to Blue Coyote. Perhaps there was a family for Mourning Dove's child yet, or at least a mother, one who wanted him.

At the end of a span of days, Basket was completely well, the camp was rested, and savages had not again been seen, nor heard. They were ready to move on. Blue Coyote had explained to the new people that they would be following the river valley for another double span of days and then setting up a winter camp. He also had made the offer that the new people were welcome to join with The People and become one camp, pointing out that together they would be a safe and powerful group; whereas separated they were open to attack. It was decided to join.

It was an overcast day when they left the cave and began to journey up the river. Far away thunder rolled, yet it did not rain on them. Basket could now walk with little strain. Star Woman and Rain Woman walked with her, as did one of the new women, the one called Raven. She looked so longingly at Chert Boy that finally Basket had spoken to Blue Coyote, and with his permission had given the care of Chert Boy over to Raven.

All day they followed the river, during the night they could still hear the distant thunder. The morning brought another dull overcast day. As the day wore on, Throw Back began to whine and she continually skewed the travois. Finally Basket got so tired of straightening it she squatted to release the wolf from the traces. It was then that she could feel the faint vibration of the ground. "Something is wrong!" She shouted to Blue Coyote. "Throw Back has been trying to tell me, but I have not listened. Feel the ground!"

The headman of the River People said something to Blue Coyote and motioned away from the river. "Get the people to high ground!" Shouted Blue Coyote, "Quickly!" He began leading travois and people to the highest point of the valley, some distance away, through heavy brush and over rocky ground.

Throw Back began to bark and leap, making the release of the travois straps impossible. Finally, Basket pulled out her knife and cut the traces. The wolf shot away, barking for Basket to follow. She carried the baby in her arms and all but drug Chert Boy after her. She was still struggling through the brush when the ground began to vibrate, the sound building. She glanced upriver and blanched. Coming directly toward them was a wall of water higher that a pair of men, one atop the other. She glanced ahead, and realized that she would not make it, not dragging the toddler with her, she screamed for help, but the water mesmerized all. She struggled, the hem of her tunic caught on a branch. Star Woman saw her predicament and ran to take the infant. Basket jerked at her tunic and just as the water hit was released. She leaped forward, but the water caught Chert Boy and tore the screaming toddler from her grasp. Throw Back shot past Basket into the now raging torrent of water and swam desperately for the child. She reached him and grasped his tunic in her teeth paddling with all of her strength toward the dry land. Men ran along beside her, shouting to her, finally she was able to get her feet on land and drag the child from the water. Someone grabbed Chert Boy, just before a rolling log struck the wolf on the hindquarters and dragged her back into the river. She gave a frightened yelp and was pulled under.

The hunters followed, eventually they returned, carrying the body of the wolf with them. Basket wailed when she saw them. Throw Back, her trusted friend and protector was no more than a limp mass of broken bones and dead flesh. Blue Coyote tried to console her, to no avail. Chert Boy was alive, no thanks to her, and Throw Back was dead, and it was all her fault. Had she just paid more attention!

"We will camp here this night," Blue Coyote directed those around him. "Please Basket, come away, there is nothing you can do for her."

"No, there is not! I have already done it. I have killed her!" She sobbed, holding the head of her old friend in her arms and adding her tears to the water-logged body. "At least I will give her a proper farewell," she rose and laid the wolf's corpse on her sleeping fur and dragged it off beyond the camp. On a high place, where the sun would touch early in the morning, she laid the wolf, wrapping her in the sleeping fur. Beside her she placed a portion of food and then said a prayer to help her spirit reached her own ancestor fires, wherever they might be. Then weeping she sat beside the body, until Star Woman came and begged her to return to the camp. Reluctantly Basket walked away forever from the most loyal soul she had ever known. She left a part of her own spirit behind.

By morning the river was returned to its original level, the flood waters from upstream passed. Basket walked numbly beside Star Woman, tears still streaming down her face. Raven carried Chert Boy. Basket had lost all of her personal possessions, except for the staff, in the flood waters. She didn't even care. She walked, day after day, for a hand of days

*   *   *

It was a mistake! Spirit Wolf admitted, *I should have warned you! The watcher was taken too soon. It was not yet her time. You are in danger so long as you are unprotected.*

"It was my fault!" Basket murmured.

These things just happen. I will find a solution. I will . . .

Wolf Spirit sadly shook her head. *Do not give up!*

"Stop!" Blue Coyote raised his hand.

Sitting in the path, directly before them was a wolf. Its head was tilted to one side, and on its face was an expression that on a human would have been described as a grin. Its ears flipped forward, its tongue hung out, and its feet were absolutely the largest he had ever seen, but for one other pup, one such as this. This one however, was completely white, and it was at the most three moons old. The blue eyes looked directly into his, and he stood silently as the animal gamboled past him and went to stand beside Basket. It whined and licked her leg, wagging its tail. Basket ignored the animal, walking on as if it did not exist. The wolf fell into step, just behind Basket and walked there the remainder of the day.

When Basket and Blue Coyote slept, the wolf watched but an arm's length away.

I have found the solution! Spirit Wolf spoke.

I don't want this wolf! I want Throw Back! Basket cried.

Look carefully, woman, before you reject my gift. Spirit Wolf said angrily, *I have broken the rules for you!*

Basket sat up and looked at the wolf, the old twinkle was in its blue eyes, and it wagged its tail in greeting. "Throw Back!" she whispered,

"Woof!" She was softly answered. She reached and ran her hands through the thick soft, ever so familiar fur. "You have come back?"

"Woof!" answered the wolf, crawling to cuddle next to her, licking her face and squirming in delight as she tickled its belly in return.

"What am I to call you? If I name you Throw Back, others will know, and they might kill you again out of fear. I must give you a different name."

The wolf wagged her tail, fanning the air.

Basket tilted her head, for if you looked really close, one could almost see through the animal, it was not, at least yet, completely of this world. "I will call you Spirit Wolf, I think. Do you like that name?"

"Woof!" was her answer.

Basket sighed and lay again to sleep, her heart greatly eased.

Thank you! She *called. I did not look closely, in my grief. Your gift is welcome.*

Take care! Heed! Pay attention! was her answer.

CHAPTER 24

Dire Wolf pulled the travois. Stone Man led the way and now, Star Child rode. She was mortally sick of traveling! It seemed that each step she took, the child inside her protested. So it had been decided that she would ride. finally, he stopped. They had followed the river for spans of days always north. Now they settled in a valley with mountains to the east and north and mesas to the west.[1]

It had not been so bad for the next pair of moons. Star Child felt much better without constantly having to move each day. She rested, was pampered and taken care of. But the child inside her seemed determined that she find no rest. Constantly the child kicked!

Stone Man helped Star Child from the travois. They had followed the river until he had decided they were safe. Here they had spent the winter, There was a spring and it had been cleared and provided water for the camp. Rain had revived the area and he had traveled to the Starving Mountains and they now were alive with game and plants. Star Child waddled across to their shelter and sank gratefully down. She would be glad when this child was born. Who would have thought that immediately after their mating she would get pregnant? But this girl was active. She could not imagine how Basket was able to continue to travel in such a condition. Star Child needed help just to go to the spring and wash.

She was glad that Stone Man had decided to spend the summer here at this place and await the birth of their daughter. He of course did not know that it would be a daughter, but Star Child did, and she had already named her Winter Rain, also unknown to Stone Man. The change in their camp was amazing. Gray Wolf had mated with Laughing Water, and they also were having a baby. Rain Woman had accepted Wind Walker and he now was the strong second hand that Stone Man had lost with the death of Bison Man. They were a large and strong camp.

Stone Man had begun to lose the bitterness and hurt he felt toward Blue Coyote, although the name was not mentioned. The time in the canyon far to the south had been healing for him. Only later it had become a place of horror for them all. Soft Wind was mourned by all, for her spirit would never be free to go to the Ancestor Fires, it would be always captured in fire. Star Child sighed. The child kicked and she shifted to a more comfortable position. It would not be long now, a hand of days at the most and her child would be born.

Star Child shifted around and tried to find a more comfortable way to rest. Her lower back was hurting almost unbearably. Rain Woman had assured her that this was indeed a sign that the birth was eminent.

When she was able to travel again, and by then it would be spring, Stone Man planned to lead the camp on north, following the river. They had not seen bison in many moons, but had returned to the way of life which the people had lived in the Starving Mountains, depending on deer, pig, elk, bear and the occasional antelope for meat and gathering heavily on the plants which grew in abundance.

With her pregnancy, it seemed that Star Child and Basket were able to communicate easily, and Wolf Spirit came to her as well. Star Child hoped that one day she would be able to talk to Stone Man about Blue Coyote. She did not want him to spend his life in bitterness. He seemed determined to avoid all the places where they might meet the other camp.

She sighed and lay back, awaiting the birth. The pains began to build, each one harder than the last, and they were much closer together as well. When it really came it was hard. She went into labor and the pains were terrible, the child was not turned properly. All of one day, the night and part of the next day she balanced, squatted in the birthing rack. It did not good. She had no more strength.

Rain Woman called for more hot water. "I am going to try to insert my hand and turn the child. If something is not done soon, Star Child will die."

Singing Serpent stood beside her, "Be sure that you clean very well, for evil spirits on your hands could harm both the woman and the child."

"I will!" She replied. "Help me lay her back onto the furs for I cannot shift the baby with her squatting!" Turtle Woman and Sage helped get Star Child back to her furs. "Now hold her legs apart. I am going to try to move the baby." Slowly she inserted her hand. Star Child bit on the rabbit fur rolled up and inserted in her mouth. She did not scream but the pain was so intense that she fainted. When she became again aware, Turtle Woman stood smiling. She had turned the child. "Now if you will help me get her back to the birthing place, I think we will get this baby born!"

Rain Woman was again cleaning her hand and arm. Star Child was returned to the birthing place and finally, with her last ounce of strength, the child was born, at precisely the same time Basket gave birth.

Evil spirits invaded, and it was only the expert knowledge of healing which Singing Serpent brought into play, which saved Star Child's life. She was ill for a long time. Star Child was unable to nurse, but other new mothers took turns, happy to share their extra milk. Star Child began to fade, but the baby flourished. Winter gave way to spring before Star Child began to recover. She had to be carried everywhere, and even the simplest of tasks was beyond her. Other women came regularly to her and nursed the baby, and Star Child weakly cuddled her the rest of the time. Singing Serpent had begun giving her powders to fight the evil spirits even before the birth. He continued to do so and very gradually Star Child began to get well. Finally she was able to take more than a few steps beyond the camp.

Her link to Basket was as weak as were her legs. Wolf Spirit also stopped visiting her dreams. Slowly, very slowly she gained strength. At her third moon, Winter Rain was named. Star Child, now finally fully recovered, smiled happily at her daughter. She knew that Blue Coyote and his camp were somewhere far to the south on the same river they had followed. She hoped they were safe.

"I think we will leave in a hand of days!" Stone Man decided. "I would find where the river leads. It had been good to us, and I would find its source. We will go north until mid-summer and then, I think, perhaps, find a place along the escarpment to spend the winter. Moon, what do your spirits say?"

"Wolf Spirit finds no fault with this plan, but he does suggest that an offering at the Sacred Spring would be welcomed."

"This, then we will do, when we go to the escarpment. Until then we will make an offering at out own spring. Would this be acceptable to Wolf Spirit?"

"I will ask!" The dreamer replied, "I will give you an answer tomorrow."

Star Child sat late that night, beside the sleeping form of her mate and tried. Nothing! Basket did not answer, nor did Wolf Spirit. She slumped back down and finally slept.

Moon, however, had no trouble; Wolf Spirit found the offering acceptable. So it was decided.

Star Child frowned at the drink. She had been taking it every mourning and night since the birth of Winter Rain. She felt fine. "I see no reason to continue with this medicine!" she protested when Singing Serpent brought it to her. "I have again begun my woman's bleeding, and I feel fine."

"When was the last time that you had a flow of the evil spirits?"

"At least a moon," She replied.

"Very well, I suppose it can be stopped, but if you discover that the evil flow begins again, or if there are other problems, let me know immediately!" Star Child promised.

Moon came to her then, "you will feel able to make an offering?" he questioned.

"I finished with my woman's blood yesterday," she answered, "which is why I am no longer in the blood shelter, and I feel fine. Is there something which I should be aware of, do I break any taboo if I make the offering?"

"None of which I am aware. Have you communicated with Wolf Spirit?"

Star Child shook her head, "Not since the birth of Winter Rain," she admitted.

"Are you still taking the belladonna?"

"What it that?"

"The medicine the healer has been giving you."

"I quit just today, why?"

"The belladonna is a spirit trapper. Wolf Spirit will not come to you as long as it is in your body."

"Then that is why?" Star Child smiled, "It will be out of my body before the offering to the spring. Perhaps Wolf Spirit will visit me before then. I will try."

"Tomorrow you make the offering at the spring." Rain Woman said "Have you completed the cleansing?"

Star Child nodded, "And I have not been near any man for the last pair of days, all is as it should be."

You might as well remain in the blood shelter tonight as well. You will be safe there."

Star Child nodded and settled back against the support to play with Winter Rain. Already the baby could hold up her head, and her blue eyes were beginning to lose the far away expression of newborns. She snuggled down to sleep, for the offering would be just as Sun Spirit fought its way into the sky.

* * *

Star Child! Where are you? Please answer me! Came the plea.

I am here.

What has happened? I have been calling and calling!

I could not hear you.

Are you all right?

Now I am. Do you fare well?

Now I do, I have much to tell you.

The savages?

They came, Journey's Far died. We are many more now, however. Where are you?

I must go now! Wolf calls me. We will talk again.

* * *

You are pleased, Woman of the Wolf? That spirit questioned. *The child fares well?*

She is wonderful! I am sorry I have not come to you. I did not know! You make the offering?

Yes, do you have any special instructions?

Burn the cedar and carry the smoke over the spring. Do this before the ceremony. There are evil spirits in the air. The dreamer gains strength.

* * *

"Why!" He banged his fist on the shelter support, "So close, but still I cannot catch her!" He ground his teeth together, the single eye glittering with hate and frustration. "Where are they?" He shook his head, the pain shooting through the brain. "They cannot be in a pair of directions! I must have more power!"

"I would speak with you Headman," Hairy Bear groveled before him, "I have exciting news!"

"Well, what is it?" White Falcon grated, "You interrupt my communing with the spirits!"

"That is why; it is a spirit thing of which I bring news!"

"A spirit thing; what nonsense is it this time? Has the Great Beast been talking to you again?" he sneered.

Hairy Bear had the grace to be embarrassed, "No headman, the hunters have just come in from the plain. They have seen a spirit animal. I came right away to tell you."

"A spirit animal?"

"A white bison; Headman."

White Falcon leaped to his feet. "Take me to it!"

"I will show you!" Hairy Bear led the way. "It is not far, just beyond the canyon."

White Falcon lay in the grass, feasting his eyes on the wonder. *I must have it!* He crawled back and joined his hunters, crouched at the head of the trail. "Bring it to me! Complete, whole, not so much as an eyeball missing! Not so much as a single drop of blood! Do you understand?"

"Yes, Headman: now?"

"Of course now! Quickly, before it gets away!"

"You do not think we should cleanse, or at least make a spirit offering first?" they questioned nervously.

"Get that bison!" he shouted at them, causing the whole herd to raise their heads and stamp uneasily. The hunters gulped and began crawling through the grass. The herd settled again to its grazing and they inched toward the white bison. It flicked its tail driving away flies, and stomped its feet as well, for they were gathering at a wound on its fore leg, the reminder of a wolf attack. The animal grunted in surprise as the first shaft was driven into it and bellowed loudly as another pierced his flesh. The herd threw up their heads and thundered away, leaving him to die at the hands of the hunters.

"The hide, I will have a robe of that hide," White Falcon decided. "Be careful! I told you, not so much as a drop of blood!" The hunters were trying to get the large animal onto a hide so they could drag him to the canyon. It was hard work. The headman gave a lot of orders, but little help. Finally they managed and a hand of them took hold of the hide while the rest kept the parts of the animal from touching the ground. By mid-day they had managed to drag it to the Home Cave.

"Get those women out of here! This is a sacred animal; I don't want it contaminated by their spirits?" The hunters drove the three women from the Home Cave barely giving them time to grab their sleeping furs as they fled.

"Someday I will drive a dart into his miserable back!" hissed Spreads Her Legs; sending a look of hatred toward White Falcon.

"If he doesn't dart you first!" Mourning Dove muttered, jerking her fur free of a snag, "I should have been content with Journey's Far. He at least did not beat me!" She stumbled from the cave and followed the others to the blood shelter, where they huddled together.

"You and you! Go and gather green-wood to cure the meat," White Falcon ordered a pair of his hunters. "The rest of you, clear out that trash and throw it out of the cave!" He directed the removal of the remainder of the women's belongings. Already he was prying the eyeballs from the animal and popping first one, then the other into his mouth. "The meat of this animal will be only for me! If I catch any of you eating so much as a bite of it, I will slit your throat!" he hissed, "Now get to work!"

For days he watched as the white bison was cured and its flesh stored at the rear of the cave. The organ meats he had cooked immediately and over the time the rest of the meat was curing, he feasted on them. He saved his own urine and mixed it with the brains and with ash from the fire. The hide was pegged out and Hairy Bear, much to his dismay was assigned the task of tanning the hide.

It took him nearly a hand of days to complete the task, and the whole time White Falcon made sure he never got near any of the women. He was not allowed a single rutt.

The head had been carefully left intact, the skull cap and front of the skull carefully broken and saved. It would be replaced, giving the completed cape the appearance of a living bison head. It was a lot of work! When it was finished, at least White Falcon was pleased.

They had been in the Home Cave for a moon before the bison vanished.

"What do you mean they are gone! They did not merely vanish! Go and find them!"

"They are not there, Headman, the tracks all lead south, but there are no bison. We have looked for a day in all directions."

"Then go out and hunt deer! Are you all so stupid that I must tell you every move to make? This is a big canyon, there are plenty of deer; go and kill a few!" He directed.

"The women, Headman," Sand Crawler reminded, "They want to return to the cave. It is getting cold at night."

"What do I care! Let them freeze."

"But, Headman, the men, they are complaining," he added craftily, "Some have spoken of leaving."

"Very well, let the women come back into the cave, but keep them away from the meat of the white bison! Make sure that they understand, or I will personally slit their filthy throats!"

"I will tell them," he promised inching backwards from the cave. He was smiling happily as he hurried to the blood shelter, each of them had promised him a full night of rutting if he got them back inside the cave. He was a happy man. Spreads Her Legs greeted him by rubbing her ample breasts against him and squirming when he boldly put his hand on her woman's place and began to explore. Mourning Dove merely smiled sourly, Sand Crawler was not much of a ride. Elsewhere stared vacantly into space and sang tunelessly as always. At least, however, they were allowed back inside the cave.

Cold weather settled in and they blocked the cave opening with hides. When the deer meat ran low the hunters went out hunting. The remainder of the time they either swilled the fermented drink that someone or the other of them always seemed to be making, they rode the women, told crude jokes or ate.

"Look over here!" Ground Squirrel called, "Another deer has been taken. There are even more tracks!"

Hairy Bear and Sand Crawler followed Hot Wind and Spider to him. All around the remains of the deer were wolf tracks, lots and lots of wolf tracks. "This makes a hand of them so far. At this rate there will soon be no deer left."

"We should tell the headman," Hot Wind said.

"All he will do is yell at us and call us stupid again!"

"Maybe we are! We follow him!" Hairy Bear grunted, "I think I will go up on the plain tomorrow and see if that herd of antelope is still around."

"I think we should kill all the deer we can now, before the wolves eat them all, or we will find ourselves starving the rest of the winter," Sand Crawler said.

"Fine, the rest of you hunt the deer, I'm going after antelope!" Hairy Bear rose and headed back to the camp. True to his word, he gathered up an extra robe, for it was cold up on the plain, and grabbing an extra hand full of darts he left the cave.

Their trail was not hard to find. The herd was large and the trail fresh. He trotted off following it. A shadow fell in behind him. Hairy Bear was breathing hard before he spotted the antelope. They grazed peacefully up wind. He discarded the extra robe regretfully for the cold was already cutting to the bone, even with his running. He went down on his hands and knees and began crawling to within dart range. He chuckled happily as he brought down first one, then another of the antelope. The herd vanished at a fast run while he shrugged his pair onto his shoulders and circled to pick up his extra robe. He found it and then headed back toward the canyon. Now a full span of shadows followed at some distance, back toward the canyon a wolf howled. Still he trudged on, the antelope beginning to get heavy. He came to a sudden stop. Before him, completely blocking the trail was a hand of wolves. He raised his atlatl and charged a few steps toward them hollering. They bared their fangs, crouched, but did not run.

Hairy Bear stopped. He dropped the antelope and reached for a dart. Even before he got in notched in the atlatl one of the antelope were moving away. He swung around and froze. He was completely encircled. More than a double span of wolves stared at him, their yellow eyes gleaming in the twilight. Behind him one raised its head and howled. At a distance another answered. He darted one, then another before they closed in. While some ripped and tore at his antelope, others stalked him. Now he had the atlatl held like a club, one leaped and he struck it to the ground. The animal crumpled with a yelp, blood spreading beneath its skull. Something struck him in the back. Teeth latched on to his arm and although he rolled onto his back and swung again and again, they kept coming, finally the atlatl broke. He began screaming, but only the wind hard him. Then suddenly he screamed no more.

The wolves lifted their heads and howled. More answered.

The people in the Home Cave heard the wolves; the hunters looked at each other, fear clearly written on their faces. No one spoke of Hairy Bear. They had brought in a hand of deer from their afternoon hunting. The next day they began drying the meat, eating it roasted, and discussing further hunting trips.

Winter set in with a blizzard. They huddled inside the cave and listened to the wolves howling outside. They were closer now. They ran out of water. "You," White Falcon kicked Elsewhere, "Go and bring more water. Take more than that!" She had picked up a single water bag, so she scrambled and gathered a pair more and wrapping an extra robe around her shoulders she slipped through the hide opening. They heard a single terrified scream.

"White Falcon threw down the meat he was eating, onto his scapula and frowned, "Wolves must have got her!" Was all he said casually and then resumed eating.

They found a little blood the next morning, but even the water skins were gone. The hunters, armed and together, gathered the remainder of the water skins and filled them during daylight. They were afraid to go hunting now. Every day the wolves got bolder, and the camp got hungrier. Before they realized it, the deer meat was gone.

Over the moons White Falcon had taken to riding the ugly one whenever it pleased him. She was inventive, he would give her that much. They were holed up in the Home Cave, there was little to do, so he rode her more and more frequently.

The hunters were forced by starvation to go hunting. But there were no more deer, only wolves, so they darted wolves and dragged them into the cave. They ate the wolves and tanned their hides. Now they understood how the Yucca Camp came to wear wolf pelts. The starving time came.

Mourning Dove watched. When White Falcon was busy, had his back turned, she sneaked a bit of his bison meat. For the better part of a moon she fed herself this way. The rest ate the wolves, she did as well. Only White Falcon had plenty of food, he still had over half the bison meat.

He sat, deep in a trance, off on a 'spirit' trip somewhere. This was the time she always picked. Mourning Dove slipped from the fur she was sharing with Sand Crawler and eased to the storage pit. He opened one eye and watched. She grabbed some of the bison meat and tucked it into her waist pouch, then returned to the fur. He rolled over and grabbed her by the throat with one hand and squeezed. "Give it to me!" He hissed. She kicked and struggled, but in the end he merely ripped her pouch free and hungrily wolfed down the meat. Then he kicked her out of the fur, "I am still hungry!" he hissed, "Get me more!"

"I dare not!" she whimpered, "He will notice if any more is gone! I am still hungry!"

"I don't care about your hunger," he glared at her, "Bring me more meat!"

On shaking hands and knees she crawled toward the storage pit. Miserably she grabbed more of the bison meat and brought it to him. Sand Crawler grinned widely and wolfed it down, tossing her a small piece. So began a ritual. Each time White Falcon took the spirit drink, Mourning Dove raided the bison meat, bringing Sand Crawler the larger share, yet grabbing a few bites for herself as well.

The rest of them ate the wolves.

It was inevitable; she had known from the beginning that she would get caught.

White Falcon went to the last container of the bison meat. When he lifted the lid anger flooded over him. The top hand of it was gone. He turned to the group laughing and carrying on as usual. His one eye flashed over the camp, taking in at a glance the frightened face of the ugly one. He dropped the lid and moved with the speed of a striking snake, his hand flashing out and his fingers wrapping like talons about her wrist.

Mourning Dove let out a squeak of protest and the cave went silent. The dreamer dragged her kicking and snarling to the middle of the cave. "He made me do it!" she screamed "It was Sand Crawler, he ate the sacred meat!" She accused.

"Me!" Sand Crawler sputtered, "I know nothing of it! I have eaten the wolves just like everyone else! It is her! I saw her do it! She waits until you are dreaming then she sneaks and gobbles the sacred meat!" He pointed and scrambled back against the wall shaking in terror.

White Falcon trusted his own senses. The sniveling Sand Crawler didn't have the brains or the guts to carry out such a brazen act, but the ugly one did! She was like a snake, ready to strike at any given time. He had enjoyed her body, but even that had become tiring. Almost casually he withdrew his knife. Now she was shaking in terror, her eyes rolling, the whites flashing. She struggled against his grip and he calmly broke her arm in a single savage twist. She screamed in agony and tried to get her feet beneath her. Smiling he released her dangling arm and with lightning speed wrapped his hand in her hair, dragging her relentlessly to the hearth. Mourning Dove moaned and twisted, but she was no match for the dreamer. He put a foot on one leg and stretched her body over a log, then as casually as though he was dining, he brought the knife to her throat and opened it, ear to ear. A gurgling sound brought a gush of blood. He caught it in a handy horn and as the body sagged in death he raised the horn to the others of the camp and drank.

"You have meat now, other than wolves to eat, he shoved her body toward the hunters, "Be careful you do not share her fate." He then turned and with a single cast embedded the knife to the hilt into the chest of Sand Crawler, saying softly, "She may have done the stealing, but you ate as well!" White Falcon walked to where the glaze was beginning in the eyes of the sagging hunter. With a twist of the knife he smoothly cut free the heart and withdrew it. He held it up for all to see, then began to eat. No more sacred meat disappeared. The camp ate what was left of Sand Crawler and Mourning Dove.

White Falcon wrapped in the white bison hide and swallowed the thorn apple drink. He could hear them, the voices, but he could not locate them.

I have a daughter. . . one said.

So have I . . . Another answered.

His eyes snapped open, "They lied!" He snarled, "They promised that one was dead! Yet both live! And now they have bred, like serpents they multiply!" He wrapped the white hide about him and thought; now it all began to make sense. Of course he felt her in more than one direction; for there was not one but a pair of them. He ran his fingers down the smooth surface of Basket's relic staff, absorbing the power and he ran his hand down the rich white hide and felt the power flow into him. Then he sighed, smiling.

They are separated! Their power is lessened! I have the sacred points, I have the relic staff, and I have the white bison hide.

Now every night he listened. Again and again the one from the south called, but the other did not answer. He smiled, maybe....

*   *   *

Stone Man and Star Child walked before the camp, Rain Woman and Wind Walker walked beside them. A happy camp followed. They were following the river, steadily going north. Spring warmed into summer and still they hunted the river valley and the mountains. There was food enough to satisfy all. Falling Water showed them how to capture fish with the nets that until now the women had used to capture quail. He also showed them how to wade slowly, downstream to where a fat trout rested beneath a rock. He fascinated them with the trick of capturing the fish in his bare hands. Others tried, but only he succeeded.

Sun Dancer watched the hunter Grass, until one day he looked back. Mid-Summer would see them mated, yet another bonding of the pair of camps. Stone Man considered having a ceremony uniting them, but so many had already cross-mated, it hardly seemed necessary. Then Running Deer and Sage and Song Bird and Falling Water paired as well.

Star Child sat on a log resting. The sun was high and warm. Below, in the little valley the camp was preparing to move on in the morning. A bird sang happily in a tree. Singing Serpent lay on his back asleep, snoring loudly. Beside him Messenger raised his head and watched a bird circling in the sky. As Star Child watched, the bird flew down and landed on a tree branch a short distance form Messenger. The animal tilted his head and the bird squawked in its raucous voice. The wolf blinked and lifted its head. The bird flew away.

Star Child frowned, not fully understanding, had she seen something or not? She tucked it away in her mind and determined to keep an eye on Messenger in the future. Over a span of days she began to realize that Messenger was indeed properly named. Finally she went to Singing Serpent.

"Did you know that Messenger can communicate with the other animals and with birds as well?"

Singing Serpent looked a bit embarrassed, and nodded, "I have known of his ability for a long time. In fact," he admitted, "I have but to tell him what I need and he finds it for me, or tells me where to look."

"He actually talks to you? You can understand what he tells you?"

"Oh yes, in fact it is little different than the way that you and Basket communicate."

Star Child paled, "You know of that?" she whispered.

"I will not tell," he assured her. "Messenger tells me many things. I have wanted for some time to share them with you, yet I did not know how to go about it. I am a healer, I do not like messing in spirit things, but there are times I wonder if I should not speak."

"What do you mean?"

"The danger!" He said softly, "I worry about the danger."

"What Danger?" Star Child sat up straighter and looked directly at him, "There is danger?" she questioned.

He nodded, "It is the dreamer," he sighed. "I did wonder if you knew, for you take great risk he has almost located you."

"What are you talking about? What dreamer?"

"The evil dreamer, the one Basket knew as Red Eagle. He is getting more powerful. He knows about you, and about Winter Rain."

"How can he know?"

"He listens."

"And Messenger has told you this?"

Singing Serpent nodded. "I must alert Basket!"

"No!" Singing Serpent said "Do not do that! You will alert him as well. You cannot speak with Basket again. There is another way, one he is not aware of. But you can take the chance of sending messages this way. It is not fast like how you have been communicating, but it is safe from the dreamer. But for your safety and for Basket's as well, you cannot communicate with her again. He will know where to find you, or her, or both of you. And if he can locate one of you, he will come to kill you and your child."

White-faced Star Child nodded, "How do I send this message?"

"Tell me what you wish to say. I will tell Messenger and he will tell messenger Raven, raven will carry the message to one who travels with Basket."

"Then tell him this: White Falcon listens to us and he knows we are a pair, he seeks to find us. We are in great danger..." Basket will understand.

Singing Serpent nodded and went to where Messenger sat. He squatted and spoke to the wolf. Messenger wagged his tail and loped off. Star Child watched and a short time later a raven flew over, going south. Singing Serpent watched as well. "The message is on its way," he said.

"How will I know if she gets it?"

He shrugged, "Maybe she will reply."

"Star Child," Rain Woman called, "Come here!"

Star Child excused herself and hurried to where Rain Woman and Stone Man stood. "What is it?" She questioned.

"That mountain over there" Rain Woman pointed, "Do you recognize it?"

Star Child studied the place where she pointed "It looks just like the mountain where we were camped when....." she hesitated.

"Where the camps split into a pair" Rain Woman nodded, "I told you!" She turned to Stone Man, "We have come full-circle!"

"We will see." He replied. He picked up his atlatl and darts and led the camp away, in the direction of the familiar mountain. A pair of days later Star Child sat beneath the tree from which she and Basket had cut their staffs. She smiled, a hand of small trees were growing in a circle around the old one. She found a container and went to fetch water. It made her feel much better to thank the old tree once again for its gift. A pair of seasons had passed since they had planted the seeds. It felt right. When the old tree died there would be young ones to take its place, the circle of life went on and on. For several days she made her way to a large boulder near the ring of small trees. Here she took out her graver and carved pictures into the soft sandstone of the boulder. Finally she was satisfied. The boulder told a story.

They would hold their mid-summer ceremony here. Each day Star Child carried water to the old tree and to the seedlings as well. They stayed in the valley for a moon longer than the ceremony, Stone Man deciding that the escarpment was where they would spend the winter. Winter Rain and Star Child were both thriving. It was good to see the healthy glow on Star Child's cheeks again.

They followed a different route to the escarpment. They went directly south, avoiding the place of stone completely. They did not need the stone, for they had an ample supply of obsidian, and the quarry was out of their way. They ambled slowly along, enjoying life. The men hunted in the rough land and the women gathered the plants and brought down birds and rabbets with their bolas. Still, the escarpment was a welcome site.

"I would just as soon set the camp up here." Stone Man indicated a series of caves, at least a hand of days north of the old camp.

"But they face into the wind;" protested Star Child "They will be cold during the winter! Besides, I want to go back to our old caves."

Stone Man frowned but led the way.

Ghosts! Must I constantly face ghosts? He shook his head as he settled his little family into the storage cave. Turtle Woman and Cougar and Rain Woman and Wind Walker moved in with them. It was crowded, but still, they were all good friends and the women helped Star Child with the baby. Winter Rain was now teetering on uncertain legs, holding on to anything handy and taking her first uncertain steps. She jabbered nonstop as well, entertaining herself for hands of time. She was a good baby.

Star Child occasionally left her in the charge of the older women and slipped off to the cave where she and Basket had lived. Stone Man turned a blind eye.

Winter was hard. Star Child became pregnant a second time, she was dreadfully ill, and she lost the child almost before they knew of it. She was depressed for more than a moon after that. Singing Serpent and Star Child spent a lot of time sitting about the hearth and talking. The two-colored eye dog of the healer seemed much in their conversation. Dire Wolf was attacked by a cougar and suffered severe damage. The old wolf seldom left the camp after that, content to watch Winter Rain grow, and keep Star Child company. Spring came and with it the rain. It rained and rained. They decided to stay at the escarpment another season. The acorn crop was going to be the biggest anyone could remember. The deer along the breaks were fat and plentiful and the birds were everywhere. A small herd of bison came to the area and they were able to secure a number of hunting capes. They held the Mid-Summer ceremony at the Sacred Spring. Star Child made the offering. They wandered southward along the escarpment and spent the next winter there many hands of days south of the old camp.

Winter Rain celebrated her first-hand birthday there.

"I think I would like to return to the northern mountains again this spring," Stone Man stretched his long legs before the fire. "Perhaps hunt on the plain for a while after that!"

"We must hold the Mid-Summer ceremony at the Sacred Spring!" Star Child said a bit sharply.

"We shall see," Stone man replied, "What does it matter where we hold it? The spring or the plain, it is all the same."

"I would prefer the Spring," Star Child replied, "This will be a particularly important ceremony. Winter Rain is a hand of seasons old, I would make a special offering," she thought quickly for a reason.

"We will see," Stone Man repeated and Star Child bit her lip but kept her peace. There was time to change his mind.

They ambled north late in the spring. The mountains were filed with plants and animals were plentiful. The men had lived for a hand of seasons hunting as in the Starving Mountains. So many times they had told tales of hunting bison, the newer members of the camp now decided it was time that they also were given the opportunity. As summer approached, they moved closer to the plain. Again they were at the valley where the camps had split.

Star Child took Winter Rain to visit the mesquite tree. The young trees were now taller than a pair of men, one standing on the other's shoulders. The old tree, however, was beginning to die. Many of its branches were dead and broken. Star Child took her stone ax and trimmed away the deadwood. She made a special prayer of thanks to the tree for her and Basket's staffs. But she knew that the circle of time was approaching for the old tree. In a pair of seasons it would be dead, its place in the sun then taken by the ring of trees she and Basket had planted. Star Child smiled. It made her feel much better that the life of the old tree would be carried on in the saplings they had planted, just as their own line would go on through their daughters. The circle of life was no longer closing in on them. But she knew there was still one final task facing her and Basket. At night, sometimes, while Stone Man lay sleeping beside her, Star Child wondered about the approaching encounter.

*   *   *

"I have decided that we will go out on the plain and hunt bison," Stone Man stated as they were preparing to leave the mountain valley. "We will circle out and go to the place of stone for a time. We need to store up on chert. Perhaps then we will go south to the secret valley, perhaps on to the Sacred Spring, we will see."

Star Child opened her mouth to speak and then bit her lip instead and held her silence. The other hunters gathered around Stone Man had a few questions, but in the end they left the mountains and headed for the Place of Stone.

It was empty and showed few signs of recent habitation. The camp settled there for a few days replenishing their supply of stone. Star Child took time to take Winter Rain to the secret cave. She showed her the drawing that she and Aunt Basket had created over the seasons and then Star Child left another. She was satisfied that her last message had been erased. Basket had been here. She wandered restlessly along the canyon, a feeling of urgency sweeping over her almost overpowering her with fear. She trembled. But still she did not bring up the subject with Stone Man again.

From the place of stone they headed out onto the plain, then for some inexplicable reason Stone Man changed his mind and they headed for the Secret Canyon instead. For several days it rained, making traveling miserable. However, they kept moving.

Star Child was feeling increasingly uneasy by every day that passed. She knew they had little time to spare. They would have to push hard now to reach the Sacred Spring by Mid-Summer Ceremony, still, she did not speak.

CHAPTER 25

Basket watched while Raven played with Chert Boy. The child gamboled about like a chipmunk, his stubby little legs pumping as he ran. Raven laughed and pushed her hair behind her shoulders. She had learned much of the language of The People over the past moons. "Come I will show you where our shelter stood," Basket called. Raven picked up the boy and followed. "I cannot believe that it has changed so much?" She shook her head, "Right there and that is where my grandmother and I had our shelter! That tree was just a twig then. And you could stand here and see the moving sand out there."

"I see only rolling hills of grassland," Raven said.

"I know, "Basket replied, "But that is what was there, and we called this land the Starving Mountains, for there was nothing to eat here."

"That is hard to believe!" Raven set the squirming child down.

"But it is true." Blue Coyote came to stand beside Basket. "It is strange, it almost feels like I have come home, yet I can remember how filled with fire I was to leave this place, to lead my people to a better life!" He gave a short laugh, "And now I am happy just to be back here. I feel like rebuilding the camp and settling down here."

"Let's do it!" Basket clapped her hands. "I would like our daughter to grow up in this place where we grew up."

Blue Coyote nodded, "Very well, we will stay in this place for a time perhaps even longer. What do you say people? Does this look like a good place to put down roots?" He shouted to the people gathered around him. Some cheered, some nodded; all were tired of traveling. Basket smiled, yes this was a place to grow, a place to heal, a place filled with memories, memories of a friendship which should never have been broken. With his childhood and youth rich all about him, perhaps Blue Coyote would find the need to repair that broken friendship.

They began cutting saplings and setting up shelter structures. In a span of days a large happy camp had been established. Blue Coyote was off with some of the new people showing them the lay of the land. Basket had helped Star Woman set up her shelter, now shared with Gatherer. It was not close to the one she had shared with Fire Dancer. Now she was ready for a break. She picked up Sun Spirit and calling to Raven left the camp. They went to a rock situated beneath a tree and Basket laid Sun Spirit on her fur to play, while Chert Boy found his own entertainment. The women sat for a while. Basket watched a bird fly high in the sky, thinking how wonderful it must be to be so free. The bird circled, and almost as if she had called to it, landed high up in the tree. It cocked its black head, blinked and cawed several times, then skittered back and forth on the branch, waiting.

Raven sat very still. She listened, she nodded, and then she turned to Basket. "I have a message and the bird tells me that it is for you."

"The bird?" Basket laughed, "You talk to birds?"

"You live with wolves!" Raven nodded.

"All right," Basket said, "What is the message?" She was still chuckling.

"I hope I get all of the words right," Raven bit her lip. "White Falcon listens and he knows that we are a pair. He seeks to find us and there is great danger."

Basket went white as a mating robe. "What did you say...?" she whispered.

Raven repeated the message. "Do you have an answer?"

"Can you send as well as receive messages?"

Raven nodded. "Then send this: The teeth must be reunited, at the Sacred Spring, mid-summer, one hand, take care.

"This is a message? I hope the receiver understands better than I!"

Basket grinned, "She will!"

The camp settled at the Starving Mountains. The men hunted, the women learned from one another, and the children grew. The seasons passed. Chert Boy Grew, and Sun Spirit grew and the pup grew.

"It is time to leave," she said one night as they lay watching the ancestor fires in the sky.

"I know, I feel the pull as well, where do we go?"

"The Sacred Spring," she answered.

He nodded, "When?"

"Mid-Summer."

*   *   *

"That is crazy Basket!" Blue Coyote protested.

"She is right," Acorn stood beside Basket, "It must be done!"

"You don't even know where to look, where to start!"

"I know the place," Jackrabbit said, "It is not something I am likely to forget! I still have bad dreams about that occasion! Perhaps this will bring them to an end."

"You can't really mean that you intend to dig him out so that you can burn his bones!"

"That is not all, for we mean to destroy that place. Remove every single trace of its magic and power. It should have been done at the time, but we did not know. But Basket is right, so long as it remains, as long as he remains, this thing cannot be put to rest. His spirit will not go away! We must go there, and we must remove every trace and burn it. We must burn his bones, commit them to fire and make sure that he cannot return!"

"When do we begin?"

He sighed, "To tell the truth, I have always been curious about that place, after all no one would talk about it, but still we did hear bits here and there. You really do remember where the cave was located?"

"I remember," Jackrabbit replied, "And the sooner the better."

"We begin tomorrow!"

"She will be fine!" Star Woman assured Basket, "I promise you, three adults are quite capable of seeing to one small girl, just you be careful!"

"Jackrabbit says it will take at least a pair of days to get to the place, a pair more to get the cave open again. Then we must remove every trace and burn it all, and then we will be back." Basket followed the men down the trail to the west.

"Are you sure this is the place?"

Jackrabbit nodded, "You see the rock way up on top? The one with the up and down marks scratched into it! That was how we marked the place, not that any of us were likely to forget!" He shivered, "I can still hear his screams echo in my dreams!" He shook himself, "Let's get to it!"

The men began the long process of removing the rocks, it probably took less time than putting them there, for they were able to pry them free and watch them crash to the ground. By evening they had nearly reached the opening. They camped just beyond and the next morning began again. By mid-day they were able to climb inside and before dark had the cave open once again. Torches were lighted and Basket followed Blue Coyote and Jackrabbit and the others inside.

"This is incredible!" she wandered in awe, "It is a shame to destroy such beauty!"

"It is evil!" stated Jackrabbit.

In the morning they began.

"Bring the container here," called Acorn, "Someone, help me get the bones inside."

Gatherer went to help. Jackrabbit brought out scrapers and the rest of the group began the process of removing every trace of the paintings from the wall. Every flake of paint was collected and dumped into another container. The ancient relic point still lay on the ledge. This Basket slipped into her pouch, it was not going into the fire. All day they worked. They finished well after dark, which did not matter for they worked by torch light any way. But no longer did the paintings cover the wall. Then Acorn and Gatherer smeared pine pitch all over the walls. Blue Coyote helped pass the containers out through the mouth where Nighthawk and Wolf Caller took them. There was not so much as a fragment of a moldering sleeping fur left behind. Then all left the cave, all but Acorn. He made a hasty prayer and lighted the pitch. The walls flared with fire, burned brightly for a time and then died. Spirit Wolf had accompanied Basket, but would not enter the cave, instead she stood at the entrance and growled, her lip curled back, and her sharp teeth snarling. Now she ran into the cave and sniffed about, barking and playing, totally unconcerned.

They started another fire before the cave. The paint scraps and everything else collected from the cave were fed into the flames; and finally, the body. All night wood was added to the fire and it burned brightly. The next morning men went back inside and made sure the cave was burned. Then the fire was allowed to die and the ashes were collected in yet another container. This they took with them back to the camp. They sifted through the ashes, removing any unburned bits of wood, the rest were poured into a specially made wolf hide container and tightly sealed.

"Make sure that you have left nothing behind which you will want. Remember, it is a long trip." Those waiting nodded. It was sad to be parting from people you had become so close too over the seasons, yet some chose to stay, and others to go. Star Woman wiped tears from her eyes and she bade farewell to her friends, she would follow her son and his family. Gatherer stood strongly beside her. Yet she smiled, for she hoped, at the end of this journey, to find a sister she had sorely missed for many seasons. Acorn waved them farewell. Dream Catcher went with them, as did Owl and Raven and Chert Boy. Willow and Moth, and Badger stayed.

Sunflower and Dog Boy followed behind Blue Coyote and Basket. Sand Digger led his wolf next, followed by Sun Woman and Whippoorwill, and Wolf Caller. Sparrow and Swift Fox brought up the rear. A hand more, were scattered through the line. This trip however, they were prepared, they carried food, water, and obsidian. They knew the route and they chose freely to go. Part way across what had once been the moving sands; they once more reached the river valley. Now, however it had water running through it. They rested here, filled the water skins and hunted.

"It is hard to believe that this is where we were caught in the blizzard. We dug into the side of the dunes and spent a hand of days caged up with our dogs, fearing it was our last resting place. Now it is a river valley filled with game," Blue Coyote mused. "I wonder if the rest has changed as well."

"Many things change: that is the circle of life. You are born, grow, have children grow old and die. The young follow after, and where once you were a child, now you become an ancestor. Yet in many ways things do not change. Look at our wolves. They are not the same wolves we stole in the secret canyon, yet no one could tell the difference, for we have done as the spirit said, we have not bred sister to brother, and they are strong and loyal companions," Star Woman answered.

"You do not change," Blue Coyote hugged his mate.

"I know," she sighed, "I am still just plain Basket!"

"You have never really forgiven me for that, have you?" he smiled, "It was just one of so many things I was wrong about as a rash youth. How was I to know that you would become the most beautiful thing in my life?"

She tilted her head, "Is that how you see me?" she laughed.

"Absolutely!" he smiled down into her eyes, and Basket could convince herself that he meant it. "You are the very best thing that has ever happened to me. I cannot imagine life without you by my side. It seems now that you have always been there when I needed someone. When I was a child, you shared your berries with me. Then you gave me courage, stood beside me when I was wrong and needed someone, and always you have given me the strength to go on. Now I will need you even more, for I face the hardest task a man can face. I must ask for forgiveness."

"I will be beside you," she promised.

"How can you? How can you, of all people, stand beside me and forever forgive me! I have done you as great a harm as I have done myself! I parted you from Star Child!"

Basket merely smiled.

That night they sat beside the campfire, "You really are sure this cleansing is going to work?"

"We carry the ashes with us, Star Child and I have the power to put the evil to rest."

"You are absolutely certain that it is White Falcon?"

She nodded.

"How can you be certain?"

"Acorn and I figured it out," she answered. "Wolf Spirit said we were right."

"And you say that by casting his ashes into the Sacred Spring you can drive him into the spirit world."

"We already have him trapped in the ashes, he has no where else to go!"

"He was already trapped in the cave, why bother to dig him out and go to all of this trouble? What are the chances that anyone would ever have found that cave?"

"Now there are none," she answered logically.

"Have you any idea where the rest of your camp is?" asked Owl.

"No," Blue Coyote answered, "But if we search long enough, eventually we will find them."

"Perhaps I could help!" offered Dream Catcher, "My spirits may know!"

"We must complete this task first," Basket cut in, "Then you will be free to find them for us!"

The next morning, Basket fell back and walked with Raven. "You are sure? That was the message?" Raven nodded.

Blue Coyote lay snoring gently by her side. *Sister!* She called. *Where are you? Why do you not answer? We go to the Sacred Spring to celebrate the mid-summer!* Basket smiled and lay to sleep. Again the next night and the one after she called and then she stopped for a hand of days, then she called again. Steadily they moved toward the escarpment.

The raven sat on a bare branch waiting. It ruffled its feathers, tilted its head and cawed at them. Raven handed her travois lead to Basket and hurried toward the bird, as she approached the bird cawed several times and flew away. Raven returned to the travelers and fell back in line. She smiled.

Again that night she sent her message.

Far to the east, the one-eyed man smiled.

"It looks just as it did the first time we came here!" Basket stood at the edge of what had once been their camp at the escarpment. You leave a place, and in no time the earth claims it back. There are not even any traces of our shelters, just blackened ground where our hearths were, yet when we left here the game had all been hunted and the plants gathered until there was nothing left. Now the cat tails grow as tall as ever and the game trails are a maze of tracks, just as it was in the Starving Mountains."

"Perhaps constantly moving is the way to live. You are never in one place long enough to devastate the land. It then can heal more quickly," Gatherer said, "It was the same along our river. The places where we kept the camp for more than part of a season died, but seasons later when we returned to them they were as rich and bountiful as this place. This is why my people moved regularly, to give the land a chance to heal."

"We lived for generations in the Starving Mountains, seldom moving the camps more than an easy walk season after season, until there were no longer any animals to hunt, no plants to gather, and the land forced us to leave," Star Woman nodded. "Yet when we returned there the land was rich again with plants and game. Will this happen to those we left behind? Will they also be forced to move to another place?"

"Probably; the spirits do not intend for humans to settle in one place, to put down roots like a tree. We were made with feet for walking otherwise, we would have roots also."

"Legend tells that the ancient ones spent their entire lives following the herds of bison which live on the great plain," Dream Catcher said. "At one time our peoples must have been one, for the tales which your story teller related are almost the same ones we have heard all our lives, and our parents before us. It must have been a long time ago that our people parted, for we had only a few words which all understood."

"I used to think that we were the only people," Blue Coyote remarked, "We did not come across signs of anyone else, even when we moved to the plain, there were no signs of others, but over the past few seasons, such signs are common. We found you, and the Heron group, and the savages seem to be everywhere to the south. There must be people in other places as well. We saw where hunters had been to the west of the Starving Mountains this last season as well."

"It doesn't look like there has been anyone here since we left!" Star Woman said.

"Well let's get settled in, there is no sense in putting up shelters for the short time we will be here, we might just as well use the caves," Blue Coyote stepped forth and headed toward the storage cave, Sun Spirit ran after him. Basket slowly followed, her eyes were sharper than Blue Coyote's, for she saw signs.

Later, after things had been unpacked and put away in the storage cave she slipped away and followed the faint trail to a tiny cave that had once been her home. She lighted a torch and shined it on the wall. She laughed at the message left for her. There were stick figures of a large dog surrounded by many puppies, pregnant women and several figures followed by a whole string of smaller ones. The other part of the camp had obviously thrived. There was a single woman with tears running down her face. "Yes, Sister, I have missed you as well!" Basked whispered. She sighed and with a rabbit skin, erased the message. "Soon," She sighed.

Basket stood at the base of the trail going up to the wolf cave. "Is that where it happened?" Raven questioned. Basket nodded.

"I have not ever been able to go back into that cave. I suppose now it is time that I do so," she bit her lip.

"Would you like me to go with you?"

"I think that would help. I know there is no logic to it, for others lived there afterwards, but the pictures are still bright in my head." Slowly she walked up the path. "That's funny;" she stood in the middle of the cave, "I don't feel a thing! It is just another cave. I can't feel his presence at all; it is as if it didn't happen here at all. I felt him stronger in the spirit cave at the Starving Mountains!" She smiled, "Thank you for coming with me. I do not know if I would have had the courage to face the ghosts by myself, and in the end there are no ghosts here after all." They left the cave, "Perhaps I am not the same person any more, now maybe the past at this place will leave me."

"Can you feel him?" Raven asked later as they sat beneath a tree, grinding mesquite beans into flour.

Basket nodded.

"Mommy! Mommy!" Small feet brought the child running to her. Basket gathered her daughter into her arms and hugged her. "Where is Grandma?" She questioned "She said she was going to take you to gather cat tails!"

Sun Spirit wiggled from her hug. "We did! I got lots and lots of them all by myself!"

"So I can see!" Basket wiped mud from her daughter's face. "What else did you and Grandma do?"

"We hunted quails! Grandma showed me how to put the nets and everything! Then we sneaked behind the silly birds and they all ran into our net and we are eating them tonight!" She finished all in a rush.

"That is wonderful!" Basket clapped, "You are getting to be such a big girl, soon you will be going off and being a mommy yourself!"

"Chert Boy and I are going to be mated some day." Sun Spirit nodded, "And I will have my very own little girl, just like me!"

Basket frowned, *perhaps it isn't such a good idea for her to play so much with Chert Boy! Wait until she meets Winter Rain, things will change then.*

"Well run off and help Grandma with the meal. Raven and I are just about finished here, and we will be there shortly. See if you can wash off some of the mud as well!" She called after the already disappearing child.

"You do not approve of her being too close to Chert Boy, do you?" Raven asked.

"He seems to be a happy enough, well-adjusted child," Basket admitted, "But I cannot get the idea out of my head that there is bad blood there, he is after all Mourning Dove's child."

"Raven frowned, "Maybe it would have been better had I stayed behind with him."

"No, I worry too much! What does it matter their dreams at that age? I had my heart set on Stone Man when I was her seasons! And look at me now, very happily mated to Blue Coyote."

"I had dreams at one time also," Raven smiled wistfully, "Impossible dreams... He was the son of a neighboring headman, so handsome and strong and beautiful! He never even knew I was alive. Poor silly Raven, I cried my eyes out when he mated, to an equally beautiful woman of high status. The messenger did what she had to do and I joined Gatherer and his group when they left. I have been careful not to dream since then."

"You no longer desire to mate and have a family?"

"I did mate, before we left, to a man who was little better than your Red Eagle. He beat me, abused me and got me pregnant. Then he got himself killed."

"And the savages killed your baby," Basket concluded.

"They killed my mate as well. Him I did not mind, but I lived for my child. When he died, it was as if a part of me went with him. But now Chert Boy has taken his place in my heart, and I am content."

"Do you not miss you family?"

Raven shook her head, "I had no family. My parents died when I was little older than Sun Spirit. My Grandmother raised me, and she died before I left with Gatherer."

Sand Digger came down the trail from the plain, his feet flying and his dart bag bouncing against his back. "Bison! He shouted; bison!"

The hunters gathered, "How many?"

"A small herd, but you must come and see; I have never seen one like it!"

Puzzled the men followed him but within a hand returned. "Basket, I think you had better come and see this. Bring the dreamer as well," Blue Coyote came to her, "There is still time before Sun Spirit vanishes."

Basket called Raven to find the dreamer and followed Blue Coyote to the top of the trail. Just beyond the trail grazed a small herd of bison. There was, perhaps a double span of them. She frowned for there was nothing particularly special about them. Then she saw it. "What do you think it means?" she questioned, "I have never heard of such a thing!" She called to the dreamer, "Dream Catcher, what do you think?"

"I have no idea! I have never seen many bison."

"I have seen lots of them, but they are always the same color. Never before have I seen one that was pure white. White is a sacred color. It must be special."

"I will ask my spirits this very night!" Dream Catcher promised.

"They will still be here in the morning," Blue Coyote said, "We will come back then."

"Do you think we should kill it?" Gatherer asked later as they sat about the communal fire.

"I think we should make an offering to it," Basket said, "If it is a sacred animal, the spirits would be angry if we killed it. It would be far better if we protect it from danger."

"How can you do that?"

"I do not know; but killing it does not please my amulet," she replied. "Bison is my spirit animal, this one is special, it was sent to us as a message, but I cannot understand the message. I just know that killing it isn't the answer. Perhaps we can keep this herd in the area and make sure that nothing attacks it."

"Well, since we are the only people here, and since only people could kill a bison of that size, perhaps it is safe."

"I will go tomorrow up to the plain and see if I can find the answer," Basket said.

"And I will seek advice from my spirit tonight!" Dream Catcher rose and left the group. Others followed and soon the camp settled into sleep.

Basket gathered up a water bag and stuffed food into her waist pouch. She left the camp and went up to the plain. The bison herd was still there, mostly lying down, chewing on grass that they had stored in one stomach and brought up again. The white one was there as well, standing, watching the trail. As she stood at the edge of the escarpment it began walking toward her.

*   *   *

Basket felt her amulet begin to throb gently. The mark on her arm sent warm thrills and the feeling began to spread through her body. Calm descended upon her and calmly she walked out to meet the white bison. Spirit Wolf stepped at her side. Behind her, following at a safe distance, Raven watched. The bison came steadily toward Basket. She and the wolf walked steadily toward it. The herd remained calm as the woman and wolf passed among them. When they were but a step apart, Basket stopped.

"You have brought a message," she reached out and touched the white head. Around them a soft blue light began to glow. It enveloped the woman, the wolf and the bison. The watcher held her breath. Basket rubbed the great bison on its face, scratched it behind the ears, and the bison laid its head against her breast. So they stood, for a long while. Then Basket handed the bison a mouthful of meal ground the evening before and thanked the animal. Then she and the wolf turned and left. Raven slipped quietly back to the camp.

Within a finger of time, the bison herd had vanished across the plain.

*   *   *

"Get those travois loaded and the animals ready to go!" The misshapen figure scurried back and forth at the edge of the quarry. It was already hot, but still he insisted on wearing the heavy clumsy bison robe. The head jiggled and wiggled atop his head as he moved. The hind feet dragged sadly across the ground stained a dirty brown from seasons of being dragged in the dirt. The scruffy group of ragged men grumbled and finally did as they were ordered. Their wolf hide tunics were stained with seasons of filth. Their hair and beards were ratted, matted and alive with assorted vermin. One casually scratched his crotch while another blew snot from his nose. The animals were equally matched. Their coats were patched with mange, and the inbreeding had begun to show. Where once had been strong, cross bred dog wolves, were now weak and cowardly. The hunters grabbed them by the scruff and dragged them yelping and whining to their places and roughly harnessed them to the travois.

"What we want to go back to that canyon for?" Hot Wind whined, "The wolves nearly killed us there!"

"The wolves won't be in the canyon, you idiot! They are out on the plains hunting bison. We go there because I say so! I need things that in the hurry of our leaving I left behind. Then we go hunting bison. I need a new hide! This one is all but worn out, it needs replacing!"

"Where you going to find another white one? We never saw another!"

"There are others! This can't be the only one. He was an adult so he must have bred, so there have to be others!"

"Be easier to clean that hide," muttered Spider as he slid into step beside Hot Wind, "Crazy dung ball!"

"I don't want to go back to that canyon. I want to forget that place and the things that happened there!" whimpered Hot Wind. "I still have nightmares about him drinking the ugly one's blood and eating Sand Catcher's heart."

"Yeh! Well I still wake up at night with crawlers, remembering that we ate them! What if we ate their spirits? What if they are in us just waiting to get even?" Spider shuddered.

"I missed Spread's Her Legs for a long time," he sighed, "But we had to eat!"

"What you miss that whore for? You got me, ain't I good enough?"

"Sure you're good enough for humping, but you got not tits! I really liked her tits!"

"Well you ate them, so what you complaining about!"

They ambled from the quarry after the headman.

* * *

"What was it like, Basket?" Raven wanted to know. "I have never seen anything so amazing in all my life. You walked right into that herd of bison, you and the wolf, and they didn't pay any more attention to you than if you had been one of them."

"Bison is my spirit animal," Basket replied, "I have a special connection to them."

"That was more than a special connection! Besides, you looked like you were actually talking to that animal, and what's more it seemed to be answering back."

Basket nodded, "In a way we were talking. I can't explain it, but that animal told me things, and I understood him."

"What sort of things?"

Basket shook her head, "I can't even begin to explain it. It wasn't words, but feelings, of comfort, of contentment. I just came away feeling at peace within my soul. It was like a time of quiet just before a storm. That is in fact what this next moon is, a time of peace, before I must prepare."

"There was another message," Raven sighed, "Not good news I'm afraid."

"What was it?"

"The messenger wolf is dead!"

Basket signed, "I am sorry for Singing Serpent, he was very attached to that animal, I gave it to him, many seasons ago. It was old."

"There won't be any more messages."

"I know. It doesn't matter now." She sighed, "I hope that Dire Wolf was able to breed another. The spirit wolf was her brother."

"Doesn't it scare you, all this 'power' and 'spirit' stuff and everything?"

"I have lived with it all my life. There was a time it made me uncomfortable, but I have grown used to living with it now."

"The Mid-Summer ceremony, it doesn't frighten you?"

"No, oddly enough, it does not; if I feel anything, I feel at peace."

"Is there anything I can do to help?"

"Keep an eye on Sun Spirit, and be there if I need you, beyond that I cannot think of anything. I must go out and collect the things that I will need. That alone will take time. Then there is the cave to prepare. I wish Star Child were here, she is much better at that than I am."

* * *

The next morning Basket left the camp with her gathering basket and staff, Spirit Wolf at her side. They wandered along the escarpment, Basket looking for the plants that she needed, Spirit Wolf chasing rabbits and squirrels and enjoying being young. Over the next hand of days they made several such trips. Then Basket carried everything up the faint path and into the small cave which at one time she and Star Child had shared.

Blue Coyote watched with concerned eyes, and Star Woman kept an eye on Sun Spirit, who missed her mother and could not understand why all-of-a-sudden she did not have time to play with her.

Basket carried bison tallow and water into the cave, and wood for a small fire. She lugged a grinding stone and pounder there as well. Then she was ready. She settled Spirit Wolf in the corner.

She spread tortoise shells around in a circle. Into each she placed the twigs of plants she had gathered especially for this. She lighted her fire and began. First, she burned the cedar, filling the cave with the smoke, nearly choking herself on it in doing so. Then she let the smoke clear. It felt right. She dug in one pouch and brought out chunks of charcoal. These she placed in a hollowed-out stone and added rendered bison tallow to them. Her pounding stone mashed the mixture into a past and she ground it smooth. It was transferred into the first tortoise shell. Then she carefully cleaned the equipment, capturing all the wash water in a container.

Her next color was white. Ash provided the base. The tallow was added, and it was mixed and put into the second shell. Then she went on to the red, it had been harder to find, but the spirits had provided. Far from camp she found a piece of red ochre, just enough for the project. She pounded it into a fine powder before adding the tallow. Yellow followed, made from the yellow ochre that was quite common in this area. Blue had been the hardest color to find. She had searched for a pair of days before she located sufficient bits of blue stone. Now she emptied them into the grinding stone and beat them into a powder as well. This took longer, for some of them were quite hard. Finally, she added the tallow. The paints were ready. This took a single day. She carried the wash water far out into the brush smiling as she remembered the difficulty she had finding the particular tree at one time. Here she dug a deep hole and poured the water into it, careful to remove all traces when she was finished. Power was very particular.

She curled up against Blue Coyote that night and slept soundly.

* * *

The next morning she was ready to begin. She found a piece of charcoal in the ashes of her fire and started beside the entrance. All day she worked with the charcoal. She frowned, erased and redid, until after a pair more days it suited her. Next came the paint. Twigs chewed at the end provided her brushes, a bison scapula her palate. Each day she worked, alone and quietly, the peace afforded by the project soaking into her like water into a sponge. Each night she cuddled up to her mate and slept.

It took her twice as long as it would have Star Child, and the result was only half as good, but it was done. The camp had been at the escarpment half a moon.

Now Basket moved into the cave. The dreamer was also beginning preparations for the Mid-Summer Ceremony, as were all members of the camp. There were animals to hunt for the new men and new women. There were bison caps to be prepared and white tunics for the girls. Spirit quests must be made and journeys completed. The camp was alive with activity.

Basket carried enough wood into the cave for her needs. She also had food and water. She arranged her things just where she wanted them, sleeping fur against the back wall, hearth in the center. She placed her special wolf skin before the fire and seated herself on it. A horn of tea waited for later and a scapula of food sat beside it. She sat quietly, clearing her mind of all thoughts. Then she ate a few bites of the plant food and drank some of the tea. Before her, touching her crossed legs lay her staff. In her lap, where her hand would rest was the tooth, and the sacred point taken from the cave in the Starving Mountains, and the owl feather, given to her when she went to bury the cleaning water. Her hands rested in her lap. Then she waited. Spirit Wolf crawled closer.

A blue glow started in the fire.

*   *   *

Blue Coyote led the hunters up onto the plain and they headed a pair of days to the east, they were after capes. A pair of youths needed them. They were gone more than a hand of days, returning as the last quarter of the moon faded away.

The youths were set to tanning the hides while the men dried and stored the meat. This would be meat not touched by women. Raven was in the blood shelter. Star Woman watched the children and Gatherer accompanied Blue Coyote. Dream Catcher had his own things to prepare. A hand of children played happily in the camp.

Sunflower's baby would be given a name. Sparrow and Swift Fox were mating, as were Sun Woman and Wolf Caller. Fawn would become a woman. Sand Digger watched Raven. He sighed and went about his work. She had no idea he breathed. Raven smiled, when she was free of the blood flow, Raven went to Blue Coyote. She left with a new lift to her step. Blue Coyote called Sand Digger to him and he left with a wide grin on his face and a sparkle in his eye. Another task was added to the Mid-Summer Ceremony.

"But why won't Mammy come out and play with me?" Sun Spirit whimpered, "Doesn't she like me anymore?

"Mommy has special tasks, Sun Spirit. I know that you don't understand now, but one day you will be responsible for those same tasks." Star Woman explained.

"Will I have to do them alone, like Mommy, or will Winter Rain help me?" Innocently the child questioned.

"Winter Rain?" Who is that, one of your imaginary playmates?"

"Don't you know who Winter Rain is, Grandma?" Sun Spirit put her hands oh her hips. "She is Aunt Star Child's daughter. She is just the same age as me, and we will do everything together!" Sun Spirit stated.

Star Woman went very pale and her hand began to shake. *Not already! She is so young!*

"I am sure that however you do it, it will be done just as properly as Mama now does it," Star Woman answered, and dug out Sun Spirits' favorite toy, a doll she had made for her of wood and rabbit fur. The child ran off happily to play.

The blue glow vibrated, almost like a living thing as slowly it grew, pulsing and shimmering. Slowly it began to encase them; the woman and the wolf at her side. Basket stroked the relic tooth, just as she had so many seasons ago in this very same cave. Then there had been a pair of them. Now there was but one, but soon, very soon! She drew the power into herself, slowly, steadily. For a long while the glow grew brighter and brighter, then it began to fade, losing the color that matched the eyes of the wolf. The fire burned to ashes, the light left the western sky. The woman sighed and opened her eyes. They glowed with a far away light, she smiled. It was done. She finished eating her meal, drank the remainder of the liquid in her horn and sat talking to her wolf for a long while, stroking her soft thick fur.

The dark of the moon arrived. In a few days it would be time to leave for the Mid-Summer Ceremony at the Sacred Spring. The camp was in a festive mood. They had enjoyed the stay at the escarpment, but the men were yearning for action. Too long they had been in one place. They longed for the open plain and the bison herds. Those who had originally been of the Yucca Camp remembered the bison hunting with wondrous tales of heroic hunts. They proudly showed their sacred dart points and wolf carriers to the others. Others could hardly wait for their very own first bison hunt. The river people had tales of strange animals with long tails, and long snouts filled with sharp teeth. They described animals that were as big as a man. Animals that had been know to eat full-grown deer; and the occasional careless man as well. They had stories of hollowed out longs, large enough to hold a hand of men. Logs that carried them along a river so huge, the big river was a simple stream in comparison. Rivers filled with strange creatures they called fish, but fish unlike any found in the mountain streams

The people from the salt sea shore had equally fantastic tales, of fish so big they would feed the entire camp for a pair of seasons; and of others, large enough to eat a man. Still stranger animals that jumped completely out of the water and called men to come and play with them. They told stories of storms, so terrible that the 'cloud which carried live bison' paled into insignificance beside them.

The camp was hard put to provide better. They had only tales of bison herds so large that a man could walk a hand of days and never see the end of the herd and could see no land beyond it. Herds which when they moved caused the very earth to shade and thunder to pale beside the sound. But they did their best.

"Why do we have a Mid-Summer Ceremony?" Chert Boy asked.

Wolf Caller answered, "According to what I was told when I was your age, long ago, when our ancestors were young, all the people of the land were of one tribe. They all walked together, hunting and living on the vast grassland. But as time went by, they forgot each other and soon they did not even speak the same language. The spirits were worried. If the people forgot each other, perhaps they would soon forget the spirits as well. So the spirits called all of the people together every season and they gathered on the longest day all in one place. Here they visited, exchanged news. Family members who had been parted were reunited. Mates were chosen from different camps and everyone had a wonderful time. They remembered each other. Soon once again they all spoke the same language. And they all remembered the spirits.

"It isn't that way with us!" Chert Boy replied, "We don't have anybody else."

"But we still have the ceremony!" Blue Coyote said, "And we still give names to the children, and boys become men and girls become women. And we still remember the spirits. We give special offerings to the spirits and ask them to help us. They make the rain come, and the grasses grow so that the animals have food.

The spirits make the birds lay eggs, and the rabbits have babies, and the wolves have pups. And the bison and deer have young. When we do not revere the spirits, they get mad at us, and maybe even stop the rain from falling.

Chert Boy giggled, "How can they stop the rain from falling?"

"It has happened," Blue Coyote frowned, "When I was you age, it happened. We lived in the very camp that we just left. But it had not rained in such a long time that all of the land between there and here was moving sand, there was no food, nor water there. The people had no food either, and we all followed the very same path that you took to reach this camp. Here the rain fell and the spirits were no longer angry, and the people remembered the spirits and did not forget them again. And always since then it has continued to rain. The grass grows on the plain. The oak trees give us acorns and the bison and deer give us food.

"Just because we have a Mid-Summer Ceremony?"

"Well, maybe not just because of that, but it is a part of it."

"Why did we have to come all this way just for it, last season we had it in the camp?"

"We need to have a special ceremony this time. It has been a long while since an offering was made to the Sacred Spring. Since before you were born. It is time to do so again, so that the rain will continue to fall and the animals will continue to provide us with food."

"But Basket made an offering last year. She could have done the same thing this year. It rained, and the animals were there to hunt. I don't see what difference it makes where it is, and this has truly been a long way to walk!" Chert Boy concluded.

Everyone laughed and the hunters again began telling stories of their most memorable hunt.

"Be sure that you do not forget to pack the extra supply of obsidian," Blue Coyote reminded Sand Digger, "Your mind is not on your work lately."

Sand Digger merely grinned. Blue Coyote smiled back. *Women!* He thought and then sobered as he remembered his disastrous past in that area. He kept on with his task. The Men had already made the wolf hide carriers for the new capes. The meat was already loaded into the distinctive carriers so the women would not accidentally contaminate it. New harnesses had been made or old ones repaired. Animals had been carefully checked to be sure only sound healthy ones pulled the travois. The hunting wolves had been separated from the rest so that no one accidentally put one of them to a travois. Pups cavorted about excitedly. Women had gathered tubers and other plants that did not grow on the plain, so that they had a variety to eat. New sacred points had been crafted and attached to the dart shafts carried all the way from the Starving Mountains for that purpose. Travois were being packed and water skins filled. The young wolves had been fitted with special harnesses to carry these, thus relieving some of the weight from the others that pulled.

New shoes had been made, and extras tucked into the packs. Extra travois poles and netting were added to backpacks. When they reached the places where bison grazed, these would be put to use for gathering bison chips for the fires. All was ready.

Basket looked around the cave one last time. Everything was as it should be. She studied the pictures on the wall. *Star Child could have done it better!* She led Spirit Wolf from the cave and rejoined the camp.

"Mommy!" squealed Sun Spirit, wiggling free of Star Woman and running to Basket. Basket picked her up and hugged her. Blue Coyote smiled at her over their daughter's head. All was well with their world.

CHAPTER 26

We staying here long?" Hot Wind questioned.

"As long as I say," White Falcon answered, as he pawed through the items he had buried in the back of the cave. "It has to be here somewhere!" He muttered. "You ever see the Ugly One messing around back here?" He questioned his camp, all standing around watching him.

"Some." Shrugged Spider, "In that spot and others!"

"Did she take anything from here?"

"Something, yeah, but she hid it from me. I didn't get a good look at it." Spider admitted. "It wasn't very big, only about the size of you hand, and it was gray, that's all I can tell you. I thought it was food at first, but it wasn't nothin to eat."

"What did she do with it?" He grabbed the front of Spider's tunic and twisted so that he was right in the smaller man's face, "Where did she take it?"

"Down the valley!" he squeaked, "Probably to the cave. She was real fond of going there!"

White Falcon shoved the other man aside and strode from the cave. A hand of time later he was down on his hands and knees feeling around on the floor of the smaller cave. "It has to be here somewhere! I would have ripped her heart from her and force her to eat it raw had I known!" he muttered. Finally, his fingers found an area where the earth had been disturbed. With a sigh he quickly excavated the spot, breathing in relief as the gray flaked edge of the sacred object was revealed. He wiped the dirt from its surface and rolled back onto his heels. It was undamaged.

They had looked long and hard for another white bison, having no success at all. Finally, White Falcon had settled for cleaning the old hide that he had as best he could. Now it was folded and stored on his travois. He put the sacred object into his waist pouch, where he now carried the other as well. The staff was rolled in a bison hide on the travois as well. "Must take care of the sacred objects, need their power to kill her!" he muttered. He rose and with an evil leer he pulled aside his breechclout and passed water on the place where the Ugly One had buried the sacred object. "Now to be sure there is nothing else buried in the other cave!" he muttered, leaping down the trail.

"I don't care if you understand, just keep digging! I want to be sure they didn't leave anything here that I can use against her!" The motley crew had dug and dragged the better part of the floor of the living cave and dumped it from the ledge. The back of the cave was lower than it had been by nearly the height of a man. Still the Headman demanded they continue. "If you find anything, no matter how insignificantly you think it is, bring it to me!" Under his breath he swore at their intelligence.

Hot Wind was down in the hole at the far back when he let out a yelp and leaped out. "There are bones down there!" he whimpered, "Human bones!"

"You find something?" The headman trotted to the back of the cave a mad gleam in his eyes.

"Bones!" whined Hot Wind, "Somebody buried a baby down there!" He shuffled out of the way, "Probably didn't send the spirit off! He shook his head, "What kind of people would bury a body in a place where people live? It ain't right! No telling how many other bad spirits are around this place! Sure some we know of! I'll bet old Ugly One is laughin at us right now!"

The headman was already down in the hole, sweeping dirt away from the burial, he reached down into the rib cage and brought out a bit of stone, turning it over in his hand. He could feel the power vibrate from it, "Yes!" He chuckled as he tucked it into his waist pouch with the other power objects. He jumped out of the pit, "Keep digging and if you find anything else call me."

"What about them bones?" questioned Hot Wind.

"Throw them out, they are worthless!" White Falcon had already lost interest. "You, over there, have you found anything?" Ground Squirrel was down on his hands and knees digging beneath an extended section of rock, which had been below the floor level when they began. "I can't tell!" He replied, "It might be more bones, but I can't be certain yet. I need something else to dig with; this scapula is so dull it doesn't do any good!"

"Use one of the deer leg bones, bust the end off so it is sharp, use it for digging and scoop the dirt out with the scapula," suggested Spider, "That works pretty good."

Ground Squirrel grunted and was soon having more success. His bones were not human, but they proved more exciting to the headman. "Here, give that to me!" He demanded. Taking the skull from the other man, he knocked the dirt from it and held it up to the light. The long canine teeth extended well below where the jaw once connected. The cranial ridge was high, serving as an attachment for the powerful jaw muscles of the great cat. He picked up a handy rock and broke the maxilla, dropping the teeth free. These also he put in his waist pouch. They had held no power that he could feel, but it could grow.

After a hand of days, there was only rock left to the floor of the cave. Beyond the lip they had dumped an extensive mound of dirt. Nothing more had been excavated however.

Late into the night, well after the ancestor fires were bright in the sky, White Falcon lay in his shelter. He could hear the grunting as Hot Wind and Spider coupled in the next shelter. He paid no attention to them. *Soon! He smiled I have more power that she can imagine! She doesn't know that I come! She can't find the other one, soon I will be more powerful that anyone can imagine! Soon I will have enough power to live forever! Soon! For I will have her power, I will kill her, eat her heart and drink her blood, and I will take her power. Already I have her staff, and the sacred objects, and now I have teeth as well. She knows nothing of the sacred white bison hide. It alone has more power than her puny object. She has only one of the pair of teeth for I have taken her staff, and I have the other sacred objects as well,* he thought. Now he pulled himself up to sit and wait. Almost every night she had called. He knew where she was now, and in less than a moon he would attack at the Sacred Spring. He had only one more object to remove from the canyon. Below the cave, sitting in the stream sat the skull of the

Great Beast. He would take the tusks in the morning. Then it would be time to leave for the Sacred Spring.

Sister! She called, *where are you? Why do you not answer? I go to the Sacred Spring for the Mid-Summer Ceremony! Sister, where are you?* The message came. He smiled and rolled into his sleeping furs.

Tomorrow, he smiled.

"What you want those things for?" Spider questioned, "They are heavy and who's going to carry them any way? Not these dogs! No way they can pull that heavy a load!"

"Then you can pull the travois on which they are loaded!" The headman replied, "Just do it!"

Spider sighed and waded into the water a large stone in his hands. He whacked and pounded, and finally busted the skull around the tusk and it fell free. It fell into the stream with a large splash, drenching him thoroughly. He and another of the men dragged it from the stream and dumped it on the bank. Then he returned to free the other tusk. "Crazy!" He muttered under his breath, "Spider, do this and Spider, do that! Never 'Thank you Spider, a job, well done!' No; nothin but orders and kickin!"

Finally, the tusks were loaded onto travois, each one on a special travois, one with extra long poles to accommodate the great length of the ivory. It was heavy, and not a single one of the dogs could pull it, so, a pair of men was required to do so. Getting them up the trail to the plain was the hardest part. Once there it wasn't so bad.

"Now what you doin?" Hot Wind questioned as the Headman returned to the valley and set fire to the brush at the base of the trail. The smoke could still be seen a hand of time later, the men could only assume that the entire valley would burn.

Then it began to rain. The sky clouded, and thunder began to rumble. The sod became water soaked and soon the travois poles bearing the tusks sunk deep into the earth, making pulling them almost impossible. Still, the men struggled on. Finally, the rain stopped, but the sky did not clear. Then black clouds began to form under the white ones, lightning flashed, and thunder bellowed, and the wind stilled into nothing. Men began to shed their tunics. The air became oppressively hot. Still they trudged on, ever westward. The headman strode well out before them, expecting the burdened camp to keep up with the pace he set. Farther and farther away he strode. Spider was the first to hear it; a funny high-pitched whistle. He looked over his shoulder and began to scream! He dropped the traces of the travois and began to run; Hot Wind and a hand of others followed him. The funnel swept down touching the ground and when it reached the deserted travois it sucked them up, tusks included, like they were no more than twigs. Then it went after the men, one screamed, his feet still running in the air as he was lifted from the ground. In a heartbeat a hand of men was swirling through the sky caught up in the vortex of the twister. Spider and Hot Wind ran, their legs pumping harder with each step. Their eyes rolled in fear and they could hear their companions screaming above them and the funnel whistling behind them. Then suddenly it was silent. The funnel pulled up into the cloud, taking everything with it. Spider stopped; unable to run a single step more. Hot Wind dropped to the ground beside him. Both lay looking up at the sky.

"Where'd they go?" Spider whispered, "The headman is going to be really pissed!"

"Look!" Hot Wind pointed, "A travois pole!" speeding rapidly toward the ground the pole struck with such force it buried nearly an arm's length into the soggy earth. "Look out!" He leaped aside as the body of one of the men crashed into the earth just where he had been lying. A white object spiraled from the belly of the black cloud, striking the earth with a sickening thud. The tip of the tusk had been driven completely through the body of the man.

Hot Wind looked at Spider, and they both began to run again. Behind them they could hear things hitting the earth, but they didn't look back until they had put considerable distance between them and the area of destruction.

White Falcon had glanced back when they began to scream. He now stood helplessly as the cloud dropped the wreckage of the travois and the bodies of the men onto the sod of the plain. The tusks had both shattered when they struck, scattering into unnumbered pieces, totally ruined, their power now scattered and worthless. He had only the staff and sacred objects which he carried on him. "The bison hide!" He screeched and began running back. Miraculously, it was still tightly bundled and unharmed. He rescued it and looked around. Spider and Hot Wind stood a distance away, shaking with fright.

"Get over here and help me find stuff!" He shouted.

"The Funnel!" stuttered Spider, "What if it comes back?"

"Get over here you fool!" White Falcon shouted, "The funnel is gone, it won't return. Go through this wreckage and salvage what you can! Those travois poles are all right; pull them free and get this stuff put back together!"

"What of the men?" Spider questioned.

"What of them? They are dead, any fool could see that!"

"Aren't you going to lay them out or nuthin?"

"No, we have already wasted enough time here. Let's get going. Be sure you don't lose that robe!" Again, he strode away, leaving the pair of men to follow as best they could without their companions, their dogs, or anything but their two legs. They had managed to salvage a pair of shelters, the spirit bag of the headman, a few odds and ends and one travois put together from parts scattered over the ground. Grimacing they searched the bodies for flint cores and tools, packing what they found onto the travois. Then they trudged after the headman.

They brought down a pair of rabbits and a hand of quail as they traveled. When the headman called a halt for the day, Spider gathered bison chips and Hot Wind put together a spit, from broken bits of equipment he had salvaged. They gutted the rabbit and birds and roasted them after the Ancestor Fires came out. The Headman claimed one rabbit and a pair of quail, and they ate the rest. That night they didn't even have the desire to hump. They lay trying to seek courage from one another.

White Falcon sat cross legged in his shelter, an empty spirit horn beside him.

How did she do it? He questioned. *How did she know I am coming?*

It was only a storm! The spirit answered, *she knows nothing! She has no power over nature, she in only a puny female. You have taken her sacred objects. She has only the tooth. Your power is greater by far than hers! You will destroy her at the Sacred Spring and then go on to find the other! Then I will make you the greatest Dreamer ever, even as great as I.*

I wanted those tusks! They would have great power! White Falcon sighed.

There are others, at the Sacred Spring. You will have those, their power is even greater, for I myself slew the beast! The spirit promised.

Can you give power to these teeth? White Falcon rubbed his fingers over the surface.

I can give power where I please! The spirit answered, *you have no need for more power than you have. Use it! Don't waste it! You have a pair of sacred points, one for each of them. Be sure that you follow the directions for hafting and casting them. They will carry enough magic and power to drive the spirit from her body. When it is done, and she is dead, be sure that you cut out her heart and that of the child as well. Eat their flesh and drink their blood. That is the power. Then you will be beyond all, no one will be greater!* Promised the spirit, *and I will be free,* it said to itself.

White Falcon smiled. He could not believe the luck he had when first he visited the Sacred Spring. It was there that this powerful spirit had first visited him. Since that time it had directed him successfully in his search for the daughters of Feather. It was the spirit that had told him that both still lived. It was the same spirit that had showed him how to listen. Now he was about to achieve his goal. The death of Feather's daughters, and their offspring, would bring to a close, the power of the spirits who guided. The circle would be closed and a new way begun, a way which he White Falcon would direct. Then only one dreamer would control, one would guide and direct, one would be the Greatest Dreamer of all time; White Falcon!

"Perhaps I will even claim the body of Blue Coyote!" He mused, "This one no longer suits me. It is not grand enough for the greatest Dreamer ever. Yes," he murmured, "Blue Coyote will do very well. I will be careful how I kill him, so that as I drive out his spirit, I may possess his body." He was actually smiling when finally, he slept.

*

"The pair in the shelter next to him woke later and looked out, the sky was clear, and the ancestor fires burned brightly. There were no signs of any clouds, not of any kind. They sighed, much relieved and returned to rest.

Far to the east Stone Man led his camp into the place of stone. He was very pleased with his camp. There were a number of children, all healthy, laughing chubby little people, his own daughter, Winter Rain, but one of them. The mated pairs were also happy. The only dampening occurrence on the camp had been the loss of Singing Serpent's faithful wolf. The animal well over a span of seasons, had simply gone to sleep and never woke again. It was sad for Singing Serpent, but Star Child had already presented him with one of Dire Wolf's last litter. The old wolf had surprised them, whelping but a pair of pups, one such as herself, to walk with Star Child on her own passing, and one to replace the faithful wolf of Singing Serpent. The two-colored-eyed pup followed the old healer everywhere, generally getting into everything, or chewing anything it could get its teeth into. Star Child spent many hands of time with old Dire Wolf, realizing that soon her old friend would walk the wind. She supposed that Throw Back and Wolf had long since passed on.

Stone Man wondered about Blue Coyote, did he ever think of them? Did he miss Stone Man? Was there an empty place in his very soul that would not fill? Late at night, when Star Child slept peacefully beside him, often Stone Man thought of Blue Coyote, and Basket! Star Child had proven to be a very competent mate, he had not complaints with her, but still . . . he wondered about what could have been. At least he had never called out the wrong name in the depths of passion; for he had been guilty of thinking . . . He closed his mind.

"Where are they?" he murmured, "I wonder if we will ever cross paths again?" He sighed and rolled over to pull Star Child closer, "Be happy with what you have!" He told himself, "You have more than most men could ever hope for!"

Star Child slipped away from the camp, making the last trip to the secret cave that old Dire Wolf would ever accompany her on. They both knew this. She scrambled more slowly up the trail, and lighted a torch. The drawings she had left were gone and in their place was the tearful rendition of a crying woman that a less talented hand than hers had drawn. She smiled and erased it. She did not leave another message, for there was no need. She was careful to keep her thoughts under strict control.

Singing Serpent was sitting beside the trail when she returned to the camp. "I tried to send a message yesterday," he stated, "A raven was near."

"Did it work?" she questioned.

He grinned and nodded. "I just received an answer while sitting here waiting for you."

"Tell me, please!" she sat beside him, her hand resting on the head of the old wolf.

"I sent a simple message, for he is still young, understand, and so I merely asked, 'How are things going?' And today I received the answer, 'As planned;' and it was a very clear message."

"That is wonderful! I am so glad for you," the pup came running up and Star Child scratched its belly, just as she did Dire Wolf's. "You give this young wolf a name yet?" She asked

"I keep thinking, but not yet!" Singing Serpent sighed, "It isn't as easy as Messenger was to name."

"Then why not simply call him Young Wolf. That is how you always refer to him."

"Perhaps, I will think on it!" Singing Serpent promised.

"I had better go and see if Stone Man has missed me," Star Child rose, "There are a number of tasks which I need to be completing while we are here."

She found Stone Man. He was sitting idly beside the quarry watching the men mine the stone.

"The raiders have been here," he remarked as she approached.

"How do you know?"

"Found the carcasses of several dogs dumped over there. They are not wolves, but badly inbred mixes. Besides no one else would treat faithful camp animals that way," he did not mention 'who' would not do so. "There are other signs as well. The place is strewn with trash, and the hearths were never properly banked and put out, clearly the work of Red Eagle and his camp."

"Can you tell how many travel with him?"

He shook his head, "Probably no more than a span at most, I would guess. There is no more than a hand of recently used hearths."

"Since you are not overly upset, I gather it has been some time since he was here."

Stone Man nodded, "At least a moon. Before that long run of rain we had in the valley. I figure they have gone on to the secret canyon." He rose and stretched, "I am going to follow him," he stated, "I am tired of the constant threat he has held over our heads for so many seasons. It is time to bring it to an end."

"So you plan to go to the secret canyon from here?" Star Child questioned.

"I plan to start there. We know that he has found it, for there were signs that he spent a winter there, probably where he inbred the dogs. If he is not, or has not been there, I will search until I do pick up his trail, and then I will follow it until I find him at the end of it. Then, my dear mate, I will do what should have been done long ago. I will punish him for all the lives he has taken over the seasons."

"It is about time that someone went after him. I have shuddered at the threat for seasons. I will be very glad when it is possible to raise my daughter without such threat."

"You do not seem to be really worried that I might suffer at his hands," remarked Stone Man.

"Perhaps I have confidence, that events will go your way, after all, if the spirits have any sense of justice, they will bring that creature to his knees for what he did to Basket all those seasons ago. You and Blue Coyote should have insisted then. Look at all the harm that man has done since that time?"

The pup snuggled its head under her hand, Star Child absently scratched it, "Now go back to your mother, Young Wolf," She instructed, thus sealing the name.

Stone Man merely raised an eyebrow and rose to go to the men. Star Child sighed and calling her errant animal, returned to the camp. She was smiling slightly, something she had done little of in recent moons. A pair of men brought in deer and the women were busy with the preparations of a huge celebration meal. It had been decided that they needed such a thing to raise spirits, although the main spirit it was designed to raise was Star Child's.

They unpacked the drum and Singing Serpent had been busy for some time brewing a fermented drink experimenting with grains and the sweetness of honey. They had found a honey tree in the northern mountains and collected a good portion of it. This was the first time that they had made it into fermented brew. Singing Serpent was not completely certain how to make it, for it had been a long time since he had helped do so, and the ingredients were not going to be the same. But he had been sampling it, the last few hands of time and already his head felt fuzzy.

Gray Wolf dragged the drum to the center of the camp. Already a lot of wood was gathered for the fire. Turtle Woman had enticed Rain Woman off to gather tubers for the event. Cougar sat at the drum and began calling the camp in. They ate, and danced and drank, and finally, long after the Ancestor Fires were bright, the drum drifted into silence and the camp slept.

The morning brought another 'celebration'. There were many headaches, sour stomachs, and general regret for the reveling. They lay around for the better part of the day, feeling generally sorry for themselves, and accusing Singing Serpent, good-naturedly, that he had poisoned them with his potent brew, yet threatening him not to forget how he made it.

The following day they began to load up for the next leg of their journey. Stone Man had definitely determined that they were going to the secret canyon. For the most part it was a relaxed and good-natured group which traveled with him.

They ambled to the canyon, and their arrival brought an abrupt end to the good humor. A silent unbelieving camp stood and looked down into the canyon. "Stay here; I am taking a hand of men down and investigating the canyon," Stone Man ordered. He then led the men down the trail. They could hardly believe their eyes. The entire end of the canyon was a blackened burned out mockery of its self. The home cave had fared just as bad. Some madman had dug all the earth from the floor, searching for something evidently. The dirt had been dumped over the edge. However, the rape had not ended there. The Great Beast, that wonderful reminder of the past that had greeted them on every return to the secret canyon, had suffered an outrage as well. The great tusks had been broken from the skull and taken. It made no sense!

The canyon itself had wept as well, presenting them with a burned out, blackened, vista. Every tree, every bush, each and every plant had been burned. Only a very few had begun to grow again. Tears ran down their faces as The People looked at what had once been such a beautiful surprise each and every time they had arrived. "It will grow again," Star Child whispered, standing beside the stream, the only part of the valley which was as it always had been.

"Why?" asked Turtle Woman, "What sort of madman would do such a thing? It is against everything that we hold sacred!"

"Perhaps that is your answer," Singing Serpent replied, "It was meant to make you weep. That is the purpose of this devastation. There was a man, along the Great River, who became angry with the tribes. He was a trader, but he was not honest with the people. He traded high for poor quality materials. Soon the tribes refused to welcome him to their camps. So in revenge he set the forest afire. I can still remember, as a child, seeing the blackened skeletons of the great oaks, sad reminders of his pettiness. It took the forest many seasons to recover, but gradually it did."

"See here, already the canyon has begun," he pointed to the flowers blooming bravely along the stream. "They will send out their message, and soon the trees will begin to grow new leaves and the grass will renew."

"But what of the deer, and the other animals which have made their homes here," questioned Grass. "When will they return?"

"If there is a season of plentiful rain, by late summer, much of the scaring will be healed. The fire burned very quickly. See here, the top of this brush has burned, but the lower part is still green. The leaves were scorched on the trees, perhaps even a few needles burned on the pines, but for the most part, it will quickly recover."

"The Great Beast will not," Star Child said regretfully.

"It will take many people hands of time to return the Home Cave to its original degree of comfort!" Turtle Woman said dourly.

"Then we had better begin quickly!" Rain Woman began unloading her travois, "I will begin loading these containers with the earth, and I will pass it up. If we make a line, you will be surprised how soon the Home Cave will be returned to its old comfort."

"First, I think we need a good cleansing for the cave," Moon stood in the opening, "Just in case there are discontented spirits here. I will arrange my things and be ready within a finger of time," he began rummaging within the contents of his travois.

"I think I will see what the rest of the valley is like," Stone Man stood from his contemplation, "Perhaps the entire valley will have need of your prayers."

Moon shook his head, "The fire did the cleansing for the valley, this cave and the other I will see to." Stone Man nodded and headed toward the lower end of the canyon. Beyond a certain point the rain had halted the fire. Even some of the trees still had their leaves. The small cave however, had suffered the same fate as the Home Cave. It was decided that they would camp outside for that night, leaving the dreamer plenty of time to complete his cleansing. When he had finished, they began returning the earth until Turtle Woman brought this to a halt.

"There are bones here!" She yelped, "Human bones! Some cruel soul has cared so little that they did not even set it to walk the wind!"

Moon came to where she stood, he stooped down and removed the tiny bundle, shaking his head, "You need not fear Turtle Woman, for this infant has been inside the Home Cave for far longer than you or I have lived. It is very old. We will place it in the very bottom of the back storage area, that way no predator will feast upon it. Whoever placed it there, cared very deeply, but the evil dreamer has stolen the spirit gifts left with the infant.

"I would give a gift for it, then," offered Kind Heart.

"And I as well," added Falling Water.

Soon almost every member of the camp had discovered some small item they wanted to gift. When the baby was gently lowered back into the cave, almost exactly from where it had been removed, it had a welter of gifts, offered by the good-hearted people of the camp. Later they also discovered the broken skull and bones of the Long Toothed cat. Star Child shivered and stroked her tooth for reassurance. But she could feel no power in the skull. Perhaps there was also no power in the teeth. She reasoned that the Mother of the People had given the teeth, which she and Basket wore, their power; power given at the time of the animal's taking. It had been the deed that produced the power. This cat had died a natural death. Its teeth would not have any power what-so-ever.

They stayed in the canyon a pair of days further, putting the Home Cave and the far cave back into order. Then they left.

"Look, look at the depth of these groves! What could have made them?" Singing Serpent squatted beside the long continuous grove in the sod. It began at the top of the trail and went as far as the eye could see.

"One thing is certain. It will make trailing Red Eagle very easy!" Stone Man smiled sadistically, "They certainly had something very heavy loaded on a pair of travois."

"The tusks!" shouted Star Child; "They have the tusks with them. They are the thieves!"

She shook her head, "I cannot think why I did not see it sooner. He plans to use the power in those tusks! He thinks to turn it against Basket and I and overpower us. He took the tusks in an effort to kill me!"

"What harm could he do against you with them?" Stone Man questioned.

"Some things have power that not everyone can feel," she replied, "The power of those tusks was very old, perhaps it has gotten weaker over the generations, or perhaps it never had much. The Great Beast at the Sacred Spring carries much more power. But this Red Eagle, he is gathering up every power object he can find, no matter how minute, to use against us." She laughed, "As though the old power can touch us! He has made one fatal mistake, thank goodness!"

"What do you mean?" Singing Serpent questioned.

"He gathers the old power," Star Child smiled, "It has no effect against us. It might have been sufficient for White Falcon to take over, but other than an ability to recognize it, Basket and I cannot be harmed by it. It was power given by the Great beast. Our power comes from Bison. It is new power, and far stronger than the old power."

"You mean that he cannot harm you, no matter how much of this 'old power' he collects?"

She nodded, "You see, when Basket lost her old staff we realized that it also carried old power. The new staffs given us by Mesquite Tree are much stronger. The only items we now have which hold old power are these teeth. And they have the greatest power because The Mother of The People gives them herself; they have no connection with the Great Beast at all. Also, they will give power to no one but one of the same line. Even if the dreamer were able to steal one or both of them, it would do him no good. The teeth are 'power' only for those of the direct line."

"What if he also has bison power?"

"Yes, but what kind of Bison Power, could he have?"

"Perhaps we should ask?" Singing Serpent suggested.

"Can you call a raven?"

"We will try," he said and squatted beside Young Wolf. He whispered in the wolf ear and the animal trotted off a few fingers of distance and then lifted his head and howled. He trotted back and walked beside Singing Serpent. Shortly a raven flew into view. "What do I ask?"

"What kind of Bison Power is there?" Replied Star Child.

"What are you doing?" Stone Man came to stand beside the pair of them.

"Uh, training Singing Serpent's wolf," she replied, "We have already taught him to howl on command. Isn't that clever?"

"Very clever," he replied, totally unconvinced, "Now come and walk with me and leave Singing Serpent to training his own animal."

Star Child went looking over her shoulder to make sure that Singing Serpent was getting the message sent. He was. She turned and spent the next hand of time walking with Stone Man, allaying his suspicions. They camped late and retired later yet. Morning came, yet no return of the messenger. Midday brought a single lone bird into view, but it was a raven and it flew true and straight. Star Child knew she had a message returned. However, it was time to settle the camp for the night before she could get away to Singing Serpent.

"What is the answer?" She quickly whispered.

"The white bison," he replied.

"White bison," she blinked, "Is there such a thing?"

He shrugged, "Not that I am aware of, but as I have said many times, I know little of bison."

Later, as she lay beside Stone Man, Star Child questioned casually, "Have you ever seen a white bison?"

"There are a great many things which I have never see, Star Child, including a white bison. It this question related to whatever it is you and Singing Serpent are up to and refusing to share with me?"

"What do you mean?" She questioned innocently.

"Just answer me, I am not blind Star Child, and while I do not see myself as the answer to every woman's prayers, I do not think your fascination with Singing Serpent lies in his male attributes, which brings me back to my question."

"Oh!" She said. "Would you believe me if I told you I was sending a message to Basket?" she asked tentatively.

"No!" was his answer.

"Then there is nothing more for me to say!" She replied, yawned hugely and snuggled and closed her eyes in sleep.

He smacked her soundly on the backside. Star Child yelped and jerked around.

"I am waiting for an explanation!" He reminded.

She rubbed her rear, "That hurt!"

He grinned, "Perhaps I should rub it better," he began to follow suit. She slapped his hand and pretended to be upset. He nuzzled her neck and very shortly both forgot what the questions or answers were. Much later she lay relaxed in his arms.

"You will be very angry with me," she confessed.

"I have never been angry with you in my life!" he protested, "Now what horrible thing have you been up too with the healer? I do not want you leading him astray!"

She chuckled, "You have little to fear from that!" She sighed "But you will not believe the truth either."

"Try me," he offered.

"You aren't going to like it, not even a little bit!" She warned.

"I am listening."

She sighed, "It all began . . ."

"When Blue Coyote and I split the pair of you up," he continued.

"Yes. Well, you see, I missed Basket terrible, and she missed me just as much,"

"How do you know?"

"I told you that you wouldn't like it!"

"I am still listening!"

"And that is exactly what I did, I listened, and she called."

"What do you mean she called?"

"It is hard to explain. I could close my eyes, particularly at night when all was quiet, and we could talk to each other."

"You What!" he sat upright.

"Talked to each other," she replied lamely biting her lip.

"You mean, just like we are talking?"

"Not exactly, and she certainly never shouted!" Star Child replied.

"All right, continue, you talked to each other."

"Yes, right up until the babies were born."

"Babies?"

"Winter Rain and Sun Spirit," Star Child replied.

"And Sun Spirit is?"

"Basket's daughter. They were born at almost exactly the same time."

"Do you mean to tell me that all of this time, while I have been tearing myself to shreds wondering where they were all of the time you have known and never said a single word?" he was shaking in anger now.

She shook her head, "I didn't know exactly where they were. Well, all right so I have known! But you weren't in any mood to listen any way!"

"So what was the thing with the wolf and the raven?" He managed to get himself under control.

"We found out that White Falcon was listening. He discovered there were still a pair of us and had we kept communicating he would have been able to track one or both of us down."

"Star Child, White Falcon has been dead since before you were Winter Rain's age."

She shook her head, "That's what everyone thought, but he wasn't. Well his body was of course, but he escaped from the cave they walled him in to and lived for many seasons inside Red Eagle. Then he began to gather the power objects, or rather he had Red Eagle gather them, until he was strong enough to kill Red Eagle and take over his body."

"And just when did he supposedly do this?"

"About the time the camp split," she admitted.

"Or was it about the time Basket lost her staff?"

Star Child sat up, "You think he has it?"

"I am beginning to think you are not entirely wrong," he offered, "But I am a long way from being convinced."

"Any Way Singing Serpent was told that White Falcon was listening."

"Singing Serpent?"

"His wolf; remember Messenger was a brother to Dire Wolf. Basket gave that pup to him the same time as I was given Dire Wolf. A raven told the wolf and the wolf told Singing Serpent,"

"And Singing Serpent told you."

"Yes," she agreed.

"So now ravens bring messages back and forth between the pair of you?"

She nodded.

"So what was the latest message? Oh, don't look so innocent, I saw you hot foot it to the healer the first chance you got."

"Oh! So much for being sneaky! I asked Basket what kind of bison power could White Falcon have."

"And she replied, a white bison?"

Star Child nodded, "Have you ever heard of such a thing?"

He shook his head, "But I have seen other animals, and have heard of still others, that perhaps one time in many generations will give birth to a pure white offspring. I saw a deer once; or rather I saw the hide."

"We make deer hides white," she reminded him.

He shook his head, "This one was born white."

"So it is possible?"

"Yes, I suppose so."

She shivered," It would have great power, far more than we do," she began to cry, "Poor Basket!"

"Why do you say that?"

"She is waiting for him at the Sacred Spring!" Star Child sobbed, "I was supposed to meet her there, but we are going to the plains to hunt bison. The dreamer will have killed her and taken her power and then he will be after me!"

"When?"

"When what?"

"When were you to be at the Sacred Spring?"

"Mid-Summer Ceremony day," she hiccuped

"When were you planning on telling me all of this?" He questioned.

"About a moon ago, but I was afraid!"

"Afraid? Of me?" He stared at her opened mouthed.

"Afraid you wouldn't believe me," she said lamely.

"Well I do believe you, ridiculous as it all sounds, I do believe you, and furthermore, if we hurry, and I do mean really hurry, we can still beat the dreamer to the Sacred Spring, and give him the surprise of his life!"

"Really?"

"Really, and in the morning we will tell the camp and see just how fast we can all move!"

"Oh, Stone Man!" She threw her arms about him, "I could not live without you!"

"You had better sleep now. You are going to need it," he nuzzled her neck and Star Child sighed and almost instantly slept.

Stone Man roused the camp just before Sun Spirit took hold of the sky. He explained that it was most urgent that they reach the Sacred Spring before midsummer. All agreed to hurry.

"How did you get him to agree to that?" Singing Serpent questioned.

"She told me the truth, as you should have from the beginning!" Stone Man answered from just behind the startled healer.

They pushed hard, for a hand of days. It was less than that until the midsummer. They still had a distance to go, but they cut straight across the plain, instead of following the herd trails. Stone Man topped a slight rise and suddenly halted, signaling the camp to stop and drop. He motioned Star Child to join him. She did, Singing Serpent tagging along.

"Look!" Stone Man pointed, "Does that answer your question?"

Grazing, is a wallow, less than a hand distant was the white bison. Star Child held her breath. The animal turned and looked directly at her. Star Child rose and began walking, almost as in a trance, Dire Wolf at her side, directly through the small herd to where the white one stood. It walked to meet her. The entire camp watched from the rise as she laid her hand on the great creature's forehead and they were enveloped with a soft blue glow. For some time she communicated with the animal and then with a sigh turned and rejoined the camp; the bison wandered off and were shortly gone from sight.

"We will be in time," she smiled, "The dreamer has fallen on hard times, already we have passed him."

"The bison told you this?"

She nodded.

"And the other camp, it is at the spring?"

"Not yet, but they arrive shortly."

"And you and Basket; are you communicating as well?"

Star Child shook her head, "We dare not alert the dreamer that he will face the pair of us."

"Wait!" He stopped, "I don't think I got all of that last little bit!"

"That is why we are going there!" She shook her head, "You don't think I plan on Basket facing him alone do you?"

"Actually I was rather thinking of *My* facing him, dart in hand, with perhaps Blue Coyote at my side. I certainly never considered a pair of women battling him."

"We have to!" Star Child stated. "This isn't a thing between men; or even between people. It is between 'power'. This is what we were born for. It has been our destiny since birth. Why do you think we have the watchers? Why do you think Bison chose us? This dreamer is not just a man, he is an evil, very strong 'spirit', he has much power, some he stole, some he has gotten from a source we do not know, but you cannot kill him, not even you and Blue Coyote together. Power must take him out, and that 'power' is Basket and me."

"Basket carries the ashes of his body. Blue Coyote and his men went to the cave, opened it and removed every trace of White Falcon. They burned everything, and they carry the ashes to cast into the Sacred Spring. That way the evil one is trapped. He cannot return to his own body, and if we can kill the one his is in; kill it with 'power', not darts, he will be trapped. And when the body of Red Eagle is destroyed the spirit of White Falcon will be forced into the spirit world, and never allowed to return."

"But it is dangerous!" he shouted, "You could be hurt!"

"I could be killed!" she shouted back, "But I don't intend to be! What would you have me do? Let Basket face him alone? Let her face sure death? He is stronger than either of us alone, but he cannot overcome the pair!" She shook her head, "This whole thing has gone wrong from the start! First the old grandmother, mistakenly thought to save one of us by separating us, but the only way we have the power to overcome White Falcon is together. We were working on it when you and Blue Coyote split up the camp. We have waited, all these seasons for the right time to come together again. Now is that time, but it will do no good if I do not arrive before the dreamer."

He sighed heavily, "Then it is my responsibility to make sure that you do so, even if it means your death."

"I hope that it will not come to that," she hugged him close.

"Come on people!" he shouted, "You heard her; we have a destiny to meet!"

The camp all rushed to follow them toward the sunset.

PART IV
WOLVES OF THE PLAINS

CHAPTER 27

I do not think you should go off and leave that cave open where anyone could enter it. There is power there, just like there was in the cave in the Starving mountains;" Blue Coyote said. The camp was preparing to leave the escarpment for the Sacred Spring, and then planned on spending the remainder of the summer hunting bison on the plain. Perhaps they would winter at the place of stone. Plans were loose at the moment, for Blue Coyote hoped to find some sign of Stone Man and follow it. They did not plan on returning to the escarpment any time soon and Basket had explained that she had prepared a spirit message in the little cave. Blue Coyote had not seen it, nor had anyone else, except perhaps Raven. He did not know, but the very fact of its existence bothered him. "It would not take long to block the entrance."

"All right, if you feel better about it, but the power drawings cannot be removed until White Falcon's ashes are offered to the Sacred Spring. We could always come back here and destroy it if it really bothers you, or you can block the entrance, but not entirely, the power must be able to escape. That is the whole idea of the drawings," Basket replied. "However, the next time we are in this area, I will remove the drawings and cleanse the cave of any remaining power."

Spirit Wolf ran her head beneath Basket's hand and she automatically scratched the animal behind the ears. Now that she was fully grown, Spirit Wolf was no longer pure white; her fur was tipped with black, giving the appearance of being silver. Basket smiled, for only she knew that in reality Spirit Wolf was her old friend Throw Back, she could tell that the body of the wolf was in certain cases, nearly transparent, but only she was able to see this. To all others Spirit Wolf was an ordinary animal. It seemed impossible that a hand of seasons had passed since the old wolf had been drowned. But just looking at Sun Spirit made her realize that this was so. The girl was like her name, everywhere, brightening the day for all with her pleasing ways and cheerful smile. Basket sighed, "Will blocking the cave cause us to be late for the Mid-Summer Ceremony?"

"Not if we hurry," Blue coyote replied, "You get the remainder of the packing done and I will see too at least obstructing the entrance." He went and called on Whippoorwill and Sparrow to help him.

"I will feel better with the entrance blocked as well," Star Woman said as she finished packing her and Gatherer's things. "Do you think we will find them?" she questioned wistfully.

"I have no doubt," Basket replied smiling, "Soon you will be reunited with Turtle Woman and I with Star Child. Sun Spirit will meet . . ." she halted.

"With Winter Rain? That is what you called her isn't it, Winter Rain?" Basket nodded.

"Sun Spirit is always talking about meeting Winter Rain," Star Woman frowned, "I do wish you hadn't filled her head with such nonsense!"

"What?" Basket looked up startled, "What did you just say?"

"I said..... Oh for goodness sake, Basket, you heard me!"

"I heard you, yes, but to my knowledge I have never said a word to Sun Spirit about Star Child or Winter Rain."

"But she goes on about them constantly! She thinks we are going to meet them for the midsummer celebration. She is expecting them to already be at the Sacred Spring when we get there. If you have not told her these things, where is she getting them?"

Basket frowned, the smiled, "She is my daughter," she answered. "Grandmother was forever hushing me at that age, for I always had knowledge about the future which I should not have. We just know things, and I cannot explain it any better than that. They just pop into the head. Remember the acorn gatherers?" Star Woman nodded, "Grandmother and I had an argument before we went on that trip. I did not want to go, for I saw the storm and I saw the people die, but Grandmother was afraid of my visions, so she made me be quiet. All I could do was insure we had warm clothing and extra robes."

"And because you did that, so did I," Star Woman nodded, remembering. "But for your determination, we would have suffered far greater hardship on that occasion. If you can see into the future, why did you not foresee Throw Back's death though?"

"I was not paying attention! She had been trying to tell me for hands of time that something was going to happen. I had my mind on other things. And it cost me the protector!" Basket sighed, "Were it not for Wolf Spirit, I do not know what I would have done." Basket referred to the spirit that visited her in her dreams, but Star Woman thought that she referred to the white wolf.

"There are times that if I did not know better, I would swear that animal is Throw Back! There are so many little things."

Basket smiled, "Well that is everything from the storage cave that I can tell; do you see anything that I missed?"

"No, that empties it. I think we can lead the animals to the top of the trail now. The men will soon be finished with their chore and already people are beginning to gather." Star Woman took up the lead on her wolf and led it toward the trail. She spoke to others along the way and soon there was a procession formed.

Raven fell into step beside her, Chert Boy and Sun Spirit chattering and laughing beside them. The little boy was a sturdy, thoughtful child, showing absolutely no indication that he was Mourning Dove's offspring. This at least gave Basket relief, although she was still determined to divert the relationship if it did not dissolve on its own accord. The revelation that Sun Spirit was fully aware of Winter Rain and Star child did not surprise her at all. She listened to her daughter's chatter.

"You will see!" Sun Spirit said to Chert Boy, "She is exactly like me. You will not be able to tell us apart. When you think that you are talking to me, you might instead be talking to Winter Rain!"

"But she could not know all our secrets!" the boy replied, "I need only say something that only you could know to tell the difference!" he grinned back "So you see, fooling me will not be so easy!"

"But we share all of our thoughts!" Sun Spirit smiled, "I have no secrets from Winter Rain."

Chert Boy thought, "But Winter Rain could not possibly have that scar," he pointed to Sun Spirit's head, where she had fallen and received a jagged scar on her forehead.

"No," Sun Spirit sighed, "She doesn't have a scar like that."

Basket frowned, "Sun Spirit, come here," she called.

She took her daughter a way away from the camp. "I overheard what you just said to Chert Boy, is it true? Do you talk to Winter Rain all the time?"

"It isn't really talk Mommy!" Sun Spirit started to explain.

"I know that it isn't, but what I need to know is, have you been sharing thoughts with her all the time! Please Sun Spirit, it is important that I know!"

The child nodded, and a feeling of dread began to fill Basket. As careful as they had been, neither she nor Star Child had thought about a connection with the children. They could have greatly underestimated the dreamer and his knowledge!" She hurried to Raven. "We must send a message quickly! I must know if Winter Rain also has knowledge of Sun Spirit! If the children have been communicating, White Falcon could know our every move. He could be waiting with a trap!"

"I will send a message right away!" Raven hurried down the trail to where the raven waited most days, for she fed it regularly. She spoke to the bird and it tilted its head and soon took wing. Now they waited.

Blue Coyote and the pair of men joined them, he checked that all were ready and then led the way toward the Sacred Spring. In a hand of days, they would be there. Spirit Wolf walked beside Basket, licking her hand occasionally and whining. The animal understood that Basket was worried. *What if after all our careful planning, the children have led him directly to us. He could be hiding anywhere along the way, waiting for either one of us!*

That evening the raven returned. 'Not since a pair of moons,' was the answer. Basket sighed. Star Child had discovered and stopped Winter Rain from talking to Sun Spirit, the rest was merely her vivid imagination, and it did not matter if the dreamer read her messages, for Basket still sent them regularly. Just so long as there were no answers! The raven however, had yet another message; '*he approaches*'.

That evening Basket again called Sun Spirit to her, "when did you last talk to Winter Rain?" she questioned.

"She won't talk to me any more," Sun Spirit's lip began to quiver, "I have called and called, but she won't answer!" she began to cry, "Is Winter Rain mad at me?"

"No, honey, she isn't mad at you, but she can't talk to you just now. Mommy can't explain, but it is very important that Winter Rain doesn't talk to you."

"Because of the dreamer?" Sun Spirit questioned.

Basket sighed "what do you know of the dreamer, Sun Spirit?"

"I know that he is bad! He wants to kill us! I have seen him!"

"What?"

"I have seen him," repeated Sun Spirit, "He sits at night, all wrapped up in his white robe and tries to find us!"

"Say that again!" Basket went pale.

"I have seen him," repeated Sun Spirit, "I already told you that Mommy!"

"I mean the part about the white robe! What does it look like? Can you describe it to me?"

"Of Course I can!" Sun Spirit huffed, "I am not a baby, Mommy! It is old and dirty and has a bison head on top. It looks silly bouncing around on his head and he is very ugly."

"Yes, I know!" *he has bison power!* She began to panic.

"What else can you tell me about him?"

"He is almost alone. Most of his camp is dead. A funny cloud ate them. He has a staff, it is like yours, but the top is different."

"Can you draw what the top looks like?"

"It looks like this!" Sun Spirit drew a long stick with three roots extending down from the top.

"My old staff!" Basket muttered, "So that is where it is!" *Well he will find that it does him little good! Perhaps its power was sufficient to let him kill Red Eagle, but it has no power over us!*

"Does he know you can see him?"

Sun Spirit nodded, "He said he was going to kill me," she grinned, "But Daddy won't let him!"

"How long have you been able to see him?"

"Last winter, when you thought I had a bad dream and I woke up screaming!"

Basket remembered the occasion. "He was in a cave with all of his people. He killed an old woman."

"You saw this?"

Sun Spirit nodded, "It was really awful. She was very ugly! She had scars all over her, and her hair was chopped off all raggedy! He grabbed her by the hair and dragged her over a log. He cut her neck with his knife and when blood dripped out of the cut, he got it in a bison horn. Then he drank her blood!"

Basket jerked upright, "How Awful!" she nearly gagged, *Mourning Dove!*

"It scared me, Mommy! He looked right at me and he smiled! He told me that he was going to drink my blood!" Sun Spirit shivered, "He is an awful man Mommy! Don't let him hurt me, don't let him hurt you either!"

"I will do my best!" Basket promised.

"Why does he hate me, Mommy? Why does he want to kill me and drink my blood?"

"Because you can see him, Sun Spirit; just like you can talk to Winter Rain, and just like Mommy can talk to Aunt Star Child. We are special, and the bad man is afraid of us!"

"But we are going to kill him any way aren't we?"

"I certainly hope so," Basket whispered. "But you mustn't say anything about any of this to Daddy, or to Grandma either. It must be our little secret! Promise?"

Sun Spirit nodded, "I like having secrets with you, Mommy. Just like Spirit Wolf has secrets!"

"And all those secrets must be kept just between us!" Basket reminded, "Understand?"

Sun Spirit nodded again.

"Now, off to bed with you!" She hugged her daughter and sent her on her way.

* * *

Wolf Spirit! She called.

I am here!

I am afraid! She whimpered, *what if something goes wrong? He has bison power. He has the white bison's hide!*

Yes. Wolf Spirit sighed, *I was unable to stop it.*

He is stronger than I?

You alone, yes, but the pair of you are stronger than he.

What if Sun Child does not arrive? Or what if she is late?

I have done what I could. Now it is up to you. The circle is open. The people have another chance. The evil dreamer seeks to close the circle and steal its power. Only you can stop him! I cannot interfere. You must draw the power from within. Basket sighed and slept.

* * *

"When we get to the Sacred Spring, I am not going to have time to keep an eye on Sun Spirit, I need you to make sure that she is safe. She cannot be running of from the camp with Chert Boy like she always does. This is very important Star Woman!" Basket worried.

"I have already said that I will watch her!" Star Woman repeated sharply, "That means exactly that Basket, I will watch her!"

"I know, I am sorry, but I am so worried! What if something goes wrong?"

"What can go wrong? It is just a midsummer ceremony, Basket! Even with the addition of throwing those ashes into the Sacred Spring, it still isn't anything to be so worried about! I will keep an extra special eye on Sun Spirit, all right?" Basket nodded.

"I don't know what to do!" She later confessed to Raven, "If I tell Star Woman why I am so worried she will alarm the entire camp. But Sun Spirit is so active, and she is always running off from the camp to play. It doesn't seem to matter how many times I tell her to stay within the camp, she always seems to forget. If the dreamer is out there, he could grab her!"

"What about Spirit Wolf? Would she watch the child?"

Basket shook her head, "she is my protector, she will not leave her post, not for any reason!"

"Then I will just have to make sure that both of the children stay within the camp," Raven promised.

"Oh, would you? That would take a lot of worry from me! I know that Star Woman means well, but she is getting old, and Sun Spirit is such an active little girl!"

"At least I do understand the danger!" reminded Raven, "I will keep her within the camp if I have to gag her and tie her to my travois!"

"I hope such an extreme won't be necessary!" Basket replied.

"Why not just tell her that the bad dreamer is nearby and is coming to get her and if she leaves the camp, he will grab her and slit her throat before she has time to so much as squeak!"

"I don't want to frighten her!" Basket protested.

"Better to frighten her now than regret it later. Besides, she probably knows something is going on any way."

"You could be right. Maybe if I tell her, well, not what you said, but explained that she needs to be extra careful to help Mommy not to worry . . ."

"You are to stay with Aunt Raven, is that understood? You are not to leave her side, not for any reason!"

"But Mommy, I need to pass water sometime! I can't do that in front of Aunt Raven!"

"You certainly can!" Raven stated, "In fact we will pass water together! That way you can protect me as well!"

Sun Spirit giggled, "I promise Mommy, I will stay with Aunt Raven. The bad dreamer won't catch me away from the camp!"

Basket nodded, accepting that she had protected her child as well as possible. She was returning to where Blue Coyote had set their shelter when she was halted by one of the younger wolves. It came to stand purposefully before her and looked directly into her eyes for a short time, there was a flicker of blue fire in its eyes and, then it walked past her and went to stand beside Sun Spirit. Basket glanced back, exchanged another understanding look with the young animal and nodded. She felt much better now; Sun Spirit had an additional protector. Spirit Wolf had provided, and Basket was as ready as she could be.

The ashes were packed on her travois. She checked to make sure they were secure. This was going to be a surprise for the dreamer. He had no idea that she would be cutting off his only avenue of escape. She smiled, Blue Coyote waited for her and they got underway.

"Sun Spirit is behaving extraordinarily well!" He commented later.

"I had a talk with her," Basket explained. "I am getting really tired of the children going off completely out sight of the camp to play, it is not safe."

"She has one of the young wolves to play with as well, calls her Woofie! Where did she get that animal?"

"I think that Spirit Wolf has also been worried. I would not be surprised if that wolf was not her idea."

Blue Coyote raised an eyebrow but did not comment; Basket was glad that he did not.

Later, when everyone was busy setting up the camp for night, Sun Spirit forgot and saw something fluttering just beyond the camp. She went to see what it was, and found her way blocked by her new friend, Woofie. The young wolf growled and would not let her pass. Sun Spirit then remembered her promise, and she returned to Aunt Raven.

They sat beside their fire after the camp had settled to sleep. The Ancestor Fires burned brightly in the sky. Blue Coyote stretched out his legs and sighed, "It is such a large plain out there. We could probably follow the bison on it for the remainder of our lives and never come across signs of other people."

"We will find them, Blue Coyote, you will see," Basket reassured him.

"You always sound so positive! I wish that I had such confidence."

"Perhaps Dream Catcher will have news when he speaks to his spirit helper."

"I do not have the confidence which you do in spirit helpers!" Blue Coyote replied.

"They have not left the area," Basket finally admitted to him.

"What do you mean?"

"Star Child has left me messages," she replied.

"Messages?"

Basket nodded, "Even though they have been very careful to erase all signs of their occupation, Star Child has managed to let me know that they have been there."

"Such as?" he sat forward now, "Why have you not shared this with me before now?"

"You have not been ready to hear," she replied, "Now you are. When we were at the place of stone, she left a message in the secret cave. She said they missed us, and again at the escarpment."

"They have been to the escarpment? Are you sure?"

"They spent an entire season there."

"And you did not say?"

"I tried talking to you when you were determined to return to the southern canyon. You would not listen to me, and we lost Journey's Far and were nearly captured by the raiders, but you would not hear me when I pleaded not to go there. There is no sense talking to a man when he will not listen. Now, you are ready to listen," she replied.

"You didn't tell me that Star Child had left you messages; you said that you spoke to her. There is a lot of difference between leaving messages and speaking across air."

"You still do not believe that she and I can communicate, do you? You are still convinced that Soft Wind is living happily with Stone Man and his camp, and you did not believe me when I told you that we were in danger of capture by the savages, yet it has all happened."

"I will believe that when I see it with my own eyes. When Stone Man tells me that Soft Wind met such a horrible death as the one you described, then I will believe. When Star Child walks up to me with a daughter exactly like Sun Spirit, then I will believe, but until then I only believe what my eyes and ears tell me is true. I do not trust in spirits!"

"And Spirit Wolf? Do you not trust in her either?" Basket shook her head, "You stubborn man! You saw that pup with your own eyes, but you did not see!"

"Basket, I have grown up watching wolves. I know how they live, that pup was born different, so the pack would not accept it. It was left behind. We were fortunate to come across it, and it certainly helped you get over the loss of Throw Back, but there was nothing magical about it, noting spirit related! Animals can sense things. Spirit Wolf probably sensed that you were upset and hurting. It is their nature to try to help members of their pack. Besides, the animal knew it was thrown out of the pack, and if it could find another pack, and after all we walk with wolves, it was natural for it to join us," he concluded.

"Look up at the Ancestor Fires in the sky, Blue Coyote. Do they not tell you that there are things that we do not understand? What happened to the visions you had as a youth? It was you who saw a way to escape the Starving Mountains; it was you who led the way, yet now you seem to be blind."

"It was also I who let a woman so blind me that I drove away the other half of my soul!" He said bitterly, "I am sorry Basket, but I no longer trust myself."

"Then trust me!"

"I appreciate that you care, Basket, but you know nothing of the working of a man's mind. You cannot understand that honor and trust between men is something that far transcends even the mating between a man and a woman. Hunting brothers are the unit that makes The People strong. When I broke that trust, divided the unit, it was the worst kind of mistake that a headman can make. The only reason that I remained headman was that there was no one else to lead."

"But now there is Gatherer, and there was Nighthawk as well, yet the camp did not select either of those good men to lead, they chose you. Why? Because you are the leader of men, Blue Coyote, because you see far and have vision, vision for leadership. What happened between you and Stone Man was awful! You said things that were I a man, I would find hard to forgive. But time has passed, scars heal, people grow in wisdom. You are not the same man who said those things. You have grown and become wiser. Perhaps then you were a young and untried headman, but now you are not!"

"I only know that somehow, I must find Stone Man and ask his forgiveness," Blue Coyote sighed, "It eats at my soul!"

Basket realized that nothing she could say would be a help. They sat, each wrapped in their own thoughts until finally they sought sleep.

She rose early, before the rest of the camp was awake. She sat quietly, holding the head of the white wolf in her hands, stroking the soft fur. She could feel the power beginning to build inside. Her fingers tingled as it ran up them and into her hands and arms. She drew power from the white wolf. She stroked the animal and cleared her mind. The camp awoke. They looked questioningly toward Basket, but no one disturbed her. Quietly they packed their shelters onto the travois, they ate the morning meal, and then they waited. Basket did not move, the wolf did not move, the blue aura still encased them. Then slowly it began to fade, and she became aware. Quickly Basket released Spirit Wolf and stretched her cramped muscles. No one said anything about the delay, Blue Coyote frowned as he led the camp away, but he did not question.

The next night Basket went to the blood shelter. She must begin to prepare for the Mid-Summer Celebration. She sat most of the night, again holding the wolf's head, and again building the power. In the morning she was refreshed, her step was firmer, her eyes clearer and her mind even more so. *The dreamer was searching for her.* She could feel him. *Could he feel her as well?*

In a pair of days, they would reach the Sacred Spring. Now Basket walked alone. Only Spirit Wolf walked near her. The rest of the camp dropped away. She was purifying for the Ceremony. No one must break a taboo by even accidentally getting too near. All understood. Basket walked as if in a daze, she sat quietly, eating by herself, and when the shelters were put up at night, she went alone with Spirit Wolf into the blood shelter. No one disturbed her. Each morning she left the shelter and now many could feel the power that she radiated. It puzzled some, for they had gone through a number of midsummer ceremonies together, but Basket had not acted like this before any of these. They concluded that it had something to do with the parcel of ashes she carried. They were not far wrong.

*   *   *

Where is she? He reached out with his mind. *Where is the child?* Again, he searched. *Why can't I feel them? I know that they are coming, and the feeling should be stronger, not weaker!*

She is blocking you! She knows that you are near. You cannot surprise her. You can only overcome her. She knows that the time has come. She begins to prepare. You must also prepare!

The one-eyed headman smiled and reached for the horn of spirit drink. The spiral began, and he was again lifted to fly over the great plain spread out beneath him. It was a favorite vision. He could see The People spread below, hunting the bison. They were a large camp, the largest that he had ever seen, and their leader, it looked like Blue Coyote, but in truth, he wore the sacred white bison cape, and White Falcon knew that it was his spirit which lived in the body, not that of Blue Coyote.

The woman was not there. Basket and her child and the abomination of a wolf, they were not in the camp; or the other one who so resembled Basket. She also was gone, as was her child and now he, White Falcon, led; followed by Stone Man and a hand of spans of other people. They hunted the bison. They had become strong. No longer did the Yucca Camp starve far to the west. They had left that life behind them. Like the falcon of his name he flew overhead, then turned and again watched as he led The People into a new way of life.

No more would they make offerings to the animals. The animals were their servants, the circle had closed. The vision changed. Now the bison spread over the plain as far as the eye could see, and the people slew them. They drove them in hordes over cliffs and ravaged the land. He controlled!

The dreamer sighed and returned. *Be careful!* Cautioned the spirit that directed him.

He rose and kicked the pair in the other shelter awake. "Make a meal!" he ordered them, and Hot Wind scurried to do so. The headman called to Spider, "I have need of relief!" he motioned. The little man nodded and hurried to kneel before him. A time later he shoved the creature onto his face in the dirt, straightened his breechclout and walked away. Spider glared at him and hurried to where Hot Wind had their meal ready.

"Someday I would enjoy putting a knife to his throat!" he whispered.

"Be careful or he will beat you to it!" Hot Wind replied. "Me, I would just like to escape, what you think of our heading out on our own? We could go back to the escarpment and live out our lives there in peace. What we need him for any way?"

"He could come after us!"

"So what? He could kill both of us now, at any time, which pleases him. The only reason we are still alive is because I prepare the meals and he humps you regularly. Not much of a life is it?"

Spider shook his head, "Remember that little cave way south along the escarpment? I bet he would never think of looking for us there."

"So what is stopping us?"

"We will be at the Sacred Spring in a pair of days, and he is up to something there! We could sneak off then and be long gone before he misses us! He isn't much of a tracker. We could pick a night when he goes into one of his trances. They always last most of the night. We could be far away before morning. The moon is nearly full. It would be easy to see at night," Spider mused.

"Well tonight will be the last chance."

"Then we do it!" Spider nodded.

They trotted along in the wake of the dreamer as always. He led them steadily westward, toward the Sacred Spring. That night, again White Falcon took the spirit drink. The pair of men loaded up their backpacks and, leaving the shelter behind quickly traveled toward the south for some time, then turned west. By morning they were a good distance away and they kept going all day. White Falcon called, went to the shelter to kick them awake, and swore when he realized that they had run off during the night. *I will find you, little worms!* He vowed *and I will suck the life from your veins!* He rummaged in his own pack and found some dried meat there. This then was his meal. He was forced to bring down a rabbit for his evening meal, but that was all right. Tomorrow he should be at the Sacred Spring, and then he would have time to prepare for her arrival. That night it rained.

All day it drizzled. He plodded on, the sun hidden by the clouds. He came across tracks and realized than that he had not traveled in a straight line but had circled around and was following his own trail. Disgusted he stopped and sat angrily inside his dripping shelter, soaked to the skin and hungry. He wrapped in his white bison cape and sat shivering. There was not even anything dry enough to build a fire. He sneezed.

* * *

When the rain began, Basket dug out her oiled rain skin and pulled it over her. The River People had shown them how to make these garments seasons ago. They were simple really, a hood was formed to cover the head, then skins were sewn together to provide a robe which fell down the back and front as well. It worked wonderfully for keeping one dry and even warm. *Now if they had something for the feet as well!* She glanced at her sodden shoes and sighing pulled them off and tossed them onto the travois, also now covered with an oiled skin. Spirit Wolf shook the water from her fur, sending a cascade of droplets over all that were nearby.

Sun Spirit marched glumly beside Raven, her wolf friend walking there also. Chert Boy sloshed along on Raven's other side. It took too much effort to run in soggy shoes, and the ground hurt the bare feet, soft from all the wet. Besides, the rain took away the desire to play. Even Woofie was not in the mood to play. Her fur was dripping and she looked more like a drowned rat than a fine wolf.

Blue Coyote called a halt finally, and the camp gratefully put up shelters and got fires started inside them. At least they had the forethought to collect bison chips and keep them dry on travois, now they could relax, drink hot tea and eat a good meal. Hunters had brought down an assortment of small game as they walked; rabbits, prairie chickens and quail. Raven helped the children get settled and then prepared the meal. She brought food to Basket as well, secluded in the blood shelter.

"We will reach the Sacred Spring tomorrow evening, according to the headman," she remarked.

Basket nodded, "I hope that I will be ready."

"Can I get you anything else?"

Basket shook her head, "I have everything that I need," she replied. "Just keep an eye of Sun Spirit and keep her out of harm's way. Let me concentrate on what I need to do without having to worry about her."

"I will keep her safe!" Raven answered.

"Thank you, my friend!" Basket sighed.

"Are you sure there is no other way?"

Basked shrugged, "I have asked myself that question many times. The only answer that I have is that power brought me into the world for this purpose. I have been moving toward this all my life. Look at my birth! The dreamer was trying to kill Feather, my mother. In a way he succeeded, for she never recovered from the attack. My grandmother, not Butterfly, but the other one, took Star Child and ran away with her. The dreamer sent men after her, and when they caught up to her, she had a girl infant with her. The child was dead, and the old woman was dead. But power saved Star Child. Rain Woman had just discovered her own infant girl dead. The old woman arrived with Star Child, and Rain Women made the switch."

"All of my life, the power has directed me. White Falcon killed Butterfly's son, my father, and he injured Feather so badly that eventually she died. He wanted Feather dead because she was of the direct line of The Mother of The People, the one that your people name Mammoth Mother.

White Falcon was obsessed with power. He wanted to steal Feather's power and make it his own. But we were born before he succeeded. Then he raped Turtle Woman, Star Woman's sister, and Fire Dancer had him buried alive in his spirit cave. Only White Falcon's spirit escaped. He hid inside Red Eagle for seasons, waiting for a chance to kill me."

"I think that Star Child and I were born to stop White Falcon. He was very powerful, that is why the spirits needed the power of twins. He had Red Eagle take the power objects from me, somehow he gained enough power to take over Red Eagle and now he is coming to kill me, and Sun Spirit. Then he will go after Star Child and Winter Rain. If he succeeds, then the circle will close, and the old way of The People will be gone forever. I have seen the destruction that will ravage the earth if he succeeds. The savages pale beside it."

"How do you plan to stop him? I mean, you say he is greater than you."

Basket shook her head. "I have only the power building within me," she whispered, "And Sun Spirit . . ."

"No!" Raven shouted "You cannot mean it! Not Sun Spirit! Not your own daughter?"

"Blue Coyote changed the balance," Basket wept, "He separated me from Star Child. Together we were enough! So the spirits gave each of us a daughter, one of the line. If the circle is closed, the people will turn away from the spirits, and they will die as well. Only the continued reverence of The People keeps them alive."

"It seems to me that these spirits think more of themselves than they do of you! What are they for after all, if not to protect you? It is not your place to protect them! You ask your spirit wolf that! You demand that they give you help! This dreamer, White Falcon, he isn't even human anymore! He is more 'spirit' than man. Tell them to fight their own battles and tell them to leave Sun Spirit out of it as well!" Raven shouted and flounced from the blood shelter.

Basket was deeply troubled. What Raven said did make sense. She had never really thought about it, but why was she expected to fight 'spirit' battles. What had the spirits ever given her? Raven was certainly right about one thing. They should at least help!

* * *

That night she called of Wolf Spirit.

I hear, she answered.

The dreamer comes near, and I can feel him. I am afraid. I am not strong enough to fight him by myself!

Call on us! We are here for you. Call on Bison, call on Wolf, call on The Mother of The People. We are all here for you, but you must call our names. We are powerless to help if you do not call.

What do I ask of you?

That must come from within . . .

* * *

It took many hands of time before Basket could regain her sense of serenity and draw on the power of the white wolf.

Sun Spirit didn't want to walk quietly beside Raven. The sun was shining, and the birds were singing. She wanted to play, to run through the grass and laugh. Sullenly she plodded along, Raven on one side, Woofie on the other, a prisoner between them. Chert Boy had gone off to play with the other children once he realized that she wasn't going to play with him. This really hurt! Sun Spirit vowed that she would never play with Chert Boy again. Perhaps she would never even speak to him again.

Tears ran down her face. Raven was being totally unreasonable. She would not even let Sun Spirit speak to Mommy! *And Mommy!* She had not even asked about Sun Spirit for a hand of days. Sobs racked her small body. Everything had gone wrong lately. *This rotten old Mid-Summer Ceremony! Who cared any way, about a bunch of naming and matings? What difference did it make?* Mommy was mad at Sun Spirit, Grandma frowned at her, Raven made her walk right beside her, and Winter Rain would not talk to her! It would serve them all right if the mean old dreamer did kill her! They didn't care! Maybe then they would miss her!

Raven squatted down and pulled the child into her arms. "I know that you can't understand all of this Sun Spirit, but trust me, we all love you very much!"

"Mommy doesn't!" Sun Spirit sobbed, "She won't even talk to me."

"Soon this will all be over and then, I promise you, Mommy will have all the time in the world for you."

"Is it the bad dreamer?" She whimpered.

Raven nodded, "Mommy must be very brave and fight the bad dreamer. She is scared, and we need to help her. We must help by being very good and doing exactly as we are told, without arguing, without being even the least bit naughty. The best way we can help is by thinking only good thoughts and thinking about Mommy, very hard." Raven smiled and wiped away the tears, "Do you think that you can do that?"

Sun Spirit nodded, "Woofie and I will think very hard," she promised. Raven sighed, and they caught up with the camp.

It was well after mid day when they sighted the end of the shinnery. Just beyond they would dip down into the very slight valley where the Sacred Spring lay. The camp was beginning to laugh and exchange stories. The Mid-Summer Ceremony was a joyful occasion that they all looked forward to. There would be dancing, fermented brew, and although no new people, no matings were to be added, there was a naming, for Sunflower and Dog Boy's child. Only Basket was isolated from the festivities. She had fallen behind the camp now, needing the quiet and concentration that the camp no longer afforded. She knew where they would set up the camp, and she would join them at the proper time. She was responsible for the giving of gifts to the spring, and she was also responsible for consecrating the ashes of White Falcon. For a hand of days she had been preparing to face the dreamer as well. He was near, but she had no idea how near, nor from what direction he would come. She had to be ready, no matter what happened. She was agitated and was having trouble focusing inward. Suddenly she realized that the camp had suddenly became silent. From beyond the rise came the lone call of a wolf, long and mournful. Spirit Wolf threw back her head and answered. Basket began to run; the travois all but bounced her belongings across the plain. She and Spirit Wolf entered the camp at full speed and almost ran into Blue Coyote as he stood still as a statue. In the place where they always camped, there was spread a large and noisy camp. It was filled with strangers. The people so joyous just breaths before stood silent and worried. Never had they come up against such a thing. Basket caught her breath and then leaped forward again running to meet the woman running to meet her. "Star Child!" she screamed and threw herself into the arms of another, exactly like herself. Another pair of people had come out from the other camp, one, an old woman, the other, tall, strong and moving with command. Star Woman trotted past Blue Coyote and was soon hugging Turtle Woman. Stone Man stood quietly beside.

* * *

Blue Coyote stood as if frozen in stone. He took in his mother and his mate and their tearful reunion. But it seemed his feet were rooted to the ground. Something struck him in the middle of the back, propelling him forward, and Spirit Wolf was smiling from ear to ear as he stumbled and then with a boyish whoop threw himself into the open arms of the other half of his soul. Stone Man clamped strong arms about him and nearly crushed the breath from him.

The camp now came forward. Raven led Spirit Wolf, Sun Spirit and the rest. Sun Spirit suddenly slid behind Raven shyly and peaked around her. Standing, beside Turtle Woman was a small girl, so like Sun Spirit that it took the breath away. Her blue eyes scanned the camp anxiously, finally lighting of Sun Spirit, then her whole face lighted in a smile which went from her blue eyes all the way to her chin. "Well go on," Raven gave Sun Spirit a little push; "This is what you have been waiting for, go and meet her."

Sun Spirit went cautiously forward, her thumb in her mouth, Woofie at her side until she stood within touching distance of Winter Rain, accompanied by the double of Woofie. Then she began to smile, "I have missed talking to you," she said.

"Mommy said it wasn't safe anymore," Winter Rain replied, "I have missed you also. She reached out and touched Sun Spirit, "I can hardly believe that finally you are here."

Sun Spirit wrapped her arm in Winter Rain's arm and the pair of them stood watching their parents.

* * *

"I was sure that I had misunderstood!" Star Child wiped tears from her face, "When we arrived and there was no one here."

"We were late leaving, Blue Coyote insisted on blocking the cave before we left."

"You have everything?" Star Child questioned.

Basket nodded, "I cannot think of anything that I forgot. Have you . . . ?"

Star Child shook her head, "Not since just after leaving the secret canyon. But he is close. I can feel him."

"So can I, but now that you are here I can quit worrying."

"We must set up our shelter and prepare, but not just yet. I would greet old friends first," she went to where Star Woman and Turtle Woman, still holding on to one another stood, dragging Basket along, for she had no intention of letting her go, not for a time at least. "It makes my heart complete," she hugged Star Woman, "to see the pair of you together again."

It fell to Gatherer to bring the camp into the presence of the other camp and get them settled. Blue Coyote and Stone Man would not have noticed if the earth had opened and swallowed both camps. Chert Boy stood beside Raven, his lower lip stuck out and a sullen expression on his face. Suddenly Sun Spirit had no time for him!

Raven saw to the setting up of her shelter; and a bit farther out, the blood shelter. Basket and Star Child could greet the other pair of women and freely deal with the pair of children, but they dare not join in the remainder of the celebration until they had finished the offering and cleansing ceremonies. Then they could join in freely. Reluctantly they handed the care of the girls over to Raven and entered the shelter, old Dire Wolf still beside Star Child, and Spirit Wolf with Basket.

Star Child eyed Spirit Wolf and then smiled, "I cannot believe it! What on earth happened to her? I was expecting Throw Back to be long gone, walking the wind seasons ago! How on earth did this happen to her?" she ruffled the fur on the silver wolf.

"I am glad that you recognize her," Basket sighed, and related the story of the drowning of Throw Back.

"And no one has noticed?"

Basket shook her head, "Only me."

In the background a drum began to sound. The Mid-Summer Celebration had begun.

"I am glad that finally you are here, it was hard always keeping my thoughts under control, and it was even harder on Winter Rain. But I explained to her how very important it was and she promised not to call or answer Sun Spirit."

"How did you convince Stone Man to come here for the celebration?"

"I told him the truth," admitted Star Child, "Or we would be chasing bison on the plain now." She sighed "He was not at all pleased that we come to do battle with the dreamer, but he has accepted that I must be here to help you fight him. What of Blue Coyote? How does he take the confrontation with White Falcon?"

"He doesn't know," Basket admitted. "I merely told him that I had to commit the ashes to the Sacred Spring at Mid-Summer. I didn't say anything about White falcon himself, or I would not be this side of the moving sand. I found your message at the place of stone," Basket smiled.

"I know, I found your reply."

"I made the painting in the little cave. You could have done better."

"I saw a white bison," Star Child smiled. Basket nodded. On and on into the night they talked and healed. They hardly noticed when the blue aura began to envelop them, but soon the vibrating power brought them back to their task. With a sigh they gave in to it, and clasping hands, their free hand on the head of Spirit Wolf, they drew forth the power.

CHAPTER 28

I looked for signs of you everywhere we went, but I found none," Blue Coyote admitted.

"We left none," Stone Man replied, "I wanted no raiders following."

"Basket insisted that you went to the southern canyon," Blue Coyote started, but stopped when he saw the expression of Stone Man's face. "It is true then, the story that Basket tells me? Soft Wind. . ?"

Stone Man shuddered, "It was truly the most horrible thing I have ever witnessed. At least they gave her some strong potion, for she did not know what was happening. Some day I intend to go to that place again and try to free her soul if possible. Its location will remain in my memory forever!"

"We were very nearly captured by the savages. Trust Basket to be giving forth with dire warnings in the middle of having a baby, screaming that they were about to attack! We lost Journey's Far to them. They had cut his heart from his body and were playing with the body like it was no more than a toy with which to amuse themselves. They had taken Chert Boy prisoner as well, and we went to free him, but we freed any number of other prisoners at the same time. Some of them still walk with me, although most elected to stay behind at the starving mountains. You would not believe that place! It is as different from when we lived there as possible!"

"There is a river flowing through the moving dune area," Stone Man said.

"We crossed it, I could hardly believe that was the place we waited out the blizzard. So much has changed." He paused and sighed, "Me most of all. I have been searching for you for seasons. The hardest thing a man can do is admitting that he is wrong, but I do so. The things which I said . . . Words cannot be taken back once they are spoken, but I would beg if necessary that you try to put those hurting foolish words from your mind and forgive this stupid man. I was not thinking, or if I was it was with the wrong head. I cannot explain the grip that Mourning Dove had on me. She was like a fermented drink gripping my soul. I was drunk with the need of her. I did not think, I only felt. She was a burning fever, raging out of control. My words were the rantings of a fool!"

"I also suffered the same symptoms, for a time. As for your words, they were forgotten long ago," Stone Man said softly. "The pain of separations was far greater than the anger over the words. I walked away, leaving a part of myself behind. I have since been searching, for the brother of my heart. I have been a long while finding him." Neither man spoke for a time, their thoughts going inward.

"I was planning on scouring the plain for you just as soon as Basket finished her cleansing," Blue Coyote stated, "I would not have stopped searching until I was set to walk the wind, no matter it took me the rest of my life."

"Basket did not tell you then, that we would be here?" Stone Man frowned.

"Basket tells me little of the things she knows, for like always, I have refused to listen," Blue Coyote replied, "Spirits know that she has tried!"

"Star Child has had little better success with me," admitted Stone Man, "You must agree that messages sent by mind are hard to accept. Were it not for the proof afterwards that she was right, I also would have refused to listen. When she told me that Basket gave birth to a daughter, at exactly the same time as Winter Rain was born, well . . . I just did not believe her."

"Basket tried as well, but as usual, I did not listen. So many times. . ." he sighed. "Fire Dancer should have named me I Do Not Listen; it would have been suitable, it seems to be the tale of my life. Perhaps now, I can change that.

"As easily as you can stop breathing," Stone Man shook his head, "You have always been hard headed, Blue Coyote, that is what led us to cross the moving sands; that is what saved The People from starvation. Agreed, at times it was extremely irritating for me, especially when you always seemed to be right, but in the end, I always followed you."

"No longer," Blue Coyote sighed, "Now it seems, you lead, and very well from the looks of your camp."

"Perhaps, but I lack imagination. I always choose the safe path, never the adventurous one."

"You are here," reminded Blue Coyote, "And if that isn't adventurous, I do not know what else to name it!"

"I am here because I knew that I would find you here, and I could only hope and pray to Spirit Wolf, that you were ready to accept my hand again in friendship at least."

Blue Coyote shook his head, "Never as a friend, only as a brother!" Again, the men embraced, another small portion of their hearts healing.

"So after all of the seasons of telling you, finally you took Basket to mate!" Stone Man grinned.

"Only because I was desperate," Blue Coyote admitted. "She is the best thing that has ever come into my life," he admitted, "Yet she has always been there. But could I see? No! I had to be forced by circumstances to take her. Why she ever accepted is beyond me! I was a pitiful thing, I admit it, but she took pity on me and has stood loyally beside me ever since. I have always known, though, that I was not her choice."

"Can you talk of it? Or is it still too painful?" Stone Man asked.

"It is not painful exactly . . . only I feel so foolish!" Blue Coyote sighed. "What is it about young men when first they get a taste of a woman? Do we all lose our heads? Is there something magical about that first one, something which causes us to lose all sense? Or was it just me?"

"If so, it was me, as well, and a hand of other also," Stone Man sighed, "She was so very beautiful . . . and so very clever. She could make a man feel he was the most wonderful . . . Well I was as taken in as you. Had it not been for the fortune of luck, I would have continued to be her slave, but then I came upon her rutting with another and had the scales ripped painfully from my eyes. I had no idea at the time that she had ensnared you as well. She played us all for fools that winter, but you had the misfortune to be next in line for leadership."

"Even as I mated her, she carried the child of another." Blue Coyote admitted. "Believe me. It did not take long for me to see her clearly! I truly received the 'gifts' I so richly deserved. She made my life a complete misery and then presented me with another man's child. Even then I was blind, and I could not convince myself that I had been so wrong.

I still looked for the illusion, until I found her in the arms of another. You . . ."

"I did what had to be done; as the tradition of The People dictates. She left the camp in a state that guaranteed that no more would a man look at her without a shudder. In that at least, I had the strength to act like a man," he said bitterly. "Then I had to go to Basket and beg her to mate with me and raise another man's son. To give her credit, she nearly said No! Had you still been in the camp she would have told me No!"

Stone Man sighed, "All these seasons, I have yearned . . . pretended . . . yet now that I see her again, there is nothing . . . all I see is Star Child. Perhaps we are all fools when it comes to women!"

"I went to where we laid Father and Bison Man, I talked to them, left gifts . . ." he sighed, "I felt better, but I do not know if they heard me."

"I did also," admitted Stone Man, "And as with you it helped. I apologized for their deaths, but I don't know . . . I could offer no closing for them."

"I did. That is the reason that I insisted on returning to the canyon. I hope that I gave them peace. At least I was able to tell them that there had been punishment for their killer."

"Do you know where she is now?" Stone Man questioned.

"Dead." Blue Coyote answered.

"You ...?"

Blue Coyote shook his head, "She made her way to the secret canyon, and joined up with Red Eagle, according to Basket, and for once I did listen; he slit her throat."

"A fitting end," Stone Man nodded. "Now, perhaps we can all put her behind us. She has caused more than her share of grief and pain. I would as soon forget she ever came into our lives."

Into the night the men spoke. They talked of many things, but Mourning Dove was no longer even a ghost between them.

*   *   *

Beyond the camp, a lone man crawled to the edge of the rise, out beyond the Sacred Spring. He was hungry and thirsty, and laying aside the white bison cape he sneaked down to the spring and filled his water skin. Then he returned to hide again. A pack rat scurried past and quick as a flash, his rabbit stick took its life. He could not afford a fire, so reluctantly he consumed the creature raw. It stopped the hunger pangs. He had arrived too late to be able to understand where people were sheltered. It was a large camp. He would have to be patient and wait . . . just before dawn he moved to a better vantage point and gathering some brush, he pulled it over the bison hide, then he settled down to watch.

The sun was high before he saw Basket. She came, and she went, and she came again and went again, yet he could not determine which shelter was hers, for others blocked his view. Before long he began to question the wisdom of his position. The bison hide was suffocating hot. The sun beat down mercilessly upon him, and to make matters even worse, he had inadvertently settled himself directly over an active ant nest. They nearly drove him to screaming. They crawled inside his tunic and bit the tender flesh of his stomach, his arm pits, and even his crouch. They got between his toes and fingers, and into his hair. And everywhere they went they bit! His head began to swim, from the heat, from the poison, he could not say. All day he lay, unable to move so much as a hand to brush the creatures away. "Should have stayed where I was," he muttered to himself. "I could have seen her shelter from there!"

"Must get to the tusks, I Need their power," he muttered.

You have power enough! His spirit helper whispered in his brain. *You must force her to come to you! Then you will be able to defeat her! Then you will be able to call down the spirits and destroy her and the child and the abomination as well! Take her power, make it your own!*

And then I will be free! The spirit added to itself.

*　　*　　*

"I can feel him near by," Basket sighed. She sat still feeling with her mind. Star Child still had her mind tightly closed so that there was no chance that the dreamer could sense her. "Tonight I will cast the ashes into the spring. But first I must give gifts! As must you, but we must be careful that we are not both seen at the same time, for he is watching."

"Will he not think it strange that you do everything a pair of times? He will not know that one of you is me."

"Perhaps once will be enough. I am sure that the camps will remain together. Blue Coyote will not easily be parted again from Stone Man, and now that they are mated to us, truly they are brothers. This bond is not one which they will find easy to break."

"It had better not be easy to break, for I will not be parted from you again, no matter what!"

"Sun Spirit is much like Winter Rain," Star Child grinned, "Were I not her mother, I do not think I could tell them apart," she shook her head. "Both are most unhappy that they must remain inside the shelter with Raven. That poor woman has her hands full!"

Outside the drum began; "It is time," Basket sighed.

*   *   *

Finally the sun spirit left the sky, and darkness came. The man was finally able to move. He crawled backwards from beneath the bison robe. His body was a welter of blisters, and he pulled unnumbered ants from his body, many of them leaving their heads still grasping his tortured flesh. He swallowed mouthful after mouthful of water, replenishing his nearly depleted system. The drum beat vibrated in his brain, mesmerizing him as it had for hands of time. He closed his eyes and prayed to the spirits for strength.

All after midday he had watched the preparations for the naming ceremony go forth. There was a welter of babies in this camp. It seemed forever before each and every one of them had been named. And Basket kept changing! First she had her hair braided over one shoulder and every where she was followed by the abomination and the next time she returned, the hair was down her back and it was a white wolf which walked beside her. Yet again, when it was time for the naming of the new woman, the wolf had changed, back to the abomination, and the hair was braided again. Now he watched her come again from the camp to the spring. The white wolf was with her, and the hair was hanging down her back.

*   *   *

Basket lifted the wolf hide container. It had traveled from the Starving Mountains unharmed. She tucked a sharp blade into her pouch and dug about for the packet of special powder that Dream Catcher had prepared for her. Then she was ready. Star Child sat back on her heels, "How will I know when to come?"

"I will call you!" Basket replied.

"You are sure this will draw him out?"

"I cast his ashes into the Sacred Spring. He will try to stop me!"

"How will he know that his ashes are in the container?"

"I plan on announcing it, loudly and clearly, so that he does know. Wolf Spirit assures me that he will try to stop me. Remember, he is as much 'spirit' as man, he will understand the meaning of my actions, at least the 'spirit' side of him will."

"And this will draw him out to attempt to kill you?" Star Child looked worried, "What if he casts a dart? You have no protection against human weapons."

"I would just as soon not consider that possibility," Basket bit her lip.

"I will be nearby, just behind that end shelter," assured Star Child.

Basket nodded and turned and left the shelter, the white wolf at her side. Star Child sat, her arms about Dire Wolf, drawing courage and comfort from her old friend. Now she could only wait until it was time for her to join Basket.

* * *

"I want to watch the naming ceremony!" Sun Spirit stuck out her lower lip and her eyes glittered in rebellion.

"So do I!" Winter Rain demanded, glaring hatefully at Raven. Raven sighed, "I will make an agreement with the pair of you. Winter Rain, you may go and watch the naming of the children of your camp, only so long, however, as you promise to return just as soon as your mother is finished. Is that agreeable?" Winter Rain considered and finally nodded. "You promise to return immediately!"

"I promise," the child nodded.

"Then Sun Spirit may go to watch the naming of the child of our camp!"

"It isn't fair!" Sun Spirit complained, "There are over a hand of new names to be given out in Winter Rain's camp, but only a single one in ours!"

"But there are no new matings in her camp," Raven grasped at straws, "And nearly a hand in ours, so, Winter Rain will get to watch none of them, and you will!"

Sun Spirit considered this "Very well," she finally gave in, but not happily. "I do not see why we cannot both watch the ceremonies together!"

"I have explained that to you!" Raven glared down at the stubborn children. "The dreamer must not see the pair of you together, or he will realize that your mothers drew him here to trick him!"

"Could I not peak from behind a shelter and watch?" Sun Spirit was not giving up, at least not easily. "He would never see me. I would be ever so careful!"

"Your mother said to keep you here," Raven stated, "and that is exactly what I am going to do! Now what is it going to be girls; my way or not at all?"

"Your way," they replied glumly, in unison.

"Very well, now Winter Rain, your mother is leaving the shelter to begin the naming ceremony for your camp. You may go."

Winter Rain shot out of the shelter on running legs.

*　　*　　*

Star Child went nervously to her place beside the central hearth. She was very much aware of the hated eyes boring into her, but she closed her mind to him and proceeded with the naming. There was a hand of children. It had been a prosperous season for the camp. She caught a movement out of the corner of her eye and saw Winter Rain settle beside her father, she frowned and forced herself back to the task at hand. Finally, she finished and hurried from the hearth.

"Winter Rain is watching the ceremony!" She reported to Basket, "I thought you said the woman Raven was dependable!"

"Only Winter Rain?" questioned Basket. Star Child nodded. "Then it will be Sun Spirit to watch the mating," she smiled, "Our daughters are proving to be a handful even for the resourceful Raven. Perhaps we should be warned."

Star Child gave her a weak smile. "He is out there. I could feel him." Basket nodded and left the shelter. She also could feel him as she nervously went about the single naming and began the mating ceremony. Spirit Wolf was whining nervously as well. She kept looking toward the Sacred Spring. Basket managed to pat her on the head and the animal understood, Basket knew!

Sun Spirit now sat happily beside Blue Coyote, the other child was nowhere in evidence. Basket sighed and completed the ceremony, glad to have it over with. The offering was going to be worse, for she would be much nearer the dreamer then.

She returned to the blood shelter. They were finished until after the hunting ceremonies were complete. The day would be far gone by then. They had decided that Star Child would do the offerings, and then Basket would carry the wolf hide container to the spring, and draw the dreamer in.

*   *   *

Blue Coyote and Stone Man led the hunters in, one from each end of the camp. They danced around the fire, and Dream Catcher and Moon each presented part of the narrative. The younger men had chosen to take the part of the bison. They pranced into the camp, pawing the earth, lowering the great heads they carried, and bellowing in their best imitation of a bison. Around and around the fire they danced, until, with a shout, the hunters rushed leaping into the camp. Bison danced away, hunters advanced. Darts were cast, and bison fell to the ground. The camp cheered and laughed. Then the bison rose, cast off their disguises and began dancing with the hunters. The fermented drink was passed around and all partook freely. The hunting ceremony went off without a hitch! A pair of small girls were able to watch through holes cut into the hide of their father's shelter. Raven could only guess what the repercussions were going to be from this!

Now the women were free to join in the celebration.

Star Child picked up the special white rabbit skin and tucked it into her waist thong. She lifted the container holding the deer antler baton and the offering tools. "I am frightened," she admitted. "This is his last chance to attack. What if he doesn't wait?"

"The wolves will know," Basket reassured her, not at all certain that her fears were not completely justified. "Besides, it is much more likely that he would prefer to sneak into the shelter long after all are asleep in order to kill me, that is what he has done in the past."

"If that was supposed to give comfort, it doesn't!" Star Child tried to give a weak smile; "A dart in the back at the spring or a knife at my throat while I sleep; some choice!"

"He will not get the choice," Basket replied, "It would be his way, however."

Star Child was as ready as she would ever be, so with a final encouraging smile she left to make the offering. Basket gripped her shaking fingers together and waited. She placed her hand on Spirit Wolf and with a sigh soon calmed. Finally, after seasons, no, her entire life, of fear from the source of White Falcon, she was about to bring it all to an end. She had no guarantee that she would survive the ordeal, but at least Star Child would and their children as well. Basket figured it was a fair exchange. She sat, gathering herself, pulling in power from the spirit of the wolf, through Spirit Wolf. When Star Child returned, the Sun Spirit had left the sky. Basket was ready.

"You were right. I could feel him, he is very angry, but he did not attack. He still has enough of humanness about him that he was afraid of the hunters. He did not dare attack while they were there, armed and dangerous." Star Child shivered, "Soon it will be over."

"Yes," Basket replied. Almost in a state of sleep-walking she rose and picked up the wolf hide and a sharp knife. Spirit Wolf whined and licked her hand. "It is time," she nodded, "We go now and make the cleansing. Stay close."

Whether she spoke to the wolf or to her twin, both responded. Star Child hurried to the nearest shelter to the spring. It was dark now, and probably the dreamer could not see her at all, but Star Child took no chances. She crouched behind the shelter grasping Dire Wolf tightly. The animal was shaking as well.

Basket walked calmly to the spot she had chosen. It was a slight rise, just above the spring itself. From here it was a simple hand cast to deposit the ashes in the spring. The camp quieted, even the drum stopped bating. The people waited, holding their breath. Raven ushered the children to their father's shelter, again they would watch through the holes she had cut through the hide. She squatted with them, a hand on each. The young wolves whined and circled but stayed by their sides. Blue Coyote and Stone Man stood together watching, just at the edge of the camp, Blue Coyote ready to welcome Basket to the celebration, Stone Man to rush to her defense in case . . . of what he could not say.

She spoke clearly. "For nearly a generation, there has been an evil dwelling among The People. An evil so vile that it has hidden its face from us, it has raped, murdered, and eaten the flesh of its victims," she paused raising the wolf hide. Around her, the blue glow began. The white wolf lifted her head and let forth with a soul rendering howl. The dreamer wrapped the white bison cloak about him and began to tremble . . . then he began to prepare.

"I have come here to this sacred place, on this, the longest day, to put this evil from us. The men of the Wolf Camp, the Dreamer Acorn, and I, Basket, woman of The People, descended from The Mother of The People, herself, have captured the evil in fire, and kept it secure in the hide of our sacred totem, Wolf."

Beyond her, the wind began to rise, above her clouds obscured the Ancestor Fires, and the moon, full and round, began to lose its light as the clouds passed between it and the ground. She lowered the bundle and with her knife cut the bindings. She knelt before the open hide and from her waist pouch removed a packet.

"With these powders, taken from the very heart of the wolf, mixed with the spirit of the dream I call the spirit of Wolf! Come to these people and take this evil from among us! Bind it with cords so strong that it cannot break through them, so hard that it cannot bite through them, and so tough that they will never rot and let it free! She scattered the powder into the ashes and with her knife stirred it in. Then she lifted a dipper, made from bison horn and scooped out some of the ashes. These she raised and poured into the Sacred Spring. The water surged and swallowed them, then again became calm. She lifted another scoop and spoke, "Spirit of White Falcon, I send you back to the spirit world!"

At her first cast of the ashes, his head jerked up and a searing rush of pain shot through his body, his guts twisted in an agony of pain, his body rolled in spasms on the ground. He struggled to his knees and then to rising and standing on the ridge before her.

"Noooo . . ." he screamed as he staggered down the slight incline to the pond. He wrapped the white robe about him and raised the ancient staff of The Mother of The People and commanded. "Strike her down!" He raised his face to the storm, "drive the dagger of the Spirit through her and giver to me her power!" A bolt of lightning came from the cloud. The ground shuddered as it struck, very close to where Basket stood. Her hair rose on end, and the wolf whined and danced as the ground burned her paws. Basket felt a searing pain tear through her body, as though it were on fire. A great ringing sounded in her ears, and the power of his strike knocked her to her knees. Again he commanded, and again the lightning responded, singing, her hair and that of the white wolf. The pain was nearly unbearable. An angry red weal ran down her arm and she could feel the skin of her back and belly blister as well. Her head felt as though thunder was striking again and again within her head. She reeled, and would have fallen, but from behind the shelter rose another and she ran to support Basket, to stand beside Basket, to at last free the bonds from her mind and call to him, and beside her stood yet another sacred wolf.

"We command you to the depth of the Sacred Spring!" Basket cast the ashes. The water rose and surged, around the tusks of the great beast casting a blue light upon it.

The dreamer pulled the white robe tighter, and he reached into his pouch and brought out the ancient point object. He held it up and with the wind shrieking and moaning he cast the object at the women. It struck at their feet and exploded into a cascade of sparks, each fragment a tiny missile, each bringing blood where it struck. Basket and Star Child fell back, each bit of stone driven deep into their flesh. The blood ran freely now from arms and legs. Then they stood and again Basket tossed the ashes. "Be gone evil one!" She called.

"I need more power!" He screeched, twisting and staggering along the edges of the pond. "I need the power of the tusk!" He looked about and located a rock and he tottered to the water's edge and began to wade in. The heavy bison cape started to hinder him, so he cast it on the bank, a rock in one hand and the staff in the other. He waded out to the skull of the Great Beast and began pounding at the skull where the tusks were attached.

"No!" shouted Basket.

He broke off a bit of tusk, and with a demented grin lifted it. This time the lightning struck. The great White Wolf whined and sank to her belly, then rolled over and lay still.

Basket looked at her friend. Anguish burned her soul, "Spirit Wolf!" She cried.

Star Child grabbed her arm, "Basket, come back to me!"

The water of the pond began to shimmer. It stilled. Basket turned to Star Child, "Help me, we will pour the rest in, but be careful not a speck can escape. Together they carried the wolf hide container to the very edge of the pond. Now the dreamer was wading toward them, the one eye gleaming in the reflected fire light. He began to raise his hand again, to cast another power bolt. He stopped. From behind a shelter stepped a pair of children, beside them walked a pair of wolves. They went to stand with Star Child and Basket, silently watching him, their minds free to laugh at him.

The dreamer began to tremble. Desperately he staggered in the water.

The twins tilted the wolf hide and poured the ashes into the Sacred Spring. Then they threw the hide in as well. "I command your spirit to the world on the dead!" Basket shouted, "Wolf Spirit!" She wailed, lifting her head and howling just like a wolf. Star Child followed suit. From the spring they received an answer.

The water began again to shimmer, and then it quivered. The man stood, thigh-deep in the pond, and he realized that the old power was nothing against them. The white bison hide lay just on the bank. It alone had the power to fight them. It glimmered and beckoned to him! He turned and began wading toward it. The waters bounced and shimmered in the reflected light of the fire. They danced and took shape.

Again, the twins wailed for Wolf Spirit!

Treadles of fur wrapped around his legs, they bound him. Sinew, building from the body of Wolf Spirit wrapped around his ankles, halting him. The water rose, and the spirit wolves sprung forth from the spring. They leaped at him, throwing him off balance and he fell backwards into the depth of the spring. Their feted breath took his away, the evil gleam of their blue eyes caused fear to quake in his soul, their snarl deafened him, and the pain rendered by their teeth, made him writhe and twist in agony. They ripped him limb from limb and cast his blood into the water.

Again, and again the dreamer screamed and thrashed in the spring, every move drawing him tighter and tighter into the grasp of the Spirit Wolves. The entire pond was alive with them, grasping and tearing at him. Again, and again he screamed. The churning, wolf ridden spring began to swirl and a vortex formed, the struggling body of the dreamer began to circle around and around, each circle taking him deeper into the Sacred Spring, the water wolves followed. And then, finally it was done. The water calmed, the clouds went from the sky, and the moon shone bright once again. The ancestor fires burned brightly in the night sky.

Stone Man released the grip he held on Blue Coyote.

Basket knelt beside the still form of the white wolf, her hand resting in the soft fur. Her tears fell, and the wolf whined, wagged her tail once, licked Basket's fingers and departed. The pond was calm and serene. The young wolves lifted their heads and howled, long and mournfully. Far away, on the distant plain, they were answered.

Star Child helped Basket lift and carry the body of Spirit Wolf back to the blood shelter. They laid her carefully on Basket's sleeping fur. Then they called the healer, Singing Serpent and he brought a balm. Basket rubbed it into the poor burned pads of her feet; she swept the singe from her fur with her hands and bid a prayer for her journey. Singing Serpent begged them to allow him to tend to their own wounds, but they shook their heads and went on with their task.

The silent camp followed as they pulled the travois carrying the wolf's body to a place distant from the camp. Here Basket said a last and final farewell of Spirit Wolf-Throw Back-Protector. She laid a charm that Acorn had created for her with the body to ward off evil. Then she walked away and left the beloved Spirit Wolf to walk the wind with her ancestors, wild and free as the ancient Dire Wolf was meant to be. In the morning, Dire Wolf was gone as well. They found her, beside the white wolf, their heads lying side by side. Now they ran with the wind together.

Acorn had rescued the white bison hide. It was purified in smoke, cleansed, and cleaned of the accumulation of grime. The hunting robe of Blue Coyote was used to form a container for it. Then it was wrapped as well in wolf hides. It would travel with them, honored and protected, as befitting a sacred object of The Bison Hunters!

* * *

In the next several moons, Basket and Star Child healed, at least the superficial wounds did. They both had faint scars where the lightning had burned them. Of the scars within, they did not speak, even to each other. The People left the Sacred Spring. They wintered at the place of stone, and spent seasons following the bison herds. They traveled north and south along the western edge of the great plain hunting the vast herds of bison that roamed there. They visited the secret canyon from time to time and were relieved when its healing was complete. They left offerings to the animal spirits there but did not linger.

Basket mourned the loss of her protector most of all. She missed the great head beneath her hand and she missed the comfort and companionship as well. The spirits did not speak to her again. Her task was completed. Now Basket became just another of the women of the Wolf Camp. She held a special place in the hearts of The People, but she held no extraordinary powers. The Spirits had released her. The camp regarded Spirit Wolf as a magical creature, one who had given her life to protect them. Many sent her silent prayers. Basket developed the habit of talking to her when she was alone. This at least did give some comfort. Her memory of the great beast, however, did not diminish with the passing of time. The loss never lessened. Basket mourned Throw Back-Spirit Wolf for the rest of her long life.

The camp grew strong. They were truly 'wolves of the plains', they were bison hunters!

There were no more threats from evil. The raiders were all dead, no 'others' bothered them, nor did spirits of any kind. The girls grew, as alike as had been their mothers. Every season they grew in the ways of The People. Sun Spirit, when she became a woman, carried the sign of 'bison' but she was never called. Eventually the camp returned to the escarpment and Basket and Star Child removed all traces of Basket's painting, and these were gifted to the Sacred Spring as well. One tusk had broken from the old skull and now lay in the water, only its tip cutting the surface.

With the passing of the seasons, as the circle expanded, Star Woman and Turtle Woman, Water Woman and Gatherer, each in their time, went to walk the wind. Young Wolf also passed in her time. The camp moved continually, from the mountains to the plain to the canyon and beyond. They followed the herds, from the north to the far south. The savages had moved off. Stone Man and Blue Coyote kept their promise. They returned to the place where Soft Wind had met her end. Here they said prayers for her and made offerings, a gentle spirit sighed and passed onward.

The wolves were carefully mated to keep their lines pure and strong, but never again was a big footed, flip eared pup born. With each litter, Basket watched eagerly, only to be disappointed. She called upon Wolf, Spirit but received no answer. As the seasons passed, gradually she began to realize that the spirits would never again call upon her. With this she was relieved. She and Star Child gradually lost the ability to communicate with their minds, as did their daughters. By the time they reached adulthood, the mind talking was just a memory from their childhood.

Basket walked beside Blue Coyote. She gave him sons, strong and true. Star Child walked with Stone Man, and they watched their only daughter grow into a beautiful woman. So the seasons passed. The memory of the evil dreamer faded into legend.

The People had returned to the place of stone and the escarpment many times. It was at the escarpment old Blue Coyote had been laid out and a season later Stone Man, at the same place. Now Basket's grandson led. They had returned to the place of stone for the winter. Grandmother Basket and Old Star Child made their usual trek to the secret cave. It was hard to climb up the trail, they were puffing and out of breath before they tumbled into the cave.

As usual, Star Child drew pictures in the soot on the walls. There were seasons of them now, depicting the various times of their lives. One whole wall was covered. Basket was content to watch her sister draw. Then they returned to the camp.

It was here, at the place of stone, many seasons later, that Old Woman Basket breathed her last. Ancient Star Child needed her grandchildren to help her up the steep trail to the cave. But here she made a final picture on the wall, that of a crying woman, then she left the secret cave for the last time.

Basket was laid to walk the wind on a high ridge, above the place of stone. It had been a good life; she was content to go to the fires in the sky. The story tellers still talk of her passing. It is said that as The People watched, her spirit rose and was greeted by the spirit of a great white wolf, the likes of which no longer roams the plain.

THE END

BIBLIOGRAPHY

Alabates Flint Quarries National Monument: https//www.nps.gov/alfl.
2018

Amann, Andrew William, Jr.; John V. Bezy, Ron Ratkevich, W. Max Witkind.
1998: *Ice Age Mammals of the San Pedro River valley, Southeast Arizona.* Arizona Geological Survey, Down-To Earth Series 6. Tucson, Az.

Andrews, Brian: *Mountaineer, CO.* Southern Methodist University, Department of Anthropology, QUEST Archaeological Research Program.
2006

Arenberger, Leslie P. and Jeanne R. Janis: Flowers of the Southwest Mountains.
1982: Southwest Parks and Monuments. Tucson, Az.

Barnett, Franklin: Dictionary of Prehistoric Indian Artifacts of the American Southwest.
1991: Northland Publishing.

Blackwater Locality #1 Site, A Brief Scenario of Life at... 2002: Eastern New Mexico Unversity Department of Anthropology. www.google.com

Blackwater Draw National Historic Site; **Roosevelt County Chamber;** 2018

Cloud, William A., Richard W. Walters, Charles D. Frederick and Robert J. Mallouf: *Late Paleoindian Occupations at the Genevieve Lykes Duncan Site, Brewster County, Texas* Center for Big Bend Studies, Sull Ross University Press, 2012

Curry, Martin F. *Barger Gulch Archaeological Site;* Grand County History Stories. https://stories.grandcountyhistory.org/articles/barger-gulch-archaelogical-site

Dawson, Jerry and Dennis Stanford: *Linger Site; a Reinvestigation.* Southwestern Lore. 41(4): 22-28, 1975 (tDAR id: 104477).

Frison, George, C.: *The Carter/Keer-McGee Paleoindian Site: Cultural Resource Management and Archaeological Research;* American Antiquity 49 (2). April 1981.

Geological Fieldnotes: Alibates Flint Quarries National Monument. 1997 National Park Service, Texas. www.google.com.

Glendo State Park 2000: Wyoming State Park Service. www.google.com

Johnson, Eileen and Vance Holliday; *Lubbock Lake National Historic and s\State archaeological Landmark;* www.tshaonline.org/handbook/online/articles/bbl13

Kris Herst, K. *Folsom Culture and Their Projectile Points;* ThoughtCo www.thoughtco.com/folsom-culture-ancient-bison-hunters-1709

Hoffman, Todd, Schultz and Hendy; *Lipscomb Bison Quarry*; Bulletin of the Texas Archaeological Society, Volume 60, 1989; p 171.

Jodry, Margaret A.: *Stewarts Cattle Guard Site: a Folsom Campsite and Butchering Locality is South Central Colorado. (tDARid: 54121)* National Archaeological Database (NADB)

MacMahon, James A.: Deserts; The Audubon Society Nature Guides: 1988; Alfred a. Knopf. Publisher.

Meltzer, David J. and Meena Balakrishnan: *New Archaeological Investigations of a Classic Paleo-Indian Bison Kill.* 2006, p 260. www.folsomvillage.com/FolsomManSite.html

National Geographic Society: *Field Guide to the Birds of North America;* 2nd edition, 1989,

Palo Duro Canyon: Texas Park Service. www.google.com; 2018
Palo_Duro_Canyon: Wikipedia; 2018

Roberts, Frank H. H.: *A Folsom Complex: Preliminary Report on Investigations at the Lindenmeier Site in Northern Colorado;* Smithsonian Miscellaneous Collections 94 (4). 1935.

Stiger, Mark: *A Folsom Structure in the Colorado Mountains;* American Antiquity, 71.no 2 (April 2006)

Tilford, Gregory L.: Edible and Medicinal Plants of the West. 1997: Mountain Press Publishing Co. Missoula, Montana.

Wendorf, Fred and James J. Hester: *Early Man's Utilization of the Great Plains Environment.*1962: *American Antiquity, Vol 28; No. 2.* Salt Lake City.

Westfall, Tom; *The Shifting Sands Folsom/Midland Site.* www.arrowheads.com/folsom/411-the-shifting-sands-folsommidland-site

Wikipedia: *The Lindenmeier Site.*

Wormington, Marie H.: *Ancient Man in North America.* Denver Museum of Natural History; 1957.

Printed in the USA
CPSIA information can be obtained
at www.ICGtesting.com
LVHW051348311223
767823LV00041B/261

9 781984 570673